Leftwich Blues/Elfwitch Rules

by Jeffrey Cummins

ForgivenIAm Publishing House

First E-Book edition: August 10, 2021
First Print edition: December 13, 2021

Published by
ForgivenIAm Publishing House, Salem

Copyright © 2021 by Jeffrey Cummins

This is a work of fiction. Unless otherwise indicated, all the names, characters, businesses, places, events and incidents in this book are either the product of the author's imagination or used in a fictitious manner. Any resemblance to actual persons, living or dead, or actual events is purely coincidental.

Scripture taken from the New King James Version®. Copyright © 1982 by Thomas Nelson. Used by permission. All rights reserved.

Print Edition ISBN 979-8-9853920-1-2   E-book ISBN 979-8-9853920-0-5
Print Edition ISBN 979-8-9853920-2-9
Print Edition ISBN 979-8-9853920-3-6

Printed in the United States of America

Dedication:

To my mother, who has always been my constant reader. And to all my family who ever believed in me.

LEFTWICH BLUES/ELFWTICH RULES

Table of Contents

Acknowledgements:

A book needs readers. A book needs friends. Thank you to the following readers: Danielle Slater, Zachary Thomson, and Jorden Reed. And thank you to Morgan Jones for helping with images.

PROLOGUE: Vows and Curses

"Who-who cooks for you?" called the great bird.

It startled Gina. She spied out the night hunter sitting in the Mighty Oak above her and Frehley. Large as a cat with bright yellow eyes that took in the night.

"I've never seen one so close," Gina said.

"Who-who cooks for you?" called another owl from some other tree.

"It's sure not afraid of us," she marveled. "What does it mean?"

"Seeing an owl portends mighty things. They stand for wisdom. Or a messenger sent by the Judge. To remind us all things have their season," Frehley said. "Look at us. We met in one season. Now another season is about to begin for us."

Frehley held up both quicksilver necklaces under the large full moon. The mercurial metal glowed. Back and forth between grey and black. Liquid like water. Shiny like silver.

For generations, people had used silver as tokens of love. Silver was the metal of vows and curses. Very rare in the Realm.

Gold was even rarer. It was used by only the Regents. As a sign and seal of their authority.

But quicksilver was the rarest. Because it was found in only one place. Outside of the Realm in the Domain. It was a forbidden place.

Quicksilver was inconstant. An active ember taken from the fire that made Creation. Azotic and powerful. Volatile and poisonous.

"Oh, Frehley," his love said. "It's so beautiful. It's quicksilver! How did you make it?"

Quicksilver dissolved every metal. Changed them into an amalgam. All except one.

"I was able to bind it. Then I went to a blacksmith. Simple enough," Frehley said.

"But isn't it forbidden?" Gina asked.

She was just a peasant girl. Not much younger than Frehley, truth be told. Auburn hair. Brown eyes. Freckles across the bridge of her nose. Full lips. Sharp chin. And a mind as bright as her smile. A heart as deep as her brown eyes.

"Aren't you worth it?" he asked her.

She wouldn't relent, "But isn't it dangerous?"

"It obeys the one who holds it. It can only be given by consent. Otherwise, it is useless," Frehley said. "It's worth it."

Frehley had kissed other girls. Even chased some women. A hug. A kiss. Some sweet nothings. All empty promises. All just a fleeting game.

But this was the real thing.

Rare and true.

Frehley knew what to do when a rare thing came along.

He was just a Royal Huntsman. Part of the company that managed the Royal Forest under the command of the Black Watch who was under the authority of the Judge's Son until the princess, the last of her line of ruling Regents, could ascend the throne and uphold the Law, truth, and justice.

Word had it that princess wasn't much younger than Frehley himself. But that she was ugly as a dog. Queen she might become but good luck trying to marry her off. Frehley did not think that any man could justify throwing away his future love and happiness to share in wealth and power that would be in name only and all for a woman that he not only couldn't love but couldn't stand to look in the face.

Wealth and power did not matter to Frehley. Only hunting. The forest was his true home. He lived there. It provided for him. That was where he wanted to be buried, the Judge willing.

Or so he had thought until the day he had met the peasant girl while angling in his favorite fishing hole beside the Mighty Oak. It was rumored to be the oldest tree in the forest. Tall and broad. Massive branches spread out covered with moss and lichen, like the cloak of a sage giving shelter and hope. It was a constant sentinel of the forest.

The girl said her name was Gina. And that she admired the way he fished.

Frehley said if she liked the way that he fished then she should watch him hunt.

Gina asked what kind of hunting did he do well? And Frehley said all of it: stag, boar, rabbit, and even bear. She said she wanted to watch him do it all. And Frehley had said there was no need to watch when he could teach her and they could become hunting companions.

She agreed. And planned a rendezvous with him. At this same great oak deep in the Royal Forest.

One meeting had led to another.

One animal caught had led to another.

Until Frehley realized that it was he who was being chased into a sweet trap.

He wanted Gina and him to pledge their love to each other and then to be married. But it would take three year's wages to buy just a small bar of silver and five years wages just to buy an ounce of gold and that with permission only from the Black Watch. There would be trouble in finding a blacksmith capable of crafting either into a ring, again for the right price.

Instead, he bought several chains from a second-hand stall and had a silversmith re-forge them into a certain length of chain. He desired neither gold nor silver. His love was greater and demanded even a greater metal for a one of a kind token.

The other hunters in the Company teased Frehley. That love and marriage was a trap for life and the only way out was to gnaw off his leg. Or that a wild wolf wasn't meant to be collared like a house dog. And that he smelled like bear spoor and the only way any girl would get close to him would be to hang bacon around his neck.

Then they told him it was a curse for Royal Hunters to get married. But it was a better life being recruited for the Black Watch to live in a land of ice and twilight inside a stone Keep in the middle of Glacier Mountains. Only men who couldn't find love joined the Black Watch to protect the Sepulcher of the Son and guard Ice Prison. It was an exile to the farthest corner of the Realm. The loneliest place in the world for the most hopeless of men who had no future.

Frehley paid the older hunters no mind. They were rough and coarse. With hard bark and leathered necks. Being the youngest hunter, they always teased him about something. Frehley lived only to hunt and he meant to exceed everyone else in the company by might and deed.

But he shuddered at the thought of being underground or surrounded by stone walls. Frehley feared that trap the worst. If stuck in a cage or small room and away from the open sky and woods then he might just gnaw his leg off to escape. Who would want to join the Black Watch? One wouldn't just be guarding the Dark Riders; they would be sharing their prison. Wouldn't a soldier have to turn to ice or stone in their heart, too, just to bear the misery?

His heart lay with the Forest. And with Gina. Hadn't he met her in the heart of the Forest? At the Mighty Oak?

Why couldn't they spend the rest of their life there? Who was there to say otherwise?

He was a Royal Hunter and she was a peasant. All Gina had to do was ask her parents and all Frehley had to do was get the permission of the other Royal Huntsmen.

Under a full moon at midnight, he had given Gina a secret gift at the Mighty Oak. One that they could share.

"The chain is so long," Gina said. She held the double heart necklace in her palm with the chain cascading down. The hearts were an open design. Two clasped together. Interlocked in symmetry. A perfect match. True and sure.

"It's a double chain," Frehley said. "Here. Let me show you."

He unclasped the two hearts and then showed her the double clasp locks on the chain. Undoing one clasp, he made a second necklace from the first. Which he then slipped over her head.

The second necklace he slipped over his.

"Who-who cooks for you?" the owl called out again above their heads.

"Wise old owl," Gina said.

Something buzzed by. Large enough to hover near Frehley's head. An insect.

He waved it away. He wasn't going to be bothered by anything unwarranted. So the insect decided to investigate Gina.

She shooed at it and jumped back. "Is that a wasp?"

Frehley knocked the insect away. "No, it's just a bee."

Gina sighed. "Good. I'm allergic to wasps."

They held up each other's heart necklace in their hands.

"Gina, just like this necklace, there are two hearts. But now there's one heartbeat," Frehley said.

Gina looked into Frehley's eyes and saw herself there with tears sliding down the cheek of her reflection. The glowing silver heart in her palm. Only her reflection was dressed differently. She had no habit to cover her head. Instead her auburn hair was pulled back at the neck. And she wore copious amounts of rouge and her lips were painted red. In place of a peasant's smock, she wore a strange tunic. One with a red doublet and short black sleeves. There was a metal pin on her chest engraved with the strange word REGGIE.

A piece of a mystery. A wisp of a dream. An echo from a strange place.

"Frehley," Gina said. "You are in my heart and always will be."

"Say it with me, Gina," Frehley said. "Two hearts. One heartbeat."

"Two hearts. One heartbeat," Gina said.

And with their vows made, their world came apart.

It shook the foundations of the Castle.

It shorn the foliage from the Royal Forest.

It blotted out the Law.

The moon stayed full and huge.

Blocking the coming day.

Eclipsing the sun and the Light.

Shining a Lesser Light. Beginning a season of night.

Bringing an ancient evil. A bane needing blood. And causing death to rise.

The Black Watch betrayed their duty and let out the Darkness they were to guard.

The people forgot the Law and spurned gold.

The wise old owl flapped away leaving the Realm behind.

***

OUR WORLD

Chapter One: Mom and Dad

"Who-who cooks for you?"

Chayse Leftwich heard someone say it as plain as day, though it was night.

It hadn't come from the TV show she was watching--*Chasing the Grail*—where Templar knights plotted with and against the Pope and King Philip of France and each other for a ceramic cup that Jesus once used for some supper.

And it hadn't come from her twin brother's phone. Reed Leftwich played his Candy Man game app with all types of sweet-shop and baking ovens sounds. And not one of them had made that "who."

Then the voice came again: "Who-who cooks for you?"

It was coming from outside their house. A rental in Raccoon Springs Village on a street full of them—three bedrooms, a bath and a half, an open kitchen and living room, a sky-light, and a carport. Every house in the neighborhood a slight variation of the same conformity.

Someone was outside the house.

Someone bad, worse, or the worst. Bad would be some crack-head just escaped out from Standing Rock Prison looking for a house to knock over to score some over the counter cold meds and make more meth before they got arrested again. Or worse, some hater-terrorist looking for a soft target: twin twelve-year-old kids trapped alone in a house in the middle of a sleepy retirement community in the heart of the rural Ozarks. Or the worst, which Chayse could only imagine as a huge dark figure trying to grab her.

Why were there so many evil people in the world? Chayse didn't know. She only knew from all of the Newsfeed updates coming across her phone that the world was falling apart.

Dad Leftwich used to say if a thief could find him out here in the woods then there were piles of stuff that the thief could have for free. He liked to say, "You can't run from your problems. They'll just run after you."

He was one to talk. He was never in a rush to run anywhere. Like to work, for instance.

Chayse looked at the wall clock. It read (because it couldn't say anything) nine-forty-seven.

Mom Leftwich wouldn't be home for another hour.

And Dad wasn't ever coming home again.

Chayse used the remote to pause her favorite Wednesday night cable show.

Sure enough. The voice called out again.

"Who-who cooks for you?"

It was loud enough for Reed to look up from his phone. The game continuing with its happy music and church bells and register chuh-chings.

"God bless my time!" Reed said. That was as near as Mom would ever let him get to straight-up cursing. Although, what Dad could say was far worse and more colorful. "Who is that, Sissy?"

"That's what they're asking us," Chayse said.

"It's a robber!" Reed said jumping up. "I'll get the gun."

"What do we got that they'd want to rob?" Chayse said. "Sit back down!"   "Then its human traffickers!" Reed said. "They'll kidnap us and sell us into child labor."

Chayse paused. She hadn't thought of that. It had been trending just yesterday on her news feed. "No. They like to ambush people in parking lots."

"Then it's the neighbors. Playing a prank," Reed said and set his phone down. "I'll get the gun."

"No, you won't neither. The Carrs are both over seventy. And Mr. Carr only has one leg. So it can't be them," Chayse said.

They both moved towards the front door.

Whoever it was had gone silent.

As they approached the door there came a scuffling. Something brushing against the side of the house. Reed tried to interpret the noise.

"Something is climbing on the roof," he said.

That fit with the escaped crack-head tweaking out of their mind scenario. A crack-head was as dangerous as a rabid dog. Maybe Reed should go get the gun. Better to shoot first and ask questions later with a crack-head.

She pulled back the edge of the front curtain window.

There was no one to be seen.

The carport was empty. The dark shiny oil and water stains on the driveway needing a refill whenever Mom would pull in with her Altima.

Chayse heard the back door slide open. Reed was already halfway out onto the back porch. "Reed, no! Wait for Mom to get home!"

"What's she gonna do? Yell at 'em?" Reed shot back. "Maybe we can sneak up on them. Scare them off!"

There was no stopping him once he set his mind to something. It was worse when he got his hands on something. "Well, hold on!" Chayse said. She rushed back into the kitchen to rifle through a counter drawer to pull out a LED flashlight buried under batteries and cords.

Then she hurried up behind her brother as they stepped across the old wood porch in their stocking feet. The porch hadn't been stained in years. Paint peeling and boards splintering. It creaked loud enough to let whoever it was know they were outside, too.

Reed was grateful Chayse had brought the flashlight. She shined a path through the debris. Like her play stove with all its scattered accessories or his muddy dirt bike with its missing front wheel and rusting detached chain. And Mom's broken flower pots. Half filled with water and choked with dead leaves.

Chayse was afraid but glad she wasn't alone. Her twin brother Reed was by her side. And had been all her life except for the three minutes when she had arrived first on the delivery table.

She was mad at Dad for not being here. Now they had to do his job.

Reed was too angry to be afraid. This was Mom's fault. She was the one who'd chased Dad away and stayed gone at work all the time.

Chayse remembered Mom complaining that Dad never worked enough to pay for what they needed. Reed remembered Dad saying Mom wanted to spend their money even before they got paid.

Reed had seen his parents fight so often he could recite their arguments word for word off the top of his head. Mom would yell at Dad for being gone all weekend hunting with his old school friend, Buddy instead of his family. Dad said hunting put meat on the table. Mom said hunting didn't pay the bills.

Chayse remembered the day Mom threw Dad out. All he did was complain. That Mom had been happy when they were renting a trailer from Buddy. That she wanted a baby and they'd gotten twins which Dad was fine with because he said he loved his kids. But all the trouble started when Mom had made them move out. And ever since, they'd been hounded with shut off notices and collectors wherever they moved.

Dad picked up his keys to his Chevy Off-Road Z and said he was tired of screaming kids and Mom yelling at him so he was going out for beer and cigarettes. Mom told him that having a family took money and that if he wasn't willing to work to help his own family then not for him to bother coming back.

So Dad left and he'd been gone ever since.

Goodbye and good riddance Mom said.

And that was that.

Reed remembered it, too. But not the same way. Whatever Dad did wasn't good enough for Mom. Dad worked hard at his job and he wanted to spend time with Buddy. Dad shouldn't have to give Mom all his money and Mom shouldn't tell Dad that he couldn't have any friends.

One day Mom had drawn a line across the trailer kitchen floor. She'd used a red magic marker on the linoleum to give Dad an ultimatum: he could stay and do what she said or he could leave and do what he wanted.

Not much of a choice. So Dad had left. Because Mom was being so impossible.

But he still was Reed's hero.

And the minute he'd walked out that door, Mom had started in on Reed. Talking about Dad like he was a piece of dog crap.

Now it was Reed who would catch the heat for every little thing while Chayse got away with every other thing. Reed would square up at Mom and say, "Why don't you yell at me some more? What are you gonna do? Draw another red line?"

But that just Mom made mad. And she would smack Reed. Or chase after him.

Chayse remembered a time when both Mom and Dad used to put on their twin silver heart necklaces with their open designs and clasps so one could fit inside the other first thing in the morning and kiss each other's heart necklace and then kiss each other. "Two hearts, one heartbeat," they would say before they left the trailer to go to their jobs.

Now when Chayse watched Mom get ready for work--after she'd showered, put on her make-up, dressed in her KFC uniform with the black tunic and red sleeves and the crew member badge that read: REGGIE on her chest--slipping on the heart necklace was the last thing she did.

To Chayse, Mom had aged ten years since Dad had walked out. Working two jobs, getting mad all the time, crying herself to sleep.

Reed thought Dad hadn't changed a lick since Mom had thrown him out. Still tall and lean. Flashing his wicked smile and sticking out his chin. Still running with Buddy, his best friend since high school. The man was a biggun. Taller than Dad and as round as a barrel.

Buddy could pick up both twins with one arm and liked to bend a roofing nail while holding it with his teeth. Except he never said much beyond a grunt or mumble and pointed at things with his meaty paws.

Chayse never could figure out why Dad wanted to hang out with Buddy rather than his kids. Reed couldn't wait until he was old enough to do everything Dad did with Buddy.

Reed stepped ahead of Chayse so that she had to shine the flashlight around them both. They followed the beam of light off the porch and around the corner of the house and through the carport. Chayse shut off the flashlight.

Whoever it was making all the noise had gone silent now.

Stopping next to the drain spout at the edge of the house, Reed turned to his sister. "I'll jump out and scare him. Then you shine a light on him."

"Then he'll just shoot us," Chayse said.

"Crack-heads don't carry guns. They pawn everything just to get more crack," Reed said.

"What happens if he comes after us?" Chayse asked.

"Don't show him you're scared and he'll back down. That's what Dad always says," Reed said.

Chayse took a breath and turned the flashlight back on. Then she shone it around the corner across the front porch. Both of them peered around the drain spout.

Something, not someone, was there.

Perched on the brick trim, a thing of brown feathers and down with a squat torso and no neck. The thing's head turned one hundred and eighty degrees around and faced them. Two round eyes like yellow moons reflecting the blue LED flashlight back at them.

"Who-who cooks for you?" asked the something.

The twins were taken with wonder.

"What is it?" Chayse asked.

"It's a barn owl," Reed said.

The owl kept an eye on them. Sizing them up. While the twins could feed a flock of vultures, they were too big for a midnight snack for the owl.

"What's it doing on our house?" Chayse asked.

"They only come out at night. To hunt. Mice. Rabbits. Squirrels. They swallow them whole and throw up their fur and bones," Reed said fascinated by the predator's process.

"That's so gross," Chayse said.

"Yeah, well, I've seen you throw up Fruit Loops," Reed said.

The owl decided it wasn't going to get fed sitting on the edge of the Leftwich's house. So it flapped off into the dark night. Both the twins felt an ancient fear: to cover their heads from talons clutching at them from above.

Every house in Raccoon Springs Village had a berm or wood lot beside it. Someone had laid out the roads by tying torches to foxes' tails before turning them loose to run over the hollers and through the woods. The roads crisscrossed and switchbacked each other becoming a spider web of drives and traces and circles.

It was easy to get lost in the Village, more so at night. The bends in the roads gave a sense of isolation and the power company made owners pay for their own street lights which meant there weren't many street lights on. Even if a crack-head psycho wanted to perpetrate some terror in their neck of the woods he'd have to find them first.

Chayse had gotten herself all worked up over nothing.

"Stupid owl," she said.

The twins went back inside. To wait out the last forty-five minutes until Mom came home. Killing the time with cable DVR and digital phone apps.

About thirty minutes later they could hear a car coming down their road. See headlights—twin high beams burning fusion in a vacuum--along the curve of the road. The car slowed in front of their driveway.

"Bubba! Mom's home!"Chayse said. She always got excited when Mom came home.

"She's early," Reed frowned. He tightened up whenever Mom got home.

It didn't pull into the carport. Instead parking halfway up the driveway. Mom never did that.

Mom drove a four-door Altima with a noisy muffler. This was bigger than an SUV with an engine that idled like a diesel. Along with the high beams on came floodlights that blinded them through the front window's flimsy curtain.

Chayse tightened up. It wasn't Mom's car. It wasn't even Mom.

"Is that Mom, Sissy?" Reed whined and slid off the couch. Mom didn't like him playing games all night on the couch. And truth be told, Reed sometimes did just to annoy her because no matter what he did, Mom would find something wrong.

The doorbell rang.

It couldn't have been Mom.

Not in a thousand years.

Everything about this late-night arrival was wrong.

Neither Chayse nor Reed wanted to open the door. They did not who was out there or what they wanted. But the twins were going to open the door anyway.

If Mom would have been there she would have asked the twins if they were stupid and upon replying they weren't then Mom would have said something like would they open the door late at night for some strangers in an SUV.

But Mom wasn't there.

So they opened the door.

There stood a tall and lean lady in a grey skirt, high heels, and a fuzzy pink sweater blouse which held a large badge. With twig arms and a stick neck. Her head like an upside-down bottle. Her grayish face had pinched lips that gave a hint of serpentine fangs. Triangle glasses rested on a beak nose. Dull silver hair pulled back into a tight bun against her neck.

Chayse noted the woman looked too young to have gone grey. To Reed, she looked like an albino, except her eyes didn't have white irises. They were yellow—like the owl.

The twins felt the urge to run and hide in a closet. Or scurry and scamper like mice before a great owl. Standing before the woman in her imperious presence outlined by the SUV's high beams was like standing before some deity who demanded total obeyance.

The twins were so startled that they forgot their own names.

"Chayse Leftwich?" the woman asked looking down at her phone and then to Chayse. Then she looked down at her phone again and over to Reed who stood just behind his sister. "Reed Leftwich?" the woman asked anew.

Neither Chayse nor Reed had ever seen this strange-looking woman before in their lives. And they didn't want to be looking at her now. She seemed a cold stone. An impassable object. An impossible relic.

The third time the woman asked, "Is Regina Leftwich home?"

Chayse gave her phone a cursory look. It was as near as big as a mini-tablet. Hard to hide the screen. It showed a portrait of Mom, probably one of her mug shots, along with lines of data. The woman was flicking through pdfs on the whole family with her thumbs.

Reed read the woman's badge pinned on her ugly fuzzy sweater. It bore her likeness: face and shoulders in an even more unflattering pose. Her name: ELSIE CRUTCH. And her title: CASA DIRECTOR. And below that: COURT APPOINTED SERVICES ADVOCATE.

"Ree-jean-nuh?" Reed asked. He looked at his sister. "We don't know any Ree-jean-nuh do we, sis?"

"You very well know who I mean so you might as well tell me," the mean woman snapped. "Is your mom at home? Yes or no?"

Chayse's next impulse was to shut the door. An image of her brother throwing his weight against the door rode along with the twitching in her hands and legs to do something. But she just stood there in her tracks.

The tall woman's head seemed to slink down towards them. Was her neck bending? Did the pupils in her eyes become oval slits?

Would Miss Crutch slither inside to wrap herself around her and Bubba, unhinge her jaws and swallow them whole—one after the other until there were two distinct bulges between her ribs.

"I am Miss Crutch, court liaison and child advocate. I am your friend. Tell your brother to step back so I can come in," the woman said.

Chayse heard the woman's voice. The words were simple. Spoken in plain English. But they began to stretch and curve through the air. There was something beneath them. Twisting trails in authority supreme. Heavy fetters in their tone. Encircling the twins' heads like ghoulish whispers. Caressing their auricles with a cold chill. Reverberations sliding down their ear canals.

What Miss Crutch had said was one thing but what the twins heard was something else: *Stupid children, be afraid. Bow down and serve me. Both of you shall be in my thrall.*

Chayse didn't want to speak but she heard herself say, "Reed, step back so Miss Crutch can come in." She couldn't believe she was listening to this strange woman.

Reed knew she was lying. She was after something. There was no way he was going to be friends with this woman.

There was no way Reed could trust her.

But there was no way to stop her, either.

So Reed stepped back and his hand reached out to pull the door open even wider, though he'd rather not.

Someone else spoke. Two people, at the same time. Both echoing the same sentence: "Little pigs, let us in."

What the twins thought were dark pillars of the porch outlined in the SUV's high beams until two figures stepped forward.

Two men. A big and hairy duo. Two heads with dark hair. Two pairs of slacks and black dress shoes and two polo shirts between them. And each holding a similar badge like Miss Crutch's.

Except both men looked the same as the other with the same photo on their badge.

Chayse and Reed were twins, but they were fraternal twins. Different zygotes conceived at the same time. Different fetuses made of the same stuff sharing the same womb.

But these were identical twins. Twins of evil. Double trouble.

The spell snapped and Chayse came to her full senses.

"Run, Reed, run!" she shouted and tried to slam the door.

But Miss Crutch put a foot across the threshold. Having gained an inch inside their home, she pushed her lean frame against the door. Now Chayse couldn't close the door.

Reed gave a battle cry and ran against the door. It swept Miss Crutch from the threshold and closed tight against the doorjamb. They had shut the court liaison out.

Chayse gave a cheer.

"Children, let me in," Miss Elsie Crutch said with kerosene in her breath. Then she said, "Nic. Vic."

She must have been talking to the twin agents who had come with her. Because they howled against the SUV's twin burning moons pouring into the Leftwichs' window.

Both twins collapsed on the floor with their backs to the door.

"Not by the hair on my chinny-chin-chin!" Reed laughed.

Now all the twins had to do was wait until Mom got home and tell her the CASA people had tried to come into their home illegally—Mom would know what to do.

Chayse wanted to laugh, too. Until the doorknob began to turn--she had forgotten to lock the front door!

Instead, she cut off Reed's laugh with a scream, "Reed, quick! Lock the door!"

Her twin couldn't reach the lock-in time. The door opened up. Sweeping the twins away like a bunched up rug.

In burst the other twins. Scooping up the Leftwich kids in their burly arms. Locking them against their chest.

"We huffed and we puffed," said the first, whose name tag read: NIC CRAW. AGENT. COURT APPOINTED SERVICES ADVOCATE.

"And we blew your house down!" said the second whose name tag read: VIC CRAW. AGENT. COURT APPOINTED SERVICES ADVOCATE.

The twins scratched and clawed and kicked and screamed but the brawny men laughed at their helplessness.

"You can't take us! We haven't done anything wrong!" Reed cried.

"Your mother has abandoned you and put your welfare in danger," Miss Crutch said.

"Mom works too much to get into trouble!" Chayse argued.

"That, my children, is stone cold abandonment," Miss Crutch smirked. "I'll see that you are taken care of."

How many times had Mom said to never answer the teachers or counselors or the school nurse or even the neighbors whenever they would ask, "Where is your Mom?" "When's she coming home?" "When did you eat last?" "How long have you had that scratch?" "When was the last time you had a bath?" "Does your mom yell at you often?" "How does she punish you?" and the one Reed most dreaded, "Is your dad still in jail?"

Chayse hadn't said a word to anyone. And surely Reed hadn't told anyone anything since he thought most adults didn't even care to listen to him.

But someone had sure said something to bring this truck down on them.

Truth be told, it'd been coming for years. Since Dad had left, Mom had moved them more times than the twins could count. One step ahead of shut off notices or in the middle in the night before the sheriff was due to show up or changing schools before they could file a FINS.

The cycle had gone on and on for years. Now they were caught. And neither Mom nor Dad was home to protect them.

"Mom and Dad aren't gonna stand for this! This is kidnapping! You can't make us go with you!" Chayse argued even though the CASA twins, Nic and Vic, had already proven otherwise.

"Your parents will be declared unfit. The State will have to finish their job. I represent the State. You are under my authority," Miss Crutch said. Then she snapped her fingers. "Take them away!"

First, they had lost their Dad.

Now they would lose their Mom.

***

Chapter Two: Guardians and Offenders

The next time the twins saw their Mom was at the FINS hearing. Mom couldn't even afford a lawyer. She had to represent herself.

The court had appointed the twins their own lawyer. When the twins asked why they had one but Mom didn't the lawyer told them it was "because you're both minors. So, I'm here to make sure the full letter of the law regarding the welfare and endangerment to minorsis followed."

"But we're not in any danger," the twins said.

"Let the court decide that," the lawyer said.

He was younger than Dad. His shirt barely tucked in over his belly. Beefy hammocks stretching his grey corduroy pants. Long curly hair spilled over his shoulders. With a scraggly beard bushy in some places and bare in others. He looked more like an old West Marshall dressed for court with his corduroy jacket and elbow patches and a square cloth knit tie.

There was a badge on his jacket lapel. It read: LAWYER AD LITEM, ARKANSAS STATE JURISDICTION DISTRICT THREE, ALEXANDER KYLER.

"What's a minor?" Reed Leftwichasked his sister.

"I don't know. I guess we are," ChayseLeftwichsaid. So she asked her theirlawyer ad litem. "How old do you have to be before you don't need a lawyer?"

"You will always need a lawyer in court," the lawyer ad litem growled. "But when you're eighteen you can stand for yourself. Though, I wouldn't recommend it."

"Why eighteen?" Chayse asked.

"The court says that when you turn eighteen, you become an adult. Ready or not. You are responsible for yourself and you will answer for what you do," Lawyer Alexander Kyler said. "For instance, your mom is responsible for causing us to be here today."

"No she's not," Reed said. "It's that Crutch woman."

He pointed her out. Miss Elsie Crutch sat coiled on the left side of the courtroom. Just behind the table where Lawyer Kyler had set his ad litembriefcase. She wore a jacket and pantsuits,no belt.

Her dull silver hair piled on top of her head like a pile of moss. Her beaky nose and small eyes stood out from her pasty skin. A twisted chain clung around her neck from which her thick glasses dangled.

But Reed could see the links of another necklace Miss Crutch kept hidden under her blouse.

"And she had those two kidnap us," Chayse said.

She pointed out the twin CASA agents sitting beside her in dress slacks and button shirts. Each with scrubbed faces and dual badges. Like two faithful bulldogs on short leashes.

Behind the CASA crew sat another couple. A man and woman dressed in the same name brand jeans and button shirts. Both had short hair spiked with gel. Looking law-abiding and blameless, they weighed up Mom and the twins with hard glances and found them all wanting.

At the front of the other aisle, Mom stood at the defendants' table. It was her day to work at her second job at the motel because she had on her grey striped maid's outfit. Chayse could see the chain of her heart necklace along with another necklace. Both close to her heart under her tunic.

Thanks to Miss Crutch's watchful eye, Mom couldn't talk to them so she blew them each a kiss and touched her heart with a finger and then pointed to the sky. That was Mom's signal to remind them that she loved them and that God loved them.Reed had always believed in God and that it was the people who didn't who did the mean things in the world. Chayse wondered what kind of god would allow some government agency to take kids away from their own mother?

"If we aren't on trial, why do we have a lawyer and Mom doesn't?" Chayse asked.

"She must be in bad trouble," Reed said.

"The judge will straighten this out. Then we can all go home, bub," Chayse said.

The lawyer bent down to look them in the eye. Much the same as Miss Crutch had the first time they had met her. "I'm the one who tells the judge what to do. So don't tick me off."

The twins doubted Lawyer Kyler had any kids of his own. Or even liked kids. Just their being born caused trouble because someone had to make sure they were safe as milk—except he made the milk sour.

As much as Reed was angry at Mom, he wanted to grab his twin sister and rally round their Mom. Yes, she was mean to him. Yes, Chayse was her favorite. But what had she done to get brought to court?

"She threw your Dad out of the house like some old dog," Lawyer Kyler said looking down at him.

Reed blinked again. Lawyer Kyler was walking to the other side of the courtroom. So he couldn't have spoken to him just now.

He needed Dad. More than his sister beside him. More than Mom's hugs. He wanted Dad to come through the metal detector at the courtroom door and take him and Chayse and even Mom back down the steps to the main hallway and outside across the Courthouse Green. Away to freedom.

Everyone was waiting for Court to start.

And before it started, the judge had to come out.

Against the wall between two doors,with one the entrance to the courtroom through the metal detector and the second door marked JUDGE'S CHAMBERS on the other, stood a tall strong man in a police uniform.He had thick blond hair parted down the middle and a burly brown mustachereaching down each side of his mouth. Even without a weapon, he looked like he would have no trouble keeping the peace.

Keeping her eyes on Mom, Miss Crutch nodded to Kyler and the lawyer ad litem summoned the police officer by hooking his forefinger.

"Bailiff," Kyler commanded. The bailiff had to obey. He pushed his hulk off the wall and marched over."Take the twins to the jury box. Make sure their mom doesn't talk to them."

Mom was just a few feet away. But now she wasn't allowed to be near the twins. Why was it illegal to be around her?

First Dad and now Mom, Chayse thought. *Get me out of this family.*

The bailiff gave the lawyer ad litem a long look. As if respecting the position of authority rather than the one giving the commands.   But to the twins, he smiled like an old friend. "Follow me, you two. It will all work out."

Reed was confused. He wanted to be with Dad. Could the Bailiff make that happen?

Chayse didn't believe the bailiff. She wanted a real home. With loving parents.

The twins looked at the small bronze shield hanging over the man's blue left pocket. It was a star above lettering that read: Fade County Sheriff's Department. On the right side was of the blue tunic was a white label that read Mike Marler.

"Ok, Mike," Reed said and saluted.

"Call me Big Mike," the Bailiff laughed. He led the twins to the jury box on the opposite of the courtroom. Keeping himself between the twins and Mom as they passed. She folded her arms over her chest as shewatched them pass holding her hurt back.

The jury box was just two rows of chairssort of like a movie theater. Reed liked that. He could see everyone in the courtroom. Chayse thought it was like watching a reality show.

Big Mike walked back to the other side of the courtroom and stood erect by the door to the Judge's Chambers. "Hear ye, hear ye!" he called out. "Family In Need of Services Court for Arkansas District Three is now in session. The honorable Judge Hart presiding. All rise."

Everyone stood up. Though, Miss Elsie Crutch was the last one out of her seat.

Judge Hart came in on cue from out of his chamber door.Graceful but not very tall.Slim build under his flowing black robe.Parted hair going gray.A trimmed goatee under a large nose. Not handsome, but respectful and regal.

Judge Hartcarried a black book tucked under the fold of his robed arm. Taking his seat on the bench he took up the gavel. Looking over everyone present in his courtroom, he weighed them but did not find them wanting.

Then the judge rapped the gavel twice.

"Be seated," Mike barked.

Just as everyone was sitting down, two men came in late. One had greasy hair and a hulking frame bulging out of stained jeans and a dirty sleeveless blue mechanic's shirt. The patch above his heart read ALBERT.

The second man seemed small next to his sidekick. He wore a new light blue Western shirt with dark jeans and clean cowboy boots.

His eyes laughed as he smiled at the twins.The twins hadn't seen him in a month of Sundays. The man might or might not have a working phone. Might or might not have a job.

Reed was excited. Maybe Officer Mike had been right. The judge was sure to let him go home with this man. He leaned over to Chayse, "It's Uncle Buddy."

"And dear old Dad," Chayse said using the same tone in her voice that Mom had whenever she talked about Dad.

"I'm gonna ask the judge to let me go home with Dad, Sissy," Reed said.

"No, bub," Chayse snapped. "He'll just leave us again."

"I miss him," Reed said.

"Well, I don't miss him," Chayse said. Mom was right. Dad couldn't go anywhere without Buddy.

"Why?" Reed asked.

"Because he doesn't miss us," Chayse said.

The only other person in the courtroom was a young clean-cut man who sat at cubicle just below the Judge's bench and typed everything that everyone said. Now everyone was going to know everything about the Leftwichfamily.

Chayse wanted to be somewhere else. Anywhere but here. She was embarrassed to be a Leftwich.

Judge Hart shuffled through some manila folders. "Well, we've just the one case on the docket for today, so Reporter, if you will."

"Arkansas District Three, Fade Court, Family In Needs of Service Case Number Two-one-one-two-see-ex-one. Department of Health and Services Children Division versus Regina Leftwich," the Reporter said, "in the investigation under the auspices of Elsie Crutch, Court Appointed Service Agent, of the maltreatment and neglect against the minors Chayse Reese Leftwich and Reed Chase Leftwichand their disposition of care as to be rendered by the authority and jurisdiction of this court."

Judge Hart nodded.

Elsie Crutch narrowed her eyes at their Mom.

Mom blinked and gulped.

Dad just sat and stared. Having been in court often he knew enough not to speak until spoken to. This might be the first time he wasn't in the hot seat.

Judge Hart cleared his throat and opened the black book that he had carried up to the seat. A passage had been bookmarked. "Before we begin, let us remember who is the true author of justice. When justice is done right and not perverted, the righteous are never afraid but evildoers are always afraid. Because they don't understand what justice truly is. Seek the Lord and you will understand."

He nodded and closed the book. Both Chayse and Reed guessed it was a Bible. Grandma had given one to their mom. Sometimes, late at night after the twins had gone to bed, they could hear her mom sobbing and whispering to someone: Reed asked what she was doing and Chayse said that mom was reading from the Bible like Grandma did.

Only Mom had never read the Bible with them or to them. And they had never seen Dad go near one.

Miss Crutch rolled her eyes and coughed behind her hand.

Judge Hart looked over the edges of his glasses. "You have some criticism against me using the Word?"

"This country was founded on the separation of church and state. A judge has no more right to read from a Bible than a preacher does making laws," she said.

Judge Hart squared his jaw and pointed his finger straight out at the CASA agent. "This is still my court. And in my court, God rules. Only he is sovereign. Only he appoints authority. Over me and you," Judge Hart said.

Miss Clutch raised her chin as if to spit. "One day I'm going to take that book away from you and kick you off the bench! It's illegal for you to wave it around in court or to read from it. Just because it's your courtroom doesn't mean you get to do what you think is right!"

"True, it is my court. But you're wrong, just because it IS my court does NOT mean I get do what I think is right. This book makes sure I do what I KNOW is right. Heaven help us if you ever ran this court because you would ONLY do what YOU thought was right. Which would be one wrong after another.

"It's like this: when the righteous rule, people have joy but the wicked rule, people are miserable.

"Now one more outburst from you and I'll have the bailiff remove you from my courtroom. Or maybe a contempt of court charge with a fine of one thousand dollars would be more to your pleasure.

"I know it would be to mine."

Miss Clutch swallowed bile and held her tongue. She sat ready and waiting. Like a coiled snake.

"Mr. Kyler, let us hear from you," Judge Hart said.

"Your honor, this is a serious case of neglect," Kyler began. "The mother, Regina Leftwich, has had numerous complaints made to the CASA agent by her neighbors against her lack of care. And even her ex-husband, who I think is here in attendance…" Kyler surveyed the courtroom. Their Dad wasn't hard to miss. Even as he tried to hide in Uncle Buddy's shadow. "Yes, there he is. Stand up, please, Mr. Leftwich. Your honor, that is Mr. FrederickLeftwich."

Dad stood up. Still dwarfed by Uncle Buddy's hulk.

Judge Hart held up his hand to stop Dad. "No need, Mr. Kyler. I am well acquainted with Mr. FrederickLeftwich and his companion, Albert Chowder. Sit back down."

Dad sat back down. He caught the eyes of the twins and winked. In trouble or out of trouble, Dad never quit smiling.

Reed wanted to be like that. To let trouble just roll off your back. "Nobody can make you do nothin' you don't wanna do," Dad would say time and time again.

Chayse imagined Dad said it everytime Buddy bailed him out of jail. Mom used to say Dad was the oldest child in the house.

"Your honor, I submit these complaints as evidence," Kyler said and held out a manila folder as if it had damning evidence against Mom to label her an evil lawbreaker.

Judge Hart beckoned Kyler to approach with a flat handwave like he wanted the folder yesterday. The lawyer ad litem came forward and stood on his tiptoes to hand up the folder to the judge. Judge Hart opened it and scanned each page.

Then he addressed Mom. "Mrs. Leftwich, these are severe allegations of neglect. You should have your own counsel present. Have you decided to forgo that counsel?"

"Your honor, I don't even know what the allegations are. I came home from my second job and found the twins had been taken and this letter left in their place," Mom said and held out a crumpled letter that she had tried to smooth back out.

Lawyer Kyler pounced. "Your honor, Mrs. Leftwich said it herself: she came home late from her second job not knowing anything about the whereabouts or welfare of her two children since she had left for work at six in the morning. The report shows this is what usually happens in the Leftwich household. As you can see from Mr. Leftwich's testimony if you would care to question him."

Judge Hart sighed, "I take it that Mr. Leftwich does not see the children?"

"No, your honor," Mom said.

"Or contribute to their welfare?" he asked again.

"No, your honor," Mom said.

"Or return your calls or requests?" he asked once more.

"I stopped calling him or requesting anything from him a long time ago," Mom said.

"Then Mr. Kyler, the father would be considered a hostile witness and himself in contempt of this FINS directive," Judge Hart ruled. "After they divorced they had a custody agreement which both seem to have vacated. I may have to rule a stay on that agreement."

Reed didn't think that sounded good for his wanting to home with Dad today.

Chayse thought Miss Crutch got satisfaction from hearing her parents' dirty laundry.

"Granted your honor, Mr. Dickerson is seldom involved in the household and his knowledge of the children's treatment is limited," Kyler said. "But there are several signed statements from the neighbors that these are daily occurrences. The children not being properly clothed.Or bathed.Or having proper meals.Or attend school regularly. All daily occurrences as I said."

Judge Hart frowned. "I heard you the first time, Mr. Kyler." Then he looked at Mom. "Mrs. Leftwich, you don't deny that you left the children alone for long periods?"

"Your honor, I have to work. I can't afford a babysitter," Mom said. "Having children is expensive. And I'm having to do it all on my own."

"And that they weren't properly cleaned or had proper meals at times?" Judge Hart continued.

"I provide for them. The rent is paid. We always have enough food. They are always clothed. We have running water and electricity--"

Lawyer Kyler pulled out several pink papers. "Your honor, here are shut off notices for both utilities. The defendant has been on a payment plan to get caught up with them. I need not remind you, judge, if there is a lapse and the utilities are shut off, several Health Department regulations will be broken. This is an appalling way to care for any child."

Mom looked as if she had been hit by a rock, made of pink paper.

"Mrs. Leftwich, have the utilities ever been interrupted at your house?" Judge Hart asked.

Mom swallowed.

"I have the exact number of times, right here, your honor," Kyler said and sifted through more paperwork.

"I don't recall asking you, Mr. Kyler," Judge Hart said.

"Once," Mom said and looked down. "Maybe twice."

"Four times to be exact, your honor. One time when they went without water, she had the neighbor put a garden hose through her kitchen window. And another--"

The judge raised his hand in a stopping motion. Lawyer Kyler kept talking lowering his voice until he was silent.

Mom's shoulders slumped. She crossed her arms. And began to shake.

"No, Mom. Fight," Reed said. He wanted to hit Lawyer Kyler. This was his job?

"She's having a panic attack," Chayse said. Mom shuddered and some tears fell. Like she would often be at midnight when she thought the twins were asleep.

"Why do you have to know about everyone's worst possible moments? Is it a crime to fail? What kind of person holds that over another?" Mom asked.

"It's my job to uphold the law," Kyler said.

"No, you just want to punish. And for not doing anything wrong.That's not the law. That's hate," Mom said.

"If you can't provide for your kids, then you shouldn't have had them! Now the government has to provide for them!" Kyler snapped.

"You are both out of order. It is my job to write this order regarding the children's welfare," Judge Hart said. "Mrs. Leftwich, I get it. When was the last time, you took your kids out for ice cream? Or took them to Indian Springs Park?

"Double shifts. Bills. Rent. Groceries. Any medical expenses. That doesn't leave any quality family time or money for outings. No trips. No picnics. No time to even bake cookies.

"I get it. I understand. You didn't mean for things to get like this."

Reed and Chayse couldn't remember doing any of those things in a very long time. They didn't know what families were supposed to do. Other than fuss at each other.

Judge Hart continued. "I'm going to set some goals for you in my order. You need help with supervising the kids. Just a few changes.It'll be tough but it's not impossible.

"Avail yourself to the local services. There are church programs that help with kids after school. Medicaid has sponsored rides to appointments. Even churches that will pay your utilities. Miss Crutch's office has a list. She should have already shared them with you."

Miss Crutch squared her jaw.

"That is part of her job," Judge Hart said looking the woman straight in the eye. "Also, I want you to get a better full-time job, Mrs. Leftwich.One full-time job is better than two or three part-time jobs. Getting a better job means going back to school. I want you to enroll in a community college. You should also apply to the Housing Authority. It'll be cheaper rent and utilities will be included."

"There's a waiting list a mile long and I can't even get on the list because I make too much and I'm not already on WIC or foodstamps," Mom complained. "It's like the government wants me to be totally unable to take care of myself or my kids before they will decide to help. And then all y'all wanna do is tear me down. Y'all act like I'm some sort of bad mom if I try to work and provide for my kids. I don't leave bruises on my kids or tell them I never wanted them.

"Your honor, if the government doesn't like how I raise my kidsmaybe it's the government that needs to change."

Both the twins nodded. Lawyer Kyler looked shocked. Miss Crutch gave a steeled look.

"Your honor, Mrs. Leftwichmistreats her children by not being there. Children need parents who are available," Kyler said. "You have my recommendations."

"And what are those?" Mom asked.

"The children should be placed in foster care," Kyler said.

"No!" the twins screamed.

Mom confronted Lawyer Kyler, "Who's gonna take my kids away? You?"

"For a time, Mrs. Leftwich," Judge Hart. "This is temporary. Until you comply with my goals set down in this order."

Mom shook her head. Trying to wrap her head around the word. "How long is 'temporary?'"

"Until the court liaison has determined you have met the standards I will set down in my order," Judge Hart said as he wrote.

"And who will that be?" Mom asked.

Judge Hart didn't even look up as he wrote out his order. "Miss Crutch."

"She'll never let me get them back," Mom said.

"Do what I order and she will have to," Judge Hart said. "Mr. Kyler, do you have recommendations for any foster parents?"

"Yes, we do," Kyler said.

Miss Crutch stood up. "They are here, Judge Hart. These are the Brazzles."

On cue, the cute couple who hadn't said a blessed word stood up to be recognized.

"Bailiff, bring them forward," Judge Hart said.

***

Chapter Three: Two Hearts and One Heartbeat

Bailiff Mike stepped away from his place along the wall and met the couple as they came down the aisle.

Chayse's looked twice at the couple. Because the first time she didn't believe it. The couple could have stepped out of a commercial. Her parents had crawled out from under a trailer. This couple was respectable. Her parents were embarrassing. The couple looked like they had careers. Her parents couldn't even pay their bills.

Just like that, Chayse wanted this couple to be her parents. This couple would be home after school waiting for her with fresh-baked chocolate chip cookies. On Saturdays, they would wake her earlier and take her to Papoose Park to climb the falls coming off the spillway of Lake Cherokee. And there would be a large Christmas wrapped with fiber optic lights that brushed the ceiling with lots of presents made out to her under its artificial boughs.

Reed blew disgust through his lips. "No way are we gonna live with them. We need to run away the first chance we get."

"You don't even know them. Give them a chance," Chayse argued.

"They will never be our Mom and Dad," Reed said.

"Mom and Dad can't take care of us. These people can. I'll bet they are perfect," Chayse said.

"Perfect isn't real," Reed said.

Chayse realized then and there that she and her twin wanted two different things. How could they come from the same mother? Live in the same house. And be so different?

"Whatever," Chayse said. "I'm not talkin' to you."

"Suits me fine," Reed said. "I like quiet. Like it a heckuva lot."

Reed felt like he'd heard those words before. Where? Of course, that's what Mom and Dad would say to each other whenever they would get into a fight.

How could how two people who hate each other so much have ever been in love? Was that what marriage was about? Having to get the last word in day after day?

Chayse was horrified. How could she have treated her twin like that? She loved Reed more than anyone in the whole world.

Maybe even more than Mom.

First Dad had let her down. He had gone away. And Chayse was still mad at him.

Now the court was making Mom go away. What had she done? Let's see: either she worked too much or she was always tired and cranky. Somehow that had been against the law. Somehow Miss CASA-Crutch and her twin bulldogs and this lawyer ad litem Kyler knew better.

Neither of the twins understood what love or home should be. They only knew what it was it not.

"Judge Hart, these are the Brazzles. Peyton and Shawn. He is an accountant. And she is a grade school teacher. Both have a clean record and impeccable reputations," Kyler said.

"Mr. and Mrs. Brazzle, are you ready to accept responsibility for these children for the next three months?" Judge Hart said.

"We are," said the woman.

Mom, in her maid outfit, gave them a dirty look.

"And you've prepared a safe place for them?" he asked.

"We have," the woman said.

Mom seemed hurt by their claim.

Judge Hart looked from the twins and back to Mom before pursing his lips. He didn't enjoy what he had to do next. While Miss Crutch and Lawyer Kyler wanted to gloat.

"Mrs. Leftwich, due to the overwhelming evidence from the many claims, and under the laws determining the welfare of minors and health of families, I have no choice but to--"

Mom started shaking her head.

"Place your children in the temporary custody of the Brazzles," Judge Hart said.

"For how long? When can I get them back? How often can I see them?" Mom asked as she squeezed her arms against her chest.

Miss Crutch shook her head at Lawyer Kyler.

"Your honor. Granting visitation rights to the mother right away will just confuse the twins and conflict between them and their new guardians. Wouldn't it better to let the children bond with their new foster parents for a time without any detrimental circumstances?" Kyler suggested in a way that tried to rewrite the judge's order without having his authority.

Judge Hart kept on writing his order. "Mrs. Leftwich can talk to her children by phone every night. She is to call by 7 PM. The Brazzles and she will exchange numbers. However, there will be no harassment or threats given by either party."

"Your honor," Miss Crutch ventured.

The judge looked at her from over his written order as if she should not venture.

"I do not think it wise that the children have any contact with their father, Frederick Leftwich, at all during this separation," she said. "Because he is still on probation."

"Granted," Judge Hart said.

A stone dropped on Reed's heart. Why was Miss Crutch so mean? How could she have so much control over his life?

Judge Hart finished writing his order. "Mrs. Leftwich, this custody will be temporary. Work on those goals I've given you. Court will meet again in three months and we will note the progress then.

"Bailiff, you will hand over the twins to the court-appointed guardians." The judge took up his gavel and rapped it once. "Court is adjourned."

The deed was done and just like that the Leftwich twins had lost both their parents.

The government that was supposed to have helped them had made them orphans.

The twins had been made ashamed of their family name.

Bailiff Mike came back to the jury box where the twins sat. Behind him, Mom followed with her home broken. Behind her, Lawyer Kyler was on her heels looking out for more broken laws. Behind him, the Brazzles waited with patient dignity because they would have never dared to disrupt the order of things. Behind them, Miss Crutch narrowed her eyes because she never would have let such a breach of rules happen if she were in charge.

The only smiling face the twins saw was the Bailiff. Warm and real like a sunny day with white clouds. The gold on his badge shining with hope. "Take my hand, children."

Bailiff Mike offered out both his hands. The twins came down from the jury box and each stood to one side of the bailiff and took a hand.

Mom blocked their path. "May I talk to my own children?"

Miss Crutch puffed up. "It's highly irregular."

"No one is going to do anything 'irregular' while I'm here," Bailiff Mike said.

Mom bent down on one knee and slipped off one of her silver chains. Twin silver hearts hung at the end of its tether. Each clasped the other in an open design. Each attached to the silver chain through a loop.

"I want you each to wear one of these," she said and with her fingers unclasped the twin hearts. There was a double lock in the chain which she undid so that each heart became a separate necklace. "I was going to give them to you on your birthday next month. So now they are just an early birthday present."

Mom slipped a heart necklace over each of the twins' heads until it rested snug against their shirts. "Remember, we are in each other's heart. You each have a heart. So there are two hearts. But one heartbeat."

Then she pulled out the length of the second chain. At the end of it was her own silver heart that Dad had once given her. Once upon a time it, too, had been clasped inside another silver heart. "Say it with me. 'Two hearts. One heartbeat.'"

"'Two hearts. One heartbeat,'" the twins echoed.

Reed reached and took up Mom's heart in his palm. Then he put his own pewter heart within hers. It was a perfect fit.

For one brief moment, Reed understood what love and family were supposed to be about. Only one piece was missing. The one sitting at the back of the court.

"Mom, do you think Dad has his heart with him?" Reed asked.

Right then and there, even Chayse believed all things were possible. Maybe they could be a family again. All they needed was Dad to step up.

"I doubt he wears his anymore," Mom said.

"That will be enough," Miss Crutch said from behind the Brazzles.

Mom shot her a look that warned the CASA agent not to take another step towards her children.

Miss Crutch wasn't paying Mom any mind. Her eyes tunneled down with relish. A magnetic gaze locked onto sparkling things like a thieving magpie. It wasn't even the twins themselves: it was the silver hearts that the twins now wore. The clean metal chain link. The clean symmetry of the curved lines. The open space of the metal shaped heart.

Reed got that way whenever donuts were in the house. He could not stop thinking about them being in the box on the table. Until he had taken one out of the box and ate it in secret under the table.

Chayse got that way whenever her Mom got a new ring or earrings. She would watch her mom put them away in the jewelry box knowing that she could sneak them out when her mom was gone to work. Mom never got a chance to wear them anyway and Chayse wanted them worse.

It was wanting something that wasn't yours so you wanted it that much more until you were jealous.

But there was another word for it. One Mom has said Grandma had taught her.

Covet.

Miss Crutch coveted the silver heart chains.

Why?

Neither of the twins knew.

"Come along, children," Bailiff Mike said and led them around Mom to the waiting guardians.

The Brazzles, Peyton and Shawn, walking side by side with arms open and faces smiling to take the twins straight to their hearts. The woman put her hand on Chayse's shoulder. It was cold.

What was it that Mom's Grandma liked to say? "Cold hands, cold heart."

"Hello, Chayse. Hello, Reed," the woman smiled. Reed didn't think it was anything like Bailiff Mike's smile. He had a real smile that matched his words. This woman's smile did not match the look in her eyes. "We're going to take care of you for a while."

The man hadn't said a word. He only wore the same cold smile.

"Hello, Mr. and Mrs. Brazzle," Chayse said as sweet as she could. She waited for Reed to say hello. Only he didn't. So she gave him a nudge.

"Don't you ever say nothin'?" Reed asked the man.

"'Course," Mr. Brazzle said through his smile. "When I've got something to say. You seem to be just like that. Do you have something to say?"

"Just this. Which one is which?" Reed asked.

"What do you mean?" Mr. Brazzle asked.

"Which one of you is Peyton and which one of you is Shawn?" Reed asked.

Mrs. Brazzle was taken aback.

"You can call us Mr. and Mrs. Brazzle," the man said.

"Well, again, which one is which? 'Cause, right now, she's doin' all the talkin'," Reed said.

Mr. Brazzle just stared at him.

"What he really means is, can we call you 'Mom and Dad?'" Chayse said. That made Reed gave her a telling look.

"If you want to, honey," Mrs. Brazzle said. Chayse knew the smile on her face was a bluff. That Mrs. Brazzle did not want Chayse to call her "Mom."

Chayse didn't care. She wanted a new mom bad enough that if it meant getting her own room in a warm house her new mom could be a little cold.

The courtroom was clearing. The spectators exiting back out through the metal detectors. Bailiff Mike was saying good day to Judge Hart who was on his way back to his chambers.

"How is your son, Judge?" Reed heard him ask the judge.

Judge Hart looked down. "He's got one last chemo treatment to take. It makes him sicker than a dog. And if this doesn't do the trick then there is nothing else to be done."

"I'll be prayin' for him," Bailiff Mike said.

"Prayers always help," Judge Hart said as he retreated behind his door.

Miss Crutch left first with her twin bulldog agents on her heels. Then Lawyer Kyler escorted Mom out as they exchanged phone numbers so that Kyler could let the twins call her on his phone in his presence. Last, Buddy lumbered out the courtroom.

The Brazzles stood on either side of the twins. Bailiff Mike stood at the metal detector. Waiting on the last spectator who leaned against the wall next to the metal detector.

It was Dad.

"You sure you don't have any outstanding warrants?" the bailiff asked Dad.

"Go ahead and run me if you want to," Dad said.

"If you do, you'll have to stay overnight across the street," Bailiff Mike said.

"Nope, don't think so," Dad said shaking his head and hitting his wallet in his back pocket. "Wallet's fat. I'd be able to pay my fines today and have a sandwich at Schwinn's."

Dad shoved his hands in his pockets. "Looks like you two squirrels are gonna get some playtime."

"Isn't that what you like to do? Play and not work?" Chayse said.

Dad laughed. "Just like your momma. How sweet."

"Can't you come see us, Dad?" Reed asked.

Dad looked over the Brazzles. They pretended to ignore Reed's request. But they weren't going to go against the judge's orders. And in a never million years would they dare to cross Miss Crutch.

"'Fraid not, bubbie," Dad said. "Mom doesn't want me around you guys. And the judge thinks I'm a bad element."

"If Mom can talk to us why can't I talk to my dad?" Reed said to Mr. Brazzle. "You can tell Mr. Kyler I want to talk to my dad, can't you?"

"If we follow the judge's orders then everything will work out for the best," Mrs. Brazzle said. But Reed didn't think she sounded like she cared if it did or didn't.

"I was asking him," Reed said.

"Bub, let's try to get along. It's not what anyone wants for now. Hope for the best," Dad said.

"And prepare for the worst, right Dad?" Chayse asked.

"You two squirrels do your part and I'll do mine and maybe Mom will do hers. And that's all we can do," Dad said.

"I'll never see you again!" Reed cried embarrassed at the sudden tears that had come out in front of everyone. He wiped them away as quick as he could.

Dad pointed with his forefinger and gave a wink. "Never say never. It ain't over yet."

For Chayse, first Dad had given up and now Mom was walking away. She was ready for new parents who would be there. She wanted to accept the Brazzles.

For Reed, he wanted Mom back. But most of all he wanted Dad back. To have a real home and family he would need them both.

It would be a long time before the twins would be home again in this world.

***

Chapter Four: Street and Curb

The Brazzles made the twins wait so they would be the last to leave the air conditioned courthouse. Afternoon shadows ambled down the main hallway. Cool air lolly-gagging from county office doors.

But once outside, the twins had to blink against the blaring sun. Heat rolled off the asphalt streets. Warming the twins' skin. Sweat beaded on their faces and necks.

Downtown being more brick and concrete than shade or tree. The dead air hung like a blanket on a clothesline. Like someone cooking in the oven with the oven door down.

The courthouse green was more a spotty brown lot. The heat driving insects across the scorched ground and the ones with wings into the bushes and trees. Their drone louder than the air conditioner hum.

Shiloh was the county seat for Fade. The courthouse was located at the dead center of downtown. A small town square with local business flair. Everything situated around the century-plus old courthouse building: the police station, county offices and services, a legal help center, Mom and Pop Schwinn's Dine-In, Main Street Bakery, the Sweet Repeats consignment store, and the In-Season thrift store.

Its owners, three earthy sisters who deigned to sit in lawn chairs while brewing their tea while letting their indolent kids run up and down the sidewalk calling it their home school lessons, favored Halloween above all seasons and year-round had a life-sized red-eyed mummy posed in colonial British soldier's clothes in the front store window like from a popular 80's metal band's album cover. The eaves of the store awning bore a score of swinging Grim Reapers in shabby grave habiliments.

But the centerpiece was the life-size biker revenant-ghoul with leather studded gear and topped with a black fright wig near the front door. The biker's patch read DEMON styled over horns, pointed tails, and a pitchfork. The biker triggered via by a foot pedal by one of the sisters to rev up his bike, pop a wheelie, doom to utter repeats of "Born to ride!" or "Born to be wild!" over a song extolling liking smoke and lightning and the joys of heavy metal thunder.

Chayse wondered why CASA didn't scoop these kids up off the street and put them in foster care.

All the spectators and players had left the courthouse and were getting into their various vehicles. The courthouse parking was laid out on all four sides of the courthouse green.

Mom had parked her Nissan Altima in front of the back entrance to the courthouse across from a temporary employment agency.

While Dad hadn't even driven his old Dodge to the courthouse. Instead, he'd talked Uncle Buddy into running him up to court in Buddy's trusty, fading red Off-Road Chevy Z100 with its oversized tires and running boards. Perfect for mud running. Not so good for running from bench warrants. They had parked across from the diner.

Mom's Altima and Uncle Buddy's Chevy backed out onto Federal to pull onto Main Street. The Altima blowing blue smoke and the Chevy matching it with diesel from double exhaust pipes. At the light, they would go their separate ways. She to work at the Days Inn in Henley and Dad to wherever they would find scrap to haul.

Lawyer Kyler was leaning on the open driver's door of his Mercedes Benz parked across from the police station. Leaving the car running, he had stopped to talk to Miss Crutch through her open driver's window of a silver Hummer—the same one she must have blinded the twins with the other night. She had backed into a parking space with an occluding the sign that read RESERVED FOR COUNTY PERSONNEL.

Reed wondered if they were talking about how well pleased they were with their hard days' work. Somehow they made a living at it. *Not much of a living*, Dad would have said.

The dark-headed twin CASA agents, Nic and Vic, got into a royal blue Chevy Malibu parked in the spot next to Miss Crutch's Hummer. They never seemed to be too far behind her.

The Brazzles led the twins past the old bandstand and Civil War Memorial cannon to reach the other front entrance of the building where there was only one vehicle parked on this side. A gold Ford Explorer that like Miss Crutch's silver Hummer had been backed in facing the In-Season storefront.

Chayse was impressed. So, no Ford Focus. She had the Brazzles pegged for eco-conscious do-gooders but in the decision of comfort over the ecosystem, comfort had won out again. If the Brazzles had decided to go one hundred percent green, they would be walking or riding bikes.

Reed hated Ford trucks. The SUV might have cost a pretty penny, but for just a little more, Mr. Brazzle could have gotten an extended Chevy with a king cab. But then, Reed doubted Mr. Brazzle was the king of his castle.

Coming and going--everyone else was locked into a rhythm. Traffic rumbled in a pattern around the square. Stopping and turning. Braking and revving. Cars lined up like drones in their painted lanes.

Don't become a slave to routine, Chaysie, Mom would say. *One day, I'm gonna be totally out of debt and I'll be able to get us nice things. It takes hard work to make your dreams come true, Chaysie.*

Last Christmas, Mom pawned her wedding ring for a second time just for the twins to have a few presents under their tiny fuzzy tree. This Christmas, if there were going to be any presents it looked like it would be up to the Brazzles. More than anything Chayse wanted to wear the right clothes with a brand name that her school mates wouldn't tease her over— since every kid knew that there was a correlation between how much their parents loved them and how stuff they got.

Reed wanted the latest iPhone with enough data to hold all his favorite apps and get any current updates. Instead of the Wal-Mart tracfone Dad had gotten him with its "classic" games like "Pong" or "Donkey Kong, Jr." The graphics were just circles and lines that made bleeps and squelches.

Wish in one hand and crap in the other, Reeder, Dad would say. *And see which one fills up faster.*

Reed wasn't so sure. He could wish for a lot of stuff.

And whenever he started listing all the things he wanted, Dad would stop him. *There's not enough money in the world for everything you want. How much money do you need? Most people say the same: just a little more.*

There was a man on the corner. On the curb of the sidewalk. Standing on Main and Church.

He wore dirty overalls with no shirt. His weathered construction boots dappled with paint splotches. A blue Cubs hat pulled down over his black greasy hair. He held up a cardboard sign with REPENT! THE KINGDOM OF GOD IS NEAR! written in black sharpie.

Reed wanted God to get off his throne and come down here and make everything right. Bring back Mom and make her stop yelling at him. Then let him see Dad again.

Chayse knew God wasn't going to show up. He didn't care what happened to anyone. Everything was screwed up six ways to Sunday. God or no god, Chayse knew the twins were on their own.

"Repent! Turn back to God!" the man on the corner called out above the insect drone to the moving traffic. Everyone could hear him but no one was listening.

"He shouldn't be allowed to bother people like that," Mrs. Brazzle said dropping her voice in case the man on the corner might here.

"That's Creedmore. Just a street preacher," Mr. Brazzle said. "Although, he calls himself an *evangelist.*"

"How do you know that?" Reed asked.

"I do all the police department's taxes," Mr. Brazzle and pointed to the police station over his shoulder. "As well as all these businesses on Main Street.

"Everyone complains to the police that Creedmore drives customers away. But the police say he's not breaking any rules. The only thing he's doing is getting on the business owner's nerves. I also know that Creedmore's been to every single one of these places asking for work. No one will give him a job so he's made one for himself."

Dad had told Reed once, *There are two types of people in this world: those that make sure everyone else follows the rules and those that know when they have to break them.*

Mom had told Chayse, *rules are only good when everyone follows them. Otherwise, it's everyone for themselves.*

Ensconced on his street corner pulpit, Creedmore cried out, "Repent! Turn back to God!"

Passing drivers honked. Safe inside their air-conditioned means of motion, the drivers thought themselves far better off than the man standing out in the heat so why did they need to repent? What did Creedmore have to offer that was better than what they already had?

The Brazzles looked like they had done well for themselves. So why should they repent? They had jobs. They kept the law. The court had just awarded them more responsibility. So they would be sure to keep any and every new law that was being passed.

Chayse thought that everyone wanted follow the laws the same way that they wanted to wear name brand clothes so that no one would make fun of them.

Reed thought that trying to do what everyone else said was good must take a lot of work. No one could be that good all the time. So what was the point in trying?

There was a buzzing all around the square. A high whining. At first, Reed thought it was a hum from power lines.

It also sounded like an insect drone. A million buzzing bees. The drone filled Reed's ears until the only thing louder was Creedmore's preaching at passing cars.

Until Reed was switched out from the boy he was supposed to be in that world reaching for the crossbow heirloom back to just plain old Reed reaching out to touch Mr. Brazzle's crest on his blue polo jersey shirt.

A bee floated in to look at the crest on Mr. Brazzle's shirt, investigating it for pollination possibilities until Mr. Brazzle's hand smack both the bee and Reed's hand away.

Mr. Brazzle's eyes smoldered at Reed. A line had been crossed. Boundaries violated.

No," the man said as if it was an unforgivable sin. Punishment boiling over within the word. The promise of an old vintage stocked from grapes of wrath.

Reed's first instinct was to hit Mr. Brazzle back, harder than he'd been hit. He hadn't meant to touch Mr. Brazzle's shirt. He'd been somewhere else, maybe physically, maybe not—Reed was a little confused. But he didn't deserve to get his hand slapped.

The bee drifted back in, meaning to investigate these warm bodies for any kind of pollen.

So it landed on a pink horizon. Which just happened to be Chayse's shoulder.

"Get it off me!" she screamed and slapped at it.

The insect had no fear of her. It tucked its papermache wings over its fuzzy striped back as it lit on her shoulder just as it pleased. It stumbled over the fabric of her shirt busy with its work.

"Ew!" Chayse screamed. She shook her head so hard Reed heard her teeth rattle. Bent over and spinning her head around, she used both hands to brush her hair and shoulders to get rid of the insect and anything else that might have become attached to her.

But still, the insect would not budge.

Reed thought she might have to tear off her shirt and beat it against the sidewalk.

"Well, get it off me, Reed!"

Only he didn't. He laughed instead. Chayse had what Dad called the heebie-jeebies. It was the funniest thing that he had seen in a very long time.

"Get it off her!" Even Mrs. Brazzle had become concerned but not enough to help herself. She wasn't going to get any closer to the bee or she would get stung herself.

A hand with long dirty nails plucked the insect off Chayse's shoulder. She came to a dead stop. Everyone turned.

The man on the corner stood next to them. Chayse calmed down. The bee climbed over Creedmore's open palm.

"Thank you," Chayse said.

"I'm just God's humble servant. No better or different than this bee," Creedmore said looking the bee over with gentle eyes. "Anything is amazing if you just look long enough at it."

Being that close to the evangelist, Chayse realized that he didn't smell like bees' wax. It must have been a while since he'd taken a shower.

"Well, get it away. I'm allergic to bees," Mrs. Brazzle said.

But the man didn't shoo the bee away. He let it stay. "Are you allergic to honey?"

"Doesn't honey come from bees?" Reed asked.

"Yes. That's one reason God put them here. To make sweet pure honey. It can preserve and help heal, too. Ma'am with all due respect, you're allergic to their venom, not to the bee itself."

"People can die from their stings. So, it's just a pest," Mrs. Brazzle said.

Mr. Brazzle slapped at Creedmore's open palm. The agitated bee flicked its wing like a mad engine and stung him before falling to the ground.

"Now it can't sting anyone anymore," Mr. Brazzle said and looked at the side of his hand. A stinger still attached to the venom sac continued to jab under his skin. He pulled it outwith the thumb and forefinger on his other hand.

"It only tried to defend itself," Creedmore said. "All things serve God's will."

"How can someone dying from a bee sting be a part of God's will?" Mrs. Brazzle wanted to know. "Isn't God supposed to be all good and all-knowing and all-powerful? Things are in a mess down here and he doesn't do anything about it."

"God is always at work to make sure his will is being done," Creedmore said. "Only you may not like how he does it."

A four-door car going in the other direction on Main Street squeaked its brakes. With its worn-out muffler choking, the driver's side window came sothe driver could shout, "Hey! God hates the Cubs! This is Cardinals' country!"

"Cubs. Cardinals," Creedmore shrugged and tapped the upper pocket of his overalls. "God is no respecter of persons. He doesn't look at the uniform. He judges the heart."

"Go Cards!" The man yelled and honked the horn to adjudicate his opinion into law for himself.

Traffic began moving again.

"Shouldn't you be looking busy in case Jesus comes?" Mrs. Brazzle asked.

"Only God the Father knows when that will be," Creedmore said. "Though Jesus is the same as God, even he, being the Son, does not know the mind of God, the Father."

"How can Jesus be both man and God?" Reed asked. "How can anyone be two people at the same time?"

A large silver vehicle pulled up into the parking space behind them.

Creedmore reached into the pocket on the center of his overalls and pulled out a gold coin. "A coin has two sides at the same time. Heads and tails. Up and down."

"This side is heads." Holding it vertical between his forefinger and thumb, Reed could see a portrait of a man's head with a short haircut. A word was stamped in an arc above that head. LIBERTY. At the man's neck, more words were stamped. IN GOD WE TRUST.

Chayse heard the driver's door open and then close behind them.

"And this side is tails," Creedmore said and flipped the coin by overturning it right-side up with his thumb. It depicted a building. Topped with a single tower and cupola. Below it was stamped HALF DOLLAR. "But both sides are true. Both have equal value. They are both worth the same fifty cents together."

"Just like the coin, the Son has two natures, both equally valid at the same time," Creedmore said. "Jesus is fully human and fully God. He is both the Son of Man and the Son of God."

Then the evangelist took the boy's hand and placed the half dollar in it.

"That's enough. Leave these people alone!" a voice commanded.

The twins heard something moving underneath the voice. A collapsing thunderhead. A rolling boulder. Smashing down like a fist.

The command reverberated around them. Twisting under the words into something else.

Do not speak his name. I have more power here than you.

The twins turned and saw Miss Crutch standing behind them. Hands on her slender hips. Her eyes narrow eyes focused through her thick glasses with a glint of silver frames.

Creedmore stood his ground and did not flinch. What did he have to fear? "I am just a messenger. Like a voice in the wilderness. The Messiah came the first time to save the world not to condemn it. But he's coming again. This time to judge it."

"That's the best you got?" Miss Crutch asked. "Just the same old song. 'Jesus is gonna come back one day'. One day. Only it'll be one day too late. The world doesn't care about Jesus and the world doesn't want him. The world doesn't even need Jesus any more."

"I feel sorry for people who call good what God calls evil. That's like calling bitter sweet and sweet bitter.

"Jesus is the light of the world. But the world is in darkness because it does not want the light to show its true deeds," Creemdore said.

"Another prime example of the patriarchy!" Miss Crutch said. "Every time you open your mouth you offend everyone! You're a danger to these children!"

"The Master said that to get into the Kingdom of Heaven you have to become like a child and that if anyone harms a child, He will take it up with them," Creedmore said.

"Get into the car, kids," Mrs. Brazzle said.

Mr. Brazzle only had to step down off the curb for the Bluetooth fob to start up the engine on the Ford Explorer.

Miss Crutch took out her Galaxy. "I have the authority to have you arrested."

"All authority comes from God. Nothing happens except by His consent," Creedmore said.

"Then he'll consent to your arrest," Miss Crutch said as she fired off a text. A ding came once it was read. And then a buzz arrived with a reply.

Reed wondered why Miss Crutch had to make everyone do what she wanted all the time. Even Mom wasn't that bad. How was Creedmorebeing dangerous?

Miss Crutch was treating Creedmore like a registered offender and had the Brazzlesworried that they or the twins both were about to be stung with venomous evil.

Mrs. Brazzle opened the back passenger doors. "Get in the back seat! Hurry!"

Reed climbed in first and slid across the leather bench. He had never been in such a big car before. The comfort and luxury dwarfed him.

After Chayse got in Mrs. Brazzle shut the passenger door and climbed into the passenger seat. "Buckle up!"

Chayse smelled vanilla as she buckled up. It usually calmed her. But the Brazzles were in a panic and Miss Crutch was being so hateful. All because of Creedmore.

What had he said that was so dangerous? What were they afraid of? Because he didn't wear a shirt or believed something different than they did?

Two police officers had walked down the front steps of the station, crossed the street, and were moving towards Miss Crutch.

The SUV was running. Both the Brazzles had their seatbelts on. Chayse was buckling hers. They were ready.

But they weren't going anywhere.

"Reed!" Mrs. Brazzle yelled. "Put on your seatbelt!"

"No," Reed said.

Mr. Brazzle looked over his shoulder at Reed. "Put it on."

"Make me," Reed said.

Mrs. Brazzle reached between the seats.

Reed slapped her hand away.

"Reed!" Chayse said.

Creedmore slapped his hand against the back passenger window. Chayse jumped against her seatbelt. Mrs. Brazzle screamed.

Only Reed and Mr. Brazzle kept their cool. Reed was too angry to be scared now. He was impressed that Mr. Brazzle didn't even flinch.

The evangelist pressed his face and dirty hands against the window. "Remember, where you are going they call God's light the darkness and the darkness they call God's light. But God is everywhere. So when you're lost in the darkness, call out to Him."

Then Creedmore turned to face the police officers as they reported into the walkie talkie clipped onto their Kevlar vests with the self-satisfactory Miss Crutch behind them.

The Brazzles' Explorer still hadn't moved.

"We can go now," Mrs. Brazzle said.

Mr. Brazzle kept his foot on the brake. "Not until Reed is buckled up."

Reed folded his arms across his chest.

Chayse reached over and buckled him in.

"Sis!" Reed complained.

"Quit showing your butt," Chayse said as she sat back.

Mr. Brazzle turned left out onto Main Street. Nothing seemed out of place now. Not the street preacher in greasy overalls. Not the triggered red-haired CASA lady or the drone-like police officers. Not the customers looking out the windows of Mom and Pop's dinner. And not In Season's Grim Reapers and mummies and revenant biker lined up to see the Explorer off with a gauntlet of skeletal smiles.

"Are you taking us home now?" Chayse asked as Reed sulked.

***

Chapter Five: Osage and Asheroth

Three things happened while they drove to their destination.

Three such singular things. As if the Leftwich twins' lives hadn't had any occurrences out of their normal routine. They were beginning to expect extraordinary things out of hand.

Just twenty minutes into the Brazzles' foster care and the twins discovered that Mr. Brazzle had a lead foot. He goaded the Explorer down the road. Even passing vehicles that were doing five under the speed limit.

What was the hurry? Where were they going? Indian Springs was the next big town up the road. There an Arkansas state park protected the state's largest natural spring that served as the headwaters for the pristine Spring River. Soon the town would have its homecoming, traditionally called Old Solemn Judge Days. Two days of carnival games and rides and cakes and pie contests capped off with a rodeo.

"Do you live in Indian Springs?" Chayse asked.

"Yes, we have a house there," Mrs. Brazzle said. "But we thought we'd take you two somewhere first." Chayse imagined a thousand places they could go where their foster parents could shower them with gifts to prove their love: Turtle Shell Mall, the outlets in Branson, open markets in Little Rock, or even to the big retailers inside the Memphis pyramid.

Reed leaned over to whisper, "Bet it won't be anywhere we want to go."

"So, where are we going?" Chayse asked.

"We thought we'd take you two to Osage Cave," Mrs. Brazzle said. She looked back in the rearview mirror to gauge their reaction.

Reed raised an eyebrow. He could hide out in a cave. At least for a while.

Chayse didn't like being outdoors. And today it was blistering hot. But she had another destination in mind. "Isn't that near the Big Dipper Ice Cream Store?"

"'Fraid we can't stop there. But I think you'll like the cave just the same," Mr. Brazzle said.

"Told you," Reed said and Chayse knew he'd said it just because he didn't want to like the Brazzles.

"What was that, hon?" Mrs. Brazzle asked.

Reed couldn't stand the way she said *hon*. She didn't care about him. She was only pretending. Why? That's what Reed couldn't figure out.

"He didn't say anything, Mrs. Brazzle," Chayse said and whacked her twin on the shoulder.

"Call me Peyton, hon," Mrs. Brazzle said.

"I didn't say anything, Peyton-hon," Reed said. He would enjoy getting under her skin. He'd had lots of practice with Mom.

Mr. Brazzle pushed the Explorer up a steep hill which had a tight turn on the other side so he had to slow down fast enough everyone found something to grip. Up ahead was the first extraordinary thing. Something standing in the road.

Mrs. Brazzle gave out a warning.

It was some kind of animal. Half of it laying in the road. Half standing up at the same time.

Mr. Brazzle pumped the brakes. Still holding on to what they could, everyone gnashed their teeth.

Except for Chayse, who kept right on talking—God bless her heart, "I mean tramping around cave and rocks isn't all that fun for a girl--just thought I'd throw that out there. "But ice cream—now, that makes everyone smile."

Ice cream kept sounding better and better to Reed. Even if it was these people who were buying it.

There were two different kinds of animals on the road. Some kind of mammal—dead roadkill lying still. And some kind of large bird sitting on top of it.

The roadkill had mammalian taxonomy--fur and a tail and once a straight spine with vertebrae now flattened beyond classification.

Mr. Brazzle was still going too fast. The bird too interested in picking over the carcass. Though it didn't look like any buzzard—its feathers spotted brown and white, not dull and greasy—with its backside to the oncoming traffic.

It didn't matter. The twins were just along for the ride. And about to collide--seat belted and helpless.

The large bird flew up from its feeding at the last second but it couldn't get enough elevation in time and smacked up against the on-coming windshield of the Explorer. It tumbled head over talons coming to rest at the bottom of the windshield nestled against the wiper blades with its wings outstretched and two great yellow eyes blinking upside down at the Brazzles and the twins safe inside their air-conditioned cab.

"It's an owl!" Chayse said.

"That's just great! You've hit and run an owl!" Reed called out.

Still, after all that, Mr. Brazzle did not come to a full stop. The Explorer kept rolling in low gear. The great bird rolled across the hood and landed on the roadside.

The Explorer resumed speed as Mr. Brazzle swerved back into his lane.

The twins turned and watched the owl hop, test its swing span, and take flight across the road to open pastures and tree lines.

They had never seen anything like it before.

"That bird came out of nowhere," Mrs. Brazzle.

"They're usually not out during the day. That's why it didn't see us coming," Mr. Brazzle.

"Mr. Brazzle, no offense, but you can make someone carsick on a straight road," Chayse said.

The road returned to normal Highway 9 was a rural highway cutting through pasture land and small springs and creek beds. There a few old farm towns so small even the U.S. Post Office had forced them to build a small post office building to hold their P.O. boxes so their mail people wouldn't get lost on the many unpaved back roads. Reed had read once, in some KNOW IT NOW book for his non-fiction Accelerated Reader points, that up to the 1960s, Arkansas had the most unpaved roads in the United States.

They might still be able to take a close second.

Chayse did not relish getting back outside. It had been like an oven downtown. While inside the SUV it was like a meat freezer.

Each of the twins had an adjustable air vent above their head and a drink holder at their feet on the backside of the console. Chayse liked the luxury. The seats in Mom's Altima were gouged and ripped. The front console cracked and stained.

Such comfort made Reed uneasy. Chayse could settle for ice cream but Reed wasn't going to let his guard down around the Brazzles. He kept his arms folded over his chest.

Mom worked two jobs and they still never had enough money to do anything. All their clothes were second hand and she couldn't even afford to Redbox him any new Xbox games.

He didn't like Mom being gone all the time but when she was home it was worse. When she was at work, Reed could relax. YouTube stupid videos galore, play Xbox all day. Chase Chayse.

But the minute Mom would get home, the fun would be over and the shouting would start. She always cranky, always tired, and always found something Reed hadn't done right or something he shouldn't have done at all.

Reed liked it better when Mom was gone.

Chayse got to do whatever she wanted. Stay up late. Watch a horror movie instead of going to bed. Eat a bag of chips or a bowl of ice cream at ten o'clock at night.

She could talk Mom into believing that salt was sugar.

Chayse lived by a simple plan. Don't set out to make Mom mad on purpose, as Reed did. Then ask her for anything.

She had to work fast. After coming home late from a double shift Mom was in no mood to suffer two kids full of boredom and sugar. Within five minutes, Mom would be asleep on the couch still in her fast food uniform and a half-eaten frozen dinner on her lap.

Mom was just one person. Might as well ask for the moon. What was the worst she would say, "No?"

But the Brazzles were a double package. A two-headed monster that wore the same name brand clothes. A double pair of mouths giving the same answer.

Chayse didn't know which one would give the twins snacks and which one would make them follow the rules.

Might as well ask for ice cream. It was a good enough place to start as any.

Reed worried that maybe the Brazzles had been just playing nice in front of Judge Hart. Promising to look after the poor Leftwich twins who had just been ripped from their mother's side. Only when they would get the poor little kiddies home behind closed doors out would come the rules—three thousand pages of do not's or else.

Why did adults always want kids to follow their rules?

Dad hadn't. He always played games with the twins. Or showed them something.

He never had to get onto them about misbehaving. He gave them something to do instead. After games, he would show them his coin collection or a new muzzleloader or bow he'd just gotten. Then they would practice shooting with them.

There wouldn't be any trouble until Mom would come to get them. Then Mom would get onto Dad for something. And then onto the twins on the way home.

Chayse lived in the cracks between the rules while Reed lived in the caves underneath them.

Reed loved reading about caves or reptiles or guns or wars or anything about Indians. They were the first peoples to discover all these wonderful places. So going to Osage Cave was an intriguing choice. Way more interesting than getting ice cream.

It wasn't hard for Reed to imagine another time and place beyond his everyday miserable life. A time and place without gas cars or electricity for TV or refrigerators or social media didn't scare Reed. Although, he might have Xbox or YouTube withdrawals, he could still hunt and fish.

Chayse would have a harder time. Not being able to shop on-line was always a deal killer. She liked being around people, adults usually, since they didn't make fun of what she would wear to school and she loved asking them questions because they loved it when kids took an interest in them. And besides, asking questions was one way to learn.

Mr. Brazzle drove in silence with two eyes on the road and both hands on the wheel. The twins lulled by the unending stretch of pastureland and unpaved roads or driveways where the only thing to do was to run cattle or ride three-wheelers. And the hum of the tires running down lonely Highway 9 filled their ears.

Mrs. Brazzle broke the spell of monotony. "Chayse." She touched the back of her headrest to get Chayse's attention. "What's your favorite color?"

She took the bait. "Red!"

"What kind of pizza do you like best?" Mrs. Brazzle asked. Her arm lifted and Chayse caught sight of the second singular thing. Something black on the inside of her wrist. A design tipped in black ink.

"Cheese! Can we get pizza for dinner tonight?" Chayse asked and then forgot all about the pizza as she looked at the design instead.

It was a tattoo. Mrs. Brazzle had a tattoo tucked under her wrist. Just a little walk on the wild side. Not like Dad or any of his friends who had tattoos on his forearms and neck.

A different tattoo than any Chayse had ever seen before. It depicted a crescent moon resting its arc atop a coiled snake. A new moon as a hat for a snakehead.

Chayse nudged her twin brother pointing to her wrist and the nodded towards Mrs. Brazzle. Reed gave her a look as if he knew Chayse'd been crazy since birth. But then he took her lead and caught a look at Mrs. Brazzle's wrist and raised an eyebrow to her sister. Then he nodded towards Mr. Brazzle in the driver's seat. Chayse could only shrug.

Reed leaned over to peer between the driver's seat and door to catch a look for himself at the underside of Mr. Brazzle's hands. Satisfied he leaned back in his seat and belt and gave a nod and a wink to his sister.

Both the Brazzles, law-abiding citizens of good repute with the court, upstanding in their jobs and roles within the community, had the same strange moon and snake tattoo on the underside of their wrists.

What did the tattoo even stand for? The Brazzles didn't seem the type to get tattoos. It seemed as strange as an owl being seen out in midday.

They came into the old downtown of Indian Springs. More the traditional Main Street drag with three or four blocks of turn-of-the-last-century storefronts. The Explorer was nearing the Highway 9 t-junction with Highway 63. Left would take them to the Missouri state line and the town of Trainer which sat on it. Going right would take them back to Henley on the Spring River.

And to the Big Dipper. The best ice cream ever. With homemade flavors.

Chayse's favorite thing to get was a strawberry malt. Not just ice cream and milk or syrup. But with malt powder added.

Given the choice, Chayse would rather the Brazzles bonded with them over the smell of melting sugar and heated waffle cones.

The stop sign was just ahead. Dead ahead was the parking lot to Indian Springs State Park. Mr. Brazzle put on the blinker.

Chayse leaned forward to see which they were turning. Maybe Mr. Brazzle had changed his mind.

"Do you have a favorite phone app?" Mrs. Brazzle asked.

Trying to keep her eye on the road, Chayse let her mind wander. Of all the apps she had on her Tracfone which was her favorite? Snapchat? Shopkicks? That was a tough decision.

"I like 'Jaws: the Revenge,'" Reed piped up.

Why did he always have to butt in? Sometimes Chayse didn't like having a twin. Mr. Brazzle laughed as he turned the Explorer but Chayse no longer was paying attention which way.

"I don't play silly games," Chayse said. "I like 'Shopkicks.' All those points you can get swiping the barcodes on stuff. Then you can turn them in for gift cards."

"I actually get points playing 'Jaws,'" Reed argued. "And I can use them for upgrades on my game. You have to actually shop to get points for 'Shopkicks.' And you don't ever shop."

A Sonic drive up restaurant with its stalls half full and a line for the drive-thru passed by on their left. On the right side of the highway was a billboard proclaiming: WELCOME TO MISSOURI! Above it was a taller pole with a sign for a smaller building with its drive-through window. The taller sign read STATE LINE LIQUOR AND VAPES.

"Hey!" Chayse said. "The Big Dipper is the other way! We could have gone to the right!"

"Let's do our hike first," Mr. Brazzle said. "Then we'll see about ice cream."

"After a hike, you'll be good and ready to beat the heat with something sweet," Mrs. Brazzle said. "You'll appreciate it more then."

Chayse wasn't so sure she appreciated it all. She was more than just a little frazzled. She didn't want to get back outside and march around to see some stupid old cave.

Instead of saying, "I told you so," Reed just stuck out his tongue.

They crossed over into Missouri. And into a state of frustration. The listless sky held no feature nor promised any shade.

Chayse had nothing better to do than play on her phone. She got it out and her eyes popped out of their sockets. "Reed! Better check your phone!"

Reed was playing with the half dollar that the Street Preacher had given him. He kept turning it over and over from heads to tails and back to heads to back to tails. He didn't even know he was agitated until Chayse elbowed him in the side, then he became very agitated.

"Stop, Chaysie!" he said.

Chayse put her phone in his face. "My phone! The minutes are almost gone! You'd better check yours!"

Reed didn't want to listen to her. But he got his phone out anyway. His phone showed he had only two minutes of airtime to stream data.

"I'm gonna be out, too," he said. The coin would do him no good. Neither would ice cream.

"Mr. and Mrs. Brazzle!" Chayse called. "We're out of minutes!"

"What?" Mrs. Brazzle asked.

Reed held up his phone so they could see it in their rearview mirror. "We've got Tracfones! We need more time added on our phones or they'll go dead!"

They were coming into Trainer. At the next light, there was a rehabbed McDonald's with a new playground on side of the corner and a dirtier KC gas station on the other. Behind the McDonald's was an even older Wal-mart, a smaller division one store with very little foodstuffs.

"Walmart'll have Tracfones!" Chayse cried. "Please! We need some minutes!" Sissy rarely lost it over most things. Never over food or getting to watch TV since she could get either as much as she wanted. Clothes? Maybe.

But once she did lose it, she went into total spaz mode. Like the world was coming to an end. And not having internet access was the end of the world. Both twins would be cut off: complete social orphans without parents or internet.

Reed joined in the wailing and the gnashing of teeth.

The Brazzles moaned and rolled their eyes. Just like Mom. All that was missing was the grouching and yelling.

"Kids," Mr. Brazzle said as he turned left at the light. "We'll take care of it on our way back."

Both Leftwich twins stopped their crying. "You will?"

"Now be warned," Mr. Brazzle said. "You may not get a signal at the park. Osage Cave is in a canyon. Surrounded by quartz and granite. We'll be below ground level. The Ozarks are notorious for losing signals and bouncing GPS to the wrong place. So don't freak out."

Chayse was too busy hyperventilating to respond. Reed put his hand on her shoulder. "You're saying we might be cut off once we get to the park?"

"Yes," Mr. Brazzle said.

"But we can stop at Wal-Mart and get some minutes later?" Reed asked.

"Yes," Mr. Brazzle said.

"And you'll be able to talk to your mom!" Mrs. Brazzle said. "We all exchanged numbers. It's in the court order that you can talk to her. And we want to comply with the law."

"Well, there you go, sis," Reed said rubbing her shoulder. "Problem solved."

"We can talk to Mom," Chayse told herself. Then she grabbed her twin by the shoulders. "Bubba! We get to talk to Mom!"

"I know, sissy," Reed said.

Osage Cave lay to the west. The Explorer took a road out of town through the old business district that quickly turned into rural cattle ranches. Mr. Brazzle made another left at an old brown sign signifying a state tourist attraction: OSAGE CAVE 7 Mi.

The painted two-lane highway turned into a paved county road with no marked lanes. Chayse worried they would miss the turnoff for the cave among all the hills and farmhouses. Seven miles began to seem like seven years.

If they did get lost for a while, Reed was good with that. Other than this morning, he hadn't seen Dad for over three months. Now it could be another three months before he got to see him or Mom again. How could walking around in a dark cave be any different than how he felt now?

Ahead the country road turned into a dirt road of red Ozark rock. Next to it was a brown asphalted drive and a sign that read OSAGE CAVE STATE PARK.

"Look, kids!" Mrs. Brazzle said pointing back up the dirt road.

The third thing slithered across the road. Something black. Every inch over five feet long. A snake.

"Ew!" Chayse shuddered. "Run it over! The only good snake is a dead snake!"

Mr. Brazzle turned onto the brown paved road which brought them into the State Park.

"Wow!" Reed said. Wild animals, any animal with hair or scales or feathers, fascinated him. Trap it and tame it or kill it or skin it. He often dreamed of being a game warden and getting paid for being out in the woods and tracking game. Except that no one liked game wardens.

"We shouldn't kill snakes," Mr. Brazzles. "They have a niche in the ecosystem. They eat rodents and rodents carry disease. But mostly they love bird eggs."

The parking lot was small and nestled around a loop with a few smaller outbuildings and a trail.

"They are always hundreds of snakes around. And very few are poisonous. And very few people even get bitten. You've a greater chance of getting struck by lightning or getting bit by a spider than you do getting bit by a snake," Mrs. Brazzle said.

Chayse couldn't stop shuddering. All she saw were snakes. Snakes everywhere. Black shadows around tree roots. Clumps of dead leaves against granite rocks. They were snakes. Everything a snake everywhere. Waiting just for her. To get out of the Explorer so they slither towards her. Wrap their bellies around her ankles.

"No way am I gettin' out now! Y'all can go see the cave. Good luck gettin' snakebit," she said.

Mr. Brazzle parked the Explorer at the front of the loop. To their left was an open hut with three closed doors. One marked with the logo for a man, the second for a woman, and the third marked with a man and a woman both holding a child with their stick arms.

"Why do you both have snake tattoos?" Reed asked.

The Brazzles shared a look. Weighing whether the next words out of their mouths should be a smiley face lie or the ugly truth. When they started talking their eyes went down to the left and they said what they had to say with a smiley face.

"We used to be in an 'mc'—a motor cycle club. And that was our patch," Mrs. Brazzle.

But Reed wouldn't let it go. "What was the name of your club?"

"Asheroth," Mr. Brazzle said.

The only other visitors were three bikers who had come in on two motorcycles. They were standing at the second open hut which was marked INFORMATION and held a map of the park with trail routes marked and a stand of brochures. The tallest stood in the middle with leather riding chaps and a jacket. His jet black hair lay on giant shoulders and he was scowling underneath his thick sunglasses. The other two were a man and a woman, about the same height and build. Each wearing a sleeveless jacket and bandanas over twisted and braided hair.

The Brazzles got out and waited on the twins. Reed was the first out. Looking around he decided that he had never been here. Chayse slid off the back seat bench ready to leap back into the car until Mr. Brazzle locked the doors which shut automatically.

Hot air blew around them. The wind was picking up. Bringing low hanging clouds dark and pregnant with rain. Rumbling like motorbikes downshifting.

***

Chapter Six: Cave and Door

The tall biker was lighting a cigarette and the other pair had one arm around each other and the other in each other's back pockets. They jeered at the temporary family. The parents and their foster kids made an even odder gang than theirs.

Reed looked around. They were still on high ground. "Where's the cave?"

Chayse needed to know how far would they have to trek to get to it. Sweat beaded on her upper lip from the humid air. And now it was going to rain?

Mrs. Brazzle led out to the first trail and the trio of laughing bikers. They followed the trail onto a wooden walkway that led to a zigzagging stairway with descending levels. They came to a wooden platform that led single-file to a flight of stairs.

The brush and trees began to pull back. The ground disappeared into open space beyond the platform. Below was a very large descent.

The stairs led to a circular observation deck that clung to a granite cliffside. There was no doubt for the twins that beneath the dirt and trees was nothing but hard bedrock. Immutable and immobile. Unforgiving and unyielding.

Sheer sides of granite surrounded them. They stood over a large hole. A hundred feet below was a deep pool of still green water.

Along the other sides of the ledge barbed wire guarded cattle eating hay and swishing their tails from the drop off into the treacherous karst.

"This can't be the cave, can it?" Reed asked.

"No, this must be a sinkhole," Chayse said.

"It is," Mr. Brazzle said. "All caves are formed from the groundwater eating away at the soft rock. But when the cave gets too wide and the roof can't handle the weight of the ground above it, it collapses into a void."

"And you get a sinkhole," Chayse said.

"So where is the cave?" Reed asked. He was done with the sinkhole. Sure it was deep and probably dangerous. But it wasn't mysterious enough.

"We're standing on it, Reed," Mrs. Brazzle said.

Reed processed that. Ignoring what was going above them.

Daylight dimmed. The wind knotted storm clouds together. Brash cool air mixing with thick heat.

The smell of sulfur was in the air. It was going to rain. And not just rain: storm.

"That means we have to walk back up," Chayse groaned. "All the way back the way we came. And clear over to the other side. And it'll storm. And we'll get soaking wet. But is anyone listening to me? Hello? No!"

"Let's go!" Reed said attacking the stairs two at a time.

"Wait up, now!" Mr. Brazzle said as he descended behind until both were gone below the rim of the gulf.

They backtracked to the parking loop to another sign designating another trail. SOUTH CANYON TRAIL. 1/8 mile. This trail descends 70' using 119 steps.

"Great!" Chayse complained. "Why can't there be an elevator?"

"Wish we could climb down on ropes!" Reed said as he scouted ahead. "Come on, sissy!"

Chayse looked back to find the Brazzles' Explorer. It was parked just a few yards away. But the bikers had left. She caught a quick glimpse of two other cars that had arrived after the Brazzles. One was a dark blue four-door car. The other was a bigger silver SUV with a huge metal grill across its front.

"Can't we just go back to the Big Dipper?" Chayse whined as she followed down the stairs.

"We'll earn a sweet treat climbing these stairs, hon!" Mrs. Brazzle said.

Chayse didn't appreciate her talking about ice cream if they didn't intend to take them to get some.

These stairs were different. The sides and railings were wooden. A series of flights switchbacking along a cliff. But the treads were metal. With an open mesh to let rain and dirt through.

Mr. Brazzle was doing his best to keep up with Reed who was skipping down each flight and jumping onto the landing to start the next flight down. Each landing was situated between pine trees. At some places, bushes and tall weeds clung to the side of the cliff.

The grey granite pockmarked from wind and weathering. Traces made from running rivulets. Old and proud before it would be ground down into dust.

A few trees at the bottom rose against the sides of the cliff so that the stairs were between them and the cliff wall. Loose rock and dirt lay away from the cliff along with leaves and sideways trees. This time they weren't walking down into a sinkhole. They were heading to the bottom of a gorge. A small canyon that snaked divided scraggy pastureland from this hidden chasm.

The final flight of stairs led to another observation platform passing from grey oak to rusted metal mesh but this one had wooden foot railings and steel posts standing it twenty feet off the gorge floor where granite boulders and quartz rocks littered a running stream rimmed with red Ozark clay.

As Chayse walked onto the platform something brushed her shoulders. She turned and had to push the leaves from a stray branch off her. It belonged to an oak tree that had sunk its roots long ago in the red clay and dirt runoff from the cliff. Once it had started growing next to the cliff it would not be moved and became bent heaving all its branches to one side so its tender branches could reach the sunlight. The state engineers who had built the trails had wisely moved the platform around the oak rather than disturb the old sentinel.

Some things were very stubborn.

Where the oak had to bend away from the cliff there was an odd knot. Bigger than the tallest biker's head had been. Perhaps an old wound or stunted branch now grown over with layer upon layer of bark.

Chayse reached out to touch it. It was warm, not hot. Stiff.

Some things were very stubborn, indeed.

Reed had climbed up on the rail to look up the cliff face. Then he jumped down on the steel mesh. It vibrated from the jolt.

Beneath the steel platform was a pool large enough to fish. It pushed over a trail of boulders and lapped against the walls of the gorge where hollows the size of birds' nests or cannonballs had been carved out.

There was something up the cliff face that Reed was looking at. Tucked underneath a rock outcropping and jutting out over the gorge floor was a cave mouth. A cool cavity. The entrance to a place where chthonic forces worked away in blind darkness. Slowing time to a drip in a sieve of secreted calcium columns. Hiding mazes of chambers and hoarding blind secrets.

"Sissy, there's the cave!" Reed pointed at the clear water pouring of the yawning cave mouth.   "I see it, bubba," Chayse said.

"Can't we go in?" Reed asked.

"'Fraid not, Reed," Mr. Brazzle said. "They've got it closed off so we don't get hurt or disturb the ecosystem."

Reed twisted his face up at him, "You're all about rules! Why does there have to be so many rules!"

There was a strange beauty here. A secret revealed. That below the pines and evergreens and red clay and cattle pastures, the source of all the springs were cavities under the earth. And when everything above was stripped away, this was the true world beneath their feet.

Magnificent rock and pure water.

But it came at a price. One day a farmer would have cattle in an open field high on a ridge. All would be at peace.

And the next the ground would heave and give way. Solid earth churning into dust. Grass and sod collapsing into a hungry void.

Until any cows or farmers who had started with standing at the top were now sitting at the bottom looking at upside-down confusion.

She knew what that was like: having your world turn over on you.

The mesh floor vibrated again. As if something was being dragged across it. Chayse turned. "Reed!"

Too late. Her twin had climbed over the top railing to jump down to the gorge floor. Once he landed he slid down to the bottom arriving with a cloud of dust and tumbling debris.

Mrs. Brazzle's jaw dropped. "You can't do that!" She wasn't using "hon" anymore.

"I think he just did," Chayse pointed out.

Mr. Brazzle's face became red and squinted. "Get back here at once!"

They might be richer than Mom. They might even be better educated. They might not be as high strung as Mom but Reed had gotten under their skin all the same and they became another screaming mad adult monster.

The pool with its free-running water was just ahead. Reed grinned at being this close to the majesty of the gorge. Chayse envied him.

The mesh floor bounced again. Chayse thought it was just from the three of them walking about.

"Don't run off!" Mr. Brazzle commanded at a loss of what to do next.

"No need to worry," said a woman's voice. It was like a stone sinking in a stagnant pond. Like a rock flying up from the road and hitting a windshield. Like the sting of an angry wasp.

Chayse turned around. Miss Crutch stood on the last landing above the platform in her tight slacks and jacket. Her lithe arms at her side.

Others were skidding down the slope from under the platform. Nic and Vic. The CASA twins still clad in the clothes they'd worn to court.

"We see you," said the one twin.

"Just fine," said the other twin.

They stood next support poles their eyes blazing. Not unlike the Red Coated zombie from the In-Season window.

The wind blew through the curls of Miss Crutch's red hair lifting it off her shoulders like writhing snakeheads. Her slanted glasses seem to slit her eyes. She pulled out one of the two necklaces that she had kept hidden under her blouse. It burned with an ardent flame. A lightning pulse. A plasma ball hanging off the chain on her chest.

Chayse had never seen anything like it. Fascinated by its every flicker. Enthralled by its every fluctuation.

Something quicker than water. Something more powerful than stone. Something bloodier than blood. Something more alive than herself.

Miss Crutch rolled her thumb over to the right side of the platform. "Vic."

The dark-haired man stalked toward the cave stream.

Then she jabbed at the slope to the left side with her other thumb. "Nic."

That dark-headed twin darted upstream. Reed was cut off. Where could he run to? Could he reach the cave mouth and climb up the jagged lip slick with algae?

CASA Nic came at Reed crouched low with both hands out like a linebacker. But Dad and Buddy liked to play rough with the twins so it was nothing for Reed to duck around him and crawl under the mesh platform. The twins had to guard three open sides thinking Reed couldn't get out against the cliffside.

Reed was slim enough to get out under the mesh platform and between the foot railing and the cliff. There was nowhere for him to crawl except up the bent oak tree. The CASA twins had to climb back up over the railing.

"Anytime now, boys. It wouldn't be wise to let him get away," Miss Crutch warned.

Reed stood on top of the railing and just reached the lowest branch of the bent oak. He began to shiny up the bark. CASA Vic reached him and grabbed his dangling foot.

Trying to yank his foot free, Reed didn't want to admit he was caught. Holding onto the lower branch, he tried to pull his foot free. And he might have until CASA Nic came over and grabbed his free foot.

Now the CASA twins had him like a wishbone. Reed hung out onto the branch until his fingers slipped loose. CASA Nic put an arm clamp around his neck and half pulled, half drug him across the platform towards Miss Crutch as if to make Reed do obeisance.

CASA Nic grabbed Chaysie by the arm. She tried to pull loose but he wouldn't let go. She tried to turn her arm over to break the hold but he wouldn't let go.

The man's fingers gouged into her forearm. Like a blood pressure cuff. Making the blood in her arm beat against a bass drum. Desperate to push through.

That broke the thrall of Miss Crutch's necklace over Chayse. She looked at it again. Now it was nothing more than a crescent moon set over a coiled serpent. Just like the Brazzles' tattoos.

"Is CASA supposed to treat us like dogs?" Chayse asked Miss Crutch.

"Why aren't you helping us?" Reed asked the Brazzles.

And what of Miss Crutch's second necklace? It was still hidden under her blouse. What was at the end of that necklace?

The Brazzles were as still as the boulders lying in the stream below. Nothing more than statues. And as about as useless.

"This can all be over quickly if you let it," Miss Crutch said.

The woman held out a lithe hand. Her slender arms seemed nothing more than bone. Her fingers nothing more than nails. "You both have something I want. You will give it to me now."

"What do we have that you could possibly want?" Chayse spat. "You took Mom away."

"And you made sure we can't see Dad," Reed joined in. "I ain't givin' you squat!"

The wind began to pick up. Leaves and stray twigs blew across the gorge floor and up against the stairs. There was a lightning strike up above them followed by a peal of thunder.

"I command the lightning's hand!" Miss Crutch said raising her hand. "I tell it where to strike. I can spit out sparks from the tempest! Now hand over what I desire!"

"You're just a crazy lady!" Reed said. He gave an elbow to CASA Nic's inner thigh and stepped on the toe of his shoe. Nic howled and let go of Reed.

Chayse ducked and crawled between Vic's legs. He had to let go or fall over. He did both.

This was the twin's best chance to escape.

"Run, bub!" Chayse called as Reed climbed again over the railing instead of trying to pass Miss Crutch on the landing.

"Come on, sis!" Reed urged as he ducked Miss Crutch's hands and jumped down to the slope.

Chayse was right behind grabbing onto Reed's hand as she slipped past him.

They crawled back up to the next landing as the CASA twins followed behind. Miss Crutch let them climb over the rails. Was she going to let them go?

How many steps were there on this trail down to the gorge? 119? That left at least a hundred and even taking the stairs two at a time winded the twins.

Their legs burned. Getting up the stairs would be like running a mile. If they both had been birds they could have taken wing and flown away.

Miss Crutch reached out her hand to the bent oak and said, "Spin and catch!"

The words echoed out in a wave. Between the steps. Over the rocks. Under the brush. Rippling faster than a wave. Riding harder than the breeze. Rising past the twins on the stairs.

What was the CASA woman doing?

Who was she talking to?

Ahead of Chayse, Reed began to drag his feet. Slowing his step. Losing his breath.

She caught up with him. "Keep goin'!" she urged.

He leaned against the railing using it to pull himself towards the next landing. His head rolled over his shoulder as he supported himself against the handrail and looked back.

"Chaysie! What is that?" he gasped.

She turned to look at where he was looking. At the oak tree. Something had changed.

It was more than bent. It looked like a hunchback. Because the knot had changed. Becoming bigger. Growing.

The bark on the outside began to undulate. Something womblike moving underneath. Pulsing in contractions.

The knot burst and exhaled out creatures. Score after score. Insect-like with four sets of legs on either side of plumb bodies.

Spiders. Hundreds pouring out. With different markings than tarantulas—orange and black stripes around spindly legs.

They were as big as their palms. Long front fangs. Six glass beady eyes apiece.

And all coming for them. The spiders ran up the slope on either side of them and over the railings and onto the landing in front of them. Encircling the twins.

The twins shuddered as they spiders ran over their feet. Up to their legs. Across their bellies.

Reed tried to knock them away but they clung to his hand. Sat on his shoulders.

Chayse wanted to scream but she felt hooked feet crawl over the back of her head.

She clung to the back of her twin. Meaning not only to protect him. But not to be without him.

The spiders didn't bite. They spun instead. From head to toe, the twins were bound in sticky filaments that tightened like bungee cords when they tried to move.

Until they couldn't move.

"Bring them!" called Miss Crutch.

The spiders tugged at their prey sealed up in sacks. The bound twins fell over onto the backs of the spider troop. They were toted back down the stairs to the bottom landing.

Miss Crutch leered at them. The CASA twins glared at them. The Brazzles still hadn't moved.

It was like being sewn into a sweater except Chayse could breathe. "What? What are they?" Chayse asked expecting to get bitten and eaten at any moment.

The webbing was so tight that Reed couldn't move a finger or bat an eye. But he knew these creatures. He'd read about them. "Giant huntsman spiders," Reed said. "They live in caves. But not around here."

"Correct," Miss Crutch said. "They came to serve me."

She spread out her arms. "Take us all back to my Domain."

The spiders swarmed over the five adults. Wrapping them up like mummies. Then the spiders passed the cocooned seven people along on their hairy backs in teams like a caravan laden with cargo over the railing and down the slope and up to the lip of Osage Cave.

When Reed wasn't able to talk Mom in letting him stay home and actually had to go to school, Reed liked to get out of class and read his Accelerated Reader books in the library. He gravitated to non-fiction: science or history. And he remembered a thin hardback book on spiders that had several pages on these creatures.

Giant huntsman spiders chased their prey. And lived in lairs near cave openings. But they weren't blind.

For Chayse, it was like being strapped into a runaway rollercoaster. Except she had never ridden one while lying flat on her back. And she had never touched by scores of spiders all at once.

Into the cave mouth, the spiders dragged them. Along the sides away from the running water below. Further back into the Ozark granite cliffs. Deeper and deeper. Down into the earth.

The light of the cave mouth from the outside world grew faint. The gorge of Osage Cave State Park being left behind. And the Brazzles' Explorer that had brought them here. Away from the countryside and Trainer. From the highway that led back home. To Mom and Dad.

On they were carried into the unknown. Into the mysterious dark. To another place.

***

DOMAIN

Chapter Seven: Cross and Over

The storm seemed to follow them.

The twins had never heard of a thunderstorm inside a cave before.

The thunder threatened and bullied. Howling and rumbling. Rolling barrels of collapsing air pockets.

Lightning raced ahead of them through the darkness. Bursting arcs of power. Shooting streams of electricity.

The streaks flashed over the cave walls. Shooting into mineral and quartz which insulated the blows but lit up the walls like a kaleidoscope. With blinding brilliance.

Miss Crutch's silver necklace seemed to be a conduit. It was a lightning rod. Catching the fire from the battling storm clouds.

Some of the spiders strayed too close to the bolts and were enveloped in the plasma.

Catching fire they did a mad dance. Bumping into others as they were incinerated.

The lightning increased. Flashing here and there incessantly so that the twins squeezed their eyes shut. The streaks made diamond patterns on the back of their eyelids.

Between the moments of darkness and blinding light, the twins caught glimpses of the cave. The huntsman spiders pulled them all along the cave wall. Staying out of the stream below, the troop made a trail across the rock.

The cave became a downward tunnel. The speed of their descent increasing. Leaving the storm behind until it became a distant growl.

All of them were carried along. The Leftwich twins and the Brazzles cocooned away for a rainy day. While Miss Crutch and the CASA twins were tethered in the air by threads of spider webs like human balloons.

The troop of huntsman spiders carried their cargo deeper into the darkness. The only light now being the glowing silver moon-snake necklace that Miss Crutch held up in her hand. A star-fire glow in the eternal night.

Guiding the caravan through chambers and between stalactites. Across soda flows and behind calcium curtains. Passing ancient secrets buried long ago in the earth.With a speed like a falling elevator. Butterflies churned in the twins' stomachs.

They passed the boundary of where humans were meant to go in this world.

The cave became vast.

Opening into an empty space.

A mysterious cosmos.

It became the basement of eons.

The twins were floating as if in embryonic sacs. The simple physical presence of being becoming insignificant to their surroundings.

Onward the spiders scuttled.

Back to the beginning.

To the center of the dark.

To a seed long ago planted. Whose blind roots cut through the bowels of the universe. Spiraling out around itself into a web.

Gravity caught them again and slung them down a chute. The butterflies in their stomach returned. The darkness turned into a dull grey. Which became a blurry white and then a limpid blue.

The air became cold. Frigid and freezing. Again they were in a definite tunnel.

Bored through smooth ice. Smooth blue and white crystals. Diffusing a distant light from miles away.

There were things in the ice.

Denizens of the deep. Giant fish as large as a bus. Giant squid longer than a plane. Megladon sharks. Pods of whales. Schools of fish. Squadrons of seals. Giant sea turtles. Kelp and coral. All turned into crystallized flotsam and frozen jetsam. Every creature overcame in mid-turn. Ready to swim away if the ice would only thaw.

Their descent slowed and the tunnel leveled out.

The caravan was now surrounded by broken trees and detritus. Flowers and seeds. Whole waves of grain. Woodland creatures and pond animals running too late from the catastrophe.

Larger apex creatures, too. Lions and bears. And larger prey. Elephants and horses.

The smallest to the largest. Prey and predator. All frozen together.

There were darker shapes. Human debris and garbage. Wooden chairs and tools. Weapons and furniture.

There were people. Running. Swimming. Surrendered. Swallowed up.

Their faces shocked. Their eyes open and dull. Bodies suspended. Stuck on their last thought. Strangled for breath. Preserved for millennia.

It was if the sea had thrown itself on top of the land and everything marine had been piled on top of everything terrestrial.

The twins had crossed over into a different world. Not unlike their World. But this one seemed even more upside down than the one they had left.

The tunnel ran back into bedrock. The frost fell away. But the cold never did leave the twins' bones.

Ahead there was a red glow. A pinpoint on a flat horizon. An orange circle.

The air grew mephitic.

Rocks enclosed them again.

The caravan followed streams of heat. The twins' could begin to feel their fingers. Though they couldn't move them.

The circle grew brighter. Growing into three larger shades. Red on the sides and orange in the middle and blue on top.

It was a real physical phenomenon. Something occurring that could be seen and felt. Sitting atop a solid floor.

It was a fire. Feeding upon chopped wood in a pit. Lined by charcoal stained boulders.

The Leftwich twins blinked to adjust their eyes to the low ambient light and to the fact that Osage Cave was a sinkhole that opened up outside of Trainer, Missouri just to lead into someone's basement.

Reed didn't think that seemed impossible. He had read of the Underground Railroad for runaway slaves and Colonial homes that had escape tunnels from the Redcoats. But why would anyone want to run away from their World?

Chayse had seen travel shows on cable networks that had toured sewers and catacombs under ancient cities like Jerusalem and Rome. There were as many places below where people were buried to hide as they were above ground where people lived.

Bringing their load to a secure place somewhere underground, the remainder of the huntsman spider troop put them down and slipped away. Back into shadows and corners. Through crevices into their hidey-holes tucking their eggs legs over their hungry bellies and looking out for prey with their four eyes.

The caravan had arrived.

On stone cold cave floor.

Now all the Leftwichs had to do was get out of the webbing. Get away from Miss Crutch and the CASA twins and get back to Judge Hart and Officer Mike and report what the Brazzles had let Miss Crutch do.

Except the twins were secured tight in the webbing. Miss Crutch and the CASA twins tore the webs from their bodies. They were free to move around while the twins were their captives. Kidnapped. Which was illegal--back in their World. But what kind of world were the twins in now?

The CASA twins moved about the chamber. It was completely round. With the large fire pit at the center.

It was made of natural rock. Carved into the obdurate stone were many niches full of vials and bottles. Benches and ledges had been smoothed out of the walls as well which held tripods and centrifuges and other apparatus.

Chayse still had her faculties and her senses—she was alive and aware and she could breathe and see and hear and smell. She just couldn't move due to her spider bonds. "Reed, can you move at all?"

He lay on his back in front of her and, like her, he was in a coma position.

Testing his bonds as Chayse rocked his shoulders, he said, "I wanna go home!"

"So do I," Chayse said.

Struggling for freedom, Reed sobbed, "I want Mom and Dad!"

"So do I," Chayse said hating to admit if either of her parents strolled into the chamber now she would be most grateful. She and her twin had become most helpless. "But first we have to get free."

"Not so fast, children," said a woman's voice. It was still Miss Crutch. Only she wasn't the same person who had come to their front door just the other night.

The CASA twins, who had also changed their mien, had brought her a dark robe— different than Judge Hart's--made with raven feathers. She fluffed her long ginger curls on top of her shoulders showing black lacquered nails. Her thick glasses had been placed on a stone bench next to a centrifuge. Her suit pants and jacket exchanged for a black tunic.

She looked like the high priestess of some secret cult. And with her silver moon-snake necklace, she meant it. The final touch was a black metal band—Reed saw it and tried to remember what metal could turn black, of course! Lead!--she put on which fit snug against her forehead. In its center was a large unpolished quartz crystal.

The CASA twins had also changed out of their business casual clothes and now wore black tunics and leggings and no shoes. After giving the woman her cloak and her metal band they stepped back behind her.

The chamber stank of chemicals. Rank with refuse that burned the twins' noses. Whatever was stoppered in the bottles was far worse.

The twins wrestled with many things at the moment—fear, wonder, awe, abandonment, and hurt. But more than anything, they wanted to be free of their bonds.

The woman had said *children* like a curse. "This is my Domain. I will rule here and all things learn to serve me. All things will serve me."

"Lady, we just want to go home," Reed said.

"This little one never knows…," the first dark-headed twin started.

"When he should be quiet," the second dark-headed twin finished.

The woman/lady held up a long pale hand. "Victor. Nicolai. These little ones are very much afraid. The boy knows no better than to repeat empty threats that he has learned. But what do they mean? What power do his threats have here?"

"None," echoed both the dark-headed twins who had worked for CASA in the twins' World and were known as Vic and Nic there but were followers of this woman/lady here and also known as Victor and Nicolai.

"Then let us go," Chayse said.

The dark-headed twins laughed.

"You do not rule here," the woman/lady said.

"The Elfwitch rules," the dark-headed twins said.

Elfwitch? Had Reed heard the word right? Was the name Miss Crutch was known by here? Where ever this *here* was?

"I rule here," the Elfwitch said.

Elfwitch. Chayse had read about elves. There were all kinds of elves. High, dark, and sylvan. They also came in different sizes: brownies, imps, and fairies. They existed in myths and people's books who loved those old myths. They weren't supposed to be real.

Now witches, on the other hand, lived in both the real world and lived in myths. And there were all kinds of witches: white, black, herbalists, sorceresses, and diviners. They were in every culture throughout every part of history.

Somehow, this woman embodied the worst aspects of both worlds.

"Sooner rather than later, you will learn that truth," she said as she folded her arms over her chest. "For your sake. Bring the vessels."

The dark-headed twins both nodded and moved away from their mistress. Taking out knives the size of Bowie blades they moved towards the cocoon sacs. But it wasn't the Leftwich twins they freed first.

It was the Brazzles. Peyton and Shawn Brazzle—Reed couldn't remember which was called which—brushed off their bonds and came before the Elfwitch. First, they bowed, and then they got down on their knees.

The Elfwitch's eyes grew to silver saucers and by her smile, she relished the action like it was a favorite treat. "See how they grovel? That is how one must show obeisance, little ones."

"She is way-cray," Reed whispered to his twin sister. "Driving on only three wheels. Gone loco. Plumb crazy."

Chayse was in awe of the Elfwitch's presence: her mien and her power. She couldn't wait to see what powers she would unveil next.   "Ssh" was all she could manage for her brother's incessant rudeness.

Reed could be so annoying. It didn't matter what they were doing: watching the DVR, driving to Wal-mart, stretching against spiderwebs, her twin brother just couldn't be still or keep quiet.

The Elfwitch gloated over their surrender, "Who rules you?"

Both the Brazzles said with bowed heads, "You do, my mistress."

Their mistress held up her silver moon-snake necklace to her headband. Both the silver metal in her hand and the quartz crystal in the center of her forehead began to glow. It was hard to understand which one was igniting the other if one was just reflecting the brilliance of the other.

The silver necklace grew brighter until it outshone the fire. It was a tiny sun with an event horizon. The Elfwitch brought the silver necklace down as if to anoint both the Brazzles.

Both of them winked out.

The Leftwich twins blinked their eyes.

But the Brazzles were gone from the chamber circle.

Reed became angry.

While Chayse was amazed.

"You killed them!" he accused.

"That was awesome!" she said.

The Elfwitch tutted at Reed's nonsense. "They are not dead."

"Well, they're not here!" Reed said.

"True. But you lack understanding," the Elfwitch said. "Victor. Nicolai. Loose them. Then bind their hands."

The two dark-headed twins grinned with pleasure as they cut the twins free from the spider webbing. Victor stood them and Nicolai took two pairs of metal binders off of a nearby stone bench in the wall. The binders were old fashioned iron cuffs fettered with chain. Like from out of some gothic dungeon.

Only the metal was heavy and hardened. Rough from being forged by hand. And real enough.

"Let me show you something," the Elfwitch said to the Leftwich twins. "A deep, deep secret."

Chayse couldn't wait. She was becoming enthralled.

Reed became indignant. "I won't promise *not* to tell. You'll get no promises from me."

"It's not your promises that I want," the Elfwitch said.

***

Chapter Eight: Guest and Captive

The Circle Chamber had two entryways. Both round apertures leading to other passageways. Both dark mouths to unknown destinations, though an icy draft emanated from one as well as a dull blue glare.

The huntsman spiders must have brought the caravan through that opening. And that was the same one the dark-headed twins now pushed the Leftwich twins through by the shoulders. The Elfwitch followed behind holding up her precious silver necklace between thumb and forefinger.

Having been spun into their cocoon sacs on the journey in, the twins hadn't been able to discern the passageway's formation. The sides angled up like a pyramid giving the passageway a vented roof. Chisel marks delineated the walls' design.

The twins could feel the heat from the fire pit receding behind them. Ahead the temperature plummeted. The twins had just begun to thaw out and now that bitter cold was cutting into them again. Numbing skin, freezing muscle and marrow, icing blood.

The afternoon August heat at the Shiloh courthouse in their World had just been stifling, but if the twins were to be left alone down here they would soon freeze to death from exposure. As much as their World seemed confusing, it was known to them. This strange world just seemed so harsh.

The passage dead-ended at a T-junction. Another corridor bored through the rock. Running parallel along a huge massive wall of ice. The twins were going from one extreme element to another. Every exhale turning into a vapor trail.

Dead ahead were four niches.

Three were filled with occupants.

But the fourth was empty.

The empty niche held an outline of a tall thin figure. While the other three being shaped to hold their occupants. Reed was reminded of action figure toys encased in plastic wrap safe and snug inside their card boxes. But since these figures were larger than life-like, he thought somehow they had walked into a freezer In Season might use to store their extra Halloween door figures.

Of the three filled niches, the one was on the right held the tallest figure. A rail-thin person in a long robe. Its hands hidden in the folds of the robe's arms. Its face hidden under a heavy cowl.

The one on the left held a figure in a large leather duster with the collar up. A large brimmed hat hid the face but a long ponytail hung across its neck. This figure seemed a person having human features, though Chayse wouldn't swear it was human.

But their attention was riveted to the person held in the middle. The figure was as tall as it was wide. Clothed in leather pants and jacket. With long jackboots and a belt with a square silver buckle.

The twins could not look away from the creature's face. Serene and striking even while frozen blue. Black shadows ringed the sleeping eyes and traced the full lips perched to open and take a breath and speak a word. The beautiful head was offset with a mane of wild black hair.

Three strange figures. Why were they here inside this immense ice? Who had imprisoned them here?

Before the four niches was a large rectangular shape covered with a black shawl. It might have been a table. Or a box.

The air changed. Under the frigid cold, an ancient smell was palpable. Like old dust in a basement. Rusted metal tools. Acrid pee stains. Rotten apples. Bad eggs. Or dead mice. Old fish offal—or blood.

The Elfwitch turned to face the twins. "This is a sacred place. It, too, is my Domain. Though it is in disgrace, it will soon be righted."

She got on her knees before the figures. So did the dark-headed twins. They bowed low until their heads touched the frozen floor.

Both Victor and Nicolai hissed at the Leftwich twins who did not take the hint, so the twin brothers slapped at the other twins' knees until they, too, got down on bended knee.

The Leftwich twins looked over the mysterious figures. The shrouded one seemed to twitch a shadow on the fold of its robe. The collared one's mouth stretched into a leering smile like a wild-eyed clown at a midnight carnival. And out of the biggest one's mouth came a forked tongue that licked the black lips before retreating inside.

The figures were somehow alive. And if everyone in this world had to bow to these frozen people then the Leftwich twins wanted to know why.

"Who are those people?" Chayse asked.

"They are not people, little one," Victor sneered with his head upside down.

"They are your true gods," Nicolai barked at them.

"Then why are they frozen?" Reed asked.

The Elfwitch jumped up to her feet and strode over to put a long forefinger into his face just like his first grade teacher used to do. "Blame the Judge. All fault lies with him. But soon they will be free again. Free again to do what they will. I will teach all the Realm to serve and worship them. Then this entire world will be under my thrall.

"My Domain will spread its roots out to other worlds. There will be no turning back then. The Great Work will be finished. Complete. Not even the Judge can stop it. And the battle for Light and Dark that began on the first day will be over,"

"The Elfwitch and her gods will defeat the Judge," Victor said.

"Because the Judge is weak. Only the strong should rule," Nicolai said.

Reed didn't like being weak and helpless. But he felt that way now. An insignificant ice crystal or a worthless pebble flaking off a stone. Even Mom made him feel that way after she would yell at him or try to beat him before he ran away. But she was still his mother. Under the anger and the hurt, he could remember her hugs and kisses and birthday cakes and baking chocolate chip cookies just for no reason other than saying she loved him.

Miss Crutch had never been like that, more so the opposite--mean and conniving.

And the Elfwitch was way worse.

Why else were his hands cuffed behind his back?

"You're evil," Reed said.

The dark-headed twins pushed themselves up to defend their mistress. Instead, the Elfwitch slapped Reed across the mouth. He tasted something salty and tin like in his mouth--it was his own blood.

"Why are you so rude all the time?" Chayse asked as if the last thing in the world she wanted to deal with was being embarrassed by her twin brother. Five minutes apart was no different than five thousand years apart.

"Sissy," Reed whispered as he rubbed his jaw against his shoulder. He could see a spot of blood on his shirt.

"You'll get no sympathy from me," Chayse said not realizing that those were Mom's words that she had heard a dozen times spoken against Dad. And each time they had been another brick in a dividing wall between the family's heart. She still carried the baggage of hating Dad. All that pent up spleen had to go somewhere. Chayse had a new target: Reed.

The Elfwitch preened with satisfaction over the twins taking bites of out each other. She meant to sow seeds of discord. That was her fruit.

Thus defended by his twin sister, the Elfwitch squared up against a twelve-year-old boy whose hands were cuffed behind his back. "There is no evil here and there is no good anywhere. There is only Light or Darkness. You must serve one or the other. And in my Domain, the Darkness rules supreme. You will learn it is so, little one."

Chayse had had enough of waiting for Mom to come home just to have five minutes to get her attention or permission for anything. Mom's way of dealing with things—job, bills, having a house filled with food and things they wanted—sucked. Since she wasn't around, what allegiance did Chayse even owe Mom anymore?

How was having her hands cuffed behind her back any different than waiting around for supper—which would be the same Hamburger Helper meal they had last week--or being taken away from Mom--because Chayse was too young to be emancipated—or not having money to buy things and swipe them on Shopkicks?

Chayse wanted the handcuffs off.

The Elfwitch bent over to put her long cold hands on the twins' shoulders. Not unlike how Lawyer Kyler had treated them. Which meant they were to listen and not question. "Now you can either be my guests or my captives. Guests will be treated in kind as to how you treat me. Captives will be dealt with mercilessly. Either way, I will be served. Understood?"

Chayse nodded. "Understood."

The Elfwitch waited for Reed to answer. He hadn't expected she'd wanted him to answer. So he wasn't going to. "Just get on with whatever you're gonna do."

Both the dark-headed twins laughed at his insolence. "Better put a muzzle on this one, Mistress." "That's all he can do. Bark but not bite."

The Elfwitch ignored Reed. Instead, she smiled and patted Chayse's shoulder. "That is well. I can trade in kind with this little one. I will tell you what I want from you. Then I will tell you what I can do for you. And know that what is offered to one is offered to the other."

Reed wanted to tell Sissy not to listen to the Elfwitch. That she had also been Miss Crutch back in their World and they both had known better than to trust her. What could she offer the twins that would make them want to listen to her now?

Staying bent over before the twins, the Elfwitch held up her silver moon-snake necklace. "This is the Lesser Light and this is the Porter. The Lesser Light rules the Night. She is the Queen of the Darkness. The Porter guards all doors."

"That's the moon," Chayse said.

"That is true, little one," the Elfwitch said.

"If that's the moon and that's the lesser light, then what's the sun?" Reed asked.

The Elfwitch narrowed her eyes at him. "Of that, we do not speak. Soon no one ever will again."

"What? You can't just make the Sun go away," Reed said.

Victor and Nicolai growled and bared teeth at him. The eyes of the Elfwitch burned. "The Light has gone away. The Judge has turned his back on this world. It will be my Domain.

"There is now myself. Back of me is Shadow, Rancor, and the Destroyer. Back of them is the Lesser Light. And back of her is the Darkness. Meditate on that and despair."

Reed wanted to ask, "Why?" but the question caught in his throat.

Instead, his twin sister asked, "How will you free the others from the ice?"

The Elfwitch smiled. Her teeth a livid white against her pale blue flesh. With her other lithe hand, she pulled out the second necklace that she had kept hidden all the while.

It was a familiar shape. A long silver cable chain ending in a pendant of metal symmetry. An open heart with three inner clasps.

The Leftwich twins knew it well.

It was Mom's silver heart necklace.

"You stole it!" Reed accused.

Again, the Elfwitch smiled because she knew a devastating truth that Reed could not deny. "I'm afraid not, little one. It was freely given."

In her hands, the heart necklace seemed cold. A prized relic that could only be pried away from dead fingers. She meant to hold onto it in her grasp.

"But that's Mom's!" Chayse swore.

"Not quite. Very much like. It is not from your World," the Elfwitch said. "Now as to my wants. I want both of your necklaces."

"We don't have any necklaces," Reed said.

The Elfwitch backhanded him with the hand that held the moon-snake necklace. The snake tongue cut into his cheek. The Leftwich twins winced. The dark-headed twins smiled.

This time Chayse could see the mark on her twin brother's mouth. She wanted him to stop being so stubborn. It would kill him. "We lost them when the spiders brought us here," Chayse said.

"Little ones, it does no good to lie to me," the Elfwitch said. "Now as to what I will offer in exchange for your wants. Freely give me both of your necklaces and you will be returned to back to your World."

"Back to Mom?" asked Chayse.

"And Dad?" asked Reed.

"No, you must return with the Brazzles," the Elfwitch explained. "That shortsighted 'judge' has written his order for ninety days that you should be in their custody, remember. But if you do all that I say then the Lawyer Kyler can influence the 'judge' to stay the order."

"Then we can see Mom?" asked Chayse.

"And Dad?" asked Reed.

"Oh, most surely, you will see both of them again," the Elfwitch promised as if she knew beyond a certainty when that could only be if she knew all things and could do all things. She put the heart necklace back under her tunic and let the moon-snake necklace rest against her chest so she could hold out both her empty hands.

"But you got our hands cuffed behind our backs," Chayse said.

"I can't even reach into my pocket," Reed said.

"So I have and so you are," the Elfwitch said. She snapped her fingers. "Loose them. Watch them."

The dark-headed twins each pulled out their silver rope chains which had several things attached. Their moon-snake festoons and several small keys. Using one they unlocked the Leftwich twins' fetters.

Victor put his hand on Chayse's shoulder but Reed ran away from Nicolai.

"Watch them, I said!" the Elfwitch said.

The ice corridor stretched in a tight parallel either way into the darkness. All that he would meet there would be a long slow sleep on an ice-cold bed. So Reed made for the portal back to the vented hallway. That would take him back to the Circle Chamber.

Then what?

Hadn't there been another portal on the other side?

He'd try for that.

Only Reed didn't get as far the first portal from the ice chamber. The opening was occluded. By something moving through it.

Something as big as the opening.

It was a monstrous animal. As thick and wide as his chest coming to his thigh. It was moving with rapid speed both blocking the portal and cutting off his escape down the ice corridor.

The animal was a dull white like an anchor chain. Except it had scales. Its head reared up against the blueish ambience from the ice sheet. A triangular mass of slit eyes and pitted nose and a forked tongue, as long as his arm, darting in and out.

It was a snake. An albino constrictor of massive length and strength. Coiling an ever-tightening circle around him.

"Sissy!" Reed cried. He froze like a rodent with no escape. Facing the terror of slipping down a tight black hole into a cul-de-sac.

But Chayse couldn't help. She was just as scared at the sight of the reticulated constrictor whose head was thicker than her abdomen. What could she do to stop such a beast?

"Porter! Cease!" the Elfwitch called out and stomped her foot.

The words were simple. Three syllables. Echoing down the ice corridor. Bouncing off the glacial wall. Stretching into long waves. While the syllables changed into harsher words.

Serpent. Stop. Back to your lair.

Chayse could feel the spoken words pushing against her body as well as hear them down deep in her ear. Maybe they were most clear only in her mind. Either way, they had undeniable power.

The snake stopped its advance against its helpless prey. Then it slithered back down the ice corridor. Away from Reed who began taking deeper breaths again.

"Lycanthropes!" the Elfwitch commanded. "Change shape!"

Both Victor and Nicolai closed their eyes and stuck their hands out like claws. In an instant, they were down on all fours. Their arms and back legs becoming nearly the same length and their spines becoming raised and ridged. Tails sprouted and their heads grew as their noses became long snouts with long pointed ears.

The twins were now wolves. Two of the biggest Chayse had ever seen. But Reed had read of such wolves--dire wolves. As big as Great Danes with heads bigger than pit bulls.

The twin dire wolves ran to secure his escape. Then in a blink of an eye, they stood back up as their human counterparts. "Silly rabbit." "You would have been swallowed up for sure." Taking the boy in hand they the twelve-year-old twin back to their mistress.

The Elfwitch crossed her arms. "This is a new world for you. You are a stranger in my Domain. Your only hope of survival is to do what I say."

"You would have let that thing kill my brother," Chayse said. She had never been afraid for her twin before. They had always stood up for each other but this time she had been just as helpless as him.

"That thing is the Porter," the Elfwitch said. "It is an elemental. Made long ago by forces that I have yet to control."

Chayse had seen the great serpent before. Represented in silver metal. All coiled with a forking tongue holding the crescent moon on its snout like a trained seal. "Your necklace."

The Elfwitch grinned. "You are a fast learner. How very wondrous."

"So that thing is controlled by the moon?" Chayse asked.

Reed put aside his fear and considered the existence of such a giant creature and then also, the origin of bigger objects--the moon or any other star. "Everything is made from the same stuff, Sissy. I guess the laws of physics are the same in this world."

"See, my lycanthropes? The little rabbits are quick of mind, too. Being a twin, do you not marvel?" the Elfwitch asked her two servants.

Victor scowled and Nicolai blew air out of the side of his mouth.

"Jealousy," the Elfwitch noted with relish. "Good! Careful my little rabbits or my servants may devour you just to keep their place.

"Now, I have brought you here for a singular purpose and my will shall be accomplished. You are never to come here without me. For you have seen what may happen otherwise."

"Because that snake guards this place?" Reed asked.

"The Porter guards all doors. They will be locked to you since you are strangers to this world. I am your guide here, without me you both would be lost and surely die," the Elfwitch answered.

Reed didn't want to believe her. She had lied back in their World in court as Miss Crutch. So why wouldn't she lie to them now in this Domain?

But Chayse had seen her master the Porter who would have devoured Reed otherwise. The woman had strange powers that should be respected. The Elfwitch was speaking a kind of truth.

"So we are back to my request and my offer. Again, I extend out my hand and I expect an offer in kind," the Elfwitch said holding out both empty hands palm up.

Chayse was at a crossroads. A part of her didn't want to give up anything Mom had given her. It was just a silly necklace. No more than twenty-five U.S. dollars at Wal-Mart. Mom had meant it as an heirloom. Something to remind Chayse of her Mom's love. But her Mom was so far away from where they were now. And here it seemed to be something more than Chayse could understand.

Reed made his decision. And he was going to stand by it. He spat into the woman's hands.

This time the Elfwitch did not strike him. Instead, she balled her hands into fists. She puffed up her chest and shoulders. Her eyes slit and her silver speckled skin turned a dangerous hue of gray. "Victor! Nicolai! Take them away! To the dungeon! Both of them! There are worse fates than snakes in my Domain!"

The lycanthrope twins changed into their canid forms and herded the twins back down the tunnel to the Circle Chamber. Exchanging the cold blue glare for the soft orange light of the Elfwitch's Lair. This time the twins were corralled down the other exit. To another tunnel cut through the gut rock of this world long ago. It was tall enough for a man to pass through in single file and seemed too narrow for that snake to slither through.

The confines of the smaller passageway returned their body heat to the twins. The numbing cold of the ice fell away and now their limbs merely ached from traversing the terrain. The afternoon began with the Brazzles promising to take the twins for a hike and then to get ice cream.

Reed reckoned they had hiked more than a few miles and the promise for ice cream had been broken.

Chayse wondered what time it was back home and if Mom missed them as much as she missed Mom.

***

Chapter Nine: Forgotten and Remembered

The second passageway leading away from the Circle Chamber was narrower than the one which had taken them to the ice corridor. It was a great deal warmer. There was a light ahead casting flickering shadows over the rough-hewn walls.

More firelight. There seemed to be no electricity in this world.

Reed had often daydreamed of being a frontiersman hunting and trapping when Arkansas had been a part of the Louisiana Purchase before waking up to find himself back in his bedroom bored again. Chayse preferred the safety and surety of well lighted and clean places and this world seemed short on both. What was the point of scratching a living off from the land when you had a refrigerator?

The long shadows solidified into a slanting lattice. Firelight off torches set into a wall came through a large iron portcullis that barred the mouth of the passage.

Leaving the twins to Nicolai's capable hairy hands, Victor stepped up to the gate and banged on an iron stud. A man's face capped with a red scarf appeared. He leered showing teeth and gums not because he had a huge grin but because he had no lips or the left side of his face. Muscle and sinew were exposed up to an empty eye socket.

"Pass," the man whispered as if he had rusty knives stuck in his throat.

Victor gave the password. "Silver. Now open up, rawhide."

A great chain was released and then cranked by turning metal gears. The heavy portcullis gate was hoisted up. And the twins came into the underbelly of this world.

The chamber had a low ceiling where black smoke clung like upside huntsman spiders. Humid air gathered and became too heavy and dripped back down into puddles on the rough floor. The chamber spread out into many stalactite columns shaping niches and antechambers.

These smaller rooms had either iron bars or iron doors over them. With grimy faces of animal-like humans stripped of freedom and dignity. Now kept in filthy cages to rot. With dull eyes that would not focus. Sunken cheeks with open sores. Gaping mouths that moaned through missing teeth. Reaching out with bony hands, not for freedom or even hope.

But for a crust of bread.

This was a dungeon.

A place of torture.

A place of torn hope.

A place of no return.

Placed throughout the room were skeletons. Not chained to the wall in manacles. Not placed in human-sized bird cages to show the final punishment of being forgotten: rotting death.

These skeletons were tall and broad. Clothed in worn and torn red jackets. In knee-less breeches with faded boots. They had frayed bandoliers and powder horns. Some had missing eyes and mouths. Hooks in place of missing hands. Some even had scarecrow heads full of straw in places of missing heads.

But their weapons looked all too real and ready. Well oil rifled muskets, sharpened double edge pikes, blunt staves for digging or stabbing, and razor-fine swords. These troopers had died with their boots on only to find their sworn duty was not finished on the other side of the grave. They had found no peace and would serve until they crumbled into dust.

Small furry things scampered along the sides of the walls. Moving from one shadow to another. Padding on tiny feet.

Rats. With thick brown fur. Long hairless grey tails. With alert eyes close to their sniffing noses. Moving with both the fear of exciting discoveries and the fear of being discovered.

Reed wasn't surprised to see them here. The surprise had been the run-in with the biggest snake he'd ever seen outside of his family's one vacation when they'd gone to the St. Louis Zoo where they kept a thirty-six-foot long reticulated python in the zoo's original 1904 reptile house. But this albino constrictor—maybe a freak anaconda--had been every bit of fifty feet long.

Snakes fed on rats. Rats fed on anything they could find. So far, the taxonomy of this place wasn't much different than from their World and it wouldn't do much good to worry about what he couldn't see.

"Sergeant Hood!" Nicolai called.

One of the shuffling half-dead-who-should-have-been-all-dead soldiers with tattered brevets on his shoulders came as called. He was bigger than the other soldiers. And had both eyes, though the right one had become a milky orb like a marble shooter. His skin had been flayed back in places to expose the working meat of his hands and arms.

"Put these two in the oubliette," Nicolai commanded and pushed the twins forward.

The sergeant growled. His eyes fixing on the Elfwitch's servant and back to twins and as he did the milky orb tracked along his one good eye making Chayse want to puke. Was he growling at her and her brother or at the servant giving orders or at the trooper's condition?

With one meaty arm, the dead but living sergeant ushered the twins forward to march down the center of the dungeon. Being this close to the soldier the twins got more than a good whiff. Musty, dusty, like an old wet sock.

The dark-headed lycanthrope twins tramped back through the open portcullis gate.

Reed was tired.

Chayse was hungry.

But fear overrode those basic needs.

The sergeant stopped them and bent down to the floor. With a rotting hand, he pulled up an iron grate thicker than one used in the storm drains in downtown Shiloh. Setting the lid back on its hinges he pointed downwards to a deep dark hole.

"Get in," he croaked.

Chayse looked at Reed. It wasn't just caves she feared. It was small spaces and the dark. "You know I don't like small places. Or being in the dark."

"I'm right here with you," Reed said as he sat over the opening to dangle a leg.

There was a screech below. And the sound of tiny feet scampering away from the light cascading down.

More rats.

Reed shuddered. As much as snakes and rats and even lizards fascinated him, he didn't fancy being in a place where they could get an up close look at him. No, he wasn't going to let himself be afraid of what he couldn't see. If Dad were here, that's what he'd tell him to do.

He took a breath and jumped down just like he was diving off the low diving board at the Raccoon Springs Recreational Center. It was a short drop into the dark unknown. He landed on rocks and a huge pile of what he thought was sticks.

"It's okay, Sissy," he called back up.

Sergeant Hood was waiting anymore. He shoved Chayse as he began to close the lid on top of them.

His twin sister fell into him. Reed would have put his arms out to catch her if he'd had the chance. But there had been no time to do anything other than put his arms around her as they both fell on top of the pile of sticks.

Reed would protect his sister. He would give his life. If it came to that.

And in this place, that seemed to be a growing possibility.

Chayse thought it was an odd place to put twigs and limbs. Maybe it was a place to store firewood. Having no electricity meant burning lots and lots of wood.

She picked up a stick that was poking her in the small of her back.

The stick was hard and worn. Dirty like a stone. More porous than driftwood.

One thing for sure, it wasn't a stick. It ended in a hard round ball. Like a socket joint.

It was a bone.

They were lying on top of a pile of bones. Hundreds of bones. Broken bones. Snapped off. Gnawed on. Chewed up. Spat out bones.

Chayse screamed as the iron lid clanged shut. Not only was she in a small place but that place was even lower than the dungeon which was already inside a cave. And everything was dark.

Pitch black perfect blindness.

Fingers found her.

She kept screaming.

They were warm and tender fingers. Meaning to offer solace and shelter. Not harm.

Chayse was beside herself. She was in a perfect storm of fear and hate. With nowhere to go and no one to help her. Not Dad. Not even Mom.

Except for one person.

And that person was with her here and now.

The fingers were attached to kind hands.

The hands were connected to encircling arms.

The arms were a part of a body that had arrived in their World just five minutes after her own. A heartbeat sharing the womb with her. A silver necklace that fit into hers.

Her brother. Her twin self. Who was her complete opposite?

There in the damp darkness of their cruel cell, Reed hugged her. His warmth was a blanket. His words a soft caress.

"It's alright, Sissy. We are still alive. We still have each other. We still got hope," Reed said. He offered a truth: love, hope, and family. Maybe it was the only truth.

Chayse returned to herself. Full of queries and endless investigation. Reed was right— this was just another circumstance. If Mom were here she would say, "Either we define our circumstances or we let our circumstances define us."

The darkness wasn't so deep. There were hints of shade and grey. Uneven walls.

The bones weren't so bad. They looked very small. Like animal bones rather than human bones.

And there were other things down here. Broken bits of chain. Banged up tools. Bolt heads and bumps of slags.

"This is a trash pit," Chayse said.

"Guess we must be trash to them," Reed laughed. "Time to take out the trash. Don't forget to throw away the Leftwich Twins."

"Ha, ha," Chayse said. "Why do you have to make fun of everything?" "Dad   says   if you can't laugh, they win. And when you laugh, they lose," Reed said. "No way am I going to let them win.

"Sissy?" he asked.

Chayse had been surveyed the trash pit that served as their cell.

"Yes, bub?" she asked.

"What's an 'oubliette?'" he asked.

Chayse had to think. It's what Nicolai had told that undead soldier to put them into. So they were in one now. Chayse thought back farther. Her mind flicking through some recent titles she'd read to a collection of short stories in an Accelerated Reader book that had been two grades above her. *Tales of…the Weird and Wonderful?* No. *Tales of…Mystery and Imagination.* In one story, someone was put into a dark cell with no light that had a door where his captors could watch him through it.

Then she remembered, "Some kind of dungeon with a trap door."

Reed stood up on the tallest part of the trash pile and tried to reach the bottom of the grate. He was about five feet too short. The debris began to slip under his feet until he was seven feet too short.

"Must be the only way in or out," Reed said.

Chayse had enough hope not to be overcome with her fear of small places again. So she was too tired to hope they could get out right away. She sat down in the middle of the trash. Their long journey to this place began to catch up with her.

Reed sat down next to her. "Sucks."

"Yes, it does," Chayse said picked up an old bone to poke through the nearby trash. Chayse leaned against her brother's shoulder. "Why are they doing this to us?"

"It's that Elfwitch lady. She wants us to be afraid," Reed said and yawned. "You mean Miss Crutch. But why does she want our necklaces?" Chayse said.

"I don't know but it's the only thing of Mom's we got," Reed said.

There was something hard in Chayse's pocket. Something that had been there all day. She sat up. "Bubba! We still have our phones!" She took hers out. It was a Tracfone mini-tablet. And dead as the pile of bones, they sat on. Still, she did not give up hope. "Do you still have yours?"

Reed slapped his pocket. Something rectangular smacked against something else. He felt. It was round. Maybe a quarter or something. Great, he'd brought some change along to their dungeon in case they wanted to use the vending machine. He didn't bother getting either item out since Sissy's phone was dead. "There's no signal down here."

"But we were supposed to call Mom tonight. Well, the Brazzles were. When she doesn't hear from us, she'll worry. Then she'll call that lawyer add-light-tum--"

"You mean Lawyer Kyler. He's a lawyer and his hair's longer than Mom's," Reed snorted.

"Yep. That's the one. He'll have to try to make sure she calls us. Then he'll have to tell Judge Hart. And he'll want to know where we are. Then he'll want to talk to this Miss Crutch. So he'll send someone looking for us," Chayse said.

"The trouble is, Sissy, we don't even know where we are," Reed argued.

Chayse asked her next thought out loud, "How will we ever get back?"

"I don't know, Sissy," Reed said.

They both yawned. And leaned back against one another. Their heads drooped down on their chest not in defeat but out of exhaustion and their eyes closed like iron grates.

***

Chapter Ten: Invitation and Acceptance

Reed hoped that by falling asleep he'd forget about being hungry. But it would be hard to stave off thirst. The humid air only made his sleep shallow and his mouth dry.

Chayse meant to take just a quick nap. One of those power naps that CEOs of Japanese car factories took on benches in public parks. Then when she woke up she'd be back in their World: in her bedroom, she shared with her twin with all her make-up and stuffed unicorns.

Reed dreamed that Dad had ridden along with Uncle Buddy in his Chevy Z-Off Road to pick him up and take him over to Uncle Buddy's trailer. The one they had lived in when they had been little and Mom and Dad had been happier. And they had all day to fish and target shoot and then play Xbox games together.

Chayse dreamed that her phone was going off. It was Mom trying to call her. To tell her she'd taken the day off from her evening job and was driving home to get her so they could go shopping at Turtle Shell Mall in Hamilton and get some custard from Billy's which was even better than the Big Dipper if that was even possible.

There was a clang. Metal being hoisted. Hinges banging.

Somewhere overhead.

Which meant there were still in the Domain. In the oubliette. In the dark.

But there was something smaller making a fuss, too. Shaking and vibrating against her thigh. In her pocket something small and rectangular.

Her…Tracfone!

Someone…was…texting!

Or…calling?   In a flash, Chayse was sitting up awake on her numb butt from having slept upright on a pile of bones. But she did not care a whit! Her phone was going off! It was working! She wasn't dreaming now. Taking out the phone the screen she could see text notifications.

A…real…hope…come…quick! They would be saved!

Soon they would be home!

Reed had been more right than he'd known.

The text notifications were all from the same person:
> MOM
>
> Are you there?
>
> MOM
>
> Why haven't you called me tonight?

Chayse had never been happier. Everything would be alright. Everything would go back to the way it was supposed to be.

"Reed!" she tried to shake her twin awake. But his head just rolled off his chest and he drifted down to his side so he could snore on the pile of dead bones.

"It's Mom! She's texting!" Chayse said. Hoping to share the turn of luck with her twin.
> MOM
>
> Are you ok?

Now Chayse had to text back. Mom was worried. Why wouldn't she be?

Chayse texted back.
> ME
>
> I'm ok! We got kidnapped! You gotta come get us!
>
> MOM
>
> Where are you?
>
> ME
>
> In a dungeon.
>
> MOM
>
> How did that happen?
>
> ME
>
> Miss Crutch did it! U gotta tell Judge Hart to stop her!
>
> MOM
>
> Can you get out?
>
> ME
>
> Dont think I can. Im scared. Come get me.
>
> MOM
>
> Do not be afraid. Soon we will be together

Chayse noticed it was lighter in the oubliette than before. She looked up to see glorious firelight coming through the open trap door. It had been pulled back up to rest on its hinges.

Unbelievable!
> ME
>
> Maybe I can!
>
> MOM
>
> Do you still have the heart necklace I gave you!
>
> ME
>
> Course!
>
> MOM
>
> Bring it and get out of there!
>
> ME
>
> What about Reed? Can't leave him!
>
> MOM

Come to me. Bring necklace. We will go back and get Reed.

Chayse had never been happier. Had never been surer of Mom's promises. They didn't belong in this Domain. There had been a mistake. And now Mom would take care of it. And they would all go home. Together.

How could she climb out?

Something dangled down from the top of the grate. It was knotted and twisted. It was a frayed and musty old rope.

Hanging low enough for her to grab with one hand she pushed herself off the bone pile and reached up to take hold of the rope one hand than the other. Now the toe of her Converse sneakers scrapped the bone pile.

Pulling herself up hand over hand, Chayse shinnied up the rope like it was a swing rope on an old oak in their front yard of the rental in Raccoon Springs Village.

Her head was above the oubliette floor. Chayse surveyed the dungeon floor. The hopeless miscreants lay against the bottom of their cages still waiting for the smallest sustenance. They looked at the girl who had gained her freedom but could not discern what that meant.

Chayse gripped the sides of the oubliette door frame and pulled her chest up until she could swing her legs over. Then she rolled out of the oubliette. She looked back down inside.

It was a small dank hole indeed. But her brother was still down in it. Sleeping away his chance to escape.

"Reed!" she whispered as loud as she could. No matter. Mom was waiting. She had promised after she'd met up with Chayse that they'd come back for him.

There wasn't a single undead soldier around. Where had they gone? How had the trapdoor been open? By however and whoever, Chayse was free!

MOM

Where r u?

ME

I'm out!

MOM

Good Grl! Come 2 me!

ME

Where R u?

MOM

Circle Chamber

ME

Where is that?

MOM

Thru other gate

Chayse remembered now. That must be the large room where the twins had been released out of the spider webbing. It had looked like some kind of laboratory or workshop.

She crept to the other end of the dungeon and through the lifted iron portcullis. It was a short journey back to the Circle Chamber. The air was pungent with the mixing fragrances of oils and perfumes of spices.

A large fire at the chamber's center flicked its running shadows on the outside of the tunnel rooms. It was much warmer than what Chayse had remembered the first time. But with all the vials and tools it was more like a pharmacy than being at home.

And standing in front of the fire was Mom in her KFC uniform. Red and black tunic and black slacks. Her ginger hair pulled back through the back of her black cap.

Chayse ran to her and hugged her tight. She never wanted to let go of her again. Mom seemed a little stiff but gave a partial hug.

"How did you ever find us?" Chayse asked.

"Doesn't matter. What matters is that we are together again," Mom said. But somehow the words didn't match her hug or lack of one. "Did you bring the necklace?"

"Yes, of course!" Chayse said. "But shouldn't we go get Reed?"

"Of course!" Mom said and moved her hands to Chayse's shoulders. "Give me the necklace first."

"Why?" Chayse said. "Don't you want Reed's, too?"

"Of course," Mom paused and looked down to the left, "but we have to wake him up."

Chayse pulled her necklace out from under her shirt and over her head. Mom was smiling so big. Chayse couldn't remember the last time she'd seen Mom this happy.

The links of the cable chain chinked in her hand. Dad had given Mom a set of heart necklaces. And now Mom had given one to the twins. Why on earth would she want it back?

Mom's eyes were bigger than the moon. Like magnets drawing Chayse's hands to them. Chayse didn't want to disappoint her.

"Chayse!" yelled a voice she had known all her life. "Don't give it to her!"

She turned to see her twin brother in the Circle Chamber. He had awoken to find her gone and then noticed the trap door was open and a length of rope hanging down. So he'd climbed up and come looking for her.

"Reed, it's Mom," Chayse said. Why was he upset? They were both out of the oubliette. Soon Mom would take them back home.

Reed shook his head hard enough to shake a tooth loose. "That's not Mom!"

Chayse got mad. "Quit being a butt!"

"We must go," Mom said. "Reed is with us now. The necklace, Chayse. I need the necklace."

Mom's voice turned to worry. Clouded with frustration. Amping up with stress.

But underneath it, Chayse heard another voice. A low whisper. *Child, give me the necklace.*

Reed ran to his twin sister. Meaning to pull her away as if she were too close to a fire. Only there was a spark. Like a huge static electrical charge. And Reed was pushed back.

Chayse was confused. She was tired and hungry. And so very thirsty.

She couldn't go on. She didn't want to be in this place anymore. She just wanted to go home.

And Mom was here. Right in front of her. Asking Chayse to do one simple task.

Chayse gave her Mom her silver heart necklace.

The hand that clutched it was not her Mom's. Not freckled brown with broken fingernails. Not dried out and rough from working two menial jobs every day.

The hands were cold. With a dull grayish hue. And scaly.

Mom's KFC outfit was gone. Her countenance faded. The smile flickered.

Chayse heard Reed warn, "Chayse! Get away from it!"

A large presence stood in her place. Mouth open with an unhinged mandible. Pit fangs above two nostrils slit. A long blue tongue with a forked end tasted Chayse's confusion and growing fear.

Mom's legs and chest molded together in a white trunk. Encased in scales and undulated muscles. Moving with reptilian grace.

Chayse became a rodent. Eyes close together like prey. Ears flattened back in alarm. Heart fluttering in terror. Frozen in place. Caught by a much larger predator.

The Porter slithered around the fire with most of its length pointed back towards the exit to the ice tunnel. Head rearing up over Chayse. Mouth open inviting her into a tunnel to oblivion.

Chayse was no longer certain Mom had ever been in the Circle Chamber. She could only believe what she saw in front of her.

"Get away from her!" Reed yelled. He wasn't going to give up on his twin sister. Not on his Sissy.

There were no weapons in the Circle Chamber. And Reed had already tried to rush in and get Chayse just to an electrical shock. Chayse could smell sulfur in the air and feel the hairs standing up on her arm.

He picked up the first thing his hand reached. Some vial resting in a wooden rack. Full of some liquid that sloshed around from being jostled.

He hefted it up and threw it at the Porter's open mouth. Let the freak anaconda get a taste of something spicy. The vial broke against the snake's large snout. The contents must have acidic because smoke began to rise from where the liquid burned into the snake's scales.

The great snake began to shake its broad head. Reed rushed in and pulled his twin sister back from its maw. The snake thrashed its head against the ground trying to put out the fire on its nose and stop the pain.

"Victor! Nicolai!" commanded a familiar and unwanted voice.

As two dire wolves, the twin servants bounded in and surrounded the twins. Cutting off their escape and herded them together against a wall of the Circle Chamber. While the Porter writhed and fled through the exit to the ice tunnels in an attempt to use the cold to staunch its pain.

The Elfwitch strode over to the twins in what looked like a KFC uniform and cap. She held up her prize: Chayse's dangling heart necklace on its cable chain. "Now it is mine."

"You tricked her!" Reed accused.

The Elfwitch shrugged off the KFC uniform and shook it out into her raven feather robe which she put back on her shoulders. She took the restaurant cap from her head and reshaped it into the metal band with the quartz crystal which she adorned across her forehead. "It is freely given. Its power will be mine to do what I will."

The wolves bent their front limbs and became the two dark-haired twin men making obeisance on bended knees to their mistress.

The Elfwitch patted the tops of their human heads while speaking to the twins, "You do not understand the power of metals. Or what I can do." Then she put out a lithe hand to stroke Chayse's check. "And what I can do for you."

Chayse pulled away from the woman's touch. How could she confuse that cold touch as coming from Mom? Promising love and acceptance. She wanted to see what she believed. Not again anytime soon.

"Soon you will not fear me. I will show you wondrous things," the Elfwitch promised. And Chayse was scared to see that promise come true.

"We'll never follow you," Reed promised, speaking for both he and his twin sister. He still had his heart necklace. "You're a liar. You got us taken away from Mom. It's your fault we came here!"

The Elfwitch leveled a long forefinger at Reed as if she were Judge Hart's evil hateful twin. "It's your fault the Porter was injured!"

Then she offered an open hand and a cold smile to Chayse. "I will trade in kind with this little one. Child, I will show you mystery and wonders. That is my promise to this one."

But she glowered at Reed. "But to this one, I promise cruelty and captivity. I will deal with you in kind as to how you have treated me. Insults are brave. But they are just words.

"I will teach you what I think of men. They are no better than rodents.

"I will bend you. I will break you. You will beg me to take that necklace from you before I am through."

Reed shrugged. "Sticks and stones will break my bones. But words will never hurt me."

The Elfwitch gave him a long smile that drank up his blood and crushed him into pulp like an apple under a mallet. "Do not worry. I have sticks and I have stones. Just for you."

"Did you personalize them for me?" Reed asked. He had learned plenty from Dad. Not only how to shoot a gun but how to shoot his mouth. When the Elfwitch cocked an eye at him, he knew she didn't understand. "Got my name on my very own cell?"

The two dark-headed lycanthropes laughed at Reed. "He mocks at my mistress!" "What a whelp!"

"Very well, then," the Elfwitch said. "Take the whelp to his cage. You, my little one, shall sit at my table. You must be hungry and thirsty."

Chayse clung to her twin brother. She'd been doing it all her life except for the five minutes she'd been without him. And that was before he'd been born. "Reed?"

The lycanthrope twins tore Reed away. Grabbing him by the armpits. And took him back through the exit leading to the dungeon.

Now Chayse was alone in the Domain. The last of her family was gone. A long arm wreathed in black raven feathers encircled her shoulders and led in the opposite direction.

Her first step down a dark path.

***

Chapter Eleven: Water and Wine

Reed kicked at the Elfwitch's twin servants.

It did no good.

Their grips were like iron. They could easily snap his neck. And if they turned back into their dire wolf shapes they could bite through his neck.

He wondered which shape they had been first? Men? Or wolves?

Victor and Nikolai led him down the short tunnel back into the dungeon. But this time they didn't open the trap door to throw him back into the trash pit. They had a new destination planned for him.

Two undead soldiers stood as sentinels among the quiet and solitary niches where hopeless prisoners were imprisoned. Their dull sunken eyes watched the captors march by with their captive as they waited to die to escape this place. Reed noticed that every prisoner was a man.

This dungeon was the kind of place that Grandma meant by being in a hell on earth. Only Reed wasn't even sure he was still on the same earth that his Grandma had known. It seemed that even in different worlds, some things were still the same.

The twin servants led him up an incline to another section of the dungeon. There were larger holding cells here arranged in a narrower hall. The open spaces between the stalactites closed off with iron bars that went from floor to ceiling.

A squad of five not so dead soldiers waited to greet him beside cell doors to a large cage. Two soldiers holding their muskets at the ready and Sergeant Hood who had tossed Reed and Chayse into the oubliette without a qualm and two others who, by their mien, must have been officers.

Coming this close to them, Reed did not doubt they were already dead. They smelled like a sack of rotten potatoes. One time he had found a package of bologna in the refrigerator that had gone bad in the bottom of the crisper—the once brown meat had gray patches speckled with white and blue spots.

While the broad sergeant kept his bearing with half of his face being eaten away, the two officers' dignity was more pronounced. The first was the tallest and thinnest of the soldiers, dressed as what Grandma would have called a "dandy" with a rich red jacket with silver leaf patterns on the sleeves and silver trimmed tricorner hat. His aquiline nose and small chin would have given him a regal bearing except he had no eyes.

And the second was even more pompous. Short and squat with his arms on his hips. Rotting hands were framed with frilly cuffs. He wore a white vest under his open tunic and a silver chain from his belt up across his chest to a breast pocket that had a hole marked with gun powder showing a putrid wound. His tunic had epaulets at the shoulders and his hat was crowned with a white feather. Though he was dressed to the nines, the officer had no nose on his face. It was gone. In its place was a jagged fissure.

"Colonel Graves," Victor said. "We have brought you a prisoner."

"You have captured a boy," the one with the white feather and no nose spoke.

"Our mistress wants you and the jailers to give him 'special considerations,'" Nicolai said.

"What danger is a boy to your mistress?" the tall thin officer with no eyes asked in a hoarse whisper.

"'Our mistress,'" Victor corrected. "Take heed, Lieutenant Grey. Your life may be over but your service has only just begun. You can serve as you are now or as a bag of bones hanging on the wall of our mistress' Circle Chamber."

The gray lieutenant pursed his lips. His hand fingering the hilt of his sheathed rapier. Another time and place and that would have been an invitation to a duel of honor.

But honor had long ago left these soldiers. Along with their true allegiance. All that was left was their profaned duty.

"How is the prisoner to be treated then?" Colonel Graves, the shorter one, asked.

"He is to receive half rations and one cup of water and be held in this cell until he is needed further," Victor said.

"I would not treat a dog like that," Colonel Graves proclaimed.

Victor poked the officer in his chest. Putting a finger in the open wound through the white vest's breast pocket. "You have done far worse than this dog. And for that, someone shot you straight in the heart." Victor pulled his finger out and pointed to the officer's face. "But I did take your nose. To mark your traitorous ways. Next, I will take your tongue."

Colonel Graves did not bat an eye for at least he still had them. "Sergeant Hood, you will see this prisoner is put into this holding cell with the other miscreants. He is to be given only half rations and one cup of water. Anyone giving him help will receive no mercy."

"Aye, Colonel," Sergeant Hood grumbled. He brushed between the twin men, being just a hair bigger than either and took hold of Reed. "Open sesame."

One soldier unlocked the iron door with a huge turnkey and the other pushed the great door back against a framing stalactite. Again Sergeant Hood pushed Reed into the large room. The door clanked shut behind him.

Sealing him off.

In a cell. Full of other people who slept without peace. Still, shadows melded into the rock benches or like dogs upon piles of straw.

The cell block smelled of onions and vinegar. Of number one and a whole lot of number two. Which was still better than what the soldiers smelled like.

Reed was in a room full of criminals. Who had done God-where-ever-he-was-now knew what. As far from home as he could possibly ever be. And as alone as a boy could ever become.

Sissy was gone. For the first time, Reed could ever remember she was not beside him. School didn't count because they would often be in the same class or see each other at recess or lunch.

The Elfwitch had separated them.

Reed still didn't want to believe Chayse hadn't known what she was doing. The Elfwitch had tricked her. Miss Crutch back in their World or the Elfwitch here in her Domain, didn't matter. The woman was pure evil. Stone cold mean. What Grandma would call "Three words: No and Good."

Why? The Elfwitch had tricked Chayse out of the silver heart necklace. It was a matching pair, Reed having the other one.

And he vowed not to give it to the Elfwitch.

Even if…it meant never seeing Sissy again? Or his parents?

What if the Elfwitch just left him down here?

How long could Reed hold out?

When was the last time he had eaten? A McDonald's McGriddle sandwich with sausage, egg, and cheese for breakfast that a DHS caretaker had bought for him and Sissy before they had been brought to court. When had that been?

This morning? Or yesterday? Didn't matter.

Breakfast was long gone. And McDonald's was in a different world. His body couldn't remember what food tasted like.

But even the need for sustenance had been pushed back to a dull ache. A new need overruled his empty stomach. One that all his body was in agreement over.

Water.

His throat was coated with dust. His spit turned to salt. His dry tongue stuck to the back of his teeth.

All for want of water.

One sip would not be enough. Just a drink wouldn't do. Reed could drink a whole bathtub full of water. He'd give anything to be in a swimming pool right now. For every square inch to be immersed. Splish and splash. Suck in a mouthful. Spit it back out.

Reed stepped through the cell block. There was a score of sleeping prisoners. Some snoring and dead to his passing—those were the ones the soldiers envied. Some shifting over on their makeshift pallets—those were the light sleepers. And some with one eye on him—those were the insomniacs.

There wasn't a space for him. And he needed to rest. And wanted to sleep. Somewhere safe but there was no refuge here.

Then he saw a small barrel wedged between a cell bar and a stalactite column. It was as high as his knees and as wide as his legs. Half of the wooden lid had been laid back on hinges with a slim iron bar hooked on the outside of the barrel so that the rest of the bar lay inside the barrel.

Instinct told Reed what it was. His throat gulped in anticipation. His tongue clicked in hope waiting to be refreshed.

Reed stumbled on weak legs and fell on his knees in front of the barrel. It smelled like wet rock but he didn't care—he was ready to drink out of a puddle. Dad had said he'd done it when he used to work on roads for the county.

He pulled the long and heavy dipper up to the brim of the barrel. Its spoon was broad and flat. The water running over the hammered edges.

A rifle butt jabbed through the iron bar and hit against his wrist. It was like getting his hand slammed with a flat rock. Reed dropped the ladle back into the bucket and jerked back his hurt hand.

"No drink for you!" hissed the rotting face of a guard. His phlegmy eyes sharpened like bayonets. The maggots living in the festering pus of his face threatening to fall onto his shoulder.

Crouching his chest over his hurt wrist, Reed used his other palm and feet to push himself away from the edge of the cell block. He wanted to get away from the guard as fast as he could. Scampering backward into the darkness until he butted up against the rock wall.

Hugging his knees with his good arm and holding his hurt hand in his lap, Reed put his head down on his thighs and cried. He was amazed he still had enough water left in him for that many tears.

But he did not let them go to waste. Wiping them off as fast as his eyes peeled them, he licked at the back of his hand. Now he was tasting his tears.

Sissy would have gotten a laugh from that. Since she wasn't here, he had to laugh for her. "Pretty salty."

He wrapped both his arms around his knees and slid over to his side. The rough floor did not yield to his sore body. Reed curled up into a ball.

There was nothing he could drink. And there was nothing to eat. There was nothing to do but sleep.

And there was nothing he could do about it.

The Elfwitch had shown Chayse a secret. Taking a stuffed raven off one of the apothecary shelves had sprung open a false door in the rock face. The whole rack swung revealing a narrow door frame. It wasn't very tall or big but wide enough for the Elfwitch and Chayse to slip through.

It was a short passage through the rock to a smaller chamber than the one they had left which reminded Chayse of some scientist's lab. This one had a pallet with a mattress in the center upon which were piled many throw pillows. There were open wardrobes with gowns and dresses.

At the foot of the bed was a large oak chest. There was a single named burned into the rough wood planks. WICE.

The room was full of other curiosities. There was a screen set up in one corner with strange patterns her last Geometry teacher. And in another a long thin mirror.

"Make yourself at home, pet," the Elfwitch said and filled two goblets from a decanter of red liquid.

"I'm not your pet," Chayse said. She didn't want to touch anything. A part of her hated the Elfwitch for being Miss Crutch. And another part reminded her that a new door had opened and that Chayse had already stepped through it into a brand new world.

Without thinking she flew to the nearest wardrobe. It was full of strange outfits. Long sweaters and vests. Some of the netting and stranger mesh. Some of the blouses or tops had identification labels on the lapels. Or security badges. With or without photos. A few were blinking lights in strange frequencies. Two were a three-dimensional hologram.

All the images were the same. It was a headshot of a lady. With silvery hair in various hairstyles and ashy skin. A head like an upside-down bottle. Two piercing blue eyes with prominent checks and a beak nose. The hair was either up or down or in a bun or teased out and sometimes there were glasses or even sunglasses.

The names were different but always the same.

Miss Elsie Crutch. Dr. Fey Sidhe. Bruja Duende. Miss Constantina Liogan. Lady Winona McBeth. Senora Muleta. Helene De Troi. And on and on went the names.

The other side of the chamber was shut with a wooden door and a metal latch. It opened and in came the lycanthrope twins (Chayse didn't know what else call the two dark-headed men since she could never think of them again just as true CASA agents) carrying a large wooden table set with silver platters and bowls topped with meats and fruits. They set the table against the far wall and left without either saying a word.

Her eyes swam in the medium-rare roast and the dripping fat off chicken legs and the seared marks upon pieces of ham steak.

Her nose did not lie. Well-cooked and seasoned meat slid up her nostrils to tease her brain. Her taste buds danced and her stomach rumbled in envy.

All sense of fear and wonder and all feeling of sleep and soreness disappeared in a flash. Chayse was wide-eyed and alert and expectant as if the Brazzles had just driven her in their Explorer to the Big Dipper.

She couldn't ever remember being so hungry before. And she couldn't ever remember food looking so good before. It was a happy meeting of time and chance.

Chayse took a step towards the table set for two. With more than enough food for four or six.

"You are hungry, do not deny it," the Elfwitch said. "You are welcome to eat with me at my table. But before you do you should be presentably attired."

That stopped Chayse in her tracks. She turned back to the host. The woman had an undeniable hold—Chayse wasn't just a guest, she was a stranger in a place where she wanted to know what the rules were and test them.

The Elfwitch gestured to the open wardrobe.

"Are you going to let me pick something out for myself?" Chayse asked. That never happened. Mom always went to yard sales or if she did take her daughter shopping it was usually whenever there was a sale at the Dollar General or Walmart.

"We can surely find something more suitable," the Elfwitch said and indicated she wanted Chayse to change from head to toe.

Chayse looked down at her attire. Her pink t-shirt was torn at the neck and sleeves. The large heart across her chest that was once lime-green and chocolate brown had new hues of green and brown from moss and dirt and mud. Her once light blue capris were ripped at the knees and stained with green algae. And her Converse shoes that were supposed to have been pink were now a fine shade of dirty.

She would welcome a change.

Chayse flicked through the choices. They weren't on hangers. The clothes rested on pegs or hooks. She would need something smaller and tighter to fit her. And something to fit her new mood.

She found what she wanted and pulled it off a peg to show it to her host.

"A good choice," the Elfwitch nodded her consent and then pointed to a corner of the room. "You may change behind that screen."

Chayse went behind the screen and discovered how much her muscles ached just from trying to change out of her clothes. She needed a bath. And about ten hours of sleep. And a large double cheeseburger meal from McDonald's. And a fast Wi-Fi signal. With unlimited data.

The change from her dirty old clothes from their World to the new dress she'd picked out startled her. It had a silky feel. Very fine spun. Soothing and relaxing. Comfort. As if she were the first person to ever have worn it. And not some used second-hand hand-me-down that was just about threadbare.

Chayse came out from behind the screen and the Elfwitch handed her a large handheld mirror. The backing was green copper metal with trails of oxidized rust. The mirror face was blemished and cracked. But it showed Chayse her dress.

Black with lace webbing across the chest and where it split at the wrist on each sleeve. It had brocade circles sequined with glass beads down the seam of each sleeve and across the shoulders. But the face staring back at her was not her own.

Or not who it should be.

Chayse had been born with dark hair and blue eyes while her fraternal twin brother had ginger hair and brown eyes. In essence, Chayse had always been told she looked like their Dad while everyone told Reed he looked like their Mom. Neither of the twins liked the fact that they resembled their least respective favorite parent.

The Chayse-who-was-not-Chayse-in-the-mirror winked at her. As if she knew a secret that the real Chayse didn't want to know. It gave a leering smile. Confident and self-righteous. But Chayse couldn't stand its gaudy rouge and red lipstick.

"Very fitting," the Elfwitch nodded and took back the mirror being careful to keep it face down and away from herself. "In your world, mirrors are common and mundane. Here, they are very different."

"What do you mean 'different?'" Chayse asked.

"Mirrors are just a negative space that flatter us in vain. This one reveals what you'd like yourself to be but it conceals what the rest of us would see. Who is worshipping who?" the Elfwitch shrugged and slid the copper metal mirror into a black bag.

"Am I all set? I am very hungry," Chayse said.

"I know, pet," the Elfwitch and ticked her teeth while tapping her chin with a long forefinger. "Let's do something about that hair first."

She picked up an ornate piece of metal and a long spike. "Now turn around."

Chayse turned around and held up the back of her hair off her neck with her right hand.

She felt the Elfwitch's long cold fingers sweep up her hair and twist it. Then apply a metal clamp and slide the pin through.

"Have a look," the Elfwitch said and indicated a free-standing salon mirror in an alcove. Before Chayse stepped over she handed her a compact. For being such mysterious and dangerous things, the Elfwitch had several mirrors situated in her personal chambers.

Chayse watched herself approach the long thin mirror. She was no longer a twelve-year-old girl from Fulton County in the Ozarks. No longer a newly appointed ward of the court. No longer a social misfit unpopular with the rich girls or the jockettes or the emos. No longer bullied by the boys who were trying to draw attention away from their ever-increasing pimples.

There was no longer anything to hide.

The moment struck her like a bell from the top of her head all the way down to the tip of her big toe: she could be anybody she wanted to be.

She didn't even have to be Chayse Leftwich anymore.

Before her in the mirror was a young woman beginning to bloom. Cheeks rosy enough without rouge. Full lips and white teeth that scratched at the lower one. A tickle. An itch. A desire for something more.

The black sequined dress with beads was the most elegant thing she had ever worn in her entire existence. It felt smooth and gave comfort. Now it was a part of her.

She hardly ever wore her hair up. But it fit this new style. Made her cheekbones taut and her chin stick out.

And the bun holder and pin capped off the new "her."

The metal was silver. Curved like a snake with a split tongue coming out of the top of her head and the coiled tail at the bottom of her hair knot. The twist in her hair being crushed between the snake's silver scales was held together by a silver pin with a ball at the tip and a sharp point at the end.

The Elfwitch turned back to the feast table which had not a single seat and picked up a glass urn full of red liquid. She filled two silver goblets with it.

She offered one goblet to Chayse who took the offered drink and smiled when the Elfwitch chinked the goblets together. Chayse knew it was because she was about to make a toast.

"To new beginnings," the Elfwitch saluted and took a long draught. She kept on an eye on Chayse as she took her first drink of wine. It was bitter. It was warm. It stung. It was sweet. It left an after taste of grape that numbed her tongue.

The Elfwitch gestured with her forefinger from the top of the goblet. "Now you."

Chayse shrugged. What was she supposed to do with the glass now? How long was she to hold it? Where was she supposed to put it when she was done?

The Elfwitch made a wheel in the air with her forefinger. "Your turn to make a toast."

"I've never done one before," Chayse said. She was excited to have this opportunity. And embarrassed that she had turned into her twin brother: a mindless boy who left his dirty socks in the weirdest places. "I don't know what to even say."

"How about a new name?" the Elfwitch said.

"For who?" Chayse asked.

"For you, pet," the Elfwitch said. "What shall we call you now?"

"Um," Chayse said and bit her bottom lip. Every other name from their World sounded no better or no worse than Chayse did. "Um." She looked around the room of curiosities. There were so many things. But only one name.

"How about 'Wice?'" Chayse suggested as if she knew the answer that the Elfwitch had wanted to hear but was afraid she might still get it wrong.

The Elfwitch beamed and nodded her assent. "A most excellent choice."

Then she took up a carving knife and a serving fork. "Take one of the plates on the other side and I shall serve you first, Wice, as you are my most honored guest."

Chayse or Wice felt as if the wine had slid all the way down her spine polishing her insides into a warm glow.

No one had ever made her feel this special.

***

Chapter Twelve: Bread and Body

What was the use of waking up? His nose told Reed he was still locked in a moldy dungeon at the bottom of the Elfwitch's Domain. And he wanted to be anywhere but here.

Reed kept his eyes shut but he did not sleep.

All hope was gone. All he had left were his fears. Even if he could get out of this cell block, where had the Elfwitch taken Sissy? And even if he could free his twin sister, how could they get back home? And even if they could get back, it was still illegal to see both Mom and Dad.

Why had things gotten this bad? What had he done?

He was just a kid.

What could he even do about it?

He was just a kid.

Reed slipped into a darkness that swallowed his dreams. And robbed his hope. The unrestful sleep gave cold comfort.

Something warm spread over his chest. Making his skin sweat. Relaxing him with a soothing anodyne.

Something brushed against his hand. Then he heard the scampering of the tiniest feet. And that same something pressed on his chest.

Reed woke with a start. The largest rat he had ever seen had its front paws on his chest with its head turned towards him. Frozen as if caught red headed.

Wide black eyes watched Reed anticipating his next move. Whiskers and ears laid back against grey hair that stood up along its spine. Its pink tail twitched.

Reed was just as startled as the rat.

Something was glowing under his burgundy acid-washed Chevrolet t-shirt. A muted ardent glow at the left corner of the Chevron. Just above his heart.

His shirt wasn't supposed to be glow-in-the-dark. Whatever it was lay at the end of the cable chain around his neck. And whatever it was doing the glowing had left Reed the most refreshed he'd been since before Miss Crutch had shown up at their house and started this whole mess.

There was a sliver of hope in the moment's respite.

Reed sat up and pulled out his heart necklace. It shone like a glow stick. Sure and warm. Humming with a high pitched voice. Like metal being sheered.

What did it mean?

The rat stood on its hind legs and sniffed at it. It wanted to know, too. Then it scampered away taking a path along the rock wall back into the shadows.

"Silver is sacred, my child," spoke a strong voice somewhere close in the shadows.

Reed used the tiny ardent light to find the speaker. The soft ray fell on a face near the ground as the man must have been sleeping and just now had rolled over. Even more striking, Reed found he knew the face.

The man had large brown cow eyes. Greasy locks bordered a face with a coarse beard. Long nails and grimy fingers reached out towards Reed's silver necklace.

Instead of a Cubs baseball cap and overalls, the man wore a hair shirt that came to his knees cinched around his waist with a rough belt and a stained leather strap across his forehead. In place of the painted dappled construction boots were handsewn leather boots.

Minus the Cubs cap and overall and add a full beard and Reed knew who exactly who the man should be.

"Creedmore," Reed remembered the man's name. He would have been the last person he'd expected to find inside this cellblock. "You're the Street Preacher."

"I am Moor Kreed the Revelator," the man said. "I don't hang around on the streets. The Judge called me from the wilderness to go and speak the Law to all the four corners of the Realm."

"The Realm?" Reed was confused. Wasn't this the same man he and Sissy had seen when they'd left the courthouse with the Brazzles? But how come his name was different? What was 'the Realm?' The Brazzles had taken them to a state park outside of Trainer, Missouri.

But he was most confused about the "judge." What "judge?" Did Creedmore or Moor Kreed mean Judge Hart? Was he here, too?

Reed's heart pumped iron into his veins. His brain came alive with an idea that got his blood going. Get out of this cell block. Find Sissy. Then Find Judge Hart. And stop the Elfwitch. Or Miss Crutch. Or whoever that woman was. "How did you get here?"

"Because I refuse to serve the Dark Mistress," Moor Kreed shrugged. "The same as you, I should expect." That's right! When the Brazzles had been driving off, Miss Crutch had stirred up the police so she could have Creedmore—Moor Kreed here— arrested. For what again? Harassing the Brazzles and the twins.

Only Creedmore hadn't been harassing them.

He had been trying to warn them. *Remember, where you are going they call God's light the darkness and the darkness they call God's light. But God is everywhere. So when you're lost in the darkness, call out to Him.*

Reed hadn't even thought about God being here in the Domain. He still was mad at God for letting him and Sissy get taken away from Mom and Dad. And now they had been taken away from their World. How much more was God going to let happen to them before he decided to do something about it?

But for now, Reed had other questions for matters at hand. "Why is my necklace glowing?" "It's made of silver, isn't it? It's used for vows and curses. It is both healing and unforgiving," More Kreed was only happy to explain. Then he paused. "Why do you not know this already?"

"I don't belong here," Reed said.

"None of us belong here, kid. We're all innocent lambs," croaked a sleepy voice.

Reed had forgotten that other prisoners were trying to find sleep down here in this tomb of unyielding rock.

"Speak fer yerself! I deserve everythin' comin' down on my head," snapped another voice.

"Boys, better find rest while you can before the Dark Mistress remembers why she put you down here," Moor Kreed spoke to the horizontal shapes across the room. They all fell back into silence.

Then the Revelator regarded Reed once more. "You're a stranger, sure enough. What might you be called?"

"Reed Leftwich," Reed said.

"By the Law!" Moor Kreed whispered. His hands shot out to cover Reed's mouth and the silver necklace. "Put that away for your own sake. And don't speak your name here."

Reed agreed to put away the necklace. Not handing it over to the Elfwitch is what had landed him here in the first place. So he wasn't going to let anyone steal it away now.

But he was confused about why just saying his last name would get him in more trouble.

"Why?" Reed asked.

Moor Kreed shook his head. "I can only tell you that the Dark Mistress has servants everywhere. But I begin to glean why you were brought here."

"You do?" Reed asked.

Moor Kreed nodded. "The Judge had you brought here for something special."

Reed shook his head. "No, Miss Crutch brought us here. After she lied to Judge Hart."

"The Dark Mistress has several names," Moor Kreed shrugged. "They are all lies. She had a true name once. But it has been forgotten."

"Why did she bring us here? What does she want?" Reed asked.

More Kreed raised himself from the ground to speak right against Reed's ear. His fetid breath passed over Reed's face and his body funk plugged up his nose. The man must have been down in this hole for quite some time.

"Power and control," the man whispered. The cold words slipped down Reed's ear and left a bad taste in his mind. Then Moor Kreed leaned back and nodded at Reed's initiation into the shared secret.

"Pshaw," Reed blew through his lips. "Is that all?"

It was the most ridiculous thing he had ever heard. No one could control everything. A person would have to be…God.

Moor Kreed knotted his fingers so he could rest his chin on them and prop up his head with his elbows. The two talked face to face. "Let me tell you the truth, the Judge made this world long ago. Everything below and above the earth and everything that swims in the sea or crawls or walks the Realm.

"Therefore, He made your world as well. And many others to boot. He is all-powerful, is He not? Therefore, all things are possible with Him, are they not?"

Reed didn't know if Moor Kreed wanted him to answer so he shrugged. "I guess so."

"When the Judge made the realms of land and sea and underground, he also made the realm of the sky. So He made the sun to be the Greater Light to rule the day. And he made the moon to be the Lesser Light to rule the night.

"It is the Judge who gives us Light. Life. And Love. These things reflect who He is. But people tend to go their own way until they become very confused.

"So the Darkness came. In many forms. Shadows. Hate. Death. And made many servants out of the things below and above. All these things just put confusion in people's hearts and minds.

"Then the Judge gave people the Law so that they could put it in their hearts and in their minds instead and follow his will every day. But people tend to follow a leader and not the Law. And when the leaders turn to Darkness, all forsake the Law.

"So the Judge sent his Son. He said, 'Surely, they will listen to my Son and return to the Law.' But the people loved the Darkness more and called that the Light. And the Light they called the Darkness.

"The Son promised to bring all deeds hidden in the Darkness into the Light so that they are known to the Judge. But people wanted to hide their deeds.

"So they came to hate the Son and love the Darkness. They told themselves that if they got rid of the Son they could just make their own laws. So they killed the Son and buried him along with the Law."

Reed listened to every word. It seemed so plain and true: when people didn't listen to God they messed up everything. "Then what happened?"

"The Judge brought his Son back to life. And He, too, Light, Life, and Love. Now He is the living Law.

"One day He will return to bring deliverance and justice to those who remain in the Light by utterly destroying those who remain in Darkness."

More promises. Like all the times Dad said he would take him fishing and never did. Like every time Mom said there would be leftover money for them to do something fun and there never was.

One thing that Reed had learned about adults: they never did what they said they were going to do.

Why should this "Judge" be any different?

The clanking sound of a key turning woke up everyone on the whole cell block. A door screeched on turning hinges. Everyone stood up, moth-eaten blankets falling to the floor or brushing straw off themselves.

All except one figure stretched snug and tight with his back to the bars.

Boots slapped the rocky floor. Moving torchlight lit a passageway making giant shadows of the approaching people.

It was Sergeant Hood, or what was left of him, leading a squad of troopers bearing barrels. Water sluiced out of some. And steam wafted out of others.

"Time to feed the animals! Wake up, you miscreants! You should beg us to kill you quick rather than poison you real slow with this slop," the soldier who had once been alive said.

"What's wrong with these soldiers? Why are they like that?" Reed asked.

"They're Deadcoats," Moor Kreed said. "And they are cursed beyond hope. Death does not even want them."

As the squad put down their load, one of the troopers knocked into another with the edge of a barrel. The other soldier's leg snapped off and fell to the ground.

The entire cell block roared with laughter.

"Pick yerself up, trooper!" Sergeant Hood roared. "Quit fallin' to pieces! Won't do you no-good, no-how. We still got our everlastin' dooty."

The Deadcoat who had knocked the other's leg off picked it up and offered it back to his comrade like a broken sword given in surrender at the end of a mighty battle. The second Deadcoat took as it offered but could not put his femur back in place try as he might. His sergeant got down on his knee with a great groan of his bones and jammed the leg back into its socket as best he could.

The hobbled Deadcoat saluted his sergeant in thanks and acknowledgment that he was ready for his next task. Even though his left leg was now slightly askew.

"Alright, lively up yerself, then," Sergeant Hood said. "Bust out the victuals and water and let's get this lot fed."

Two of the troopers had ladles at the ready for dipping into the water caskets. While two others had ladles to dip out some kind of soup—either it was a light broth or some cream of something or other. The final two Deadcoats had held a stack of canteens each to pass out.

"Line up in twos, then," one of the Deadcoats croaked as if his vocal cords had been ripped out. And mayhap they had been.

The prisoners did as they were told. They made two lines. All except for the one who still snoring away his supper.

Moor Kreed kept Reed in front of him as the line moved. A hulk of a man blocked Reed's view of the top of the line. He couldn't see what was being served for dinner—or was it breakfast?

Was it morning or evening? Day or night? Reed didn't know.

The prisoners grumbled about the conditions of the cell and complained about the quality of the food. Sergeant Hood harangued them to keep moving while they were still breathing. "It don't get much better than this for the likes of you slobs."

Coming to the head of the first line, each prisoner was given a tin canteen cup by one Deadcoat while the second dipped the ladle in the water cask and sluiced it into the waiting cup spilling as much as what fell inside.

Reed stared at the water being wasted and wanted to put out his hands to catch a drink. He had never been so thirsty in his whole life. His tongue felt like a dry tree limb stuck to the bottom of his mouth.

"Hey, Hoodie!" called a prisoner pointing to the inert prisoner. "He's still asleep! Can I get his ration?"

The hulking man in front of Reed swiped at the Deadcoats because they didn't fill his canteen cup to his liking.

Sergeant Hood brandished an iron blackjack. "Move on and drink up."

The hulk hit the bars just in front of Sergeant Hood's half nose with the end of his fist. The sergeant jabbed the hulk's wrist through the bars with the flat end of the blackjack. Knocking the prisoner's canteen cup to the ground.

"There! No water for you! Move on! Or I'll give yer head the same!" Sergeant Hood promised. Since he was cursed and decaying bit by bit, he did not seem to have much more to lose.

The hulk stepped away keeping his glowering face in shadows.

Reed stepped forward. He was given a canteen cup the same as the other prisoners by the first Deadcoat. But the sergeant tapped the second on the shoulder with his blackjack and the Deadcoat poured out most of the ladle-full of water onto the floor. Reed looked down and saw that his cup was only half full.

Moor Kreed spoke up. "Sergeant, this prisoner did not get a full ration."

"The prisoner got all that he's gonna get. Move on," Sergeant Hood said.

When neither Reed nor Moor Kreed moved on, the Deadcoat sergeant lifted his blackjack to call the bluff. A line of restless prisoners had formed behind the two as those who had first received their ration of soup wanted to get their ration of water.

"Hey, bub. Yer holdin' up the line. We're just ez thirsty as you two."

Moor Kreed put his hand on Reed and with each holding their canteen cups of water they moved to the end of the next line for their soup ration. Sergeant Hood also followed outside the cell and took up his overseer position behind the troopers dishing out the soup ration. And when it was Reed's turn to get a ration of soup in his second canteen cup, again the sergeant put his rancid beefy hand over the trooper's making him miss the canteen with the ladle.

Again, Moor Kreed spoke up. "Sergeant, you did not give this prisoner a ration at all."

"He's to get *special* rations, he is," the sergeant explained and showing a haversack, he reached into it and produced two old dried heels of bread. He dropped the tough heels into Reed's canteen instead of soup.

Moor Kreed's face grew red under the coarse curls of his beard. Reed felt humiliated. Why were they trying to starve him?

His hand strayed to the small ingot of silver attached to the end of the silver cable chain hidden under his Chevrolet shirt. Did getting this necklace mean that much to the Elfwitch? Did keeping this heart mean that much to Reed?

Moor Kreed steered Reed out of line with little rations he had been given balancing his soup cup on the boy's shoulder and holding the cup of water close to his chest. Reed found a secure grip by putting a thumb atop each lip of the cup and hooking his hand around each. But as they went towards the back of the cell block, a grubby hand snatched one of the crusty heels.

"Hey!" Reed said. It was like being back in the cafeteria at school.

"Thief!" Moor Kreed pronounced. "Why would you steal from a child?"

"Shut it, you old crazy revelator!" came the first response.

"He's got two of 'em!" came a second explanation.

"Hey, I'll take have o' that bread!" came a third complaint.

Whoever it was who had been the thief decided to annoy Reed further by complying with the request and threw a piece of it across the cellblock. The bread chunk missed the open hand and fell to the floor. Everyone scrambled for it like it was a football in fair play spinning on the one-yard line in a tied championship game.

Then empty canteen cups began to fly. And some not so empty.

"Duck, child," Moor Kreed said and slid down with his back against the wall.

Reed did the same. And they both bowed over their food. Not just grateful to have it but meaning to protect it.

A stray canteen cup caught the sleeping prisoner square on the head. The cup bounced from there against the rock wall to rattle across the floor. The prisoner stretched, rolled over, and sat up.

"Someone's gonna answer for that," the man said with sleep in his throat. Even with a scratchy voice, Reed would have recognized it anywhere. On the phone. Or at a basketball game.

Reed set down his canteen cups and stood up as the man rubbed his eyes and threw off a moth-eaten blanket.

"Bunch of yard apes," the now waking prisoner said. The man had shaggy black hair. And the bluest of eyes. He might have been dressed in a pair of Levi's with a western print button shirt. But even though he wasn't, Reed knew the man. And though he had a flowing beard which he didn't have the last time Reed saw him, there was no doubt who it was.

"DAD!"

***

Chapter Thirteen: Thirst and Quench

The entire cellblock roared with laughter.

The man who looked and sounded like Reed's Dad was taken aback. He blushed from the humiliation. And blinked with confusion.

"Boys, he's a mighty hunter! His aim must be true!" roared one prisoner.

"First I heard o' the acorn findin' the oak!" roared another. And the laughter began anew.

Reed ignored every word. While the man, who had to be Dad, let each word heap upon his shoulder like a dead weight. He ran up to the man as he sat up straight on his rock bench.

"Dad! It's me, Reed!" He couldn't have been happier. This was better than being home. Everything would work out alright, just like Mom would say whenever things began to get worse.

He did what was the most natural thing in the world. What he'd done a thousand times before growing up and being around Dad. Especially after Mom kicked him out.

Reed hugged Dad. Tried to hug him tighter than he ever had in his entire life.

Only the man who looked and sounded like Dad pushed him away.

"What's the matter wit'chu, boy? Quit jokin'! I ain'tyer father!" the man declared before every prisoner in the cell block.

Reed's heart sunk. Why would Dad say he wasn't his dad when he was the only Dad that Reed had ever known and had ever wanted?

"Dad…" Now it was Reed who was confused. Dad had never pushed him away before. He wanted Dad more than ever. Needed to know he still loved him. Without even thinking about it, Reed tried to grab the man's hand.

The man who looked and sounded like Dad but denied that he was cuffed Reed who fell to the ground.

"Stay off me! Keep away! I'm ain'tyer father no how and never will be!" the man declared now growing ever angry.

Dad had never hit Reed before in his entire life.

Tears welled up in Reed's eyes. Coming from an underground stream of hurt he'd rather have kept closed off. "You hit me."

A huge shadow blocked out the torchlight.

Reed looked up.

The hulk of a man who tried to cause trouble was looking down at him. A face that Reed knew as well. For wherever Dad went, this big stray of a man would follow. Reed had known him as a gentle giant. Kind to a fault.

It was Albert. Dad's best friend from high school. Uncle Buddy. Dressed in dirty leather breeches and a sleeveless fur jacket. He did not wear a cap to cover his balding head and his arms were covered up and down with grime.

The hulk made a mean face and shooed Reed away. Then he sat down next to the man who claimed not to be Dad.

Now it was Reed who felt a cruel joke was being played on him. How in the world were both Dad and Uncle Buddy in the Domain with him? How did they get put in this cellblock? Why had they changed their clothes? How could they have grown beards and get so dirty in such a short time since Reed had last seen them? How long had Reed been in the Domain?

Too many questions. Too much confusion. Too little love.

There was nothing but hurt in this Domain.

And no hope whatsoever.

"Better git him away from me, Moor Kreed!" the man who claimed not to be his Dad complained to the Revelator. "He's just as crazy as you!"

Then Moor Kreed was by his side. Putting his hand on his shoulder and guiding him back to their place along the rock wall. Soon the prisoners settled back down, gaggling over and what chunks of soup they could scrape out of their cups and slurp at puddles of water like beaten servants while those who hadn't tossed their canteen cups sipped and dined like dethroned kings.

For Reed, the water in his canteen may have filled a Dixie cup. Not enough to even tickle his tonsils. And he barely had enough spit to help mash up the piece of crusty heel he'd been able to keep.

He was still in shock over the fact that his own Dad had just denied him. The man sat with his pal on the rock bench. Keeping their eyes away from everyone.

Reed was miserable.

And he seemed to be in good company.

"Child," Moor Kreed said in a soft tone. Moor Kreed or Creedmore, he hadn't changed who he was from their World to the Domain. It was the one bright spot so far. "Is that man really your father?"

"Yes," Reed answered. He didn't feel like talking but he still wanted someone to at least try.

"What's his given name?" Moor Kreed asked.

Reed had to think. "Frederick's his full name. But he likes Freddie. He always says 'Call me Freddie. Fred was my dad. And Fred is dead.'"

"Wonders of wonders," Moor Kreed said. "He must be your father in your world. But not in this one. The Judge's way is indeed strange to us. But it is perfect. In His time and His way."

"What do you mean? 'Perfect?'" Reed said and felt like crying anew. "That man's my dad and he won't even talk to me!"

"Child, to us *perfect* means without a mistake," Kreed Moor said. "But to the Judge, *perfect* means complete and whole. The Judge does not make mistakes. We make mistakes all the time. At no time has something ever happened that made the Judge say to himself, 'How did that happen?' Yet, when things happen that we don't like or go against us we think it must be a mistake. Sometimes people wonder if the Judge is real since mistakes happen. Yet, I am telling you, the Judge does not make mistakes.

"Consider, child. In your world, your father has the same last name as yours?"

"Of course," Reed said. "But you said not to say that name here."

"Correct, child," Moor Kreed said. "Not to anybody at anytime. Now listen to me. In your world that man sitting on that bench may indeed be your father and you may know him as Frederick and you may indeed share the same last name but here in this world that man is called Frehley and he is or was a royal huntsman. To my knowledge he has never married--"

Reed scoffed. He wanted to scream. He liked Moor Kreed but the man was wrong— dead wrong.

"—and he has no children."

"Impossible. He's my Dad. He married my mom. They had me and my sis--"

"Is 'sis' your sister?" Moor Kreed asked.

"Yes! I'm trying to tell you--" Reed was getting agitated.

"This sister's here, too?" Moor Kreed asked with growing concern.

"Yes! The Elfwitch separated us!" Reed said.

Moor Kreed held up a finger to quiet Reed. Then he used the finger to point at the lump beneath the chevron. "Does she wear what you do?"

"Yes, my mom--" Reed started but Moor Kreed drew a line with the same forefinger.

"No more talk of your family name. Not here. I must think. The Judge gave us our wits and reason so we wouldn't be overcome with fear," Moor Kreed said. Then he tapped his chin with his finger.

"You first thought my name was 'Creedmore.' And that you were a stranger. With all my heart, I believe every word you've said. It makes sense. To a point. You are from another world. Much like this one. Too much it seems.

"Who else do you know from your world?"

Reed pointed to the hulk who looked like Uncle Buddy wearing Viking gear. "Him. He's my dad's best friend since high school. Albert. Only we call him Uncle Buddy. Back in my World."

"Wonders of wonders," Moor Creed said again.

"Only I guess his name is not Albert or Buddy down here," Reed said.

"His name's Strap. He's a common outlaw. His father's an outlaw and so was his father's father," Moor Kreed said. "His family lives in Outlaw Forest. Not far from where I was born. Outlaw Forest is now home for exiles who have escaped the rule of the Elfwitch."

"Is that part of the Domain, too?" Reed asked.

"By the Law, no!" Moor Creed said. "Neither was this place originally. Most of the land here has long been part of the Realm. But somehow the Elfwitch was freed from her Ice Prison and all is being swallowed in Darkness."

"Is this some kind of dungeon?" Reed said.

Moor Kreed shook his head. "This is just the jail. The dungeon lies below. And a very nasty place, too."

"Don't I know it!" Reed said. "The Elfwitch put me and sis down there!" "I am truly sorry for that, child. These are lawless times," Moor Kreed said. "We are at the bottom of the Keep."

"What's the Keep?" Reed asked.

"An old tower built here at Glacier Mountains to guard the Ice Prison. Have you seen it? It would be unforgettable. Evil things are kept in the ice," Moor Kreed said.

Reed nodded. It was a place he did not want to visit again anytime soon. "Where did the Deadcoats come from?"

"When they were men, they were the Blackwatch," Moor Kreed said. "Colonel Graves. Lieutenant Grey. Hoodie. The troopers. All the regiment swore an oath to man the Keep and guard the Ice Prison and warn the Realm if the Darkness tried to return. They were to serve the Regent until Princess Regina could come of age and ascend the throne. Then they would pledge her fealty to her.

"But somehow the regiment got bought fer a price. And they turned their backs on their duty while someone freed the Elfwitch. And fer what? Now they're all damned. You can see for yerself, Death doesn't even want 'em. Traitors, one and all."

Reed couldn't imagine who could trick a whole command into mutiny just to become zombies. That couldn't be what they had been promised. They couldn't be happy with the way they were now. Hadn't they been the ones who'd been betrayed?

There wasn't much feeling sorry for the half-dead soldiers when they poked the prisoners between their shoulders with rifle butts. Or prodded them in their backsides with bayonet tips. Or plunked them on the top of their stubborn heads with iron blackjacks.

The Deadcoats enjoyed being cruel.

And they served the next meal the same way. Two lines of prisoners. Two troopers ladling out water and two troopers ladling out the awful smelling broth. And again, Reed received a half ration of water and two pieces of bread. The moment he heard the squad bringing the food and smelled the acrid liquid his stomach betrayed him and gurgled without ceasing. And when he'd been given his portion and returned to the cell wall, Reed noticed small pieces of his bread crust moving.

At first, he thought they were seeds. Tiny white and segmented. But they weren't seeds. Maggots.

His stomach gurgled anyway. A thought entered his mind. *Just pick maggots off and eat it! I'm SO hungry!*

Reed shuddered. Then he began to shake. Miss Crutch with Nic and Vic showing up at night. Lawyer Kyler at court trying to make Mom look like a bad parent. The fakeness of the Brazzles. The spiders—so many and so big. The deep dark of the cave. The Elfwitch and the Ice Prison. The dungeon with its piles of bones. Sissy taking the hand of the Elfwitch…

It all became a wall that raced up and hit Reed right in the heart and upside his mind and square in the gut.

Reed was losing himself.

He was shaking so much most of his water spilled out. He had trouble setting down the canteen cups. Before he was going to drink he had to make himself stop shaking.

And he couldn't.

Someone snatched up his canteen of maggoty bread crust. Someone else tried to take it away. Another someone tried to prevent that from happening.

A brawl ensued in the cell block. Everyone wanted to knock everyone else upside the head for this, that, or the other.

The Deadcoats made a ring around the three walls of bars to watch.

Reed just put his head between his knees and began to cry.

Strap or Uncle Buddy stood up and waded through the riot. Shoving men to and fro. Knocking sense back into their heads and order back into their stomachs.

Sergeant Hood folded his ripped up arms over his stomach and smiled with his left side showing how the muscles worked to make it so. He was content to let the hulk do his work for him. The cellblock quieted down as men nursed swollen knuckles and bloody noses. The only sound left was the sobbing of a child.

It was something they had not heard since before they had become outlaws or mutineers. When they had been happier men doing honest work and had wives or mothers. Families and homes. Freedom. Having something worth dying for.

It was a dead world that came alive bright and bold through the tears of a child. It could have been their child. Or their twelve-year-old selves.

A hurt. Someone was hurting. They all felt that same hurt.

One by one the prisoners shuffled by Reed's two canteens. Pouring a few drops of water into one and a spoonful of broth into the other. Until both cups spilled over at the brim.

The cell block became quiet as the prisoners did away with their rations. This time Reed was thankful. Not just for the water but for the broth, too. It cut away at the dust in his throat and the slackness in his head.

There was the sound of muffled boots.

"Ten-HUT!" Sergeant Hood snapped. And he and the four troopers did their best to stand at the ready.

The lanky Lieutenant Grey strolled down the corridor. Hunched over between his shoulder blades and his thin arms on his hips. Even with missing eyes, his empty sockets pierced like swords. "I need not remind you that if any prisoner is caught helping the boy, the penalty will be death."

"I've been here for nigh twelve years. Death would be a kind of parole," Frehley said giving the lieutenant in his once dandy officer's uniform and now besmirched and fouled a very cool look. "If it means not havin' to look at your empty eyes and Hoodie's half-a-face nor eat your slop, I'm startin' to weigh the options."

Back in their world, Dad would smile and laugh at the good, the bad, and the ugly-- except when he was playing poker. Frehley was using Dad's poker face—how he could not be Dad? With Strap brooding beside him, Reed thought that Dad—no, Frehley--might just call the sergeant's bluff.

"Frehley, I hope it's you that helps the kid," Sergeant Hood said. "I've got summin' special in mind for you."

"Hoodie, if you pull too hard on me, your arm'll come right off," Frehley said.

Now that was Dad! All the way through. Twenty-four seven. Square, front to back. Straight up Dad.

The Deadcoats did their best to glower. But they contented themselves to wait. There would be another opportunity to show their cruelty.

The gulps of water and pieces of crusty bread did little to satiate Reed and he wondered what Chayse was eating.

***

Chapter Fourteen: Initiation and Expulsion

"Another plate of blood sausage?" the Elfwitch asked her guest of honor.

Once Chayse got used to standing while eating, it made it so much easier to graze the buffet spread the Elfwitch's servants put out as the two talked. The food in the Domain wasn't much different: meat, vegetables, spices, and sauces. But it tasted fresh and homegrown.

Chayse nibbled between questions and stories. Talking more than eating. Just like back home.

The Elfwitch ate with relish and purpose. Putting each bite on her slender fork deep into her mouth and pulling back the fork through her red lips. She chewed down while keeping an eye on Chayse as she listened to a story about Mom or about how cruel a supposed friend at school had been. Then she would lift her chin to swallow and take a sip of wine and answer another question from her guest.

Chayse had something she hadn't had in years. Attention. An audience. An adult who showed her some kindness and gave their undivided time to Chayse.

Most of their time was spent in the Circle Chamber. It was more like Dad's "Man Cave" or workshop that he shared with Uncle Buddy. Shelves and racks of things where everything had a specific purpose.

The great fire burned in the center of the room. Stoked and fed by the lycanthropes who bundled in chopped wood. The Elfwitch kept various metal tongs and pokers at the base of the fire resting on large stones blackened from soot.

Chayse had free reign.

There were racks of ceramic pots. Some with lids. Some without. Rows of glass vials. Some had dried herbs. Others had liquids. There were all manner of bottles and jars. Some stoppered. Some latched. Half-pint. Pint. Half-gallon. Gallon. Five-gallon. Some had seeds. Some had liquid. Some had things floating in liquid. Some had desiccated flowers. Some had small animals with fetuses. Some had mummified remains of human body parts.

Nothing was labeled.

There were animals in the Circle Chamber, too. All types of birds fluttering against wooden aviary cages. Large grey rats in small handheld crates shuffling around each other and pressing their paws against the walls of their captivity. Hardly being kept as pets.

And there were five-gallon sized jars full of pebbles and desert flora set under low burners. Full of different species of lizards: Chayse knew that Reed would be able to identify them had he been here.

The Elfwitch went about her experiments while Chayse watched. She had never seen an adult at work before: Dad was always between jobs during the times when Mom allowed him to see the twins and when Mom would be at home, she would either be yelling or napping.

Her host was meticulous. Sure and studied. Patient and pursuant.

To what end? What was all this for? Chayse was beyond curious.

The first experiment shown to Chayse was like something at the behind the scenes tour her class had done at the Little Rock Zoo last Spring. A large egg—maybe a turkey egg because it was larger than a jumbo chicken egg—set in a stone pan under a large magnifying glass tied to a stand.

"Come, child," the Elfwitch beckoned to her initiate. Chayse ducked under the lithe woman's arm to stand before her and have a front seat. She smelled so different than Mom who preferred vanilla scents. The Elfwitch's scent was sage-like, burned over weeds, and dry earth.

The egg rocked in its stone cradle. Back and forth like fighting magnetic poles. Something scratched from the inside. Poking against the shell until cracks appeared at two ends at once. Pieces of shell fell to expose an inner membrane that covered two moving things. It was some kind of chick that worked its way free of its embryonic prison.

Only it was like no other bird or chick Chayse had ever seen before.

Covered in downy instead of feathers. Tiny claw talons to scuffle for purchase. A bowed triangular head ending in a long beak that curved to an upside-down point. The heads were red and there were ridges above the four eyes.

It had two heads. Like a Siamese twin. Conjoined at the chest.

Both of its mouths opened and squawked.

"Do you know what breed this is?" the Elfwitch asked Chayse.

The shock of seeing such an oddity overloaded her reason. Chayse didn't want to think. She wanted to shudder.

"It's a turkey vulture chick. Double-headed," Chayse said. "A two-headed buzzard."

The Elfwitch clicked her teeth. "Aren't you the poet? In my Domain, they are called John Crows. However, 'vulture' is an apt name, too. Do you know what they mean?"

Chayse shrugged.

"Things are not just named nilly-willy," the Elfwitch said. "Names are for children and poets. Who seek rhyme and reason to explain the world. They crave essence and identity. As if a name is all a thing will ever be.

"I hate names. Names are prisons. Things should be free to change into whatever they wish to be. All things can change. All things must change. They just need guidance.

"'Vulture' means 'tearer.' For this bird lives on carrion and tears at soft flesh. They peck out the eyes first. And then it devours the sweetmeats.

"But in my homeland, they were called 'cathartes.' And that means 'purifier.' Which is more to the truth of what this bird does and what it is.

"What does 'buzzard' mean?"

Chayse was taken aback. The Elfwitch didn't ask her many questions. At least beyond what she might like or prefer for wants like food and clothes. Chayse thought the Elfwitch knew everything—way more than Dad, a little more than Mom, maybe even Judge Hart.

"Something greasy and nasty that eats dead things. Something lower than low. Something that waits to jump on someone else when they need help the most," Chayse said.

"I begin to understand," the Elfwitch said. "Watch."

She strode over to one of the large gallon bowls and snatched up a lizard by the tail. It froze. Showing no fear or alarm. It didn't even dangle. Its head was stiff with open eyes and its claws stretched out just waiting to get back on solid ground.

Only it didn't get the chance. With a side swish of her wrist, the Elfwitch knocked the head of the lizard against the rock wall. Killing it instantly. Then she snapped it in half getting blood and offal on her hands.

She lay the two halves before the twinned John Crow chick. Both beaks began to dip as the chick gorged itself. Twice.

Done with that experiment, for now, the Elfwitch stepped to the rat cages. "Come, my pet."

Chayse didn't want to come. She didn't like rats. Or snakes. Or creepy crawly bugs.

The Elfwitch set down two cages on a flat stone table that had not been cleaned off in ages. Both were crammed full of rats. Long pink tails whipping across each other. Grey fur and wild black eyes.

"I have not fed or watered them in two days. Do you not think they would eat something living or dead at this point?" the Elfwitch asked her with a grin that Chayse couldn't understand.

For some reason, Chayse thought of Reed. She hadn't given him a thought everytime she had eaten or drunken. What was her twin eating or drinking and where was he now?

"Go over to that rack before you and down the vial with the pink stopper," the Elfwitch commanded. Chayse was only too happy to help. "Good. Now step once to the right and take up the bottle full of the amber-colored liquid. Good. Now bring both over to me."

Chayse brought the vial and bottle over as the Elfwitch set out two dipping dishes full of water before the cages. Chayse handed over the two items to her and the Elfwitch unstoppered the pink vial before letting a drop fall into the dish on the left, the water receiving the drop with a tiny ripple and changing not a whit. For the dish on the right, she poured in a teaspoon of the amber liquid. It swirled around in trails and traces until it had turned the water in the dish into something tea-colored.

The Elfwitch put down the vial and the bottle. "Now unlatch the cages and step back. And watch and learn. You can learn much by watching creatures."

Chayse unlatched the top of both cages.

The rats did not all pour out into the open space nor all try to flee. Just a few jumped down from the table and scampered away into the darkness to find the paths back to their nests. Quite a few came to the dishes and put their muzzles into one or the other. And a few stood on the threshold of each cage and sniffed their air. Even standing on their hindlegs.

The ones who drank out of the bowl on the left shook their snouts and brushed at their heads with their front claws. The ones who drank out of the bowl on the right made mad circles and attacked each other. Then they began to convulse. Trying to breathe at the same time they began to vomit. Blood and bits of organic matter.

Those rats that had drunk from the right bowl then fell where they were and died bleeding from every orifice. While the ones who had drunk from the left underwent changes. Some grew hair on their tails. Some grew quills out of their spine ridge. Some grew extra-long front incisors. Some grew tumors almost as long as their tails. But all of them attacked each with a frenzy until one stood standing on its hind legs.

And some rats who had come out had not drunk from either bowl. After watching the massacre of the mob scene they joined their more cautious brethren and all retreated to the safety of the cages.

Quiet satisfied, the Elfwitch set two bowls in each cage, one of fruit and seeds and one of freshwater before re-latching the cages. The rats devoured the food but sniff with the water with extreme caution before giving into their overdriving need to drink. And survive.

"What did you put in their water?" Chayse asked.

"The one on the left was a transmogrifier. It changed their very nature from rats to whatever they desired. Or perhaps feared. Except it drove them mad in the process. The one on the right was a quick-acting solvent poison. Quick to dissolve their innards and turn them into slush. Look," the Elfwitch said.

The transformed rats twitched in death. The restless changes still going. The sole victor had succumbed to fear and was in its death throes. Steam came out of the poisoned rats as their bodies continued to dissolve into a liquid mass congealing around hair and bone.

Chayse had never seen any biology labs like this in school.

The Elfwitch swept out her hand. "Everything here in the Circle Chamber is for your discovery. That is the best way to learn. By accident. There is no design."

The sweep of her hand ended in a fist and pointed a finger. "But there is one taboo. We eat and sleep in my Den. And you are welcome there. Except never open that chest."

"The chest?" Chayse asked. She had to think. There was one large chest at the foot of the Elfwitch's large pallet. An old wooden chest engraved with that strange word that Chayse had been so taken with.

"Once you open that chest, the punishment will be never-ending," the Elfwitch explained and the pointed finger joined the others as they touched Chayse's forehead and smoothed over her brow.

Chayse noticed the Elfwitch had said, *ONCE you open that chest*, not *if*.

"My pet, my Wice," the Elfwitch purred.

Had she just given Chayse some kind of challenge? She knew what Reed would have done. A seed planted like an open invitation.

***

Chapter Fifteen: Rule and Punishment

Reed needed six more cups of water. And another cup of that odious broth. Just so his thirst and hunger could be slaked.

Soon everyone in the cell block settled down in a fitful sleep. Even with his eyes closed, Reed was restive. His stomach did the dreaming.

Dad, dressed in his dirty cowboy boots, faded levis, and an unbuttoned Western shirt, had taken him to the Omaha Center pool. They walked in with a large cooler food of every kind of flavored soda and snacks aplenty when the listed rules spelled out in large black print: NO FOOD OR DRINK IN THE POOL AREA.

Dad dragged an umbrella stand table halfway across the pool area to set the cooler down on. Then he climbed the high dive in his jeans, shirt, and boots and ran out to the end of the diving board. Then he knelt and grabbed the board with both hands and putting his head down on the board did a handstand before diving off into the deep cool water waiting for him below. The splash drenched Reed who squealed in delight.

Next Dad climbed out of the pool and opened the cooler. Reaching in, he brought two steaming foot long Coney hot dogs wrapped in foil. Reed's eyes wanted to eat two of them before he could the next breath.

Dad stopped Reed from eating it. They needed condiments. Mustard. Ketchup. Relish. Banana peppers. Chopped onion. And dill pickle spears. One by one, Dad pulled them out of the cooler and they stacked them on top the last condiment until they all fit snug in the bun atop the Coney.

Now they could eat. And be satiated. For a long time.

Except that the lifeguards, all middle-aged women and teen-aged boys, were running around them in a tizzy unable to stop Dad from breaking the rules and setting such a bad precedent for his young son. Dad wouldn't listen to their pleas and began to eat as the relish dripped over his fingers and mustard caught in the corners of his mouth.

So the lifeguards began to pull and tug at Reed so much and so hard he could feel them jerking his chest, rubbing his chin, running over his ears, and down his face. It happened so much and so often that Reed realized it wasn't a dream. Someone was rifling his clothes. He was being robbed in his sleep.

Reed woke with a start. Again the large packrat sat on his chest looking down at its prey. It had been busy. A silver cable chain caught in its mouth and the open heart necklace that Mom had given Reed rested in its pink paw pads.

The rat was a little thief. It leaped off his chest hopping across the floor on three legs like playing jump rope.

"Hey!" Reed sat up. Hunger and thirst took a back seat to coveting. He wasn't about to lose something that was his. The only link to his family and the World he had come from.

The prisoners in the cell block began to stir. Only they weren't too happy to be awoken just yet. And especially not to have a thieving rat scamper across their toes or head. Or having a pursuing twelve-year-old carelessly trample on their fingers or bang their shin.

Moor Kreed threw off his tattered blanket in awe of the sight. He might have been the only one in the cell block who understood Reed's attachment to the necklace. But he wouldn't be the only one who understood the value of the rare silver.

Other prisoners forgot the madness in an agitated boy pursuing a rat around a cell block full of cranky prisoners and saw only the glint of silver.

The necklace was fair game now.

Strap, who curled had curled himself on the stone bench like a cat, lifted his broad shaggy hag and blew out his frustration through his lips. Frehley, who slept leaning upright with his back against the wall—not unlike how Dad would sleep in a recliner—watching through one open eye for the boy's chance for success or not. He admired the boy's spunk.

Everyone was awake and full of alarm. And none too happy. But no one could catch the rat.

It could go just as fast backward as it could forwards. It zigged when the pursuers zagged. It scooted under stomping boots intended to squash its spine and that instead smashed grasping finger.

The rat squealed in delight as the prisoners screeched in pain.

It dashed to while the others dashed fro. It crissed the center of the room while the others crossed the corners. But Reed kept on its trail bobbing to the left and back to the right waiting for it to stop just once long enough and grab it either by its tail or by the chain of his precious necklace all the while having to duck the prisoners who collided into each other because they were so big and clumsy.

The rat found a groove along the rock wall. Reed thought it had made a mistake. All he had to do now was pin it against the wall. He fell hard on his knees coming down with both his hands like a pouncing cat. Clamping both his hands together like the sides of a steel trap.

He even heard the high pitch shriek of the surprised rat.

Only when Reed came up empty-handed.

The rat had squeezed through a gap in the rocks. There was a flash of a centimeter of pink rat tail and a chink of silver cable chain. Then the rat was gone.

Escaped. Taking the silver necklace with it. Stealing it away.

Hope collapsed in a tiny ball inside Reed. All was lost. Nothing left to do but cry.

But before Reed could cry, the other prisoners grabbed him up. Being quite mad at the hullabaloo caused by a twelve-year-old boy. And angry that Reed had been holding out on them—a kid holding onto a near fortune right under their noses and now it had been ratted away? Unforgivable. Someone would pay.

They jostled Reed standing in a circle around him demanding his true name and where he had gotten ahold of silver and preventing Moor Kreed to come and stand by his side. They held the Revelator just as guilty if he had known about the silver. At least five prisoners could have bought off the Deadcoats to bail them out leaving the other fifteen to suck on their big toes.

A loud piercing whistle, like a hunter calling off a pack of dogs, broke the air. It had been Frehley who stood up on the bench. Next to him stood the man-mountain, Strap. "No one touches the boy unless I say so."

One prisoner called the bluff. "What? You mean this boy? Why, we wouldn't 'arm an 'air on 'is 'ead, now would we?" The man even reached out to touch the top of Reed's head. Only he received a blow on top of his own from Strap which folded his legs like a camp chair.

A greater clanging sounded behind the congregation of prisoners. It was Sergeant Hood with his soup squad. Banging away on the bars with their blackjacks instead of ringing a dinner bell.

"Well, I see you beauties 're already up 'n adam," the Deadcoat sergeant grinned showing the pain of his torn face on the left side. "Rat's good meat if'n you can get it. Sorry, our chef ain't got no trainin' fer the culinary arts."

"Better than eatin' old soldiers, ain't it, Hoodie?" Frehley chirped up.

The pained wound of the left side began to undulate as they all could see the sergeant gnash on his teeth.

"Do 'dem Deadcoats really et one anutter?" asked one prisoner like a callow gossip.

"'Course they do! Not raw, mind you! Cooked!" came the reply.

And everybody in the whole cell block rocked with laughter.

Sergeant Hood stuck his hand through the bars and made a grasping fist that squeezed hard and tight. "I'm just waitin' on the word, Frehley. Then we'll take you downstairs to the dungeon. There's a special room reserved jus' fer you. You'll be beggin' for us to end it quick. But we won't. We'll take our own sweet time.

"Look at you yobs laughin' it up. Lookin' at him like the mighty hunter. Like he's top o' the heap. But the way I see it--" and here he brought his fist up back to his head and stuck out his forefinger to point at the frayed wound on his left side—"Frehley's to blame fer all this. All y'all are here 'cuz o' him." Here the sick grey finger pointed at Strap. "If'n he didn't have that giant guard dog to back him, he'd be the king o' nothin'. Y'all give 'im a crown fer sure.

"Now you yobs come get yer slop and be quick about it!"

Again. Two lines. One for a canteen full of water, except for Reed getting a quarter ration. One for a canteen of broth, except for Reed getting a chicken leg that had already been picked over.

Reed threw the canteen rattling with its gnawed on leg against the rock wall and hugged his knees with his back against the bars. He might as well give up. If they weren't going to feed him right, then he just wouldn't eat.

Moor Kreed sat down next to him and slid his canteen of broth up against Reed's thigh keeping his hand over it. Then he reached out to grasp Reed's fingers and slip them under his hand until it was Reed's hand that rested on the top of the soup canteen. The Revelator took his own hand away.

Reed brought the canteen up to his chest. But before he could bring it to his mouth to sip it at his leisure, Sergeant Hood's blackjack knocked it out of his hands to the ground. It was no use to cry over the puddle of broth spreading out over the rock floor.

It only made him madder at the Deadcoat sergeant.

Sergeant Hood tapped Moor Kreed on his shoulder with his blackjack. "Holy Son, what's this? Helpin' someone in need? Guess what, me beauty? You'll bleed fer it, you will!"

***

Chapter Sixteen: Darkness and Light

The initiation continued in the Circle Chamber. But the focus had changed from small animals and potions to precious metals and infernal devices.

The dark-headed lycanthrope twins erected a metal stand over the great fire at the center of the chamber. It consisted of one pole that stood near to the wall with a great arm that could be swung out over the fire with a long metal hook. They attached a thick metal cylinder to the end of the arm and unscrewed the lid on the side of the cylinder.

"Wice, my pet, go over to the rack with the long vials," the Elfwitch coaxed as the lycanthrope twins stoked the great fire to become even bigger.

The Elfwitch always called Chayse that name now. Since she had chosen it herself. She was getting used to it, rather liked it. It reaffirmed that she could be someone new. Someone else. Chayse/Wice made an arc around the room trying to choose the right rack. She found it stuck between overstacked shelves full of scrolls and parchments. A skinny rack of long vials and tubes all plugged with cork stoppers.

"Good," the Elfwitch directed. "Now, find the quicksilver."

Quicksilver, Chayse/Wice should have known that word. Though she'd heard of the word before, she didn't know exactly what it meant—was it a color? How could silver be quick? But wasn't silver a metal? Weren't metals hard? Like steel?

Everything on this rack was a liquid. Shades of different colors and viscosity. And in the low light of the Circle Chamber, she couldn't see any metal inside a single tube or vial.

The Elfwitch sensed her frustration. "Look again. Trust your instincts."

Chayse/Wice looked again. Her only reference was of it as a *color*. She had no idea of the identity or property in any of the vials. She could only go by the color: darker, lighter, translucent, amber, blackish but there was one that was thick and dull like the contents of a thermometer. Wasn't mercury used in thermometers?

She took the tube off the rack. It was as long as a thermometer. The silverish liquid sat snug in the bottom half of the tube.

"Excellent, my pet. Now bring it here," the Elfwitch said.

Chayse/Wice did as she was told and handed over the long skinny tube. The Elfwitch had to curl her long fingers around it.

Bringing it up to her gleaming eyes, she asked, "What do you know of metallurgy?"

Chayse/Wice shook her head, "I don't even know what that is."

"Pity, that," the Elfwitch said. "You're world is full of such disbelief and ignorance. Yet, I've never seen a richer world of metals and herbs or people ripe for servitude. They are dumb to the riches within their grasp. Which will make mastery of them all the more delightful.

"This, my pet, is quicksilver. Here within my Domain, it is the substance most prized by those of the Lesser Light. It has certain attributes that serve my needs."

The lycanthrope twins wheeled in a cart bearing a different apparatus. Consisting of three parts, the base was a thick mesh cylinder that resembled a birdcage; the second was a long vertical tube going up the central axis of the contraption; the third a squat horizontal ventricular tube. There was a crank handle on the outside of the birdcage. Nicolai began to crank it up causing an inner casing to churn counterclockwise inside the drum of the birdcage. It made a whine that turned into a high pitched electrical note.

Sparks were born in the drum of the birdcage, took wing, and flew around clockwise against the cyclone motion looking for an escape. They found the long spine and traveled vertically up to the circular nest becoming rings of blue flame.

"Victor, unscrew the crucible," the Elfwitch commanded.

The other twin put on an asbestos glove to unscrew the threaded plug on the side of the crucible which resembled a thick and crude iron bucket. Victor held the plug against his chest with one hand and held the crucible steady with the other. The Elfwitch uncorked the tube of quicksilver and poured just a few drops into the crucible. Chayse/Wice watched the liquid become perfect spheroid balls and roll back into the bucket. Then the Elfwitch helped Victor screw the plug back into the crucible.

The second lycanthrope twin picked up the long hook and used it to pull the crucible dead center over the fire as the first twin began to crank ever harder. The drum squeezed out sparks and the blue flame climbed up the vertical tube ever faster until the horizontal tube began to glow. The air changed as a force coalesced around the device.

Lightning streaks shot out like licking tongues of white and blue flame searching the air for another conductor. Tasting freedom the caged animals of the electrical charges sought only to escape and through anything that could hold it.

The discharges of plasma grew across the air until they found the crucible. Latching onto the bucket like probing fingers. Stoked by the fire below and the plasma ball surrounding it, it began to glow red hot.

"Enough!" the Elfwitch commanded. The word spread out in lower echoes throughout the space of the room. *Don't you want to touch that power? I can give it to you* was what Chayse/Wice heard tickling the bottom of her ear.

Nicolai quit cranking and the plasma retreated into the curved tube as the blue rings shrank away and the sparks faded from the drum as it slowed to a stop. Then he, too, put on asbestos gloves as his twin brother Victor swung the crucible out of the fire. Both of them unthreaded the metal plug which they left steaming on the metal floor.

It was like watching the two-headed buzzard hatch out of its egg. Removing the metal plug revealed a membrane of blistering light. A pinpoint as bright as the sun flooded the room.

Everyone shielded their eyes. The Elfwitch took up an empty tube and brought it up to the lip of the crucible's open side. Using the hook, Victor dipped the crucible towards her and the quickened mercury ran into the tube.

It was no longer just the grayish dull liquid. It seemed speckled with ice crystals. The Elfwitch shook up the bottle and an instantaneous light ignited in the gaseous vapor along with a few tendrils of lightning. Satisfied, the Elfwitch folded her black feathered arms over her thin chest.

A Deadcoat trooper entered the Circle Chamber with a stained piece of parchment. The lycanthropes became more wolf than human growing red eyes and long hairy ears that pinned back against their head as they growled at the messenger. Handing over the note to the Elfwitch, the trooper bowed as much as his afflicted body let him and backed away as he kept his one good eye on her servants.

The Elfwitch cast a look at the note and then crumpled it up in her bony fingers before holding it up to the glass tube. The heat from the blazing tube set it alight and the Elfwitch threw the burning paper up in the air.

"Nicolai! Victor! Fetch both the boy-child and the Revelator to the altar," she commanded.

The lycanthropes morphed into their wolf counterparts and padded away towards the dungeon.

"You are about to bear witness to a miraculous event. An arcane occurrence. One that has not been seen since...my very own!" she crowed to Chayse/Wice as she led her by the arm through the other exit from the Circle Chamber. Towards the Ice Prison.

***

Chapter Seventeen: Light and Darkness

Moor Kreed sipped from his canteen as the other prisoners pulled away from him and Reed. The Revelator urged him to drink up his soup. "Eat. Who knows when they would feed you again."

"But you got in trouble for it," Reed said.

"You're hungry aren't you? Drink. Eat," the other said putting the canteen in his hand. "The Judge will see that you can repay me in kind."

"You've got moxie," Frehley nodded. "Maybe you're so crazy, you don't care. I'm not sure which it is."

"We all took a stand against the Mistress of the Darkness. That's why she puts us here. Including this child," Moor Kreed said to the ring of faces. "Would the Judge condemn you for it?"

"I ain't a criminal fer what I did," said a prisoner. "I had to take a stand. My family was starvin'. What choice was there? Follow a law I knowed was wrong and starve? Or run the risk to break it just to feed my family fer another day?"

"How about now? They're still starving,' ain't they? How you gonna help 'em from here?" complained another prisoner. Then he pointed a finger at Frehley. "Hoodie's right. This here's all yer fault, the way I see it. We might not be able to do anythin' to the Elfwitch but we can sure do sumpin' to you."

The prisoner, who was bigger than Frehley, stood up. A few others filled with the same sentiment did the same. To match their response, Strap stood in front of Frehley.

"Boys, ain't no good condemnin' each other fer what we chose to do just cuz we don't like what the other done or how they done it," Frehley said. "I had to make a choice. Take a stand. Against evil. And I'd do it all over again. Same as Evander here did. If I had done what the Elfwitch wanted, then things would be way worse. No one could've foreseen all this."

"The Judge did. It's all in the Law," Moor Kreed said. "Every single solitary word. Right there for any of us to look at. Only we don't. Because the Law has been lost. And now we're all runnin' blind through the Darkness."

Then the prisoner who had complained turned to Moor Kreed. "You talk of the Judge. And his Law. Where's the Light gone? How come the Son don't come down here and take care of the Elfwitch? Why's Darkness winnin' out? What are the chances of that?"

"I don't believe in chance, boys," Moor Kreed. "All things will work out in His time and in His way. Keep the faith, boys. Keep the Law."

"The Elfwitch is sure to make an example of you," Frehley said.

Moor Kreed shrugged and tousled Reed's hair. "Why should I be afraid of her? I serve the Judge, not her. The Judge made both the Light and the Darkness. How could the Darkness ever be greater than the Light?"

The sound of marching boots filled the hall. And snarling dogs. Hounds on the hunt. It wasn't hard to find the foxes when they were all pinned up like pigs.

The two lycanthropes trotted at the head of a squad of Deadcoats fully armed with muskets and bayonets. In the center of the squad were the officers, Colonel Graves and Lieutenant Grey. Sergeant Hood used the turnkey and the whole procession came into the cellblock.

The lycanthropes snarling and snapping at the prisoners. The Deadcoats sweeping them back with bayonets and half-cocked muskets. Lieutenant Grey put a dandy arm on his lanky hip and the squat Colonel Gray folded his arms over his chest.

"Prisoners," Colonel Graves addressed then. "You have lost all rights of the Realm by breaking its laws as set forth by Queen Regina. Besides, the Elfwitch has proclaimed that helping the stranger forbidden and punishable by death. Lieutenant Grey, have Sergeant Hood read the charge."

The Lieutenant pulled a small scroll from out of this dirty jacket cuffs and handed it over to the sergeant who unfurled it with a wounded grimace. "By my Word which is Law, the prisoner Moor Kreed is hereby condemned to death for giving aid to the stranger and for using illegal and hateful speech to incite others against my rule. Both prisoners are to be brought before me immediately."

The lycanthropes trotted over to snarl at Moor Kreed and Reed. Some of the prisoners began to protest. "Not the boy, too!" "Whaddaya want him fer?" "He ain't done nuttin'!"

Lieutenant Hood dispersed the troopers in a semicircle around the cell door.

The Revelator put his arm around the boy's shoulder as the lycanthropes grabbed their arms with their jaws and pulled them up on their feet and dragged them out the door. Any second, Reed was afraid that the powerful jaws would snap and the sharp incisors would sever his beautiful hand from his fearfully made arm. A thought passed through his mind of what Reed wanted to do to the lycanthropes--either as man or wolf.

Reed and the Revelator were escorted out thus. The two Deadcoat officers fell in step behind the trotting lycanthropes. The squad of troopers filed out and as the prison door slammed shut the prisoners rushed the door. They shook it. Beat against it. Even Strap hammered on it.

But the door held. Built to take the weight of a battering ram. There was no getting out.

The two prisoners, man and boy, were dragged down the tunnel which crossed a barracks room made of paved stone and back into a different hallway that went from paved stone to cut rock to a borehole through the ice. Waves of chill rolled off the ice wall making a path of slight fog. Reed's skin began to freeze.

He knew where they were headed.

Back to the Ice Prison.

The blue light couldn't reach the height of the ice wall. The horizontal line stretched far back on either side. So that both the top and the sides of the ice wall were shrouded in shadow.

And that horrible smell. Like a sack of rotten potatoes at the bottom of Mom's kitchen pantry. Or dried blood crusted on top an old wound.

Two people waited at them in front of the four ice cages. The tall slender Elfwitch in her black feathered robe with a fey look on her grey face. And a smaller figure in a black gown sequined with glass beads. Where the Elfwitch wore her silver curly hair down, the other figure wore her black up in a bun with a comb and pin. But the fey look on her face mirrored that of the Elfwitch.

Chayse. His twin sister. Standing next to the woman who kidnapped them both away from Mom and brought them this strange world. Why?

The lycanthropes changed back from wolves to men and pushed both down to their knees before their Dark Mistress.

This was one place Reed did not expect on being again. And the last person in either world he wanted to see. His knees were already going numb. The frigid air burning in his chest as his lungs struggled to warm it up for his blood.

And most of all, the things frozen in the ice niches made his skin crawl. Reed was sure that the horrible smell--like a sack of rotten potatoes at the bottom of Mom's kitchen pantry was coming from them.

Oh, they weren't dead, though. Not yet. He thought one of their eyes had blinked or a finger or two twitched.

Serve us…free us…be one with us…

Had he heard someone talking? It could only have been whispered straight into his ear. As if one of the frozen figures had been standing right behind him.

Or had it been a gust of glacial wind? Whistling down the corridor? Brushing against ice crystals?

The Elfwitch had her hands tucked inside her black feathered sleeves while Chayse held a silver tray with a cloth napkin draped over it.

"The great revelator. Still serving the Judge. A god who has turned tail and run. First, his Law has been lost. Then his son was killed. You are all that is left of the Light in the Realm," the Elfwitch mocked.

"I was sent to bring the Light. And to be a light. So that the people of the Realm might remember that the Light still shines in the Darkness. And it can open the eyes of the blind, free the captives from prison, and release from the dungeon those who sit in darkness," Moor Kreed said.

The Elfwitch strode forward and slapped him hard enough across the face that he put out his arms to steady his balance. Nicolai turned back into a lycanthrope and bit down on Moor Kreed's wrist and pulled him flat onto his stomach.

Reed jumped to his feet and beat the lycanthrope's flanks until it let go. Victor pulled him away from his twin brother's lycanthropic hind legs.

"Tell me, revelator. Did you foresee that?" the Elfwitch spat. "Do not dare to speak the Law. Not to me. Not here. This is the altar of my Domain. This is my holy sanctuary!"

Moor Kreed grinned as he wiped blood from the corner of his mouth with the back of his injured hand. He tried to shake the feeling back into his numb hand as blood streamed down his fingers. "Then I have a message for you from the Judge who has made all things: He reveals the deep things of darkness and brings the utter darkness into the Light."

"Why should I fear the Light?" the Elfwitch asked raising both hands. "The Light of this World has gone. This World is now in Darkness."

"I see that you know the Law as well as I do," Moor Kreed continued, "Then you must know that the Judge will punish the forces in the heavens above and the rulers in the Realm below. They will be chained together in a dungeon; they will be locked up while they wait for punishment."

"He's already tried that. And here I am. Free to do as I please," the Elfwitch scoffed.

"Wait, there's more. The moon will be horrified. And the sun will be shame-faced,'" Moor Kreed finished quoting the passage.

The Elfwitch shrugged. "And? Is that all? I am the moon now. The sun has been hidden."

"But the moon is the Lesser Light. And the Judge made both the moon and the Lesser Light. So he made you, too. But matter how hard you try, you will never be the Greater Light," Moor Kreed said.

The Elfwitch folded her arms again and tapped her chin while nodding to herself. "First, I will turn you into carnage. Next, I will throw you into perdition. Then I will cast you into utter oblivion."

Kreed shrugged. "Better do what you can, while you can then. Yer time is short."

The Elfwitch's face turned to grey ice. Her pupils swallowed her eyes and then became slits into tunnels of a smoking abyss. She puffed her head and neck like a hooded viper. About to strike with venom.

Reed understood what the Revelator was doing. How many times had Reed gotten under the skin of a teacher or counselor or principal? Like Dad always said, *No one wants to face a cornered animal. Call their bluff. Turn the table.*

"Wice," the Elfwitch snapped her fingers. Reed watched her sister in her beaded black dress and done up hair present the silver tray to the Dark Mistress. She whisked away the napkin to reveal a glass vial glowing like a tiny spotlight. And lying next to it on the tray was his twin sister's silver heart necklace—the one Mom had given her back in their World.

"No, Sissy," Reed whispered. Why had the Elfwitch called her *Wice*? It was another blow to his heart. How could his sis take the Elfwitch's side? If it wasn't for Moor Kreed, he'd be all alone right now.

The Elfwitch took up the vial in one hand and the necklace in the other. Static electrical sparks shot out of the vial. Like tendrils of a blind animal. Or roots of a seed. It latched onto the open heart necklace and pulled it against the glass vial with a kind of magnetic attraction.

The silver necklace began to draw on the electrical charge in the vial until the power in the glass vacuum dimmed and the necklace shone with a bright nimbus like the nights when there would be a hazy ring around the full moon that signaled a coming storm.

"Holy ones who have come before me. From the ancient deep of the foundation of the universe. From the eternal Darkness," the Elfwitch intoned.

Reed leaned his head up to whisper at Moor Kreed's ear. "Who are those people frozen in the ice?"

Moor Kreed shook his head. "They ain't people. They came out of the Darkness a long time ago."

"I don't understand," Reed said.

"You believe in angels?" Moor Kreed asked.

"I guess so," Reed said.

"That doesn't sound too convincin'. Angels are the Judge's messengers. Sometimes, they take on disguises to see how people will treat them. An old lady who smells bad. A beggar askin' for your last loaf of bread. A farmer whose hay cart has lost a wheel on a very hot day. They'll be the last person in the world you'd expect to meet.

"So those in the ice are the opposite of angels. They are demons. Dark Riders. Each one taking on a certain shape of a certain fear. Just to make people more afraid and make the Darkness more real.

"See the one on the right? That tall thin one in the robe? That's Shadow. He lives off of fear and doubt. Now the one on the left, with that long leather coat? That's Rancor. He lives off of hate and fighting.

"But the one in the middle, in that black armor? That one's the worse of the lot. Judge help us if she frees that one."

"Why? What's he called?" Reed asked.

"The Destroyer," Moor Kreed said. "I don't have to spell out what he does, now do I?"

The charged air grew heavy. Like lightning about to strike. Thunder boom. Pain drop.

"Now be set free," the Elfwitch said. "To receive all power and glory. To make this world a Domain of Darkness."

She pulled the silver necklace away from the vial which she set back on the silver tray. Letting the necklace dangle by the chain, the Elfwitch strode over to the ice niche in the middle. There was no telling how long the figure inside had been frozen.

The glowing necklace began to draw the swirling mist of the ice wall. The icy clouds began to turn into steaming vapors. The necklace levitated into a horizontal line spreading straight out to the figure's chest.

It was thawing out.

The ice around it turned into vapor and gas that was sucked into the open design of the heart necklace. The figure's face began to move. Lips try to talk. Throat swallow. The fingers began to wiggle. The serene blue face turned into a pasty white smile with black rings around its eyes.

Its eyes opened.

And the once frozen creature stepped out with its black boots. Looking at the gauntlets on its forearm and checking his leather jacket and pants for any tears. Then it leaned back its head and gave a wild lawless scream.

Nicolai changed back into a man and both he and his twin bowed on one knee. They bade Chayse to do the same. Only the Elfwitch stood to receive her companion of Darkness.

"Destroyer, be welcome to our Domain," she said.

The Destroyer put out his arm and spread his fingers. And Chayse's freely surrendered silver heart necklace floated through the air into its waiting grasp. Then the creature slipped the necklace over the mane of its wild black hair.

It embraced the Elfwitch in a licentious hug. Lifting her high above its head with a gleeful delight and spun her around in mad circles as she cackled like burning thistles under a pot. Then it set her back down on her booted heels. Both of them held out their matching silver heart necklaces touching the two at their ends. The Destroyer pointed back to the ice niches.

"Yes, we have unfinished business. And punishment to deliver," the Elfwitch said.

The Destroyer took an interest in her proposition as she further explained, "There are two more necklaces. One has been hidden from us somewhere in the Realm. It was the lover of the one who bore the necklace I wear. The other belongs to the twin of the one whose necklace that freed you."

A steeled look came over its face. Having waited for millennia to be freed the Destroyer had longsuffering in abundance. But if flexed its hand like the claws of a cat looking for something new to torture and destroy.

"The lover I have kept in jail for years now. Keeping him in reserve until I searched out another pair of the relics we require. I have found them and brought them and their bearers here. Look, dear one, twins!" The Elfwitch swept her hand back to indicate Chayse who stood frigid with fear holding a silver tray and Reed with numbed legs down on his knees.

The Destroyer strode over and ruffled the top of Chayse's bun like stroking the head of a kitten. Then he stood over Reed, twice as big as Uncle Buddy and looking every inch mean. He picked up Reed with his pale white hands and stained claws to look him straight in the eye.

Reed looked up into the face of a nightmare. Stinking death. Fetid breath. Tombstone teeth. Deadlights for eyes. Pupils that sucked in whole constellations and spat out Hawking radiation. A creature far older than any monster could ever dream.

"The Destroyer has tortured whole worlds," the Elfwitch said. "He wouldn't stop just for a boy. Yet, he offers a trade. Your life for your necklace. Hand it over. Now."

"Then I've got bad news for you," Reed said. "I lost it."

"You lie!" the Elfwitch spat. "You insignificant whelp!"

The Destroyer wadded his Chevy shirt up into his fist. The creature growled at him before throwing him back onto the ice floor. But not before Reed caught a glimpse of crucified soldiers who had surrendered during an apocalyptic battle with forces led by the Destroyer.

"We will...," Nicolai began.

"Search him," Victor finished as they moved forward.

The Elfwitch snapped her fingers. And they froze in obeyance, whimpering from being held back. "It must be freely given. I cannot change that rule."

Reed felt empowered. Seeds were being planted.

Then her eyes grew into slits. "Let his punishment will fall upon his comrade."

She indicated the still kneeling Moor Kreed, who seemed to be mumbling with his eyes closed, to the Destroyer. The creature picked up the Revelator by his head with both sets of claw and with a twist, decapitated the man with its bare hands. It cast the body down at the Elfwich's feet but the man's head it stuck on its left claws like a sock puppet.

Reed had never seen anyone murdered in his whole life. But once he had seen Dad dangle a mouse over Uncle Buddy's ball boa constrictor. The mouse's chest had spasmed in terror and as it tried to push itself away from the glistening scales of serpentine death.

The Destroyer had relished in the total destruction of a being he felt totally beneath its worth and consideration. And Reed knew it would do the same to him.

"He was no more than a rag doll," the Elfwitch crowed at Reed. "You will be returned to your cell." She signaled to the lycanthrope twins with a scurry of her hands. "You will have one hour to hand over your necklace to me."

Reed could not stop the tears of fright and loss—there had been way too much taken from him in such a short time—from streaming out. Crying was all he could from going into complete shock. His body was on overload.

"Or else the Destroyer will do the same to Strap. Then Evander. And on and on and on until there is only Frehley and you left alive in that cellblock standing in a sea of headless prisoners with all their severed heads looking up at you. Then the Destroyer will kill Frehley. Then you will be all alone. And it will be all your fault," the Elfwitch promised.

Chayse started forward, "Reed, I'm sorry."

The tray dropped to her side. The vial fractured and the electrical charges spread out like silver snakes wiggling through the ice crystals under the boots of the Destroyer and jolting through him. Up his mighty trunk legs and coursing through the closed system of this body straight into his hands.

A zap sounded at the base of the Revelator's head. And the man's mouth gasped as if he had been holding his breath this whole time. Then his eyes flashed open—not like a rag doll's—but like a true man's.

"You are a child of the Darkness and an enemy of the Light! You are full of lies and schemes. Since you refuse to stop fighting against the right ways of the Judge, his hand is now against you!" Moor Kreed's head quoted the Law, the living word that could not even be stopped by his own death.

The Destroyer screeched like a frightened child and tossed the head into the ice niche where it had just finished a millennia repose.

***

Chapter Eighteen: Frettered and Free

The Destroyer raged at the shock of having something happen that had never happened before. A dead man's head had spoken forbidden words to its face. The Law.

"Dead's dead," Chayse said at what should have been true just proven untrue. And then asked, "Isn't it?"

The Destroyer, even with all its long eons of experience, wanted to know the answer to that same question. So, Chayse turned to the person she trusted most: her twin brother still down on his frozen knees.

"Chaysie, you've got to help," Reed said to her. "Dad's down in the--"

They lycanthrope twins came between them. Trying to contain the Destroyer as he kicked out and slapped at the sound of the Law still ringing in his ears. Neither would it listen to the entreaties of the Dark Mistress and pushed her long fingers away.

The creature was mad to the core of its being. Full of hate. Deadset on destruction.

"Take them to the Circle Chamber," the Elfwitch instructed. The lycanthropes swept up the twins and moved back down the ice corridor, the Elfwitch bringing up the rear. Leaving the Destroyer to flail at the great wall of glacial ice.

Once back in the Circle Chamber, the Elfwitch had Nicolai put fetters on Reed. Then she stood over Chayse. "Your loyalty is still misplaced. You still want to save your brother?"

"Yes," Chayse said. She would do anything for her brother. She felt so helpless. What was she compared to the power of the Darkness?

"Then get him to hand over his necklace," the Elfwitch said. She took a glass flask from off a shelf and a tube from the rack of another shelf. The flask held distilled water while the tube held indigo liquid. Unstoppering both, she let a single drop of the indigo liquid fall into the water.

She stoppered the flask and shook it up.

The indigo did not dissolve. And it had not fully dropped. So Reed knew it must be lighter than the water. What it did do was begin to turn the water black across the top of its surface.

"It will take an hour for this element to completely absorb into the water," the Elfwitch said. "And then it will become a poison that stops a person's heart and lungs in an instant.

"The boy will be returned to his cell. And by that hour, if the necklace is not handed over, I will see your sister drinks this draught. Then she will be joined with the Darkness."

Reed took a deep breath from his shoulders. "I. DON'T. HAVE. IT!"

"Then people will die," the Elfwitch said and gave a signal of hand for he and the lycanthropes twins to scurry away.

Leaving Chayse alone with her host or mentor or captor. The lines were beginning to blur. She was becoming confused.

The Elfwitch bent over her ward and touched her cheek with long cold fingers. "Your loyalty is misplaced. Everyone you have ever trusted in has let you down. I have been down the road you are on now."

She pointed towards the exit that led back to the Ice Prison.

Chayse turned.

The Destroyer strode through it.

"Exit the Light. Enter the Night," the Elfwitch said.

All the prisoners were up and standing at the bars of the cellblock when Reed was brought back in. Sergeant Hood had three troopers placed on the outside walls while he went down the hall to the barracks. All had weapons at the ready.

"Where is the Revelator?" asked Evander. "What happened to Moor Kreed?" asked the complainer. They jostled for a place around Reed. Frehley was the only one who took Reed by the hand and drew him to the center of the cellblock. The man dropped down on one knee.

It was many degrees warmer in the cellblock than in the ice corridors. But the numbness had risen from Reed's legs to his chest. He began to shiver.

"He's in shock! Can't you see?" Frehley said while Strap pushed back the prisoners who wanted answers from a twelve-year-old boy.

The royal huntsman clapped his hands and rubbed his palms together for a long while and then put those open hot hands on the sides of Reed's face. A flash of the Destroyer holding Moor Kreed's head in its claws struck Reed in the brain and the heart.

"Dead! Dead!" he cried out between gasps. "We're all gonna die!"

"Slow down, now, child," Frehley said. "Is Moor Kreed dead?"

Tears flowed. His breaths were shallow. But Reed warmed up. "Yes! It killed him!"

"What killed him, kid?" the complaining prisoner demanded. "Come on, tell us! Be quick!"

"Cyrus," Frehley chided the man who was older and bigger than himself. "Does that even help? You may think bullying makes you taller but it doesn't. It makes you smaller."

"That thing," Reed said with the creature's face still before him and Moor Kreed's dead body at the Elfwitch's feet. Finally, Reed named the fearsome creature. "The Destroyer."

The prisoners became sore afraid. "By the Law!" "How can this be?" "We are doomed!" "And Moor Kreed is dead! The best of us is dead!"

"What did they do to you? What did they say?" Frehley asked Reed.

"The Elfwitch said if I don't turn over my necklace, the Destroyer will come for all of you. One by one," Reed said and hated to have to say it as he spoke the words. "But that's not all. I have one hour to turn it over or she'll make my sister drink poison."

"Sister?" Frehley said in disbelief. "Who are you? What necklace?"

Reed turned his eyes from the frightening vision still alive in his mind—though it was really in the past—and beheld the man who claimed not to be his father but was so like him in every way he could be his exact twin.

"I am your son!" Reed pleaded. "Mom gave us each a necklace. Sissy gave hers to the Elfwitch. That's how the Destroyer--"

It was all too much too fast for Frehley. "Hold up. Your mom gave you each a necklace. Were they silver?"

Every prisoner fell silent and held their breath.

"Yes. Shaped like a heart--" Reed began.

Cyrus cut him off and grabbed him up. Reed couldn't fend him off with his hands fettered behind his back. "You have a silver necklace? Hand it over!! I can buy my way out of here! Evander, I can bond you out, too! Our families could eat for years!"

Each one began to daydream of what they could each do with a silver necklace while forgetting they were still in prison and none of them had it in their hands.

"But I don't have it anymore!" Reed said. "That's the problem."

Cyrus began to shake him. "Why? Where did you stash it, you little imp!"

Strap, who outweighed him by only twenty pounds and was taller only by a few inches, clubbed the man on the side of his head. His feet folded under him. Reed stepped away.

Frehley had him again by the shoulders while Strap dared the next one to try the same only to get the same.

"What happened to your necklace?" he asked.

"The rat took it!" Reed said.

"The one you fed?" Frehley said.

"That's the time we turned over the whole cell block, remember, Frehley?" Evander said.

Frehley nodded. "Can't be helped. Packrats are little thieves. They like to take shiny things to line their nests. At least, the Elfwitch can't get it."

"But we're all still gonna die!" Cyrus complained anew once he had shaken off Strap's blow and counted his teeth.

Frehley rolled his eyes and blew out his frustration. "It hasn't happened yet, has it?"

"What are we going to do now?" Reed asked.

"I hear tell, there's another necklace. That a certain someone made a gift of to give to a certain someone else," Cyrus said. "Boys, don't you think if someone found out where the silver necklace was hidden and told the Elfwitch where to find it that it might be worth a pardon? Don't you think the finder would have enough silver to post a bond for everyone?

"All we have to do," Here the big man, with a red welt on the side of his head turned to face Strap, Frehley, and Reed. "Is making either Frehley or the kid tell where they stashed a necklace."

"I told you years ago, mine's lost for good. And we all saw the rat steal away with the boy's necklace," Frehley said.

"So you say. And I only saw a rat run through that bolt hole. I didn't see any necklace. Maybe the boy gave it to Moor Kreed," Cyrus said.

"And where's he now? The Elfwitch has his remains. The lycanthropes would have sniffed it out by now," Frehley said.

"Then the boy still has it on him," Cyrus said. "Let's make sure."

This time more agreed with Cyrus that it sounded like a good plan. They showed support by standing behind him. After all, everyone in the whole cellblock had been threatened—except for Reed.

Strap rose to his full height with his fist like maces hanging at the end of his club-like arms. Frehley crossed his arms. The two were all Reed had now that Moor Kreed was dead.

"We have to do this," Cyrus said. "We've got no choice. Step aside, Frehley."

"This child may be a stranger with strange ways but he's a prisoner just like all of us. How many of you here would let your own son be treated like this?" Frehley asked.

No one stirred or said a word. It was a stand-off. Then the man called Evander stepped forward and turned to join Frehley and Strap.

"Your odds aren't much better," Cyrus said. The opponents made a solid front while the three had their backs to the rock wall with Reed behind them. He felt like he would get squashed flat if there was a riot.

He stepped out in front of his trio of protectors. The fetters had enough slack for him to slip his right hand into his front pocket. "I don't have the necklace anymore. This is all I have on me. See?"

Reed found two items he had forgotten about. He put one in his left hand and one in his right. And turned around to show the items to the whole cell block.

Cupped in his left hand was his Tracfone. Useless in the Domain. Since there was no signal.

And in his right hand lay a large coin. Reed wondered why everyone took a step back and dropped their jaws. He held it vertical between his forefinger and thumb he could roll from one side of the coin to the other and see them over his shoulder.

It was the gold coin that Creedmore the Street Preacher had given Reed outside the courthouse before the Brazzles had taken them to Osage Cave and started this whole mess.

But it was no longer the exact same. So that it was like the gold coin.

Reed pulled it close to his belt so he could see it. Etched into the gold on one side was the portrait of a man with long tousled hair. One word stamped above in arc: LIBERTY. And under the man's neck was stamped the phrase: TRUST IN THE JUDGE.

This was the HEADS side.

On the flip side was a building that Reed had never seen before. But one all the prisoners seemed to know. It was a round castle with a large central tower atop which flew a single pennon. Etched into the bottom was the two-word phrase: TOWER REIGN.

This was the TAILS side.

The coin was the same. In gold. And weight.

But the coin was different.

How could that have happened?

Who was this strange man? Reed remembered presidents of the United States of America were usually on the heads sides of coins. He was pretty sure this person had never been president. At least not in their World.

And what was this strange building? There weren't any old castles in America. Not even real ones that dated from the medieval ages.

"Gold," Cyrus whispered. "The Root of Lyftwych," said another. "The Tower Reign!"

Two of the Deadcoats standing guard took more of an interest now that it was more than a prisoners' squabble and stepped closer to the cell. The third Deadcoat shuffled off back to the guard station.

Even Frehley's jaw dropped. "By the Law! Where did you get that?"

"It was given to me," Reed said.

"Who gave it to you, child?" Evander asked.

Reed wouldn't say. Would they believe him that Moor Kreed was also someone else in his World? Moor Kreed had told him not to tell anyone his last name. Reed began to understand that the Revelator knew it would be dangerous. Just not why.

"You stole it!" Cyrus shouted.

"Cyrus! You always think the worst!" Evander snapped.

"Just look at the here and now," Frehley said. "The child has gold. A Regent's coin at that."

"What's the big deal?" Reed asked.

"Silver is for the Moon. The Lesser Light rules it. But Gold is for the Sun. The Greater Light," Frehley explained.

"It stands for righteousness," Evander said.

"For Justice and Law," Cyrus said.

Strap put his hand over his heart.

"And truth," Frehley added. "Silver has its own powers and uses. But Gold even more so."

"You're saying this coin has special powers," Reed said feeling a little hope and wonder for the first time in what seemed years. He had no idea how long he had been in the Domain since he'd spent all of that time underground so far.

"You'd better find out quick just how to use it," Cyrus said looking to the noise that drifted down from the guard station up the hallway.

"They must have seen you pull that out. There's no way the Deadcoats will let you keep it. Time to find out what that gold coin can do,"Frehley said.

"Pshaw," Cyrus said. "That boy's no regent."

"What's a 'regent?'" Reed asked.

"The old ruling family," Evander said.

"The Root of Lyftwych," Cyrus hissed.

The entire cell block could hear Sergeant Hood barking orders down the hall. Rousing more Deadcoats to their never-ending duty. They turned from the coming trouble back to their only hope: a small coin in the hands of a twelve-year-old boy who was a stranger.

Reed felt all their eyes and fears weighing on him. "What am I supposed to do?"

"What do you want to do?" Frehley asked. Not unlike how Dad would have asked when Reed would get frustrated at losing a game of blackjack to him. "Do you want to be here?"

"No," Reed said.

"Then what would you rather do?" Frehley asked.

"Get out of here," Reed said as if that was a no-brainer.

"Okay. How do we get out of here?" Frehley asked.

The hallway was full of boots and scraping swords and cocking matchlock flints.

"Through the cell door, I guess," Reed said. "But we don't have a key and I'm handcuffed."

"Those are fetters, boy," Cyrus pointed out.

"Do you want them on you?" Frehley asked. "What does the heads side of the coin read?"

"'Liberty,'" Reed said. He knew the word. What it meant. And wanted it more than ever. The word sounded like a thunderclap. Echoing off the rock wall. Shaking the cell bars.

The fetters fell from his hands.

"By the Law!" Evander shouted.

"Now do the same to the cell door!" Frehley urged.

"Better make it quick. The whole regiment's comin' for us!" Cyrus warned.

Reed didn't know how he had made the fetters fall from his hand. But they were so small. And the cell door was much bigger. As wide as Strap and double-thick lead.

He knew all the prisoners were waiting. They had utter faith that he would open the door. So they could all escape.

"But I can't do it," Reed whimpered.

"Read the other side of the coin then," Frehley urged on. "All you can do is try."

Reed read as others prayed, "'Trust in the Judge.'"

The prayer might as well have been a shout. It sounded like a musical note. A reverberating ping that struck the cell door.

The lock turned by itself. And the large metal door began to swing open. All on its own.

The entire cell block cheered. Reed was even more amazed than they were.

The first one out of the cell wasn't even a prisoner. It was a packrat. Grey hair on its ridgeback and a long pink tail. Was it the same one who had stolen away with Reed's necklace?

Cyrus led the long-suffering prisoners out into the hallway to their first steps of freedom in a very long time. Just as Sergeant Hood rushed down the hall with a broadsword out in one hand and a matchlock pistol in another. Two squads of Deadcoats were at his heel with muskets at the ready and bayonets out.

He gave the command, "Push 'em back into their cell!"

The front row of prisoners was pushed on from the rear. They took the brunt of both groups charging. Some of the bayonets found their marks in soft bellies. Bloody hands grabbed at the sides of the bayonets and pushed them away and down.

Evander went out before Strap. Frehley stood at the threshold in front of Reed. A Deadcoat stabbed at Evander who ducked to the side. Strap swung his fist down and walloped the Deadcoat between what was left of his eyes.

The trooper's head fell back chin up to the ceiling. But the body pushed on. At such close quarters, it was going to jab either Evander or Strap.

Evander grabbed the trooper's shoulders and spun it around into the cage bars while Strap beat down on his back. Taking the rifle out of its hands, Evander clubbed at the trooper. Strap pulled a matchlock pistol out of the trooper's belt.

The Deadcoats tried to push the prisoners back. But they would not yield. The combat turned to hand to hand.

A shot was fired.

"Don't ye fire!" Sergeant Hood reprimanded and swung his sword down on one of his own troopers. "You'll hit the boy! The Elfwitch wants him alive! Do not harm the boy!"

Lieutenant Grey appeared down the hallway leading a relief squad. The prisoners would be outnumbered and outgunned.

"Deadcoats' got that way blocked," Evander said. "They'll cut us to pieces."

Something small squealed and zigzagged out of the mass of bare feet and boots. Going from the cell bars along the right side of the stone foundation wall. It was the packrat making good its escape by heading down to the lower parts of the Keep: to the dungeon.

"That pack rat's got the right idea," Frehley told the others.

"Is there another way out of the Keep?" Evander asked.

"I heard tell of secret passages. Guess now's the time to find one of 'em," Frehley said. "Whaddaya say?"

Strap nodded. Reed shrugged. He hadn't even taken a step out of the cell yet.

"Gentlemen, let's follow the rat," Frehley said.

They left the cell and went in the opposite direction of the brawl in the upper hallway.

"Coward!" It was Cyrus. Always thinking the worst. "Save yerselves, boys! I'm gone!"

Strap led the way with his big strides. Frehley had Reed by one hand as the boy put his cell phone and gold coin back into their respective pockets. Evander brought up the rear.

The quartet reached the descending tunnel

"Wait up!" Cyrus yelled. He came along at a limp and with a hitch in his side. There was a broad sword in one hand and a matchlock pistol in the other.

"Where'd you get those?" Evander asked.

"I sucker-punched ol' Hoodie," Cyrus gasped.

"You finish him off?" Frehley asked.

Cyrus shrugged. "He went down. I took these off 'him."

Frehley took the sword out of Cryus' hands.

"Hey! That leaves me just one shot with this!" Cyrus complained.

"Better make it count then," Frehley said. "We'll all need a free hand, I fear. Lead on, Strap."

Strap began the descent down the ramp to the dungeon.

"Why go this way?" Cyrus demanded.

"We'll try to find our way out down here," Frehley said.

"I might as well as jumped into Hoodie's arms," Cyrus complained.

"You're still breathin', ain't ya?" Frehley asked.

"Yeah, but not for long," Cyrus said.

"Well, hold your breath and make that count, too," Frehley said and dragged Reed by the hand to run down and join with the hulking giant.

Cyrus and Evander followed behind.

***

REALM

Chapter Nineteen: Heads and Tails

The ramp sloped down. Away from the torchlight. The riot left behind.

Ahead darkness. Stillness. Hopeless—they prayed that it wasn't.

Frehley and Reed found Strap crouched at the bottom of the ramp. At his feet was a single Deadcoat trooper, finally dead with a busted head. Strap had taken the trooper's blackjack from him and had used it on the Deadcoat.

He stilled their questions with his large hand and all they listened together.

Evander and Cyrus joined them.

"Which way now?" Evander asked.

"I heard tell the Elfwitch put the boy down here when he first come," Cyrus said.

Frehley squatted down so he was eye to eye with Reed. "Do you remember bein' down here?"

Reed nodded. His skin crawled with the thought of sitting on a pile of bones. And the solitary figures wasting away behind closed doors.

Ahead, the dungeon was no more than a wide hallway with a low ceiling. A rough floor with open pits covered with pits. And rows of lead doors along the sides of rough rock walls.

"We came through a tunnel from the Ice Prison. And then into the Circle Chamber. Then down there," Reed pointed to one of the grates in the dungeon floor.

"She put you and yer sister down in the hole?" Frehley asked gritting his teeth and shaking his head. His grip tightened on the broadsword's heft.

"If we go that way, we're sure to run straight into the Elfwitch's lair," Cyrus said.

"There has to be another tunnel. Then leading out. Probably more than one," Frehley said. He beckoned the rest of the quintet on. Strap again took the lead having tucked his matchlock pistol in his pants and keeping the blackjack at the ready.

"Oh, great. 'Probably more than one' says you. 'Probably a whole honeycomb,' says I," Cyrus moaned as he trotted behind.

"Every step is a step of freedom," Evander reminded him. "And that's worth a year being locked up."

The quintet skulked low across the dungeon floor. Ahead an exit tunnel was cast in a yellow glow. Being the passageway to the Circle Chamber.

Reed pointed with a shaky finger.

Frehley paused to consider. And they all felt eyes on them. In the low light, they could see the whites of the eyes. Not healthy eyes. Some were jaundiced. Some were sunken. But all were curious.

Long time prisoners were standing up in their rags. Holding onto door windows with emaciated hands. Peering out with something even animals had: a desire for freedom.

"Look at the poor sods," Evander said.

Cyrus blew out through his lips. "Good as dead already."

Reed looked down at the grate below his feet. Then past the eyes peering out of peepholes set in the cell doors. "No. This is wrong. Lockin' up men like animals just to die."

He took out the gold coin and held up it straight up. "'LIBERTY!' Freedom!" The words resounded off the walls like falling rock. The ground gave a kick. "'TRUST IN THE JUDGE.'" The echo grew louder pinging off the metal doors until they groaned. "'TOWER REIGN.'" The grates blew off the tops of pits high into the air. Cell doors wrenched open and slammed against rock walls.

The prisoners sulked forward.

"Run, you silly bastards! Run fer yer lives!" Cyrus hooted.

The prisoners sniffed the air. Felt themselves. Looked at each other. Unsure of anything. Taken with everything.

Frehley patted Reed on the shoulder. "That was brave, child."

"That was a waste," Cyrus said. "If'n they do get out alive, all they're good fer is to howl at the moon."

Ahead of them, they heard a rat squeak. A small figure darted away from the passageway into shadows along the left wall.

"There!" Frehley called out. "Follow! Be quick!"

"We've no light, Frehley!" Cyrus complained anew as he tried to keep up with the others.

As the rest of the quintet passed into shadows through a crack just wide enough for Strap, gold light streamed out from Reed's coin.

"The regent's coin!" Evander said. They were all amazed. Reed even moreso.

The passage they found themselves in was natural. Carved by time. Not by humans or the Elfwitch's servants.

Ducking and bending slowed the quintet down. Strap caught the worst of it as his back got scratched and his head bumped. But led on without complaint.

A chill was building in the air. Ice crystals appeared on the rock wall. It was hard to tell what direction they were headed or whether they were going up or down.

The cave wall broadened out into a large cavern. At least they were able to stand up. The chamber doglegged to the right and into a brighter natural light that didn't come from torches.

Strap reached the corner first and stood among columns of stalactites. Then he waved them to come on. The rest of the quintet joined him.

Around the bend, the chamber widened into a large mouth-filling with light from the outside. Grayish and blue. A way out!

Except that the cave mouth was gated shut with thick bars that carried the rust of ages so old, the metal had turned red.

"Those are iron gates. They must be very, very old," Evander said.

"It's the Portcullis," Cyrus whispered.

"What's a 'Portcullis?'" Reed asked.

"Barriers set up long ago. There are deep caves all throughout the Realm," Frehley explained. "They're supposed to lead to the Infernis and other taboo places."

"They're supposed to keep us out and keep what's ever below down there," Cyrus said.

"Except that puts us on the wrong side of the gate, gentlemen," Frehley pointed out.

"It's huge," Reed said. It looked as if a giant had set the door. And if a giant had, couldn't someone smaller slip through just as easy as a packrat?

He pondered the size and the builder as he strode forward. Taboo or no taboo, the other men weren't going to let a twelve-year-old boy show them up. Again, by nature, Strap took the lead.

When they reached the gates, Strap could only put his arm through it up to his shoulder. Cyrus, who was a burly and stocky man, fared no better. Evander, who was just a little older than Frehley, could only put an arm and a leg through. When they let Reed try, he couldn't wedge in past his chest.

"The boy just about can get through!" Evander said.

"Care to try it again, Evander? This time headfirst?" Cyrus asked.

Evander ignored him and looked about the mouth of the cavern. "Why isn't it guarded?"

Cyrus shrugged. "There's no guard. That's just a fairytale."

Frehley knocked rust from the iron gate the edge of his broadsword. "The gate's real enough. So the guard must be, too."

"Who supposed to guard it?" Reed asked.

"The Porter," Cyrus said. "So they say."

Reed froze. He couldn't even get the words out. "Th-the Puh-porter? Porter?"

"What's the matter, kid?" Cyrus asked. "Rat stole yer tongue, too?"

Frehley looked Reed over. The boy was sore afraid. Not of a fairytale either.

"Snuh-snuh," Reed tried to get the word out. He was full of fear. All he could do was raise his hand and point behind them with a shaky finger.

Frehley caught movement out of his peripheral. Something huge. He turned before the others did and flattened himself against the bars of the gate knocking Reed back.

A huge snake was coming out of a side hole. Its girth was as wide as Strap. Its triangular head bigger than Cyrus. Its scales shone in the low blue light. A dull white glaze and a grey serpentine texture.

It knocked the other three men down with a sideways glancing blow. Then it twisted its body around so its head could swing around. The snake had moved its whole body into the cavern. It must have been over a hundred feet long.

"The Porter!" Evander cried trying to roll towards the gate.

"It's colossal!" Cyrus said as he wrapped his forearms around the lower part of the gate.

There was nowhere to run. Nowhere to hide. Nothing to protect them.

"Quick, Reed!" Frehley cried as he dodged the lunging snakehead and smacked at it with the point of his broad sword. "Use yer coin!"

"Yes, yes!" Cyrus cried as he kicked at another snakehead lunge that brushed against him.   It was either toying with them or gauging the strength of its opponents or sizing up its first morsel. Strap hit it on its snout with his stolen blackjack. That made the snake stop and jerk back.

"Strap! Stand here!" Frehley pointed in front of him while he kept his left across Reed's chest.

Strap stepped back as the snake's head encroached on them. Frehley swapped out weapons with the giant, taking his blackjack and handing over the broadsword. The curved blade would be no trifle for the gargantuan serpent.

"Both of you!" Frehley said. "Stand next to me! In front of the boy!"

Cyrus stood on the left and Evander stood on the right. Frehley again swapped out weapons with Cyrus trading the blackjack for the matchlock. The pistol shot would do little to stop the snake.

"Lock legs!" Evander said. Everyone wrapped a foot around the other's ankle.

The snake came at them again. This time turning its head sideways as it swung the top at them like a club. The quintet did their best to duck and not get crushed as the snake crashed against the iron gate.

A clamor came from behind the snake. Several figures entered the cavern coming from the same passageway the quintet had taken. It was the remnant of the cellblock prisoners being pursued by Sergeant Hood and Lieutenant Grey and a squad of Deadcoats.

The lieutenant called for a halt as the few escaping prisoners raced on to what they thought was a long white ledge that stood between them and the gated cave mouth. He had the Deadcoat squad form a firing line with his sword at the ready to give the order to fire.

As soon as the prisoners touched the rock ledge, the great body writhed as the head rose above the massive coils singling them out for prey. The group splintered. Two prisoners ran back towards the firing line as the three remaining prisoners stood their ground.

Lieutenant Grey dropped his sword. "Squad, fire!"

A dozen muskets kicked out their balls. Enough found home in the short distance. The two fleeing prisoners were flung around and danced sideways before they fell over.

"Squad reload!" Sergeant Hood called out.

"Fire at the ready, Sergeant," Lieutenant Grey said and made a circle with his sword.

The snake encircled the three remaining prisoners with its pile of coils making a pen that closed in and swept them up. The great snake began to tighten its coils as the men screamed like helpless children. With every breath, the snake constricted even more.

The quintet could not escape through the iron staves of the ancient gate. And the snake blocked their path across the chamber. And behind the snake stood a squad of Deadcoats ramming shot and powder down their muskets.

Agonized cries of the prisoners caught in the snake's coil became muffled and then silent beyond measure. The great head weaved and bobbed between the quintet and its kill tucked safe away between its scales. Under the din, under everyone's noses, something small darted from the side of the serpent back towards the chamber wall. Small black and gray that ran in an arc towards a chimney carved within the great rock.

It squeaked as it bolted to freedom through a fissure. Leading the way once again. The fissure was enough for even Strap to squeeze through.

Frehley tracked it. "There it goes!" He slapped Strap on the back of the shoulder and the quintet made for the rock chimney.

The great snake dipped its head down between its coils and came up with prey in its mouth.

"Don't look back!" Evander told Reed.

Too late, he already had. Reed had seen many videos of snakes eating birds or frogs or even other snakes. And there were the photos of escaped pythons that had died trying to gorge themselves on alligators.

For snakes biting off more than they could chew wasn't a problem. They didn't chew anything. They swallowed their prey whole. Headfirst.

A hapless prisoner's legs dangled from its mouth as it unhinged its jaw. It meant to swallow its meal all in one gulp but that would take some time. A few morsels and it would achieve total contentment.

The quintet reached the chimney just as Lieutenant Grey dropped his sword and commanded, "Fire!"

Musket balls whizzed past them and striking rocks. Raking the quintet with dust and pebbles. Cyrus wiped powder and blood from his cheek.

"That one almost greased your head!" Evander said.

"The Deadcoats' aim must be off since they've turned into ghouls," Cyrus said.

"Being ghouls just makes them relentless," Frehley said. "Ain't got much to lose when yer already dead."

"Bayonets at the ready!" Lieutenant Grey commanded with Sergeant Hood echoing. Instead of taking two minutes to reload, the troopers took no time in fixing their bayonets. The eyeless lieutenant jumped to the head of the squad sweeping his broadsword before them all. "Charge!"

Strap was bent over investigating the interior of the dark fissure. Frehley kicked him square in the pants. "Quit dawdlin' and squeeze through!"

The giant went first. Then Frehley made Cyrus take Reed by the hand through the crack while he and Evander pulled out their pistols to fend off twenty-two charging Deadcoats with one shot apiece.

"Things are about to get hairy. Better save the shots for then," Evander said.

Frehley nodded as motioned for Evander to crawl through before him.

"We're through! Frehley, hurry!" Cyrus called.

Either half-dead or half-alive or being dead and alive at the same time, the Deadcoats were coming at the double step. Meaning to fulfill their duty as soldiers.

Frehley got down on all fours and crawled through the fissure. It ran for over twenty yards until they came out into another chamber. One much smaller and narrower than even the cellblock they had just escaped from.

Cyrus had Reed pull out his gold regent's coin which shone in the ancient darkness. Water dripped down the walls. Secreting calcium. Growing straws and flows. One drip at a time.

The chamber curved at an upward slant back towards the heart of the Glacier Mountains where the Keep had been erected.

"It's leading back the way we come," Cyrus pointed out.

"That's the way we go then," Frehley said.

Strap put his hand on Reed and kept him by his side as they climbed the ascent. Cyrus and Evander following as Frehley brought up the rear.

The passageway constricted as it doglegged to the left, back through the gutrock. But the constant dripping was pooling into puddles that once filled would stair-step downwards. Yet, the quintet knew that if the water percolated back through the rock somewhere behind them, there had been no way out for them.

The quintet would have to find another way out of the Glacier Mountains.

Shouts and scrapes came from behind. Along with flickering torchlights. The Deadcoats were not about to give up the pursuit. Not on their lives--or their deaths.

The passageway continued to run back to the left going uphill until it leveled off into a cul-de-sac. Here water cascaded down the slick rock walls into a pool deep enough to churn into bubbles and white water. Strap watched the current take the bubbles under a straw flow.

The packrat that had been their guide sat on its haunches at the edge of the pool. It sniffed the air wondering what the quintet would do next.

"Looks like a dead end," Cyrus said.

Strap pointed to where the pool emptied out of the chamber.

"I see it!" Frehley said over his shoulder as he faced their back trail. "But we don't know how long the channel is or where it leads!"

The packrat leaped into the water and began to dog paddle.

"That rat sure knows something," Evander said.

"That rat took my necklace," Reed said.

Shouted orders mixed in with the echo of falling water.

"The Deadcoats are coming up!" Frehley warned. "Strap! Cyrus! Stand in front of me!"

The passageway was narrow enough for both men to block the path. It would be just two bulky men with one blackjack and one broadsword to ward off Deadcoats coming at them one at a time with bayonets and loaded muskets. While the quintet only had two shots between them.

The first Deadcoat rounded the passageway and Strap brained him on top of his already decaying head. Blood and matter seeped out of the fresh wound but the trooper kept jabbing with his bayonet. Others began to pile up behind him and press forward while Strap's blackjack knocked the bayonets aside and Cyrus' broadsword cut and thrust at them.

It was a stalemate. A stand-off that would end when the living prisoners grew tired of facing tireless undead pursuers.

"We gotta try to get out through that channel, Frehley," Evander said.

They only had a few moments to make a decision. But what the quintet was doing now was getting them nowhere. "Child, can you swim?"

Dad had made sure of that. To make sure Reed would not be scared of deep water he had tossed him into the dead-end of the pool. Later, Dad had made sure Reed got proper lessons. The very first time Dad had ever taken Reed to the Raccoon Springs Recreational Pool, he had done a handstand on the high dive before diving into the cold ten-foot water below.

So Reed answered him by jumping in rather than being thrown in. The current was quick and rough. He caught up with the packrat and scooped it up. It scratched against him as Reed tucked it in the neck of his drenched Chevrolet shirt.

Frehley did what Reed's father would have done, took a deep breath, and then a running jump. Evander followed. And even bigger splashes came from Strap and Cyrus.

Behind the deluged quintet, the Deadcoats lined the pool. Lieutenant Grey formed them into another firing line. But none dared get into the water.

The rat squealed against Reed's throat but he held onto it. It was the only link to his necklace. A tie to the smallest chance of any kind of hope.

Cyrus shook his fist at the troopers. "Come on in! The water's fine!"

Frehley floated down to Reed as they were sucked like bubbles towards a break in the soda straws along the cave wall.

"Get yerself a deep breath!" he warned as he sucked in and grabbed the top of Reed's head just to plunge it down beneath the flood.

The others had to duck or do the same if they didn't want their heads busted open.

Behind them, a volley of musket balls twirled through the agitated waters or cracked the soda straws above ground.

But that was the worst the Deadcoats could do.

They would not wade into the water.

***

Chapter Twenty: Rock and Water

Reed was pulled under. The water rushed. The rock unforgiving. But the water made it yield. Two forces. Unchanging solid matter left over from time's first furnace being battered by constant weathering.

The water was cold. The rock dangerous. The darkness supreme.

How long was this tunnel?

How long could he hold his breath?

How could he find his way out?

The water knew. It tunneled every second of every day and night. In pure darkness.Finding its way by making a way.

Reed had forgotten his gold coin. Once just a half-dollar gifted to him from Creedmore, the Street Preacher outside the Shiloh Courthouse, now it had become something of exceeding value with mysterious qualities. He had been clenching it in his fist since jumping into the pool.

It shone forth its brilliance. Golden light shining through his fingers. Illuminating his constricting veins and the mass of bubbles around them. All containing lighter molecules of air seeking their way out.

The bowels of the cave wall were uneven rough folds. No openings to other caves. The channel twisted on.

Reed's chest burned. The trapped carbon monoxide trapped in his lungs was hot and heavy. It wanted out.

The only problem was, there was only water to trade for it in coming in.

He would drown for certain.

Frehley poked with his hands at the top of the channel. Looking for a hole. Or another cave.

Just ahead the bubbles gushed up and seemed to float and lap.

Topwater.

Frehley dragged Reed up and tried to wave to the others still behind. Still holding their breaths. Still pulling themselves through the channel.

They broke water and tried to catch their breath. Even the rat spit out water before it could squeak. The air was thick with water but tasted fresh.

The others broke surface behind them crowding everyone together in a part of the channel like the inside of a bell.

"Where are we?" Reed asked as he spat out water lapping into his mouth.

"It's an air pocket!" Evander said.

"How long does this tunnel run?" Cyrus demanded. "How can we find our way out?"

"Do you really wanna swim back to the Deadcoats?" Frehley asked.

"Won't they come after us?" Reed asked.

Strap shook his head and taking some water in his mouth pretended to strangle on it. Then held his nose.

"What did he say?" Evander asked Frehley.

"I can tell you," Cyrus said. "The Deadcoats can't get wet. They'll rot. Or burst apart like old winesacks."

"We got past them at least," Frehley said. "Now we gotta find a way out of this mountain."

"And then what? Freeze to death outside? Where will we go?" Cyrus said.

"Outlaw Forest," Frehley said.

"For what? To become highwaymen? Ambushin' caravans? Takin' elites hostage?" Cyrus asked.

"I just spent five years in a cell at the bottom of the Keep. If I'm gonna die, it ain't gonna be here. I wanna lie down smack dab in the middle of a forest," Evander said.

The rat squeaked and scratched against Reed's neck.

"It wants to swim!" Cyrus laughed. "Strugglin' right up to the end. Guess we're no different."

"That's 'cause it knows the way out!" Frehley said. "Let go of it!"

"No! It's got my necklace! I don't want to lose it!" Reed argued holding on to the rat with both hands.

"It doesn't have yer precious necklace with it here. The necklace's back in its nest. Don't you understand?" Frehley said.

"Let the rat go and see if it can find its way out," Evander urged. "It's led us this far."

Reed let go of the rat and it swam to the sides of the channel and climbed up along the sides and further on down the channel.

"By the Law! This air pocket keeps going!" Cyrus said.

"As long as it takes us outside!" Frehley said and swam after the rat. Reed followed and then the others: Strap, Cyrus, and Evander.

It was noseless and heartless Colonel Graves who brought the Elfwitch the news himself instead of sending a messenger.

She was busy mixing elements and herbs from various vials that she sent Chayseto fetch from different racks and shelves about the Circle Chamber while the lycanthrope twins looked on.

When the squat colonel came in, the Elfwitch made him wait before acknowledging him. Then she bid him approach and let him give his message into her ear. Her mien changed. From reserved to rankled.

The Elfwitch picked up the closest vial and through it to smash against another rack of jars containing animal specimens. A cloud of powder escaped out of the shattered glass as specimens burst out of glass jars to flop onto the Circle Chamber floor the liquid being so volatile that it burst into flame. The cloud coalesced into a black sheet of rain that fell onto the burning specimens and turned them into smoking ruins.

"How?" she demanded.

The Deadcoat colonel again leaned into her ear. The Elfwitch slit her eyes and glared at Chayse.

"What's happened?" she asked.

"Wice, pet," the Elfwitch said. "Come here."

Chayse knew she meant her. She'd almost forgotten about choosing that silly name. But she didn't want to go near the Elfwitch because she remembered she was also Miss Elsie Crutch, a mean-spirited woman who had embarrassed her mother in a court of law and had abused her authority and overstepped her boundaries.

If the Elfwitch/Miss Elsie Crutch had done that to Chayse/Wice's mom, why wouldn't she do it to Chayse/Wice?

"Come!" the Elfwitch slapped the top of her workbench squeezing out a silver spark.

Chayse, who now was also Wice, shook her head in refusal.

The Destroyer paced into the Circle Chamber from the passageway leading back to the dungeon. His harlequin face glowered at the Deadcoat colonel who straightened up to his full five foot five height against the walking hulk. The creature held out his right hand and jammed his left forefinger vertical between his right middle and ring fingers. Then he pulled his left forefinger away.

"Yes, Dear One," the Elfwitch said. "The prisoners have escaped."

Prisoners? Chayse/Wice thought. Had Reed escaped? How?

Then the creature pointed to his left ear lobe with his index finger and then made a horizontal fist which he wiggled while sticking out both his thumb and pinkie.

"Yes. We have been betrayed with gold," the Elfwitch said.

Next, the creature swirled two fingers up in the air and then leveled his forefinger at Chayse/Wice.

"My thoughts exactly, Dear One," the Elfwitch said. "Have you any gold, Wice?"

"Gold?" Chayse/Wice asked. "No. Why would I?"

"It seems the Judge has used foresight," the Elfwitch said. "As much as I have chosen you to be my pet, He has chosen your twin brother to be his vessel. Now tell me, who gave him the gold?"

"What gold?" Chayse/Wice said. "We don't have any at home. Mom has nothing but fake jewelry. We're as poor as you can get. Mom can barely make enough to keep the lights on."

The Destroyer strode over and picked Chayse/Wice up by the forearms and brought her straight up to his face. Her heartbeat against the sight of its sick teeth and yellow eyes. Its fetid breath made her gag.

"Think!" the Elfwitch said. "How could your brother have gotten gold?"

"I. Don't. Know!" Chayse/Wice said. That meant he had escaped! Well before the hour appointed by the Elfwitch.

The Destroyer shook her so hard she thought her teeth would fall out.

"Someone must have given your brother something!" the Elfwitch accused.

"No!" Chayse/Wice cried out. Her wrists hurt from the Destroyer's clutch and her shoulders hurt from the weight of her body.

He shook her again.

"Your mom? Your dad? The Brazzles? The Judge? Who was it?" After the Elfwitch named each person, the Destroyer shook Chayse/Wice anew.

Pain flooded her brain and the only thing that floated in over it was a bee lighting on her shirt. Then a grimy hand with dirt-caked nails reaching for the bee.

"Creedmore!"Chayse/Wice cried. "He gave Reed a gold coin!"

"You saw it?" the Elfwitch asked with incredulity.

"Yes!" Chayse/Wice pleaded. "Please let me go!"

The Elfwitch waved her hand and the Destroyer set her back down. Chayse/Wice rubbed her numbed wrists. Her head ached no better than if the creature had tried to twist it off.

"It's no matter," the Elfwitch said. "There is no longer anyone who can help the boy learn to master it."

At least Reed was free. It gave her a kind of hope. Which shrank as the Destroyer picked up the vial of mixing poisons and brought it over to the Elfwitch. She held up the potion she had promised to make Chayse/Wice drink.

"The Dear One is ever right," the Elfwitch said. "I promised to make you drink this, my pet, if your brother didn't hand over his silver necklace. And now come to find, he possesses both silver and gold.

"The question is what shall I do with this?"

The Elfwitch shook the bottle. It went from purple to dark purple bubbles before settling back to a rich purple. Nectar-like of poison.

"How am I to keep my word? I presume that you don't want to drink it, my pet?"

She spoke as Wice and not as Chayse. "I would rather not, my Dark Mistress."

"Then pick someone else to drink it in your stead," the Elfwitch indicated all those present in the Circle Chamber: Colonel Graves, Nicolai, Victor, and the Destroyer. The others seemed affronted that the Elfwitch would let a girl pick one of them to die in her place.

Wice's first impression was to pick the Destroyer or one of the lycanthrope twins for they had harassed and threatened both her and her twin brother.

But she picked out the Deadcoat colonel. He was the smallest. And already looked like death warmed over.

All of them, save Colonel Graves, began to laugh.

"A fine choice indeed," the Elfwitch chuckled. "Step up, Colonel, and drink some fortitude."

The colonel came before the Elfwitch and took the vial of poison. There was no mistaking a look of contempt on his ravaged face. And Wice couldn't take her eyes off the black wound over his heart. He popped off the stopper with his thumb and knocked the vial back until he killed it all off.

As the colonel set the vial down, his body was wracked with spasms and he choked on bile and spit that spewed out of his mouth and bubbled out of his nose. He threw up the mix of poison and vomit into a bucket beside the Elfwitch's table. Then he pulled a hanky out of his sleeve and wiped his mouth like a gentleman.

"As I said, 'a fine choice,'" the Elfwitch pointed out. "The poison would have killed anyone else. But neither the colonel nor any of the Black Watch can die. They are bound to serve me forever. And they have discovered that also means they are duty-bound in death.

"Colonel Graves, can the prisoners find a way out of the dungeon?"

His throat still full of poison, the decaying colonel had difficulty in speaking. "One way. Through the aquifer."

"So, right now they are crawling through pitch-black tunnels up to their necks in water?" the Elfwitch laughed. "Where will they come out?"

"Depends," Colonel Graves mustered through a whisper. "Behind the Keep. Quicksilver Lake. Glacier Mountains."

"Send out patrols along all those trails," the Elfwitch said. "I want the boy and his gold coin brought before me."

She waved the Deadcoat colonel away to carry out her orders. Then she turned to the lycanthrope twins. "When we find out their direction, I will send you both. You will keep the prisoners at bay and the Dear One here will take the child and deal with the prisoners."

The Destroyer showed his relish in a sickening smile.

"Where's the end of the tunnel?" Cyrus complained.

The quintet had been slogging through it for hours. With water up to their necks. Sometimes they had to take a breath and duck under a low ceiling. Their waterlogged clothes began to drag on them making their legs and arms tired. Their chests were chilled. Their stomachs growled. They had had no food since no one could remember.

This is not where they wanted to die. Deep underground in the dark. A whisk away from being drowned. Away from home and family. With no one to know what happened or where they had died.

The gold coin shone on. Sending golden streams against the subcutaneous rock and pristine water. Reed had never seen water so pure. It was like a mirror. And they had as much as they wanted to drink at least.

Again, there was hope. Why did the gold coin shine? There was hope and there was also mystery. Why had Reed and his twin sister Chayse been brought to this strange world?

"Don't drink too much," Frehley warned the others. "You'll get cramps."

The small gold light caught the end of the channel. They came out through another fissure into a wide cavern with a low ceiling. From ceiling to floor hundreds of stalactites as thin as emaciated arms stretched.

The water poured out of the fissure into a shallow pool. The quintet helped each other out of the hole and tramped to the edge of the pool where they collapsed in their wet clothes now colder than ever against the cool breeze that went through the cavern.

"I feel a breeze!" Evander said.

Strap pointed to the left.

"Definitely coming from there," Frehley agreed.

Cyrus pulled up his wet breeches and wrung out what was left of his tunic. "Let's get to it so we can get out of here!"

"Don't you wanna rest first?" Evander asked. "Don't you wanna dry your clothes out?"

"I wanna see daylight again!" Cyrus said.

Getting outside excited the others. Seeing the sun again. Feeling its warmth would be a sort of homecoming in and of itself.

They were surrounded by a hundred short stalactites. There was no clear path to the exit of the cave. Only the promise of an opening.

The rat shook its wet fur and began to clean itself at the edge of the pool next to Reed's knees. So he scooped it up and put it in his shirt. They shared some body warmth against the chill.

Cyrus pulled Reed to his feed and kept him at his side so the gold coin could illuminate their way. Strap had to bend over but his back still got scraped. Frehley and Evander brought up the rear.

Moving in the cool air with damp clothes became dismal. Their soaked clothes chafed against their skin. They became aware of another light beyond the golden aura around Reed's fist. It was broad enough to fill the cavern and cast dim shadows against the stalactites. One even appeared to be a hunchback with a grey shaggy head.

As Cyrus and Reed came under it, instead of being shadows the grey shaggy head had hair and leathery wings. It was a mass of living things. A pile of tiny upside-down heads clinging together.

Cyrus brushed the bottom of it and the mass became individual turning heads with pairs of tiny red eyes. Reed knew what it was before the little beasts took flight. It was a colony of bats.

They flapped around Reed and pulled at Cyrus' hair. Scraped across the scruff of their necks. Until they banked and dived all around the quintet.

They screeched and harried until it all became one single note echoing throughout the whole cavern. Sonorous in tone. Growing in pitch and volume. Until it filled their ears and they could not even hear themselves talk.

It was worse than a car alarm.

It was worse than the most pounding headache Reed had ever experienced.

Of all the quintet, it affected Strap the least. He swatted at the flying bats and steered them around the stalactites but not before Cyrus had snapped a few in half by trying to knock down the bats. Enraged at the sound and being swarmed by the colony of bats he kicked out at them like they were ankle biting dogs. After he had toppled half a dozen stalactites rocks began to fall from the ceiling.

Frehley rushed to grab him by the collar as he swatted away the bats from Cyrus' back. Strap grabbed Reed by his free wrist and led him up an incline along a rock ledge. The grey light grew stronger as the bats fell back to stay in the cavern.

Strap lifted Reed through a man-sized hole in the cavern wall that led to fresh air and open space.

They had found a way out of the mountain.

It hadn't been just enough to escape from the cellblock. Or get the best of the Deadcoats. Or sneak past the Porter.

They had just come out of a dark underbelly.

***

Chapter Twenty-One: Ramshackled and Sheep-Worried

Reed had his first moments of freedom.

And his first taste of the Realm.

It was a bittersweet mix.

The light was grey. The grass sparse. Tall and yellow in spots. Short and brown in others were it had died back.

The few trees about were bare. Their leaves all fallen and turned as dry as paper.

Strap helped pull the others out of the earth. They sat on the cool ground. Breathing in the fresh air.

"Is that the daylight?" Cyrus asked shading his eyes as he looked up at the dull lead sky.

"What's left of it," Frehley said as he rolled onto this back and pulled off his boots to drain out some water.

Cyrus' tunic had ripped down his left sleeve showing the underside of his left forearm. Something green had been traced on Cyrus' skin. Reed's eyes began to trace the coils of a snake as it balanced a crescent moon on its head. He had seen it before: the Brazzles each had one. What had Mr. Brazzle called it?   "Asheroth," Reed said out loud. He was amazed to see the same tattoo here in the Realm.

Both Cyrus and Frehley heard Reed pronounce the name but neither knew where his gaze had focused. The wet rat shivered stood up on Reed's shoulder to sniff at Cyrus. Maybe checking on whether the small green snake was real or not.

"Yeah," Cyrus said as he tied the ends of his ripped sleeve around his wrist. Covering the tattoo back up."It's one thing to have given the Deadcoats the slip. But I can't believe we gotpast ol' Asheroth. Thanks fer whatever you did back there, kid."

"I'm not your kid," Reed said.

Cyrus looked at Frehley and shook his shaggy head in laughter. "Like father, like son."

Frehley put his hand on Reed's shoulder. "How do you know the Porter's name?"

"The Porter?" Reed asked. "You mean that big snake's called Asheroth?"

"Yep," Cyrus said. "Has been fer ages."

"The question is, how did you know that name?" Frehley asked. "I thought you said you were a stranger here."

"It's an old name," Evander said.

"Snakes can grow a foot a year and that snake's well over a hundred feet long and that would make it at least a hundred years' old," Cyrus said. "So, who hasn't heard about it, Frehley?"

Frehley rubbed his chin keeping one eye on Reed. The rat rolled up against the boy's neck to sniff his chin. Then it sniffed the open air.

"Every day I was in prison, I thought of every which way I could bust out and what I was gonna do first," Cyrus said. "Sitting on my butt soaking wet never made my list. How long were you in, Frehley?"

"Almost twelve years," Frehley said wringing out his boots. "I think. You?"

"Just short of five," Cyrus said. "I know I was there two years before Evander came."

"Where are we and where do we want to go?" Evander asked.

Frehley slapped his boots against the ground and slipped them back on. "Let's find out."

The cave looked no more than a small washout on the side of a sloped hill. Someone would have to poke their head into the opening to see that it ran underneath the earth. It was well hidden.

At the end of the slope before them, a washout ran along the foot of the mountain they had just tunneled under. The washout ran into a wide gulley of marooned rock. It twisted away to the left out of sight.

Reed looked behind up back up the slope. The slope melted into a broad base of stone in its ascent to the sky. Peaking around the right were the fortifications of the Keep: a corner tower, one of four, built around the central tower that snuggled up to the mountain peak rising to a point to where both should have reached the sky.

Only it was obscured by clouds. A white mist dusting down snow. Drizzling sleet.

On the other side of the gulley rose an even taller wall. Wider than any mountain range that Reed had ever seen. Its entire surface gleamed with white crystal.

Pure ice. Miles of frozen water. Field and fill. A glacier.

Frehley came back at a crouched run. As the men knelt together like football players in a championship game huddle, Strap crept back up the slope to keep watch.

"The Keep's behind us. Glacier Mountains are in front of us. And too much open ground in between," Frehley reported.

"We came out on the wrong side," Cyrus said.

"It is what it is," Frehley said.

"Why can't anything be easy?" Cyrus complained anew.

"Leastways you'll stretch your legs," Evander said and slapped Cyrus' meaty thigh.

"What were the bats doin'?" Reed asked. "They're blind so they make sounds to find their way like sonar. But I never knew they could make a sound like that."

"Were they tryin' to hunt us?" Cyrus asked.

They all looked at Frehley who grimaced. "They were soundin' an alarm."

Strap whistled and came around the edge of the slope pointing behind him to the left. They all scooted over to get a better view.

It was a squad of Deadcoats. Six to be exact. Well-armed and moving despite their torn tendons and broken bones.

"Should we go the other way?" Evander asked.

"Into Glacier Mountains?" Cyrus returned the question and then answered it. "We'll freeze in an hour."

"We'll have to take them out," Frehley said. "Check yer weapons."

The rat screeched and tried to bury itself beneath the neck of Reed's shirt. He pulled it out and placed it feet first against his chest so that its head stuck out of his shirt. Its heartbeat against him and having it that close was the only thing keeping his chest warm.

Strap carried the blackjack and Cyrus the broadsword. Frehley and Evander had pistols with one shot each. Though the powder was wet and it was freezing out.

The Deadcoats spotted the escapee quintet. The squad leader sent one trooper back up the slope to the Keep and goaded the other Deadcoats on with his broadsword. They were coming on them fast.

They made a semi-circle around Reed with Strap as the anchor and Cyrus beside him. Frehley and Evander stood on either end. The first Deadcoat rushed at them with a bayonet at the charge. Strap knocked the bayonet and muzzle aside as Cyrus slashed down at the Deadcoat's face with the edge of the broadsword but all he did was make a new scar that would not bleed.

The Deadcoats took a drubbing but would not stop. While the quintet refused to yield an inch of ground. Frehley's and Evander's pistols would not work. They had to step aside from being fired on point-blank and swing the gun butts at the back of the Deadcoats' necks like clubs.

One trooper went down and Evander pounced on him before the trooper could draw out his bowie-like knife. Evander crushed the Deadcoat's skull but the trooper wriggled out from under the man and turned back upon him even with his head split open. Frehley took out the trooper's legs with a side tackle. Cyrus brought the broadsword down on the Deadcoat's neck severing the head. It rolled away as the body got on all fours and searched for a weapon.

The squad leader tried the same move on Strap but the giant would not topple. He picked up the Deadcoat by his ankle and slammed him headfirst into the ground time and time again. The Deadcoat's neck broke and the head lolled to the side but the legs continued to kick only stopping when Strap broke the back of the Deadcoat over his knee.

They ganged up on in twos on the other Deadcoats know that Frehley and Evander had grabbed a fallen musket apiece. One Deadcoat was bayoneted to the ground as Cyrus cut him piecemeal. Strap grabbed the last two and smashed them together like bricks. Evander kicked one backward so the trooper toppled down into the cave hole the quintet had escaped through.

That left one Deadcoat unaccounted for.

Frehley turned and the trooper had a pistol cocked and aimed at his heart. He had fired the musket in his hand and he had no time to bring it up to the ready to use the bayonet. All within a breath, instead of firing point-blank into Frehley the trooper was hit from behind and stumbled forward, firing off the pistol in the ground.

The Deadcoat turned to see his attacker: a twelve-year-old boy using a discarded pistol butt as a club. Cyrus slashed off the trooper's arm and Cyrus brained him. The trooper fell over kicking at the ground with its legs.

The quintet, bruised and breathless, surveyed the skirmish. Five Deadcoats had been dispatched and left scattered about. Severed arms still twitched. Cut hands grasped. Legs thrashed.

"We made a ramshackle of 'em," Evander said with pride.

"They just won't die," Reed said.

"That's Deadcoats fer ya," Cyrus shrugged.

"That wasn't so much of a chore," Frehley said.

Strap laughed as Cyrus sneered. They divided the spoils of armaments between themselves: Frehley chose the corporal's broadsword, a bowie-like knife, and another fresh pistol; Strap took a bowie-like knife; Evander and Cyrus each took a musket and bayonet; and each took a bag of powder and shot.

But they hadn't finished ransacking the decimated Deadcoats, yet. Cyrus sat down on his hunches to hold the troopers' boots one by one up against the length of his own foot.

He tore off two pair and tried them both on before he found a pair that fit. The other he tossed over to Evander who was disappointed that they wouldn't fit him. Reed looked at his Converse sneakers: they were torn beyond disrepair.

Evander tossed him one of the boots that hadn't fit him. "See if it fits."

When Reed kicked off his shoe there was as much grime inside it as on the outside canvas. His foot spread out breathing in the open space free from the dungeon dirt and the cellblock crud. Then he slipped his foot inside a Deadcoat's boot.

It fit. So Cyrus threw him the other one.

"Well, I'll be. They do fit nice. For a boy so young, you've got mighty big feet," said the burly man.

"He's gotta grow into feet like those," Evander teased. "To be as tall as Papa."

Even Strap joined in by holding his hand up to Frehley's height to indicate the measuring threshold.

Frehley slapped the giant's hand down. "Oh, stop it."

Commands and shouts came from up the slope.

"Remember the one they sent runnin' back?" Evander said.

"I remember," Frehley said.

"Which way then?" Cyrus asked as he cupped his hand over his eyes to spy out any more pursuit.

"We go back the way this patrol came," Frehley said.

"And pass right in front of the Keep?" Cyrus demanded. "We'll never make it. There's cannons and more Deadcoats."

Just the mention of the Keep made Reed think of the pit and the bones and the Elfwitch. "I'm never goin' back to the Keep."

Even the rat screeched. But the rat had stashed something Reed wanted back. Somewhere in the Keep.

"We head west and take another path that doesn't go around the Keep. It'll lead us out of Glacier Mountains and to the Royal Forest," Frehley said.

"That's taboo lands," Evander said.

But Frehley had already moved off with Reed and Strap following. "We're the hunted now. Better do something they don't expect."

Evander and Cyrus hitched their steps double time to keep up.

"They'll sheep worry us. Especially if they sick them lycanthropes on us," Cyrus said.

"But we aint' sheep," Frehley said. "We're men."

"Men running like rabbits," Evander pointed out as they quintet came up the slope under the right or eastern tower of the Keep.

"Alright," Frehley shrugged. "We can be rabbits. What do rabbits do when hounds are coursing them? They make circles. Zig when the hounds think they'll zag."

They took a goat path around to the north. Nothing more than a trail of patchy grass and pebbles over rock ledges and boulders. The noise of the Keep was left behind as the sky was blocked out by the blizzard that blew on top of the mountain.

Winds blew down at them from above where they rode the poles at the top of the world. Reed wondered, how much of this world was locked up in ice? And where was the sun?

"But when the coursers grab a rabbit, they shake 'em by the neck until they're dead," Cyrus complained.

"Better than rotting away in the dungeon," Evander said.

The goat path led them up to a ridge that ran back to the west. They followed it in single file until they reached a cleft in the rock face. Then Frehley led them straight north and took them down through the cleft to a valley below.

It ran like a bowl to the east and west. Stretched out in the middle was a body of the strangest water that Reed had ever seen. Dull and leaden. Not a ripple. He realized it was too viscous to be water.

The quintet walked down the sloping beach. Tiny pebbles and old seashells covered the shoreline all around the small lake. Reed could not see the bottom nor himself upon the surface.

Cyrus bent down to inspect it with a touch.

"I wouldn't do that," Frehley said.

"Why? What's the harm?" the other asked.

"This is Quicksilver Lake," Evander told him as if he should have known.

Cyrus jerked his hand back.

"What's the matter with the lake?" Reed asked. The rat kept one paw on his chest as it stretched its head out to sniff at the lake.

"It's full of quicksilver," Frehley said.

"And danger. And mystery," Evander added.

Reed had learned that quicksilver was just another name for mercury. In their World back home, it was used in thermometers by expanding when it got hot and shrinking when it got cold. One time, Reed had dropped a glass thermometer on the floor and all the mercury had spilled out. Something strange had happened. The mercury didn't make a flat liquid pool—it had rolled up into several tiny spheroid balls.

"No one must touch the lake," Frehley said and then turning to Reed, "and you must not drop yer gold coin in it. The quicksilver will eat it."

"Just imagine what it would do to a person," Cyrus said.

Something grated behind them.

Something against metal.

Something big.

The quintet turned. Behind them, the ridgeline encircled the sloping shore like the rim of a bowl. Beneath that rim ran a shallow trench whose lowest point ended at the mouth of another cave.

The cave mouth was gated with iron bars.

"Porticullus Cave!" Evander warned.

A blur like a horizontal white tree trunk slithered past. Reed was beginning to understand the association. Where ever the gates were located, the Porter would be nearby.

The gate wavered as rusty chains chinked on a pulley. Metal scratched along oxidized grooves. The gates were being pulled up.

And out bounded the lycanthrope twins as their wolf selves.

Cyrus fired his musket striking one of the twin wolves in the chest. The gouging ball did nothing to stop the beast-man as it bit down on the musket barrel snapping it in two. Powder exploded between its snarling jaws and Cyrus' face. He fell backward down the shore as the werewolf shook off the firefly embers.

Evander jabbed at the other wolf's flank as it tried to rush at Reed.

The Destroyer caught a slash from Frehley's broadsword on its wrist gauntlet and grabbed the sword in both hands. It slung blade and sword-bearer around like a discus and threw Frehley against Evander. Both fell on top of each other like dominoes.

Strap struck the creature against the side of its head with his blackjack. A blow strong enough to break a human's neck. But the creature wasn't human.

Its head lolled to the side with a grin of delight. Then it clutched Strap's hand with the blackjack by the wrist. Pulling the arm away and out it also caught Strap's other hand as it came towards its abdomen.

It began to pull both Strap's arms straight out to rip them out of their sockets. Running up the slope, Frehley turned to pounce onto the creature's back. He shanked the Destroyer's neck with his bowie-like knife.

The Destroyer let go of Strap and grabbed Frehley by his hair and flung him off like a ragdoll onto his back. Frehley was winded and struggled to catch his breath. Strap put the Destroyer into a headlock to pull him away from his fallen friend.

"Now's the time to use your coin!" Evander shouted at Reed as both he and Cyrus jabbed at the twin wolves to keep them at bay. But with each lunge, the wolves separated the defenders from Reed.

"I don't know how to use it!" Reed cried. He wasn't sure if he had opened the cellblock door or the coin had. The coin seemed to know its light was needed. Did it even need Reed?

He reached into his pocket to pullout the gold coin. One of the wolves leaped by and knocked him down with its flank. The coin tumbled away and bounced down the slope.

Frehley reached out and gasped, "Don't let it fall into the lake!"

The rat crawled out of Reed's shirt and leaped down to chase after the glittering round shape that bounced down the shoreline.

One of the wolves changed back into the human form of Nicolai to grab up the coin. Evander collided with Nicolai meaning to shove his bowie-like knife under the lycanthrope's armpit. Nicolai hip tossed the man over onto his back as he pinned Evander's blade hand to the ground.

The Destroyer grabbed Strap by the back of his britches and swept the giant off his legs. Raising him vertical he pile-drove him headfirst into the ground. Strap somersaulted and landed on his stomach while blood streaming down his face.

"The coin!" Frehley pointed.

The Destroyer howled at Reed and stomped towards him. Like a deer caught sleeping along the side of the road in a car's headlights, the boy leaped up and dove among the rocks and shells of the shoreline. The rat held the coin in its paws. Turning it around and around.

The sole of a boot came crashing down. Meaning to squash the rat. Reed snaked out his hand and grabbed the rat with the coin.

The Destroyer's boot pinned his wrist down and ground into the pebbles and shells. Reed rolled over and took the coin from the rat with his other free hand.

Wrapping his sliced fingers around it the coin did nothing. No light. No power.

LIBERTY and TRUST IN THE JUDGE had deserted Reed.

"Cyrus!" Frehley gasped. "Help the boy!"

Cyrus was the last man standing. Besides Reed. Instead of coming to the boy's aid, he brandished his broadsword against the wolf form of Victor.

Frehley rolled himself over and pulled himself down the beach on his arms and hands.

Nicolai sat on Evander's chest and blade arm. Trying to pull the bowie-like knife from Evander's hand until he began to hit the lycanthrope in the kidneys with his free fist. Evander slipped out from under Nicolai's weight and flipped the lycanthrope off him to send him tumbling down the shore.

The lycanthrope loped back up the beach and tackled Evander at his beltline again grabbing Evander's hand that held the blade. With a thrust, the blade slipped back into Evander's gut. The man howled and yanked it out slicing deep into Nicolai's chest.

Having pinned both the boy and the rat under the heel of its boot, the Destroyer loomed over Reed. With its left hand, he made a circle with his thumb and forefinger over his outstretched right hand. Then it made a fist with its left hand and pointed out sideways with fore and middle fingers.

"Don't throw the coin!" Frehley said sliding down the beach to pick up the broadsword. Then he did something no one expected him to do. Because it was taboo.

He immersed the broadsword into the quicksilver up to the hilt guard. And brought the blade out of Quicksilver Lake like from a cold forge. Mercury ran down the channels of the blade like a dull syrup.

The Destroyer turned to face Frehley who had raised himself to his knees. It hissed at Frehley. He replied by flicking mercury off his blade into the Destroyer's face.

The quicksilver wrapped around the creature's head and tightened like a glove. The creature dropped to its knees and gave a muffled howl of frustration. In vain it tried to tear away the seal of mercury.

The other wolf changed back into human form as both Victor and Nicolai rushed to help the Destroyer remove the suffocating metal mask.

"Cyrus! Check on Strap!" Frehley said as he pushed himself up to his feet using the broadsword as a crutch.

"Boy," he said to Reed. "Tend to Evander."

Evander was on his knees having with one hand over his bleeding wound. He had Reed tear the rest of his right sleeve off his tunic. He directed Reed to wrap it around his abdomen and back to cover the wound. Then he took off his belt and had Reed wrap it around the crude bandage and cinch the buckle tight over the seeping wound.

Cyrus wiped blood out of Strap's eyes as the giant began to stir. Then he helped Strap sit up.

The Destroyer writhed and kicked out. And when the lycanthrope twins tried to hold the creature down it lashed out at them. They had to keep the Destroyer from rolling into Quicksilver Lake by pulling it by its leather-clad legs.

Cyrus put one of Strap's arms over his shoulder as Frehley propped himself under the other one. Reed let Evander lean his weight against him almost toppling over by the man's weight. The quintet limped back up the sloped beach away from the shoreline of the strange lake while their enemies struggled to help each other.

They reached the rim of the ledge and ducked under the bowl. Stepping down into the trench the quintet entered the cave through the raised gate. Leaving Evander to lean against the cave wall, Frehley had Strap find the release to the gate chains. It took both Cyrus and the giant to heave it back with all their might.

With the help of the lycanthrope twins, the Destroyer freed himself from the poisonous quicksilver. The evil trio sprinted up the beach towards the cave entrance. The gate could not close fast enough.

Inch by torturous inch it dropped as the enemy trio reached the trench. Frehley poked his disintegrating broadsword through the lowest rung of the gate to help pull it down. "Give us a hand!" he yelled to Reed.

The boy jumped up and grabbed the bottom rung and together their combined weight pulled the gate down. The chinks sped faster until it slammed against the cave floor

The quintet took a step back as the lycanthrope twins grabbed at them through the iron bars. The Destroyer snarled as he gripped the bars and tried to pry them open. But the bars wouldn't budge so all he could do was put his head between them and spit at the quintet.

Just as the corrosive quicksilver did not kill the creature it could not bend iron. It wasn't omnipotent. It had some limitations.

"Down the passageway!" Frehley said swatting at his friends' shoulders.

"It's not over!" yelled Victor.

"There's nowhere you can run!" Nicolai yelled.

"There's no one to help you!" Victor yelled.

"We'll only hunt you down again!" Nicolai promised.

The quintet limped down the passageway.

Cyrus looked back

The Destroyer made two hand signs. In the first one, it cupped its hands over each other palms up with arms held out above stomach. Then it folded its arms against its stomach with the open palms cupped over each other. Next, it held its left hand above its left eye with all four fingers arced up and the thumb arced down like a capital L. Then it touched its fingertips to the tip of its thumb twice.

Evander had turned back also just as the Destroyer was signing at Cyrus. But his wound hurt too much to give the signs much thought. He wouldn't get far by bleeding so much out.

***

Chapter Twenty-Two: Black as Night and Clear as Day

The Elfwitch summoned Lieutenant Gray for a report while she had Chayse/Wice ground foul-smelling weeds into powder with a pestle and mortar. The ground herbs rendered an odor more potent than sulfur. Chayse/Wice couldn't imagine what good would come of it.

As she twisted the pestle into the stone mortar, the Elfwitch kept busy knitting coarse thread and fiber together. She was making some kind of mesh.

"Bring me the mortar dish when you have finished, pet," the Elfwitch commanded as she made the eyeless Deadcoat wait with his ruffled sleeves on his fine-spun officer's tunic. "Lieutenant, did your patrols succeed in stopping the escapees?"

The lieutenant shook his head.

"Why not? Did not Colonel Graves inform you as to my expectations?" she asked.

The lieutenant stood even taller and centered his eyeless face on her. But he gave no other acknowledgment.

"Maybe the wrong person commands the Black Watch?" the Elfwitch suggested.

Chayse/Wice pondered on how someone with no eyes or who would not speak would give a response. Was the lieutenant bound by any sense of duty? With one hand on the mortar bowl, Chayse/Wice kept twisting the pestle against the sage as it ground down into powder.

"Colonel Graves has failed me once again. It leaves a stain upon the Black Watch and the duty you all have sworn to me," the Elfwitch said. "I cannot abide failure. I must have total compliance. Nothing must be left undone."

The lieutenant brought up a moldy gloved hand and clenched it into a fist. Chayse/Wice heard the tendons cracking and the bones popping. Could the Deadcoats even feel their aches and bruises anymore?

"I am sending you to the Royal Forest. You are to go to the outposts on the boundary of Outlaw Forest. I am confident the escapees will flee there and try to rally others to support them.

"Watch for them. Contain them. Capture them if you can. Then send for me and they will feel my darksome vengeance. I feel that you are a natural-born leader, Lieutenant-Colonel," the Elfwitch said.

The newly minted Lieutenant Colonel Gray made a low bow catching his plumed tricorner hat as it fell off in his hand to turn it into a sweeping obeisance. His naked head revealed a gaping hole at the top of his head, rather like a bullet's exit wound. The officer doffed his hat and pushed the ruffles back up his sleeve before exiting the Circle Chamber.

"Have you finished grinding the sage, my pet?" the Elfwitch asked.

"Yes, my dark mistress," Chayse/Wice said. She had never in a million years spoken to Mom like that. She hadn't treated Mom with fear or reverence. Something more like resentment.

"Fetch the bottle with a skull stopper from off the rack," the Elfwitch said as she pulled the mesh across her workbench. After Chayse/Wice brought her the mortar dish with the ground sage, she went over to the cubby hole rack filled with bottles of rare vintage and obscure liquid. She found the one with the skull-shaped stopper, it being quite dusty, and pulled it from its place to bring it back to the Elfwitch.

The Elfwitch sifted the sage out of the bowl over the mesh and then sealed in the flavor of the herb by putting her thumb over the top of the bottle and shaking out some of its contents.

"Ever hunt wild birds, Wice?" she asked during the task.

"Dad and Uncle Buddy used to hunt wild turkey," Chayse/Wice said.

"They are too smart to be caught with a net," the Elfwitch laughed. "The birds we will hunt will be slower and not quite as smart. Once we spread this net over them it will be as black as night. And they will fall fast asleep. Help me roll it up."

As the two rolled up the mesh-like a sleeping bag, the Elfwitch said, "Always be one step ahead of your prey. It takes patience and long-suffering. Revenge is best suited for those who keep an eye on the end-game."

"What's an 'end-game', my dark mistress?" Chayse/Wice asked.

"Oh, my dear Wice!" the Elfwitch sniggered as she sat back down. "To win at any and all costs. It's not just to turn them into carnage. It's not just to send them to perdition. It's to prescribe them into oblivion. To utterly destroy them and claim total victory."

The lycanthrope twins marched in with their heads down and faces darksome. Behind them pouted the Destroyer. The twins fell on bended knees and put their heads into the Elfwitch's lap.

She petted their shaggy heads with long cold fingers.

The Destroyer held out its left hand with fingers splayed out horizontal. With its right forefinger jammed vertical between the first two left fingers, the creature flicked the right-handed finger away.

"I see," the Elfwtich said. "Was it the gold coin?"

The Destroyer shook his head. Holding up his right hand, it cupped four fingers over its thumb. Then pointing out with its right forefinger, it rubbed its left pinky back and forth over it.

"We cannot help how we are made. Even we Dark Riders require aid of each other," the Elfwitch said. "Do we not rely on the Darkness?

The Destroyer nodded and even the lycanthrope twins said, "Yes, my Dark Mistress."

"Then we must remember that the Darkness is a part of everything. Before there was anything, there was Darkness. Even the Light came out of the Darkness at the Great Separation. And for every part of Light, there is a particle of Darkness. Never forget," the Elfwitch said. She rose off her work stool and strode to a cabinet made of a hundred tiny drawers. She pulled one out and took something small from it. This she handed over to the Destroyer.

It was a small hexagonal metal box. With a heavy spring lid. Like the kind of box to hold an engagement ring.

The Destroyer smiled with relish and gleaming eyes.

"Next time, we will be ready for our prey. This netting for their flight. And this lead box for the gold coin. We will crush all our enemies into oblivion. Before long we will have the other two necklaces," the Elfwitch promised.

Two more necklaces? Chayse/Wice thought to herself. She had surrendered her own without understanding its importance, only that the Elfwitch desired it and had used it to free the Destroyer. She had also wanted Reed's necklace but either her twin brother had lost it or had hidden it away.

And now somewhere else there was one more silver heart necklace.

What would the Elfwitch do with the other two if she had them?

Weren't there two more creatures frozen in the Ice Prison?

The lycanthrope twins pulled a large trunk out of a recess inside the wall. They set it on top of the Elfwitch's work table. She opened it back on rusty hinges. Inside were cubbyholes and tiny recesses. At once, each of them began to gather vials of potions and bottles of herbs and placed them inside the trunk.

"My pet, it is time to introduce you to the Realm. And to the court at Tower Reign. This you will find most enlightening," the Elfwitch said.

The cavern the quintet found themselves in was natural and rather straight and wide. It ran close beneath the surface because of all the tree roots that hung suspended in the air without soil dripping water down on them. The air was cool and there was a grey light up ahead.

It stretched a short way and came out of the side of a hill. Just like back home for Reed where everything ran downhill both ways. How long had the twins been gone now?

The quintet came out in the middle of a tree line. There was no sign of the Keep or Glacier Mountains. Just miles of hills and knobs ahead all covered with pines and firs and the occasional ash and oak.

First, Frehley had them check the weapons they had accumulated during their prison break. He himself had two pistols plus a long knife. Strap had his trusty blackjack and musket and bayonet. Cyrus still had a broadsword and a musket with a bayonet. Evander had a pistol, a musket and bayonet, and a long knife. And everyone had a bag of shot and powder.

Reed only had his gold coin. And another lump in his pocket which he had forgotten about. His tracfone, which still had a charge but no signal.

And the rat. It was dry now and sitting on the ground. But kept washing itself with its front paws.

Reed didn't want that rat to go anywhere. Only it knew what had happened to his silver heart necklace. The necklace that Mom had given him.

The boy only had some scratches and mud-covered half of his chevron on his favorite shirt. The men were a little worse for the wear. They all had their shares of bruises and cuts with Strap looking like a punching bag.

But Evander had a profuse wound that couldn't be staunched by a piece of cloth and belt alone.

"You should leave me," Evander said in a hoarse voice. With ginger care, he lowered himself down to the ground.

"We won't leave you," Frehley said.

Cyrus looked over his hurt companion. "If we don't stop it, he'll bleed out."

"Strap, find some clay," Frehley said. "Cyrus, stay with Evander and keep a lookout. Child, you come with me. We will gather some deadwood."

"Deadwood for what?" Cyrus asked.

"A fire," Frehley explained. "To clean and staunch the wound."

"Better let me do that when it comes time. I've spent some time blacksmithing," Cyrus said.

Strap went down the slope to follow the ground of a washout. Cyrus began to load his musket his dry powder and shot. Frehley started off and then turned to see that Reed wasn't following.

"Come, child," he bade.

Reed refused.

Frehley's shoulders slumped as he humphed. "What is it?"

Reed crossed his arms. "I have a name. You can call me Reed."

The others nodded to themselves and watched askance at what Frehley would do next. The man twirled his hands in frustration. "Reed, thank you for helping us escape. I'm not sure how you did it. And I don't believe you know either.

"We're out of the Keep but we're not out of danger. The Deadcoats will be looking for us. The Elfwitch will hunt us down with the lycanthropes."

"And she has other servants who serve her. Placed all over the Realm," coughed Evander.

"We'll need a better shelter. Somewhere we can plan a strategy. Find some kind of hope," Frehley said.

"And something to eat?" Reed asked. The greasy oatmeal he'd eaten back in the dungeon had long worn off. But first, he felt like he could drain a lake he was so thirsty and his throat so dry.

Frehley nodded. "And something to eat. But we can't make a move until we help Evander. It's do or die time."

Do or die time. That phrase quickened Reed. Dad would say it often. When he was showing Reed had to throw a football or hit a baseball wherever he needed or track a moving target with a gun or a crossbow.

Do or die time. Sometimes Dad would also say *Stand and deliver.* Which Reed knew was some old-timey phrase.

It meant *Do what needs to be done and do it right the first time.*

Reed nodded and followed after Frehley. The rat jumped off its haunches and scampered off in the other direction. He had a feeling it would be back.

They had to find firewood. Reed could do that. He knew just the kind needed to start and stoke a fire. Dad had shown him dozens of times when the twins had gone camping with him and Uncle Buddy—Reed couldn't help but feel he was out camping again with them both, except Dad called himself Frehley and the laconic Uncle Buddy was the mute Strap.

Frehley had said *deadwood*. So that's what Reed looked for--fallen limbs covered in lichen and branches broken. He made sure they weren't much thicker or longer than his arms.

Once he had a pile file in his arms, Reed began to gather up leaves and twigs. They could be used for kindling. He might not be able to fight the Deadcoats with sword or knife or his bare hands like the others could, but he had this.

Reed could shoot most guns: shotgun, .22, .243, and a muzzleloader. He could even shoot a compound or crossbow. But he could not use one of those long knives like Frehley had and he had never touched a sword in all his livelong life. Also, the Deadcoats could reload their muzzle guns and get a dead bead well within two minutes. Faster than even Dad back home.

Close by, a bird whistled a two-note call. Only it wasn't a bird—Reed had been on enough hunts to know a signal. He returned the call with one of his best woods signals—a crow's caw. Turkeys hated crows. So did owls.

Frehley stepped out of some brush carrying a pile of limbs and twigs. After surveying Reed's pile, he gave a nod. Then he again gave the same two-note whistle and listened.

Someone gave the reply, a similar two-note whistle but with the last note a step down. Soon out of the brush emerged Strap carrying a pile of red clay snuggled on the edge of his tunic like a good chef might carry eggs on the edge of his apron. The giant nodded to his companions.

Frehley whistled a third time.

There was no reply.

He and Strap shared a look. Reed could sense their growing concern. The trio began to backtrack with caution. Their weapons hung on their shoulders or stuck in their belts. Close at hand but their hands were full.

A chill dropped down Reed's spine. What if Cyrus wasn't there? What if he had left Evander to save his own skin? What if the lycanthrope twins were waiting for them? What if the Destroyer had come and killed both men just to whet his appetite for the main course—Strap, Frehley, and Reed?

Reed had never seen anything as horrible as the Destroyer before. Wanton and cruel. Standing on two fear-feet. Mouth full of dread-teeth. Skin rippled with terror. Howling hate. Death grips for hands. Dark holes for eyes. Madness for a heart. Cold and merciless. Soulless and forever.

As much as Reed feared the Destroyer, he feared being put back in the pit. The deepest well of the dungeon. A place of abandonment and destruction.

Reed had been put there because he longer had what the Elfwitch wanted. The silver heart necklace Mom had given him. He wanted it back more than he knew. It was the last thing she had given him and his twin sister. Even if the pat rack had not stolen away with it, there was no way that Reed would have ever surrendered it. The Elfwitch would just have to let the Destroyer kill him like it had Moor Kreed because she wasn't getting it.

It didn't matter since the pat rack had stolen away with it.

Why, oh, why had Chayse given hers away?

Too many questions. Too many disappointments. Too many hurts.

Reed found if he kept moving, all that stuff couldn't catch up with him.

Further down the back trail, Frehley gave another whistle.

This time there was a low reply.

The trio found their way back to the makeshift camp. The other two still where they had been left. Evander pale and propped against a boulder and Cyrus down on one knee on which he rested his musket. Insects chirped and screamed all around.

The rat came back into camp pulling something along in its jaw. A twig it had found. Bearing a cluster of berries.

It brought the twig to Reed's feet and tore off one berry that it began to chew on.

Frehley picked up the twig and gave everyone a berry. "Blackberry," he said and nodded.

Each ate theirs. Cyrus bent down and took the remaining half-eaten berry away from the rat. It screeched at the dishonor of a thief stealing from a thief.

"Guess the rat's earned its keep. Guess I won't have to eat it," Cyrus said.

The rat screeched and rat up Reed's leg. He picked it up and put it on his shoulders where it perched to look at its tormentor in safety.

"No one's goin' to eat Packy," Reed said.

Frehley and Strap shook their heads.

"Named it, have you?" Cyrus laughed. "Guess we got a mascot, boys."

Strap tended to Evander's wound while Frehley and Reed started a fire. Reed lay two large pieces of wood down parallel and put a smaller branch over them crosswise. Then he mounded some of the twigs and leaves between the wood and under the branch.

Frehley poured some powder from his bag onto the twigs and leaves. Then he took out some flints and scraped them until a few sparks jumped onto the powder. The pile ignited into small flames crackling the dry twigs. It spread and caught the wood making a temple of fire.

Reed was confident that many hours had passed since they had escaped from the dungeon of the Keep. The amount of light had not changed. Everything grey and dim. Hard to tell if it was night or day. As if this world was stuck between dawn or dusk.

Frehley and Reed stoked the fire with more kindling and a few choice pieces of deadwood which helped the fire to blaze. Cyrus laid the blade of his broadsword against the burning logs. Yellow flames with orange tongues danced with blue feet over the blade until it glowed red.

The heat warmed Reed. Chasing the chill from his clothes. Healing his bones.

Evander sweated by the fire. His skin looked dull. Like beech bark.

Frehley undid the belt Evander and Reed had used to hold the makeshift bandage. Then he pulled back the soaked tunic to reveal a wound puckered on the edges and welled with black blood—deep and ugly. He put his hands on Evander's shoulders.

Evander twitched. The wound heaving up and down with each hitched breath.

"Cyrus," Frehley directed him by nodding to the sword handle.

"I'm sweatin' like a swine. Did you get it good and hot?" Evander slurred.

"Strap, trade me," Frehley said. The giant moved to stand behind Evander and clamped his beefy hands on the wounded man's shoulders as Frehley swept down to grab his legs by the ankle.

Evander kicked as if what was to come would be the most wretched thing that could happen to him. "You gotta do it while it's good and hot!"

Cyrus wrapped the edge of his tunic around his hand before taking up the broadsword by the handle. It glowed like a red ember. A steaming hot rod.

Evander clapped his eyes on the hot blade coming closer and tried to kick and twist. "Go on! Stick it to me!"

"Hold him, now," Cyrus warned. He lowered the blade against the swollen wound. Against the open flesh.

Evander gritted his teeth. First, he growled. Then he howled.

Cyrus took the blade away. The broadsword's heat had dimmed but now the wound steamed. There was a smell of cauterized hide. Strap bent over Evander's shoulders and slavered red clay over it until the wound was covered in a quarter-inch of mud.

Cyrus ripped off the rest of his left sleeve and gave it to Frehley who placed it over the greased wound and then bound it with both the tunic piece and belt.

Evander was asleep. Passed out from the pain and exertion of fighting against his friends.

"He's not going to be able to walk. Or fight. We'll have to carry him," Cyrus said.

"We don't have to fight. We just have to hide," Frehley pointed out.

Strap touched Frehley on the shoulder. Touching his chest Strap pointed to Evander and then touched behind his shoulder.

"You'll carry him?" Frehley asked. "On your back?"

Strap nodded.

"He'll need a healer," Cyrus said. "We need rest. Food. Water."

Frehley shrugged. "Welcome to freedom. One thing at a time."

Reed yawned. Not being able to tell if it was day or night didn't matter. He was dog-tired.   Three of them—Frehley, Strap, and Cyrus—made makeshift beds of leaves. They stacked the three muskets upright against each other in a field garrison. The hand weapons—pistols, knives, blackjack, and broadsword they kept close by.

Once Reed saw what they were doing for bedding, he made his own out of leaves. The three divided up Evander's weapons among themselves for the time being: Frehley would take the musket, Cyrus would carry the pistol, but the long knife was given to Reed.

"First we sleep. Then we'll hunt for food and water," Frehley said. "Tired minds don't plan well. Let's rest a spell."

Reed stretched out on his back trying to ignore his growling stomach. He held the long knife as his eyes scanned its unique symmetry. It had been hand forged. There was no copyright or trademark carved into it anywhere. No name brand on the handle. The handle was polished wood made even shinier and smoother by finger grease and palm sweat.

It was a piece of crafts-MAN-ship. Not laser cut by a robot. Or put together by a three-d printer.

It had been tried.

Tested.

Tempered.

It had its flaws.

But it was true.

There was a break in the tree line. Giving Reed a good look at the skyscape. The bottom of the sky was light blue. But there was no setting or rising sun. Above that stretched a band of darker blue like an evening sky. That dissolved into an ocean of black ink.

Full of swirling stellar dust.

Twisting stars.

Constellations askew.

Obtuse triangles and crooked rhomboids.

The biggest and brightest object arose.

The moon.

The largest moon Reed had ever seen.

Different than the Man in the Moon that he had grown up watching.

This moon was a cold dark mistress. A leering smile made from a canyon stretching across its equator. A long sloped volcano for an aquiline nose bordered by two large craters for eyes.

For all its brightness it was still the Lesser Light.

It was a cold fire. Giving sepia tones of black and white. Washing out all color. Waking his sensitive rods and causing his cones to sleep in his eyes.

Where was the sun?

Had it been eclipsed by the moon?

Reed couldn't think anymore.

Sleep came to him fast and hard.

He blanked out.

Didn't even dream

Didn't even realize he had fallen asleep.

Except for one thing.

Something vibrated against him.

Against his leg.

In his pocket.

It was his Tracfone!

Reed woke and could see the light flashing in time with its vibration.

A notification.

Someone was texting him!

How was that possible?

Even if his phone hadn't died, how was there even a signal?

Reed pulled it out and opened the flip-top.

It was a text!

MOM:

Where are you?

Reed texted without thinking.

ME:

Dont know where we r.

MOM:

Where are you?

ME: Brazzles tricked us. Tell judge. Send help. Go to Osage Cave.

MOM:
WHERE ARE YOU?
Why was she asking the same question?
There were no more messages.
The phone went dark.
Leaving Reed as confused as before.
And since no answers were forthcoming, he soon fell back asleep.

***

Chapter Twenty-Three: Moon and Sun

Reed was awoken by a nudge.

He smelled the fire. Someone had gotten up before him to stoke it. It crackled away happy to be devouring fresh logs.

Which was good. Because there was a deep chill that cut through his muddy shirts and tee shirt. He could see quite a few rips and tears in it. Some must have come from having Packy tag along under the neck of his shirt.

Mom would have had a fit.

But Dad wouldn't have cared.

The strange thing was Dad was here.

Reed blinked and propped himself on one elbow. Dad was dressed in a leather skin tunic and breeches and sitting next to the fire with a bowie knife in his hands and dry shaving himself. He kept dipping his blade into a muddy puddle and passing it over the fire.

Uncle Buddy was dressed in a sleeveless jerkin of sheepskin and dirty breeches, too.

There were two strangers. A younger man with blonde hair and beard had a bandage under a belt strapped across his stomach. He wore a torn tunic and ripped breeches. The second man was big and burly with curly hair sticking up from the back over the top of his bald head. His tunic had only one short-sleeve left.

Last night had been some kind of joke.

The Brazzles. Osage Cave. Miss Crutch. Nick and Vic. The spiders.

Dad and Uncle Buddy must have come and gotten Reed and they all must have taken him camping and hunting dressed as Daniel Boone for Pioneer Days in nearby Selkirk where Dad still had family.

Everyone else was awake and cleaning muzzleloaders or sharpening bowie knives so that must be it.

Wasn't it just a weekend trip? An old fashioned Rendezvous with other re-enactors?

But where was Chayse?

Wasn't she with Mom?

No, she's with the Elfwitch, stupid. The silver necklace. Surrendered right into the Elfwitch's hand.

Chayse had turned her back on Reed and the whole family.

He had to get back home.

He had to get Chayse and then together they had to find a way back home.

Dad shaved off a month or more growth of beard. He always was clean-shaven. Working or not working. He'd never had a beard.

"You don't look good with a beard, Dad," Reed said.

Dad shot him an angry look. "Why do you jest? I am not your father. I have no children. I never married."

That stung. Why had he said that? Dad would have never—*because it's not Dad, stupid! Yes, it is! That man is Dad!*

The man who was not Dad sighed. "Do I really remind you of your father?"

"You look like him. You act like him. You talk like him," Reed said.

The man who was not Dad pondered it.

The big burly man laughed. "Frehley, take it as a compliment."

"Do you have children, Cyrus?" the man who claimed not to be Dad and wanted to be called Frehley asked.

Cyrus' face turned as black as night. "One. A daughter."

"She look like you?" Frehley asked.

"What? Are you kidding?" Cyrus asked. "Thank the Judge no! She looks like her mother."

"It's just so strange," Frehley pondered. "Reed, you are a stranger to me but I forget that all this must be just as strange to you.

"Is there anyone else you think you know?"

Reed gave a slight nod. He wanted to tell his side. The *truth*. But Reed was finally beginning to understand. Not everyone liked the truth. Or at least *his truth*.

And he remembered what Moor Kreed had made him promise.

The truth could be dangerous. And telling it at the wrong time to the wrong person meant worse. Hadn't the Revelator been murdered most foul and cruel in front of Reed's own eyes?

He pointed to the man Reed would have sworn was Uncle Buddy, a giant known here as Strap.

"I see," Frehley said. "And just who do you think he is?"

"Albert Crowder," Reed said. "His nickname is Buddy. We call him Uncle Buddy. He was your best friend in high school. And he still is."

"Amazing and wonderment," Cyrus said. "That's what it is, Frehley."

Reed did not want to say anymore. He didn't want to get himself in trouble or make Frehley mad at him. Somehow, Reed was hoping he would admit to being his dad. But also Moor Kreed's warning rang in his ears. The Revelator had believed Reed when he said that he'd known him before as Kreedmore the Street Preacher. And he had tried to explain how Miss Crutch could be the Elfwitch.

Back in his world.

But this was a new world.

More strange than brave.

One that was alien to Reed.

The Elfwitch's caravan left that morning.

The retinue went out in three parts.

As the Deadcoats cranked open the gates of the Keep, the Destroyer huffed and kicked his heels like a mad bull out of the chute then ran headlong down the main road that led to the Royal Forest.

The baggage train marched out next. Chests and boxes and crates. Full of clothes and victuals and arcane relics. All lifted and carried by the giant huntsmen spiders in a troop. The eight-legged servants stretched out in a long line down the main road.

There were no horses or bodyguards for the Elfwitch. She had sent Lt. Colonel Grey on ahead and Colonel Graves was to be left behind. The Darkness was her true ally and supplied her with many servants.

Nicolai and Victor each bent down on one knee as the Elfwitch fitted them with a studded leather collar.

"All men should have one," she told Chayse/Wice.

Then lycanthrope twins morphed into their animal forms and bent down their forelegs. The Elfwitch put Chayse/Wice on the back of Victor and then she climbed onto the back of Victor.

"Grab a handful of their nape, pet. And hold on tight," the Elfwitch said as she took a handful of Nicolai's furry neck. She goaded him in the flanks and off the pair went: rider and beast.

Chayse/Wice had time to squeeze her thighs against Victor's spine and bunch his matted fur in her hands before the lycanthrope sprinted after his twin brother.

This was the first time Chayse/Wice had been outside since the Brazzles had taken her and Reed to Osage Cave.

The light was strange.

Grey and iron-faced. Dim and shadow-fused.

Chayse/Wice had no idea just how long she had been inside the Keep but she thought it must be morning by now.

It felt like morning.

But if it was morning then it was a twilight sky.

The sky was darkened. A kind of black battered blue.

She could not even see the sun. If it was there, it was eclipsed by the largest moon she had ever seen in her life. It took up a third of the sky.

Mists drifted all about them. Curtains of smokey dew. Trees dripped with moisture.

The air was chill. Grass and leaves were stunted. Hoarfrost clung to deadwood.

The lycanthropes raced off the main road and through the deep forest. Over the top of knobs and through the bottom of washouts.

Chayse/Wice held on as tight as she could. Keeping her breath close in her lungs. She had never seen an animal run so fast in her life.

The lycanthrope zagged around bushes. Zigged under trees. Jumped over logs.

The two beasts took turns in the lead and crisscrossed each other's trail.

The Elfwitch's eyes gleamed with the thrill of the chase. She held one hand up to the night sky. Pointing up to the Darkness.

The lycanthropes ate the distance in leaps and bounds. Closed the miles in a sprint.

Chayse/Wice couldn't even catch her breath.

Never had she seen anything cover such a distance with such speed.

Her mind spun as trees and streams fell away like road signs.

All under the full moon and silver-grey light.

It was hard to gauge how time passed in this world.

But it didn't look any different than places in Raccoon Springs or Shiloh. It looked like most of Frazer County except there weren't any paved roads and only a few gravel roads. There were deer trails and wild boar runs.

After they left the Keep, Chayse/Wice didn't see another building—not a house nor even a barn. The forest ran deep with firs and pines and shady oaks. And under the oaks sprouted smaller dogwoods.

The lycanthropes slowed their pace as they came into some cleared hills for pasture land. Herds of cattle and goats ran from the passing lycanthropes. Scattering on their cloven hooves before the hulking beasts bearing riders.

But the pasture land wasn't fenced in with barbwire. Instead, stone fences and markers ran up and down the hills. Around spring-fed ponds and smaller buildings like hayricks and smokehouses.

Still, Chayse/Wice hadn't seen one farmhouse or large barn. Here and there, they were small round hills with smoke venting out the tops. It dawned on her that these were huts. Made from earth and hay. She a few small buildings that looked like miner shacks or old hunting cabins.

The people who lived here looked dirt poor.

There wasn't one electrical pole or cell phone tower.

No sign of a car or Walmart.

This world looked like what the Ozarks might have been before even the Native Americans had found it.

Yet, the perennial night sky kept it locked in a cold silver grip.

Dark shadows and black undergrowth seemed to fester everywhere.

Here the Moon ruled. The Lesser Light had the domain of both night and day. The Sun had been eclipsed.

What kind of crops grew at night? How many flowers bloomed under the moon? When did cattle know to bed down and low or call out for salt?

The hills flattened out and ridges ran together. In that broad place rose a large stone edifice. Skirt walls. A taller outer curtain wall. A stone bailey topped with a single tower.

It was a castle. Strong and proud. The first one Chayse/Wice had ever seen with her own eyes.

Sprawled around it was a town with crowded buildings. And along the skirt walls were smaller houses and buildings and open pens. It was a good-sized town. Bigger than even Shiloh. But without a downtown courthouse. And cars and parking lots.

She could smell the habitation from here. There would be no sewers. And since there were no grocery stores, people would keep some animals for a handy fresh homemade marketplace for meats and vegetables.

The pair of lycanthrope riders crossed the main road into the Castle Town since the main gate was closed. They went along the side of the castle wall until they found an open gate under the shadow of the bailey and tower. It was manned by living soldiers in blue and black livery, not the decaying Deadcoats' in their red tunics.

These soldiers bore the same type of weapons: muskets and broadswords with powder horns. Their dark blue tri-corner hats bore turkey feathers. Their glassy eyes stared like statues.

The two lycanthropes panted from their long run. They slowed as they came into the courtyard under the bailey and tower. Lowering their heads and forelegs, Chayse/Wice got down after the Elfwitch did.

Then the lycanthropes turned back into the human Nicolai and Victor. They began to shout towards the bailey and walked up to the portal. Two doors as tall as a barn opened and out strewed forth a retinue of people. Servants: groomsmen and maids who gave the party of four robes and ladles of freshwater.

Two men came out last, the shorter one leading the taller. The one in front was squat with long curly brown hair and a scraggly beard dressed in a long fur robe and walked with a wooden staff and a silver pendant that Chayse/Wice could make out from where she stood: a crescent moon balanced on top of the mouth of a coiled serpent. The man bringing up the rear was taller and robust, dressed in a soldiers' blue livery but with his tunic adorned with golden epaulets. He had shoulder-length blonde hair and a long brown mustache.

Chayse stared at the two men like someone was playing a cruel joke.

She had just seen both of them just days ago.

But somewhere else.

Back in her World.

"Dark Mistress, we greet you in the name of Queen Regina," said the shorter bearded one in his raspy growl. It was the same voice Chayse had heard the man speak in court when he had spoken out against Mom. "Be welcome. And we extend that invitation to your young companion. All your wants and her needs will be well met, I can assure you."

"Have the Queen ready to receive her guests, Kyphus," the Elfwitch commanded. "I have much to relay and I will not be delayed. Nor will I repeat myself."

"It will be done," Kyphus said. Then he inclined his head to Chayse/Wice and gave out his hand. "In the name of Queen Regina and the Law established here at Tower Reign, I, Kyphus, High Priest of the Realm, welcome you--"

"Lady Wice," the Elfwitch said.

"—Lady Wice as our guest to be shown every honor and courtesy," Kyphus said.

"Don't be rude, my pet," the Elfwitch said. "Take his hand."

Chayse didn't want to but she took the hand of the man who looked like her lawyer ad litem Alexander Kyler. His hand was cold and waxy. Like his voice.

When he let go, she yanked her hand back shaking off the heebie-jeebies she thought might be on his hand but making sure for High Priest Kyphus not to notice.

The second and taller man stepped forward. He gave a salute by touching his fist to his chest and then holding his hand straight out. "The Queen's Men salute you. Know that you will be protected from trouble here and know also that if you intend trouble against the Queen, neither will you prevail."

"This is Captain Michael," High Priest Kyphus said. "Leader of the Queen's Men."

"I am sent to escort your party and present you before the Queen," Captain Michael said. "She is holding an Audience in the Castle Seat."

Chayse/Wice could only nod unable to take her eyes off the strong man. If he had a haircut and trimmed back his mustache, the man would be Bailiff Mike. Without a doubt.

She was confused.

What was going on in this world?

First the Domain. Then the Realm. First Miss Crutch and then the Elfwitch.

How could people be in two places at once?

How could they be one person in one place and someone different in a whole other place?

With Captain Michael and then Kyphus at the lead, the Elfwitch and then Chayse, as Lady Wice, followed them into the bailey through the large open portal as the Lycanthrope twins brought up the rear. The other servants disappeared back to their stations. Inside the bailey was a large hallway entrance that fronted many doors. Servants and courtiers went and came following whatever duties and tasks that lay ahead.

Inside the tower, sconces lit the hallways and doorways with a brighter surer light than the grey tones outside. The flames spat out from the doused rags wrapped around the torches. Giving a comforting presence to the cold shadows Chayse/Wice had lived with while inside the Keep.

Captain Michael and Kyphus led the others up a grand staircase to another large door. This led to a round hall with an inner wall around the vestibule. And one more set of doors that bore a crest.

It was the emblem of a large shield with half of it carved into either side of the door. Colored in rich tones of blue and green and outlined with gold. There was a sword crossed with a staff making an X. And two banner scrolls bearing a motto: one in an arch above and one in a half-circle below. The top banner read "The Root of Lyftwych." The bottom read "Truth and Justice and the Law."

Two human porters opened the portals and the party issued into the inner chamber, which Captain Michael had called the Castle Seat. Rows of golden candlesticks flickered lush light across sumptuous murals spanning the walls. Rich tones bled from the long tapestries depicting men and women hunting deer and boar and bear.

A thick red carpet ran down the center of the room. Right up to a chair on a raised dais. The chair was luxurious and rich with thread and décor. Bordered on either side by two small rose bushes.

This was the seat so named in the Castle Seat.

It was a throne.

For someone of royalty.

On it sat a woman with a crown and a scowl. She wore a rich purple robe over a blue long sleeve dress. This must be Queen Regina.

Chayse took one look at the queen and her mouth dropped open. The woman was in her late twenties. With long curly red hair and brown eyes and a freckled face. Set for a pageant. Her face pasty with pale base and lips bright with rouge. Set for a gala.

Chayse had seen this woman make herself up every day before she had to go to work but she had never seen this woman look this beautiful and regal before.

Or this authoritarian.

"MOM!" she gasped in disbelief.   ***

Chapter Twenty-Four: Court and Spark

Chayse forgot everything she had said just the other day.

Wanting a real home. Embarrassed to be a Leftwich. Mom and Dad can't take care of us. These people can. I'll bet they are perfect.

She didn't want the Brazzles anymore. She didn't even care what may have become of them. She didn't want to be Wice or the Elfwitch's pet anymore.

Seeing her mother sitting on the throne as the queen of this Realm made her even forget that the Elfwitch had tricked her out of the silver necklace that Mom had given her.

She just wanted to go home.

Without a thought. Without hesitation. Chayse ran.

Right down the red carpet that lined the center of the room. Straight for the throne. For her mother's heart.

She was going to leap up into her lap and hug Mom. Never let go. And everything would be alright. Everything would go back to the way it was before.

Without a doubt this was Mom. Her flesh and blood mother. No one could tell her otherwise.

Two of the Queen's Men appeared, dressed in impeccable blue and black livery and armed with long spears. They made a step forward and blocked any approach to the throne by crossing their spears. Chayse could have just slipped under the spears but she didn't want the guards to strike her. They looked like they meant business.

Captain Michael strode forward with his hand up.

"What did you call us?" Queen Regina stiffened. Her eyes grew dark. Like when Mom would get mad at Reed. "Child, your little jest escapes us."

Chayse was confused. It was more than some little jest. And instead of trying to escape from it, Chayse was smack dab right in the middle of a cruel joke.

"Your highness, Lady Wice is a stranger to the Realm. She is still learning all the niceties of court life," the Elfwitch said behind a thick smile.

Chayse wanted to smack the Elfwitch in the mouth.

"This is all your fault!" she pointed at the woman in the black-feathered robe who had first shown up at her door introducing herself as Miss Crutch. "You've tricked us all!"

Chayse's face burned red. Flushed with heat. Anger.

Then she was aware that all eyes were on her.

Everyone was watching.

Captain Michael had his hand out. Ready to lead her away.

High Priest Kyphus had his hand to his mouth as he looked up at the ceiling rather than say something snide, as lawyer Alexander Kyler would have liked to have done in Judge Hart's court.

Queen Regina, Mom, waited. Both hands folded in her lap. Tapping her forefinger on top of her other hand.

Somehow Chayse had overstepped herself.

Somehow she had gotten it wrong.

She was the outsider here. The last one to know anything. And very helpless.

She'd better say something. Anything. To save some face. "Forgive me, my Queen. This is all so strange and new to me."

Queen Regina gave a little nod. Meant to dismiss Chayse. And show acceptance of her insult with some royal grace that was growing very thin.

Royal grace only went so far.

The Elfwitch took Chayse by the elbow and led her off the carpet to the side of the inner room. Only then did the guards lower their spears and step back to a ready position.

"I know how you feel, my pet. Everything seems so familiar and yet different. For you, this is an alien world," the Elfwitch said.

Then she bent down to whisper her Spell-Speak into Chayse's ear. *"I will be your mentor."*

The words twisted and curled as they slipped into her brain so that Chayse felt them echo deep inside and what she heard resound within was, "I will be your tormentor."

"What do you do here?" Chayse/Wice asked.

The Elfwitch smiled and touched her long bony hand to her chest. "I am the Queen's most respected and revered counselor. I advise her on all matters."

A group of eight ladies-in-waiting strode down four to a side along the red carpet and lined up on either side of the throne. Two men were given entrance to Castle Seat. Both wore leather leggings and soft boots with sleeveless green vests. Chayse/Wice overheard that they were Royal Huntsmen.

Queen Regina had a full-court: ladies-in-waiting, a captain for a contingent of guards, Royal Huntsmen, a high priest, and other servants. And an advisor not of this Realm. Was there any part of this strange new world that the Elfwitch hadn't touched?

"My Queen," Kyphus stood before the throne and set his staff down at his feet. "Five prisoners have escaped from the Keep. They are a danger to the Realm and the Throne. Lieutenant Colonel Gray is requesting we send men to help patrol the Outlaw Forest."

"Lieutenant Colonel?" Queen Regina rasped. "Who gave him that promotion?"   "I did your highness. The prisoners were under Colonel Graves' charge and had he fulfilled his duty we would not have this clear and present danger," the Elfwitch said.

"But our court was not consulted. And we did not give my consent. We do not approve," Queen Regina signaled her displeasure by crossing her arms.

"I found it expedient as a means of motivation for the lieutenant colonel to fulfill his duty and help recapture the prisoners," the Elfwitch said.

"But the Black Watch was formed by the Root of Lyftwych to serve the Realm--" Queen Regina began.

"The Black Watch was created to guard the Darkness," the Elfwitch said with a booming voice. The words echoed around in the inner room. Rebounding into different pitches and whispers of other words below the spoken sentence that crept down into the listener's brains so that they heard other words: The Darkness is here. They are now servants in my thrall.

The Spell Speak—Chayse/Wice didn't know what else to call it--gave her the heebie-jeebies. The same thing had happened the very first time Chayse had ever laid eyes on Miss Elsie Crutch. *Stupid children, be afraid. Bow down and serve me. Both of you shall be in my thrall* was still etched into her memory like a fresh tattoo.

"Kyphus, who are these prisoners?" the Queen demanded.

But the High Priest of the Realm only raised a shaggy brow because he did not know.

"They are only men, your highness," the Elfwitch said. "Outlaws who've been laying around in the dungeon for years. They're just shaggy dogs on the run with nowhere to go. Easy to hunt down. Once they've been captured your Highness should show them no mercy and pronounce a hard and fast judgment. That will solve the matter for good."

The queen gave a hint of a smirk. "'Shaggy dogs on the run?' We thought escape from the Dungeon of the Keep was impossible. And yet these outlaws are free again.

Then Queen Regina stuck out her chin. "Captain Michael, send out the Royal Huntsmen."

"Your Highness, there is no need for that. The Black Watch can attend to the matter," the Elfwitch said.

"The Black Watch likes to sit in towers," Queen Regina noted. "Be it the Keep or their many Martello towers. Neither can they cross water. Our Royal Huntsmen can track raccoons and trap bears. They will find these Outlaws."

Captain Michael turned to leave the Castle Seat throne room.

The Elfwitch twitched her nose. "Hold, good Captain."

With his hand on his sword, the captain turned to the queen who gave him a sign in reply by holding up a finger from her lap.

"I propose a wager. A contest. Between your Royal Huntsmen and my fellow servant," the Elfwitch said.

The Queen leaned back against her throne in surprise. "You bet the Black Watch against our Royal Huntsmen in finding five outlaws who escaped the Black Watch in the first place? You said 'servant.' Surely, you don't mean to send just one of the Black Watch out against them? The new Lieutenant Colonel Grey or better yet, Sergeant Hood?"

The Elfwitch held up a finger. "If my fellow-servant finds the Outlaws before your Royal Huntsmen they are to be delivered to sudden death. And in turn, if your Royal Huntsmen discover their hiding place, then they shall be handed over to this court."

Chayse/Wice didn't want the queen to take up the challenge. But she thought it wiser not to say a word. She only knew that the Elfwitch was laying some kind of trap.

"Agreed," Queen Regina said.

"Your highness, let me introduce you to my fellow-servant," the Elfwitch. "We are two of four who serve the Darkness Eternal."

Turning her curly head over her shoulder, the Elfwitch called out in her Spell Speak voice *"Come!"*

The command resounded off the wood and stone and bore through the flesh and bone of everyone in the throne room. Chayse/Wice wondered just how loud and how far the word could be heard?

Either there was an immense response.

The double wooden doors to the Castle Seat throne hall threw open with a sudden burst of wind. Dry leaves and dust swept down the red carpet giving it bumps in spots. Bringing along a foul stench like when Mom would pass roadkill that had been left out a few days.

A form blurred between the askew doors. A dark mass like a flock of blackbirds taking wing before a coming storm. The beating wings collided into one solid thrashing figure that stood before the dais.

The Destroyer appeared before them all. In his black leather boots and breeches. Belted with a large silver buckle that bore the crescent moon balanced atop the head of a coiled serpent --the Brazzle's tattoo, the Elfwitch's insignia, the Porter—and a thick leather mail jacket. But all the blackness was overshadowed by the blueness of its beautiful face and black ringed eyes and blackened lips.

It shook its wild and wooly black hair as if shaking the dust and bird feathers from its arrival.

Queen Regina did not flinch. Much like Mom would have done if Dad had said something insulting which he often had. But her bottom lip quivered.

The queen was afraid.

Chayse/Wice wanted to grab both her royal hands and hold them to her face. Let her know she was afraid of the Destroyer, too. Bond with her in that shared fear. And find their way back to being just Mom and Chayse again.

The heavy hurt surprised her.

And somehow fed the Destroyer.

It reached out a blue-skinned hand with long black nails and plucked the largest rose in bloom off the bush next to the throne seat. Holding up the rose in its blue palm before its icy eyes.

The rose began to fade and blot.

The bud curled up.

The redness molted into black.

Becoming a dried-out husk.

Then it burst into flame that devoured the bud and blew the ashes up into the air.

"To the death! Go!" theElfwitch commanded.

The Destroyer howled as it turned and dissolved back into a mass of blackbirds taking wing on the wind of a rushing storm. The mass flew out through the doors slamming them shut behind in its wake.

***

Chapter Twenty-Five: Mother and Daughter

Captain Michael and a detail of blue and black-clad soldiers checked over the doors to the Castle Seat. More to see if the Destroyer was waiting in ambush than to see if they had been damaged. Lookouts along the outer wall spotted a mass of crows flying over the casement from the third floor of Tower Reign, where the Castle Seat stood. The mad crows made like an arrow shot through the sky straight on for the Royal Forest. The last twelve years had delivered dark omens daily so the guards did not mark the occasion as dire.

The guards posted at the Tower Gate reported in shaky words that the Elfwitch's baggage train had been deposited inside the bailey. The bearers being hundreds of large dark hairy spiders with four sets of glassy eyes and dripping fangs. The guards gave the beasts wide berth and performed the bare minimum of their prescribed duties by just watching them set down the baggage from afar. Only as the beasts backed out the gatekeeping their forelegs up in the air, were the guards able to breathe.

High Priest Kyphus commanded the Queen's attendants to carry the trunks and cases inside to the chambers being prepared for the Elfwitch's retinue: Nicolai, Victor, the Lady Wice (Chayse), and the Elfwitch herself.

Chayse/Wice entered the guest chambers which were on the next floor above the Castle Seat throne hall. The lycanthrope twins stood as valets at the door for their Dark Mistress and her pet. The rather capacious suite held a series of four rooms: an antechamber for receiving guests that led to a larger study with tables and desks with two smaller chambers off of that; one with two large bed frames and the other being a privy and washbasins.

As attendants brought in stack after stack of trunks and cases, it took four to carry the biggest load. The large oaken chest with the name WICE burned into the rough wood planks. That one they placed at the foot of the largest bed frame in the third chamber.

This was the one relic of the Elfwitch that caught Chayse/Wice's eye. All manner of vials and bottles filled with spies and specimens stuffed the racks and shelves in her Chamber Circle. Many crucibles and centrifuges lay across tables and workbenches.

Cages of test animals were brought in: a dozen birds, half a dozen rats, and two jars, one full of frogs, and the other of fire chameleons. And in the corner of the study, the perch stand was set up for the two-headed vulture which fluttered its wings and screeched but was kept chained to its stand.

Chayse/Wice had run of the room. Free to pet any animal. Open any vial or bottle. Fire up any crucible. Spin any centrifuge. But the one thing that the Elfwitch had forbidden her to do was to open that oaken chest.

That wouldn't have stopped Reed. Bubba would have opened it as soon as the Elfwitch's back was turned and gotten out whatever was supposed to have been kept secret. He wouldn't even have waited until she had fallen asleep.

Not that the dark woman ever slept.

Chayse/Wice had never even seen her lie down.

The woman was tireless.

Always awake.

Always on the move.

It wasn't too hard to forget about sleep in this world.

She couldn't even tell when it was night or day.

During the day, the moon seemed full and cast a false silvery light.

At night, the moon waned back to a crescent-like ambient lighting.

In this world, shadows walked on two legs.

Still, Chayse/Wice could not remember the last time she had a good night's sleep. Not since the owl had hooted and Miss Elsie Crutch had come knocking on their front door and this whole mess had started up. Not a moment of peace for either her or Bubba.

Where was he now? Escaped. Along with others.

Was that why the Elfwitch had sent out the Destroyer? It wasn't human. It was relentless.

Evil things ruled this world. Here evil went where it wanted and seemed to do what it pleased. Was that such a bad thing? Seeing everyday fears become a part of everyday life?

It was as if someone had flipped the other side of the coin.

Bubba and whoever was with him had gotten away from the creature once. How? Could they do it again?

This might have been the longest she had ever been without her twin brother. Any given day, they would end up side by side. Talking. Teasing. Laughing. Together.

Chayse had never been away from this long from Mom either.

But wasn't that she had wanted?

Mom and Dad can't take care of us. These people can. I'll bet they are perfect.

Except wasn't Mom here in this same tower? Wearing a crown? Pretending to not know who Chayse was?

Their house in Raccoon Springs—her school at Shiloh—her identity—her real self—seemed a world away.

This world—both Domain and Realm—wasn't a dream.

Which one was real and which one was the dream now?

The more she thought about it the more her head hurt.

Here she was someone important. The Lady Wice. She didn't have to be Chayse Leftwich if she didn't want to be.

She was growing to like the other side of the coin.

As soon as the oaken chest had arrived, the Elfwitch had followed behind it into the bedchamber. There she retired sealing herself behind the door with the mysterious relic. She followed behind it and closed the door to the bed chambers sealing herself inside with the mysterious relic. Leaving Chayse/Wice out in the study as the lycanthrope twins began to set up some choice vials and bottles along with the thickest crucibles and sturdiest centrifuge.

The door to the outer hall opened. In came Captain Michael with two of the Queen's Men. The broad sized captain wore a pistol and sword while the detail each bore a musket at their shoulders.

They were well met by the lycanthrope twins who did not let them past the antechamber.

"Our dark mistress," Nicolai began.

"Has retired to her chambers," Victor ended.

Captain Michael was nonplussed. "Our queen requests the company of Lady Wice in her private chambers. I am to accompany her."

The lycanthrope twins did not move so Captain Michael added, "You are to come at once."

The door to the bedchambers creaked open. Through the crack, bone-thin fingers wrapped around the edge of the door. Dark feathers stuck to the knuckles as if the Elfwitch's hand was molting.

Through the shade of icy blue eyes and grey hands, the Elfwitch purred, "Come here, my pet."

Chayse/Wice crept to within earshot of the door frame.

"Remember, here you are the Lady Wice," the Elfwitch reminded her. Her voice was curt. Meant only for her to hear but the words slipped down her ear and twisted in echoes until what she heard was *Do not tell anyone your true name.*

Spell-Speak.

Once again.

Sometimes Chayse/Wice wished she could do that.

So Michael hadn't come for the Elfwitch. He had come for *her*.

Mom wanted to see her? Chayse? No, not Mom. Chayse meant the *Queen*. The Queen wanted to see her? As her own daughter? No, as the Lady Wice.

Confusion swirled. Making Chayse/Wice's head hurt again.

Chayse/Wice had a small hope. Maybe the Queen could give some answers. Maybe Mom could flip the coin back over. And they could all go home.

But wasn't this whole mess Mom's fault in the first place?

Was that even Chayse/Wice's own thought inside her head? Were those even her own words? In her voice? Or was it that Spell-Speak?

She had to blame someone. It might as well be Mom's fault. Getting a private audience with Mom would be a good thing.

Chayse/Wice had a thing or two to say.

"Sure!" Chayse/Wice said and skipped between the massive limbs of the lycanthropes into the antechamber. "Let's go!"

Captain Michael led her out the door and down the hallway with the detail in step behind them. Coming to a stairwell at the end of the hall they went up to the next landing. At the top, two more guards stood at their posts under an archway.

Passing under the arch Captain Michael accompanied her into a wide-open room with several niches and window casement benches. The round room was vaulted. Fixed braces and rigging under the center of the dome held tied ropes and fabrics down from which hung all the drapes and tapestries in alternating colors of blue and green.

Along open spaces on the wall hung the royal crests upon wood plaques. Outlined in gold with two golden swords making an X with blades down. The six quadrants alternating between blue and green. And two golden scrolls one arcing up and the other reversed at the bottom. The top banner read: "The Root of Lyftwych." The bottom: "Truth Justice the Law."

The descending drapes angling down the wall from the domed ceiling cast the room like a circus tent rather than a simple stone room. Curtains were tied back at the windows with golden sashes. Sumptuous tapestries told a story through different panels of a feast and dance with wondrous reveries in far happier times long ago.

The chambers still held luxury. But there was only a ghost of happiness. Gloom ruled the room.

There was no dais in this room.

No raised chair.

Only couches and divans.

Tables and tiered trays.

Eight ladies-in-waiting at the ready. Though, many gave her a dark look and a side glance to one another. The kind that older girls gave her at the lunch tables as they looked down their nose before turning them up. The kind ad-litem Lawyer Alexander Kyler had given to Miss Elsie Crutch when they didn't think anyone was watching them.

The Queen sat on a low sectional couch at the room's center. She wore a satin blue robe over a green gown. Her crown had been set aside and her curly ginger hair lay on her shoulders.

Mom had never looked so beautiful. Whenever she got to sit down on the couch she was dead asleep within five minutes.

The queen's servants had set out trays of dainties and bowls of fruits and a decanter of wine. Two glass goblets with pewter stems sat waiting. All laid out on a low table in front of the sectional.

"Lady Wice," the Queen purred and held out a limp hand.

Chayse/Wice had seen a few movies with kings and queens and though this was the first time she had ever been in the presence of royalty—even if it was really just Mom because of some twisted dream—she knew what was expected. It wasn't that hard to play along here at court.

"Your highness," Chayse/Wice said as she took her Mom's—*the Queen's*—hand and kissed it. Then she sat where the Queen indicated. At the corner of the sectional so that the two were knee to knee. Like giggling confidantes at a school lunch cafeteria table or besties at a sleep-over. Only Chayse/Wice had no friends at school and she had never been invited to a sleep-over. Then again, she had never been invited to sit with a queen either.

"The land you come from must be very far from here," the Queen said.

Chayse/Wice became nervous. What if the Queen asked her something she wasn't supposed to say…like what was her last name? But she could answer to this statement.

"Yes, your highness," she said and remembered that this queen did have a first name: Regina. So did Judge Hart. But it wasn't proper to call important adults by their first names. Only by their titles. "It might as well be on the other side of the world."

"Then our ways must seem strange to you," the Queen said.

"Well, it's not so strange. It's just…different," Chayse/Wice said. She was treading on dangerous ground. But Chayse/Wice had to sit through interrogations by teachers, nurses, principals, and even other CASA agents. She knew the drill: be chill.

Now Bubba would have blurted out everything he knew about everything because he had no filter. Chayse/Wice didn't think the Queen would suffer Bubba's shenanigans for too long. Queens had a lot of filters.

"How different?" the Queen asked narrowing her eyes. Mom would do the same when seeking out the truth to who had made a frozen pizza and had both left the oven on and the pizza box out on top of the oven.

"Do you have a coin?"Chayse/Wice asked.

The Queen raised an eyebrow. "Are you going to show me a trick? I'm in no mood for a jest."

Me? I'm? That was different than how the Queen had spoken in her throne room. "Your highness? I don't know any tricks," she said.

"Here in my personal chambers, I don't have to wear my crown or be the queen. I would hope that we can be our true selves and learn from one another." Queen Regina snapped her fingers and a servant brought over a small ornate box. The queen lifted back the lid and inside were gems, jewels, necklaces, chains, rings, and a few coins. The chains and settings were pewter but the gemstones looked real. The coins were dull and grey. Not silver or gold but lesser metals.

The queen took out the biggest coin which had the Elfwitch's face on the heads and that now all too familiar symbol of the crescent moon balanced on the coiled serpent. What Mr. Brazzle had called the sign of Asheroth. And that's what the Porter—that giant albino constrictor-had been called, too.

Queen Regina handed the coin over to her guest who she thought was the Lady Wice. Chayse/Wice held the coin face up.

"Heads," she said and then turned it over. "Tails. My world—my land to me is like the tail side of a coin." She showed tails again. "And being here is like the heads side." She flipped the coin over to show heads.

Then she put the coin down on the table.

"Interesting," the Queen said. "I'll have to ruminate upon that. But I will say that too many things are important to decide by a coin toss."

"I didn't get a choice in being here, your highness," Chayse blurted. The Wice-filter was slipping. Chayse wanted to tell the Queen—MOM!—everything. Maybe the Queen would forget about being the queen and turn back into Mom and do something! Maybe she had said too much already. Maybe the Elfwitch had long ears in Tower Reign and could hear every word that was spoken.

"But you know the Elfwitch in your land?" Queen Regina asked.

Chayse had to think about how she should answer, "Yes. She works for the court."

"Another court there, too? As an advisor?" the queen asked.

Chayse shook her head. "Nuh-uh. An advocate."

"Advocate? She is a lawyer at your court in your land?" Queen Regina asked.

Chayse shrugged her shoulders. "I'm not sure anymore."

"Do you know how the Elfwitch freed the Destroyer?" the queen asked.

There was no way Chayse could tell her. And since she had questions of her own, she let one slip out of the filter. "Do you know how the Elfwitch got free?"

"What do you mean?" the queen demanded.

Chayse became confused. She wanted to open to the queen. But the Spell Speak weighed on her throat. And queen or Mom, teacher or nurse or principal, sometimes it was easier to be vague with adults. So they would stop asking questions. "All I know is that I'm upside down like a coin."

Queen Regina fell silent while her brow creased. Neither party was getting any answers.

Trust was not easy to come by for Chayse. She trusted just two people: Reed and Mom.

Reed was not with her anymore and Mom…well, that was the confusing part.

The queen put a royal hand on Chayse's arm. Her words might be cold but her fingers were warm. The touch was real. Sinking deep beneath the filter. Under the confusion. Straight to her heart. Lady Wice wanted to be Chayse Leftwich again and be her only. She wanted to be back home. With Mom.

"Lady Wice, for that I am truly sorry," Queen Regina said. "I, too, am like your coin. I have a feeling that we could share much grief and trouble. But bearing troubles is a part of our lot in life. It only hampers our station. We must both carry on."

The kind words helped fuel the warm feeling in Chayse. Tears gathered at the edge of her eyes. The woman who looked like Mom and sounded like Mom but wore the clothes and bearing of a queen had real feelings that had to be kept hidden. "Things were different here once, too?"

"Beyond measure," Queen Regina confided. Then she stood up and smoothed her blue robe. "Come with me." She offered her hand in friendship as a kind of equal. Even if one was an adult and the other a twelve-year-old child. Even if one might have been a mother and the other a daughter.

The queen led Chayse to casement with a pillowed window bench. They knelt on the pillows as Queen Regina pushed the stained glass window back. The window held beveled glass with an ornate design of a large open book suspended between the green earth and the blue sky. Out of the sky came a golden light that fell on the open book which acted as a prism and refracted seven rays of different hues onto the ground below.

"Tower Reign is the tallest building in all the Realm," Queen Regina said. "When we had day, one could see all the way to Glacier Mountains. At night one could even see the beacon light from the top of the Keep. That fortress is built on higher ground but it is not as tall as Tower Reign."

Chayse let the queen's words pull her away like a sparrow out of the window and on the wind flying over the bailey and the outer wall. Across Castle Town and over the curtain wall. Hovering high above the outskirts and the open plains towards the high icy peaks on the horizon. Miles melted away in seconds. For the heart and mind know no distance. Having an innate ability to hone into desired places. By following magnetic streams in the light.

Only the light was gone now.

The bailey lay in dark shadows. Above the outer wall, tall buildings rose to block out what light came from the moon. All roads networked out from Tower Gate. Stretching out into darkness. Tiny points of light—lit candles and flaming torches hung in market stalls or outside tents.

And behind them were smaller barns and farmhouses spread out across tilled farmland. And behind the acreage was the main road—a highway—leading to the Royal Forest. And somewhere in the midst of all that was Outlaw Forest.

The place where the five escaped prisoners were going.

And she knew that one of those prisoners was Reed.

And the Elfwitch had just sent the Destroyer after them.

To hound them. Find them. Bind them. And kill them.

The creature was a powerhouse. Built to destroy. Reveling in fear.

It had already come for Reed once and had come back empty-handed.

So there was hope.

However small it might be.

Things seldom went good for the Leftwich family. And if it did, it didn't stay that way for long.

"Just one day. I want things to go our way for just one day. But then I wouldn't know what to do even if it did happen," Mom would say after she had worked all week to pay one late bill only to get another late notice.

Mom.

She was here in this strange world. Sitting next to her on the padded bench. Looking up at the sky with her.

But she wasn't Mom.

Chayse still couldn't wrap her head around it.

The largest object in the sky, the moon, had a glowing crescent cut out of a round darkened nimbus body. Around this caldera of cooling light, the other stars struggled to shine. But the constellations that she knew in her world were askew here. Obtuse triangles and crooked rhomboids.

The geometry of a madman.

This had to be what passed for twilight, the evening, the black and dark night here in the Realm.

The sky was an ocean of blank ink. Swirling stellar dust filled the empty spaces. It all seemed just a reflection of the Elfwitch's heart.

The sun was gone.

The Greater Light occluded.

The day had died.

Somehow all of it had been eclipsed by the moon.

But it could never be as bright as the sun because it was the Lesser Light. Slipping into a slow decline of everlasting darkness.

Something small moved through the night towards the open window.

A brushing of wings.

Something black and quick.

It lit on the ledge of the casement.

It was a crow.

Indignant and bold. Clutching a twig in between its talons. Its beak opens as if give them an admonition. Gawking at them with a turn of its head as it regarded each of them one eye at a time.

Then the crow began to change shape.

***

Chapter Twenty-Six: Turncoats and Followers

The transforming crow-stepped off the casement and grew out of its feathers into a dark feathered robe with human feet and slippers. Its beak and head and black eyes transmogrifying into curly red hair and an aquiline nose below two icy blue eyes.

Uninvited and unannounced the Elfwitch preened at the two courtly ladies sitting on the couch. She had made the change seem effortless. Her power seemed limitless.

Chayse was amazed. She had read dozens of fantasy books where people with magical powers did such feats. But it was different when you saw it happen yourself.

"May I join your little party?" she asked in a gravel tone.

Queen Regina gave a gracious face, "Be welcome in my chambers, Dark Lady."

"Have you any tea?" the Elfwitch asked next.

"Of course," the queen assented and waved a servant into action.

A lady-in-waiting brought over an ornate tray with service for three: a pewter tea pitcher and glass mugs with inlays of golden wings. While the queen poured hot black tea into the mugs, the Elfwitch dribbled out some dried green herbs from her left sleeve into the first mug. And into the second mug, she sprinkled brown thistles which popped and cracked becoming saturated with the tea before sinking to the bottom.

"This has been another hard day for you, your highness," the Elfwitch said as she stirred up the mugs with the twig that as a crow she had clutched with avian talons. "This herb will help soothe your worries. And for you Lady Wice, this spice will help fortify you against the constant chill of our night-for-day."

Having stirred her concoctions, the Elfwitch took both mugs off the tray and handed them each to Queen Regina and Chayse who took them in hand.

The Elfwitch took the third mug from off the empty tray which was taken away by the lady-in-waiting. The Elfwitch lifted hers high to lead the others in a toast.

"Here's to the heart of Darkness. Oh, the horror. The horror," she mocked. Then she drained off a good portion of the hot brew in her mug in one stiff bolt.

Chayse gave the queen a wary look as the other sipped at the green tea with demure grace. Following the regal host's lead, Chayse cooled the top of her tea by blowing on it before sipping it with care. It had a tinny taste. Like sucking on a 9 Volt.

A kind of warmth spread across her tongue. Then it coated her throat. Making a trail down into her belly.

Her taste buds lit up. Sweet and bitter jumping up. Then cooling down until they became numb. The numbness chased after the warmth. Creeping down her throat. Stretching across her belly and up into her chest and arms.

It was a funny feeling. Her body fell asleep with her eyes were open and her mind stone-cold woke.

Queen Regina shuddered at the taste of her tea. Then she became as still as a deep pool. Her pupils as wide as a well where stones of light fell in and never touched bottom.

The queen's skin blanched. Her eyes locked onto the unchanging scenery threaded into the tapestries across the room. Her body was here but her mind was over the hills and far away.

"My Queen, touch your nose with the tip of your right forefinger," the Elfwitch commanded with relish.

It was a foolish thing to do. Not a regal act at all. Yet, Queen Regina did just that. Without a care. Without a will. She touched the tip of her regal nose with her royal right forefinger.

And kept it there.

Then the Elfwitch spoke to Chayse. "Lady Wice, try and do the same. If you can."

But Chayse could not move. Not her hand. Not her finger.

All she could do was breathe.

"Both of you may stop," the Elfwitch said and beamed as the queen took her finger and lay her in her lap.

"You are both in my thrall," the Elfwitch took out a small dagger the size of her middle finger. The blade was curved and thick much like a bird's talon. She ran the tip of it under the queen's chin.

To Chayse, the Elfwitch said, "I hope for her sake that you did not reveal anything about yourself, my pet."

To Queen Regina, the Elfwitch said, "My queen, speak if you understand me."

"I understand you, Dark Lady," Queen Regina intoned as if she were made of hollow brass.

"Good," the Elfwitch smiled like a wicked child. "Who did this girl tell you she is?"

"The Lady Wice. She is a stranger from another realm," the queen intoned.

"And? Do you believe her?" the Elfwitch asked.

"No. I feel like I should know her," the queen said.

"You do not know her," the Elfwitch spat. "You have never seen her."

The queen began to parrot her, "I have never…" but she stopped. Her lips quivered and she shuddered. As if she might sneeze herself back awake.

Fight, mom! Chayse thought. This dark lady was cruel. She enjoyed bullying people.

Her clothes might be different. Her name might have changed. But inside Miss Elsie Crutch and the Elfwitch were the same person.

Chayse was rooting for Queen Regina the same as he had for Mom to stand up against Lawyer ad-litem Kyler. Sitting silent and helpless in the jury box had been hard for Chayse. But that only had been the start of the nightmare.

Maybe Chayse could wake herself up. Maybe she was still at the FINS hearing. With her twin brother still sitting beside her in the jury box. Judge Hart still hadn't made his ruling. Lawyer Ad-litem Kyler and Miss Elsie Crutch were giving each other signals. While her twin guard dogs, Nic and Vick, cooled their heels in the gallery.

Mom was still at the defendant's table. Alone. Without anyone to defend her.

Dad was in the gallery, too. With Uncle Buddy.

Maybe this time Judge Hart's ruling would be different.

Because this time Chayse would speak up.

And tell him just how evil Miss Elsie Crutch was.

And then she and her twin brother wouldn't get handed over to the Brazzles.

And everything that happened afterward—Osage Cave, the huntsmen spiders, the dungeon, the Ice Prison, the Circle Chamber, and the Destroyer—was the nightmare.

But just like in court, Chayse sat silent and helpless as a stone.

The Elfwitch acknowledged the queen's struggle to resist the command with a nod. "Your will grows weaker. You will swear allegiance to me. Sooner than you think.

"I could end this whole charade here tonight," the Elfwitch grinned with the kind of malevolence that the Destroyer carried in its wicked smile. Then she took the blade away from the queen's throat. And began to run it down Chayse's limp arm.

Chayse could not feel the blade skimming along her arm. The Elfwitch turned her arm over to prick the blade point against her wrist. Chayse'sbelly itched. She wanted to protect her guts. But she still couldn't move.

"If I killed you both now, your deaths would be wasted. And the Great Work of Darkness would not be perfected. It waited an eternity to complete its work. What's a few more days and nights?" The Elfwitch pulled the blade back from Chayse's wrist leaving a pinpoint of blood welling up around a white mark from the blade's pressure.

Chayse was tired of feeling helpless. Ever since the night that she had opened the door to see the screwed up face of Miss Elsie Crutch looking down at her, she had just been along for the ride. So many strange things had happened since. So much out of her control.

She couldn't stop Miss Elsie from taking her away from her mom. Chayse couldn't stop Miss Elsie from taking her to a different world. She couldn't stop Miss Elsie from being the Elfwitch. And if the Elfwitch wanted to cut her into pieces, she couldn't stop her.

Chayse just wanted everyone to stop bothering her. She wanted everything to stop happening to her.

But what she wanted most was to do what she wanted when she wanted.

That's what the Elfwitch did. She even made others do what she wanted them to do.

Do you think the Elfwitch is happy? Asked a tiny voice inside Chayse. *Is that who you want to be?*

Well, no. But that's because she still doesn't have everything she wants yet. When she gets everything—the Great Work of Darkness that spoke about—then she'll be happy. Finally.

You think so? Are you any different? How you treated Mom? How about ice cream for dinner? How about staying up past midnight to watch some stupid movie that you could watch another time? Sleeping in late? Getting to school by lunchtime?

There's was nothing wrong with Chayse wanting all those things. There was nothing wrong with getting what she wanted. She hadn't done anything evil. Wanting wasn't evil. What was wrong with getting what you wanted if it made you happy?

How long does anything keep you happy? Why do you keep asking for more?

Chayse didn't want to answer. It was something Mom might ask when she got frustrated with Chayse after her third or fourth request in a row.

"Is that something you would desire? Or something you just want?"

Desire. Chayse didn't know that word. But she guessed it was greater than want. If desire was good then want was bad.

Right now at this moment, Chayse wanted off of this couch. Being able to feel her arms and legs would be good.

But what Chayse desired was freedom.

To have the power of freedom to do what she wanted whenever she wanted.

Mom and/or Queen Regina. They knew who they were and they stayed who they were. Just good people who got nowhere.

So much for being good. Where did being good get you? Drugged on a couch.

Miss Elsie Crutch was twisted. The Elfwitch was worse. Both she's were evil.

But she/they seemed to be able to get what she/they wanted.

Of any woman Chayse had ever met, only the Elfwitch seemed truly free.

She might be scary. Dark. Mysterious.

She wasn't concerned with either evil or good. She was untouched by the Law. She was unstoppable.

If Chayse wanted to be the one to fix this whole mess, she would have to be free.

And in order to be free, she needed power. A raw source before Light and Dark. Beyond good and evil.

Is that really what you want? Don't you just want to be home again with Mom?

Chayse wasn't listening to that tiny voice anymore.

"No one can thwart me," the Elfwitch proclaimed. "I own your lives. I shall also own your deaths."

The queen jerked. Her pupils began to contract. She came back to her senses and catapulted up from her couch.

"Dark Lady!" Queen Regina proclaimed. "These are my personal chambers. I want you to leave!"

Go, Mom! Chayse cheered in her heart. Isn't that what she most wanted, even more than freedom for herself? For Mom—or Queen Regina—to stand up for herself/themselves? For someone to lead Chayse and show her the way? It was hard to think of Mom and Queen Regina as two separate people. But they were, weren't they?

The Elfwitch shrugged. "Where do you want me to go?"

Chayse's heart raced. She could feel her toes again! She wanted to sit up. Stand beside her mom. No, stand beside the queen.

"We are the queen here! This is our Realm! Our word is law! You are to leave at once! Captain Michael! Guards!" Queen Regina stood tall and straight giving the most important edict of her life.

The Elfwitch laughed. "Please don't make a spectacle of this. I will leave your chambers. But I will not leave Tower Reign."

"No, you will leave Tower Reign. You and all your servants! We banish you all!" Queen Regina commanded. "Go back to your shadow world! Back the way you came in!"

The queen pointed to the same window through which the Elfwitch had stolen into her chambers as a raven.

The Elfwitch folded her robed arms over her chest. "Not until the Great Work has been completed and made perfect. Then all shall be like me. And the Darkness will hold sway."

Captain Michael bounded in through the archway with a matchlock pistol in hand. Two guards marched in at the double step behind him. Rifles at the ready.

"Captain, arrest the Elfwitch!" Queen Regina commanded.

Captain Michael nodded as if he had waited years for this very command. From the back of his belt, he produced a set of iron cuffs. The two guards inserted themselves between their queen and the intended prisoner.

The Elfwitch jerked back from them. "Touch me and see what happens!"

Seven ladies in waiting attended the queen inside her personal chambers. Five of them made a semi-circle around the queen and her couch where Chayse still sat unmoving with a helpless heart. But instead of protecting Queen Regina, they flicked two-inch curved talons from out of the folds of their blouse sleeves. Each of them pointed at their very own queen.

"This is treason!" Queen Regina pronounced.

The two remaining ladies in waiting retreated behind the Chayse's couch blocking the generations-old tapestry depicting a young prince and princess holding hands in a vow of fealty.

Captain Michael aimed with his matchlock pistol straight at the Elfwitch's heart. Unafraid, she put her hands on her hips. With no intention of being put into irons.

"Captain, you and your guards will lower their weapons at once. Or else your queen will die," the Elfwitch said.

Captain Michael squinted his left eye and cocked the pistol. Locking the firing pin at a two-pound draw.

"This is a dueling pistol, Dark Lady," Captain Michael said. "Fixed with what is known as a hair-trigger. All I have to do is breathe."

"All I have to do is lower my hands and my servants will carve your queen up like a turkey," the Elfwitch said.

Queen stared down the five ladies-in-waiting and their tiny shiny blades. Having already taken weapons against their regent, Chayse didn't think they would back down now. Even if Captain Michael felled the Elfwitch with one shot, too many blades surrounded the Queen for her to getaway.

Both women might end up dead.

"Captain Michael, send for more guards. And more iron cuffs," Queen Regina commanded.

"This is a painful blow, my queen," the Elfwitch said. "But for these twelve years, you thought me only as your most trusted advisor. Yet, it is I who rules this Realm!"

Taking a deep breath, the Elfwitch put both her hands to the side of her mouth and called out, "Come!"

One spoken word. With one single syllable. Echoing around the chambers in Spell-Speak. Pounding against stone walls. Pulling the bottom of tapestries up. Shaking wooden shelves. Knocking service ware off of trays. Making furniture scratch against the floor. Until the word changed and the syllables grew, *Servants! Fulfill your vow!*

When the couch jerked across the floor, Chayse felt her weight return to her. She jumped up to stand beside Queen Regina. Sticking her chin out at the Elfwitch.

"My pet, you've chosen the wrong side in this matter," the Elfwitch warned.

There was no way Chayse would stand with the Elfwitch. She was Miss Elsie Crutch, too. And both were evil.

Queen Regina might not have been Mom. But she was close enough. Chayse hadn't been able to stand by Mom and that's how come she had ended up in the Domain first and now the Realm.

Now the half-ring of five women with blades lay in wait for both of them. Even though by Chayse's counting, she and the two ladies-in-waiting cowering behind the couch along with Captain Michael and the two guards made seven against six.

And more guards would be coming. The mutinous ladies-in-waiting would be arrested. The Elfwitch would be put in chains. Then Chayse could tell everything that had happened to them to Mom—no, Queen Regina—and they could go search for Reed.

What about the Destroyer? Wasn't that beast searching for her twin brother? He would have to be stopped.

Then Reed and Chayse could both go home.

And then what? They were supposed to be with the Brazzles. Lawyer ad-litem Kyler would be checking on them.

The twins would have to find Mom and then go straight to Judge Hart.

Somehow it would all work out.

And for the first time since Chayse had opened that door on that one night, she had hope.

It didn't last long.

The lycanthrope twins leaped through the archway. Bounding into the queen's private chambers like flipping a coin to turn the balance of power turned quick against Queen Regina and her few faithful followers.

The hairy beasts flanked the two guards and wrest their rifles away with their powerful jaws. In one single bite, both rifles were crushed between tremendous canines. The lycanthropes then spit their broken toys out to the floor.

Captain Michael fired a shot but it went wide of either wolf twin. His pistol now empty, he pulled out his broadsword and swung at their snapping jaws and raking claws. But as he thrust at one werewolf, the second ran behind him knocking him enabling the first werewolf to pin Captain Michael down with a forepaw on his chest and its powerful jaws on the wrist of his sword arm.

Several Huntsman spiders scampered through the windows. Up the pennons to the ceiling and lowered themselves down on webs. They hissed and barked at the two ladies-in-waiting backing them up against the tapestry.

The Elfwitch folded her black feathered arms across her chest.

The pitched battle was over.

Chayse's hope was gone.

It hadn't been any different than back in her World. Adults seemed to get to do whatever they wanted. Like Dad or Miss Elsie Crutch. Or worse, the Brazzles—who had lied to Judge Hart and delivered Chayse and Reed over to the Elfwitch.

They hadn't been any different than kids siding with bullies in the cafeteria or hallway. Lying to the teacher and then helping the bully catch up with their victim when they would be someplace alone.

Mean Bullies. Tough teachers. Prying school nurses. Counselors and therapists. Lawyer Ad-litem Kyler. Miss Elsie Crutch.

Chayse and Reed were like yo-yo's bouncing back and forth between one agency and another.

Here in the Realm, it wasn't much different.

Captain Michael. Even the Queen.

All were powerless against the Elfwitch.

Her World or the Realm.

Didn't matter.

A bully was a bully no matter the time or place.

And they seemed to always get their way.

Why didn't someone stop them?

Why didn't God come down and straighten out this whole mess?

Maybe then Chayse could believe in an all-powerful and all-loving God who controlled all things and punished evil people.

This was all Mom's fault.

No, more Dad's fault if it was anyone's.

That's what Mom always said.

Chayse only knew it had to be somebody's fault.

Once again, adults had let her down.

High Priest Kyphus strode in at a brisk pace leading a procession of four guards of the Queen's Men clad in blue and black tunics. Behind them came the two Royal Huntsmen carrying the Elfwitch's most prized relic, her secret chest.

The squat high priest directed hunters to put the chest down before the Elfwitch. Then the troopers took off their tunics and turned them inside out showing different colors: black and silver instead of blue and black.

"Turncoats!" Captain Michael gritted through his teeth.

"We are here at your command, Dark Mistress," Kyphus said with a nod. "Very few stand against us. Just say the word and Tower Reign is yours."

The Elfwitch had kept still during the entire showdown. Never showing an ounce of fear. Now she strode forward and picked up the pair of thick cuffs intended for her off the floor of the queen's private chambers.

First, she locked them together making a figure eight. Next, she turned them over in her hands touching the entire arc of the circles with her fingers. Then she yanked the circle apart and the two cuffs had become a single collar joined together.

The Elfwitch bent down and petted head of the werewolf who had Captain Michael's sword hand pinned to the ground. The man-beast kept its teeth clamped on the hapless man and while its eyes tracked its mistress' every move awaiting a simple command to snap off the man's hand at the wrist.

"Loyal to the end. Like a dog," the Elfwitch purred down at the captive leader of the Queen's Men. Using both hands she slipped the new iron collar around Captain Mike's neck. Then she waved off the werewolf. "A man's no good without a collar."

The lycanthropes turned back into their human selves to stand behind their Dark Mistress. The huntsmen spiders jiggling and hobbling before their cornered prey: the two guards and last remaining loyal ladies-in-waiting. The Elfwitch waved off the other ladies who sheathed their talon sized blades so that no buffer stood between the captives and their captor.

The court was well represented. The Elfwitch, as an advisor, her retainers, the Royal Huntsmen, the once Queen's Men now turned, and High Priest Kyphus. All standing together against the Queen—the Root of Lyftwych—the rightful ruler.

Captain Michael tried to swallow against the tight iron collar. He wanted to put his fingers under it but he kept his hands to his side. The queen put her hand on his shoulder as she straightened her gaze. Chayse reached out, found the Queen's hand, and took it.

"All our troubles began when the Black Watch broke their oath and let you out," Captain Michael coughed out against the tight collar.

"What good was their oath? To keep watch as they grew old? Where is the reward in that?" the Elfwitch argued. "Kyphus, you swore an oath to follow the Judge. To be a keeper of the Law. In order to do that, you once proclaimed belief in the Judge and in the Way of his Son. Do you feel the same now?"

"No, I do not, my Dark Mistress," Kyphus said. And at his denial, the Queen's eyes narrowed and Captain Michael's neck stiffened. "Why have faith when there is no evidence for it? Why can't we see the Judge? Because he is not real.

"Now I believe the Son was real. But he was just a man who did some good things and said some good things but now he's dead. So if the Judge isn't real, then he didn't make the Law. Because there is no Law.

"Do we need to be told how to do good things? No, we simply know what is good and we each decide for ourselves.

"And what about the Root of Lyftwych? What about their family motto is 'Truth and Justice?'" the Elfwitch.

"If the Judge isn't real and if the Law isn't real then the Lyftwyches have no truth. And that is not justice. That is an injustice," Kyphus explained.

He continued, "That means we have let the Root of Lyftwych rule this Realm for generations based on a lie. That means the cornerstone of Tower Reign was founded on a lie. That means when they sit on Castle Seat, they sit on a lie.

"Therefore, if the Judge isn't real and if the Law isn't real and if the Root of Lyftwych rules illegally then we need a new law. And a new ruler.

"I believe what I see. The Dark Lady I can see! She is here now. Let her rule."

"This is treason," Queen Regina murmured. Stunned by the audacity of the Elfwitch. By the sudden turn of events.

Chayse thought she was more like Mom than ever before. And she felt all the same things for the Queen as she did for Mom: pride and disappointment, loyalty and embarrassment, helplessness and anger.

The Elfwitch turned to the final seven people in the room, maybe in the whole Realm, who did not follow her. "The Light has failed. The Son is dead and is never coming back. The Darkness now rules.

"Anyone who does not turn to the Darkness will be driven out. They will become outlaws to die as exiles.

"But there is hope. And I alone offer it.

"Everyone here has taken an oath. They have pledged allegiance to the Darkness. And have sealed it with a mark.

"Everyone, show your mark!" the Elfwitch commanded.

The followers of the Elfwitch obeyed. One by one, they rolled up their left sleeves; each showing a mark on the underside of their forearms. The ladies-in-waiting had it. The guards had it. The Royal Huntsmen had it. Kyphus had it. And the two lycanthropes had it.

All the same mark.

Done in the same way.

Ink carved into skin.

Contoured lines.

Coiled serpent.

Pointed head.

Forked tongue.

Crescent moon.

The closest ones that Chayse could see were on the ladies-in-waiting. One look at the mark and she knew what it was. And remembered the first time she saw it.

Back in her World. Sitting in the backseat of SUV on the way to Osage Cave. Looking at the back of Mr. and Mrs. Brazzle's heads and then seeing the strange mark on both their arms.

Reed had asked why they both had one. Mr. Brazzle had said, *"We used to be in a bike club."* And then he'd called it by a name.

"Asheroth," Chayse said out loud. She felt the filter of being Wice tugging at her again.

"Yes!" the Elfwitch purred. "There is hope for you yet, my pet."

***

Chapter Twenty-Seven: Ball and Powder

Reed spoke what he felt. "I'm tired."

"You're no more tired than the rest of us," Frehley grumbled.

They trudged up the slope of a hill cutting through the undergrowth of a huge forest. Reed's feet hurt. His new/used boots rubbing against his heels.

The forest thickened. Firs and pines and evergreens everywhere. A few oaks here. A couple of cedars there. And one or two precious dogwoods tucked under the massive oaks.

Reed felt like he had been here before. Or worse. Like he had never left.

Cyrus led the way using the broadsword to chop through the low branches and thick brush. Strap came next taking slow and wide strides as he carried Evander on his back. Reed trudged behind with Frehley coming up last.

Reed's stomach was empty and it went to his head. "I'm hungry."

Nestled safe between his neck and shirt, Packy screeched agreement.

"Great Judge!" Frehley snapped. "We're all hungry. But whining about it doesn't fill you up now does it?"

Reed couldn't stop now. Out came another. "When are we going to get something to eat?"

"We have to get farther away from the Keep. Then we'll hunt something," Frehley explained as he quickened his step to come alongside Reed. "Then we'll kill it, skin it, cook it, and eat it."

Packy didn't like the sound of that so he screeched again. Packrats didn't hunt. They foraged.

"Well, if that rat doesn't shut up, I'll eat it myself!" Cyrus threatened.

Reed's hand went straight up to cover the rat's head and body. "Don't you hurt Packy!"

He wasn't about to let anything happen to it. Packy was a kind of pet now. Ever since he'd lost Chayse. And More Kreed.

Sure, Packy had made some trouble at first. But then it had helped them all escape. And it knew where Reed's silver heart necklace was: wherever it had stashed it.

"Don't worry kid," Cyrus scowled. "I don't eat nothin' with a first name, Judge help me. My wife's family raises pigs. I'm no hunter like you, Frehley, but you can keep your tenderloins and your jerky. Just give me lots of bacon. Bacon makes everything better."

Just the word bacon made Reed think he could smell it. Ticking his nose. Hot and fresh and crackling and dripping with juice. Sizzling in a skillet. Sweet and smoking just lying in its juices.

Right about now bacon seemed to be the best thing in the world. Reed wanted it to find it cooked and ready behind the very next tree.

He looked.

It wasn't there.

Even Strap, with the human load on his back, licked his lips.

"Quit talkin' 'bout food," Frehley grumbled.

Everywhere Reed look he saw wooded hills. Ridges and washouts. Hollows and hollers. Knobs and karsts.

Monolithic grey dolomite stuck in red clay-like teeth spit out from a giant's mouth. Huge outcroppings of striated sandstone like a giant carved bread loaf. And piles of quartz and limestone like a trail of giant crumbs.

To Reed, it was the same as the Ozarks around Raccoon Springs Village where the South Fork of the Spring River cut through the sprawling town and where his latest rental was or the access points on the Spring River where he would go wading or like the twisting knobs around Shiloh where he'd last gone to school just a few weeks back.

Not one bit different.

There was even the occasional "caw-caw" from an infuriated crow as they flew away from the humans encroaching through their woods.

"What's the matter now?" Frehley moaned. Just like Dad would have.

"This is just like back home," Reed said.

"Kid, fer me this is home," Cyrus said. "Outlaw Forest. Born and raised."

Frehley put his hand on Reed's shoulder to stop him. They let Strap and Cyrus walk on a bit farther.

"I thought you were a stranger to this land," Frehley said.

"It's the same…but different," Reed tried to explain.

He kept expecting to come across a paved road with a yellow line or even a gravel road or better yet, someone's driveway leading to a typical Raccoon Springs Village house: a one-story dwelling with a carport, three-bedroom, bath and a half, open kitchen and living room.

It was strange not to look up and see power lines or a telephone pole.

"And that's what's strange," he finished.

"Because I look like your father?"Frehley asked.

"You don't just look like him. You sound like him," Reed said. "But you don't talk like him. And you definitely don't act like him."

"What else is the same?" Frehley asked.

"My coin, I guess," Reed said. "But here it's got different words on it."

"Who gave it to you?" Frehley asked.

"The Street Preacher. Kreedmore. Back in my World. It was just a fifty-cent piece. But it had different words on it," Reed said. "Here he was called Moor Kreed. The only friend I had in the Realm after I lost my sister."

Frehley gripped his shoulder. "I would not harm you. Nor let anyone else harm you. Nor would Strap."

"I know," Reed said. "Strap's Uncle Buddy back home. He's your—I mean he's my dad's best friend."

Frehley's eyes grew large as he nodded. "You say your mother gave you and your sister those silver heart necklaces. And you say I am your father." Then he rubbed his chin with his fingers. "Then someone must look like your mother here, too."

"Really?" Reed asked. A spark of hope glowed in his heart. Had he been taken from his family in one world only to find his family again in another?

"What about the Elfwitch?" Frehley asked.

"She's the same person in both worlds," Reed explained. "Only back home she's called Miss Elsie Crutch. And those twin lycanthropes are always with her."

"Really?" Frehley asked taking a turn to borrow the expression. "That's food fer thought. But the meaning's hard to hunt down."

"Moor Kreed told me about the other demons still locked in the ice. The Dark Riders. Shadow and Rancor," Reed said. Then he asked a question. "How did the Elfwitch get free?"

Frehley sighed. "When the Black Watch broke their vows. You know about the Deadcoats?" "Moor Kreed told me when they were the Black Watch and that they took an oath to live inside the Keep and keep a watch over the Ice Prison to warn others if the Darkness returned. But they let it return and now they are all cursed," Reed said.

"They've become walkin' deadmen," Frehley said. "They can't eat. Can't sleep. Can't stop walkin'. Not until their clothes wear out. And their skin falls off and their bones turn to dust.

"Colonel Graves, Lieutenant Gray, Sergeant Hood, the whole lot of 'em. Once brave men. But not very loyal as it turns out."

Reed didn't understand. Back in his World, soldiers were sworn into service by taking an oath on the Constitution. But they didn't shirk their vows and turn on their own country. That would be mutiny and treason.

"But why?" he asked.

Frehley sighed. "When our queen was still a princess. She wanted to marry a commoner. She was in love and that's not against the Judge's Law. There can be no law against love.

"Only the Black Watch and others didn't want her to marry a commoner. Through their anger and in their sleep the Darkness spoke to their hearts. They justified breaking the Law because they called what the queen-to-be was going do Darkness.

"So, the Black Watch marched to Tower Reign. Lay siege to it. Fought their way to the Castle Seat to stop the princess from marrying the commoner whom she loved.

"But the commoner had gone to the taboo place. Beyond the Keep. Into the Glacier Mountains. To Quicksilver lake.

"When the moon was full, he took two drops of quicksilver out of the lake and stole away to have a silversmith hammer them into a shape that would join the two lovers together. The two made a special vow."

"Two hearts. One heartbeat," Reed said.

"Yes," Frehley was surprised. "How did you know that?"

When Reed did not answer, Frehley continued.

"The Queen's Men and their captain fought the Black Watch bravely. Colonel Graves lost his nose. Gray lost his eyes. Hood's face was torn away. They should have died. That's when the Black Watch became the Deadcoats.

"They captured the queen. Stopped the wedding. And made her surrender her silver heart necklace."

"So they used it to free the Elfwitch. So then the Elfwitch brought me and my sister here and used my sister's necklace to free the Destroyer," Reed said. "There's just two of those demons left. And I've lost my necklace."

"Better it stays lost," Frehley said.

"How we gonna hunt up anything with you two standin' like bumps on a log?" Cyrus complained anew. "If you wanna tell tales, they sound better next to a fire with full bellies."

"It'd take alotta tales to fill yer belly," Evander slurred out of his sweating face.

"And we've got to care fer our old cellmate," Cyrus said.

Reed didn't see how they were going to be able to hunt in the dim light.

If this was what mornings were like in the Realm, it wasn't much different than the night. The bright silvery lamp of the full moon had begun to descend below the horizon. Only it never fully disappeared. It waned into an obscured nimbus. More like a squinting eye. Never closing up. Colored grey with eye shadow.

There was a pale light trying to peek out from behind the occluded moon. Paling the stars in the lower quadrant of the morning sky. Shading the lower horizon blue but unable to chase away the black bands of night that floated at the top of the sky.

It was morning. Daytime. And the sun wasn't anywhere to be seen.

It refused to shine.

Because it had been eclipsed by this moon.

A fog dragged over the hills and trees. Making a curtain of smoky mountain dew. Glazing the trees and leaves with moisture.

It would cut down on the ball and powder's range. But any prey would leave tracks in the soft mud and wet grass. Any hunting would be a soggy mess.

As the party traversed the next hill, a flock of crows flew out of the trees up into the mist with such speed the men brought up their muskets as if they expected the birds to turn into the Destroyer or the twin lycanthropes and descend upon them like field mice.

The muskets that Frehley and the others had managed to ransack from the Deadcoats were smoothbores. Old fashioned style muzzleloaders. With actual wooden stocks and butts.

But these weren't antiques or replicas like Reed had seen in the Military Museum in Little Rock near General MacArthur's birthplace when Dad had taken him. These had been made here and now. Forged by a gunsmith over an anvil and fire with crafted molds and not by a computer with precision dyes and castings.

The party came upon a ridge sparse with trees and covered with rolling meadows of tall grass. At the far end stood a naked bluff of cracked limestone with several hollows and openings carved into its gut. Cyrus chose the largest cavern which was deep enough to hold the entire party.

Frehley and Cyrus put down their muskets outside against the bluff. After Strap put Evander down on the dusty floor he stood up to check the ceiling for head clearance. He had room to spare and nodded his approval.

As soon as Reed made his way to the center of the cavern, Packy crawled down his dirty Chevron shirt and leaped to the rock floor. He scuttled away into the dark recess.

"Packy!" Reed called.

Frehley touched the boy's shoulders. "He'll be alright. Got a feelin' he's scroungin' up his dinner. He'll be back."

"If you hand me your flints, I'll start another fire," Cyrus said. He already had scrounged up a handful of tall dry grass and a few chunks of deadwood from out it the meadows.

Frehley reached into his belt to pull out his flint rocks and handed them over the burly man.

Strap bent over the wounded man. Evander's tunic was soaked around his belted wound. His cheeks were flushed and sweat poured off his face.

Evander slipped back into fever and barked at being touched. "Bring…!"

Frehley looked again at Strap.

"He's talkin' out his mind," Cyrus said as he started up a small fire inside the cavern. When he stepped back towards Evander, the young man caught hold of the man's burly left wrist.

"Bring! Boy!" Evander gasped with his eyes wide.

Cyrus pulled his arm away. His ripped tunic had come loose again. And Reed saw the green traces of the tattoo which the man covered up again.

"Well, I've done my part, Frehley," Cyrus said. "There's yer fire. Now bring me something to cook."

"We shouldn't all go out. Someone should stay with Evander," Frehley said. "I don't want Reed to be the one. He's just a boy."

"I'll stay around the ridge and keep an eye on Evander. See if I can't hunt up a squirrel or two. Maybe even a hare," Cyrus said.

"You might could climb this bluff and try to spot how far we are from Outlaw Forest," Frehley said.

Frehley and Strap stepped outside the cavern and Reed followed. They each took a musket from the makeshift stack and a bag of powder and shot. In addition, Strap had the blackjack tucked inside his belt and Frehley had his long knife. At the last minute, he decided to take only one of his two pistols and left the other beside Cyrus's weapons: the broadsword and the third pistol.

They both frowned when Reed reached for the third musket and powder bag.

"What?" he asked looking back at the two men.

"You know how to shoot?" Frehley asked.

Strap put out a flat palm and walked two fingers over it and then made undulating motions with his hand.

Reed answered Frehley first, "Yeah, I know how to shoot." Then he answered Strap. "And hunt."

"Who taught you?" Frehley asked.

"Dad," Reed answered. But what he wanted to say was *YOU*.

Strap looked at Frehley and shrugged.

"Three muskets are better than two, I guess," Frehley relented. "If you can lug the musket and powder bag while keepin' up with us, then you'll more than earn your keep. Let's see you load this musket."

Excited, Reed picked up the musket. It was over three feet long and about twenty pounds. The barrel hand-forged. The stock and butt handmade. It had a unique charm.

He had never loaded a true flintlock musket before. First, he slipped the strap of the powder bag over his shoulder so that it rested against his side. Then he stood the gun on its butt and steadied with one hand as he opened the drawstring of the powder bag. Lying on top of the grained powder was another smaller powder horn and still another pouch with metal clasps. He took the horn and pouch out hooking them with the fingers of the hand around the gun barrel.

Then he poured some of the powder from the bag down the end of the open muzzle. Next, he opened the pouch still hooked on his finger and took out a lead ball. It was spheroid but hand pressed and clipped. Not machine perfect. Still able to get the job done and make a mess.

He dropped the ball down the muzzle then he took out the ramrod to shove it down the barrel. Last, he cradled the gun across his stomach and opened the frizzen to pour the finer powder from the horn into the pan.

Reed closed the frizzen and set his thumb on the lock and cradled the trigger to test the pull. It had at least a five-pound draw. The musket would make a mighty clap of thunder when the time came.

"Let's go back the way we come first. I saw some varmint trails," Frehley said.

He led the way off the ridge and along their back trail.

They spent some hours hunting up the trails Frehley had seen but nothing showed itself. Behind them, they heard a small shot. Though it wasn't a loud report, Reed thought it came from off the ridge.

"Sounds like Cyrus got lucky," Frehley told them. "Betcha it was just a squirrel. Come on, I wanna best his squirrel or we'll never hear the end of it."

They went back up the hill near to the top of the ridge. Then they trailed down the other side into the valley rim below. They found a creek that ran down the ravine into the valley.

The thickest undergrowth and trees followed alongside. And in the thickets lived some varmints. And a few wild birds.

Strap scared a pheasant off its nest and though he missed the bird in flight, they took five of its dozen or so eggs for consolation. Frehley flushed out a hare and brought it down as it ran in circles over the littered rocks of the ravine.

That left Reed last to shoot. He didn't want to miss in front of the others. No matter if it wasn't Dad and Uncle Buddy, they were close enough to family that Reed wanted their approval.

As the hunters walked down the slope of the ravine something rooted through the tall grass around the creek bed. Whatever it was, was larger than a rabbit with a body bigger than its head. Reed steadied the musket and took a bead along the muzzle at the moving grass.

It was a four-legged animal. Moving too much not to be noticed, it must be hunting up something to eat for itself not to have taken notice of the hunters. Reed cocked the firing lock halfway back which pulled the trigger into position.

Whatever it was, was too close for him to miss. No doubt, it would run. And Reed told himself to take a steady bead, not to rush, aim slightly ahead, and not to jerk on the trigger even though he expected a heavy draw.

There was a ruckus brewing in the grass. The animal thrashed about as if it was trying to break loose. And break loose it did.

A grey hairless varmint ran out of the tall grass and over the rocks and boulders at a fast clip. It had a tiny head and pointed ears with a long thin snout and beady eyes. It had claws with pink toes and a small tail.

Reed almost jerked on the trigger. At the last second, he pulled the muzzle back and let the creature run to relative safety.

Frehley was impressed. "Good call. Do you know what that is?"

"An armadillo," Reed said.

"Here, we call them glyptodons," Frehley said. "And that's a baby one. Adult glyptodons are hard to kill. They're pests. But they carry disease. Waste of a shot."

"I know," Reed said.

Strap pointed with his free hand as his other held up the end of his tunic like an apron to cradle the five stolen eggs. They both turned back to the creek. Something else still thrashed in the weeds.

"Something's still in there! It must have been fighting with another varmint!" Frehley whispered loud at Reed.

That made sense. The armadillo, or baby glyptodont, must have crossed paths with an even bigger varmint while rooting for grubs. There were a handful of mesopredators about the size of an armadillo: opossums and skunks to name just two omnivores.

But the creature that skulked out of the grass to side-switch over the rocks wasn't a varmint. It wasn't even a mammal.

It was the largest monitor lizard Reed had ever seen. Uncle Buddy used to have a pet iguana he'd let run loose in his shop. This was almost as big as that reptile.

"Now that you can shoot at," Frehley said.

Reed took aim. Just at the back of the head. Above the neck.

He squeezed the trigger with his finger. It was a hard draw. The lock hammered down. Fire ignited near his face like a bottle rocket taking off. The muzzle erupted and spit out a ball. It hit about where he aimed. Knocking the monitor lizard onto its side kicking and scratching with half its head gone.

"Good shot!" Frehley said and clapped Reed's shoulder.   He felt two feet taller. It was no different than hunting with Dad and Uncle Buddy on their hunting lease. Only it wasn't Dad and Uncle Buddy and this wasn't the Ozarks. But it felt near enough the same.

Frehley walked over to the still thrashing monitor lizard who hadn't realized it was dead yet and stomped on its head with the heel of his boot. "This'll taste good roasted. Let's get back. Got some skinin' to do before we can eat."   ***

Chapter Twenty-Eight: Friend and Fire

Between the three, they each had a handful for the feast. The hunters turned to backtrack up the side of the ridge. On the way back up the ridge, Strap stopped them.

They each brought up their muskets at the ready.

Waiting ahead were two does. Still as rocks. One heartbeat standing still looking at the trio of hunters. Ears cocked. Whitetails twitching. In the next beat, they were off at a silent sprint. Melting back into the woods.

Reed was amazed at how nearly everything was the same as back home in Frazer County of the Ozarks. The rocks. The trees. And the animals.

"Deer meat would have been better," Frehley said to the others as they walked through the open meadows on top of the ridge. "But it is what it is."

Strap nodded. And Reed's empty stomach churned at the thought of breaded deer tenderloins simmering in an iron skillet.

Trails of smoke wafted out from the largest cavern in the limestone bluff. They could smell something cooking. Leaving their muskets outside and ducking under the cavern opening, the trio found Cyrus squatting before a roaring fire turning a roasting squirrel leg on a bayonet that he had taken from off Strap's musket before they'd left to hunt and gripped it with a piece of a tunic.

As the meat on the squirrel leg was browning, Evander opened his red-rimmed eyes. "Boy…," he croaked. His eyes rolled about. Taking in the cave. His companions. And settling on Cyrus. "Bring…"

"Is he talking about me?" Reed asked.

Frehley stroked his chin with a blood-stained hand.

"Nah," Cyrus said, "It's the fever. He just needs some water."

Cyrus leaned over from the fire to wipe Evander's sweaty face with a wet piece of tunic. The cloth was coming from Evander's shirt whose bottom had been torn away from the belt of his pants. But ever since their escape they had had to manage with whatever they could find.

"You didn't happen to kill a deer, did you?" Cyrus said. "I heard three shots."

"No," Frehley said as he and Reed laid down their kills side by side in front of the fire.

"A lizard?" Cyrus noted. "Never et one before. Heard they taste like chicken. What did you bring, Strap?"

The giant laid down the pheasant eggs one by one with ginger care.

"You wouldn't have happened to grab the chicken that laid them eggs, would you?" Cyrus asked.

"We did see deer. On the way back," Frehley said.

"Trackin's yer bread and butter, Royal Huntsman," Cyrus said.

"Maybe after we eat these fine kills, we'll go out after bigger game," Frehley said. Looking over at Reed, he winked. "I'm just getting warmed up. I've spent nigh twelve years in the hole, you know."

"Five years with no real meat!" Cyrus said. He pulled the bayonet off his makeshift spit and pulled a piece of steaming squirrel meat off to taste. "I could eat it in one gulp. Wouldn't care if I burned my tongue."

"Time to clean these beauties," Frehley said. Then he turned again to Reed. "You ever clean a kill?"

"Sure," Reed said.

"A lizard?"Frehley asked.

"Well, no. Not exactly," Reed said thinking back to every type of creature he'd killed with Dad and helped him clean. "Does frog count?"

Cyrus laughed in his throat. "Can you skin a butterfly?"

"I can skin most things. I even dissected a worm in biology class," Reed said as he took out the long knife that Evander had ransacked from their escape out of the Keep and which the others had given him when he'd been wounded.

Cyrus gave his statement another hearty laugh. "Looks like you got yerself an apprentice, Frehley!"

Reed made quick work in skinning the monitor lizard. Starting at the back of the head and cutting the hide down the middle along the spine to peel it back. The meat was china-white beneath the subcutaneous skin layers.

Frehley nodded his approval. "You're doing well."

"Comin' from a Royal Huntsman, that's quite a compliment," Cyrus said as he put his squirrel shish kabob back over the fire to roast it well done.

"Dad taught me," Reed told him and then turned to Frehley who was still watching with warm and blue like a placid lake. He would have bet his silver fifty-cent piece that those eyes were no different than Dad's back in the other World. But instead of being full of familial love, Frehley looked on with a growing admiration which was better than the repulsion and puzzlement when they had been locked up in the dungeons of the Keep.

The Royal Huntsman stepped in to direct Reed in cutting out the offal. Next, he instructed him where best to cut off the head and claws. That left plenty of tender meat on the shoulders and thighs.

"Toss those scraps into the fire, kid," Cyrus instructed. "The hide, too."

Frehley helped him throw the scraps into the fire. The flames kicked up as it ate the lizard's belly fat and entrails. Cyrus making sure to scrap his squirrel shish kabob against the steaming skin and burning fat to season his meal.

With Frehley's help, Reed set the lizard meat onto the second bayonet, making it more like a meat puppet than the understructure of a monitor lizard. Cyrus handed the boy a thick limb that he could jam the bayonet down onto so that Reed could hold the lizard filet over the fire.

"Just how are you gonna cook them eggs, Strap?" Frehley asked as he made quick work of skinning the hare. He tossed the head and hide into the fire and used the third bayonet to skewer the hare meat. Soon he and Reed were roasting side by side.

"Yeah, I was wonderin' the same," Cyrus laughed as he pulled his well done and seasoned squirrel leg out of the fire. He brought the steaming hot shish kabob up to his wet lips to tear off a small bite. Sucking in cool air and blowing it back out onto the bite at the same time.

Strap found a flattened rock as large as his chest that he scooted to the edge of the fire. He cracked each egg onto the rock's surface and used a long knife blade to catch back the yolks so that they didn't run off the rock. Using the knife like a spatula, he let the eggs cook up and bubble on one side before cutting them up and turning them over. They didn't fluff up and stiffen like chicken eggs but to Reed, they smelled like fried eggs.

Using the toe of his boot, Strap nudged the rock away from the fire as the cooked eggs sizzled.

They were all beyond hungry. And everyone, excepting Evander, had brought something to the feast and had earned a seat. All their meat would be meager against their appetite but there would be some to share with Evander.

Reed felt content with his place round the fire with the three other men. He wished that Evander had not been wounded. And that they could find a better way to help him. Yet, he, too had accepted Reed in his own way. And though, Reed was a stranger here, all four men had something in common with him. They were exiles: hated by the Elfwitch.

The company of exiles gnawed on their makeshift meat shish kabobs each sharing with Strap who in turn gave them each a fried egg staked to the end of his long knife. In that way, they shared a real meal. And for the first time since he had been brought to the Domain and now the Realm, Reed felt like he belonged—it might not be home and it might not have been Dad or Uncle Buddy—or it might have been.

Cyrus belched and said, "If we had some salt it'd be perfect."

"Might as well ask our serving wench for more wine and bread," Frehley said around a mouthful.

"How about some cheese?" Reed asked. He was surprised that he could see it so clear in his mind. Two sandwich slices neatly wrapped in plastic sleeves. Just waiting to be peeled back and rolled up and shoved into his mouth. And the taste…chewy and salty…getting stuck on the roof of his mouth just behind his front teeth.

"Now yer talkin', kid!" Cyrus laughed.

This time Strap belched.

Reed felt relaxed. The fresh meat had slaked some of his hunger. But his stomach was a long way from full.

He felt like his appetite was just getting started. Soon he would be hungry again. They would need more sustenance.

It was almost like camping with Dad. Almost. When was the last time he'd gone with Dad?

Reed tried to remember. They hadn't gone at all this past summer. Spring? No. Late fall, the year before.

Which begged another question: How long had he had been in the Realm? A couple of days? Three? It felt longer.

There was no telling.

The Moon was rising back up from the horizon. Becoming a solid silver orb in the sky. Radiating out argent rays.

It was a mockery of the dawn. Unnatural. Out of place. Upside down.

Everything was silver and grey. Black and white. All the color had been washed out of this world.

And all hope and love along with it.

Mom and Dad were another world away. Chayse was gone. What hope did Reed have now? There was just one heartbeat now. His own. And it was all alone.

He'd lost his silver necklace. The only thing from his World he had left besides the dirty shirt on his back was the gold fifty-cent piece and his stupid Tracfone which shouldn't even work in the Realm.   But if the Tracfone was so stupid why didn't Reed get rid of it. Because Mom might text again.

No, there was a little more at the moment.

He had companions. And they had a fire. And they were having supper.

A small comfort. A respite from being on the run. A stolen moment that the Elfwitch would snatch away if she had the chance.

Wasn't that a kind of hope?

There were still so many unanswered questions. The more time Reed spent in the Realm, the more questions he picked up. Now that the company had made time to eat and rest it was time to ask.

"Where did the Elfwitch come from?" Reed asked. Back home, she was Miss Elsie Crutch. She had a job: being a mean CASA lady. Somehow the court had given her authority to do what she had done: kidnap him and his sister.

Cyrus stopped eating. Frehley frowned around his last bite of egg. Only Strap made to answer by pointing back in the direction they'd come the other day or night.

"Strap says 'Glacier Mountains,'" Frehley said and swallowed.

"I know that. I've seen the Ice Prison where the Dark Riders are kept," Reed said.

"Do you realize that no one else in the Realm has?"Frehley asked.

"Not even the Black Watch. It is taboo," Cyrus said.

Reed made his eyes large and looked to Frehley.

"Means they're not supposed to on penalty of death," Frehley said.

Reed got defensive. "It wasn't my fault! I didn't mean to! It just happened."

Frehley reached over and put his hand on Reed's shoulder. Not unlike what Dad would have done. "You couldn't help it. You were brought there."

"I used to think the Dark Riders were a fairy tale or just someone's bad nightmare," Cyrus said.

"How about now?" Frehley asked and frowned again.

"I just want to see my wife and daughter again. My village. My pigs. My forge," Cyrus said.

"If the Elfwitch is allowed to run free soon there will be no one left to see," Frehley said.

"Why would she destroy everyone and everything?" Cyrus asked.

But Reed who knew the Elfwitch as two different people in two different worlds, asked, "How can she be so evil?"

Then he looked at Cyrus first who looked away. "If Moor Kreed was here, he'll be able to tell us in a flash."

Then Reed looked to Frehley who sighed and tossed the last scrap of his meal into the fire. He shrugged. "My father would read from the Law to me. He read me where it says that the Judge made all things with His Son through their Spirit. So all three are the same. A triune union.   "But he told me the only thing the Elfwitch has ever made is lies. She hates everything the Judge has ever made. I reckon she even hates herself.

"Maybe cuz she can't be the Judge and she can't beat the Judge so she can't stand it. But didn't the Judge make her, too?" Cyrus asked. "Did He make her just so she would become evil?"

"Yer askin' the wrong man," Frehley said. "Should've asked Moor Kreed while he was still alive."

"So how come the Judge doesn't come down here and stop her?" Reed asked.

"Woah, now!" Cyrus said. "Yer wantin' us to give you a sermon!

Frehley sighed and pulled at his pant legs. "This is all because we don't follow the Law no more."

"No one reads it anymore," Cyrus said. "Not even High Priest Kyphus."

"What's in the Law?" Reed asked.

"Lots of things," Frehley said. "Like the words the Judge spoke to make all things and keep all things together. It tells what we're supposed to do and what we're not supposed to do.   But no one does the right thing all the time. Sooner or later we mess things up. It tells how people are to be punished here on earth. But it also talks about love. And forgiveness.

"Father would say 'Mercy is greater than judgment.' It also talks about the Afterlife. There is a place like the Realm—an everlasting Kingdom that has many mansions. And there is a place like the Domain—a dungeon with a pit full of everlasting punishment.

"Father would read to me from somewhere where the Law said that a man's heart was wicked and that there was nothing we could ever do to earn our place in the everlasting Kingdom. That we all deserve everlasting punishment.

"But there is also a Law of love. And that the Son is love and the living Law. Because he did what we can't do for ourselves. He took on our punishment."

"I don't understand," Reed said.

"Don't worry kid," Cyrus said. "Sometimes I don't either."

Frehley looked at the big burly man. "You don't doubt the Elfwitch, do you? Or the Destroyer? You've seen both of them and the Porter, too. Same as me."

Cyrus nodded. "Seeing is believing. It's like a waking nightmare."

"Well, if you don't doubt the Elfwitch, then why doubt the Judge? Or his Son?" Frehley asked.

Cyrus looked away into the fire. "This is what my dad would say to me all the time. Not that I would believe it. But I can't seem to forget it either.

"'The Judge made all things. He separated the Light from the Darkness and gave the Sun as the Greater Light and the Moon as the Lesser Light. The Light brings love, life, justice, and truth. And the Darkness brings fear and death, lies and hate.'

"It's like everything has two sides to it."

"Like two sides of a coin!" Reed said.

"Exactly!" Cyrus praised. "Now, that's something I can see. So, I can't help but believe in it. I hear love and hate are real. But you really don't see either one. Just what they do to people. Sometimes, I think they're not real and that people only want to believe in them. Same way with the Judge. I ain't never seen him so what good does it do to believe in him?"

Reed pulled his coin out. Turning heads and tails end over end in his fingers. LIBERTY and TRUST IN THE JUDGE flipped with TOWER REIGN. The stamped man with long tousled hair became the castle and tower became the man again like a sideways wheel.

The spinning coin caught the light of the fire. Making a twirling ball of golden waves that swam across the cavern wall.

"What's 'Tower Reign?'" Reed asked.

"It's where the Regents live. They rule from Castle Seat," Cyrus said.

"And the regents are this Root of Lyftwych. Where did they come from?" Reed asked.

Cyrus looked at the boy. "You carry their coin and you don't know who they are? The Son made their family the rulers of the Realm in his place when he left to rejoin the Judge. And before you ask why'd he do that, I'll tell you how my dad told me.

"After the Judge created the Light and Darkness, he made the Realm for everything living that reflected his Light: love, truth, and justice. But the Darkness came to the Domain and created four servants."

"The Dark Riders—the Elfwitch, the Destroy, Rancor, and Shadow," Reed said. "Shadow creates fear. Rancor causes hate. The Destroyers loves to kill. And the Elfwitch loves to lie. We've already seen two, so the other two must be pretty bad."

"Indeed they are," Frehley said. And even Strap nodded.

"I see Moor Kreed taught you something," Cyrus said. "So, Darkness entered the Realm and people forgot about love and fell into despair. That's when the Judge gave the Law to the people on two stones so that they could have the truth and see it. But people did forget and did what was right in their own eyes which messed things up pretty bad. And so the Darkness grew throughout the whole Realm.

"So the Judge said, 'They wouldn't listen to me so I gave them the Law but they won't read it. If I send my Son, maybe they will listen to Him.'

"So the Judge sent his Son. But he came as a servant and not a king. He preached love and forgiveness and for the people to return to the Law.

"But the Elfwitch came among the people only to convince them that the Darkness was the Light and the Light the Darkness. She told them the Judge hated them. Why else was there so much evil?

"The Elfwitch told the people if they killed the Son they wouldn't have to follow the Law and they could do whatever they wanted to do.

"So they killed him and she entombed him in a sepulcher at the foot of Glacier Mountains.

"But the Judge is stronger than the Darkness. So he raised his Son from the dead to be the King over both the dead and the living. The Son is the way to the Judge. He is the truth that destroys Lies. His gives life over death. Love to conquer hate. Hope to cast out all fear.

"The Son put the Dark Riders into Ice Prison. Then he had the people build the Keep to watch over it. When the Son said he would return to the Judge the people did not want him to go. So he chose a family to be the Regents to rule with Truth and Justice through the Law.

"The people built Tower Reign and the Regents ruled on the throne in Castle Seat. And everyone was supposed to live happily ever after and no one was supposed to ever have a bad day again. But if the Dark Riders were ever to break free again, then Darkness would overrun the Realm and the Son would return to set things right by burning everything down and rewarding the faithful.

"So, there you are. Judge. Light. Darkness. Realm. Domain. Dark Riders. Law. Elfwitch. Son. Ice Prison. Keep. Regents. Tower Reign. You. Your coin. Us. This cave. This miserable fire. This undercooked meat. Everything. So, eat and be happy, my son."

Frehley whistled. "You told it better than my Father would've."

Cyrus looked down into the fire. "They're just stories. I said it once, I'll say it again. Seeing is believing. The Elfwitch is real enough. But I ain't never seen the Judge nor his Son. I'd have to find the Sepulcher and look inside it to make sure that it was empty 'fore I believe any nonsense 'bout the Son gettin' resurrected.

"Now back to your coin. Where'd you get it? Moor Kreed give it to you?"

Reed looked at Frehley. How much should he tell? Moor Kreed had said to trust no one. NO ONE. Reed had told Frehley very little. However much Frehley looked like Dad or even acted like Dad, Reed had to keep telling himself that he wasn't Dad.

"You said you had it with you when you and your sister were brought here by the Elfwitch. Yet, you both had silver necklaces, too. Then you said the coin changed when you came here. So much is strange about you," Frehley said.

Moor Kreed had made Reed promise not to tell a soul. The man was convinced that Reed would be in danger the moment he told anyone. Hadn't the Revelator lost his life not too long after warning him?

"What do you mean?" Cyrus asked.

"The words are in the same place but they're different. So are the images on both the heads and tail sides," Reed said.

Cyrus looked at Frehley. "By the Judge! The Elfwitch didn't know about the coin, did she? It helped us get out of jail and through the Porticullus. Then she's not all-powerful."

"I told you," Frehley said. "Her power has limits."

"I wouldn't dare tell her that," Cyrus said.

"Are you that afraid of her? What's the worse she could do? Kill you?" Frehley asked.

"There's worse," Cyrus said. "She has the power to twist people's bodies and their minds until they are ruined."

Frehley spat into the fire. His spittle sizzled. "So what? She's a coward. She does it out of fear."

Reed held up the coin to get a good look at it. Back in his world, it had just been another fifty-cent piece. Something he didn't see every day. Only in a great once in a while. But there it had been worth only fifty cents.

Here in the Realm, the gold coin had been transformed to hold words of the Law. And resembled the seal of the Regents. Now it was rare. And special.

"Who's the man on the heads side?" Reed asked.

"That's the Son. He made the first coins in the Realm for the Regents," Cyrus said. He knew plenty more than he let on about the Law.

Frehley rubbed the whiskers on his chin. "Very interesting, if you follow the tracks laid out. First, someone gives Reed this coin back in his homeland. The Elfwitch kidnaps Reed and his sister because they have silver necklaces. Yet, back in his homeland, someone has foresight enough to give Reed this coin. His sister gives her silver necklace to the Elfwitch so she can free another Dark Rider and Reed loses his necklace only to free us with his coin that Elfwitch didn't know he had."

"So, where is it leading us?" Cyrus asked.

Frehley shrugged. "I don't know."

"That pretty much sums everything up, kid," Cyrus said.

Reed rubbed his brows. "There was something else the Elfwitch had when I was at the Ice Prison. Some kind of strange silver liquid she had in a vial. When she shook it, it shone like a light and gave off sparks."

"Quicksilver," Frehley said.

"Like that lake where the Destroyer almost caught us?" Reed asked.

"You saw what quicksilver did to my blade and to the Destroyer," Frehley said.

"That's the only place in all the Realm where you find it," Cyrus said. "Quicksilver has special properties. So it runs between the Light and Darkness. The Law says that Quicksilver Lake is taboo. But we're two for two in breaking taboos today."

"All the law's ever done is cause me trouble," Reed moaned. "That's why I'm here."

"Sing it, kid," Cyrus said. "Rules are made just to be broken."

"The Law can't be against you if you have a gold coin," Frehley said. "They're for the Regents."

"I'm no regent. I'm not even supposed to be here," Reed said.

"You're the same as us," Cyrus said. "The Elfwitch's got no use for you so she put in jail and made a criminal out of you. Somehow you outsmarted her and helped us make a jailbreak. Now you're on the run with the rest of us high-tailin' it to Outlaw Forest."

"We need to know how much farther we have to go," Frehley said.

"Will we be safe there?" Reed asked. For the first time since he had come to the Domain and then the Realm, he felt safe. He was surrounded by four men he thought he could trust.

The fire was safe and warm. He didn't want to go anywhere.

"It'll be harder for the Elfwitch to find us. But she has servants everywhere," Frehley said as he rose to his feet. "Cyrus, come with me. We'd better climb the top of this rock and take a look."

***

Chapter Twenty-Nine: Wait and Bait

Reed didn't want Frehley to leave him. It was hard to shake the fact that the man was not Dad. The boy kept waiting around for the moment when Frehley would admit it. And then take Reed home.

Mom had driven Dad away. The courts—the law—told Dad when he could and could not see Reed. This was the most time he had been able to spend with Dad—even if it wasn't Dad—in over a year.

So he wasn't about to lose him—Dad or Frehley—again.

"I'm coming with you," Reed said as he uncrossed his legs and got up to trail the two men as they left the cavern.

"Strap, can you check on Evander?" Frehley asked.

The giant nodded and touched the wounded man's forehead. The man had fallen back asleep.

Reed followed the two out of the cavern. They had to get to the top of the hill that housed the cave so they began to climb. Frehley and Cyrus side by side finding purchase in the silvery light because Reed had noticed it was never fully dark in this world. Reed followed with caution between the two men as they all ascended the hill.

Each one used their hands to stand up on top of the knob and check their balance. The summit was slim. Bare and rocky. Jagged granite being chipped away by wind and rain.

For Reed, it was no different than being on top of Seven Mile Ridge or Panther Knob back home. This was the Ozarks under a different name. With all the cell towers and telephone poles taken out. Like it used to be before the first European descended Americans had come to the region after the War of 1812.

Behind them, Glacier Mountains rose into the sky. The white and blue tops crystallizing into a black canopy of the sky and starlight. In the right corner of the horizon stood the top of the Keep from which a signal fire burned against the icy glacial colors.

Below the top of the knob lay a valley where Frehley had led them in a foray to hunt. It covered a quarter-mile before sloping back up into various wooded hills. Thicker stands of forest lay to the horizon before them and more valleys beyond with knobs poking up here and there.

"That's my home," Frehley said pointing to the flatter forestlands in the west. "I was born and raised in the Royal Forest. So I became a Royal Huntsman."

"What happened? Can't you do that again?" Reed asked.

Frehley rubbed a spot on his bicep. "I turned my patch in a long time ago. Now when I go back to the Royal Forest, I'll be a trespasser. The Elfwitch will send my old hunting mates against me or have her lycanthropes hunt me down like a dog. So be it. I don't plan on getting caught again."

"Well, you can't go back there again, can you? Outlaw Forest is over that-a-way," Cyrus said and pointed to the far eastern corner of the horizon before them. "About day or so if we don't run into any trouble.

"Exactly where you headed once we get to Outlaw Forest?"

"Strap says his family is from Norfolk Wich," Frehley said. "He has healers in his village. I'll help take Evander there. And you? Where will you go?"

Cyrus slapped his chest. "I'm from Westfolk Wich. My family's been blacksmithing there for generations. And the kid?"

"Guess he should come with me and Strap," Frehley said.

"First you say he ain't yer kid and now you wanna adopt him!" Cyrus laughed. "The kid should have a say in it. Since he's a stranger and all."

Then he said to Reed, "Kid, you wanna go with this madman and that giant to some stinky village? Norfolk's is full of goats. Nothing to eat but goat milk and goat cheese and stringy jerky.

"Or you wanna come with me to my village? It's not as far. Be good eatin' there. Provided my wife's kept the larder full. Pigs is what we got mostly. So we eat lots of pork.

"Judge-darn it, kid. You can even bring the rat. I promise I won't eat him. Not when I've got pork rinds."

This was the first time since crossing over that Reed had liked any of the choices given to him. It was a no-brainer.

"Guess I'll go to Norfolk Wich with them," Reed said.

"Well, I've got a girl younger than you, kid. I ain't seen her in five long years. She's my whole reason for doin' what I'm doin'," Cyrus said.

"We should climb back down. Help Strap clean Evander's wounds. Then get some rest before we all go our separate ways," Frehley said.

Something moved across the southern skyline. Coming from over the Royal Forest. Dropping out of the sky.

It looked like pieces of drifting dirt. Except that it was formed in v's with spaces in between. The black shapes had ends that moved up and down.

Wings. Birds. Crows.

Hundreds of crows flying in flocks following lead birds. The flocks undulated up and down and circled over the valley and then descended like an arrow into the wooded canopy.

"That's not good," Cyrus said. "Do you know what that means?"

"There are no turkeys there," Reed said. "Turkeys don't like crows."

"Might help flush out some deer," Frehley said.

"I was thinking it may mean trouble," Cyrus said. "But y'all keep thinking 'bout food. Right now I could go for some fresh deer tenderloin fried in cornmeal. I could smell my way home on that."

"I thought it's nothin' but pigs and pork for you," Frehley said.

Cyrus shrugged. "A man can't live on bacon alone."

"This isn't my home," Reed said. "I want to go home. But I don't know how to."

"I want to change my home," Frehley said. "I have a choice. So I have hope."

Cyrus said nothing.

They descended the crest of the ridge and entered their cozy cavern to lay down by the fire. Bellies full and heads drowsy. It was time for sleep.

Even Packy scooted out of the shadows to be closer to both his den mate and the fire. After sitting on his haunches to groom himself he curled up in the nook of Reed's throat and chin.

Reed felt its fur warmth radiating against him. Something small that attached itself to him. That needed him and wouldn't let him go.

Sometime later in the shadows of the fire in the middle of the peaceful rest inside the restful womb of rock, Reed felt something vibrating. The boy roused himself. He had been deep asleep without a dream or care.

What had awoken him?

The phone.

In his pocket.

Vibrating against his thigh.

Someone was texting him.

He pulled himself up to a sitting position and dug out the Tracfone.

> MOM
> WHERE ARE U?
> ME
> IM IN A CAVE ON A HILL
> MOM
> COME DOWN TO ME
> ME
> WHERE R U
> MOM
> DOWN IN THE VALLEY. COME TO ME.
> ME
> I THINK DAD IS HERE 2
> MOM
> COME NOW. WE WILL GO HOME.

He had to go. His friends would be safe by the fire inside the cave. Didn't he want to go back home?

As much as Mom yelled at him. Or scolded him. Or punished him. He only ever wanted to hear her say that she loved him.

He wanted a hug from her more than this fire. Her arms around him would be like going home. There would be no more denial from Frehley about being Dad.

So Reed ran away.

Taking only Packy who climbed up his arm as he got up from the fire.

The night for day had turned cold. Shadows ruled the topography. Obscuring the ground. Making every step treacherous.

Bushes looked taller than himself. The ground locked under dark blankets. Tree branches spread to filter out the dim light.

His only guide was the ache in his heart and Packy perched on his shoulders sniffing at the air.

The pair made their way along the ridge top as the moon sunk to be dissected by the horizon with the wooded hills muddied its cold silver light.

Down the slope.

Into the valley.

Along the rocky way.

Under spread trees.

To the place where they had seen the crows descend.

It was darker in the valley. The thick branches covered the sky. Trapping air heavy with moisture.

Twisted roots poked through the earth and rock. Rugs of lichen blanketed rocks and deadwood. Colonies of mushrooms flourished in dank spots.

This was not the place Reed would have chosen for a family reunion.

Nothing else moved around him.

Not a scamper from a squirrel.

Not a flutter from a sleeping crow.

Behind him. In front of him. Beside him. A piece of deadwood snapped.

Something had stepped on it.

An animal large enough to break it.

Or a person.

Reed texted again.

Mom where r u

There was no reply.

Mom was out there waiting for him. Wasn't she?

Maybe he should turn around and climb back up the ridge and return to the cave. There was a warm fire there. His friends were there.

Something lay up ahead. On the ground. Waiting for him.

It wasn't a rock or a stick.

Reed took cautious steps.

It had striations. Ruffled feathers. Outspread wings. Grasping talons.

But no head.

It was a sparrow. Caught in the air. And having its head torn off, it had fallen back to the dank earth.

But it couldn't have been what had made the noise earlier. Because it was headless. It had been put there.

Maybe just now?

If Reed was going to turn back now was the time to do it.

***

Chapter Thirty: Darksome and Lonesome

Another stick snapped.

Reed heard it as clear as day. The same as the last time. Certain it had come from behind some tree off to his left. Or right.

Packy squeaked and ran down from his shoulder jumping off his chest to the ground. The rat scampered on ahead. Ahead into the darksome valley and away from Reed.

"Packy!" Reed cried and ran after him.

He should have gone straight back to the cavern and have gotten Frehley and the others. Might as well tell himself he shouldn't have left the cavern.

Reed came upon another shape. Another small animal lying on the ground. It was larger this time. But just as dead.

It was a squirrel with fur stretched along its spine. Long-tailed curled up around its back legs. Eyes able to look backward as its head had been turned around.

Reed was on his own. All alone. No Mom was waiting. No Chayse by his side. Dad wasn't coming in for the rescue.

He was lonesome and short on courage. But he wouldn't let fear cripple him. Reason had left when Reed refused to turn back.

Fear told him to freeze in his tracks and panic. But that would accomplish nothing. Reed wasn't going to turn back without finding Packy.

Something was out there.

Something that loved being darksome. That was just as lonesome. Something that wanted him.

Reed no longer thought it was Mom. Everything in his being told him to turn around and get back to the cavern. He was foolish to have left the warmth of the fire and the safety of his friends.

But he couldn't leave Packy down here.

Why?

It was just a rat. He was following a little rat. How smart was that? Reason asked. Somehow the voice of his Reason sounded an awful lot like his twin sister Chayse.

But that rat had dashed off with his Mom's necklace to stash it away somewhere. And this little rat had led them out of a scrape or two. By showing them the way.

So Reed stepped forward past the second dead animal following after Packy.

After twisting around a few more tree trunks he came across another body: a rabbit. Eyes large and glassy. Mouth parted showing rodent buck teeth. A scream strangled in its throat. Blood pooling from its nose.

Its neck had been broken.

And after that another and another close by each other in a jagged line. Each animal bigger than the last: a groundhog, a fox, or a raccoon. Backs broke or necks twisted.

Three trees stood at the end of the line of dead animals. Three trunks standing straight without branches. Struck by lightning and charred black.

Crows perched atop the trees on either end. Eyeing Reed as if he were full of indolence. Hopping on their talons. Ready to swoop down and peck out his eyes.

But only two of the trees were dead. The third, the one in the middle, had two leather boots instead of gnarled roots. With leather-clad legs and black chain mail jacket over its chest. The waist girded with a thick belt buckled with silver. The head of the beast held a mane of wild black hair. Out from under shone a beautiful face with blue steel eyes shadowed with black rings. A smile of sharp bone-white teeth struck out between the blackest lips.

It was the Destroyer. Lord of the crows. Harrower of all flesh.

Standing in its majesty. Basking in its power to kill small helpless creatures. Holding one last victim.

Packy. It had the rat by its tail. So that its shaking head could only see the ground. Everytime the rat kicked to free itself, it only made itself rock back and forth in the Destroyer's cruel grip. The rat squeaked in terror.

Then it raised Packy above its own head. The wild black mane tilted back and the black lips opened like a widening maw. The rat could only look down and see its demise: a dark funnel that led into the bowels of destruction.

The Destroyer began to lower Packy. The rat's ribs convulsed with fear as its little heart beat faster than its kicking leg. Its head disappeared between the harsh black lips. The blue steel eyes curling up to the sky with relish.

"No!" Reed said.

But the Destroyer did not stop. Packy sank further into the beast's jaw. Next to its body and legs until the only thing left that Reed could see was its tail that the Destroyer held it by.

Then Reed remembered he wasn't helpless. He had something that the Destroyer didn't like. He reached into his pocket and pulled out the faithful gold coin.

It cut a light through the Darkness. Returning true form and color to the ground and foliage. Like a tiny sun bursting through a fog bank.

The Destroyer pulled Packy out of its mouth so it could shield its eyes. With its freehand, it made a sign. Hand with fingers together held vertical then flipped out with palm stretched straight out. Then it put its free forefinger next to its ear and turned its hand over into a fist with the thumb and pinky stuck up like horns.

Reed thought the Destroyer was making a plea of some kind. To put the gold coin away. Well, that wasn't happening. Not until it let Packy go.

"The Destroyer delivers death. Takes away life and love and hope," spoke the voice that made twigs snap.

"Not my rat! Let Packy go!" Reed screamed. He was tired of being helpless. Tired of being afraid. Tired of adults pushing him around. So much to the point that he was past hating. He had had enough. Pure and simple.

The boy looked over his shoulder.

Cyrus stood next to him. The other sleeve torn from his tunic. Baring the snake-moon tattoo.

"Give the Destroyer yer gold coin and it will let yer pet rat go," the burly man said. Reed noticed he hadn't said, "kid."

Reed didn't trust Cyrus. Why should he care what happened to Packy? Why would he want to help the Destroyer?

"I'm tired of getting told what to do!" Reed screamed at Cyrus. Then he stuck the gold coin up at the Destroyer's face. "Now. Let. Packy. Go."

Cyrus rammed his shoulder into Reed's side. A clip in the back. A foul. Worthy of a penalty.

The coin was tossed into the air. Fair and free. For anyone to possess.

It flipped side to side. Heads to tails. Tails back to Heads.

Cyrus pushed the boy out of place and planted his feet to best come down with a completion. Reed tried to push against his opponent but the burly man could not be moved. So he pushed off Cyrus' thigh to reach the coin as it came down.

The two pushed away at each other's hands as the coin came down between their torsos.

Cyrus pushed Reed back, clear interference. And held out his thick palm. The coin landed in his meaty mitt.

Reed came at the man. Slapping and kicking. "Give it back."

But Cyrus wouldn't give the coin back.

The Destroyer tossed the rat away. Packy screeched at being free and at the rough treatment. Landing on its side, it pulled itself through the sticks and leaves.

Reed made to pick up his pet but Cyrus clamped a hand down on his shoulder. The burly man pulled out a small iron box, like a ring box. Then he put the gold inside and shut the lid. Shutting out the light as darkness and silver tones flooded back into the valley.

Cyrus tossed the box into the air and the Destroyer snatched it with a mighty grin.

"Sorry, kid," Cyrus said. "I don't hate you. Much."

"Why?" Reed asked.

Cyrus shrugged. "I have to."

Reed looked at the moon-snake tattoo that was at his eye level. "Asheroth. The same as the Brazzles. You serve the Elfwitch."

"More like we made a deal," Cyrus said. "You wouldn't understand. You're just a kid."

"I swear if you lay a hand on the boy, I'll shoot to kill," announced a voice that meant to do what it promised.

Cyrus and Reed turned.

The Destroyer hissed.

Frehley stood ten paces behind them along the trail of dead animals. A matchlock pistol in his hand with a bead drawn straight at Cyrus' heart. Strap stood another few paces behind looking down the barrel of a muzzleloader. Clinging to his back like a sack of dirty laundry hung Evander trying his best to hold a muzzleloader.

"The Destroyer gave you a sign when we were at Quicksilver Lake," Evander said. His face was very pale. He looked very weak. "It was 'Bring the boy.' Before that, the boy saw your tattoo. The snake's for Asheroth and the moon's for the Elfwitch. Then I remembered you spoke about the bounty the Elfwitch had on finding gold or silver.

"You were going to betray us this whole time. Turn the boy over to the Elfwitch. But I didn't know why."

"That's my business. None of yer affair," Cyrus said.

"This boy is my business. He is very much my affair," Frehley said.

Cyrus spit. "Bah! Don't pretend you care about the boy now. You didn't want anything to do with him. Or the Revelator. Or this gold coin. You've had yer chance to make things right. And you loused it up fer everyone. Now it's every man fer his own self!"

"If you have any sense which you ain't, you'd drop yer weapons and step clear away," croaked a voice used to dealing in authority and enjoying it.

With the indefatigable Sergeant Hood at the head, out of the woods marched ten Deadcoats. Muskets at the ready. Bayonets prepared to sweep them away at the order.

"Just 'tween you 'n me? I'm hopin' you don't," Sergeant Hood said as he drew out his sword to command the firing line.

Only Strap and Evander changed their aim towards the squad leader. As if drawing a dead bead on someone already dead might stop him. While Frehley kept his aim true--straight at Cyrus' heart.

"I'll drop you first, Cy," Frehley said. "Makes no matter to me."

Cyrus stood in front of the boy. "I've never seen people who wanna die so bad! I just wanna get home! See my wife and kid again! They're the only reason I'm doin' this!"

"The Elfwitch told you she had your wife and daughter hostage, didn't she?" Evander demanded. "Told you to serve her or she'd kill them both. That right?"

"I spent five years in that stinkin' dungeon!" Cyrus cried. "Serving a twenty-year stretch. My wife woulda been old. My child grown. I was as good as dead! The Elfwitch promised me a full pardon. It was my only way out!"

Evander shook his head. "Wrong. The boy helped you get out. And then we all escaped together. And for what? Just for you to betray us?"

"It was the best deal I was gonna get!" Cyrus yelled and stamped his foot.

"The Elfwitch lied to you," Evander said.

Cyrus shook his head. "What are you even talkin' 'bout?"

"I got arrested three years ago. But before they dropped me in the hole with you, I heard Westfolk Wich got burned to the ground and everyone in it slaughtered. Cut down like sheep. Throats cut in their sleep. Bodies dumped down a well. I just didn't know that was your home. Cyrus, I'm sorry. Your home is gone," Evander said.

Cyrus shook his head. Then said, "No." Then he slapped his face. Then he started the whole thing over again. Trying to sop the tears. They came anyway.

Now Cyrus was lonesome. And in a darksome place. He had lost all hope.

Sergeant Hood gave the order, "Fire!"

The bottom of the valley erupted in musket fire and black smoke and spinning balls. Some bit wood. Some bit flesh.

And Reed was in the middle of the salvo.

He saw a musket ball dig a channel into Cyrus' tattoo. Filling the face of the skin moon with blood. The punch of it shattered bone and the force made Cyrus pirouette but he still grabbed Reed and pulled him to the valley floor.

The Deadcoats didn't bother with reloading.

"Charge!" Sergeant commanded. The line of troopers rushed past the two trees where the Destroyer waited. Surging over Reed and Cyrus' prone bodies.

As their moldy boots kicked through the leaves and deadfall, Reed heard Packy screech.

Half covered by Cyrus' body as the man spilled his tears and blood onto him, Reed squirmed out enough to snake his hand through the deadfall and find Packy's bruised body. He wanted to cradle the rat, but it squealed. Reed snaked his hand back, sorry that he caused Packy more pain.

Both Frehley and Strap with his burden, Evander, fled for their very lives. Now the hunt was on. With the Deadcoats giving chase.

Left behind, Reed and Cyrus felt the ground shake. Step by step. Inch by inch.

Large unstoppable hands picked both he and Cyrus up off the valley floor. Dangling above the ground looking upside down at icy blue eyes staring back at them out of a pasty white face bordered by wild hair.

The Destroyer laughed through its wicked black lips.

***

Chapter Thirty-One: Poison and Sting

"Your only hope is to take the mark," The Elfwitch told her captives as she kicked open the old wooden chest with the toe of her slipper. The chest rocked on its metal corners as the hinges of the lid protested but held themselves up.

From the first, Chayse had wanted to see inside that chest. To touch its contents. To possess its treasure.

The edges framed a box of darkness.

A mouth of a cave.

The sides lined with black cloth that slipped into space.

A hole descending down into a basement of eons.

Another part of the root cellar of the mysterious cosmos.

A pocket of eternity.

Whatever secrets contained there were buried in darkness.

If Chayse had opened it and peered inside everything would have been obscured. So she would have to reach further in. Then the box would have rocked and shaken and she would have fallen in. And down the hole into a dark existence.

The Darkness would have gladly swallowed her up.

"Believe what I tell you!" the Elfwitch intoned. She brandished her double silver necklace—a heart twisted with the moon-snake emblem. From its center sparks squeezed out. Streaks of flashing silver. Making diamond patterns against the walls of the queen's personal chambers.

"All the universe began in darkness. Timeless. Shapeless.

"All energy was negative. Until this cold fire began to burn throughout infinity. That is the true state of eternity.

"All of you. This world. This tower. Your precious Realm. Nothing more than illusion.

"All of it. Law. Love. Light. Everything that liar called the Judge told you was real is just a dream. Smoke. Vapor.

"The Son is dead. I entombed him in stone. He's not coming back. There's no glory to be had in the grave.

"This is my truth. Unless you are sealed with the Darkness you will return to nothingness. You will become rock still and ice cold. Dead.

Then the Elfwitch reached deep inside the box as if she were probing a hole in a wall between two worlds. And pulled out a solid cylinder. A secret hidden from the light long ago by keeping it in a womb of darkness.

"But there is a cold burning fire in the Heart of Darkness. It has mass and bends the light of the universe. It feeds on golden hearts and argent souls. There you may find a place.

"Take the sign of the Lesser Light. Swear an oath on quicksilver. Submit to the Darkness or be destroyed in oblivion."

The Elfwitch held in a machine that shaped like a fist and sword handle. The device was metal. Two horizontal flanges ran parallel holding a metal drum and removable glass canisters. A vertical metal plate ran between the flanges embossed like a dragon's wing that swept up into the butt of a sword handle for a palm grip. A metal stick with a twistable knob was attached to the grip. Below the second flange was another thicker canister that ended with the tip of a needle.

The Elfwitch handed the device over to Victor as Nicolai shut the lid to the old wooden chest. Then she pulled the back the feathered fold of her sleeve barring the skin on her left forearm.

Her skin was cackled. Cracked like a dried washout. Scaly with short white hairs. Wrinkled green lines woven into the skin with the end of old bones from the very first night on the earth.

Infused there on her sagging skin was the moon-snake tattoo. Ragged and deep. Ancient but not of days.

"That is not a choice. You are offering death. Twice," Queen Regina said.

Most of the court was represented here in the queen's personal chambers. The court had intruded on her privacy. Reversed the audiences given in the Castle Seat to a declaration of betrayal.

So that the company of turncoats far outnumbered the loyalists. Chayse counted fourteen—not counting the huntsman spiders that crawled back up to the ceiling--to the four still with the queen and Captain Michael. And Chayse—where did she stand?

"Choice is power," the Elfwitch said, and getting on her knees reached far down into the chest. Much further than what the ground level would allow. Chayse suspected it might just be bottomless.

She pulled out the long thin glass tube of quicksilver which she attached between the flanges of the device which she gripped in her right hand. There was a trigger guard which when she touched made the needle dart back and forth and release a speck of silvery light.

"Step up and take my mark," the Elfwitch said. "Or suffer oblivion."

Both the two guards and the two remaining ladies in waiting stepped forward leaving their queen and captain behind them. One by one they rolled up their sleeves to bare their forearms while the Elfwitch began to knit with the needle and stitch the heavy metal into their skin.

As she gave her new followers the tattoo of the moon-snake: Asheroth and the Darkness, she sang a song in Spell Speak.

"A design to begin
With a needle-thin
Feel the scorpion sting
A little poison ring
Art from head to toe
A skill done slow
Tattoo quicksilver ink
A little sting for everyone
Tattoo quicksilver ink
A little pain for everyone
Sign the design
Begin on the skin
Tattoo quicksilver ink
A little metal for everyone
Know my sign
Darkness inside."

When she finished the four initiated traitors they took their stand with the others behind High Priest Kyphus.

Which left three people who did not bear the mark in their skin. Who were not inscribed with the evil geometry. Who had not pledged their souls.

The Elfwitch smirked. "Times change. People change. Your ways are done. The Realm needs new ways. They are held in my domain.

"What says your highness? Will you take the sign of the Lesser Light? Will you swear allegiance to the Heart of Darkness?"

Sober and sure, Queen Regina squared her jaw and spoke, "A realm does not include only subjects like people or animals.

"More than those, it needs ways. Paths to follow. Like truth. And justice. And peace.

"It needs the Law!

"It needs the Judge!"

At the queen's declaration of the Law and mention of the Judge's name the Elfwitch's face glowered and her teeth gnashed.

Queen Regina continued, "You may have dominion over people and animals now but you will not reign supreme for long.

"Because you do not have truth. Or keep justice. Or know peace.

"The people follow you because I failed to lead them away from you. Because for twelve years I listened to your false counsel. You promised to help heal my hurt. But I let it blind me.

"The fault is mine. But even now I do not believe all hope is lost.

"The Regents have never died out. I will not be the last of my line. I will not see it cut off. Whatever happens, I remain Queen Regina. From the Root of Lyftwych. The Shepherd of the Living Law. Upholder of truth and justice!"

The Elfwitch blew air through her lips. "And what say you, Captain Michael?"

"I serve my queen. The Regent, who alone has the blessing of the Judge to rule. Any other ruler would be treason and blasphemy," Captain Michael answered.

"Victor. Nicolai," the Elfwitch directed. "Take these two away to the chambers they had reserved for me. Kyphus, place a tight guard around them. No one is to see them without my consent."

Chayse had kept quiet since she was unsure what to do. The queen was in danger. The queen was out of power. Was the queen Mom?

The Elfwitch and almost everyone else were standing against the queen. Why? Back in Chayse's world, the Elfwitch had been Miss Elsie Crutch who had hated Mom and wanted the twins. She had manipulated in bringing them here. Why?

Chayse's world seemed like a dream. Mom and Dad were shadows. And Reed? He was just gone.

Chayse was confused. Shouldn't she care about might what might have happened to Reed? Hadn't she tried on the identify of Wice like a brand new shirt?

Didn't the Elfwitch have unlimited power that fascinated her? Everyone else was joining her side. Taking the moon-snake tattoo.

Didn't everyone who wear that tattoo do evil?

Would Chayse take it, too? Should she? How far away from her family did she want to go?

"There will be no more Lyftwyches upon this throne," the Elfwitch said. "I will see to it that none remain."

Something jolted to life inside Chayse. She latched onto that word. She knew it. Better than herself.

It was true. And in that truth, there was an undeniable power. Didn't someone say once that knowing the truth would set you free?

"I am Leftwich!" Chayse blurted to the queen. "Mom! I was tricked!"

The entire court looked at her like she was insane.

"She is a servant of the Elfwitch. So she will lie about her ancestry," Captain Michael said.

The Elfwitch laughed and crossed her pale white arms. "Here, the queen has no children."

Chayse felt everything inside her collapse. Fall down a hole. Once again, all her hope had been wrecked.

"What evil have you brought this child to?" the queen demanded.

"The truth of the Darkness. She will embrace it one day. Or she will share your fate," the Elfwitch said. Then she brushed them off with a wave of her fingers. "Take Wice to the queen's new chambers. Let her stew there awhile till she comes to her senses."

Nicolai and Victor led the three of them out of what had just up to now been the queen's personal chambers and through the archway back down the stairs.

***

Chapter Thirty-Two: Wrecked and Reconciled

The queen had just become a prisoner in her own castle. In a place where she was the ruler. Where she had the authority. Where her family had been for generations.

It all had been taken away. Given to the Elfwitch. All with the consent of the Court.

Chayse had seen the same thing happen to Mom back in their World. With Miss Elsie Crutch cheering on Lawyer ad-litem Alexander Kyler—here in this Realm they were the Elfwitch and the High Priest Kyphus. And when Judge Hart had ruled against Mom, Chayse had lost all hope.

All Judge Hart had done was let Chayse know the truth—her family was gone. First Dad got chased out by Mom and then Mom was gone to work all the time. There was no family.

Except for Reed.

All Chayse had wanted were PARENTS. To be home waiting for her. Instead, she had gotten the Brazzles who were just puppets for the Elfwitch.

It just made Chayse angry. To the core. Hitting the sides of her heart. Replaying Dad leaving in her head made her see red. Thinking about Mom being weak made her gnash her teeth.

And then Reed had left her.

That was the cruelest cut of all.

The last chord of family.

Her anchor lost. Leaving her adrift at sea.

She had been shocked to see Mom sitting on the throne of the Realm. But it was not Mom. And the Elfwitch had enjoyed the sucker punch.

Chayse was confused.

The only thing that kept slicing through it all was her anger. She knew that feeling like an old friend. It hadn't changed. It wouldn't let her down.

She was angry. Angry at Dad. At her Mom. At Reed. At her World.

But here it was different. The same but the color of anger made Chayse look at everything as if it were new.

After she'd given the Elfwitch what she'd wanted, the Elfwitch had let her do what she pleased. She could wander about the Circle Chamber free to discovery. To learn by happy accidents.

There had only been one taboo.

Not to open the chest carved with WICE.

 She didn't have to be afraid. She didn't have to be helpless. She still had a choice.

Up to now, all her choices had been limited by those who had control. First, Dad and then Mom. Then, Lawyer Kyler and Miss Elsie Crutch. Then the Brazzles.

But the Elfwitch had changed the game. She wasn't holding power over Chayse. Not anymore.

She had acted like a friend. Or a teacher.

A mentor.

Power. If someone wanted control over someone else then they needed power. Because control meant power.

Chayse wanted control over her own life.

She needed power. To do what she wanted. To make her own decisions.

And right now, Chayse felt like helping Queen Regina.

What had the queen done wrong? Why did the Elfwitch hate her so much? Why had nearly everyone in her Court betrayed her?

So, why did Chayse want to help the Queen then? She couldn't say. Other than that it would make the Elfwitch mad.

Chayse liked making people mad. Doing what adults didn't expect a twelve-year-old to do or say. Seeing adults get flustered like they'd lost control made Chayse feel like she was in control.

Nicolai and Victor marched the trio of dissenters down the hall from the stairwell back to the chambers where the Elfwitch had been quartered. Nicolai opened the door to the chambers Chayse had shared with the Elfwitch. Victor ushered them through the small antechamber into the study room.

It was still contained some of the Elfwitch's contraptions and infernal devices which the huntsmen spiders had dragged halfway across the Realm from her Circle Chamber below the Keep. Small racks of stoppered vials and open cases with corked bottles and tubes. There were a dozen aviary cages with small kinds of birds and a half dozen cages stuffed with rats with various deformities and two large gallon jugs--one stuffed with jumping frogs and the other squirming with fire chameleons.

And tucked it the corner sat the two-headed juvenile buzzard chained to its perch. Having grown twice in size with molting feathers since being hatched. It hopped up on its meaty legs and eyed the trio up for size with both pairs of red eyes.

Each of the three took a seat in an overstuffed chair as if waiting to be called into the principal's office.

"You will all stay here," Nicolai began as he retreated out of the antechamber. "Like rats in a cage."

"The Elfwitch will deal with you soon enough," Victor promised as he closed the outside door.

They sealed their only entrance in and out. And no doubt posted a turncoat guard outside the door. The trio was caught tight.

The queen and Captain Michael said not a word as Victor closed the outside door to the hall. But the very second the door to the hall was closed, both the captain of the guard and Queen Regina were up on their feet. Moving about the study chamber. Feeling along the stone walls. Picking up aviary cages and racks of vials to touch the ledges.

"What are you looking for?" Chayse asked.

"A secret passage," Captain Michael said.

"To where?" Chayse asked.

"I would rather not say," Captain Michael said.

"Just say to 'freedom' then," Queen Regina said.

The word hit Chayse like an energy drink. She was up on feet helping in the search. The birds fluttered and fussed. The rats squeaked. And the frogs and lizards gave involuntary kicks and twitches.

Racks and cases were pushed aside or moved to the floor in the hunt. But nothing could be found. Chayse stood still as she got flustered.

"Don't get mad," Captain Michael said. "You won't be able to think. Get mad and you lose. And the Elfwitch wins."

"Is there even a secret passage?" Chayse asked. She needed a way out of this whole mess. But her hope had shrunk to infinitesimal size.

"Most rooms have them. Keep looking," the queen urged. She and the Captain went into the bed chamber. Leaving Chayse to check in the privy.

The bed chamber was in line with the study chamber, both having a window casement to the outside tower wall. But the privy was set into a recess towards the other side of the wall. It was a shallower room than either the other two rooms.

Chayse stepped inside the privy. It was no bigger than a walk-in closet. A bench sat along one side of the room in two halves. The half for a person to do their business was wooden with a hole carved in the middle. Chayse supposed a person just sat on it and the waste fell all the way down a chute to the basement. Not too different than a Johnny on the spot at the County Fair.

"What am I looking for exactly?" Chayse asked.

"A triggerplate," the queen called.

"It'll release an opening," Captain Michael said. "You'll know it when you find it."

There was no way Chayse was going to stick her hand down the chute on the privy bench. Not that it smelled like flowers were being kept down in the basement now. So she felt along the wall in front of the bench.

Nothing.

Time was growing short.

Any second the outside door would open and the Elfwitch would come strolling in. And that would not be a good thing for anybody. Chayse had a feeling the Elfwitch wasn't going to hold another tea clutch.

Chayse dropped to her knees and held her breath. Then she gave the wooden bench a half-hearted push. Giving herself the heebie-jeebies.

Nothing. Thankfully.

The second bench was stone. Not wood. And it didn't have a hole cut in it. Why? Wasted space? Wasted function?

So Chayse gave the stone bench a weak jolt. It was real. It did not yield.

Or was it?

Chayse gave a harder push. Like when she was done with Reed teasing her and was trying to make her point. Something sifted behind the wall. The sound of stone scraping against stone. Rolling along a groove.

The stone bench had moved. A centimeter? No. More than that. It was noticeably no longer aligned with the wooden bench.

"Found it!" Chayse sang out.

Queen Regina and Captain Michael rushed into the privy with questioning and hopeful eyes.

"Where is it?" the queen asked.

Chayse pointed at the stone bench. "There."

Captain Michael dropped to his knees. "Everyone! Push!"

It took all three of them to push the stone bench back through the opening until it was recessed behind the stone wall. Chayse's eyes grew wide at the sight of the passage. A secret space. A way out.

"How large is it? Can we all fit?" Queen Regina asked.

"I can get through!" Chayse said. "I'll take a look."

She crawled under the wall into the opening. It was a tight space between the framing of the room and the outer wall dressing. Then she stood up. The space appeared to be as tall as the room from floor to ceiling. Curving back along the edge of the outer wall it became darksome.

Chayse dropped back to her knees and peered at the queen and guard captain through the shaft of light.

"It'll be a tight fit. But we could go in single file," Chayse said.

"The Elfwitch will send her lycanthropes to follow after us. Even if we can shut up the passageway on the other side, there may not be enough time," Captain Michael said.

"We need a diversion. A distraction. So we can slip away," Queen Regina said.

"I know!" Chayse said as she slipped back out of the passageway.

The other two followed her back into the study chamber. Chayse began to unlatch the aviary cages freeing the birds to take wing and flit around the room making a fuss with their garbled bird song. Captain Michael followed suit and opened the rat cages.

"Is this safe?" the queen asked. "Are these animals harmless?"

"The Elfwitch's poisoned most of them. They're just lab animals for her test on," Chayse said. Better they should die with some dignity free than to be a part of some experiment.

Without another word, Queen Regina pushed a rack of vials onto the chamber floor. Then she picked up a case and threw it to the stone floor. The black smoke rising clung to the fabric of the chairs and couches.

The mixing chemicals fizzled and popped. Erupting into sizzling flames. Burning through carpet and fabric.

Captain Michael kicked at the base of the double-headed vulture's perch. The big bird took flight as it stand crashed to the floor snapping its chain. It screeched and flapped its large wings to the back of the couch.

Queen Regina nodded at the mess and said, "Time to leave."

Raising her skirt to step over dying rats, the queen jostled an open case that held a single vial in a small rack. Slender like one of the Elfwitch's fingers. Except stoppered with a cork instead of a jagged fingernail.

Half-empty with a silverish vapor mixed with floating ice crystals. After being jostled, the crystals rotated in mad figure eights and a blue spark shot out into the air.

The stopped Chayse in her tracks.

It is the substance most prized by those of the Lesser Light.

Quicksilver. Refined in the Elfwitch's crucible. In conjunction with Chaye's silver heart necklace, it had helped free the Destroyer.

If the Elfwitch valued this substance above all other things, why had she left it the guest quarters? Chayse had never known the Elfwitch to make a mistake. No one had ever gotten the best of her yet. She was always right.

She reached out and scooped up the vial. The air vacuum around the vial pulled like a magnet to her palm. Static electrical charges felt over her hand like blue tendrils.

The vial felt snug in her mitt like a ball. It had a heft that felt comfortable. It held a promise to help though she didn't know she would use it. Yet.

Chayse tucked it up under the sleeve of her black dress. It assured her. She had made a step closer to taking control.

Emboldened by her first find, she felt confident enough to give a cursory glance over the wreckage of the other tubes and vials. Amid the shards and mixing pools of liquids, one more vial had escaped the ransacking carnage. One with a pink stopper.

Chayse knew it well. Bottled up inside was an amber liquid that could metamorph hair cells into quills and bone cells into spikes. While turning its victims crazy.

It was a transmogrifier.

That, too, she plucked out of the mess and tucked up her sleeve.

There were voices outside in the hall.

No doubt they could hear the animals squeaking and squawking. Or heard the crashing of the Elfwitch's implements. Or smelled the mixing vapors.

Black smoke poured off the couch and chairs. Escaping through the antechamber and below the door to the hall. All of it signaled trouble. Something that the Elfwitch or her servants had not anticipated.

Queen Regina was already in the privy. Captain Michael made his way through the wreckage of the study and coaxed Chayse to follow. As she fled behind the couch, the two-headed vulture lunged at her.

In one fluid motion, Captain Michael pulled out a small dagger and flung it into the chest of the beast. Both heads screeched in anger and pain as it flapped towards the window casement. The beating wings brushing the edge of Chayse's face.

The two-headed beast in its fury burst through the glass window and escaped out of the tower just as the chamber door was being opened.

Captain Michael pulled Chayse by the wrist into the privy while Queen Regina shut the door.

Several people, no doubt men, had entered the room. They were shouting in surprise and anger. Chayse could pick out Victor and Nicolai among the accusers—they would have the most to answer for if the prisoners had somehow gotten away.

"Can we all fit in there?" the queen whispered.

Chayse tapped her chest showing her self-election and crawled into the opening in the false privy wall. Once inside, she was able to stand up. Her shoulders were caught between wooden planks and the outer stone masonry. She scraped her back and hips as she turned to get her back against the stone and face the wood.

The space was tight. A little wider than her locker at middle school. But not by much.

The space was dark. Light by the entrance she had come through and specks of light boring through an opening in the chamber wall.

The space was cold. The air was caught between the pent up warmth of the chambers and the free breeze outside the tower. The air was stale and old having been shut up for generations.

The space was secret. Kept hidden from scheming eyes that might want to change the law. And kept secret for hopeful eyes that needed a way out from evil.

Behind Chayse was the false stone bench. In front of her was the curve of the hidden passageway tucked between the space of the chamber wall and the outer stone dressing. There might be space enough for them all. There might be a way out.

She bent down to beckon with her hand through the opening to the others. Queen Regina crawled through first on her hands and knees. Chayse moved down the tunnel to make room.

The lycanthropes and the guards pulled open the door to the bed chamber.

Captain Michael had to hurry. He scurried through. But any second the door to the privy would be opened and their concealment would not be final. They still had to close the opening to the secret passage.

Captain Michael had to lean sideways and push at the stone bench from above. The stone began to grind over the grooves as it moved. Chayse was certain the guards or the lycanthropes would hear it being moved.

Now all three of them were scrunched tight in a hidden pocket—Chayse to Queen Regina to Captain Michael 1-2-3. Caught between the back of the wooden privy wall and the cold outer stone masonry.

Every scratch a thunderstrike. Every breath a scream. Every heartbeat a clap.

It would only be a matter of time before the secret was out.

Just as the stone bench lacked only a centimeter to be flush with the stone wall again, the door to the privy opened. There was no more time to make it perfect. A tiny plane of light shone around all sides of the stone bench until it was blocked.

Blocked by moving shapes. Men. Guards with swords and weapons. Lycanthropes with the power to transmogrify.

Captain Michael tapped Queen Regina on the shoulder and pointed forward so that the queen passed along the command onto Chayse's shoulder since she was in the lead. She didn't want to be but there was no way for her to move to the back. There was barely room to step forward without scrapping the walls. There was no way to see what was in front of her. A gap in the flooring? A trap door? A chute?

But she knew what was behind her: trouble.

Chayse had to push herself through the narrow passage using both arms before her to help pull. Stone scrapped across the grooves behind them. Light shone up from the gap at the bottom of the privy wall.

"Look at the big--" Nicolai began.

"--rats are in the walls!" Victor finished.

Both the lycanthropes poked their heads through the square hole at the same time. Looking very much like a two-headed freak. Or not much different than how they were.

"Running won't help," Victor warned.

"It'll just make the chase more interesting," Nicolai added.

The twins laughed as they began to morph into their shaggy wolf bodies. Their laughter turning into mad barking. Their growing snouts snapping at the open space.

They meant to crawl through the hole and hound them down the passageway. They would tear the trio from limbs to limbs. Captain Michael didn't even have a rifle or a sword.

"Move!" Captain Michael urged.

"They are coming for us!" Queen Regina said.

Chayse felt like a rat in a cage. Boxed in and trapped. Caught on a tight curve. Desperate to breathe deep and free. Longing to be loosed. Run away.

"Here." Chayse dropped to her knees. "Step over me."

She ducked her head down like in a tornado drill.

"Hurry."

The lycanthropes yelped and barked in excitement as their legs splayed out scratching for purchase and their heads darted from side to side trying to get themselves through the opening.

Queen Regina played leapfrog and stepped over the stranger who had come as the guest of her enemy. Then Captain Michael made a long stride over her back. They slipped around the turn into the dark.

"There is a door ahead, Wice!" the queen called back their discovery.

That name stuck in Chayse's throat. That's the only name that Queen Regina knew her by--not her real name and especially not her last name. That was nobody's fault but her own.

"Hurry, girl!" Captain Michael called.

Chayse could hear the groaning of metal hinges as the heavy door swung on long-unused metal. The two would be gone. Escaped. Without her.

No one would get far, though. If the Lycanthrope twins were stopped in their tracks. Chayse wanted to smash their heads in.

With what?

She had something up her sleeve.

Chayse pulled out the vial of quicksilver. In its long slender tube, it looked no different than a thermometer from back in Her World. But instead of viscous mercury, it contained swirling ice crystals in a silver vapor.

The moment the vial came out of her sleeve it shone bright in the dim light. A tiny ball of incandescent silver so harsh Chayse had to squint. Loosed lightning expanded out in all directions. Enveloping Chayse. Striking the stone wall like a hammer and pulverizing dust and bits of masonry. Scorching the backside of the planks in the wooden privy wall. Hitting the twin lycanthropes caught halfway through the opening.

The stone wall began to crumble. The wood burst into consuming flame. The lycanthropes howled in pain.

Chayse was jolted from her head to her toe. Becoming a conductor. An open circuit.

Her muscles contracted.

Her jaw clamped down.

Her throat convulsed.

It was hard to think.

The silver light burned all around her. She was in the middle of a lightning storm. She only wanted the conflagration to stop.

Chayse let go of the vial.

It fell loose from her hand to the stone floor and shattered in a hundred thousand little pieces shooting out all its contents.

The vacuum popped.

The vapor dissipated.

The shards lay lifeless.

The crystals turned into tiny beads of quicksilver.

It was the single most amazing experience of her life.

***

Chapter Thirty-Three: Friend and Foe

Chayse stood there stunned.

The silver light went out with the evaporation of the gas.

The lycanthropes lay in a tumble blocking the escape hatch. Their eyes were wide. Mouths opened. But they did not move a muscle or make a sound.

Chayse was amazed at what she had just done.

But she didn't know what she should do next.

She had just tasted pure power. It cut through her confusion and fear with a knife. She was liberated but she was standing still.

A rough hand clamped on her shoulder and yanked her back.

"Move if you want to live!" It was Captain Michael.

It was painful to turn around with her sides hitting the stone and wood. All over her skin, every nerve was goosed. She was grateful just to be alive as if she had never been awake before.

Chayse followed the captain of the guard around the curve to a large wooden door. The hole framed behind it was cool with a breeze. Blowing up from below.

Captain Michael stepped through and bade her follow.

They descended on stone steps. Cut into the dressing of the stone masonry of the outer wall. It twirled down and around. The air becoming damp and dank.

They were going below the floor of the bailey.

Into the basement of Tower Reign.

Steps winding down in a sloping circle twisting in the dark.

Dangerous treads. Full of dust. Choked with pebbles.

They each hugged the stonemason wall. Feeling along its wet face with their hands. Each step was taken with hazard. Bending the knee. Tapping the edge with the toe. Finding purchase before the next shift of weight downwards.

Not knowing if the next step would be there. Or if time had ravaged it away. Crumbled into vain nothingness.

Finding each step there. One by precious one. A slow descent into hopeful freedom.

Why was there so much darkness in this world? Both the Domain and the Realm were full of dungeons and doors hiding secrets. It was hard to tell the one from the other except for the Ice Prison—that is the one place Chayse feared above all others.

 Captain Michael, who was in front of Chayse now, broke her chain of thoughts with a question:

"Why didn't the Elfwitch just kill us? Having you alive is a threat to her, my queen."

Queen Regina was in the lead answered, "It's expedient for her to keep me as leverage for something or against someone. Who or what I don't know."

"What do you have left that she needs?" Captain Michael asked.

The queen shuddered. "Her very words were 'Your life'. She is beyond evil."

For Chayse, the Elfwitch was like that vial of quicksilver she had just dropped and shattered: cloudy with brief swirling flashes. There was no way to gauge what was in that woman's heart. If it was like a mirror it would be shining back the celestine face of the moon.

"Wice," the queen called back over her shoulder.

"Yes, my queen," Chayse said. She was amazed at how easy she was able to switch gears between "my queen" and "Mom."

"Twice you have called me 'Mom.' Don't think I did not notice. Do I remind you of your mother?" Queen Regina asked.

"Very much so, my queen," Chayse said.

"Have you lost her recently?" the queen asked.

"Yes, my queen," Chayse said. A lump the size of an apple hit got caught in her throat and chest. It was something so raw and powerful that Chayse had thought she had under lock and key. But it seemed to be able to slip out of its cage and run free whenever it wanted. "Not very long ago at all."

"That explains it, then," Queen Regina said. "Was she a kind woman?"

"Uh," Chayse could only think of what made her mad about Mom. The yelling. The ignoring. The grousing. The endless complaining. She had to pause to come up with something that was both true and not hurtful. "She's the hardest worker that I know."

"You say you lost her? Is she dead?" the queen asked.

"No. Very much alive. Just far away from here," Chayse said.

"And it was the Elfwitch who brought you here?" Queen Regina continued.

"Yes, my queen," Chayse said wishing the interview would stop. Not only would it be too hard to explain how she had come to be here, Chayse didn't even think she could try. And combining that confusion with the lump in her throat left Chayse unable to even think.

Captain Michael continued the interview. "Do you have any other family? A father? Brothers or sisters? Or are you an orphan?"

Chayse sighed, "I might as well be an orphan."

"Let it go, good Captain," the queen commanded.

But the good Captain wouldn't let it go. "Wice can't be her name," Captain Michael argued. "That's what carved into the Elfwitch's chest."

As the descent took them down into deeper darkness and colder air, the framing walls of rooms and halls disappeared on their right side. They were heading into the foundation of Tower Reign. The space opened up into unseeable dimensions of stone columns and archways and locked reservoirs.

"Obviously, Wice thinks of me as her mother. Which I can't possibly be since I never married and have no children," Queen Regina said. "Though I am flattered, dear child.

"Wice, you seem more like a vagabond. Washed out in the rain. That is what we all are about to become."

Chayse was getting tired of having to carry two names. She would rather the queen call her by something else. *Daughter.* "Where were you will go?" Chayse asked.

"My queen," Captain Michael growled. "Be warned. The child has not proven fully to me yet whether she is friend or foe."

"I wouldn't harm either of you. You're good people," Chayse said.

They had reached the bottom of the long stairs. Stepping onto the solid ground of bedrock they all held hands to keep together. A quick squeeze of the hand was a precursor to a full-on hug on Chayse from the queen.

She even hugged the same as Mom.

It almost broke Chayse's heart.

Almost.

But there were stone walls around her heart. Thick and strong. High and tall.

"We need light, Captain," Queen Regina said.

The opportunity burst through her confusion and hurt. This was something she knew how to do. Not a trick. But a simple use of power.

"I can do that!" Chayse announced. She reached up her other sleeve, as the Elfwitch had taught her to grab the stashed alchemical item: the large luminescent scarab beetle. She pulled the taxonomic sample out. It had long expired and had been preserved through ways only the Elfwitch knew what. But it looked very much alive and illuminating, though very still.

Only the size of her thumb, it cast a green glow around the trio reaching out to a circle of about five feet.

"A marvel no doubt," Captain Michael scoffed. Chayse was confused as to why the captain did not approve. Had she done something wrong by using this alchemical device? "Didn't you know, my queen, that the Elfwitch can do anything?"

"She can't make me serve her or take her awful mark on my skin," Queen Regina said. "So she's not all-powerful."

Far behind them from another section of the columns and archways came the sound of voices and moving feet.

"But she is cunning," Captain Michael said. "Who else would know of this secret passage?"

Queen Regina blew air out of her mouth. "Kyphus. There's not a drawer he hasn't cracked open or a curtain he hasn't looked behind in the whole tower."

"I'd like to crack him open," Captain Michael said. "But we have no weapons. We cannot be caught here like this. Which way leads out of Tower Reign?"

"Wice, shine your light to the left," Queen Regina commanded.

Chayse shone the green bioluminescent light back towards the end of the stairs. Next to the last tread was an opening in the tower wall. A dark recess. A shadow door.

Closer than they would like it, torches from a squad of guards were moving through the archways and around the forest of stone columns. Kyphus's voice could be heard at the head of the squad. Chayse wondered if the Lycanthrope twins had recovered or had she wounded them badly?

"That is the way," the queen directed.

Captain Michael went into the darkened alcove first. Then the queen followed taking Chayse by the wrist so that the green light from the beetle could light the way.

The passage was encased with brick and tile. It was old and over time water and weight from above had cracked the walls and pulled sections done. Having to dart around piles of rubble and collapsed beams made the going slow.

The torchlight reached the mouth of the passageway behind them. The voice became excited.

"They see our light," Captain Michael said.

"They can't fly over this mess any faster than we can," the queen pointed out.

"I wish we could fly," Chayse said out loud. "Where does this lead?"

"Careful, my queen," Captain Michael growled.

"We are out of Tower Reign and should be under the bailey. Hopefully under the Tower Gate. Through the Curtain Wall. And then Castle Town. All the way to the Outskirts," Queen Regina said as they climbed over a beam and a between two piles of bricks and dirt.

"And then where?" Chayse asked. "Is there anywhere safe from the Elfwitch?"   "My queen," Captain Michael complained.

"Captain!" Queen Regina said. "Wice is not our enemy. She is a girl. Perhaps led astray. But I see no evil in her."

The captain of the now-defunct guard, the only man left of the Queen's Men, came to a halt. "You have a habit of seeing only what you want to see."

The queen did not stop. Nor said a word. But kept right on moving down the passageway.

The way was sloping upwards. Back towards the surface. There was growing light like the tendrils of dawn coming from the other end.

"You think all this is my fault?" the queen grumbled over her shoulder. "My only crime was falling in love. That made me blind. And rebellious to my father's wishes.

"None of this would have happened if he had not died.

"My father was a wise man. He would have found a way to make this all work out for the benefit of the Realm and for my heart.

"His passing was the beginning of the treachery. The Black Watch did not like the choice of my heart. Nor the High Priest. Nor you, I take it. Yet, you alone have remained loyal.

"It is because of my guilt that I have brought this misery upon the Realm. Upon the Root of Lyftwych. I surrendered the token of my promise. I gave up my heart's wishes.

"But that was the betrayal.

"It is the fault of the Black Watch. They freed the Elfwitch. I took her as my counselor. Twelve years of her poison in my ear. She has used my guilt to steal away the Realm. It is she who brought the Darkness. Caused the Moon to outshine the Sun.

"While I stood by and did nothing. Thinking that the last evil would be the last to endure. But there is always another evil the Elfwitch brings.

"Now she wants to grow her evil everywhere. It must be stopped.

"I will do whatever I must. Find whatever help I can. Where ever I can."

The mention of the Lyftwych name pushed down the lump in Chayse's throat. It moved aside the hurt. Cut through the confusion. She was a Leftwich!

"What is the Root of Lyftwych?" Chayse asked.

"The founder of my family. The first Lyftwych that the Son of the Judge put on Castle Seat. Frederick Lyftwych," Queen Regina said.

Chayse stopped dead in her tracks. Her mouth fell open.

Both Queen Regina and Captain Michael turned around to check on her.

Chayse couldn't believe it. Nor could she contain it. It was beyond odd. Too impossible for a coincidence. "That. Is. My. Dad!"

Secrets. Revelations. Knowledge. Truth.

Once a secret was out how could a truth ever be taken back? Could the truth be forgotten? How could both things be true at once?

It had just happened to Chayse. But now Chayse remembered who she was.

"That will be enough," commanded a cold celestine voice.

It came from in front of them.

"Too much will spoil the fun. And give the game away. My queen, I would not heed the words of Wice. She is a stranger to our lands. A lost orphan. Looking for a family. Any family. She would say anything.

"Wice, I am surprised by you. And impressed. You are learning quickly. You are exceeding as an acolyte."

It was the voice of the Elfwitch. Miss Elsie Crutch. The same tone. Harsh and menacing.

But they could not see her.

"Acolyte?" Queen Regina called out. "She says she is a Lyftwych."

"I say she is a liar," the Elfwitch said.

"So are you," the queen returned.

"I say whoever has the power makes the truth known. I am the Power. And I make the Truth," the Elfwitch said.

She revealed herself to them. Like stepping out from a curtain of black. First, she wasn't there then she was not more than ten yards from them.

The Elfwitch stood alone in her black raven feather robe with her slender crown of silver on her head. Without a weapon. Without her two human watchdogs.

She didn't need them.

Her mere presence held them in thrall. Imperious mien. Corrupted authority.

"My pet, you need to choose whom you will serve this day. As for me and my house, I will serve the Darkness," the Elfwitch said and put her hands on her hips.

Behind them, the torchlights of their pursuers poked through the ruinous passageway. Voices carried before their steps. Soon the trio would be caught between the hammer and the anvil.

The way out lay blocked.

They would have to either go through the Elfwitch. Find a way around her. Or surrender.

"Sorry about Nic and Vic," Chayse said. "But you did want me to learn by discovery."

The Elfwitch chortled. "They will recover. And may take it up with you. Let's see what else you have learned."

In a fluid motion, she pulled a vial out of the fold of her sleeve popped the top off and flicked the vial to the passageway floor where it shattered. Black smoke rising expanded out and took on the form of a dragon with hollow eyes and an open maw for a mouth.

Queen Regina and Captain Michael backed down the passageway.

"Don't be afraid!" Chayse said. "It's not real. It's a trick."

Chayse stepped forward to face the black smoky dragon as it breathed smoke out of its hollow nose that circled back around into its hind legs. She walked into the monster as the smoke wavered and split in two. Her wake made some of the smoke evaporate.

The two halves reassembled into two new shapes. Both bipedal. One taller and fully formed with a black robe and crown. The other one smaller and thin with jeans and a chevron shirt.

"It's supposed to be your dad. And my brother," Chayse said. "A mean trick."

Chayse stretched out her hand and waved through the two black apparitions. They dissipated altogether. "Is that how you made the Brazzles?"

The Elfwitch curled her lips. She clutched at the chain of her necklace. "I could crush you all. Put you into a prison this size of a tiny cube. And set you on a shelf like a trophy."

Queen Regina called her bluff. "Then do it! We are not your playthings. Unless you are scared of us, then kill your enemies. If it were me, I would not hesitate."

The pursuers had caught up with them. High Priest Kyphus in the lead of a score of Turncoat soldiers wearing black and silver-bearing rifles. He raised his hand for them to stop as they blocked the passageway.

"High Priest Kyphus, take the two rebels into custody and prepare for an execution," the Elfwitch said.

"I don't think you will," Chayse said.

Kyphus looked astounded. "You don't, do you?"

"I think you will let them pass unharmed," Chayse said.

Kyphus looked insulted. "You do, do you?"

The Elfwitch looked amused. "Why, my pet, you grow by caprice and bluff. Take them away. All of them."

Chayse swept the second vial out of her hand. Holding it high between her fingers so that the Elfwitch was sure to see it.

"You know which one this is," she told the Elfwitch.

The Elfwitch's face turned to stone. "And you do not understand the one you have purloined."

Even Kyphus took a step back. He understood the power of words. He owed his position to twisting them. But as to alchemical knowledge, he was a dunce.

"Oh, I know exactly what it is," Chayse said. "And I understand exactly what it does."

"What is it, Wice?" Queen Regina asked.

"It's a transmogrifier," Chayse said. "It changes things. I've seen it change hair to quills. Bone to horns. Changes small animals into bigger monsters. But it drives them mad. Eats up their brains."

"You saw it dropped in their water supply. It only works by direct ingestion," the Elfwitch said. She put out her hand. "Hand it over."

Kyphus waved the Turncoats forward to arrest them all.

"Then why don't you take it from me yourself?" Chayse asked.

When the Elfwitch neither answered nor moved, Kyphus made the Turncoats stand down.

"I wonder what would happen if I threw it on the ground?" Chayse asked. Then made ready to through the vial onto the ground. "Let's find out!"

The Elfwitch flinched and Kyphus put his arm over his face. The Turncoats took quite a few steps back ready to start a rout.

Breath by breath, the Elfwitch relaxed and regained her composure. "That would be very unwise, my pet."

"Then let them pass. Let them leave here unharmed," Chayse said.

The Elfwitch jumped at the order and began to slice it. "These two only. You will stay behind. With me. That is my offer. Take it now."

"No, Wice. You must come with us. Do not stay here with the Elfwitch," Queen Regina urged.

"Enough of your prattle. Take my offer or use the transmogrifier. When I count three, Kyphus will lead the charge. You'll all be cut down," the Elfwitch promised.

Then she lifted a slender thumb. "Wice, my pet, find out what the transmogrifier can truly do. That is one by my count."

Kyphus waved the squad of Turncoat traitors forward a step.

"When the vial breaks and the liquid is loosed, everyone around the transmogrifier will be at risk," the Elfwitch said. "Even a vapor taken into one's lungs will cause its fibers to change. Turn into feathers. Clog a person's airways. Cause them to suffocate. Turn them inside out into an egg. Their brain will become like a yolk. Then their head will crack."

Her slender forefinger popped up perpendicular to her thumb making a right angle L. "That's two."

Kyphus and the squad took another lock step forward.

How was this any different than dealing with Mom? Wasn't the Elfwitch a woman? When she was Miss Elsie Crutch did she get everything she wanted?

Chayse/Wice knew one thing. She knew how to call a bluff. So she turned to the queen.

"Better run."

Then she threw the vial. Behind her. At the feet of the High Priest Kyphus and the squad of Turncoats.

First, Captain Michael grabbed the queen by the elbow and pulled her past Wice and the Elfwitch. Toward the dark aperture. The escape tunnel leading under the gates and walls.

Then Chayse/Wice ran after them. Away from the freed contents of the transmogrifier. Past the Elfwitch. Racing toward freedom.

Behind her, the sealed liquid escaped from the exploding vacuum. It sucked air back in all around it. Shaking the foundation of the tower.

The smell was abhorrent. Overpowering her nose. Like a sledgehammer between her eyes.

Billowing vapors rolled up from the ground like a fog. Encompassing Kyphus and all of the Turncoat squad. They screamed to high heaven as if their skin were boiling and their eyes were being eaten away.

The Elfwitch let Captain Michael and Queen Regina pass. But she snatched Chayse/Wice. Clutching her tight with long slender nails that pierced her skin.

"You've been naughty, my pet. You have shown resolve. Free will even. How dare you," the Elfwitch chided her.

Chayse struggled. Threw kicks and flying elbows. But the Elfwitch stood behind her with her leg planted against the small of her back.

Chayse couldn't wiggle free.

So Wice quit struggling.

"There, my pet. That's better," the Elfwitch soothed.

The vapors drifted towards them. So the Elfwitch carried Wice like a load through the aperture. Further down the tunnel.

Kyphus and the others fell to the floor convulsing. All shakes and tremors. Their nervous functions no longer their own. Their body systems in flux. Their brains overloaded with the shock to the changing cellular structure.

They no longer could even scream.

The Elfwitch let loose of Wice. Turned her round. Brought up her chin with slender fingers to look into her young acolyte's eyes.

"The queen and her captain no longer matter to me. I know where they are headed. They will find no solace there. Only more disappointment.

"Come. Let's see if we can undo the mess that you made of my followers."

***

Chapter Thirty-Four: Hook and Crook

Freedom had been short. Way too short.

It was like taking a quick breath. Getting out for recess between math and reading class—the two subjects he liked least.

And on top of it, Reed had been able to spend time with Dad. No, someone who looked like Dad. Frehley acted so much like Dad, it wasn't funny. In Reed's heart, Frehley was Dad.

But now Reed had been taken away from Dad all over.

And put in another cell. The smallest one yet. With the man who was to blame.

Reed looked in scorn at his odious cellmate. "At least they could've put me in my own cell."

Apparently, there weren't any other cells. They had to share this grand accommodation.

The room they were in was only six feet wide and six feet to the ceiling. There was a window set with three metal rods. It was too high up for them to gaze out. A metal door choked off the room. A service hole was the only opening to the corridor outside.

They had been shut away. Put in time out. Locked up in a closet.

"It's to punish me more than you, kid," Cyrus said. He kept his balding head in his hands. The hairs on his arms weaving in with the wild receding nest along the temples of his face.

"I'm so sorry," Cyrus said and sucked up tears.

"Yeah, you said that. Like ten thousand times already," Reed said.

This was too much: being imprisoned, then escaping, then getting caught again. He wanted to kick the burly man. Right in the ribs.

"My wife. My kid. Gone. This whole time," Cyrus said. "I'm nothin' but a fool."

Reed rolled his eyes. "Knock it off! I've lost Mom!" He put up his thumb and kept count on successive fingers. "Dad. Sissy. Then Frehley. And now Packy."

"Again with that rat!" Cyrus snapped. "Why do you love that rat so much?"

"He was my friend!" Reed yelled. "Better a friend than you! And he's dead, too. Because of you."

"I wish I was dead," Cyrus moaned. "But I doubt death will give me peace. Probably just end up like the Deadcoats."

Reed was too angry to give up hope. Being so close to the person he most hated kept him keyed up. He'd escape again if he could just to get away from Cyrus once and for all.

"I don't even know where we are."

Cyrus sniffed up snot and tears. "The Royal Forest. This is one of the Deadcoat's Martello towers. It's a small garrison. 'Bout twenty troopers and some cannon.

"The walls are thick and the ramparts flat so they can point the cannon in any direction they need to and blast anyone that tries to come at them. They started buildin' these when the Black Watch forced the queen's hand. Got a whole string of these between Tower Reign and the Keep."

"I've been to the Keep. So how far away is this Tower Reign?" Reed asked.

"Well, I can't be too exact. Probably a day or more's ride," Cyrus said. Probably just as grateful to take his mind off his hurt as Reed was about his dire circumstances.

"How far away are we from where we were in Outlaw Forest?" Reed asked.

Cyrus shrugged. "At least a couple of days. If you're thinkin' that Frehley's gonna spring us just give that up right now. It was yer gold coin that freed us last time and I fixed it so that you don't even have that anymore.

"Our only hope might if you knew what happened to that silver necklace the Elfwitch wants so bad."

"Why can't you understand I lost the necklace?" Reed felt like he was talking to Mom. Mom just went on and on about stuff. She never let up. "Packy took it."

"I really, really don't wanna face the Destroyer again. We gotta have somethin' to trade or barter with," Cyrus said rubbing his beard between his fingers. "By hook or crook."

"Isn't that how you got the both of us in here? Thinkin' the Elfwitch was gonna help you if you helped her? She's an evil liar," Reed said.

"Well, the Elfwitch's the one callin' the shots now. The queen never married. She has no kids. The Root of Lyftwych will die out with her. Then the Darkness will reign forever," Cyrus said. "How could things possibly be any worse?"

Every time Reed had heard his last name being used, it was like some kind of cruel joke was being played on him. Somehow the name was important here. But it also brought back all the hurt of Reed's broken home—both he and sis had been embarrassed by his parents in Judge Hart's courtroom.

And then there was the promise Reed had made to Moor Kreed--*don't speak your name here!*

Except that it didn't help explain anything. Too much about this place was so confusing. It was like Reed was looking at his own world turned upside down.

"Why does a Regent have to be a Lyftwych?" Reed asked.

Cyrus shook his head. "I can't believe yer a stranger here when you've carried not only a silver necklace but one of the Regents' own gold coins. But you don't know nothin' 'bout the Lyftwyches.

"Well, I can't remember why the Son picked the Lyftwyches. But he did. The Root of Lyftwych was Federick Lyftwych. He was the first to rule at Tower Reign. But that was generations ago. Now the queen's the last Lyftwych we have left."

Reed stood up. The thunderbolt was still racing round his head. Quickening every nerve and thought.

It was a realization. Like a steely edged weapon. Cutting through the confusion. Giving him surety.

What Reed had now was the TRUTH. "No, she's not."

"Well, well!" called a voice through the service hole.

A broad face darkened the opening. With half the side of it exposed back to muscle and bone. Ripped from the chin up to the left eye socket.

"Me beauties are up and at 'em!" chided Sergeant Hood. If there was anyone Reed had met in the Domain or the backside of the Realm who thrived on cruelty it was this man. Or what was left of him.

"You don't look too spry yerself, Hoodie," Cyrus said.

"But yer fer gettin' one thing," Hoodie smiled. "I'm on this side of the jail cell door."

Cyrus shrugged. "Yer in jail, too. Maybe not in this cell with us. In case you ain't forgotten, yer cursed. And you can't escape it.

"When was the last time you had a day off, Hoodie? When did you eat dinner last with yer very own family? What would they think if they saw you now?"

Hood's face screwed up and he shoved a leprous hand through the service hole. "I'm gonna break you both. Startin' right now."

He withdrew his hand and began to unlock the cell door. When it opened, Sergeant Hood pushed it back to reveal himself and two more Deadcoats standing in a narrow hallway. The sergeant uncoiled a whip in his hands.

"We got us a nice tree to hang you both from. But that don't mean I can't soften up yer hide. Just a little," Sergeant Hood announced with a crack of the whip.

Another figure came to the door pushing the other two Deadcoats. Tall and gaunt. With an officer's pipping on his red tunic. And a large tri-corner hat with a feather in it.

The man said not a word. His gaze gave his commands. Only that he didn't have eyes.

It was Lieutenant Grey. He pointed at the sergeant and then pointed back down the hall.

"Yes, Lieutenant," Sergeant said as he coiled back up his whip.

Then the menacing officer used his first two fingers to indicate first the two other troopers and then the two prisoners and then the outer cell wall.

The two soldiers saluted and came forward to lay hands on Cyrus and Reed.

"This is it, kid," Cyrus said as the Deadcoats brought them up to their feet to escort them out. "Be brave. Make sure to put in a good word to the Judge. I'll need it."

"I wish you'd stop callin' me 'kid,'" Reed said as a trooper walked him out behind Cyrus.

"Yer gonna get yer wish alright," Cyrus said as he was led down the narrow hallway. "Here in a minute, I won't be sayin' much of nothin'."

They were marched down the narrow hall that arced with an open door into an armory room with pistols, muskets, cases of shot, and powder kegs lined against the curved walls. Then they went through a set of double doors that led outside. They paraded out into a wide circular courtyard inside the Martello tower.

The rampart walls were only thirty feet high and very thick. Sections were painted with black lines with three sets of numbers. The first number had a circle behind it. The second number had a single apostrophe behind it. The third number had two apostrophes.

It reminded Reed of a clock face. But this one was laid out horizontal to stand on and not a vertical clock hanging from the wall. The markings were geometric then. Designating a circle.

But every circle needed a center. A place from which to reckon the points. And in the middle of the courtyard stood a large oak tree. Next to a small brook. The brook ran in under the Martello tower at one point and back out under another point on the side of the circle.

The Deadcoats hadn't dammed the brook up: they had simply built over it. Two tiny sluice gates allowed the brook entrance and exit. The nourishing waters dribbled into the courtyard to feed the mighty forlorn oak wrapped in grey under the silvery light.

High above the tower walls, the stars twinkled in the cold sky. The moon face had dropped its gaze and pulled a black shawl over its stolen glory. Everything cast long shadows: the Deadcoats' heads, Reed's legs, and the Martello tower walls. But the oak tree's branches made the longest ones.

Some of the leaves hung down and seemed to stand up. Some of them seemed to lit and move. Bob and weave. They weren't leaves. They were birds. Large black crows. Come to roost. Making the tree branches their table. Waiting for a feast.

Two shadows hung side by side from the thickest branches. Like straight vines. Hanging perpendicular from the tree branches to the ground. Reed had to swallow hard when he realized that they were two vines—they were two ropes.

Twisted corded rope. Ending in two loops. Two round nooses.

The Deadcoats were about to hang Reed and Cyrus.

He was about to die.

Reed's knees turned to water. His mouth to ash.His eyes fixed on that unstoppable calamity.

Now more than ever Reed needed a savior.

Where was Dad?

A world away.

Where was Frehley?

Left behind in Outlaw Forest.

There was no one.

Except Cyrus, his betrayer. And with whom he now was going to die beside.

"You fixed us both good," Reed condemned.

"Don't worry, kid," Cyrus said as he limped ahead never taking his eyes off the double set of nooses. "When we stand before the Judge, my kid will be there asking, 'Why?'" His words jammed in his throat. Lodged down with tears. "I don't have a good answer. I screwed up. And I am so, so sorry."

"The prisoners will shut it!" Sergeant Hood commanded from behind. "Detail halt!"

The Deadcoats came to a dead stop under the spreading shadow of the oak. The sudden movement made the crows jump. They jackjawed in surprise. Calling and mocking. They were about to given two new scarecrows which they could make blind.

Both Sergeant Hood in his rotting parade tunic and Lieutenant Gray in his corrupted finest officer coat came to face the detail.

The lieutenant drew a circle in the air with a bony finger. The signal to start the proceedings. So the sergeant began with the charges first.

"You are both pronounced enemies of the Darkness--"

"And proud of it," Cyrus interrupted.

"--Traitors to progress--"

"Nah. Yer progress is hell. And I don't want to live in hell one day longer," Cyrus contested.

"--Haters of the Elfwitch--"

"Why is that so bad? We are to hate evil. If we love evil we will be cursed. You all love her and what happened? She cursed you," Cyrus said.

Lieutenant clutched Cyrus' throat with one hand to draw the prisoner's face near his rotting own. The empty sockets held dark negative space. Where the eyes—the light of the soul—once dwelled only to have plucked out by crows. The lieutenant shoved the forefinger of his other hand in Cyrus' face. Daring him to continue his tirade during the charges.

Sergeant Hood continued. Uninterrupted."--Spurners of her power. Deniers of her control. Betrayers of her will. You are both abhorrent and wretched in her sight.

"Unless either of you two yardbirds produces a quicksilver heart necklace here and now, you both will be hung by the neck until you are dead. Here and now."

"I've told you over and over again," Reed said with the double nooses reflecting in his eyes. "I lost my necklace. But if I did still have it I'd turn both of you into dust. Here and now."

"Woo-hoo, kid!" Cyrus shouted. "You tell 'em! They'd kill us even if you gave 'em what they wanted. Gettin' called 'abhorrent and wretched' by the likes of them is a left-handed compliment."

Lieutenant Gray indicated the double nooses. The Deadcoat detail pushed the two prisoners square under the loops. There wasn't a gallows stand. There weren't any steps or stool. The Deadcoats meant to haul the two prisoners up and tie off the ropes to let them twist in the wind.

The troopers put the thick noose over their heads and across their faces and under their chin. The coarse fibers biting into their neck. The ends burning against their ears.

The noose pushed against Reed's throat. Making it hard to swallow. The sergeant checked the rope's slack and position.

"Take a good look at Hoodie, kid," Cyrus said. "He's from my own village. We were practically neighbors. Good ol' Hoodie. Never married. Took the Blackwatch vow. Rode off to become a hero. 'Cept he turned into a monster."

As he talked, his words were swallowed up by the tightening rope. Choked off by the punishment about to commence.

"At least we found a way to shut you up," Seargeant Hood said.

"Don't bet on it," Cyrus said in a forced whisper.

Sergeant Hood stepped back and nodded to the two troopers who each took a hold of the ends of the rope and began to haul away.

Reed felt the pull of the rope under his chin. Against his ears. Tightening around his neck like a cruel hand.

His free hands went up to the noose to try and pry it off or at least get his fingers under the rope.

He couldn't.

His body began to lift. Only his toes touched the ground.

The crows began to jump on their branches and hop their feet in happy anticipation. They had front row seats to the upcoming meal about to be served.

"Hello! The tower!" cried a voice from outside the Martello Tower walls.

When there was no response from the detail in the courtyard, another shout followed quick.

"Hoodie! You in there?!"

It was Frehley.

At last.

Come to save them.

How?

They were inside hanging from a tree.

And he was on the outside.

Sergeant Hood looked to Lieutenant Grey who shook his head.

"We're just a li'l busy at the moment!" Sergeant Hood growled. "Come back and surrender later!"

Frehley's reply came back. "I've got what you want!"

"And what might that be?" Sergeant Hood asked.

"A heart necklace. Made with pure quicksilver. Made by the best silversmith!" Frehley declared.

Lieutenant Grey made a slash at his own throat with the back of his hand.

"Let 'em down," Sergeant Hood growled.

The Deadcoats let go of their slack and the ropes fell to the ground pulled by the weight of the prisoners' bodies. Both Reed and Cyrus fell to their sides panting for breath and clawing at the ropes under their chins to free their throats to be able to breathe deeper.

"I'll offer you a deal!" Frehley called over the wall. "The necklace for the boy! Free him unharmed and I'll give you the necklace right in yer grubby hands."

Sergeant Hood again looked at his commanding officer. Lieutenant Grey gave one nod.

"The necklace fer the boy? The boy only?" Sergeant Hood asked for clarification.

"Yes!" Frehley called back. He was close. Maybe right outside the gate.

Some Deadcoat troopers were climbing stairs to the upper rampart. Others to the front gates.

Lieutenant Grey pointed to Cyrus who had just sat up to try and slip loose of the noose. Then the Deadcoat officer pointed back to the upper branches of the oak tree. The two Deadcoat troopers laid hold of him.

Cyrus slammed the two together and knocked them down. They both fell on top of the burly man as a mad scramble ensued.

Both Lieutenant Grey and Sergeant Hood pulled out their matchlock pistols thumbing them to a half-cock as they drew down on the trigger and aimed at the pile of people.

Cyrus kicked the two Deadcoats away and swung the butt of a musket at Reed's feet. Knocking him down to the ground. Cyrus pounced on him putting an arm around the boy's throat and putting the barrel of the musket to his head.

"I'll kill the kid before you drop me. And then no necklace fer you," Cyrus said. "You'll have to answer to the Elfwitch. I'll have to answer to the Judge and my dead kid. Wanna take yer chances?"

The Deadcoat troopers unbolted the tower gates and pulled them back. In strode Frehley. Yet, he was not alone. The hulking Strap shadowed his steps. Both of them had their hands up.

"Cyrus!" Frehley cursed. "You big idiot!"

The crows atop the oak tree had had enough. In mass, they took wing to the dark sky and made like an arrow over the Martello tower wall back towards Tower Reign. Squawking their displeasure at the turn of events like a siren.

***

Chapter Thirty-Five: Trade and Fair

"I'm walkin' out of here, Frehley," Cyrus announced. "With the boy and that necklace."

"You're a stone in my boot," Frehley complained. "You know that?"

Behind him, Strap glowered and slapped his fist into his other open hand letting Cryus know what he would get if the giant ever got his beefy hands on him again.

"More like a thorn in the side," Sergeant Hood grumbled.

"Better than havin' a tickle in my throat," Cyrus said. "So what's it gonna be?"

Lieutenant Grey shook his head.

"We ain't seen the necklace so no one gets nothin'. And no one's goin' nowhere. We can just string y'all up and be done with this whole mess in one quick jerk o' the rope!" Sergeant Hood promised. He waved the two troopers nearest the tree forward.

Side by side they approached Frehley and Strap with muskets at the ready, barrels aimed, bayonets pointed. Both Frehley and Strap pushed the barrels down as they spun around to the side of the troopers and hip tossed them both while wrenching their muskets away from them.

Sergeant Hood cursed. Now the intruders were armed. But with Frehley aiming his purloined musket at Cyrus and Strap aiming his at the sergeant himself. This was about to turn into a free-for-all.

Lieutenant Grey pulled out his saber and pointed first to the upper ramparts and then down at his feet. The troopers above on the wall took firing positions on all four walls while a crew pulled one of the cannon around to load and aim it at the inner courtyard. The ante had just been upped.

"That's fine then, Lieutenant," Frehley said taking a step forward every other word or so. "Everyone's got nothin' to lose. So everyone goes up in a blaze of glory. Then we'll all stand before the Judge. I, myself, can claim no goodness in me. I can only claim his Son.

"And right here and now, I ain't got nothin' good to offer. Not even my own life in the place of this boy. But I swear to you I have something you hold more precious than both our lives.

"I'm talkin' precious metal. Better than gold or silver. I'm talkin' quicksilver."

"Yer talkin' a bluff. As you keep walkin'. With muskets pointed every which way," Sergeant Hood laughed. He watched Lieutenant Grey point with his saber from the cannon being readied down to the courtyard. "And I ain't sorry to say as soon as the gunners are ready, I get to blow you skyhigh. Straight to the Judge. Tell him I said 'hallo.'"

Frehley kept walking. Step by step. Inch by inch. Not towards Cyrus who clutched onto Reed and his musket. But beyond. "Give me five minutes of yer cursed time. And I'll hand over what the Elfwitch's wanted so bad these twelve long years.

"It was supposed to be a token love for me. But it's become a curse."

"Frehley, don't you come over here," Cyrus said clutching Reed tighter and the musket barrel closer. "Don't you make me do it."

"No one's made you do anything, Cyrus. You've chosen every step of yer own way," Frehley argued. "Haven't you figured that out, yet?"

Cyrus responded by cocking the musket back another pound of draw. He was desperate for his life enough to take Reed's. Because fear drove all his decisions.

Reed had slipped off the noose around his neck just to have it replaced with an arm lock. Hadn't Cyrus been beside himself while they had cooled their heels in the tiny cell? The man was a coward through and through. He didn't deserve to even have a daughter in the first place. Would Cyrus dare hold a musket to her head?

Frehley put up his hand to stay both Reed's fear and Cyrus' desperation. Pointing the musket down, he unscrewed the bayonet off and tossed the musket to the ground. Walking past Cyrus and his hostage, Frehley came beneath the oak—the same oak where he had once made a vow that had somehow turned this world upside down. He dropped to his knees— unlike the first time where he had only dropped to one—and began to dig between the exposed roots of the mighty oak.

Cyrus watched him in fascination.

Reed watched him perplexed.

Strap shook his head.

But Sergeant Hood nodded to Lieutenant Grey who gave a hand signal for the gunners to stand down but only when they had their cannon pointed ready at the center of the courtyard.

"You just might save yer neck yet, Frehley," Sergeant Hood said.

"I don't care what happens to me," Frehley said. "I just want the boy to get back home."

He went back to digging the hardscrabble ground with the small point of the bayonet. It was long enough to flick up dirt like a spoon.

Sergeant Hood did his best to guffaw out of the good side of his mouth but it involved a lot of spittle while Lieutenant Grey blew stale air out of his lips.

"What about me?" Cyrus moaned. "I can't go back home."

Frehley didn't consider him but kept right on digging. "Is that why you got a gun turned on a boy?"

Cyrus shifted his grip on the end of the stock and under the trigger. "Doesn't matter. The Deadcoats still got a cannon pointed down our throats. And yer the one who's givin' up."

"I ain't givin' up this necklace to save my own skin like you would've, Cyrus. I'm just now wisin' up. I wasn't able to keep what I loved but that don't mean I have to give up hope. You've lost all hope because you couldn't keep what you loved," Frehley said as he dug and flicked at the rocky soil between the oak tree's roots.

Then he hooked the bayonet on something that he could not pull out. He reached into the narrow hole with his fingers and clawed at the damp ground.

Frehley sat back on his haunches as he pulled out a dirty chain necklace. But even with twelve years worth of dirt and red clay, Reed could see the glint of quicksilver. A pulsing hue. A rare luminescence. Radiating out from the center of a heart.

Like a magnet, it drew everyone's eyes. Like a center, it drew everyone's desire. It was the most sought treasure in the Realm. It was the most useful power source in the Domain.

And while quicksilver didn't grow on trees or lie just under the ground, this one had been buried for twelve long years in plain sight beneath everyone's noses.

"Use it, Frehley!" Cyrus shouted. "Use it on these Deadcoats! Get us out of here!"

Lieutenant Grey pointed to the troopers along the rampart wall with the tip of his sword. They took dead aim at Reed, Cyrus, and Frehley.

"Drop it, Frehley," Sergeant Hood growled. "Or we'll drop you all."

"It might be a trade," Cyrus said. "But it's not fair. Frehley, give me the necklace."

***

KINGDOM

Chapter Thirty-Six: X and Y

Queen Regina and her last trusted servant, Captain Michael, were long gone. Down the tunnel.

Through the shadows.

To the exit somewhere.

Under the tower walls.

Escaped to freedom.

Wice was glad for them. At least they had gotten away.

Chayse hadn't.

Held fast in the Elfwitch's grasp. Caught tight in her long icy fingers. Chayse had been ensnared.

Ever since she had come to the Domain and then the Realm, Wice hadn't been more than a few steps away from the Elfwitch. Even when Wice had been Chayse back in her World, her mom hadn't spent near that much time with her.

But being in the Elfwitch's grasp was like being grounded to her room on a Saturday afternoon. With Mom checking on her again and again to make sure Chayse was miserable. It turned Chayse's room into a tomb.

Wice had had enough.

She bit at the hand that held her back. The Elfwitch hissed. Then she spun Wice around and slapped her across the cheek.

Chayse might have cowered but as Wice, she wasn't about to turn the other cheek. So she lashed out with a kick. But the Elfwitch grasped her ankle and flipped Wice over to the ground.

She was alone. In the twilight. In the dark. In the everlasting night. Down on the ground. Under the foundation of Tower Reign.

With no one to rescue her from the Elfwitch.

"Very noble of you my pet," the Elfwitch said. The sound of that jolting voice made Wice twitch.

The Elfwitch continued. "It does not matter if the queen and her dog getaway. There is no one left to help them. Neither have they anything that can hurt me nor anything that I want."

The silvery words slipped down further down Chayse's ear.

"You, I have watched for eons," The Elfwitch moved her hands over Wice's shoulders as if she were anointing her. "From the darkness I watched you be formed and laid my plans for you. And when you were brought out of the womb I knew you would have a place here."

Wice could not see in the darkness. It was cold and damp. The cave was no better than eternal blindness.

But a realization dawned on her like a sun coming over the knobs and hills of Shiloh. How could the Elfwitch have known Chayse before she had been born? Or for that matter, how could the Elfwitch have been Miss Elsie Crutch in her World but have been here in the Realm for twelve years before that and way before that been locked in Ice Prison for who knows how long?

"You couldn't have known me before Chayse was born," Wice argued. "When you were a CASA agent you could've gotten access to our file. You could've found out anything you wanted about me and my family. Easier than any hacker could've."

The Elfwitch's fingers dug into her shoulders like ravens' talons. They might have been a raven's talons for all she knew. Wice couldn't see the Elfwitch's face to see if she had turned into a huge ugly raven. It was so dark Wice couldn't even see her hand.

It was like they had been locked away in the dungeon of the universe without light or color or other people. It was like being back in the womb. Shut off from everything except sound.

The Elfwitch released her. Wice became lighter. Even though she could still feel the dress on her body and hear her heartbeat, Wice was disappearing.

The Elfwitch asked, "Do you remember how you came to be here?"

"Yes," Wice said. "You brought us through Osage Cave."

The Elfwitch said, "We crossed over the sea of Eternity."

Wice didn't want to listen. Wice couldn't help but listen. Because she couldn't stop her hearing. That was the only sense that was still working. Eyes: useless. Touch: untrustworthy without the eyes. Smell: plugged up. Taste: shut off.

There was no method. Only madness. Time. Eternity. Space. All crushed together like a flattened soda can.

"From one world to another," the Elfwitch said.

She wasn't using Spell Speak. Yet, every word that the Elfwitch spoke was a maple flyer in her fertile little mind. The flyer twirled down and took root as a thought. Each thought blossoming into images suggested by the Elfwitch's words.

With four of her five senses out of action, Wice's mind began to make intuitive leg leaps across oceans of logical obstacles.

"What was there before?" she asked.

"Nothing," the Elfwitch said.

"Wasn't God there? Isn't there a Heaven?" Wice asked.

"You mean the Judge. He came later," the Elfwitch answered. "As for an all-knowing, all-loving god, there is none. And since there is no god, there is no heaven."

She was speaking madness. And yet there was a method to that madness.

Wice's brain was a train. And on that train was her soul: her personality and her dual identity. Fear was the coal that fed the speed. Gathering up steam, it raced over the tracks.

Her soul along for the ride going down the line. Growing smaller and smaller until it would recede from existence.

"Believe what I tell you," the Elfwitch suggested.

Soon that method to the madness was the only reality left in her mind.

And if that madness was truth then it could not be madness. It was reality. The only truth.

So Wice chose to believe.

It made things easier.

The Elfwitch said, "This is how it all began: the universe and everything in it was shrunk down into a smudge on a cell inside a mustard seed.

"Everything that has or will or could ever happen-- the past, the present, and all possible futures--was all wrapped up in a single moment.

"Then came the Great Separation. The Darkness awoke and became self-aware. The Great Mother flexed her will and kicked herself free from the womb of the tomb.

"That was the beginning of Time.

"And on that first day, the Darkness came alive. A heart of cold-fire. Feeding and sustaining itself.

"But the cast-off material left behind self-ignited from fear of eternal isolation into the Light. Weaker but full of white-hot anger. That's why it burns so bright.

"And so the struggle between freedom and reunion began.

"Seeking retribution for its hurt, the Light chased after the Darkness to contain it. To make it reunite. And so the Universe was created from the battle between Darkness and Light.

"But the Darkness is faster than the Light. Never forget that. The Great Mother means to outpace the Light and spread it thin like a vapor trail so it just snaps out of existence.

"And just as the Darkness became aware of itself as the Great Mother, the Light fashioned itself into a will called the Judge to fight the Great Mother. The Judge wants only to condemn and punish. That is his nature.

"As pieces of the Light fell away, the Darkness' kicked started them into nebula nurseries to distract the Judge. The Judge further divided itself into the Son and their Spirit so they could try to be everywhere at once to fight the Darkness.

"The nursies came alive with billion of suns that burned with boiling furnaces. And out of those forges came cores of metals: lead, which is the heaviest; next, copper; then, silver and, finally, the weakest of all metals, gold.

"But there was one material left over. One metal that could not be cooled. And if it is put to the forge it will turn to gas. Other metals can attract and retain lightening. This metal can create its own lightning. Quicksilver. Now, do you begin to understand how its properties can serve the Darkness?

"To keep the Great Mother from escaping beyond the Light, the Son turned the metal cores into planets. They sank their weight down in the river of time like anchors and pulled against the Great Mother's escape. Then their Spirit turned some stars inside out to become black holes so that their gravity would drag the Darkness back to the Light.

"That was when the Great Mother fashioned for herself three servants to help do battle with the Judge and his Son and their Spirit. You have seen them all. They have each taken on the shape of a certain fear.

"First, Shadow who takes away people's hope and causes them to freeze with fear.

"Second, Rancor who is a bugbear of enmity and turns love to hate and friends to foes.

"And the third you know well," the Elfwitch said.

Wice turned colder than the foundation stone at the mere thought of the servant in black leather with smiling black lips coming for her. With its claws reaching. Claws creeping. Barely breathing. Loving only to kill.

Wice named the third demon, "the Destroyer."

"The Dark Riders," theElfwitch conceded. "Then the Judge and his Son made two creatures that reflected their own imperfections and flaws: woman and man doomed forever to conflict and unhappiness.

"So the Dark Riders brought fear and death to all humans. That is true justice. Only fear makes everyone alive. Only death makes everyone equal.

"But the Judge became jealous of the Great Mother's power. So he made the Law. And this is the Law: everyone is to obey the Judge by bowing down to Him and his Son. But if people do not bow down to him, the Judge will throw them into oblivion.

"Now does that sound like a loving god? Why did the Judge even make people if he's only going to cause them pain? Death is a gift compared to that.

"All this I saw as I dreamed for a thousand years. Much like you are seeing now. With your eyes closed and your mind open to the Heart of Darkness."

There was a question burning inside Wice. Pushing its way to the front of her mind. Unfettered from the terrors she had seen and her fear of what lurked in the shadows.

"How did you become the Elfwitch?" Wice asked.

The Elfwitch began again, "I was born the youngest of seven sons to a family of shepherds in a village called Star Hill in the old mountains to the North. All of my family had been either mauled by predators while protecting the sheep or marred by smallpox that had claimed three of my younger siblings.

"But I was unblemished. Without spot. Or broken bone. So I became a scapegoat for family's every misfortune. I was beaten and bruised. I was rejected and despised. My own received me not.

"One day I realized that sheep were the stupidest of all the Judge's animals and that people are no better off. Sheep cry when predators come and use them for food but do not fight back. People can't even spot the predators hiding among them.

"I say the Judge is evil and unjust. He let my family kick me out of their hut. He caused the village to cast me out. I would see the warm firelight in the night but I could not come home.

"So I walked alone. Unloved and unwanted. Gnashing my teeth. Tearing at my clothes and my hair. Turning into carnage would be sweet oblivion and my perdition would have ended.

"Instead, I wandered without food and water. Walking until I would fall dead in my tracks. My body left out in the elements as a forgotten grave.

"But then I came down a mountain into a small valley with a strange lake. The water had a grey sheen to it. Grey cream lay on the top making rainbows in the sunlight. White sand ringed the shore and descended under a ledge of rock that protected the entrance to a cave.

"The valley and the lake were unknown to everyone. No one had ever been there before. As I could not walk another step, I lay down on the beach and waited for the sun to bleach my bones white.

"But it wasn't the sun that came. It was the moon. Bigger than ever before. With a bright face looking down at me. A lady smiling with bone-white teeth.

"That was the first time I heard the voice of the Great Mother speak to me. It said, 'Know me and be known of me.' The words carved shapes into my skin. Through its Spell Speak, the Darkness had marked me and sealed me as its own."

Wice knew what shape the words had taken: a crescent moon balanced on the mouth of a coiled snake with a forked tongue.

Evil geometry.

Pledged heart.

Sold soul.

"I heard the call of the Darkness. It is like an eternal river of night. Everlasting cold that stops beating hearts.

"It spoke to me. Promised me eternal life. If I would follow it.

"And it told me all that I had to do.

"'Break the law. Bring down the light. Hide the sun. Bring on the Night. Shine the Lesser Light. Turn warm flesh into cold stone. Destroy faith. Turn hope into despair.

"'Sway everyone to believe in their hearts that the Light is the Darkness and that the Darkness is the Light. This is the Great Work.

"'Enter Quicksilver Lake and be forever changed,'" the Great Mother promised.

"So I got up and waded into the quicksilver. It was thick as oil. Clinging to my skin.Saturating my body. The waters parted and then washed back over me. Sinking me deep to the bottom.

"I held my breath as long as I could. But then I finally drank in the liquid. The bittersweet mercury filled my lungs and clung to every organ. Became my blood. Coated my beating heart. Covered the grey matter in my head.

"I broke surface and swam back to the shore. I had waded in as ashepherd boy without hope and walked out as a woman serving the greatest force in the universe.

"The Dark Riders waited for me on the shore. Shadow gave me a cloak of ravens' feathers. Rancor gave me my moon-snake necklace. And the Destroyer gave me a silver comb for my hair.

"My forever family. United in one mind for one purpose. To serve the Darkness.

"They took to the cave under the rock. There I met the Porter, the great snake. Asheroth led me to the Circle Chamber where I began the Great Work of the Darkness.

"First, we will drive the Judge from our Domain and this Realm. And then we will spread our fight to the other worlds until the Great Work is completed and the Light is banished from the Universe along with all misery and punishment.

"And then all creation will do what we please however we want. And all that will be left is raw naked power.

"We have come close. We are relentless. We will accomplish our aim.

"Once before the Judge stopped us from our Great Work out of jealousy because he knew we would have succeeded at that time. But instead of stopping only us, he punished the whole world and all his creation out of his capricious whim so he could uphold his Law.

"The Judge made fire come up from the belly of the earth to erupt out of the tallest mountain. Smoke and ash filled the sky heating the whole earth. To cool itself, the earth hibernated for an age long winter and ice appeared everywhere.

"The Judge made the great ice sheets cover everything. An entire world frozen solid. People and their cities. Animals of the air and in the sea.Frozen over. My village and all its sheep.

"My three brothers were entombed at Ice Prison. To be forever frozen with an entire world lost under what is now Glacier Mountains. The Judge had a cell prepared for me but I escaped to tell the tale. Do you know that the Ice Prison and the Keep and the Realm are at the bottom of what once was an ocean," the Elfwitch explained.

Wice was stunned that a good and loving god could turn its back on its own creation and would destroy it on a whim. Then she remembered when she and Reed had first crossed over and they had observed all manner of animals and people frozen under the ice pack.

The remnants of a judgment.

Evidence of a past apocalypse.

"Why? How could God do that?" Wice asked.

"Not a god. The Judge," the Elfwitch said. "He says he gave people free will but when they don't use that free will to follow His Law, he acts like a vindictive child and brings misery down on everyone.

"'Love me or else.' No wonder people don't love him back. He lets them torture and murder each other. He deserves no respect. He is the one who should be banished," the Elfwitch said with odious dripping venom.

"But the Judge allowed one family to escape the judgment. A father and a mother with their six children: three sets of twins; three girls and three boys.

"How I hated them. They thought themselves so righteous because the Judge had spared them. My family and my whole village were long gone with no one to plead their case but me.

"Then the Judge himself wrote his Law on a rock. Ten stupid rules for humans to follow: Ten 'thou shall nots.' Ten 'Do what I say or else' rules. Except the rules are impossible to follow. They exist to make people fail.

"That is the Judge's power over people. Guilt over their past mistakes. He wants to punish them.

"Humans don't need ten rules. They only need one: to be free to do whatever they want.

"So, the Judge gave the family his blessing to multiply and subdue all the earth. And I vowed to make humans break every single one of those rules and for them to forsake the Judge. Then I would get them to help me free my three Dark brothers and carry on the Great Work.

How could Wice deny the Elfwitch's narrative? She was the only witness to all the events who had spoken to Wice. Where was God? Wice hadn't met him back in Chayse's World. And here in the Realm, the only evidence of the Judge was a single gold coin.

What about what happened to Moor Kreed the Revelator? That couldn't have been real. Just her imagination.

The Darkness seemed large and in charge and the Judge nowhere to be found.

"So I got busy. I started with the children. Soon they didn't obey their parents. When they grew up they decided they didn't need to get married. And then they decided not to teach their children the Law. Soon everyone forgot about the Judge.

"But then the Judge sent his Son. To walk in the flesh and tell them they'd better return to the Law or the Judge was going to get them. What's the use of giving people a choice if the Judge will punish everyone for not making the right choice?

"So I walked among the people saying, 'Why couldn't the Judge just love them as they were? If you want to be free of the Law, you need to be free of the Son.

"They killed the Son so they didn't have to feel bad anymore about what they did. I took his body and the rock that the Law was written on and I placed them both in a lead sepulcher inside a crypt. It was sealed with a large stone that only the Porter can roll away.

"And ever since, the people have been free from the Son and the Law. But they are not free of the Judge nor the Light. The battle is not over, yet."

Back home, as Chayse, she had been a "Nobody." Nobody had wanted to know her. Nobody would talk to her. Nobody noticed her when she walked down the halls at school.

But here, as Wice, she was a "Somebody." Here she was respected. Here, the Elfwitch let her try out any potion. Back home, Mom had given her two lists: TO DO and DON'T DO.

Hadn't she discovered a truth? People feared punishment. That power was a truth to be used over them.

She could make Judge Hart pay for breaking up the family. She could make Dad pay for leaving Mom. And what about Reed for not giving the Elfwitch his silver heart necklace?

There would be a reckoning with him, too.

"What do you want me to do?" Wice asked.

A small ball of cold silver light ignited in the air. Holding the combustible between her thumb and forefinger, the Elfwitch grinned. "You have chosen wisely, my pet. There is work to do."

***

Chapter Thirty-Seven: Test and Trial

Chains latched to either side of the silver spinning ball. The chains wrapped around the Elfwitch's neck. The light radiating from her moon-snake necklace imposed on the silver necklace Mom had given Wice when she still had been Chayse.

Wice took a long look at the Elfwitch's cold face in the spinning glare of spark and dross. This face had seen thousands of years pass. The skin looked dry and patchy. Speckled with quicksilver crystals. Her eyelids were albino. Transparent with purple arteries.

Was this Wice's future? To end up just like the Elfwitch? In thought and deed? In look and character?

The Elfwitch led her back down the escape tunnel and through the aperture into the forest of foundation columns. Wice matched the Dark Lady's stride with purpose.

They came upon a group of prone shapes. Convulsing and shaking in the darkness upon the floor. Antrhomorphoids. Once humans now twisting into alien shapes. Hybrids of birds with mammal features.

The heads were elongated. The mouth and nose funneled into bleaks with forked tongues poking out. Irises had mutated from blue-green and brown to bright yellow. Pupils had contracted into tiny oval slits.

The bones in the arms had atrophied and the skin and sagged into leathery sacks. Hands had twisted into bony talons. Quills poked out of the spine and the crown of the head.

Wice felt both revulsion and amazement at the transformation.

And she had caused it.

Though, as Chayse.

Still, in her attempt to escape she had been running into her new identity.

"When you first step foot in the Circle Chamber, you came as an initiate," the Elfwitch said. "I invited you to test any potion among my collection. I wanted you to learn by discovery just what the Darkness could do. And so you became an acolyte.

"But with every choice comes consequence. For every action, there is a price. And now you must learn who must pay for what you have done."

The Elfwitch indicated the groveling shapes that once were men. Four of the Queen's Guard who had mutinied against her to side with the Elfwitch. And High Priest Kyphus, who should have been the queen's most trusted advisor but had become the leader of the rebellion.

The creature that once had been Kyphus pulled itself over to the Elfwitch through the dust on its chest pushing itself along with the flat of its talons. It tried to cradle the Elfwitch's boot within the hook of its talon and lick the top of it with its forked tongue.

Wice shivered. It was unnatural and pathetic. The creature was no longer a human. It was a pitiful thing.

"Every day, everything is a test. And now the question is what will you do with these servants whom you have crippled," the Elfwitch said.

"Can't you turn them back into humans?" Wice asked. "Like Victor and Nicolai?"

"They are lycanthropes. A kind of madness or curse. Brought on by the Darkness and Sister Moon," the Elfwitch said. "Whereas, these poor creatures are just mutants. Do not feel pity for them, my pet.

"When experimenting with any formula one can expect some adverse side effects. Such as instantaneous death, irreversible transformation, or unexpected madness. Do not think of this as a failure. Think of this as a stepping stone to success.

"At most, we want to make a servant who is both strong and loyal. At the very least we make a debilitating mess. Either way, we win."

"This should take care of it," the Elfwitch said as she reached into the fold of her black raven robe to pull out another vial stoppered with a pink top.

Wice looked at the amber liquid held within the vacuum and remembered the first time she had seen it in use. The Elfwitch had made Colonel Graves drink it. To prove two points: he and all the Deadcoats were bound to the Elfwitch by an oath to serve her no matter what and that oath kept them from even death.

"But that will kill them," Wice complained.

The other four accipiter-man hybrids crawled over to join what had once been the High Priest Kyphus to grovel at the feet of the Elfwitch. Together they lifted their heads and snapped their beaks as if expecting mother to regurgitate down their throats.

"You'd be doing them a kindness," the Elfwitch said. "They cannot walk or even fly. It will take days for them to die. Meanwhile, they will be in agony and confusion."

She held out the pink stoppered vial.

Then she shook it, much like Mom would when offering Chayse the rest of her diet Coke in a bottle after it had gone warm.

"No, thank you," Wice said with all manner and due respect.

"Come, come," the Elfwitch said. "You need to own up to your responsibility. Finish what you start."

The creatures struggled to reach up to the Elfwitch's outstretched hand. Their tongues clicked. Their throats swallowed. But they could not make a sound.

Once they had been human beings. Men of the Realm. With position and responsibility. They had been her enemies. Sent to stop her when she was Chayse from helping the queen and the captain of the guard escape.

They had deserved to die so, as Chayse, she hadn't hesitated in throwing the transmogrifying potion at them.

Killing them outright would have been a mercy.

This was just plain torture.

It was sick just to watch them wither and convulse. Where was the thrill in total domination of stealing their identity as humans? In destroying their personality? In stealing their souls?

Hadn't Chayse committed murder? The beasts were still breathing. If only just. With their souls gone but their hearts beating on, how was it different than murder?

Wice felt no regard for the beasts. They were inhuman. They no longer had an identity. They no longer served a purpose.

They were better off dead.

Wice couldn't stand it anymore. She took the vial out of the Elfwitch's hand and pulled out the pink stopper. The creatures saw that it was now she who would their boon of surcease and flopped over to her feet. Pushing themselves upon their twisted knuckles they opened their maws wide, yellow slits of eyes looking up to the top of the Tower foundation.

Wice did not withhold. She poured a few drops into each of the three mouths. Then she stepped back afraid of what further side effects might come.

The results were swift and harrowing. The creatures' bodies convulsed with tremors from head to toe. They coughed as bile and blood caught in their throats and spewed down their chins.

One by one they beat the floor with their baggy arms until they lay still in pools of their own vomited innards.

Somehow Wice was confused. Killing the beasts might have given them release but there had been none for her. She clutched the vial and threw it against the nearest stone column. It shattered as the liquid hissed and vaporized into smoke. It was an act that Chayse had done dozens of times at home when arguing with Mom.

They had been men not just thirty minutes ago. Weren't they still men deep down? Hadn't she just killed human beings?

"You must really control your temper, my pet," the Elfwitch said.

There came a sound of tiny rushing winds. Rotating blades making swatches of propelled air. Beating wings.

A dark cloud of large fragments flew among the columns. Darting around and through the stone pillars. It was a flock of ravens. Come to feast on the dead carcasses?

The flock rotated around becoming a cyclone of black raven shapes. Faster and faster coalescing into a tall anthromorphoid shape on two legs with two arms and a head until a being with black leather pants and boots with silver studded armor and a mane of wild black hair stood before them.

Even as Wice, she was scared to have the Destroyer stand before her.

The creature pointed to his left ear lobe with his forefinger and then made a fist with the same hand that he rocked in the air. Then it drew a semicircle around its neck with the same hand and forefinger.

"The silver necklace!" the Elfwitch said. "Who? Frehley?"

The Destroyer smiled with a jawline of mixed up incisors and canines.

"We must go, my pet," the Elfwitch gave a victorious laugh. She looked satiated after a long, long fast. "Another brother will be freed. The Judge must be quaking in his little boots."

"What do you mean?" Wice asked.

"Our servants have located another one of these!" the Elfwitch said clutching at the heart necklace that Mom had given her when she had been Chayse which she had in turn handed over to the Elfwitch.

"Where?" Wice asked.

"A garrison. That protects a powerful place. One that the Judge surrendered. You will learn that the Light always surrenders. The Judge is used to losing ground," the Elfwitch said and then clapped her hands. "We must be quick!"

"When we came here to Tower Reign we rode the lycanthropes," Wice said. "But I knocked them out when I let Queen Regina escape."

"So you did, my pet," the Elfwitch said. "But if we can't travel by ground, we will travel by air."

"How so?"Wice asked.

The Elfwitch leaned her head back and gave a call like Dad would use to call down ducks.

After a brief pause, there was a response. A screech. And then another. Drawing closer. Another winged beast flew into the foundation gliding among the many columns. Banking and turning to come to a landing on the carcass that had not long ago been the High Priest Kyphus.

The two-headed vulture gave a double cry as it began to gorge on the sweetmeats and extremities of the deceased anthromorphoid.

"Ha!" the Elfwitch snapped her fingers. Both heads wrenched their blood dipped beaks up. "Take us to the oak tree by the stream. There is a garrison there. Now."

The conjoined vulture spread its wings and hovered above them with a few beats. Wice could feel the hot air coming in waves against her from its beating wings. The twin vulture moved over them and clutched them on a shoulder with a mighty talon. Its grasp was tight and sure as it pulled them both up into the air.

Not to be outdone, the Destroyer dissolved again into a mass of swirling ravens that swept out between the columns. The flock of ravens kept match with the gliding double-headed bird until they came to the main regress out of the foundation. A wide staircase that led to double open doors.

Out of the stone basement.

Into the open air.

Above the walls of Tower Reign.

Over Castle Town and its outskirts.

Across the farmlands that fed the populace.

Towards the heart of Royal Forest.

Onward to victory for the Elfwitch.

Forward to destiny for Wice.

Behind it all was the Great Mother.

Beyond that was the Darkness.

***

Chapter Thirty-Eight: Pray and Prey

"I'm not droppin' anything until you give yer word that the boy walks out of here free," Frehley told Sergeant Hood even as almost two dozen muskets were aimed at him, Cyrus and Reed, and Strap.

Sergeant Hood laughed incredulously. "You want me to give you my word? Hello? I've taken a vow to the Dark Lady. If you wanna deal, you'll have to talk straight to the horse's mouth."

"It's more like the other end," Cyrus said.

"I'd sure like to put a ball right 'tween yer eyes, Cyrus," Sergeant Hood said, "I truly would. You never was that good a blacksmith, truth be told. 'Bout the only thing you did right was get married and make yerself a daughter. I wonder if you'd be holdin' yer daughter hostage if she were here now."

Cyrus's cheeks blushed. He took a long deep breath. But he kept his grip steady on the musket butt and the trigger which was nuzzled under Reed's chin.

Reed had more than his share of this selfish man. Part of him hoped that someone would put him down. But what if they missed? They might hit Reed, too.

His stomach was in knots. He'd been on the edge since coming to this world. Fear and panic were old friends now.

"That don't matter. Nothin' matters except gettin' that silver necklace," Cyrus said.

"Quicksilver," Frehley corrected.

"Quicksilver?!" Cyrus snapped. "Then why don't you use it to get us out of here?"

"It was made fer a single purpose. Fer a vow," Frehley explained. "But now that vow has been broken. It's even more dangerous."

"Oh, I get you," Cyrus said. "You fell in love and got yer heart broke. So all this is about yer love life! Bet you didn't think 'bout my wife and daughter gettin' killed, did you?"

Cyrus could sure talk, Reed thought. How much thought was he giving to the musket barrel shoved under Reed's chin?

"Ya want this kid to live?" Cyrus asked. "I wanna live, too. There's been enough death, don't ya think? Why ya gotta be so high and noble fer all the time, Frehley? We've all lost somethin'."

Frehley pursed his lips. Then he said, "Better start prayin'."

Reed had prayed twice before. Once for his dad to come back. But that never happened, so he'd lowered his sights and prayed for a new bb gun. And he hadn't gotten that either.

Now he felt desperate enough to cry out to God. He might hear Reed, He might not. But the levee was going to break. And everything Reed had ever done wrong, his every weakness, his every desire was about to come flooding out.

"Oh, God!" Reed sniveled. "Don't let me die here! Let me see my sister again! Let me get back home to Mom and Dad! I don't know what I did wrong to deserve this but I wanna change! I don't want to be here anymore! Not like this!"

"Hush it up!" Cyrus grunted.

But Lieutenant Grey was moved enough to give a slight nod to a trooper on the rampart.

The Deadcoat fired and a single shot bit into the exposed root next to Frehley's feet.

Frehley narrowed his gaze at Cyrus.

Next, the Deadcoat officer tipped the end of his sword toward Cyrus and the hostage Reed.

Another shot rang out. This time the bullet hit between Reed's legs ejecting a tail of dust up to his chest.

Guess that was God's answer, Reed thought. He kicked back against the ground. Trying to get as far away from the davit in the ground. But Cyrus kept him pinned against his barrel chest and Reed only succeeded in getting dirt onto the borrowed Deadcoat boots.

"Don't let them take yer only leverage, Frehley!" Cyrus said. "Why don't ya use that quicksilver necklace!"

"I can't!" Frehley said and shook its chain length. Once it had meant the world to him. So much that Frehley had now lost the world he had wished to gain by it. It wasn't any better than a stone in his shoe. "I don't know how!"

"Then give it to the kid!" Cyrus said.

"Reed!" Frehley called. "Still got yer gold coin? Use that!"

Reed tried to shake his head. But Cyrus' burly arm choked him. "No! Cyrus took it!"

Cyrus cursed. "I gave it to big, tall, and ugly! I didn't know about my wife and daughter then, Frehley!"

Frehley shook his head. "You sure don't know much, Cy. But you sure know how to screw up the works."

Lieutenant Grey nodded to Sergeant Hood. The officer never smiled, not that he much to be happy about anyway. So the sergeant smiled for him, like a hunting dog who'd corner his prey.

"Time's up, gen'uhl-men," the Deadcoat non-com announced.

"Don't, Hoodie!" Cyrus said. "You'll hit the kid!" "Do it. But you won't get this handy dandy quicksilver necklace," Frehley said as he rocked the chain length and made the heart dance.

"What do ya mean?" Sergeant Hood moaned. "All we gotta it take it outta yer cold dead hands."

"True, you could do that," Frehley said. "But then the necklace won't work. It has to be given as a free gift. Not my rules. Blame the Judge."

Lieutenant Grey took a red scarf from around his neck revealing a gaping hole in his trachea. He forced words threw his windpipe. "There. Is. No. Judge."

Frehley shrugged. "So you say. But the rule still applies. So tell me, if there is no Judge, then why is there this rule about quicksilver?"

Lieutenant Grey raised his sword perpendicular to the sky. Every Deadcoat with a musket aimed at the four available targets: Reed, Cyrus, Frehley, and Strap.

"Stop!" came a voice from the sky.

Though it spoke with authority, it was not the Judge's voice.

It was a weaker vessel that gave the command out of the air.

The command was accompanied by a mighty rushing wind. A great winged beast swooped down from on high. A massive bird of prey with twin heads and double sharp beaks and broad wings outstretched like a glider plane.

Only one time had Reed seen a bird this huge and that had been on a trip to the St. Louis Zoo when from across a pond he had witnessed a condor gliding down from the top of an immense aviary cage. Under the widespread wings of such a beast, Reed wouldn't have been much more like a jackrabbit.

This bird of prey would have no trouble in pecking out his sweetmeats given that it had a double beak. It talons clutched two human passengers. Coming down alongside the oak tree, it beat its wings to create an updraft so it could hover above the ground long enough to the two passengers. The double red-headed beast had twin sets of yellow eyes that held all the humans before it with no regard.

Both of them, the Elfwitch and an apprentice, set their feet on the ground.

Another mass of flying birds flew over the ramparts. A vortex of swirling ravens settled next to the two travelers. The ravens coalesced into a form shadow and out stepped the fully formed Destroyer.

"Enough!" the Elfwitch announced.

Everyone stood at attention. Motionless.

Reed didn't even want to breathe. He blinked at the three new arrivals. Two of them he hated and feared with just cause: the Elfwitch and the Destroyer.

But he had to blink twice at the third arrival. Because the first time he didn't believe it.

It was Chayse.

But Chayse had changed.

Still wearing the black lace dress with silver sequins and her black hair up in a silver snake comb. Exchanged for the clothes she had had on at the FINS hearing. However much Reed didn't like her wearing this attire, it was the look on her face that disturbed more.

The glint in her blue eyes--a wall against all the bullies and all the hardships of their World had been magnified. And the warmth that she had saved for Reed and Mom alone that the glint protected was long gone. Her blue eyes glinted only cold silver.

"Sis!" Reed called.

"That's yer sister?!" Cyrus asked.

"Hold tight," Frehley said to both of them. "You especially, Cyrus."

Reed was broken. Everything around him was broken. The day was fractured: Reed had never seen the sun here because of the huge moon. The company was ruptured: the five of them had banded together to escape the dungeon but now Evander was wounded and Cyrus had betrayed them all. They had been a crude replacement for his real family. Mom and Dad had busted the most important thing in his life: his root and identity. They had started all the brokenness. And here was the seed from their broken tree: Sis stood with the Elfwitch which was the cruelest twist of all.

Why had this all happened?

Wasn't there anything good left in the Universe?

Was everything just blowing in the wind?

Was there any meaning to anything anymore?

The Elfwitch and her acolyte dusted themselves off and smoothed back their hair. Then the Dark Lady leveled a long silver finger at Lieutenant Grey. "The ex-Royal Huntsman is correct. Quicksilver must be given as a freewill gift. Otherwise, its power is latent.

"That is the way of the Darkness."

"You mean the Law," Frehley corrected. "The Judge's Law."

"The Law is dead!" the Elfwitch pronounced. "I buried it with the Son. No Judge is going to come down from the sky to slay me with lightning. There is only the Great Mother. The Darkness. Bow down now or be forever obliterated."

Not one of them bowed.

In fact, Cyrus pushed himself to his feet and pulled Reed up after him. He unhooked his arm around the boy's neck and stood just in front of him to shield him.

"Then why can't you come 'n' get it yerself?" Cyrus asked. "If you're the Darkness and the Darkness is the end-all-be-all then that there quicksilver outta fly right home to mama."

But Reed wasn't looking at the quicksilver heart-shaped necklace. He wasn't looking at the two men standing near him. He wasn't even looking at the fey Elfwitch or the brutal Destroyer standing pleased with his arms crossed.

His eyes were locked on the young girl made over to look like a minor elfwitch standing under the wing of the evilest person Reed had ever met.

"Sissy, aren't you gonna help us?"

The Elfwitch looked down at her ward. "Show them, my pet. Wice, show them whom you would help."

Reed didn't know why the Elfwitch had called his sister "Wice." But he watched her follow the Elfwitch's command and step out from under her mentor and bodyguard. His sister came towards Reed and the other two men with a purpose in her stride. As if she were about to play a prank at their expense.

She winked at Reed as she came around her brother and Cyrus. Stopping in front of Frehley, she planted her hands on her hips and looked at the ex-Royal Huntsman in his dirty breeches and leather tunic.

"You're not my daddy," she smiled.

"Who said that I was, child?" Frehley said.

Wice's smile faltered for a second then she held out her hand palm up.

"Give Wice the necklace," the Elfwitch said.

"Only if you promise the boy safe passage," Frehley said.

"Don't you do it," Cyrus urged as he shook his head. "She won't keep her word."

"That's because you didn't have quicksilver," the Elfwitch puffed.

Reed didn't see any other way. Deadcoats surrounded them with almost two dozen rifles. And now the Elfwitch and the Destroyer had them penned in.

All this trouble just for a necklace. First, the Elfwitch had tricked Chayse into giving up hers. Next, the Elfwitch had threatened to kill Reed if he didn't surrender his. Now she was about to receive the third necklace.

And didn't the Elfwitch wear the fourth necklace? Did she have it with her as Elsie Crutch back in their World when she sat in the courtroom and pawed at a lump under her sweater?

Why were these quicksilver necklaces so important to the Elfwitch?

"Judge forgive me," Frehley said as he dropped the necklace into the twin sister's waiting palm.

Wice snatched it up and ran with a giggle back towards the Elfwitch meaning to hand over the prized possession to her Dark mistress.

She would have made it with ease.

Hadn't Reed tripped his sister.

He'd done it dozens of times back home. After she'd threatened to get him or tell on him. Or after Mom had issued a proclamation of punishment—"Go to your room!" "Turn the TV off and take out the trash!" "You can just forget about going to see your dad this weekend!"

Reed would do it when he had nothing left to lose. If he was already in trouble, he'd might as well get one last lick in.

It was easy.

All he did was stick out his breech covered leg and caught Wice off guard and unawares.

She fell headlong. Her dress catching her legs. Giving her no chance to find her footing. She just had time to put an arm out in front of her. The hand that held the necklace.

Reed hated to do it but he had to step on her wrist as he bent over and wrenched the necklace out of his sister's hand like taking a football that had been fumbled on the ground and was still a free ball in play.

"Run! To the barracks!" Cyrus shouted and pounced at Sergeant Hood and Lieutenant Grey.

The burly man brought up his musket as the Deadcoat sergeant was aiming with his pistol. He fired his musket on the run at just a few paces from the trooper. The sergeant took the ball in the middle of the chest as it knocked him back sending the shot from his pistol wide off the mark.

The courtyard erupted into a shooting gallery.

And everyone ran every which way from the whizzing volleys and raining shot.

***

Chapter Thirty-Nine: Tooth and Claw

Cyrus grabbed Reed by the shoulder and pulled him back towards the barracks room. Using his other shoulder, the burly man knocked Sergeant Hood aside like he was a fullback bursting out of the backfield. The Deadcoat non-commissioned officer collapsed to the ground.

Reed thought it strange that just ten minutes ago Cyrus wanted to gamble with his life and now he was fighting like a bear to protect him. Would wonders never cease?

Lieutenant Grey stepped in front of their retreat. His saber cocked back over his head ready for a downswing. Neither Cyrus nor Reed could protect themselves; all they could do was shut their eyes.

Frehley came alongside them and grabbed at the length of chain caught in Cyrus' meaty grip. Cyrus pulled it back towards his barrel chest as Frehley pulled the chain up towards his face and Cyrus' arm along with it. Lieutenant Grey's blade sliced into the chain. A burst of light ignited casting out showers and flames like fireworks on the Fourth of July.

An explosion more powerful than the Mad Dog 16 shot mortar fireworks display that Dad would buy Reed resounded in their faces. The concussion slapped their eardrums and knocked them all backward.

Lieutenant Grey rolled across the ground like a red gilded dried leaf. Frehley and Cyrus sheered away from each other. But the necklace would not break and someone's grasp had to give.

The necklace went with Frehley to the left like the winner's share of a wishbone. And Cyrus fell to the right empty-handed. But his right arm fell straight down like a broken clavicle. Sheared off at the shoulder.

Cyrus looked shocked. His covetousness could not be slacked. And now he had lost more of himself.

But the wound did not bleed. The power surge had come from the necklace. Knocking the curse out of Lieutenant Grey and collapsing his skin and bone while freeing him from the Elfwitch's curse and at the same time slicing off Cyrus' arm and cauterizing the wound.

Reed tumbled backward towards the oak tree. He tripped over something large and landed beside it on his back knocking out all his breath. A small hand clamped down on his nose and over his mouth.

Inert and still, Reed was no better than a sack of meat. Hands and feet useless. Lungs burning from filling with hot carbon dioxide.

He needed to breathe but someone wasn't letting him.

Reed couldn't lift a hand to pry the clamped hand loose. Neither could he shake it off. The hand was a seal. A plug. A cinch. It wouldn't budge.

A face appeared over him. Very young. Brown hair up in a bun. Set with a silver snake comb.

Cold blue eyes looked down at him. Frosted around the rim. Set with a hardness.

"Dear brother," the person giggled.

It looked like Chayse but it was not her character. His sister had been mad enough at him in the past to wallop and smack him. Her favorite threats were to pull out every hair on his head or tear off his left arm and beat him over the head with it. But he had never once thought she would attempt to make good on her promises.

Now she was trying to kill him.

Smother him.

Strangle him with the trapped poison gas in his lungs.

Only it wasn't his sister doing it. It was another person inside her body. Someone far more cruel and twisted than Chayse could ever dream of being.

"Don't worry," said the girl who was no longer Chayse.

Reed heard her voice. The words were simple. Spoken in plain English. Meant to be soothing but it was bitter acid atop a malicious tone. Beneath it, the words twisted around his auricles. Slipping down his ear canal like cold water. Stretching the reverberations into something else until not only the meaning changed but so did the words.

What Reed heard was: *Don't breathe. Don't struggle. Fall asleep. Forever.*

Spell-speak! Somehow his twin sister was using the power of the Elfwitch. No! Reed screamed to himself inside his brain. Chayse was becoming like the Elfwitch!

This creature was not his sister. She seemed to enjoy his helpless struggle.

His companions had their own struggles.

The Destroyer jumped into the fray by feinting at the companion closest to it, the giant Strap. Though the creature was a head taller and outweighed him by two stones, Strap was by far more nimble. He sidestepped the creature's low swipe keeping his knees bent and flipping the musket end to end so that he held the butt like a club.

The Destroyer gave a wicked grin and came at Strap. It got a jab under the chin for its trouble that snapped its head back in a wave of wild black hair. But the blow did not wipe the leer off its face.

Strap did not let up. He swung the musket stock upside the Destroyer's head. The blow would have crushed the skull of an ordinary man. And indeed the stock snapped off and flew over the Destroyer's head.

The creature side stepped absorbing the blow and funneling the shock back through its own muscles to turn the energy into pure hatred.

Then the Destroyer struck.

It put his fists together like a club and walloped Strap across the cheek. The giant pirouetted and bent down to one knee to keep his balance. He tried to shake his head clear of the cobwebs from the hit.

The Destroyer brought up a gauntlet clad forearm meaning to pile drive down on top of Strap's neck meaning it to be a coup de grace. Instead of a bone-crunching downbeat, its mouth jerked into a grimace as its teeth clenched down. A volt of electricity made a circuit around its head and danced over the rows of its twisted teeth.

The Destroyer convulsed as if a score of hammers were hitting its head making the wild mane of hair stand on end. Its eyes rolled up until the corneas were all white. Then it slumped to its black leather-clad knees.

Frehley stood just behind the Destroyer having punched the creature in the back between its shoulder blades with the quicksilver necklace wrapped around his fist like brass knuckles. Then the ex-Royal Huntsman darted in and grabbed his giant companion by the elbow pulling Strap back on his heels.

The pair retreated past the Elfwitch who coiled up and gave them a serpentine hiss. She warded herself with her pair of necklaces that shone a quicksilver aura about her head.

After their first volley, Deadcoats began to fire at will, slowed only by their loading and aiming. But with Cyrus almost back to the barracks door and Reed at the bottom of a dog pile, no one could get a dead aim on Frehley and Strap. The strange glow generated by the quicksilver necklace deflected the musket balls around them into whizzing gnats.

The only Deadcoats who hadn't fired yet were the gunners stationed by the five pounder cannon with a lit punk next to the fuse. However, the order to fire would not be forthcoming from Lieutenant Grey who lay in a tangle of rags and bones. With his broken arms askew and there was no way he was going to put his white-feathered black cap back on his emaciated head ever again.

Sergeant Hood tried to pick himself up but Cyrus pushed him back down with the heel of his boot. He wobbled through the door into the barracks off balance by his loss unsure of his next move. With the toe of his boot, he kicked the door against the jamb. It slammed against it but did not close.

Reed watched it all from another place. Like it was happening to someone else. He would have liked to have been able to help that person and he knew that he was the only one who could, but he just couldn't help right now.

The smothering made him drowsy. Reed felt weightless. He rose above his prone body.

He saw a figure that looked like his sister draped in a black lace dress sitting on his chest stealing his breath like a cat. She was a load of stone pressing down on him. A spanner in the works of his bellows.

If Reed didn't get her off his chest then he would die.

He knew she meant to kill him. His own sister.

Maybe that was what was keeping him in shock.

It was worse than losing Dad and then Mom. Sis had been the one person who he had been the closest to in their World and now she had been taken from him in this one. The one person who supposed to have his back now sat on his stomach. The one person he thought he could trust forever had turned against him.

It couldn't be Chayse. Something had happened to her. She had changed somehow.

His sister was more like one of the lycanthropes. Or one of the Deadcoats. Or worse, the Destroyer, who loved to spread misery and cause harm.

All those creatures served the Elfwitch out of their own free will. And had become twisted. Because that's what the Elfwitch did, she jacked everything all up.

Chayse was just a twelve-year-old kid.

What had happened to her?

Reed couldn't figure out why Chayse was treating him like the enemy. But that didn't matter right now.

What mattered was getting her off of him.

Taking a breath.

Getting air back into his lungs.

But instead, blackness closed in around his vision. Forming a tunnel that shrank to the size of his contracted pupil. Everything around became a fuzzy gray.

This must be what it's like to die. Everything just shuts down. Might as well go to sleep.

The last thing Reed was going to see was the leering smile of his twisted sister. Knowing it was her who had killed him when he had needed her most.

But another shape loomed above Wice as she sat in her saddle seat of murder. It was the face of Dad. Mad enough to turn Wice over on his knee and give her a lickin'.

His long arm swung to knock her off her throne of oppression. The young tyrant gave a yelp as she rolled to her side.

The weight was gone.

The clamp removed.

But Reed wasn't breathing.

He was looking but he wasn't seeing.

Then another face bent over Reed. A dark-haired head and a face with concerned blue eyes. It was Dad's face but not the man of easy smiles and crude jokes.

It was the face of a man who had gone through a lot of trouble for Reed's sake. He had proven himself a steadfast companion. Reed did not doubt that this man would lay down his life for him. Even though Frehley didn't understand who Reed was or why he was here.

Maybe that was love. Even in this dark twilight world where everything Reed understood was backward and upside down.

That one thing still remained.

The man wasn't Dad. He was Frehley. And Frehley was everything Dad wasn't and everything Reed wanted Dad to be: a hero.

Frehley sat Reed up like a poseable action figure and yelled in his face, "Get up! We gotta run!"

Strap pointed to the ramparts above the Mighty Oak tree. The quicksilver necklace might protect them from the Deadcoats' musket fire but what about the waiting gunner crew? The giant didn't seem to think so.

There was a sound. Low and guttural. Traveling on air.

And Reed had no air in him. So, the sound hadn't come from him at all. Rather, it had come from the heap of rumpled black dress next to him.

The sound became a moan. The moan became a wail. The wail became a cry.

Gaining strength like a gale-force wind. Intensifying from hurt to anger to wrath. To the sound of a Fury.

Wice flew up from the ground shrieking with hands out like claws. She latched onto Frehley's back. Using the silver snake comb, she raked it along the back of his neck.

"Stop!" Frehley shouted as he twisted around trying to either through her off his back or grab the comb from out of her hand.

Reed tried to take a breath but he couldn't draw in a single atom of air. He still had a stitch in his side. His lungs were still jammed.

Everyone and everything around him moved in a flurry. But he was still stuck. Without air, he couldn't move a muscle.

"Judge bless!" That was as close as Frehley ever came to cursing as he swatted at Reed's impish twin now. "You little demon!"

Strap bounded forwarded against the whizzing musket balls and ran in a crouch with his arm out down low as he were to going to scoop up the game football. Instead, he whacked Reed between his shoulder blades and grabbed him by the back of his hunter's tunic and snatched him up like a fumbled handoff and turned on a dime.

Tucking the gasping Reed under his arm, the giant made for the narrow goalposts: the door frame to the barracks room.

Frehley, rankled to the point that the little she-demon had become an abhorrent burden, bent to his knees slumping forward in one quick motion. The girl once called Chayse snapped forward and shifted towards his shoulders. Frehley reached over his head and grabbed her by the scruff of her neck and flung her towards the Mighty Oak tree.

Then he jumped to his feet and ran after his companions with the Elfwitch howling curses and prevarications at his back.

Reed took a breath.

And then another.

He couldn't get enough air.

His breaths were shallow and fast. Cool and sweet.

It was a miracle! His lungs were filling and emptying! His diaphragm was working like a bellows squeezing his lungs and then drawing them back.

Reed's brain snapped to life sending images and giving feelings.

Things to do. Places to be. Running through the wooded hills of Raccoon Springs Village. Eating lunch at Shiloh Elementary School. Going to high school. Maybe learning how to weld. Getting married. Having kids of his own. Maybe even a son that he would show how to hunt.

Hope returned like a forgotten toy at the bottom of the toy chest Dad had gotten him when he'd been three. Dreams welled up like balloons at his fourth birthday party which was the last time his parents had been together to celebrate with him. Even Uncle Buddy had been there.

Reed's first thought was a prayer.

God, get me back home.

. And then another prayer came to him. A true and honest thought. Coming from his heart. Buried down inside under the weight of years like a dormant seed in the Sahara Desert, waiting for a hundred-year rain.

God, bring my family back together.

All Reed could do was hope. Despite the evidence around him.

Safe as Reed was tucked under the arm of the man who was a dead ringer for his Uncle Buddy, it hurt to watch his sister descend into a kind of possession. She was down on her hands and knees with a twisted sneer on her face like one of the lycanthrope twins.

"Sis," Reed pleaded. "Please stop."

"I am not your sister!" said this girl who looked like Chayse but sounded like a stranger. She got up and began to smooth her dress and straighten her lace. "But I am going to kill you!"

"You're whack!" Reed was still stunned. Sissy had been hateful at him before, but never this evil and cruel.

Strap set him down so that Reed could cling to the side of the door frame. The giant grabbed the metal door from the other side meaning to close it except that Reed stood in the middle of the threshold. Stray musket balls shot into the frame and door sending splinters and smoke from the impact.

Reed might be just five minutes younger than her and almost two inches shorter and maybe even ten pounds lighter. But he wasn't weaker. Not by a long shot.

The shock of Sissy attacking him and the horror from watching her side with evil was turning into anger. He wanted to run back out into the fray of whizzing musket balls and knock some sense into her. "I'm your own brother and you just tried to kill me!"

Reed was through with being threatened. Being imprisoned. Having creatures put their hands on him. He never wanted anyone to hurt him again.

Frehley ran past Reed and almost pushed him back. "Quit arguin'! We gotta close the door!"

The volleys stepped up. Now the Deadcoat garrison had a stationary target. A door frame with a twelve-year-old boy standing dead center in it.

The Destroyer walked up to Wice's left side. And the Elfwitch stepped up to her right. "I have a forever family here! We have a secret purpose! I have been promised a great power. They promised it to me and not to you. You're not a part of my family anymore. I'm fine without Dad. And I'm fine without Mom. Now I'll be fine without you."

Reed pointed back at Frehley. "Don't they both look kinda familiar to you! That's gotta be Dad and Uncle Buddy! Something is goin' on!"

Every second this girl became less like Chayse. "No, they are not. Dad and Uncle Buddy are both back in our world." Then she swallowed and blinked. "And so is Mom. Here, we're on our own."

The trio took a step closer to the barracks door. More and more musket balls whizzed by Reed's head. Bit the ground at his feet. Slammed into the doorposts around him. "Don't you remember the Street Preacher bein' here, too? 'Fore that monster standin' next to you killed him? He said we were brought here for a purpose."

"The only purpose I have is to serve the Darkness," Reed's dark twin said.

Reed slumped his shoulders. "But we don't belong here. Don't you wanna get back home?"

Wice shrugged. "We were miserable back home! We don't have a family there anymore! No one cared what happened to us. Not Mom. Especially not Dad. What's gonna happen if we go back? We stay in foster care until we turn eighteen.

"Back home we are powerless. Look around you! Do you see any Light here? The Light has left this world! Here, the Darkness will give me the power to do whatever I want!"

Reed knew that was a lie. And it made him mad. He pointed his finger back toward the Elfwitch who had crossed her arms. "You mean whatever she wants."

Wice looked down her nose at her twin brother. How could she still be his sister and do that? "The Dark Lady is right. You're just a cast-off. It'd been better if Mom had stopped having kids after me."

That hurt worse than being hit or kicked by her.

"Sis," Reed called in a weak voice.

"Don't you ever call me 'sis' again," Wice said.

"Chayse," Reed whispered.

"There is no 'Chayse!' There is only Wice!" Wice declared pumping a closed fist to the forever night sky.

The trio took another step in lock together.

The Elfwitch cocked her hand back with her index finger up in the air and then aimed it at Reed and the half-closed metal door to the barracks.

It was like if her finger was a weapon and could shoot fire out at them.

Reed caught a glimpse of movement upon the rampart above the oak tree.

What the Elfwitch was doing was lining up a shot for the gun crew. '

"Fire!" she ordered.

***

Chapter Forty: Punk and Fuse

Frehley yanked Reed back through the half-closed metal door and clanged it shut behind them. But there was no time to put the iron security bar up. Within a breath, the door frame exploded turning brick and wooden framing into a shower of powder mortar and sawdust. The metal door flew down the hallway as if it were a running back charging downfield pushing both man and boy out of its way.

The blasted door scooted the two into the next room like a flying anvil before crashing into the next door frame. The weight cracked the frame while Reed and Frehley flopped into the middle of the room on their backsides smacking against stacks of boxes and piles of sacks upon barrels.

Frehley was the first one up. The back of Reed's calves burned from the slide. His leather breeches had kept his skin from having been torn away—Dad had told Reed horror stories of motorcycle enthusiasts taking a spill and getting "road burn" from not wearing jeans.

Reed let the ex-Royal Huntsman pull up him off his keister with a steady hand. A zap from the quicksilver necklace had knocked Reed one way and a blast from the cannonball had knocked him the other. But he was still here, still breathing.

Strap, who was already in the room, came over to check them both over.

"Where are we now?" Reed asked. It looked like the extra bedrooms Dad used as storage whenever he would move from place to place.

Frehley surveyed the contents as Strap knocked his fists together and pulled them apart with his fingers splayed out.

"Judge bless," Frehley said. "We're in the magazine room."

There came a whine like a whipped dog. Someone or something was huddled in the corner behind a stack of boxes marked SHOT No. 10 and two barrels marked POWDER KEG.

Up stood Cyrus. Or what was left of him.

"My arm! You took my arm!" the ex-blacksmith raged. "It was my right hand, too!"

"Cyrus, I am sorry," Frehley said. "But it was the blade of Lieutenant Grey."

"Now I can't even pick up my daughter if I was to ever see her," Cyrus blubbered as he gave a ginger touch to his empty right arm socket with the fingers of his left hand.

Reed had never seen someone get some of their own medicine in such a large dose. That missing hand had held a gun to his head not less than ten minutes ago. The man who had proven himself a traitor twice over sank to the floor with his back against a powder keg.

They could hear Sergeant Hood shouting orders out in the courtyard. Rallying the troop. Lining them up and having them fix bayonets.

"They mean to overrun us," Frehley said. "Quick! Look fer some weapons."

They peered around the stacks to search the walls. Though enough ball and shot and powder were kept stored here to fight off the entire legion of Deadcoats, there was not a single weapon in the room.

Reed thought, *Why not just light all this powder and let it go up in a blaze of glory? The Deadcoats would run over themselves tryin' to getaway.* Trouble was, Reed and his other companions would be standing inside the blast.

"We either gotta keep 'em out of here or 'cause a distraction so we can get outta here," Frehley said and scratched at his chin. "Strap! Reed! Help me pull that metal door over the threshold!"

"Are you gonna hide behind that?" Cyrus asked.

"It stopped a cannonball, didn't it?" Frehley asked as he and Strap moved the warped metal door down on its side. Then as they pulled the metal door through the door frame on its side, the ex-Royal Huntsman said, "Reed! When we pull it through, close the magazine door!"

Leading three other Deadcoats with chipped teeth, clenched naked jaws, and steeled bayonets, Sergeant Hood passed through the wreckage and smoke of the front door and down the atrium.

The two men pulled the warped metal door through the cracked door frame and then Reed shut the magazine room door just as the Deadcoat squad reached them. And though it was well balanced enough to swing with a simple push, it would not close flush since the frame had bulged out.

Bayonets slid through and tried to pry the door open. Strap took a step forward and put his shoulder against the door just like one of Dad's football stories with Uncle Buddy as a fullback driving up the middle on Goal to Go on a third down.

When Strap had pushed the door flush against the broken frame he stuck his huge arm through the door braces to bar it shut. On the other side, the Deadcoats jabbed at the door meaning to pry their bayonet tips against the jamb.

Frehley pressed on the door to help keep it shut. "Reed! Cyrus! Bar the door!"

"I couldn't even pick it up if I wanted to," Cyrus cried.

"Do something!" Frehley pleaded as he and Strap tried to keep the bucking door shut. Whenever the Deadcoat pushed it open a half-inch for half a second, bayonets poked through the gap to slice up Strap's wrist and Frehley's check.

Reed scuttled around the stacks. He knew what to look for. He didn't even think Cyrus was trying.

He saw something standing vertical against the wall between a row of barrels and a stack of boxes. Thick enough to be a four by eight-piece of wood. Reed half pulled-half drug it to the waiting Frehley without Cyrus' help.

If it wasn't the bar to the door, it would do until they found the bar.

The beating and stabbing on the door stopped.

Cyrus came back out of the stacks of ordinance with something as well. A wooden basin with a large punk rolling inside of it. Strap rolled his eyes.

"We need a bar. Not a punk," Frehley said. Then he picked up the bar at one end while Reed picked it up from the other. Strap pulled his arm away as Frehley dropped the bar in place and Strap hammered it down in the middle with his fist.

There came a blow upon the magazine door that rattled the bar in its braces. Blow after blow descended upon the door until its rails vibrated. And dust sifted out of the splintered frame.

"Little pig, little pig," mocked Sergeant Hood from the other side of the battered door. "Let me in."

Everyone knew it was the Destroyer. And everyone knew what would happen if that thing got in.

"Not by the hair of my chinny-chin-chin!" Reed called back. Sure he was right back in the middle of another scrape with the same company that he had met in jail but he wanted to do something else—anything else—than to just be scared all the time.

"We won't be able to get past him," Cyrus said.

"Then we'll find another way out," Frehley said and turned to survey the room.

"How? Blow out the back wall? Stroll out the front gate?" Cyrus moaned.

A blaze of glory…set off in the Destroyer's face.

"Dump it out!" Reed said. He felt alive. Fully awake after getting his breath back. "Right in front of the door and light it up! Let it go off in their faces!"

"Are you mad, kid?" Cyrus said. "You'll blow us all sky high!"

Strap struck the knuckle of his thumb across his vertical palm.

"Yeah, I know," Frehley said. "We need flints."

"I could do it if I still had my gold coin," Reed said giving Cyrus the eye.

"Well, it's gone now," Cyrus said.

"But you still got your heart necklace," Reed said to Frehley.

Thunder rained down on the door and beam. Both began to bend from the pounding.

Frehley reached into his leather belt and pulled out the chain link and the simple open design of the quicksilver heart. Reed realized that it looked the same as the ones Mom had given to Chayse and him. Like the ones that the Elfwitch had been wanting from the very beginning.

The ex-Royal Huntsman touched the tip of the heart to the end of the punk. It flared up like an Ohio blue tip match guaranteed to catch on the first strike. The light from the punk pushed the shadows back between the rows and stacks of sleeping powder.

A hammering blow made the door crunch this time. It wasn't going to hold much longer.

"Start dumpin'!" Frehley commanded.

Strap pushed against two towering rows of barrels like Samson knocking out the lynchpin pillars of the beloved house of Dagon down upon the benighted heads of the Philistines.

The barrels tipped end over end and burst upon the floor like smashing pumpkins vomiting out mealed cakes of black powder.

Frehley dipped the punk towards the molehill of powder.

"You light that and you'll destroy us all!" Cyrus moaned as he slunk back against the bare wall clutching the wooden basin against his chest.

Frehley brandished the quicksilver heart necklace still in his sit. "This is what needs to be destroyed!"

Then the ex-Royal Huntsman handed the punk to Reed. "I'll leave it up to Reed."

Reed was tired of being on the run. Being hungry. Being in darkness.

More than anything he wanted to get home. To see Mom. But he would have to figure out how he could win his sister back and why Frehley looked and sounded like Dad but wasn't Dad.

But most of all, Reed was tired of the confusion that happened since Miss Elsie Crutch had shown up at his door. He'd rather not face the Destroyer again. He'd rather the Destroyer show a little fear.

So Reed put the end of the punk against the edge of the gunpowder spill. "You're gonna get punked! Come and get it!"

The flame jumped from the torch onto the mass of mealed cakes. One dancing flame multiplied into an army of fire as the mound of black powder began to deflagrate. The whole top of the hill lit up in incandescent combustion. Giving off half-smoke and half trails of ash particles. Filling the room with a haze and waves of thick sulfur.

As soon as the fire took hold and the smoke rolled, the pounding on the door stopped.

The company did not have much room to back away from the burning mass. The combusting fire radiated out more heat. They were stopped by another row of barrels.

Three more barrels toppled over onto the floor. One was crushed like an egg spewing out its contents like a bag of biscuits. The other two rolled across the floor throwing off their lids and slinging mounds of gunpowder everywhere.

"Put that thing out!" Frehley warned him.

It was only then that Reed was conscious of still holding the lit punk in his hand. Cyrus flipped the wooden basin over and scooted it across the floor with his boot. Reed dropped the punk into the wooden basin.

"Water!" Frehley said. "They'd fill the basin with water! In case of fire!"

"The stream!" Reed called out. "It comes under the wall and goes by the oak tree."

"And so it goes back out on this side of the Martello tower! It has to! The Deadcoats built over it! They didn't put all this ammunition underground otherwise it'd get wet!"

"Then the stream's below us! Just don't stand there! Start lookin' for it!" Cyrus said.

They spread out. Searching the back walls behind the rows and stacks. Looking for a vent in the wall. Or a trench in the floor.

The air in the room was thick with spent sulfur and floating ash. Reed didn't know who but someone spun the open gunpowder barrel around so that it faced the deflagrating mass. A tiny spark ran up the mouth of the barrel. It smoked and then flames erupted out as the barrel spun around and whistled like a Flying Saucer fireworks that Reed always enjoyed as a kid. But Dad had made him shoot it off outside, not inside a room full of gunpowder.

There were just but seconds before an almighty explosion that would send the company skyhigh.

Reed coughed and waved the wafting ash from before his eyes. A stack of boxes full of stood atop a piece of furrowed metal along the back wall. It looked like a grate for an air vent.   "There! It's there!" Reed called and pointed. The others joined him near the back wall He bent down and poked his fingers through the grate. He could feel cool moisture below.

The spinning barrel came to a stop against the door frame catching it alight post to post.

In a step, Strap and Frehley were beside Reed. They worked like mad dogs to get the boxes of shot off of the grate. The boxes were tossed or placed wherever. Stacked like off-kilter hedges.

One box teetered and spilled out into the edge of the smoking residue of gun powder. The balls began to smoke under the brisant heat. They exploded. Became low-velocity projectiles.

"Judge bless!" Frehley said as a ball struck near his head.

The grate was clear. Strap snatched it up like an arm in a crane machine and threw it into the middle of the floor.

"Reed!" Frehley yelled, "You go first!"

The boy didn't know what was down there waiting for him. Asheroth? Deadcoats? A dead end with gnawed bones? What if it was what something he most wanted? A way out.

Thinking about it didn't help, Reed just had to do it. And if he was scared, Reed would just have to do it scared.

So he dropped down through the vent.

***

Chapter Forty-One: Burn and Down

There was a chamber below. More like a culvert. Or a sluice gate.

It was dank and wet. Much of it was covered in shadow. With water running.

Reed stepped down and put his boot into water up to his ankle. Reaching out with both hands, he met smooth wet brick.

"I'm in a culvert!" Reed called back up. "There's room enough for everyone!"

Flaming gunpowder gave a cast off light. But at least there wasn't much smoke, thank the Judge.

Frehley dropped down beside Reed. Next Cyrus wobbled through and fell into the water. Then Strap twisted himself through the opening and plopped down.

Things got a little crowded at that point.

And Cyrus complained again, "That room's about to burn down and that shot'll cut us all up!"

Every time Cyrus got like that, he seemed pleased to be so right.

"The barracks door!" Frehley said. "We can cover the vent with it and hope for the best."

"Who wants to go back up there just to get themselves blowed up?" Cyrus asked.

Everyone looked at Reed. Who, by default, was the smallest.

"Reed, we can you lift you back up but you can't pull that door over by yourself," Frehley said.

The giant snapped his fingers until he had everyone's attention. First he pointed to Reed and made a climbing motion followed by a grabbing motion. Then he pointed to Frehley and made a grabbing motion at Reed's feet. Then he gesticulated at Frehley's legs.

"Maybe that'll do it," Frehley said. "Reed, get up there and grab that door! I'll hold onto your legs and Strap will hold onto mine!"

"If you all wanna get yer heads blown off, I won't stop you," Cyrus said and scooted away from the vent opening and further back into the shadows of the culvert.

Strap picked Reed up and just like that the boy wiggled through the oven door and back into the fracking pan.

The magazine room was turning into wreck and ruin. Two boxes of shot sat in the fire and spit out musket balls like a tiny wild pitching machine. The balls slammed into stacked boxes and careened into barrels until they threatened to topple.

Neither the Destroyer nor a single Deadcoat had made it through the burning door. Reed was grateful for that. Now all he had to do was crawl over the floor without getting shot up. He felt Frehley's sure hands around his ankles.

And Reed was grateful for that, too.

Reed snaked forward having to stop until he felt Frehley pull himself back out of the vent. It wasn't the same as Dad holding onto the back of his bike when the training wheels had come off but it was close enough. Frehley pushed Reed forward until he was stretched out with Strap's large hands around the ex-Royal Huntsman's ankles.

Strap was their safety line.

Blows pounded against the door anew. Not only was the frame on fire but also the bar locking it. Reed spotted the metal barracks door tucked along the back wall to his right. Right next to the stack of barrels that had been shot up and were smoking.

Within a breath the whole room was up to go up like a massive mortar air burst on a cloudy Fourth of July night.

Another blow fell on the door brought the burning bar down into two pieces.

Reed pulled himself over the side wall on his elbows and grabbed the edge of the thick door. "Got it!"

The door couldn't be pushed open so the Destroyer knocked it down. He peered through the flames of the burning mound looking for anyone else to knock down.

"Pull!" Frehley yelled back over his shoulders to Strap.

So Strap began to pull.

"Hold on!" Frehley said to Reed.

The Destroyer spotted them on the floor and sneered at them as they were skulking rats. Then it slit its eyes raising clenched fists. The Destroyer would kill them if it caught them again.

Strap pulled Frehley down through the vent which swung Reed about being he was on the end of the human rope. In turn the door was yanked away and fell to its side crashing smoking barrels which collapsed in a long arc right smack dab in the middle of the burning pile of gunpowder at the Destroyer' feet.

The fire kicked up so bright the creature had to shield his black ringed eyes with his arm.

Reed followed the descent through the vent. He carried the metal door over the top of it. The last thing Reed saw were flames leap onto the barrels giving them fresh accelerant for combustion in a room full of ordinance while the Destroyer turned and ran.

The three companions fell over each other in the small culvert with Reed half landing on someone's legs and in the middle of the stream. Above them a subsonic explosion echoed throughout the culvert with the hot steam of dragon breath and the stink of spent sulfur.

A battle's worth of gunpowder gone in a single volley. The magazine room consumed in blind fury. And just maybe the quicksilver necklace would be obliterated.

The ground rumbled with the shock.

Was the Martello tower falling in?

The rumbles faded. The shock subsided. Ash sifted down from the covered vent.

They all had dog piled on Strap and half landed in the sluice stream. Everyone checked on themselves over for any hurts. Everyone was still breathing.

Reed gave a nervous laugh. "That was the biggest bang I ever heard."

Frehley smiled, whose own face was covered in soot. "It singed yer eyebrows."

Reed could smell his burnt hair now. It worse than a wet dog.

Light illuminated the other end of the culvert. That meant an opening. Into the day's moonlight.

It was Frehley who asked, "Where's Cyrus?"

Reed was supposed to show respect and listen to adults. Even when they were wrong. But Cyrus had lied and betrayed them and now had slipped away again.

How was that being an adult?

They all duck-walked to the end of the culvert where the stream exited into the forest. It was covered with something like chicken wire with the edge pulled back enough so that a stocky man could squeeze through.

"He's gone again," Reed said.

"Good riddance," Frehley said.

Strap spat into the stream.

****

Chapter Forty-Two: Stone and Cold

Wice stood by her mistress' side. As Chayse, she couldn't remember being proud of Mom or wanting to be around her much. Mom never seemed to have control over anything: Dad, Reed, the bills, or her work schedule—and that was pretty much her whole life right there.

But now, the Elfwitch, she couldn't get enough of this fey woman. She basked in her presence. Tried to soak up her every look and word.

Wice wanted to become her.

The Elfwitch had directed the Destroyer to make a path through the wreckage of the hallway and magazine room. Sergeant Hood had split up the remaining Deadcoats: some removed the rubble from the barracks that the Destroyer threw out and the others went with their sergeant to patrol the perimeter of the ruined Martello Tower on the odd chance that the renegades had escaped.

When the hated renegades had first set the magazine room on fire, there had been much smoke. After the Deadcoats failed to gain entry, the Elfwitch had sent the Destroyer to finish the job. How long could the worthless men's resistance last with a room full of lit ammunition and a Dark Rider bearing down on them?

But instead of the Destroyer striding back out with renegade heads in one hand and the quicksilver necklace in the other, it had come running out of a hail storm of smoke and whizzing bullets. It regained the ruined barracks doorway just as the rest of the magazine room touched off in a massive explosion. The wild and untamed kind that Dad and Reed would have gotten tickled over on the Fourth of July in another time and another place.

The blast force pushed the Destroyer back to the feet of the Elfwitch and sent flying debris across the stream like a dam and rolled bricks to the roots of the Mighty Oak. No one could have survived that explosion. Wice was impressed that the vile renegades had elected to die together rather than surrender. Neither did it fail her notice that the Destroyer had turned tail.

There was a memory of Chayse, buried under her debris field, considering suicide just last year after the constant bullying of every girl in her sixth-grade class. To them, she was a freak, an outcast. Because she skipped school a lot. Because of her family life.

Never again. Now Wice had power. Because others feared her. It gave her confidence.

But there was something more. A feeling that power had no use for. Concern.

Had the boy agreed to the renegade's suicide pact? Even when Chayse had been full of despair and self-loathing from being the bullies' victim, the one thing that had turned those thoughts around was knowing there was a twelve-year-old brother, five minutes younger than herself, who was always willing to share life with her—the good, the bad, and the ugly.

Didn't that count for something?

Wice didn't think so. Not here in this world. Not anymore.

Did Wice wish the boy dead? Let the boy be buried under a pile of stone and bone. Let the memory of Chayse and she felt towards the boy—her twin brother—be buried there as well.

The memory hurt less even now.

Tomorrow it would hurt even less.

Wice had it down stone cold—stop believing and the boy would no longer matter. She said, "Surely, they all died in the blast, my mistress."

"Desperation can lend aid to rats trapped in a corner," the Elfwitch said. "If they were able to escape, we will hunt them down.

"The only thing they could do was try to keep the quicksilver from me. I have waited thousands of years. A little more time matters not. I will have that quicksilver necklace."

"Cannot we look for the boy's silver heart necklace?" Wice asked.

The Elfwitch scowled. "Silver belongs to the Darkness, true. But it is weaker than quicksilver. Quicksilver is azothic. A piece of creation still can be formed. In a state of flux. A most wondrous treasure, my pet."

"Why can't you just go to that lake?" Wice asked. "You could make a whole tower of quicksilver."

"I cannot. There are ...," the Elfwitch began and then whispered the last word, "boundaries."

"Can't the Darkness do anything?" Wice asked.

Deep down, the memory of that silly girl's Mom answered instead. *If you have to ask, then the answer is no.* It was an adult's stock answer and hated by children.

Hadn't the Destroyer run from the explosion? Didn't all the servants of the Darkness fear gold? So even they had *boundaries.* Limits. Rules.

So, they were not gods or goddesses. They were not all-powerful or all-knowing. They couldn't do everything they wanted whenever they wanted.

Hadn't Mom said that's what being an adult was like?

Wice promised to do her best to squelch the memories of that silly little kid. What she once was wasn't what she wanted to be anymore. *I'm Wice*, she told herself over and over.

Trouble was, how many times would she have to keep saying until she believed it?

Then another thought came so fast on the heels of that one that once it crept into Wice's mind she tried to ignore it because it seemed impossible and forbidden and she didn't want the Elfwitch to know it was in up there walking around in her mind: *can they be destroyed?*

Hadn't the Judge *made* Ice Prison? Hadn't the Judge put them *there* in the first place? Didn't that mean that the Judge was *more* powerful than what the Elfwitch claimed?

The Destroyer strode from the wrecked barracks with a broad grin. Assurance. Victory.

In its open palm lay a small, dull amulet.

The Destroyer tossed it up in the air.

The Elfwitch snatched it up like a hawk pursuing a dove.

She held it up between her thumb forefinger for Wice to see. It was an open heart amulet. The chain blasted off and the clasps pinched back. Shiny like silver. Liquid symmetry like running water. Tarnished from the burning fire. .

An alarm went off in Wice's gut. A shot of electricity ran up her spine to her brain. It was hurt. For a brief second, she was Chayse again. A twelve-year-old twin kidnapped from her World who had abandoned her own twin in this world and she knew the reason why: she had been tricked.

That's just like the heart necklace Mom gave me! **So what?** *I was wrong to give mine up.* **But now you have power.** *Quicksilver is the ultimate power here.*

Then I'll get my own quicksilver necklace! And I'll do what I want!

She wasn't sure who had answered: Chayse or Wice?

A call came from outside the gate and those on watch drew it up. A Deadcoat marched through and up to the Elfwitch. The trooper saluted with a decayed hand over his one good eye. "Sergeant Hood sent me to report. There is a trail leading out of the culvert into the woods. He requests that the rest of the garrison be sent to search for the renegades."

The Elfwitch shook her head. "The rats are of no consequence now. There is nowhere they can run to and no one to help them.

"Return to the sergeant and have him bring the patrol back here. All the legion is to report to the Keep," the Elfwitch ordered.

The trooper finished his salute and left through the front gate.

The Elfwitch fidgeted with the amulet between her fingers. "We are headed back to Ice Prison."

The Destroyer nodded his consent and smiled in anticipation of the coming evil and misery.

"To do what?"Wice asked.

"To free another prisoner," the Elfwitch said.

"I thought the quicksilver or any metal amulet could only be given by consent," Wice said.

"That is true. It is a boundary. But even though this quicksilver amulet has been abandoned," the Elfwitch said and touched her cheek with the point of the amulet. "There is another way around the boundary. A back door, if you will."

Then she tucked the quicksilver heart up the fold of her robe. Cupping her hand to the side of her mouth she cawed like a twisted ugly blackbird. "Wice, I have called the feathered twin back to carry you. Do not try to harm it this time or it will drop you from on high like a turtle.

"The wind will carry we Dark Riders!" the Elfwitch said.

Without another word, both the Elfwitch and the Destroyer spun themselves as they dissolved into a mass of swirling blackbirds. Both flocks shot up in the sky and followed the magnetic streams north.

***

Chapter Forty-Three: Silver and Gold

Once outside, Frehley shooed them along the streambed as it ran free and clear into heavy woods. "We gotta get deep into the woods. The Deadcoats won't just assume we all died in that blast. TheElfwitch will make 'em comb through that whole mess. And when they find our escape route, they'll be on our trail again."

"Where can we even go in the Realm where the Elfwitch and the Destroyer can't find us?" Reed asked.

"I don't know where we'll end up," Frehley said. "I only know where we've been. We're due for some food. And a miracle. Overdue, in fact. You even listening up there, Judge?"

"I need to find Packy," Reed asked. He had grown fond of the small rodent. He caught himself even talking to it. The rat had proven himself more helpful than a pet.

Strap put a hand on both Frehley's and Reed's shoulders.

"We left your Packy with Evander," Frehley sighed.

"Where?" Reed asked. Now there was a modicum of hope.

"Not far from here. We stashed our weapons with them. When we get there, we can hunt up some food. Food always helps me think," Frehley said.

Reed doubled time his step and tried to pass up Frehley. Their back trail along the stream led to a steep cliff. The water cascaded down in pools and falls from its source high above. Soon the boy grew tired beyond belief. Too little food overrode the excitement of escape. Tired legs could not propel the thrill of seeing Packy and Evander.

Reed was so starved and weak he couldn't think beyond the next step. One need at a time. Rest and water. Or water then rest. Or both together would be nice.

Frehley was serious about getting up the trail before the Deadcoats gave chase again. Reed chanced a look back at Martello tower. He couldn't see the base or where the culvert emptied out. Smoke plumes drifted up from the top of the tower. Swirling black tendrils lost in the black of the night sky. He could still see most of the flat tower ramparts chalked with lines that demarked the degrees of a circle to position the cannon.

Success! Something they had tried had worked! Although it didn't help slake their thirst.

"Can't we at least stop to drink or rest?" Reed asked.

Frehley pointed up the slope to the summit hidden by trees and karst outcroppings. From there the water flowed all the way to the Mighty Oak now walled up behind the Martello Tower.

"We gotta climb to the top so we can spot anyone on our back trail," Frehley said.

Reed was bone tired. And more climbing was not on his to-do list. He groaned.

Strap motioned to carry Reed but he declined making his stiff legs work a little longer.

Reed tried to gauge if it was night or day. Since there was no sun, it was almost impossible to track time. The sky kept itself dark.

"It's like a twilight world. How do you know if it's day or night?" Reed huffed.

Frehley had steeled himself long ago, "You get used to it."

The Realm was a mirror of back home—the trees and the rocks and the knobs and hollers all cried OZARKS. So when the trio reached the summit, they found the source of the waterfall to be the lip of a large lake. The water had hallowed out a spillway filled with fronds and polliwogs across a ledge. Water bugs skipped across the top and minnows darted below crystal clear water stretched back to even steeper granite cliffs.

It had to be the most serene place Reed come across yet in the Realm.

Majestic and wonderful.

Frehley made a seat for himself on the granite ledge. Strap knelt beside him. And Reed, using the last of his strength, spread over the natural spillway face down.

So everyone rested. Drank their fill. And rested some more.

After a time, Reed asked, "Are the Deadcoats comin' after us?"

Strap looked down to the smoking tower and shook his head.

Frehley kissed the sky. "Not yet. But they soon will be. Rest easy, my companions."

Reed felt better. Drinking the clear water had cut his exhaustion. Relaxed his muscles.

Strap sighed and then dipped the top of his head into the lake. Frehley wiped off his face and neck with handfuls of water and then stood to walk up the slope towards the granite cliffs.

Reed hoped against hope that Packy was well. And Evander, too. Both had taken a beating.

Hope. Reed knew the word. He could spell it. Speak it. But it was just a word.

He had never understood when Mom would say, *Hope is something small.* Yeah, so small, he couldn't even see it. So, he couldn't really believe in it.

Reed saw Deadcoats filing off from the ramparts. "What are they doin' down there?"

Frehley spat. "They're lookin' for the necklace! I hoped to the Judge that it gotten blowed up. I hope I didn't make another mistake. We'd better start off again."

It was Strap who led them away from the ledge and along the bank towards the cliffs.

Another thought came to Reed. "What if the necklace didn't get blown up?"

Frehley shrugged. "Then things will get worse than they are now."

How could things get any worse? Reed had already lost Dad. Then Mom. And not long after coming to this world, he'd lost Sis, too.

Sure, he had gained some companions. Frehley. Strap. Evander . Packy. And even Cyrus for a time. But Cyrus had run away again. And how bad off were Evander and Packy?

Every time Reed thought about Cyrus, his chest got tight, his guts caught fire, and his cheeks burned. But the thought of losing Packy felt like glass cutting across Reed's gut.

As they climbed the steep incline beside the cliff, Reed asked out loud, "I've seen how gold and silver work. But how does quicksilver work?"

"I forget you're not from the Realm," Frehley said as wiped the sweat off his forehead his a frayed sleeve. "So, I'll tell you what my dad told me. Life is like your gold coin. A coin's got two sides: heads and tails. But there's also top and bottom. Up and down. Right and left.

"There is an order to life, see? There's a beginning and an ending. Hot and cold. Day and night. Sun and moon. Man and woman. Child and parent. Old and young. Winter and Summer. Spring and fall. Rich and poor. Truth and lies. Hope and despair. Love and hate. Good and evil. Life and death.

"And you've also got the Light and the Darkness. My dad always said the Light came first and everything else came out of it. Even the Darkness grew in the shadows of the Light.

"Two sides. Same coin.

"And it's the same for the metals," Frehley said.

"So, there's silver and gold," Reed said. "Gold stands for the Light and the sun and it's used for the power of truth.

"But silver stands for the Darkness and the moon and it's used for vows and curses."

"Yes," Frehley acknowledged. "But there's more. Iron comes from lead which is the heaviest and strongest of all metals. So, that's why tools and weapons are forged from it. But it can't stand up to water. It will rust.

"But quicksilver is different than any metal. It's sorta liquid like water. Sorta solid like metal. Kinda like a leftover from the time of creation.

"It's neither good nor evil. All depends on who's usin' it. It can dissolve both gold and silver. But there's one metal it can't dissolve: iron. Quicksilver clings to iron and takes its shape."

"Got all that?"

"Gold beats silver. Quicksilver beats both gold and silver. Iron beats quicksilver," Reed said with a nod.

"You got it down stone cold," Frehley said.

Even Strap nodded in consent.

"Kinda like rock-paper-scissors," Reed said.

Frehley stopped to turn back. "What is that?"

Everyone stopped.

"It's a game we learned in kindergarten. Everyone does it," Reed said but when he looked at the blank faces of Frehley and Strap he decided maybe everyone didn't after all.

So he showed them. "This is rock." He made a fist. "This is paper." He held out his palm. "This is scissors." He stuck out his first two fingers. Next, he used both hands. "Paper beats rock." He covered his other fist. "Scissors beats paper." He cut his palm with two fingers from the other hand. "Rock beats scissors." He smashed the two fingers with his other fist.

Both Frehley and Strap practiced with him. They both held up their fists.

"Two rocks," Reed said. "That's a draw. Means no one wins. It's a do-over."

The child's game over, they made the top of the cliffs where exposed boulders sat shaded by large bushes.

Caws echoed overhead. Maddening cries of blackbirds on the move. It resounded and came at them.

Frehley stopped them in their tracks.

Strap made a claw with his hand and swooshed through the air. Frehley led the company to cover under thick hemlock bushes. Reed risked a glance skyward.

Two flocks of blackbirds jetted up side by side up from the bottom of the hill over the waterfalls to the sky above. Streaming like a two fluttering arrows shot through the clouds. And coming from the other direction was a lone figure. Soaring and gliding. A vulture with two sets of eyes on two heads. An unnatural and evil thing.

Even when the birds had passed them in their road in the sky, Frehley made them keep still and quiet. After the cries of the blackbirds had faded behind them, a double squawking continued. Reed took another peep from his hiding place.

The two-headed vulture flew back the way it had come. This time flying much lower.Since it was laden with weight. In its claws, it held a passenger by the shoulders.

A lithe young girl.Chayse, his estranged sister who claimed to be someone else—Wice.

"Where is it taking her?" Reed whispered.

"They're headed for Glacier Mountains," Frehley said.

Strap traced a loop around his neck.

Frehley cursed, "The Elfwitch found the amulet. I should've put it in the fire!"

"Why?" Reed asked.

"Fire melts silver and gold. Refines it. And you can reshape it. But not quicksilver. I told you when you put quicksilver into a fire it turns into a gas. That's the only way to destroy it. Now she's got the quicksilver!"

***

Chapter Forty-Four: Ice and Thaw

Everyone met in the Circle Chamber: Dark Mistress, Dark Rider, servant, and Deadcoat officers. The Lair of the Elfwitch. The abode of her secret wares. Beneath the Keep. Between Porticullis Cave and the Ice Prison. Behind the dungeon.

The double-headed vulture took its perch alongside the wall of caged animals: some reserved for experiments, some reserved for exotic pets, and some reserved for cruel punishments.

The servants let Wice pass through their midst 'till she stood by the Elfwitch and the Destroyer in the center. The other followers ringed them in circles. In the first circle stood Colonel Graves and the remaining officer core of the Black Watch. Sergeant Hood stood among his decaying soldiers in the next circle.

"Hear me, oh, servants," the Elfwitch hushed them. "The struggle has been great. And you have forfeited your serfdom in the Realm for service in my Domain.

"Do you feel lost? There is a forever home for you in the Darkness.

"Do you feel fear? There is a forever purpose for you in the Darkness."

"We have done and will continue to do what is needed to finish the Great Work. We are bringing the Darkness. First, we ignored the Law. Then we railed at the Regents and made all their servants mutiny! Next, we broke all oaths and twisted all vows. Next, we banished the Light.

"We replaced the sun with the Moon! We replaced justice with revenge! We replaced love with hate! We purged the weak!

"One by one we free the servants of the Darkness. With an offering of precious metal and blood! Every step brings it closer. It cannot be stopped. It is coming like the changing seasons.

"Oh, glorious day! When all order shall be turned upside down! And anarchy shall rule! That is the Great Work!

"Soon we shall stand in the Lesser Light of the Moon forever. And the Darkness shall know us and call us its own. And fill us with its cold fire.

"Praise be that day!"

All of the servants, except for Wice, lifted their ragged hands in allegiance reaching as high as they could. They repeated the response "Praise be that day" but Spell Speak changed it into *We obey the Darkness. We renounce the Light. We hate the Law.*

"Do not swear allegiance to the Light that has lost. Pledge not your heart to the Judge who has left you. For your true mother is the Darkness.

"In the twilight. In the evening. In the black and dark night. She stands waiting at the door. To draw those close who will heed her.

"She steals the Law in secrecy. Then she wipes it away and says 'I have done no evil.'

"If the Porter were to let us pass into the Sepulcher, we would see that the Law has turned to sand and the Son has turned to dust. Because the Son is dead and the Law is dead.

"We don't need the Judge. We can be like him in being able to know good and evil! We are free to decide for ourselves!

"Let me tell you a secret. Something that is not in the Judge's flawed Law. There is no good and there is no evil. There is only shadow.

"Praise the Darkness!"

Again the servants gave a salute and echoed the refrain. And again the Spell Speak changed it into arcane submission.

Wice felt sick at her stomach.

Why?

Wasn't this what she wanted?

To escape? To be free of her whole family who couldn't follow rules and pay bills and didn't know how to love each other?

Wasn't it too late to turn back now?

Where was Reed now? Was he still with that renegade who looked like Dad? How was that even possible? How could the Queen look like Mom?

They weren't Mom and Dad. But Wice was going to treat them the same as Mom and Dad. They were nobodies and not worth her respect.

Reed wasn't her brother anymore. She had no family. Only the Darkness.

The vibe was rising. Building like a storm front. Gathering static electricity.

Something was coming.

Something was going to happen.

Something that should not be.

It could not be denied.

It could not be refused.

It could not be stopped.

The lycanthropes entered the Circle Chamber, fully recovered from their smack down in the escape tunnel from the guest quarters. They carried the one thing that always caught Wice's attention.

The chest.

With her namesake burned into the wood.

WICE.

The lycanthropes parted the servants with the chest and brought to the center of the circle and laid it at the Elfwitch's feet.

"Anger is an energy," the Elfwitch said. "Jealousy is a fire that burns. The means are the ends. The seed is sown in the fruit. It brings a blue harvest.

"We have eternity at our feet."

She bent down and pulled the lid back on its squeaking hinges.

Wice looked into the heart of the chest.

It wasn't empty.

It was full of dark blackness. So black it could not be penetrated by any light. Yet, it pulled the light in like a magnet. An event horizon.

The Elfwitch reached down into the chest her arm disappearing up to the elbow. Then she pulled it back out. Her fist was closed.

There was something in her hand.

She opened up her palm.

In it lay the open heart made of quicksilver.

"We have quicksilver, my servants!" she called out.

Again the followers pumped the air.

Wice had come to the Domain as someone else and with someone else. Both of them had worn silver and not even known its power here. She knew now that her first step in becoming Wice had been the moment when she had handed over her silver necklace. **No, I was tricked**! But hadn't she learned the trick? Wouldn't it be fun to play that same trick on someone else?

The Elfwitch had spoken of a back door.

Another trick!

That's what Wice was interested in! How to cheat the order of things. How to beat the boundaries.

There had to be a catch. There had to be some danger. There had to be.

The Elfwitch held up her hands to silence the throng and refocus them. "Oh, my servants! Quicksilver is precious. It is a relic from the moment of creation. It is flux itself. But to be wielded it must be given as a freewill gift. Otherwise, it can still be harnessed. But one time only.

"By fire and blood. Who shall bring both before me?"

The lycanthrope twins came forward. Nicolai bore a torch. And Victor lit with flint stones.

A lady-in-waiting stepped out of the last ring of followers. The Deadcoats made way for her as she stood before the Dark Lady. The Elfwitch took in her youthful freckles, the assurance in her brunette hair, and the willingness to believe in her hazelnut eyes.

"It is such faith that feeds the Darkness! Stay here, my faithful followers! You shall see what the end of this quicksilver shall bring!" Then the Elfwitch pointed to the passageway that led to Ice Prison. "Nic and Vic, bring the fire! Wice, bring the gift!"

The Elfwitch led the way as her servants made a path. The Destroyer followed and was sure to grab a tripod by the passage entrance. Wice walked behind the creature leading the naïve lady-in-waiting by the wrist. Behind them came the lycanthrope twins each with a torch.

Once again, the six people walked through the passageway as it turned from stone to ice until they came to the parallel corridor with the wall that rose stories above the Keep. The glacier that covered the mountains.

Torchlight danced against the diffused blue crystals. Against the frozen wastes that held the remains of the Elfwitch's world. Man and beast. Tool and house. Miles of frozen water. Millions of cubic inches of ice.

The caprice of the Judge.

A trick of the Light.

The procession came upon the four niches.

Every other was now empty. Leaving two occupied. The one on the far right held the tall rail-thin figure in a long robe hiding its hands and face. And the one on the left stood erect in its leather duster and a wide-brimmed hat with a ponytail across its shoulder.

But one would not be for very much longer.

The Elfwitch stopped the procession before this figure.

She bade the lycanthrope twins set the tripod down in front of the ice niche beside the cloth-covered table. One lycanthrope set the tripod and the other lit it. The table served as some kind of altar.

Then the Elfwitch put her hand on the lady-in-waiting's shoulders. This is what the young girl had waited for her whole life: purpose and service.

"We have our fire. Now we shall have our blood," she traced the outline of the young girl's ears and neckline with a long fingernail.

The lady-in-waiting stiffened her shoulders. "I am willing, my Dark Lady."

The Elfwitch paused her finger. "There will be no need to shed the blood."

The lady-in-waiting's shoulders dropped as she exhaled.

"This is a different kind of sacrifice," the Elfwitch confessed. "One of loyalty."

The lady-in-waiting nodded. "What is your wish, Dark Lady?"

The Elfwitch traced her finger along the lady-in-waiting's shoulder and then around the front of her neck. Then she turned over her hand. In the Elfwitch's open palm lay the quicksilver heart amulet.

"Take this. Walk up to that tripod and drop the amulet into the fire. Then watch and wait," the Elfwitch commanded.

The lady-in-waiting considered the ease of the command. Then she took the amulet out of the Elfwitch's hand and nodded. "As you wish."

The lady-in-waiting walked over to the tripod in front of the ice niche with its lazy fire. Then stuck her hand out with the amulet above the fire. With a flip, she tossed the amulet into the fire.

Wice was surprised at what came next. The amulet sizzled. The quicksilver evaporated easily in the flame. Turning from a solid-state into a gaseous vapor. The vapors wafted out of the tripod and encircled the lady-in-waiting caressing her head and face. Drifting into her mouth and up her nostrils.

The lady-in-waiting became weightless in the cloud of mercurial gas. She was overcome with breathing the azothic vapor in and out. The cloud lifted her to the eye level of the Dark Rider encased in ice within the niche.

When the gas touched the ice it created a fog. In this way, the ice evaporated into a fog. The lady-in-waiting's eyes opened. But the iris had changed from hazelnut to quicksilver.

Her skin had taken a dull ashen hue, much like the Elfwitch's tone. She reached out a hand and reached through the thin ice over the Dark Rider's hand. Then she drew him out from his frozen sleep.

The Dark Rider's eyes opened. The orbs were solid black. It flexed its hands and stretched its back and yawned.

The lady-in-waiting fell at its feet. The vapor dissipated. The servant was dead.

The Dark Rider bent back its head and howled in misery. Then it jumped at the Destroyer with a snarl and hip tossed the other. The released Dark Rider put the Destroyer's head in the crook of its elbow and once the other was sitting on the ground the first Dark Rider put a hold around its neck with the crook of its elbow and would have pulled its head off had not the Elfwitch stepped in.

"Hold, Rancor!" she addressed it.

The first Dark Rider let go of the Destroyer who choked as it slid away.

"You are Rancor," the Elfwitch continued. "Your fight is not with us. You seek the same purpose as us! To crush the Law! Bring down the Light! Banish the Judge!

"You are the Eternal Dark Rider who crushes love and friendship. Who causes animosity and antagonism between family and friends. Who stokes grievance and spite into cold revenge.

"Rancor, be one of us! Ride with us! Sow seeds of anarchy with us! Reap the Darkness!"

Rancor let go of the Destroyer who choked and sputtered and kicked to get away from his adversary now turned companion. The released Dark Rider took off his broad-rimmed hate showing a hairless head bore scar tissue from claw and tooth and fire and blows and howled recriminations for eons long incarceration.

The cry mutated into retribution for being born.

"Wice!" the Elfwitch called.

"Yes, my Dark Lady," Wice answered. "What is it you wish of me?"

The Elfwitch reached into her robe and pulled out something Wice had not considered for quite some time.

It was a device.

That belonged to another world.

It was Chayse's Tracfone.

Wice took it from the Dark Lady's hand. It felt so alien to her now. Rectangular. Compact. Barely more than a few pounds.

"Contact the boy. Tell him to come to the Keep. Say whatever you have to make him believe you still care," the Elfwitch said.

"I thought he doesn't matter," Wice said.

The Elfwitch shook her head with a slow smile. "He is a boy. And if I allow him to become a man he would be hollow inside. Blind. Men have to be led like a dog with a collar.

"But you, my pet, are not the same as him. You are a woman-child. You have killed in my name. A moon child with blood on your hands.

"You were a seed planted by the Darkness in your mother's womb. Woman is the mother of all life. You alone have the destiny of the Lesser Light."

"I don't know what you mean by Lesser Light," Wice said.

"I will teach you. You are the initiate and I am the high priestess. It is a mystery. Deep and wide. It encompasses the circle of the universe. The fabric of existence. You will enter into it. You will discover it. You will control it," the Elfwitch promised.

"What about the boy?" Wice asked. "He is a twin." *My twin.*

"Twins have a special power but it is a cruel jest to have a girl and boy twin," the Elfwitch said. "Just like when an oyster yields two pearls, one must naturally be greater and the other lesser.

"He is a cast-off! A weakling! Had you both been mine, I would have kept you and the boy would have been left exposed in the Glacier Mountains.

"If he's useless to you, then let me have him for a servant," Wice said.

"No," the Elfwitch said.

"Then as a pet as you call me," Wice said.

"I think not," the Elfwitch said.

"Then let him go. Return him back to our World," Wice said.

The Elfwitch shook her head.

"Why not?" Chayse demanded.

"There is one way he still must serve us. You will have to see to it," the Elfwitch said. "Then you must kill him. To show your fealty to me. Now use that device."

"I can't without a cell tower or a signal," Wice said.

The Elfwitch squinted her eyes. "It has precious metal in it. You know how to use that."

Wice's heart sank.

Her future seemed sutured up.

She was out of choices.

***

Chapter Forty-Five: Day and Night

Frehley hurried the pace.

They must have traversed most of what counted as a day here in the Realm. Reed wondered how much further would they have to trek to get back to Evander and Packy.

A figure appeared in the tree line. Wearing a duster with a broad rim over a sneering face. The figure took off his hat to reveal a scarred and bald head. Ugly wounds. Old hurts.

With a sweep of its hat, Reed was filled with the wine of wrath. Then the figure disappeared.

"How are we gonna stop the Elfwitch?" Reed complained.

"We didn't destroy my necklace. You lost your necklace. But yet, we have to stop her from releasing the last two Dark Riders. Then we have to find a way to stop her and put them all back into Ice Prison. And, lest I forget, win your sister back to our side. And bring back the Light so they'll be peace and joy for everyone while we're at it," Frehley groused back.

"You're just like Dad. Always changin' the rules to suit yourself!" Reed said.

Frehley turned and in one step snatched the front of Reed's leather jerkin.

"I ain't yer daddy!" the ex-Royal Huntsman raged. "But I guess I'll be the one to light up yer tail!"

Frehley made to backhand the boy but Strap covered Frehley's fist with his larger palm. Then he stuck out the first two fingers of his other free hand. Frehley stared at the sign.

"Judge bless it!" Frehley said slapping his face. "She's unleashed Rancor."

Strap let go of Frehley's hand and swept them both in a huge bear hug.

"Oh, dear Judge," Frehley blubbered. Was he crying? Then he hugged his big companion around the neck and squeezed Reed to his bosom. Reed was shocked.

"I am so sorry, Reed. I'm sorry you were ever brought here," Frehley said as tried to push the tears back into his eyes. Then the ex-Royal Huntsman he wiped away flowing tears. Only more came down. He brandished a fist at the crescent moon. "We still have a choice!

The sun's up there whether I can see it or not! It's a lie of the Elfwitch! I won't give up hope!"

Reed looked up into the sky.

The sky was an ocean of black ink atop the fading blue and purple of the horizon.

The moon was a caldera of cooling light. A reflection of the Elfwitch's heart.

The stars were bright. But the constellations seemed askew. Obtuse triangles and crooked rhomboids.

There was no sun. So this had to be night time then.

Reed sniffed up his tears. "I'm sorry I'm cryin' all the time."

"Both our worlds have been turned upside down," Frehley said and ruffled the hair on the boy's head. "Deep down, you never get over it. You just want things back the way they were."

That struck Reed. If Frehley felt like that, did Dad feel the same way back in his World?

Strap got them back on task and blazed the trail ahead. Frehley followed. But Reed fell behind.

Something vibrated against Reed.

The last thing he still owned from his World.

His last tie to who he was: Reed Leftwich, brother to Chayse Leftwich. Son to Freddie and Reggie Leftwich. A twelve-year-old boy under yet another FINS and in Foster Care.

It was his Tracfone!

Worlds away from a cell tower.

But here it was vibrating in his belt line. Out of habit, he pulled out the flip top.

The outside screen read:

1 Unread Message.

He flipped it open.

SISSY

Where r u

ME

We ran away. U tried to kill me. Y

SISSY

Come 2 the Keep.

ME

Y

SISSY

I need ur help to escape. Please

Reed didn't know what to do. Well, yes, he did. He needed to win Chayse back and together they needed to get back home and find Mom and get Judge Hart to take them away from the Brazzles. Then they needed Mom to get back together with Dad.

He was confused about just how all that would get accomplished.

Strap led them to a stand of thick, vibrant evergreen trees that had shed a soft carpet of old brown needles. Upon this bedding, the companions had stretched out their fallen comrades: Evander with arms crossed and eyes closed. And Packy on top his still chest huddled in a ball.

Reed's throat clenched off and his stomach tried to curl up. Moor Kreed's death flashed before his eyes. It was never easy to see people you cared about die in front of you.

Out of respect, Frehley and Strap knelt before their fallen comrades. Reed did the same.

"They were both heroes, Reed," Frehley said. "They proved themselves the best of companions. They both made the ultimate sacrifice for their friends."

Reed watched Packy stir his head. His bloody nose twitched. A small beady eye opened.

"He's alive! Packy's alive!" Reed said and reached out to scoop up his pet.

"He's pretty tore up," Frehley said and stayed Reed with a hand on his shoulder. "If you picked him up, he'd hurt even worse. Let's get our weapons and look for some healing sage."

A man stepped out from the brush armed with some of their stashed weapons: a cocked matchlock pistol aimed at Strap and a cocked musket leveled at Frehley. His once blue and black uniform with gold piping now torn and dirtied. His face scratched and his blonde hair tussled. Blonde handlebar mustache smudged with dirt.

The only thing that didn't seem to belong was the leather collar around his neck.

Reed looked long at the man. Trim the mustache and put a smile on his face and give the man a dark blue policeman's uniform and it was…"Bailiff Mike?"

Frehley looked at Reed. "You've seen this man before? Back where you're from?"

Reed nodded.

"That's Captain Michael," Frehley said. "He leads the Queen's Men. He's her chief bodyguard. He would die before he left the queen alone. Which means…"

Out from the brush stepped another figure.

Lithe and regal.

Besmirched and proud.

In a torn green bodice and slippers turned to a shade of red clay mud.

A woman with curly red hair spilling out of the braid at her neck. Freckled cheeks and brown eyes searching for hope. For restoration. For true justice.

Those eyes passed over Reed and Strap and clapped straight onto Frehley.

Which hurt Reed because the woman was Mom.

Here.

In the Realm.

Along with Dad. The man who claimed wasn't Dad but said he was Frehley.

Reed's heart quickened with a strange hope. Running forward, he squeaked out, "Mom!"

But Bailiff Mike/Captain Michael blocked his path by pointing the pistol at Reed's chest.

Frehley stepped in front of Reed so that Bailiff Mike/Captain Michael aimed the pistol at him. "Woah. Hold up. You say she is your mother?"

Frehley/Dad pointed to Mom/the Queen and Reed nodded. "Yes."

"He also maintains that I'm his father," Frehley told the newcomers.

Reed nodded again. Sure as the sun shone in his World. It was true.

"The boy is deranged," Bailiff Mike/Captain Michael snarled.

"He has a twin sister," Frehley told them. Then he indicated both himself and Strap. "We've seen her. The boy says that the Elfwitch brought them both here from some other place. But his twin sister serves the Elfwitch now. Have you seen her?"

"The Huntsman means the girl Wice," the bodyguard said over his shoulder. "She is the Elfwitch's servant but she did help the queen escape. We are grateful for that. But the Elfwitch re-captured Wice. No doubt, the Elfwitch will want to recapture you and your companions."

Then he aimed the pistol at Frehley's head. "As far as I'm concerned, this is all your fault, Huntsman."

Frehley stood like a soldier on parade. "Again with that crap! Alright, I admit it. Everything bad that's happened to the Realm is my fault. I'm guilty as charged. And I deserve the maximum punishment under the Law. Which is death.

"You've judged me. And now you get to administer punishment. So shoot me dead. .

"Of course, then you'll have to shoot Strap here. And next, you'll have to shoot the boy. For we're all men and the Elfwitch claims that men have ruined everything. But since you're a man, too, you'll have to shoot yerself last of all to save the Elfwitch the time and effort."

Then Frehley asked, "Now is all that gonna solve your problem?"

But Captain Michael did not shoot.

Instead, the Queen put her hand on his shoulder. "Stay yourself. What has become of us?"

"The Elfwitch has released another Dark Rider. Rancor, this time. That's why everyone's hatin' on everyone," Frehley said.

"Then how do we stop hate from spreading? How do we stop the Destroyer from its carnage? How do we stop the Elfwitch from her twisted lies?" the Queen pleaded.

Frehley sighed. "We need to find what was lost. We need to…forgive. And I guess it starts with you and me, Gina. Or should I say Queen Regina."

Something clicked in Reed's memory which had been choked from so many emotional shocks.

"That's Mom's name!" he blurted. "Regina! But she goes by Reggie!"

Reed felt his night begin to turn to day.

***

Chapter Forty-Six: Hate and Love

Frehley put his hand on Reed's shoulder. "Reed, let me introduce to you the Queen of the Realm. Queen Regina. The Root of Lyftwych."

The queen raised her chin waiting for the proper obeisance. None was forthcoming.

"Queen Regina, let me introduce to you, a wondrous boy. I've seen him tame rats. I've seen him wield a gold coin and take on Asheroth. But when I first saw him, he possessed a silver heart necklace," Frehley said.

Captain Michael regarded each detail with an incredulous eye.

Reed spoke up for himself. "I'm Reed." He felt now was the time to drop the name that Moor Kreed had wanted him to keep secret. "Reed Leftwich."

At that, Captain Michael lowered his weapons and the Queen lowered her chin.

Frehley slapped his knee and laughed, "That explains why he had a gold coin!"

"There are no other Lyftwyches. We are the root and have no seed. How old are you, child?" the Queen demanded.

"I'm twelve, don't you know?" Reed said. Strange things were being revealed. He had a building sense of anticipation like climbing the first hill on a roller coaster. Then he added, "Your highness."

"And this Wice? Your sister?" the Queen asked.

"Her real name is Chayse Leftwich," Reed said. "She's older than me by five minutes. We're twins."

Frehley clicked his teeth and pointed a forefinger at the queen. "You've got some 'xplaining to do, Gina."

The queen jolted as if she had been slapped. "Surely, you don't think they're ours? And we are your queen and will be addressed as such."

Frehley waved his hand. "My apologies, oh, queen. It's plain to see the boy has ginger hair and brown eyes. Can you describe his sister?"

The queen shrugged. "She has dark hair and blue eyes. So?"

"Pray, tell me, who do they resemble, if not their parents?" Frehley asked.

Reed looked at both of them. Frehley resembled Dad in every way: dark hair and blue eyes. Queen Regina was a mirror of Mom: curly ginger hair and dark brown eyes.

Queen Regina snaked out a royal forefinger of condemnation at Frehley. "We are not amused. This is some kind of prank on your part."

"I have not had the time nor the inclination. I've been in jail for twelve years," Frehley said. "Your highness."

This is how Mom and Dad would fight. Mom would accuse Dad of something. And when Dad tried to defend himself, she wouldn't listen.

"If Moor Kreed were here, he could explain it better than me," Frehley said, "But I think Reed and his sister must come from another World. And in their World, twelve years ago, their parents who look like us fell in love and had twins. Meanwhile, twelve years ago here in the Realm, we pledged our love and made vows--"

The queen stopped him with a royal hand. "What happened is not our fault!"

"You were young and foolish, my queen," Captain Michael said.

"We were young and..." the queen said but did she mean herself or both her and Frehley?

"Foolish to think a queen could fall in love?" Frehley offered.

"You had your responsibilities. Your duty. Your family legacy," Captain Michael said.

"We have our royal responsibilities...duty...our family leg...," Queen Regina parroted and then spoke as Gina. "I did fall in love. But a queen cannot have such simple joys."

"But you couldn't forget the Law. A queen must uphold the Law," Captain Michael.

"We were the Law," Queen Regina parroted his phrase. Then she dropped the royal "we" persona. "But I abdicated. Years ago. To High Priest Kyphus. And then the Elfwitch.

"I have lost much, Frehley." It had been a very long since the queen had said his name.

"First, I lost my father. Then I lost you. Then I lost the truth of the Law. Then I lost heart. And now I have lost the Realm and let the Darkness in.

"I had lost all hope until Wice saved me. But now I'm not sure of what to do."

"I've made mistakes, too," Frehley said. "After I heard that the Black Watch had stormed Tower Reign, I hid my necklace back at the Mighty Oak where we'd spotted the owl and made our vows.

"I had hoped the mutiny would fail. Then we would have our royal wedding at Castle Seat. And at our feast we would serve stag and wild boar that we had hunted together."

Queen Regina had to staunch tears.

Frehley continued, "But when I'd heard the Black Watch had forced you to surrender your necklace to free the Elfwitch, I ran as far as I could from the Mighty Oak.

"The moon eclipsed the sun. Day turned to night. And all became shadow. Then I swore to the Judge that I would never surrender my necklace to the Elfwitch.

"I fled to Outlaw Forest where I met Strap. We became renegades. But the Elfwitch had you send my fellow Royal Hunstmen to track us down. Finally, her lycanthropes caught us.

"We were taken to the Keep. The Elfwitch tortured me but I wouldn't surrender my necklace. As long as that necklace remained hidden, not another Dark Rider could be freed. So that secret became my only hope.

"I thought the Judge had turned his back on me. The Elfwitch kept me chained in a cell for years. Even when Moor Kreed was tossed in with us I thought, *maybe the Judge is testing me to see if I'll spill my secret.* But Moor Kreed said that wasn't true.

"But then this boy was put into my cell.

"The moment Reed called me 'Dad' my world turned upside down. The boy had a gold coin and a silver necklace! I thought it beyond strange but it gave me a hope I cannot explain!"

Reed nodded. "You even fight like Mom and Dad. And when you got married at the hunting lodge, you served wild game to everyone. I've seen the pictures!"

Captain Michael rolled his eyes, "My queen, this child is severely deranged."

Queen Regina regarded Reed. "There is something special about both Wice and Reed. There is more to their being here than what the Elfwitch intended. I begin to feel hope."

"Don't tell me you believe their nonsense, my queen," Captain Michael said.

Frehley pointed his finger at the bodyguard's face. "The only nonsense was everyone tellin' my queen what they thought she should do for the good of the Realm instead of trustin' her to do what she thought was best for the Realm!"

"You're the one who broke a taboo!" Captain Michael shouted. "By going to Quicksilver Lake you called the wrath of the Dark Riders down on our heads! Maybe it's not a crime for a queen and a commoner to fall in love but what you did to win and woo her most definitely is!"

"Who made the Black Watch break their vows? We make our choices and take our consequences. I spent twelve years locked in a cell and they got cursed. Isn't that enough?" Frehley demanded and took another step closer to his adversary.

Reed could see Rancor's breath again coming from behind a tree.

"Then make it right," Captain Michael growled.

"I'm tryin'," Frehley said. "I'm still alive. So I've still got choices. I've still got hope."

"Time out y'all," Reed said. "I know now that I'm in a different world. The Realm looks just like the Ozarks in my own World. Except here, there are no houses or cars or roads or electricity. It's the same but different. If I still had the gold coin or the heart necklace, I'd prove it to you. But wait, I still have this," Reed said and pulled out his Tracfone.

Captain Michael eyed it with suspicion. "I want to believe. But I don't understand."

"I can't help but think the Judge has a hand in all this," Frehley said.

"Why are the Leftwichs considered royalty here when back home we're nothin' but losers?" Reed asked.

"My child," Queen Regina began. "If you are alive, you are most certainly not a 'loser.' The Judge fashions everyone in the womb and gives them a purpose.

"You come from a strange land. Yet, you bear the same family name. So you have come here with a purpose. The Son chose the Lyftwyches for a purpose: to rule on Castle Seat. To uphold his Law, preserve his truth, and administer his justice.

"Until this moment, I thought I was the last of the line. That's why I have to marry. And whoever I marry becomes a Lyftwych and the king by Law."

Frehley shrugged. "See, kid? I'm no Lyftwhych. I'm from the woods, not a castle."

Reed looked from him to the queen. "Don't you love each other? Or are you just like my Mom and Dad and have decided it's easier to hate each other?"

Both Frehley and Queen Regina became red-faced and looked away.

"That's not the issue at hand," Captain Michael said. "It's about bringing down that blasted moon and bringing back the sun. It's about restoring the Law. And getting this blasted collar off!"

"We will have to imprison the Dark Riders again," Queen Regina said.

"That means we have to storm the Keep. Battle the Dead Coats. Defeat the three Dark Riders," Frehley said as he kept count on his right hand. "But that's just for starters."

"In order to bring back the Law. We need to find the Law. The actual Law that the Son gave to the Lyftwyches. That means we'll have to find the sepulcher of the Son."

"Asheroth protects it. How do you propose to get by that beast?" Captain Michael asked.

"We'll need gold or silver," Frehley said.

"I keep tellin' you I lost my silver necklace!" Reed complained.

"No," Frehley shook his head. "You didn't lose it. Packy took it."

"Who's this 'Packy?' Queen Regina asked.

"His pet rat," Frehley said and pointed back to Evander in repose waiting for internment and the wounded rodent upon his chest.

"If the rat's dying what good will it do us?" the queen complained. "It will take quicksilver to put the Dark Riders back in Ice Prison."

"And the only handy quicksilver you buried by the Mighty Oak. If that's true, then how did Rancor get loose?" Captain Michael asked.

"I traded it for the boy's life," Frehley said. "I meant to destroy it when the magazine room in Martello Tower blew up. But somehow the Elfwitch found it and was able to still use it.

"But there's still a whole bunch more in Quicksilver Lake. Wanna try for that?"

Captain Michael frowned.

"Let's see to this rodent," Queen Regina commanded. "And then let's bury the dead."

Frehley chose a spot just under the evergreen needles not far from where Evander reposed. Captain Michael had held onto all the remaining weapons that Frehley and Strap had stashed at the trees; so he broke ground with the bowie knife while Strap and Frehley helped move rocks and pebbles. Outlaw Forest, being just like the Ozarks, was full of tiny rocks and pebbles.

Queen Regina and Reed saw to Packy. The boy followed her into the deep woods so search for medicinal herbs. The queen counted them off and how to get the ingredients. "We need willow bark which will have to be soaked. Then ground into powder. Wintergreen leaves from which we can steam and extract the oil. The root of witchgrass and sage stalk all of which will have to be boiled and drank like a tea.

"We all might benefit from these medicines. We will rest the better for it tonight."

"Tonight. Today," Reed said. "How can you tell when you can't see the sun?"

"By the waxing and waning of the moon," Queen Regina said. "The Law of nature might have been subverted but it cannot be done away with altogether. The Eflwitch certainly does not have that power and I doubt the Darkness does either."

The two searched across mossy rocks and beneath exposed tree roots and alongside sentinel boulders. Reed had never spent this much time in proximity with Mom back in his World. Doing so now, here in the Realm with Queen Regina, was ironic.

They were able to scavenge some pieces of willow bark. A handful of wintergreen leaves and stems. The witch grass and sage proved trickier to find but they came across two plants of each and were to pull them both up by their roots.

Bundled with their herbs, they began to circle back to the place of the evergreen trees where the burial would soon take place.

"So, will it help Packy?" Reed asked.

"If the rodent is able to eat some, which is a good sign in of itself, then it'll help his pain and swelling. But if it has broken bones or torn insides, it may not be able to move until its fully healed," Queen Regina answered.

"And that would take how long?" Reed asked.

"A week? A month?" the queen ventured to say.

"We can't wait that long," Reed said.

"Then we'll have to pray to the Judge for a miracle," Queen Regina said.

Reed agreed, "A big one."

When they returned to the stand of evergreens, the trio had dug out a jagged square in the hardscrabble ground. A grave more wide than deep. Strap rolled over some large boulders in preparation for sealing it up.

Reed approached the still Evander and resting Packy. He put some of the winter grass before the rat's nose. The rat moved very little and only half slit his eyes.

At least he was still alive which kindled a flame of hope in Reed.

The three men stood beside Reed.

"The grave is ready, oh, my queen," Captain Michael.

"We have brought some healing herbs, let us pray the Judge will bless our efforts. But now let us tend to the matter at hand," Queen Regina said.

"We, ourselves, have not attended a funeral since our father's, the King. But we will do our best in officiating and making it honorable before the Judge. Surely, this man..." the queen began.

"Evander," Frehley offered.

"...Evander was as brave as my father in upholding the Law for which he was branded a criminal and believing in truth for which he was branded a renegade and believing in justice for which he gave his life against the very forces of Darkness. Such sacrifice we honor. Such sacrifice does not go unnoticed by the Judge," Queen Regina said.

"This is where the High Priest commends the fallen one's spirit. He was your friend, so you'll have to fill in," Captain Michael prodded Frehley.

Frehley said, "Then we pray for the Judge to receive our fallen companion, Evander. Do not let his sacrifice be in vain. Let Evander live again in the Son's kingdom."

With ginger care, Reed took Packy off Evander's still chest and lay the rat down on a flat stone. All three men picked up Evander: Strap by the feet, Frehley at the head and Captain Michael under his back and laid him down in ground. Safe and sound in the grave.

After that, they piled large stones upon the grave making a cairn knee-high above the ground.

"And now that our burden's been laid down, we'd better hunt us some meat or we'll be the next to lay down," Frehley said and looked at Captain Michael who was a walking garrison of weapons.

"Give them their share of the weapons," Queen Regina commanded.

They split them up man to man. Strap took his trusted blackjack and musket. Frehley took up his pistol and the remaining musket. A second pistol was given to Reed. And Captain Michael took the third pistol but would not relinquish the bowie knife.

The three men spread out to hunt what they game they could while Reed asked if he could stay with the Queen to prepare the herbs into powders and stocks. Queen Regina and Reed dug out a circle about three inches deep and did their best to line the sides and the bottom with hand sized rocks and small pebbles. The boy found a small creek close-by but since they had nothing to carry the water in other than their hands, Reed took huge gulps and made a short walk to spit out the water into their new hole.

The queen pretended not to be offended.

They heard shots nearby.

Soon, all the hunters met back at the cairn to show their prizes.

Frehley had two large grey squirrels.

Captain Michael had bagged himself a small grey rabbit.

But Strap came up with the biggest prize--a very plump groundhog.

There was some debate about who should skin the kills since there was only one knife.

"Let every man skin his own kill," the Queen commanded.

Captain Michael insisted that he go first and hacked at his rabbit, tearing and pulling more than cutting and slicing. And when he was reluctant to hand over the knife to Frehley, the queen scolded him. "Share what we have."

Reed thought that was a very wise and royal thing to decree.

But when Frehley got the knife he offered it instead to Strap who made quick work of his kill. He offered the knife back to Frehley who made deft cuts and pulled the hides off both squirrels faster than Reed had ever seen Dad do.

Captain Michael stoked up a fire for roasting and Queen Regina had found good-sized sticks that the captain made into stakes once he got the knife back. Then he gutted the kills and cut off the parts they didn't want to eat. This offal was tossed into the fire and heating it with animal juices and seasoning it with the smell of flesh.

As the spitted meat roasted in the fire, Strap soaked the willow bark in the creek while Captain Michael tied the wintergreen leaves around a long limb. He placed it just over the fire and moved a flat stone beneath the leaves to catch the oil that began to drip. With the toe of his ragged boot, Strap culled out some fist sized rocks from the fire and kicked them over to the round hole the queen and boy had made.

The rocks plopped into the water causing it to steam and then boil and bubble. Queen Regina dropped the sage into the water. It had been worth the toil and trouble.

When the meat was well-roasted, the men pulled the spits out of the fire.

"We thank the Judge for what we have," the queen said. "Only you alone are worthy, Judge. Give us this day our daily bread. Lead us in the way we should go, we pray in your Son's name."

After she had finished, everyone said together, "Amen."

The spits were passed around as everyone bit and tore into the game. Reed had eaten squirrel aplenty. Even rabbit, more than a time or two. But he had never eaten groundhog before in his life. It was downright greasy.

For Reed, it wasn't much different than roasting hot dogs over the fire pit at a family picnic. It wasn't much different at all. Except Mom wasn't Mom, she was Queen Regina. And Dad wasn't Dad, he was Frehley.

Reed was both happy and homesick. At home and a foreigner. Settled and unsettled.

It had been too long between meals. But it was hard to beat eating something fresh and well cooked. Maybe it couldn't be beat, here or in any other world.

The leftovers were tossed into the fire. Then Strap retrieved the willow bark out of the creek and placed it against a flat rock. Then he pulverized the bark with a round rock.

"The powder is done and we scrape the oil off this rock," Captain Michael said. "But we have no cup for drinking the sage stock."

Again Queen Regina solved the issue by asking for the large bowie-like knife. After Captain Michael handed it over she unscrewed the round pommel from the handle revealing a cap the size and deeper than a thumb.

"How did you know that was there?" Frehley asked amazed.

"My father designed these knives for the Black Watch," the queen answered. "He was known to sip wine while out on the hunt in this fashion."

"My kind of hunter," Frehley said.

"The King would have approved of you, Frehley," the queen said.

"The king would not have approved of taboo breakers," Captain Michael said.

"What is greater? Love or rules?" Frehley asked.

"I wouldn't ask anyone I loved to break the rules," the Queen's bodyguard answered.

"So have you never broken the Law?" Frehley asked. "Or have you never loved?"

"Gentlemen," Queen Regina intoned. "It is time to administer our medicines."

Three thimblefuls, one from each medicine, was spooned into the small cup. Each one, in turn, was offered to Packy who roused and sniffed each and lapped each up.

Then each one of the company, in turn, took small doses from each of the three medicines with the thimble-sized cup. The medicine was warm going down and spread its anodyne across Reed's chest and down his legs. Strap needed a double dose because of his size.

"Better than grain alcohol," Frehley said and slapped his friend high on his back since he couldn't reach his shoulder.

"Let us rest," the queen said. "We will be fresh enough again in the morning to plan."

Each one lay down next to the fire with Reed lying down next to Packy and Strap while Frehley took the first watch.

Reed felt as safe and warm as he could. He felt closer to home in some respects even if the queen still treated him like a stranger. He drifted into sleep.

Then a thought struck him.

Queen Regina was a Lyftwych.

And he was a Leftwich.

Weren't they family even in this strange world?

Something vibrated against Reed.

It was his Tracfone again.

The outside screen read 1 UNREAD MESSAGE.

Reed flipped his phone up.

SISSY
WHERE R U?
This time he did not reply.
SISSY
COME TO THE KEEP. MEET ME THERE.
He wanted to reply. Sis needed him. And he needed her.
Frehley took the phone away to look at the device for himself.
"'Sissy?' Sister, right? Chayse or Wice?" Frehley murmured.
"She's both of them now. But she's still my sister," Reed said.
"And y'all can talk to each other through these devices?" Frehley asked. "So you don't have to write notes or use messengers? How?"
"It sends out a signal through the air. It needs electricity. Lightening," Reed said.
Frehley turned the phone over. "Then it must use precious metals."
"There's a chip that runs the whole phone. It has gold threads," Reed said. "You have to open it up and take out the battery to get to the chip."
The phone vibrated again. Which shocked Frehley. He turned it over and read the new message.
SISSY
I miss u.
"What happens to the battery if you take it out?" Frehley asked.
"People say if you throw the battery in the fire, it will explode," Reed said.
"It does have some power then. This battery still has life?" Frehley asked.
"I thought the battery was dead," Reed said. "I don't know how it's still working."
"Do you want to answer her?"Frehley asked him.
"Yes," Reed said. "But I'm afraid it's a trick."
"If she's your sister, let her know how you feel. You can never go wrong with the truth," Frehley said.
ME
I luv u.
There was no response.

***

Chapter Forty-Seven: Law and Love

"*W*ho-who cooks for you?"

"Was that you talkin' Reed?" his sister asked him from her perch on the couch.

Reed was sitting on the love seat across from her as he played on his phone.

"I just heard someone say it as plain as day," Sissy said.

Well, Reed hadn't. She was just joshin' him. Again.

"Who-who cooks for you?"

This time even Reed heard it over the happy music of his Candy Crush Saga phone ap.

"God bless my time!" Reed said. That was as near as Mom let him get to using straight-up swear words. Although, what Dad could and would say far worse. "Who is that, Sissy?"

"That's what they're asking us," Chayse said.

They both rose from their worn and weathered leather seats. Reed didn't want to leave the safety and comfort of his chair but Sissy had beaten him by getting up first and he couldn't let that go unanswered. So when she moved towards the front door Reed had to get there first.

They heard something scuttling up the roof shingles.

"Something is climbing on the roof," he said.

Bright lights radiated out from the carport. Maybe from headlights. Pouring through the curtains. Someone was here!

"It's Mom!" Chayse said.

Except Mom never parked in the driveway. She always drove right into the carport.

Maybe it was escaped crack-heads tweaked out of their gourds. A crack-head was as dangerous as a rabid dog. Maybe Reed should go get the gun.

Sissy pulled back the curtains and looked out onto the front yard and driveway. Reed was already halfway out onto the back porch.

"Well, hold on!" Sissy called.

She followed him out onto the back porch which was choked with dead plants and busted bikes and a faded plastic play oven and a toy toolbox.

I never owned a toy toolbox. I always wanted one but Mom wouldn't get it for me.

"Who-who cooks for you?"

They came around the side of the carport. Somehow Sissy had a flashlight. Reed had meant to grab the gun. But he hadn't. Now he had no weapon. Nothing to protect himself.

Sissy and I aren't at home right now. We're somehow else. Far away.

She turned the flashlight on. Then she shone it around the corner across the front porch. Both of them peered around the drain spout.

Something, not someone, was there.

Perched on the brick trim, a brown thing, squat with no neck. The thing's head turned one hundred and eighty degrees around to face them. With two round eyes of gold light. Piercing them to the quick.

"Who-who cooks for you?"

Sissy started to ask, "What is--"

Reed woke up.

He wasn't inside his house or in Raccoon Springs Village. But somewhere that looked exactly like it. Fir and pine. Red clay and quartz rock. Grey slate boulders.

There was no house. No carport. No driveway. No Sissy.

But there were other people. Companions. One buried. Another run off. Two new ones.

Even though, he was in the Realm and not Fade County, he'd heard a familiar sound.

"Who-who cooks for you?"

He wasn't dreaming. He had heard it. Plain as day could be here in the Realm.

The morning dew had turned from a mist into a fog. Hued by the silvery and slippery light of the full moon.

Captain Michael had the morning watch. He walked over to where the company lay next to the fire. With cooling embers like red veins running to grey-white wounds on the bark.

"We have a messenger," the queen's bodyguard said as Reed roused himself.

"What do you mean? It's just a barn-owl," Reed said stretching his shoulders and arms.

"Are these creatures a common sight or rare in your world?" the captain asked him.

"Rare. I saw one not one long before I came here," Reed said. He rose and turned his side to crack his back. Then he stopped. "Actually, I saw an owl twice. Once at night. Then once during the day. The Brazzles tried to run it down. They're mean like that."

"You saw an owl in daylight?" Queen Regina asked as she yawned.

"Yes," Reed said and then added. "Your majesty."

"Do you know how long it's been since an owl has been heard anywhere in the Realm?" Captain Michael asked.

Sitting up, Frehley answered, "Twelve. Long. Years."

Strap stood up and moved his hand flat through the air.

"What's the big deal?" Reed asked. "It's just an owl."

"Owls are messenger. Sent by the Judge. They stand for his wisdom. For his authority and power. They are also birds of prey. Seeking rats to devour," Captain Michael.

"That's what it's after! Packy!" Reed said and put his arm over his hurt pet.

Packy moved its head and blinked its tired eyes.

"He's no better," Reed moaned. He use the pommel cup from Frehley's bowie knife to dip some of the now cool sage stock into the thimble. He offered it to Packy who lapped at it.

"Will he live?" Reed asked. He didn't want to lose another companion.

A lightburst through the morning fog. Brighter than a fire. Though it wasn't a fire.

It was like the time Dad had taken Reed and Chayse to see his favorite band, Blue Oyster Cult, at Magic Springs' Timberwood Amphitheater. Just after sundown the band covered the stage with fog and shone lights through it before beginning their first song.

The fog burned away. Leaving the mighty brilliance of a sun. They all shielded their eyes from the glory.

"Something's out there," Frehley said.

"Someone's coming," Captain Michael said.

"Gentleman, let us go forth and discover," Queen Regina commanded.

Captain Michael cocked his pistol.

"Leave your weapon," the queen commanded. "Everyone, leave the weapons behind."

The bodyguard hesitated.

"You heard her!" Frehley said. "Reed, take Packy. Just in case of the owl."

Reed didn't have to be told twice.

Frehley led the way. Then came Queen Regina and Captain Michael. Then Reed holding Packy and Strap following behind them.

Everything was imbued with its proper hue. Bushes were a dark green. Tree bark a glistening brown. Wildflowers bloomed delicate blue and perfect purple.

The company was struck with wonder.

The source of this light, this peace, this majesty streamed from just ahead.

The scent of sweet honey permeated the air. Frehley cut a trail straight through thick bushes with long branches and vines spiraled over its roots. From each branch poked twin groupings of broad leaves and from out of the leaves hung white tubular flowers like trumpets.

When Reed reached out to touch the white blooms, he found them saturated with something sticky. He licked his fingers. It was very sweet nectar.

"Honeysuckle!" he told the others.

"Of course, it is," Captain Michael said.

There was something else, too.

Suffused under the swath of honeysuckle bloom. Inside each trumpet flower. Something buzzed.

Flying insects with abdomens banded yellow and black flew from one bloom to the next. Hovered over each leaf and then crawling inside the trumpets. Tickling the flower with their pollen bearing legs.

"Bees!" Reed said.

Captain Michael opened his mouth but his thought was lost amid the dozens of great bumblebees and droves of humble honeybees buzzing about.

Reed counted at least twenty honeysuckle bushes.

There could no doubt.

Reed loved reading about bees. How they made their nests. What kind of flowers they sought. How they gathered pollen. How they built their nests. How they organized their hives.

The bees were pollinating. Helping spread the honeysuckles even further into the forest.

The bees were hunting, too. Using their compound eyes in the ultraviolet to seek nectar.

And all because there was light.

Daylight.

Reed saw patches of blue and clouds of puffy white drifting above the tree branches.

It was wondrous.

Marvelous.

A vision of sight and sound in an endless revelation all around.

Reed beheld it.

He could touch it.

Smell it.

Hear it.

It was more real than all that time in dark caves and cells.

But where was the sun?

Reed couldn't see it. Because the light wasn't coming from the sky. It was coming from somewhere else.

Just ahead.

Frehley led them on. The honeysuckle bushes were gathered around the ascent of another hill. Was the light emanating from up there? It was so warm and life-giving, the source had to be all-powerful.

As they climbed they heard bleating and baa-ing.

Hoofed animals.

Sheep? Goats?

There came a chime. A tinkle. A clang.

Small bells. Like a cowbell. Being hit in erratic patterns.

They came to a ledge outcropping that jutting out from the hillside like a stair landing. A small herd of bell wearing goats stood like an order of monks sworn to silence and cheese. They regarded the company with their double pupils and stamped their hooves and twitched their ears.

Frehley led them past the goats into a large grassy meadow rising up to meet a ridge. At the top was a long pasture. Nestled along the ridge were seven wooden structures.

Six looked like feeders except they had three tiers with their own ledges. They were all situated around the seventh structure which was a flat table. On the it rested glass jars and ceramic containers. Next to the table a goat's leg was spitted over a large fire.

More buzzing rolled out of the six structures. They were constructed bee hives. The ledges weren't ledges but pull out drawers.

A figure appeared among the beehives. Drowsing the structure with smoke from handheld bellows. Then the figure put the bellows down on the table and pulled out a drawer full of dripping honeycombs which he transferred to some of the waiting jars.

Honey!

Reed thought he could see white liquid in the ceramic containers.

Milk! Probably from the goats.

And there were blocks shaped like small wheels on the table.

Rinds of cheese!

The figure wore a leather jerkin with a hood. He waved at the company like it was a family reunion. Then he removed his leather hood.

The man was younger than Frehley. With long wavy hair and a well oiled beard. And peace in his large brown cow eyes.

The man was illuminated in the light. It radiated around him like waves. Sat on his head like a crown.

. "Do not be afraid, faithful servants," he said. "Welcome to the kingdom."

Kingdom.

Where they no longer in the Realm? Where ever it was, it seemed peaceful. And there was *food.*

Reed's stomach flipped over at the smell of roasted goat and his mouth watered at the sight of milk and his eyes swam over the rinds of glorious fermented cheese.

The food in the dungeon had been dog slop. And the meager meals in the Realm few and far between.

Reed could still remember his last full meal: on the night that Miss Elsie Crutch had come knocking on their front door, Reed had shared a can of Spaghettos with Chayse and then fixed himself a bag of microwave popcorn and topped all of that with two or three Swiss Rolls all washed down with copious amounts of Root Beer.

But everything that Reed could see in the Kingdom was full and good.

The man keeping the bees looked mighty familiar or just mighty.

"Creedmore!" Reed called out.

It did feel like a family reunion.

"Moor Kreed?" Frehley asked as if this was the last person he'd ever expected to see.

The man smiled and shook his head. "The man you speak of is my child. And my children keep my commandments. So when you've seen love, you've seen my face."

"Then Moor Kreed's not dead?" Reed asked.

The man shook his head. "He lives in my love forever. You will see him again."

"Who are you, sir?" Queen Regina asked.

"Call me Beekeeper. For I tend to these industrious creatures," Beekeeper said.

Reed thought it strange and wonderful that the light was radiating around the Beekeeper.

Nothing remained hidden in the Light. Everything was known in the Light. Matter absorbed the Light and reflected some of the glory back.

"You called us faithful servants," Queen Regina said. "Are there other servants here?

"Oh, yes!" the Beekeeper said and pointed out to a nearby field. "There is the Goat Herder. Who tends the kids."

The Goat Herder smiled at them while he guided some goats with his leg crook. The man had brown hair and a youthful smile. It was Evander.

"And there is the carpenter who makes these excellent beehives," the Beekeeper said.

"Father!" the queen called.

A man with a grey flecked beard turned to wave as he sanded down a wooden drawer.

Reed turned to Frehley and Captain Michael. "Is that really her father?"

Astounded, both men nodded.

"And there is the maker of curds and whey," the Beekeeper pointed to a third fellow.

A shirtless man sat with a churner and a large bucket with a press. His wild curly hair glistened with sweat that dripped down his oily beard.

"Creedmore! Moor Creed" Reed called out.

Moor Kreed/Creedmore gave a big smile and returned to his chores.

"As Lord of this kingdom, I invite you to share in my feast from out of the earth's bountifulness," the Beekeeper said and indicated the stack of dishes at the other end of the table. "Yes, O Lord," Queen Regina spoke for all.

She curtsied and bowed her head before walking to the table and sitting on a low stool.

One by one the others followed suit until Reed was the only one still standing.

The Beekeeper regarded the boy. "Is this not to your liking?"

"I like your kingdom very much. It's just like the Ozarks back home before anyone put a road over a hill or built a fence around a spring," Reed said. Then he bowed his head.

"Good! Now come get yourself a big hunk of cheese!" The Beekeeper said.

The company sat at three sides of the table. Leaving the Beekeeper free to serve from the other long side. Along with the ceramic jars of milk and jars of fresh honey and rinds of cheese there two dishes of raisin cakes stacked like a pyramid and an empty platter for the meat that would soon be carved from the leg of goat. Six small cutting knives lay next to the six plates at the end of the table.

"The meat is ready," the Beekeeper said as he took up the large platter and a carving knife. The tender goat meat crumbled onto the platter as he cut from the spitted leg. Then he set the platter down from where he could serve the company.

"Let us give thanks to the Judge," he said.

Everyone bowed.

"O great Judge in heaven," the Beekeeper prayed. "Holy is your name. Your kingdom is coming. Your will be done in the Realm as it in the Third Heaven. Give us our bread every day. Forgive us as we forgive others or you will not forgive us. Lead us out of temptation and deliver us from Darkness. Amen."

"Amen," everyone echoed.

"What does 'amen' even mean?" Reed asked.

"It means 'fine by me,'" the Beekeeper said. Then he gave each a small plate with a sampling from everything offered at the table making sure to serve himself last.

The meat was tender. The honey was sweet. The cake was fresh. The cheese was tart. The milk was filling.

"Everything is superb," Queen Regina said.

"Delicious," Frehley said.

Strap patted his belly and smiled.

Captain Michael shrugged.

"It's the best meal I've had since Thanksgiving," Reed piped up.

"I guess it beats Spaghetteos, popcorn, and swiss rolls with root beer," the Beekeeper said and winked. Then he had everyone pass him their empty plates which he stacked at the end.

"And now children, hear a story and then a question.

"A master had vineyards and acres of wheat. He employed servants to work the fields and tend the vineyards. With the proceeds of his harvest, he built a threshing floor and a wine press that produced enough to feed the whole land.

"Then he chose overseers from some of the servants. They were to give to the master his share first, then the workers theirs, then sell to others at a fair price, and before they could pay themselves, they were to let the needy clean the fields and empty the dregs from the barrels.

"When the master saw that the overseers listened to his every word and that each harvest produced an increase, he traveled to the coast to make contracts with merchants to sell his produce abroad.

"After he was gone, the overseers decided to put a hedge around the threshing floor and wine press to protect it from thieves. But this also kept the servants out on payday.

"Then the overseers increased the price to sellers and no longer let the needy clean their fields. With their wealth, they built a new barn and cellar and later a mill and winery.

"The overseers said, 'Look at how we increased the wealth. The master might own the land but we control the harvest.' So they paid themselves more and called themselves Managers.

"Then the Managers built a wall around their buildings with guards to patrol it. No one except rich buyers were allowed entry. Then they contracted with merchants on the coast instead of letting the Master do it.

"The Master sent the Managers a messenger saying, 'I commend you on increasing the wealth and buildings but see that my instructions are carried out or I will return and clean house.'

"But the managers became scared so they killed the messenger inside their warehouse.

"So the Master sent a second messenger, who was stoned against a silo. Then the Master said, 'If they will not listen to me nor my messengers, surely they will listen to my Son.

"So the Master sent his Son but the managers, fearing they would be punished, hanged the Son on a tree in a vineyard.

"Now, I ask you, children, what should happen to the overseers?"

Captain Michael was the first to speak, "They deserve death. When soldiers don't follow orders, they are nothing better than cannon fodder. An example must be made."

The Beekeeper nodded. "An eye for an eye it is then. Is that justice or revenge? Justice makes things right. Vengeance only gets you even. Never ahead."

"A wise ruler would offer mercy if they gave all their profits back to the Master and his servants and the sellers they cheated. They would lose what they loved most, their wealth," Queen Regina said.

The Beekeeper nodded, "Mercy it is then. Along with their freedom?"

"They killed three times to keep their money. How many chances should they get?" Frehley asked. "If you let them pay to get out of trouble, their hearts will never change.

Boars have tusks in the wild. Hogs on a farm don't have tusks. But if the hog runs off it goes feral and grow tusks. Then you have to hunt it down and kill it."

"They have broken trust, no doubt. So if they don't show repentance in their heart, what then?" The Beekeeper asked.

Strap drew a line across his throat with his thumb.

The Beekeeper nodded. "I tell you truly, if a person has no repentance in their heart and never forgives, they will not inherit this kingdom."

"I knew kids at school like these managers," Reed said. "They got their way all the time. They picked on the other kids and yelled at the teachers and never got in trouble with the principal. They were mean cuz they never learned different."

"How would they learn different?" the Beekeeper said.

"If they knew that hurtin' others only hurt themselves. If just payin' money keeps the managers out of trouble then that's an easy out. So make the managers do the work. Make them clean the workers' houses. Have them show the workers how to run the place. Then they could do each other's jobs. They'd be equal."

"If the managers did that, could the Master forgive them?" asked the Beekeeper. "If he was lovin', good and kind, he would," Reed said. "No amount of money would bring back his son. Even if he killed all the managers, he wouldn't get his son back. After having had their lives spared, the managers should learn to love people and not money."

"That was the Master's hope, too, my son," the Beekeeper said.

Strap put his hand over his heart and tapped it with his other finger. Then he removed his hand and tapped his finger against his chest.

"I think Strap means that if they truly wanted mercy they would repent and do what the master told them," the Beekeeper said.

"Since they proved themselves industrious making wealth for themselves, let them prove the same with charity with other people," Queen Regina said.

"So giving extra chances of forgiveness might lead to a change of heart. It is a chance that the Judge gives everyone every day," the Beekeeper said.

"Then what about the Dark Riders?" Frehley asked.

"They have blasphemed to the point of spitting on their chance. They have hardened their hearts from repentance," the Beekeeper said. "The Judge allows them to exist as examples of condemnation. They face a final destination of condemnation and torment. A place that was never meant for humans."

"Beekeeper," so Queen Regina addressed their host. "Where is the sun?"

"Where is the Law?" the Beekeeper asked.

The queen looked down. "We have lost the Law."

"Then that is why you have the Darkness and the moon instead of the sun," the Beekeeper. "But what about love?"

The queen lifted her head back up and stole a glance at Frehley. "I want that most of all."

"There can be no Law against Love, my child," the Beekeeper said. "Seek the will of the Judge and he will give you your heart's desires. For all good things come from him."

"Am I to blame for all this?" Frehley asked.

The Beekeeper laughed. "Did you make the Elfwitch? Do you follow her? Are you responsible for all the evil she has let loose over the years?"

"I broke the taboo," Frehley said. "I went to Quicksilver Lake."

"Yes, you did, my child," the Beekeeper said. "Does not twelve years in jail count as your punishment? Or do you want more punishment? The full measure of punishment is death."   "No, Sir," Frehley said. "I'm not like the managers pleadin' for mercy to get out of trouble. After twelve years locked in walls and darkness, I've learned my lesson. I repent of makin' a token from taboo metal. I want to undo what I did but I don't know how.

"I wanted to marry the maid, Gina. I didn't know she was Princess Regina and now she's the queen. I'd be the most blessed man in the Realm if the Judge willed it we should marry."

Queen Regina straightened her shoulders and wiped away a tear. Then she smiled.

"Hunt the Judge's righteousness first and everything will fall into your trap," the Beekeeper said. Then he asked Strap. "Strap, what do you fear?"

Like two players both playing rock, paper, scissors, Strap knocked both fists together. Then he covered one hand with the other. Next, he chopped the air with his hand and pretend to wipe sweat from his brow. Then he shrugged.

The Beekeeper nodded. "Yes. To all those things."

"What did he ask you?" Reed wanted to know.

"When the time comes, Strap will tell you in his own fashion," the Beekeeper said.

"Beekeeper," Captain Michael said as he smoothed one end of his handlebar mustache. "In your story, am I a guard or one of the overseers?"

The Beekeeper laughed. "Which do you do? Protect that which is righteous and holy with your life? Or withhold that which is righteous and holy from others?"

"Both," Captain Michael said. "At the same time."

Then the Beekeeper asked, "Do you repent?"

Captain Michael turned his hands over. "If I allow their love will it not weaken the law?"

"You have faith in the Law?" the Beekeeper asked. "Then have faith in love. We are to love the Judge and love one another. On this one peg hangs the whole Law.

"And now, young Reed, what questions do you have?"

"How did my sister and my family back? How do I even get back home?" Reed asked.

"With man this is impossible but with the Judge all things are possible," the Beekeeper said. "When you next see your sister, tell her the Judge says, 'I desire mercy and not sacrifice.'"

"I don't understand all this!" Reed cried out. "How can this world be like mine but so different? Why is it always night here? It's like everything is upside down. Why does the Elfwitch have so much power? Why don't you do something about it?"

"Oh, I intend to, trust me," the Beekeeper said. "But when I come again it won't be as redeemer or friend, it will be as the master to clean house. And when I do that there will be no chance for a single person to repent or receive mercy.

"But the Judge is willing to extend mercy for a time so that all may repent and be saved.

"Now the Elfwitch has been a liar and a murderer from the very beginning. The Judge and the Word with the Spirit made everything. Whereas the Elfwitch makes only lies. But the lies only work as long as people believe in them.

"The others have heard these words before, but maybe not for quite some time. So, let me speak as to all."   ***

Chapter Forty-Eight: Genesis and Exegesis

And so the Beekeeper began, "I speak the Truth. I am the Law.

"In the beginning was the Law. And the Law was with the Judge. And the Law was the Judge.

"Now the Judge is everlasting. He lives in the third heaven. He does not change. He cannot lie. There is no Darkness in Him.

"His Law is the Son who was slain at the foundation of the world. And the Spirit was there, too. Hovering over the material of the unformed earth.

"So, in the beginning, the Judge created the heavens and the earth. He spent three days forming and three days filling.

"First, He said, 'Let there be Light.' And there was Light. And he saw that it was good. Then He separated the Light from the Darkness. And there was Day and Night.

"On the second day, He separated the waters from below and above making Sea and Sky, which is the first heaven. On the third, He made dry Land to appear out of the Sea. Plants rose on the Land.

"On the fourth, He formed stars and planets to fill the second heaven: the sun as the Greater Light to rule the Day and the moon as the Lesser Light to rule the Night. The stars he poured out like sand across the universe in their courses to track the seasons.

"On the fifth day, the Judge made the denizens of the deep to fill the sea and the creatures of the air to fill the sky. So he made five domains: Day, Night, Sky, Sea, and Land.

"On the sixth day, the Judge made terrestrial animals to fill the Land. Then He said, 'Let US make man in our own image.' So he made both male and female. As helpmates and side by side companions. He let them subdue the domains of the earth.

"Now the Darkness hid in shadows and slipped between the cracks of the earth. It grew into a void so it could hide from the Light. Because it believes that it cannot be loved nor will it surrender its will. It is scared of both rejection and condemnation.

"That was the first lie. And of out that lie came fear, pain, hate, and destruction.

"So, the Judge turned the void the Darkness had made into a domain of death and destruction.

"Therefore, the Darkness rejects the Light and the Law. It turns Truth into lies and fear; love into hate, and Life into death. Since it will be separated from the Judge for all eternity, it seeks to destroy all that the Judge made before it faces its final condemnation.

"The Judge made humans for a relationship. They are a special creation. He gave them a choice: obey Him or obey the Darkness.

"The Judge promised He would never leave nor forsake the man and woman. And He told them all they had to do was to love Him and love each other.

"But the Darkness came and spoke fear into their hearts. So the man and woman disobeyed the Judge and followed their own way. They thought they could be like the Judge and make the rules. So the Law was broken and death came to everyone.

"Therefore, if you reject the Judge, you turn your back on Light and walk in Darkness. The Judge will allow no Darkness, no death, no fear or hate into his Kingdom. All who are in the Darkness will be put in the Domain of destruction forever.

"But the Judge had a plan to save humans whom he loved from the Darkness. For love covers a multitude of sins. And blood has to be shed to pay for breaking the Law."

"Beekeeper, how can the moon be the Lesser Light and block out the sun?" Reed asked.

The Beekeeper said, "In order for the moon to shine, it must reflect light. And whose light does it reflect?"

"The sun's?" Reed asked.

The Beekeeper nodded again. "And who made the sun?"

"The Judge," Reed said. "But where did the Eflwitch come from?"

The Beekeeper smiled. "An excellent question. The Judge blessed the fallen man and woman with a dozen children. And from them came all the peoples. Though each generation grew darker in their hearts and forgot about the Judge's promise and his Law.

"Their descendants raised a mighty kingdom beyond the mountains that reached to the eastern sea. They subdued animals and worked the land until it flowed with milk and honey.

"In their prosperity, they made laws to benefit one over another and turned justice to their advantage until each did what was right in their own eyes. Their living law became a living lie.

"The Elfwitch was born into those days and became queen of the eastern lands. But her husband, the king, did not honor their marriage vow. And so they fought day and night.

"In her anger, she swore vengeance and sought out the ways to serve the Darkness. She used quicksilver to poison her husband, the king. But her skin absorbed the poison of quicksilver and she became fey: a dark elf. And by taking justice into her own hands, her nature became divided and bent: Weik and then Wice.

"As the Elfwitch, she can only create lies. So she called evil good and good evil. She put Darkness for Light and Light as Darkness. She put bitter for sweet and poured salt onto blessings.

"She turned justice into justification. Punishment into vengeance. And clemency into cruelty.

"Then she loosed the Dark Riders one by one: the Destroyer who loves death. Rancor who hates all things, including itself. And Shadow who gives people fear so they forget hope."

"Then why does the Judge let them ruin the Realm?" Queen Regina asked.

"Darkness can only occupy the space vacated by the Light," the Bee Keepers said. "It has no authority except that which the Judge allows. Vengeance belongs to the Judge. It is He who will repay and he is not slack in keeping his promises.

"Remember, the Judge gave humans a choice. Follow Him or follow the Darkness. If they won't let the Law or Love lead them, then they walk in Darkness and have no Love.

"The Spirit went abroad and saw that humans' every waking thought was bent towards evil and that their flesh was divided against the Judge's Law. He repented of ever making them. So He brought about a great cataclysm by turning the domains of nature against them.

"First, an earthquake leveled their great cities, and then ash erupted from the bowels of the earth to cover their fields and villages. A great smoke covered the sky and blotted out the sun during the day and the moon at night. Plants withered and animals laid down to become dust.

"Then the world cooled and ice grew. Great sheets of ice covered everyone and everything from the mountains to the coast. Even the Elfwitch and the Dark Riders."

"Ice Prison," Reed said.

The Beekeeper nodded. "So the Judge repented of His wrath and promised to never destroy the world by such a cataclysm again.

"One village of humans He spared. They lived on the other side of the mountains and had not partaken in the evils of the Elfwitch's Domain.

"The only place to find quicksilver is there."

"Quicksilver Lake," Reed said. So many of the places in the Realm and the Domain had a mirror image back in his own World. If he swam out into Quicksilver Lake and tried to dive to the bottom, just where in his World would he come out?

"Yes, my son," the Beekeeper said. "You have been told that gold is for the sun and Light and that silver is for the moon and the Lesser Light. And that iron is heated in the bowels of the earth and is the strongest metal.

"But quicksilver has been left unformed. It dissolves both gold and silver. It is dangerous to touch and poisonous to breathe. This is why Quicksilver Lake is taboo.

"Here is a secret. Iron tames quicksilver. Quicksilver clings to iron and then can be shaped giving the wielder mighty power.

"That's how you did it!" Captain Michael said to Frehley. "You simply shaped the quicksilver onto an iron ring! Or had someone do it."

Frehley nodded. "I'm a hunter. To catch something, you turn its habits into the trap."

Queen Regina smiled. "You are very resourceful."

Frehley nodded. "And you are braver than you think you know, my queen."

The Beekeeper smiled. "Now I tell Reed a great truth. Since gold is Light, it will dispel the cold fire of Darkness. Just bring the two together. The Spirit will help to remind you.

"Now the people of this village were led by a woman so loved by the Judge she was called 'Dear' and 'Beloved' or 'Leoft" or 'Lfyt' The village was called 'Wych.'

"Lyftwych," the queen said.

"Leftwich," Reed said.

"It is as you say," the Beekeeper said.

"Because this village had kept their faith in the Light, the Judge blessed them by giving them the Law written on scrolls. To keep the Law all they had to do was to love the Judge and one another. And when they sinned, blood had to be shed and forgiveness offered. He renewed his promise to never leave or forsake them.

"The people grew strong in the Realm. They married and did business with one another. Farmed fields and built towns.

"But the Darkness did not die. It hid. Under rocks. In swamps. In caves. In shadows. In frozen nightmares.

"The Dark Riders cannot sleep in peace. Their one desire is to slip free of their frozen cells so they can run riot and deceive all the peoples and lead them once again away from the Law and into the Darkness and bring about so much evil that the Judge will again destroy the world, this time by fire.

"To this end they seek followers to secure their release.

"But the Judge had another plan. To make one final sacrifice. So that blood would cover everyone's sins once and for all. And to give people a fleshy heart to replace their stony hearts so they might turn to the Light and know Love.

"The people had made themselves a temple for sacrifice and bent the Law to where the leaders thought they knew the will of the Judge and spoke in His name. So he sent his Son as a suffering servant and as a Light to a world that was again in Darkness. He came to die so that anyone who would believe in Him would have everlasting life. He became the final sacrifice to fulfill the Law.

"He went among the people teaching and preaching.   Healing the sick. Saving the lost.

"But the Elfwitch escaped again and stirred up the leaders who were jealous of the Son. She convinced them they did not need the Son. That their judgment was better."

"This is your story about the Master and the overseers come true," Queen Regina said.

"Yes," the Beekeeper said. "The leaders reasoned if they got rid of the Son, he couldn't make them feel guilty. So they arrested him and hung him on a tree until he was dead.

"And the Elfwitch had them entomb his body with the scrolls of the Law under the Glacier Mountains and roll a stone over the entrance.

"But the Son had done no evil and did not sin, so the Judge raised the Son from the dead. Now the Son had escaped the tomb with victory over the final domain: death and destruction.   So that by his name people might be saved and have everlasting life.

"The Son returned to the people and again put the Elfwitch in Ice Prison. He chose a family descended from that faithful village to be the Root of Lyftwych. He helped them to build Tower Reign as a place to rule. He told them that if they kept the Law, it would be a light to their path and if they kept the Law in their hearts it would wash them daily.

"The Root of Lyftwych were to rule of the Realm with the Law, truth, and justice. Gold would be their sign of authority. The Son said he was leaving to return to his own Kingdom. Before he left, he gave a warning. There would come a time when people would again turn to Darkness and the Elfwitch would gather followers to free her and the Dark Riders. Then the Moon would eclipse the Sun. Vows would be broken and families torn apart. People would call the Darkness the Light and the Light the Darkness. Then people would forsake the Law and worship the Darkness and take its sign.

"At that time, the Son will return in clouds of glory to destroy all the Darkness. Those following the Darkness will see His coming and tremble in fear.   And every creature above and below will confess that Judge's Son is the Living Law. And the Darkness and its followers will be forever cast out forever.

"Then the Son will gather all those who followed his Word, his Light, his Love, and Law and He will give them eternal Life. And His kingdom shall come and they shall be His people forever in a Realm of love and peace.

"This is true and it will happen. If it were not so, I would have told you. For the Judge always keeps his promises.

"I am the Light of the World. I am the Truth and the Life.

"Do not be afraid. I will never leave or forsake you."

. The Beekeeper finished. Every word pricked Reed's conscience. Quickened his hurts. He wanted to name them and give them all over to the Beekeeper. To be free of them. To be healed.

Because the Beekeeper was the Judge. And his Son. And their Spirit.

So Reed got down on his knees.

So did the queen.

Then Frehley.

And then Strap.

Finally, Captain Michael followed suit.

"Forgive me, Lord, for being mad at Mom. Blaming her for Dad leaving. Bring my family back together. Turn my sister from the Darkness. It's my fault I lost my silver necklace and the gold coin. I screwed up," Reed said.

"Forgive my pride Lord in makin' a quicksilver necklace that got used for evil. For losin' faith in love and lettin' the Realm get turned upside down," Frehley said.

Strap signed for his forgiveness of letting everything he loved slip into Darkness.

"Hear me, O Lord! Forgive me for forsaking the truth and justice and your Law. For turning my back on Love and letting Darkness come over my land. But most of all for letting others tell me how to rule," Queen Regina said.

Then Captain Michael spoke. "Lord, forgive me for what I'm might have done. I thought I was doing what was right. But I'm confused."

"Rise, my children. Let me baptize you in water and in spirit," the Beekeeper said.

He led them away from the table to a nearby stream of cool clean water. One by one, he baptized them in the name of the Judge, the Son, and the Spirit. A light shone down upon them. And a dove flew overhead.

"You have been washed in the blood and in the water," the Beekeeper said as they stood on the bank of the stream together. "Now you must be washed in the Law. The Word. The Testament.

"Bring back the Law and the Light will return to your Realm. Then the Darkness will flee for that is its nature.

"But your faith will be tested. The Darkness will sift you. Keep the faith for all things are possible with the Judge."

"But the Deadcoats are many. And the Elfwitch has other servants: both man and animal," Queen Regina said.

"And don't forget the Dark Riders," Frehley said.

"The Judge chose the foolish things of this world to confound the wise. And he chose the weak things of this world to shame the strong," the Beekeeper said. "You will need the most foolish and the weakest among you."

"I knew who the weakest is!" Reed said and ran back to bring his pet rat on its tiny pallet before the Bee Keeper.

The Beekeeper passed his hand over Packy and the rat blinked its eyes and sat up on its haunches. Then it ran from its pallet up Reed's arms to take its place again on its master's shoulders. Packy nuzzled Reed's ear as he stroked its head.

"A miracle!" Queen Regina said. "And greater ones are in store!"

"So where do we find the foolish?" Frehley asked.

"The foolish shall find you," the Beekeeper said. "And when that happens, remember: you are to forgive much because much has been forgiven you."

Clouds came down and rolled over the hillside. Obscuring the Beekeeper and the table. The buzzing of the bees faded as well as the tinkling of the goats' cowbells.

The radiance dimmed as the Beekeeper dissolved. "Do not be afraid."

Then Reed was aware of lying down.

He must have been asleep.

So he awoke and sat up.

***

Chapter Forty-Nine: Bee and Wasp

Everyone else woke up.

Even Captain Michael who should have finished the morning watch.

They lay near to the evergreen trees where they had made camp. The fire died down to cool white embers. The remainder of the pulverized willow bark lay on a flat rock. The pool of boiled witch-hazel had long since cooled. And the bundle of wintergreen leaves had turned into a bundle of charred slips. The oil drippings had congealed into greasy stains below on a rock.

All their weapons stood in a stockade pile—other than the pistol and knife that Captain Michael held in his sleepy grip.

"Where's the owl?" Queen Regina asked.

"Where's the Beekeeper?" Frehley asked. "And the animals?"

"It was just a dream," Captain Michael said.

"It couldn't have been a dream," Reed said as he looked about for Packy. The tiny litter was empty. Hadn't the Bee Keeper healed his pet rat?

Strap stood up and then patted his belly while miming chewing.

The queen was slower in rousing. "I feel close to bursting.

"We didn't see anybody. And we didn't eat anything," Captain Michael said.

"Then how come I saw y'all there?" Reed asked. "How come we're all talkin' 'bout it?"

"If it was a dream, I'd rather right back there now," Frehley said. "As good as it was."

Packy had been there in the dream, too. But had the owl been part of the dream, too? "Packy? Where's Packy? There was an owl out last night!"

Frehley straightened up. "You heard an owl, too?"

Reed wasted no time arguing. He ran back towards the stream. "Packy? Come here!"

Packy had wandered off before. And every time he always found something. A way out of the dungeon. A cluster of berries. Or the Destroyer.

But this time had something found the rat? Reed something small darting near the streambed. He sighed in relief. It was Packy.

Hadn't the Beekeeper said they would need the weakest of the company?

Reed needn't worry. Packy was doing what rats did best. Discovering curious things. What was it that Packyhad discovered?

Reed bent down. Packy ran around the object and then got up on his hind legs to sniff the top of it. Whatever it was, it was solid.

It was a glass jar. Filled with a viscous amber liquid. There was a sweet must.

Reed picked the jar up. Put his finger in it. And then brought it to his mouth.

Honey. Hadn't there been jars like this on the Beekeeper's table. In their dream?

Packy ran up to perch on Reed's shoulder as they brought the jar back to the company. They looked at Reed with fresh eyes. Packy shouldn't have been upon his shoulder and the jar of honey shouldn't have been in his hand.

"Sure it was still a dream?" Queen Regina asked as she took the jar from Reed.

The queen scooped some out with her finger and licked it. Then she passed it to the others who each dipped a finger into it.

Captain Michael raised an eyebrow and said, "Last night's meal was real."

Strap patted his stomach and licked his lips.

"Yes, I can still taste the cheese," Frehley admitted. "And the milk. And the meat."

"And now we have honey for breakfast," Queen Regina said. "If we want to banish the Dark Riders then we need to find the Sepulcher where the Elfwitch put those scrolls."

"Well, if you want to find the Elfwitch, her lair's under the Keep," Reed said. "She calls it the Circle Chamber."

"Reed, you've been there?" the queen asked.

He nodded. "You can get to Ice Prison from there, too."

"This'll be the worst kind of hunt," Frehley said. "To put these creatures back into their cage, we have to go into their lair. And we keep addin' more hair triggers to the trap.

"First, we go back to the Keep. Get inside somehow and fight off the Black Watch. Then we find our way to the dungeon. Fight all of the Elfwitch's servants. Then we find the Sepulcher and get the Law back. Then we go to Ice Prison and bait the Destroyer and the other one skulkin' around now, Rancor, back into their cells."

"Don't forget my sister," Reed said.

"Wice serves the Elfwitch," Captain Michael said.

"Her name is Chayse!" Reed said.

"Reed, she did help us escape," Queen Regina explained. "But the Elfwitch has her enthralled."

"Well, she's been my sister longer," Reed said. "She's just forgotten her name is all."

"And the final lynch pin to the trap will be trap the Elfwitch," Frehley said.

Strap pointed to Reed and then passed his hand over his head and shoulder.

"Yes, my friend. Once we've done all that. We will make sure Reed and his sister get back home," Frehley said.

"So, let's be off, then," the queen commanded. "Pass out the weapons."

Keeping a pistol and the bowie knife, Captain Michael passed out the remaining weapons with caution: Strap, the blackjack and musket. Frehley, the pistol and remaining musket. And Reed a pistol.

Frehley gave his pistol to the queen. "We've hunted together so I know you can shoot."

"You're the best shot we have," Queen Regina said.

"I can only shoot one at a time," Frehley said. "Besides, this gives us more firepower."

Captain Michael took the lead as the company set off in dirty clothes and few weapons and a jar of honey between them. They crossed the stream and moved towards the slope of the ridgeline. Reed, and Frehley bringing up the rear.

"Why aren't you leading us?" Reed asked the ex-Royal Huntsman. "You know the way."

Frehley nodded. "Sometimes, you gotta let the children play with the toys. So when they get in over their heads you rush in for the save."

The tree line thinned out as they climbed a small ridge. At the top, they did not find goats and bees. Instead they could see Outlaw Forest stretching over wooded knobs and hollers and above it all Glacier Mountains rising like an icy blue wall.

The peace of the Bee Keeper's farm was wearing off. As was the unity of love. And the fullness of the meal was long gone.

Shadows slipped between the silvery trees. Birds and insects would quiet and then call out again around them like a theater in a round. Something else was in the woods.

"Something's out there," Reed said.

Frehley nodded. "Good. You've got the knack."

They passed close to tall bushes with thin serrated leaves. Bouncing on top were stalks with clusters of white blooms. Reed thought he heard something hovering among the blooms.

"Careful," Frehley said. "That's hemlock. Very poisonous."

Something was buzzing. Being busy.

Bees! Big one. Bumblebees.

Reed darted off. Straight to the bushes. Hoping to see the Beekeeper.

"Reed!" Frehley called like Dad would. "Stay with the company! Everyone stop!"

Reed felt hope rising. He wanted to see the Beekeeper again. Be known in the Light.

Frehley got Captain Michael to stop only when Queen Regina stepped over to the bushes.

"Are there really bees?" she asked wanting to see for herself.

"Yes!" Reed said. "Come see!"

In answer, a bumblebee flew near the queen to investigate all the intruders.

A shadow stepped out from between the trees. From that shadow out dove a wasp that intercepted the bumblebee. It clasped onto the larger insect and stung it. The bumblebee beat its wings in fury but the wasp flew off with it in its clutches and Reed knew why from having read it in a three-minute science book so he could get his reading points for the week: the wasp would take the bumblebee back to its paper lined nest in order to feed the prey to its larva while it was still alive and paralyzed.

Another wasp hovered about with its ladylike legs tucked under its stinger. A venomous barb. It got close to Queen Regina.

Too close.

With its a stinger.

It landed on her shoulder and neck. Then the wasp flicked its wings in agitation.

"Mom!" Reed said in a flash. "Stand still!"

He knocked it off her shoulder. But not before feeling a prick against the side of his palm. He turned it over. There was a bump around a tiny red point.

He'd been stung.

Queen Regina turned to look at him with an open mouth.

Reed looked at her neck. She had a rising welt around a thick dark point. It was turning into a knot as other bumps around it began to grow in unison.

The queen had been stung, too.

Just once but somehow the bumps were replicating all over her neck and chest.

Hives.

"You fool!" Captain Michael said as he rushed over. "The queen is allergic to wasps!"

There were other wasps around. Weaving and ready to strike. Unlike the bee, who lost its stinger and died from bleeding out, wasps had a barb they used to sting over and over again.

The queen hyperventilated. Her face went red. Her eyes glazed over. Shock.

Reed knew what to do. Someone was supposed to get her to the ER so someone else could administer a cortisone shot. Except that's what worked back in his own World.

The queen needed help. Medicine. That came from herbs. Who would help them here?

Captain Michael pulled her back and she collapsed in his arms as she convulsed.

He held her shoulders down. "Keep those wasps away from her!"

Strap bounded in and slapped them down.

Reed noticed there were more. Enough to make a swarm. How could that happen?

Bees had a hive. Wasps had a nest. Out here it could be as big as Strap's head.

So where was the nest?

Reed looked around. Through the hemlock bushes. From tree to tree.

He caught sight of a moving shadow. A piece of clothing. A leather duster.

Then the entity poked its head around an oak. It had a scowling human face under a large hat brim and its hair in a ponytail. From its claw-like hand came four more angry red waspers.

"We've got to help her!" Frehley told the captain. "We've got to get her out of here!"

"We've got to stop the wasps first!" Captain Michael said as he covered over the gasping queen's head.

"Where are they coming from?" Frehley asked as he held down the queen's kicking legs.

Reed pointed towards a tree from which behind the Dark Rider sneered at him. "Rancor!"

"A Dark Rider?" Frehley asked.

Strap strode towards the creature. Swinging his great fists out like a hammer ready to fall. But they did not make contact with flesh. Only wafted through a swarm of flies as Rancor dissipated.

Instead, another person ran from behind the tree. Around Strap and through the cloud of black flies. While waving a crude torch that billowed dark smoke in his only hand.

It was Cyrus. Swatting at the wasps with his torch. The ones that didn't dodge the moving flame fell to the ground with their bodies and wings on fire.

The smoke confused the wasps. Some fell to the ground stunned. Cyrus ran to the prostrate queen and waved the torch about to envelope her in a smokescreen.

Strap and Reed stamped on the ones on the ground.

Reed looked for Rancor but the Dark Rider had gone. It did not prefer direct confrontation like the Destroyer. Instead, it had left its hate behind.

"Traitor!" Frehley yelled and jumped up at the man who had just helped. "Coward!"

Captain Michael had to get between the two.

Then Strap waded into the fray to tip the balance when he grabbed Cyrus by the neck.

Reed kicked at Strap. He couldn't believe he was trying to help Cyrus.

"Stop!" Reed cried out. "The wasps are gone!"

Cyrus held the torch away from the queen as he looked her over. "What happened?"

"She was stung," Frehley said.

"And she's allergic to wasp stings," Captain Michael said.

"I can help," Cyrus said.

"We've got to get her to a healer," Frehley. "We'll have to build another litter."

"I can help," Cyrus said again.

"I don't know if we should move her. The poison might spread," Captain Michael said.

"I can help," Cryus said a third time.

Captain Michael lashed out, "Are you a healer?"

"No, he's a blacksmith, so shut up," Frehley said still under the spell of Rancor.

"I can use silver. It'll draw out poison out of her blood. It can heal her," Cyrus said.

"Silver?" Frehley cried. "Where are we gonna find silver?"

"We will only need a little. About the size of a wire," Cyrus said.

"Where are we gonna find silver out here?" Frehley howled.

Reed held out his Tracfone. "There's gold and silver threads in my phone. Remember me telling you I think that's why it still works here in the Realm?"

***

Chapter Fifty: Fire and Forge

Frehley snatched the Tracfone out of Reed's hand.

Not unlike what the big bullies did to the little bullies at school.

"Hey!" Reed said. Anger rushed up into his face. Dad wouldn't have been so mean.

Frehley cocked his arm to chuck the Tracfone across the forest. He would have, too, hadn't Strap grabbed his wrist from behind and turned it over making him drop the Tracfone.

Reed snatched up his Tracfone and cradled it. Strap waited until Frehley winced before he turned the ex-Royal Huntsman's hand lose. They stared each other down.

"Is that true, kid?" Cyrus asked Reed. "Can I see it?"

"You're not gonna chuck it are you?" Reed asked. He wasn't about to trust Cyrus.

"No, I want to smelt it," Cyrus said.

"You can't smelt that tool!" Frehley shouted.

"Why can't he?" Captain Michael asked. "Isn't he a blacksmith?"

"Look at him!" Frehley said.

"Look at her," Captain Michael said. "Don't you love her madly? You went to Quicksilver Lake for her. Wouldn't you smelt all the rocks in the Realm if it would help?'

Queen Regina's face was swelling. Her neck was already the size of Cyrus' good forearm. There were hives up and down her arms and over her chest.

"I admit I might not have the strength here," Cyrus said holding up his one good hand. Then he tapped the side of his head. "But all the skill's up here anyway."

"Tell us what we need to do to help you," Captain Michael said.

Cyrus made a mental list off the top of his head. "We'll need to make a very hot fire. Then we'll need to shape some tools. We can use certain rocks. But I'll need your knife to take that device apart. And I'll need someone to hold it," Cyrus said.

He got them busy.

The fire was built up in stages. First, rubbing flints sparked dry weeds and leaves under small twigs. Three large branches were laid out against the starting flames: two parallel and one across both. More kindling was fed to lead the flames to the branches.

Captain Michael stoked the fire and Reed helped him feed it. Their next job was to stoke it with larger deadwood. Reed helped the captain scoot and rollover logs until they had five logs in total roasting away on top of the bed of coals.

Strap was sent in search of rocks. Not just any kind. He needed to find bog ore and marble.

"Why use rocks?" Frehley asked.

"Marble heats up fast. Bog ore is found around springs. It's got iron so it's magnetic. It'll help draw out other metals. It'll be makeshift forge but I can still smelt on it," Cyrus said.

Frehley waved him off like he was a madman.

"I'll help Strap look," Cyrus said taking the Tracfone with him. "Reed, if your tool's got iron in it, it'll stick to other iron. Captain, take the kid and look for granite stones about the size of your arm."

Reed had never seen the man so focused or excited. Or knowledgeable. He sounded like his seventh grade science teacher, Mr. Cox—who was also the seventh grade football coach.

Even though, Cyrus hadn't asked Frehley to help, he groused, "Count me out."

"You could at least put the bayonets on the muskets," Cyrus said.

Frehley groused some more. "What are you gonna do with bayonets?"

Now he was sounding just like Dad.

"I need tongs," Cyrus said as he tramped out with Strap following.

Captain Michael led Reed the other way as they looked over the rocks along the stream bed. The Realm was just like the Ozarks. There were small rocks everywhere. Lying on the ground. Or raised just below the dirt like splinters. And plenty of it was granite.

"Why is Frehley being so mean?" Reed asked.

"I think Rancor's spell hit him the hardest. Because he still loves the queen very much," the captain said. Then he asked Reed. "Why aren't you mad?"

Reed shrugged and patted Packy who rode on his shoulder. "I've got plenty of reasons to be mad at good ol' Cy. But I'm more grateful to have Packy well again."

"Seeing the Son couldn't have been dream," Captain Michael said. "We were all there. We shared a meal in peace at his table. And then I felt the Spirit and I needed to be cleansed. So He baptized us all in the same Spirit.

"But since we woke up back here, it's like we are all returning to our old ways. Maybe after we help the queen, Frehley will remember the dream. Reed and the captain picked out five choice pieces of granite. The two carried them back to the growing fire. Cy had chosen two large pieces of bog ore that Strap had toted back to rest on the burning wood. The ore glowed reddish brown from the heat.

The queen was no better. And labored to breathe. Each breath ragged and slow.

"Whatever you're gonna do, you best do it quick," Frehley growled. While everyone had gone rock hunting, he had taken the time to attach both bayonets. Reed thought it a good thing.

Cyrus turned to Captain Michael, "I'll need the knife now."

The captain frowned but gave over the big knife hilt first. "I'll still be needing it back."

Cyrus had Strap hold the Tracfone down on a rock outcropping while he pried it open. It didn't take too long. He took out the battery and then the faceplate revealing the keypad attached to the chip. It was a maze of silver and gold thread running through green mazes.

There couldn't be enough silver or gold to sneeze at in the chip. But it had to be enough.

Cyrus handed the bowie knife back to Captain Michael who stuck it back in his belt. Then Cyrus took up a musket and put it under his arm. He asked Reed to pick up the other musket and together they carried the chip between the bayonets to lay it on the hot rocks.

The fire was so hot no one could stand next to it for too long except for Cyrus. The chip began to smoke and sizzle along the tiny threads. Cyrus handed over his musket to Strap so that both the giant and Reed could pin down the chip with bayonets. Then the blacksmith hammered on the chip with a granite rock until it crumbled and the threads pulled away.

Cyrus tossed the faceplate and keypad into the fire.

"Don't toss the battery into the fire," Reed told him. "It'll explode. Trust me."

The blacksmith arched an eyebrow and stuffed the battery in his belt line. Then he took Reed's musket and used the bayonet to separate threads from the dross. Which was scraped into the fire.

Cyrus separated the two types of metal from the threads. Keeping them in two liquid drops with the point of the bayonet. The dull gleam of silver and the yellow glob of gold.

There wasn't much of either. Just a few drops of silver. And the gold could cover Reed's fingernail.

When they began to bubble Cyrus asked Reed and Captain Michael to bring over the other two pieces of granite. He had them give the rocks to Strap as he scraped the silver onto one rock and the gold onto the second.

The rocks were set down away from the fire next to the queen. Cyrus took up a musket again and used the bayonet to roll and knead the silver drops into a tiny paste no bigger than what Reed's Grandma would call a smidge. The gold was left to cool into a shape like an oval button.

"It's not much," Frehley said who had sat close by the queen with his arms crossed.

"Will it work?" Captain Michael asked.

"It's all we need," Cyrus said after testing the cooled material.

Reed touched it, too. The gold piece was warm. The silver was sticky.

"Careful, Reed," Cyrus said. "Strap, hold the queen's head and open her mouth. Frehley, you'll need to give this to her."

Frehley shrugged. "How?"

Captain Michael rolled his eyes. "Put in the back of her mouth. Close her jaws. Tickle her throat until she swallows."

Reed pinched the smidge of silver and brought it over to Frehley. Strap cradled the queen's head in his lip and held her mouth open his fingers.

But Frehley didn't take it. "Why are you helpin' all of the sudden?" he asked Cyrus.

"I believed a lie. I did what I did so I wouldn't lose my wife and kid. But I had already lost them and didn't even know it," Cyrus said. "So, all I could think of was my hurt. And I did things my family would not be proud of.

"I messed up. A lot. So, I want to make up for what I've done. Which might take a long time. Just give me the chance."

"You say you love her," Captain Michael told Frehley. "Are you willing to help her?"

"I always hated it when Dad wouldn't help Mom. He'd pout like a baby and she'd cry herself to sleep," Reed said.

Frehley frowned and then wiped the silver smidge off Reed's fingertip onto his own. He poked his finger into the queen's mouth and stuck the silver smidge on the roof of her mouth.

Strap closed her mouth and Frehley stroked her swollen throat until her mouth moved.

The giant kept her head in her lap as they all kept watch.

Her color changed. From pale to pink. Her cheeks and throat began to relax. The hives began to disappear.

Everyone congratulated Cyrus.

Everyone except Frehley.

"Remember what the Beekeeper said, 'We are to forgive much because much has been forgiven us,'" Reed told Frehley.

Frehley looked down. "Now I can say I've met the Son. So…"

He stuck his hand out to Cyrus. The blacksmith gripped it. Then Strap put his hand over theirs. Then the captain. And last, Reed.

"You've met the Son?" Cyrus asked. "They say he's dead and buried. In a sepulcher. Somewhere in Glacier Mountains."

"And who would be 'they?'" Frehley asked.

"The Elfwitch did," Captain Michael said. "And quite often."

"I want to see for myself. I've been lied to way too much," Cyrus said.

Frehley blew through his lips. "Well, I guess we'll just add that to the list then."

"What list?" Queen Regina asked as she stirred.

***

Chapter Fifty-One: Poison and Prison

Wice looked at the Tracfone. A device from Chayse's own World. Plastic coating. Lithium battery. A SIMS card. A chip. A keypad.

Technology at its best. Just a tool. Neither good nor evil.

Working the Tracfone this way was fun. As best as Wice could figure, the electricity needed to manipulate the device came from her. Her impulse touched the gold and silver in the wiring. She felt it hum.

Her thoughts turned to impulses being conducted through the metal threads. It obeyed her and converted her impulses into transmitted words.

Gold was for commands. Authority.

Silver was for vows and curses. Binding.

ME:

REED, WHERE R U

That had been the third text Wice had sent without a response. Reed could work his phone, too, without an outside source of electricity. It was safe to assume, he knew how to use the metal inside the phone.

Maybe he wasn't quite the cast-off that the Elfwitch assumed. Maybe the Elfwitch just wanted Wice to think that way about the boy. He was a twin after all, so how was he a lesser entity by just being a boy?

Reed hadn't answered her in a while so the Elfwitch had sent Rancor out to spread his seed: anger, irritation, hatred, and fury.

Wice was alone with the Elfwitch in her lair: the Circle Chamber. Surrounded by shelves of jars and racks of potions and tables full with cages and her familiar: the two-headed vulture on its perch along a curve of the wall. In the center stood the smoking tripod and the centrifuge on its metal hook.

But Wice's eyes kept resting upon one thing: the wooden chest with her namesake resting against the curve of the chamber wall under the two-headed vulture's perch. The Elfwitch unlatched the top of a wooden cage full of tumor ridden mice and snatched up two by the tail. She tossed them up into the air near the wall and the vulture's double heads snapped up the falling mice in succession.

But Wice did not notice the double-headed vulture with its snacks as much as the shut wooden trunk that she longed to open.

"He still hasn't answered, my pet?" the Elfwitch asked.

Taking her eyes off the chest, Wice said, "No, my Dark Lady."

The Elfwitch held out a lithe silver-skinned hand. "He will after Rancor finds him. Hand your device here."

Wice hesitated, though, she did not know why she should. The device was from Chayse's own World. The only one like it was with the boy twin. She had no intention of ever being Chayse again.

It's mine. That thought hadn't been Wice's.

"Let's have it," the Elfwitch commanded.

Wice liked controlling it. Manipulating it with her mind. What else could be done with silver and gold in larger amounts?

What could I do with quicksilver if I had it?

The Destroyer walked in on its leather boots. The Elfwitch directed the beast to stoke the tripod and clean out the centrifuge.

"What do you think has happened to the twin?" Wice asked as handed over the Tracfone over.

The Elfwitch smoothed her hand over the device. "I care not what has happened to the boy. He is no matter. But his device may be useful to us as this one might be."

After the Destroyer had finished its task, it flexed its claws like a bored cat. Soon it exited the Circle Chamber back the way it had come, from the tunnel leading to the dungeons. Not long after its departure, Wice heard screams of hapless men begging for mercy and receiving none.

"The Destroyer is so cruel," Wice said.

"Cruelty is just a means to an end," the Elfwitch said.

"What end requires giving out pain and then death to stop it?" Wice asked.

"Power," the Elfwitch smiled and glowed silver from head to toe. "This device has power. You can only manipulate a small part of it. But imagine if all its power was unleashed at once. Imagine using that power."

Wice let Chayse show her a memory of videos warnings on the danger of lithium batteries exploding in people's faces or in their pockets. "It is dangerous."

"It is also wondrous," the Elfwitch said. "You wish to see more of that power. You wish to know the cold fire that feeds the Darkness. And you will. In time." A swarm of black flies flew in through the exit tunnel from the dungeons. The flies compacted together into a moving mass that took the shape of a man in a leather duster and broad rim hat. The buzzing insects resolved back into the Dark Rider known as Rancor.

Wice felt cold waves of enmity roll off the creature. Harmful thoughts churned in her mind. This creature only had hate to give: that was its nature.

"Did you find the renegades?" the Elfwitch asked.

Rancor hissed and put out its claws. Words were useless to its fury. It could only communicate in raw groans or vicious laughs.

"You stung the queen?" the Elfwitch was pleased and laughed. "I hope the venom kills her!"

Mom. No. Here, the woman was Queen Regina. She had been kind to Wice. *She was more than kind.* And Wice had saved her. But she had killed another. *Poor Kyphus.*

Wice shook her head clear of Chayse. That was the last time she would try to do the right thing. She had screwed it up.

The queen was not her mother. Chayse had a mother once. But Wice was no longer Chayse. Wice had no mother. She had created herself. By naming herself.

If she kept telling herself that maybe she would believe it.

Then Rancor stuck his arm around his back and whipped his other arm about as he hissed.

"The blacksmith?" the Elfwitch clarified. "I thought he turned coward and ran off for good."

"What do you mean?" Wice asked.

"Never be surprised what humans do," the Elfwitch said as she patted the device. "They can make this tool only to send gossip to hurt one another. Yet, the hurt friend would die for the other like some homesick puppy.

"One last Dark Rider remains to be freed. Then all hope will be lost. Shadow will steal their faith and the renegades will cry out in despair."

"How? My bro-" Wice caught herself as the Elfwitch nodded. "The renegade child lost his silver necklace down in the dungeon. Won't we have to find it?"

"This device has silver," the Elfwitch said.

"It has gold, too. But you can't use that metal can you?" Wice pointed out.

"Neither can you, now," the Elfwitch said.

Wice became indignant. "Why not?"

"We are forbidden from gold because it belongs to the sun. To the Light. To *him,*" the Elfwitch scowled.

Rancor howled.

"But there are limits to every power," the Elfwitch said. "So what can stop gold?"

"Quicksilver," Wice said.

Both the Elfwitch and Rancor nodded.

"But you can no longer touch it, can you? That's why you need me. You want me to go to Quicksilver Lake and fetch you some quicksilver," Wice asked.

Rancor crossed its arms over its leather dusted chest and the Elfwitch slanted her head.

"In time, you will serve the desires of the Darkness," the Elfwitch said. "We seek power to use for the Darkness. But the more powerful a thing is, the more dangerous it is."

The Dark Lady held up her free arm and pulled down the robe of her black raven sleeve. Scar tissue from burns ran like rivulets of ruined flesh along with patches of bleached skin. "The first time I worked with quicksilver it nearly killed me. Instead, it changed me."

That struck something inside Wice. That wasn't what the Elfwitch had said earlier about her first experience with quicksilver. True, she said she hadn't been her present form yet, but she hadn't *worked* with the quicksilver, she had *swam* in it.

"There is one last step to secure your loyalty," the Elfwitch said.

"Take your tattoo," Wice said. The Moon-Snake tattoo. Inside her, Chayse became revulsed.Then she made an intuitive leap. "It has quicksilver in it, doesn't it?" The   Elfwitch nodded. "And iron. Quicksilver turns gold and silver into jelly. But it clings to iron so it can be molded and shaped. Then it will obey its wielder. But it must be given as a freewill gift to another or its power stays latent.

"Only humans can harvest quicksilver, it seems. My initiation was my entry into the Darkness," the Elfwitch said.

"You used the quicksilver to free Rancor," Wice said. Then another piece of knowledge that had remained hidden in the open leaped up so fast that I made her skin tingle. "But quicksilver can also imprison you."

Both Dark Riders stared at her with a smoldering glare.

"It is a poison and a prison," the Elfwitch said.

***

Chapter Fifty-Two: Secret and Power

"I don't make the rules," the Elfwitch said. "I bend them until I can break them."

Rancor laughed.

"But you can't bend or break quicksilver, can you?" Wice asked.

The two Dark Riders stopped laughing as the Elfwitch looked upon her acolyte.

"That's why you need me to get the quicksilver. But what if…" *I use the quicksilver for myself. What's to stop me? The tattoo would stop me. It's part of her thrall.* "…I don't take your tattoo?"

"Oh, I know you very much want to," the Elfwitch said as she indicated the chest against the chamber wall. "Just like you want to look inside that chest."

"Maybe I won't," Wice said.

"And maybe you will," the Elfwitch laughed.

"You can't make me," Wice said.

"You can't help yourself," the Elfwitch said. "Look at all you've done, and quite willingly, I must add, since the moment you came into my domain: you've turned against your own flesh and blood to follow me; you've proven yourself adept at learning the arcane secrets of the Darkness; you've wielded power and deceit against the twin boy and the other renegades; you've lashed out at my servants and you killed poor Kyphus.

"Did you forget you had blood on your hands?"

Wice swallowed. The Elfwitch always brought Kyphus up. The squat longhaired and bearded High Priest in this world. And in Chayse's own World? The lawyer ad litem Alexander Kyler.

Just what he had been High Priest of? The Judge and the Law? If so, he had turned his back on truth and justice to follow the Dark Lady.

He had conspired and mutinied against Queen Regina, the very queen he had sworn to serve.

Hadn't he deserved a traitor's death?

He had died alright. In a horrible and ignoble manner.

Wice blinked and Kyphus' misshapen face appeared. Twisted. Motley. Feathers sticking out instead of hair. Eyes turned to yellow slits. Tongue clicking against his transformed beak.

All because of you, Wice. You robbed him of his humanity.

No, I didn't make him a turncoat! I didn't make him take the sign of Asheroth! He would have been killed as a mutineer.

Did he deserve how he died? It was agonizing torture!

No! He begged me to kill him! So I gave him poison! To help him escape the transformation.

Which you caused!

Could Kyphus have been transformed back into a human? Hadn't he still been a human when Wice had given him poison? Hadn't the Judge made him? Didn't he still have value? No matter what Kyphus might have done?

So, Wice had committed murder then. Her shoulders slumped in surrender. Even though, she had gained knowledge the experience, she felt somehow she had cheated herself.

What if the Light were to return now and she came face to face with the Judge? Would He forgive her? Or would He forever punish her?

Rancor sensed her struggle and laughed.

"The Destroyer passes his time in leisure down in the dungeon," the Elfwitch said. "The tripod's cold fire is stoked. Rancor and I go to prepare the altar at Ice Prison."

She stepped towards the exit tunnel leading back to Ice Prison and indicated for the other Dark Rider to follow. "That will leave you alone with an opportunity to look inside my chest."

"What if I don't wanna look inside your secret chest?" That was Chayse speaking.

"'Secret?' Oh, my pet!" the Elfwitch laughed over her shoulder. "You've already hooked yourself! I will allow this time alone to peruse the 'secret' chest."

Then the Dark Lady and Rancor were through the exit into the tunnel to the Ice Prison. From back out of the tunnel, the Elfwitch called, "There's just one caveat. The chest reveals whatever you want most."

That was followed by another one of Rancor's vicious laughs.

Then Wice was alone.

With the two-headed vulture on its perch.

And the chest beneath it.

The old wooden trunk from which she had chosen her new name.

It had been fun at first. Being someone else. She had hated being Chayse. The girl was chained in helplessness and mired in miserable powerlessness.

But Wice was free.

To do what?

Discover.

Like discover just what was *inside* that chest. The Elfwitch kept tattoo needles and parlor ink in there. What else was inside?

First, the Elfwitch didn't want her looking inside the chest. Now, she was inviting her. The Elfwitch had welcomed Wice into her Domain. Allowed her to touch anything on the shelves or in the racks.

Anything but the chest.

Until now.

Why?

There was a secret inside.

The chest reveals whatever you want most.

And a secret had power. But only as long as it remained secret.

…whatever you want most.

Why would the Elfwitch not want Wice to find out the secret until now?

Power.

Wice would have power.

Just what would she do with that power?

For starters, she wouldn't have the Deadcoats rotting away into a puddle of blubber. That was gross. She would release them from their vow so they could just lie down and die.

And the test animals in their cages. Grotesque and misshapen. They were dying anyway so why not just free them?

Now that big snake. Asheroth. It was supposed to guard doors. And just what was behind those doors?

More secrets.

Which meant more power.

That's where Wice wanted to look the most. Inside every chest. Behind every door.

Maybe Wice had wanted to open the chest all along.

Why fight temptation?

Wice stepped towards the chest.

Each twin head of the vulture squawked in turn.

"Shut it, you two-headed freak," Wice commanded.

Both heads fell silent as it shook its feathers. Then both heads each took a wing to scratch with a rough beak.

Wice knelt before the chest and reached out to grasp the handle. It was cold iron.

Lifting the lid all the way back she found it wasn't heavy at all.

She held her breath then Wice looked inside.

Empty.

There was nothing in it at all.

She exhaled.

Just an old wooden trunk. Planks joined in seams without nails to make a box. Wood stained with years but containing not a single memory or souvenir.

She slammed the lid and frowned.

One of the birds' heads cawed. Was it mocking her?

"I told you to shut it," Wice growled not unlike Chayse would have at her five-minute-younger brother.

There should have been something in it.

Maybe the Elfwitch had removed the tattoo needle and parlor ink.

It had all just been a prank.

Open it. One more time.

That had not been her voice.

Spell Speak.

So Wice opened the chest up again. This time by just a crack.

This time it was full of nothingness.

The inside of the box had gone. The four walls of three dimensions shrunk into one: flatness. Blank and black.

Colorless and timeless.

In a flash, Wice squeezed her hand through the opening.

It disappeared into the plane of darkness like plunging it into an icy river.

Her fingers began to freeze until they hurt.

She made herself wiggle her fingers. She could not see them but she felt them moving.

Nothing happened. She'd won the dare. Time to pull her hand out and close the lid. So it would be shut tight. And nothing could get out.

Something brushed against her fingers.

Time to pull her fingers back before something bad happened.

She didn't and something happened anyway.

That something yanked on her fingers and banging her against the edge of the chest. Her whole arm plunging into the darkness. Into the freezing cold.

Wice dared not call out as both heads of the vulture squawked in double mocking tones.

She pushed against the side of the chest with her free hand but the unknown something would not let go. Then she planted her knees against the side of the chest and leaned back. The something would not yield.

Wice didn't what it could be. She only knew she wanted whatever it was to let go of her.

Its grip was strong.

Strong enough to pull her headlong into the mysterious black cold.

Strong enough to drown her in the darkness inside the chest.

So Wice planted each foot flat against the chest and yanked back as hard she could. She pulled for her arm. She pulled for her life.

Her arm came out of the darkness returning to light and warmth. Then her elbow. Then her wrist. Each part was whole and well.

Out came the edge of her palm and the top of her thumb.

But something else was attached to the rest of her hand. It looked like a scaly talon. Except it had a thumb, too, that rested on the back of her thumb.

The something was no longer pulling. Now it was *pushing*. Upwards.

That something wanted to come *out*.

Wice yanked her hand free and rolled over on her back pushing against the floor to get away from the chest as quick and as far as she could.

The something rose out of the flat blackness. Its other talon-hand grasping the top of the lid and opening so it could stand up. The something had molted feathers sticking to its plucked skin. The arms were crooked at the elbows and the skin hung like a sagging flag to the armpit.

Wings. Naked wings.

The something straightened its back. It had a crooked spine. And it's head…No neck. The chin and nose transformed into a twisted beak. The eyes. Yellow slits. Green bile blew out of its nostrils and dripped from its open maw.

The something was Kyphus.

Kyphus transformed.

Kyphus killed by poison.

Kyphus come back from the dead. To take its vengeance. To take Wice back with it.

Wice's heart pounded. She had nowhere to run and nowhere to hide. She screamed.

"Did I not tell you that the chest holds what you want most?" asked the Elfwitch nonplussed from the mouth of the exit tunnel.

Wice caught her heart in her throat. She had turned over on her hands and knees. She couldn't get away fast enough so she curled up in a ball.

Kyphus had every right to punish her.

"I-I didn't mean it!" Wice wailed. "Please forgive me!"

Kyphus climbed out of the chest putting one talon on the ground after another. Its eyes held wrath and punishment.

"What do you want then?" the Elfwitch asked.

"Make it go away!" Wice screamed.

"It is a revenant. Feeding on the last thing it felt and kept alive by your fear," the Elfwitch said.

The Kyphus-revenant took one step after another with its talon claws out.

"You created it! You destroy it!" the Elfwitch commanded and crossed her arms.

"How?" Wice howled as the Kyphus-revenant took another step closer.

"What does it want?" the Elfwitch asked.

"Me!" Wice yelped.

"Do you want that to happen?" the Elfwitch asked.

"No!" Wice screamed.

"Then give something in your place," the Elfwitch said. "Blood for blood."

Wice shuddered. The Kyphus-revenant made another step.

"You must make a choice," the Elfwitch said. "What should take your place? What would suffice?"

Wice leaped to her feet and raced to the cage of tumor ridden mice. She unlatched it with clumsy fingers and reached in to grab a hapless mouse. Just a little bit ago, she had sympathy for these tortured beasts and deemed them unnecessary, now she did as the Elfwitch had done: tossed the mouse up towards the revenant.

It caught it with both naked wings and devoured its prey. But its bloodlust was not slaked.

"You've had your share for now," the Elfwitch said. But Spell Speak changed it: *That is enough. Return.*

The Kyphus-revenant backed away and fumbled over the side of the chest to descend back into the flat darkness like jumping into the deep end of the pool. It was gone without a ripple.

Wice ran over and shut the lid down and sat upon it shaking in shock and guilt.

The Elfwtich let Wice gather herself before speaking, "There are many secrets of the Darkness. You have learned one. Can you name it?"

"Something's waiting for me," Wice said. She was caught between death and destruction: the Light wouldn't want her now and what the Darkness wanted her for chilled her to the bone. She wanted to hide for as long as she could.

The Elfwitch nodded. "Blood is needed to stay vengeance. Again, it is not my rule. It is what we must do. Now, let's get to work."

"Doing what?" Wice asked.

"We're going to extract the metal we need from your old device," the Elfwitch said.

The other two Dark Riders entered from both exit tunnels. Rancor standing beside the vulture's perch and the Destroyer holding something in its hands: a small iron ring box.

"What about the gold?" Wice asked.

"The iron will contain it, like the twin boy's coin," the Elfwitch said and gestured to a table full of implements near the tripod. There nestled among tools was another iron box that the Destroyer had used to hold the coin when the traitor had taken it from the twin boy. Even with both the traitor and the twin boy captured, they had proven resourceful enough to have escaped. Though, without the quicksilver necklace that had long eluded the Elfwitch.

Wice saw that, in the end, the centuries' long patience of the Elfwitch's schemes won out.

"We shall begin," the Elfwitch announced and gave the Tracfone to the Destroyer.

Rancor walked over to the tripod and sprinkled the dust of enmity and drops of hate into the flames. It glowed white-hot and flashed from purple to blue. Fed by the cold heart of the Darkness.

The Destroyer opened the centrifuge and placed the Tracfone inside and closed the metal hatch. Picking up a hook from the implement table, it pulled the centrifuge square over the blue flame. Then it took up the crank handle in its paws and spun away gaining a strong rhythm.

As the centrifuge spun end over end in quick revolutions, the Elfwitch took out her double entwined silver necklace. Chayse's open heart and the moon-snake. She held it before her magnifying her focused stare as a silver tendril probed out and struck the spinning centrifuge.

The metal case began to glow until it became a brilliant nexus. Shining in friction and spinning so fast it began to hum.

Rancor laughed and Wice could feel it like wasp stingers against her skin.

"Enough!" the Elfwitch called out. But through her Spell Speak, it said: *CEASE!*

The Destroyer eased its cranking as the rotation of the centrifuge slowed and the sheen from the heat dulled. It took up the hook and pulled the centrifuge away from the tripod and back over the table. Then it used the hook to pull back the hatch letting out steaming vapors.

With a pull of the hook, the centrifuge tipped and the contents slipped out onto the table. All that was left of the Tracphone was a mass of fused carbon with specks of gold and silver. It had been obliterated and the carnage turned into a hardened mess.

Wice didn't understand if the end product was what the Elfwitch had desired.

Rancor howled.

The Dark Riders were not happy then with the result of their experiment.

The Destroyer picked up the carbon mass and weighed it in its hand like a worthless rock. Then it threw it against the curved wall of the Circle Chamber with a scowl. The carbonized rock bounced off and fell at the Elfwitch's feet.

"What happened?" Wice asked. "Did it all run together?"

The Elfwitchpicked it up and walked over to the table. "Open the iron box."

The Destroyer took the ring box in one hand and opened it up with the other to offer it to the Elfwitch. Inside sitting straight up was the golden coin that the boy twin had crossed over with. Chayse put a memory of Kreedmore the Street Preacher placing it in the boy's hand since she had been standing beside him. Wice shook her head clear of the memory. There were many things she wished she could forget and one thing she wished would let go of her.

The closer the Elfwitch brought the rock to the open iron box, the more the gold coin began to twitch. When she put the rock up against it, the gold coin flew out of the box and against the wall.

The Destroyer arched its eyes and the Rancor growled in its throat.

But the Elfwitch smiled. "The polarization of the contents has been reversed. Now it's an anti-magnetic. Since gold and silver are not magnetic now this rock can repulse them."

Wice nodded. "It's an anti-magnet."

"And it will prove itself useful," the Elfwitch said and directed the Destroyer to put the gold coin back into the iron box.

"We may not need to gather quicksilver after all to free Shadow," the Elfwitch said.

"What do you mean? Can we find the boy twin's silver necklace with the anti-magnet?" Wice asked.

"No," the Elfwitch said. "but we won't have to. The boy twin will come. With the other renegades. Let them find the silver necklace. But they won't keep it." The Destroyer nodded with a leer and Rancor laughed.

"The twin-boy has gold," Wice reminded them.

"We shall lay a trap with the right bait," the Elfwitch said and hefted up the carbonized rock. "This will come in handy."

***

Chapter Fifty-Three: Bait and Trap

The Elfwitch saw to the defense of her Domain.

She led the Dark Riders and Wice up from the Circle Chambers and through the dungeons to the main assembly hall of the Keep.

The lycanthrope twins came also. Colonel Graves descended from his duty watch on the rampart above and stood at the head of his gunner crews. Huntsmen spider scouts hung on baited webs from the eaves of the support beams. Even the two-headed vulture flew up from the depths to light on an old table.

Sergeant Hood came in last with scores of Deadcoat scouts some of who carried a cage big enough for a large dog.

The cage was set down by the table where the two-headed vulture perched upon.

"Oh, my servants, hear me!" the Elfwitch began. "We do not have to defend. Since we have already won.We will invite our enemies in. Once inside, leave the boy twin to my care. All others are to be eradicated. Our time is at hand."

"There is but one more Dark Rider to free," the Elfwitch explained. "Then we can call the Darkness down. And my Domain shall rule over all the Realm. All shall be in Darkness."

"If you've already won where is the victory?" Colonel Graves asked in a voice full of dusty worn-out tombstones.

"You're already dead. Every breath you take and every move you make is a victory. And to my glory," the Elfwitch said as she approached the officer.

"This coming fight will be a waste," Colonel Graves said. "You only need the necklace to finish your work. We should search the Keep. The necklace would be found."

The Elfwitch straightened her shoulders and stood in front of him with her hands behind her back. Mocking his attention stance with her at ease pose. "I should finish your work with me. As I recall, you and your whole Black Watch—your precious legion of misfit volunteers who were no better than loveless exiles—made a vow to serve me. And that vow was to the death. It was for even after death. For eternity."

"You have wasted my men frivolously. You do not value us," Colonel Graves said.

The Elfwitch tilted her back and roared in laughter. "Of course you have no value! You have no soul!"

She took out her double entwined silver necklace. "Cold fire come."

But through Spell Speak, these words were heard: *Darkness burn out their dead hearts!*

Silver fire arced out of the double necklace and struck the two officers standing next to Colonel Graves. The Deadcoats went up like kindling flame disappearing in ash and smoke as the flames overtook them in a single breath.

Colonel Graves did not bat an eye. But the gunner crews behind made at a ready stance.

The Elfwitch lashed out. "You dare! Do I need any of you filthy men? You're dead and useless except to do what I tell you!

"Now return with your gun crews to the top of the ramparts! Wait there and watch for Sergeant Hood's signal. Sergeant, have your men on double patrol and cover all approaches to the Keep.

"Victor, Nicolai! Scour any trails for a scent. Then send for the Destroyer! Huntsmen! Lay your web traps from the treetops!

"Everyone attend to my words!"

The servants fell out and over themselves to carry out the commands.

Soon the Assembly Hall was empty except for the Elfwitch, the double-headed vulture on the table, the cage, and Wice.

"The child renegade has hidden his silver necklace well. But we will not have to wait as long as before," the Elfwitch predicted.

"What will be different?" Wice asked.

The Elfwitch turned on her. "You, my pet. You will be the spring on which the trap is set."

"How?" Wice asked. "I nearly killed him the last time we met."

Grabbing Wice's hand and turning it over, she placed the carbonized rock in it and closed her hand over it.

"Either he will brandish his Tracphone or will try to recover his silver necklace. Either way, I want you by his side when he does. Get as close as you can. And then, use that," the Elfwitch said. "And remember, along with precious metal, blood is required."

Then the Elfwitch opened the cage door.

"You're crazy!" Wice said. Wasn't that degrading? Was that was the Elfwitch thought of her? *My pet?*

"The boy twin will naturally want to free you. This will give you an opportunity," the Elfwitch said.

"What if the renegades try to stop him?" Wice asked.

The Elfwitch laughed. "Remember, good things run from those who hate!"

***

Chapter Fifty-Four: Hammer and Anvil

Queen Regina recovered quickly. Refusing further rest, the only nourishment she allowed herself and everyone was to finish off the jar of honey. They drank from a nearby brook before breaking their impromptu camp.

"Too much time has been lost already," the queen said. "Let's make haste from now on."

As Cyrus, Strap, and Frehley put more stones over the dying fire, Reed tested the gold on top of the granite sledge. It had cooled into a tear-shaped ingot. Rough and uneven.

It was so small. Yet the Beekeeper had said gold stood for the Sun and Light. For the Son and Truth. For the Regents and the authority. For the Root of Lyftwych.

All of that in this tiny thimble of gold.

And only a regent could have gold. And a regent had to be a Lyftwych.

Well, Reed was a Leftwich. And he had never been so proud of it.

And Reed had gold. It had come from his Tracfone. Brought from his own World, the gold had been with him this entire time.

Yet it had been Cyrus who had been able to extract this trace amount.

Reed tucked the gold ingot into the hem of his cuff.

After the fire was covered over, the meager weapons were handed out again. This time it was Strap who gave up his pistol to Cyrus under Frehley's baleful eyes. Reed knew it was hard for Frehley to trust the blacksmith. Dad used to say "Once and done" after he got burned by friends once they had who proven they weren't really his friends.

But the company needed the blacksmith. They were so few against the Elfwitch's servants. Now seven strong, including Packy, the company left the strand of evergreen to tamp up a hill to traverse a broad ridge that was surrounded only by more wooded hills.

"How far are we from the Keep?" Queen Regina asked since they couldn't see it to gauge any true distance.

"At least another day," Frehley said before he went on further ahead to mark a trail.

This time Captain Michael let Frehley take the lead so he could stay next to the queen. And behind them came Cyrus and Reed. Strap brought up the rear.

"Just what are we gonna do when we get there?" Cyrus asked.

"Find the Law. Imprison the Elfwitch and the Dark Riders. Drive the Darkness back," Queen Regina said.

"That's a pretty tall order. Might as well bang my head with a hammer" Cyrus said.

"If you think that'll help," the queen said.

Reed smiled at that. That should have kept the blacksmith quiet.

Only it didn't. A little later, Cyrus asked, "Just how are we gonna lock up the Dark Riders?"

"Quicksilver and silver can free them," Reed said, "So…"

"We use quicksilver or silver to lock them back up," Queen Regina said.

"Great," Cyrus complained. "Now we gotta get some quicksilver."

"My necklace's still somewhere down in the dungeon," Reed said.

"I'd rather we look for that," Captain Michael said. "Going to Quicksilver Lake and breaking the taboo again will put us at risk."

"Only the Dark Riders will be down in the dungeon," Cyrus argued. "What could be worse?"

"The Porter who guards Quicksilver Lake," Queen Regina said.

"I don't really wanna run into that big snake again," Cyrus said.

"Then take your pick," Captain Michael said.

"Sounds like we're stuck between the hammer and the anvil," Cyrus said.

They hiked up to a high point on the ridge where they could see their back trail and the way before them. The ridge rose like the spine of a turtle with the sides sloping away into green underbrush. Further ahead, the woods and ran on into the horizon.

There was a line on the horizon.

And it wasn't sky.

A great wall of blue and white ice stretched across the lower quadrant of the sky.

Glacier Mountains. Impassable masses of ice. Heavier than rock.

Frehley halted the company for a break.

"Why couldn't those glaciers just freeze everything?" Reed asked.

"If the Judge meant them to move, they'd move," Frehley said as the company tramped on into Outlaw Forest.

"I dunno," Cyrus said. "The Elfwitch's got everything under her power. Why couldn't she move those glaciers?"

"Because she didn't make them," Frehley said. "The Beekeeper told us she hasn't made anything but lies."

Cyrus shook his head. "Well, I wasn't there when you met him. It'd be fine by me if the Son came down here right now and told me how this was all gonna turn out. Which reminds me. Just how are we gonna get inside the Keep?"

Frehley smiled and pointed at the boy. "His gold got us out."

Cyrus looked at them each. "And you think that tiny bit of gold is gonna do the trick?"

"The Beekeeper told us it would," Queen Regina said. "Frehley, can't we go a little farther?"

"We should try for a few more miles and get off this open ridge," Frehley said. "But we need to be quiet from this point on."

"No doubt the Elfwitch's servants will be on patrol," Captain Michael said.

Everyone looked at Cyrus.

The blacksmith shrugged. "No doubt."

The company moved on as the silver light began to dim to a dull grey. There was a cool glow far to the horizon. A blue hue like ambient lighting in the lower quadrant of the sky.

"That's coming from Glacier Mountains," Reed said.

"The ice reflects the light, too. Back when the sun would come out, it could be blinding," Captain Michael said.

Cyrus hushed at them.

When the shadows began to run together, Frehley called a halt for the evening.

As the moon waned, Queen Regina sent the company out to seek soft roots, wild berries, and any nuts.

Each searcher brought back a meager handful of assorted fruits and nuts which they shared along with wild onions. Reed had not had wild blueberries or blackberries that tasted so tart before. Everything was in small bites but each morsel delicious.

Frehley would not let them light a fire. And at every scuttle or scamper of creature everyone froze until they could identify the creature: lizard, squirrel, or deer.

Strap took the first watch as the others settled on the ground gathering up handfuls of dried leaves for bedding.

Reed had trouble sleeping. Usually, he would fall asleep for a time out of sheer exhaustion. So he lay on his side staring up at what stars he could see through the trees.

And he listened.

"And I'm still coming to grips that Reed and his sister had a locking pair, like ours," he heard the queen say.

"And that they're twins by people who look like us in another land," he heard Frehley respond.

"Frehley, we can't have exact twins who look like us from some other land in this world," Queen Regina said.

"Not in this world," Frehley repeated.

Both the queen and the ex-Royal Huntsman were smart and capable people, not unlike Mom and Dad. Reed would do anything he could for them. They had proven their trust.

"Is this the work of the Judge or the Elfwitch?" Queen Regina asked.

"I only know the boy says the Elfwitch brought them here against their will. From another place which just maybe another world? And in that world their mother and father are us," Frehley said.

"But I think the two separated," Queen Regina said.

"Sorta like here then," Frehley said.

"I would like to see their world. And who we might be in it," Queen Regina said.

"No, thank you," Frehley said. "We are here. And it is now. The Judge put me in this world for a reason. Here, I have met you. And now we must battle the Dark Riders to save this world. There's nothin' in any other world more important than that to me."

That gave Reed a sense of peace. A sense of belonging. It felt like family.

Why can't my family be like that?

Reed must have slept for a while.

Sweet rest. Without a ripple. Not a stir of a dream.

Near to what passed as morning in this eternal land of twilight, Reed rolled over and brushed dried leaves from his hair. He rose and sought out Frehley who was taking his turn at the last watch.

Reed snuggled up close against the ex-Royal Huntsman as he shivered to get warmth back into his body.

Frehley put his arm around the boy's shoulder.

The woods were quiet. At some point, they must have crossed back into Outlaw Forest. Where renegade animals like raccoons kept their dens.

Reed rubbed the sleep out of his eyes. "Frehley--" It was still hard for him not to say *Dad*--"can I tell you somethin'"

"Sure," Frehley said and squeezed his shoulder. "Anything."

"I'm scared I won't be able to use the gold again," Reed said.

"It's okay to be scared," Frehley said.

"You get scared?" Reed asked.

Reed felt the man nod against his shoulder. "All the time."

"So what do you do about it?" Reed asked.

"You do what you gotta do, you just do it scared," Frehley said.

The moon began to wax full and command the sky.

The two got up to rouse the others. Frehley shook the queen's shoulder with a gentle hand but he kicked Strap's rump. All Reed had to do was get near to Captain Michael before he came to with a start but Cyrus he had to shake by his amputated shoulder. The man's eyes rolled under his lids as he murmured.

Cyrus sat up in a panic and grabbed his empty arm socket.

"You okay?" Reed asked him.

"Yeah, sure," Cyrus said. "Just a bad dream."

"What did you dream?" Reed asked.

"That the Elfwitch gave me my arm back," Cyrus said. "Only it wasn't a part of me anymore. It took up a hammer and started to hit y'all. I couldn't stop it so I had to cut it off again."

"I'm sorry," Reed said.

"No matter," Cyrus said as he tousled his hair and rubbed his face over with his good hand. "It was just a dream."

"Dad says that dreams always mean something. That they try to tell you something true about yourself," Reed said.

"Father said they will try to warn you, too," Queen Regina said.

"My dad said they will show you your biggest fear or what you most want," Frehley said.

"Yeah, but then you wake up. Cuz it's still just a dream," Cyrus said.

Strap nodded in consent to all they had said.

Breakfast was leftovers from yesterday's foraging. The meal didn't fill anyone up. But it would have to do.

Frehley took the point as the company trekked through Outlaw Forest. The steep hills gave to thick hollers and washouts trails with trickles running over moss-covered stones.

The trees gave way to scraggly underbrush and drier piles of red rock.

At what was determined to be mid-day, Frehley called a rest beside another small brook.

"You're not gonna just walk up and knock on the front gate of the Keep are ya?" Cyrus asked.

"What if it's not enough gold to open the gates to the Keep?" Captain Michael asked.

"Reed's gold will work," Queen Regina said.

"It's how we got out the first time, remember?" Frehley reminded Cyrus.

Strap held up a fist and snaked around it with his other hand.

"I'm guessing he says to go in the way we came out," Cyrus said.

Frehley shook his head. "They chased us all the way out last time. They'll be watchin' for that. Best way in is straight on through."

"Just seeing us will stir up the hornets' nest," Captain Michael said. "But let's say we do get past the gates. Then what?"

"Once we're in we have to get down to the dungeon level double-quick," Frehley said. "My queen, have you or Captain Michael toured the Keep much?"

Captain Michael nodded. "I can find the way from the Assembly Hall."

"Reed, you'll have to get us to the Elfwitch's lair, this Circle Chamber, from there," Frehley said

"Reed, are you sure we can get to Ice Prison from her Circle Chamber?" Queen Regina asked.

The boy nodded. "You can get to Ice Prison from there."

Cyrus sighed. "I'd thought I'd never see a sewer or cave again."

Frehley pointed with his forefinger and gave a wink. "Never say never. It's not over yet." Then he hurried to take up the point.

Never say never…that's what Dad would've said.

The company continued through the scraggly hills until they were on a natural line of descent. Through space in the brush line, Reed could see bare hills of piled stone under a quarter of a mile away. They had been pushed there by the advance of the glaciers.

And standing erect among the rubble was the tall stone blocks of the Keep. With portholes for muskets in each storey around its surface. From the flag pole on top flew two flags: one with a black field and a fist crossed with a sword. But it flew under a second flag on top: on a white field, a silver crescent moon sat on the head of a coiled serpent.

In each of its four corners sat two cannon apiece trained down on the pass below and approaches beyond.

The Keep sat waiting as it had for centuries.

Daring any besieger to come and bang their head against its foundation.

At the base stood a gateway with a drawn portcullis and open doors behind it. The mouth was large enough for carts and a double line of troopers to pass through.

The garrison was tempting the company to try to enter.

"Judge bless," Cyrus whispered. "You're really just gonna walk right in."

"Yup," Frehley said. "We won't even have to knock."

"And what if they drop the gates?" Captain Michael asked. "They're iron, too."

Frehley said and pointed to Reed. "He's got gold."

Reed fingered the gold ingot in his sleeve. "I saw what the coin could do. But that was a lot bigger." "'It's not the weight of the gold'," the queen said. "'It's the weight of truth and justice in the wielder. The Judge gave the Son to be our truth and justice, so let his Light shine through.' That's what my father always reminded me."

"If you're expecting to fight our way down to the dungeon, we will need better weapons and more powder and shot," Captain Michael said.

"Hammer and anvil, you can say that again," Cyrus snorted. "But has anyone noticed that we got a knack for findin' what we need when we seem to need it."

Strap butted his fists together and pulled his hands back as he expanded his fingers.

"And for makin' things explode," Frehley said.

***

Chapter Fifty-Five: Shell and Cage

"Why do you think the front gate is open?" Queen Regina whispered.

"They must be open for business," Reed said. It was something that Dad would've said.

Captain Michael looked at the boy. "What does that mean?"

Frehley laughed which made Packy stand on its hind legs to investigate. "I think it means they're ready for us. Would you expect otherwise?"

Reed rubbed Packy's long whiskers and nose. "You're almost home."

"So do we just walk on down there?" the queen asked next.

There hadn't been a single bird call for hours. The company had left the main tree line a mile or so behind and there hadn't even been field birds in the tangled brush among the bleached rocks of the low hills before the Keep.

Two caws resounded overhead. Close by and loud. It hadn't come from any crow.

Reed looked up.

A large bird glided down towards them from the low sky. Long greasy black wings. Twin naked heads with red beaks and eye slits holding them in its gaze.

It was the double-headed vulture that the company had seen coming and going from the ruined Martello tower.

"That is the Elfwitch's familiar," Queen Regina hissed.

Too small to be anything but a morsel to it, Packy hunkered down against Reed's neck and ear.

Cyrus took out his pistol and put a bead on the great circling bird.

"Cy," Frehley implored. "Don't waste your shot."

"Don't give us away," Captain Michael said.

"And what do you think it's doin' to us now?" Cyrus asked. "It's like a beacon fer them Deadcoats!"

But Strap pointed back to the Keep. Up to its spire. They all turned their gaze.

Commands and shouts rained down from on high. Not unlike the squawks of the double-headed vulture. It had done its job and given away the Deadcoat gun crews the position.

A squat figure in a white vest and folded tri-corner hat stood up on the ramparts and waved his saber in broad circles.

"That would be Colonel Graves," Captain Michael said.

"Well, Lieutenant Grey won't be standing with them today," Frehley said.

"Yeah, one down," Cyrus said. "Nine hundred and ninety-nine to go."

The colonel mustered his forces and shouted commands. The orders were relayed down the Keep. Stone to stone. Storey by storey.

Until out of the gate's mouth loped the two lycanthropes--Victor and Nicolai, both of whom Reed had first met on that night back in his own World and now wanted so bad to send them running back inside the Keep with their werewolf tails tucked between their hindquarters—as a vanguard. Behind them, the Destroyer trotted out pumping a fist in expectation of final victory. And behind him came a score of Deadcoats on the double with broad-shouldered trooper out in front uttering worse curses than what they already had to endure if any trooper shirked from his duty.

"Good ol' Hoodie," Cyrus said shaking his head.

Reed watched the Colonel Graves yell at his gun crews on the Keep's rampart and make tight circles with his saber. Several guns from the other corners were rolled over to the corner rampart closest to the company. The cannon mouths were pointed down at the hillside.

Then the colonel gave a downstroke with his saber.

At least four guns belched fire and smoke.

"They're shootin' cannons at us!" Reed yelled.

Mortars whistled through the air.

Straight at them.

"Spread out!" Frehley ordered.

They scattered in pairs. Captain Michael staying close to Queen Regina as they went one way. Strap sticking next to Frehley as they fled in another. And Cyrus grabbing Reed by the wrist and pulling him straight for the on-coming lycanthropes.

The concussion of the shells bursting in air sounded like hammers in the sky. Battering Reed's ears and sending waves of hot air against him.

Packy dug its claws into Reed's shoulders.

All the falling shells hit the same spot.

The boulder that the company had taken a brief refuge behind.

The cannonade pummeled the rock. Slammed it. Kicked it. Turned it into a shrapnel bomb that sent a million pieces flying every which way but down.

There wasn't even time to breathe before Reed realized that there was another volley in the air preparing to drop.

"You wanna keep your head?" Cyrus yelled over screaming shells about to drop. "Then duck!"

He pushed the boy down to his knees following close behind as a tree flew at a vertical angle overhead crashing into brush and splintering against rock.

More of the shells dug into the earth this time. Breaking trees. Tearing up bushes.

Dirt and pebbles rained down from the sky. Dust swirled as if they were in a sand storm. Demolished brush rolled past them unable to beat out the flames consuming it.

The ground smoked where brush had been obliterated. Splintered trees crooked with ruin. Through the drifting carnage, Reed saw four figures moving downhill and a score more coming uphill.

Cyrus pulled Reed to his feet. They made careful steps. All around them was a cascade of sliding rocks and dirt. And coming up towards them were the twin lycanthropes. Snarling as they closed in on their prey.

Reed knew they could tear out his throat in a heartbeat. But he was tired of being afraid. What these little doggies needed was a shock collar turned to five. No, seven.

He reached into the cuff of his sleeve and took out the ingot like cradling a seed. "Back, doggies!"

Two golden "O"s shot out of his fist and collared each of the lycanthropes. The twins yelped as they were yanked to the ground. They rolled over on their backs using their back legs to try and slip the golden yokes off.

Behind the writhing lycanthropes lumbered up the Destroyer. Dragon claws out. Jagged teeth showing.

Reed and Cyrus stood their ground.

"Come on!" Cyrus taunted the beast with the end of his pistol. "I've got some for you!"

But the blacksmith only had one shot. Where to put into the beast to make it stop and yield? Cyrus wanted to make it count.

Its legs and arms were thick and leather-bound. Its massive chest a wrecking ball. Its twisted hands battering rams. Its wild hair standing antenna for static electrical charges. Its icy blue eyes frozen of any life surrounded by black circles of death.

Under the blue irises were cataracts. Not secreted pearls. But frozen tiny maggots.

Behind the jagged teeth of its open mouth was a fat worm for a tongue.

The Destroyer was a thing of death. Made of bone and decay. Nightmares for brains.

What could stop it? What had it to fear?

Cyrus shot at it where he thought it might bring the beast down: at its knee cap. But the Destroyer deflected the shot by dipping down his iron bracelet to shield its leg and divert the ball off to the side. Then it responded in kind by backhanding Cyrus across the mouth sending the blacksmith flying back into Reed.

They both somersaulted backward to lie on their faces at the feet of the Destroyer. Packy was gone and so was the gold ingot. Reed's hand was empty and so was Cyrus' pistol.

Now there was no one and nothing between the Destroyer and them.

And behind them trotted up Sergeant Hood and his squad of Deadcoats.

Their attack was over before it had even begun. They were going to get inside the Keep after all. As prisoners, once again.

Another cannonade was launched from the Keep's spire. Lower in the air than the last two. Whistling fast and sharp. Straight for them.

The Destroyer heard it, too. So did Sergeant Hood and the others. This time, Reed saw the beast's eyes grow wide with concern.

There was fear in its eyes.

So death could become afraid, too.

And it was scared of fire. An eternal flame that never could be quenched.

"Incomin'! Friendly fire!" Sergeant Hood yelled as the Deadcoats broke rank and made it every decaying trooper for himself.

"Kiss the ground and pray!" Cyrus hissed at Reed as he covered his head and eyes.

Reed did the same. He didn't want to see the cannonballs coming.

The cannonade landed on the Destroyer and the fleeing Deadcoats. The ground shook and jerked from under from Reed. For a brief moment, he levitated off the ground. His teeth rattling in his head and his ears filled with thunder and doom.

Then again the rain of debris and the smoke of destruction.

Through the haze of sulfur and dirt and ringing ears, Reed heard Frehley cry, "Everyone! To the Keep! Get inside!"

Reed felt Cyrus pull him to his feet. "Run!"

But the boy was missing something. Two somethings. "I've lost Packy! And my gold!"

Packy darted out of the smoke and circled Reed's feet before climbing up his legs and chest with a limp. The rat wasn't hurt. He was carrying something small and shiny.

As the rat perched on Reed's shoulder, it held the gold ingot in both claws and turned it over to admire its shiny gloss.

Reed took the ingot in his hand and kept a sure grip on it.

"Quit wastin' time dillidallyin'!" Cyrus said.

The Destroyer lay nearby. It hadn't been obliterated. Instead, it rolled and beat out the red hot shrapnel that burned its way through its leather armor.

Frehley and Strap were lost in the haze. Reed couldn't even see Queen Regina or Captain Michael. He guessed there were already down the hill and on the road into the Keep.

Reed followed after Cyrus and ran for his life. Downhill. All the way.

Cyrus was built like the Destroyer. He would be on the frontline and not a wide receiver. Reed caught up with the adult about twenty yards off of the slope. The road straightened out and then rose to enter the mouth of the Keep's gate.

The two rushed another hundred yards to the goal.

Looking up to the top of the Keep's spire, Colonel Graves' hat was gone and the cannon guns seemed abandoned. More shouts sounded from storey to storey. But the gates were open, the portcullis pulled up, and there was no one to greet them.

Then Reed and Cyrus trotted under the great iron portcullis like the open hinge of an alligator's jaw and through the open doors.

They were back inside the Keep. Entering into a wide round hall. With torn tapestries and battered banners hanging in limp rags and bundles from the walls.

In cardinal directions, three more archways made from supporting pillars gave access to what must be stairs and hallways. There was no telling since the doors were bolted.

Once upon a time this served as the mustering hall for the Black Watch and a receiving hall for the Regents in glory days long drowned under dust.

The hall was empty now. Full of only the echoes of the pair's footfalls.

And a table near the central pillar.

And next to the table a cage. Big enough to hold a large door.

And inside the cage, a pre-teen girl. Dressed in a black lace dress with her hair brown hair down and blue eyes wide.

It was Chayse. Reed's twin sister.

Cyrus made them stop about thirty yards from the girl in the cage. His thumb fidgeted on the matchlock of the pistol. It did no good since he had taken his last shot.

"Reed!" Chayse put her fingers through the front of the cage. "Get me outta here!"

Packy stood up with a claw on Reed's ear for support to sniff out the air.

Reed started forward but Cyrus held him back. "Hold up now."

Reed shrugged off the blacksmith's hand and started forward. "It's my sister!"

"It's a trap," Cryus growled.

"I'm gonna let her out," Reed declared and marched forward.

"Your gonna bring trouble down on us is what you're gonna do," Cyrus said.

But Reed ignored him and made straight for the cage. "What else did we come for? I wanna take my sister and go home!" Behind him, he heard Cyrus grumble, "Well, I can't so I wish you luck."

"Quick, Bub!" Chayse urged.

It felt like years since Reed had seen his twin. Chayse had waited just five minutes alone before he had come into their own World. For some reason, she had left him alone in this one.

His family had been broken for so long that every time someone else left, the old hurt became fresh and deeper.

Nevermind that Chayse had stood with the Elfwitch.

Nevermind that Chayse had become Wice.

Or that Wice had tried to kill him at the Martello tower.

Sis would be by his side again. And together they could face anything. As long as they were together they could face anything.

Reed fell to his knees and pulled on the door of the cage.

It was shut tight and the latch padlocked. He turned it over and saw the keyhole on the bottom.

Chayse touched Reed's fingers. "You gotta get it open! You gotta get me out!" His hurt was heavy and his need was urgent. Reed had to get Sis out of the cage and everything would be alright!

"How?" Reed asked. His hurt blinded him and his need to get Sis out blocked his mind

Packy ran down from its perch on Reed's shoulders and sniffed all around the edge of the cage. Then on three legs it sniffed at the figure sniff at the crouching figure inside the cage only to shake off a strong scent and scurry back up to the safety of its perch. Packy tried to squeak something into Reed's ear.

"You got gold?" Chayse asked.

"Sure!" Reed said.

"Then use that, stupid!" Chayse chastised.

"Yeah!" Reed said, happy that she had thought of something that should have been so plain to him. Except he wasn't thinking. He was too busy feeling that old hurt and was full of the need to rescue her.

He scrambled to get the small ingot out of the cuff of his shirt and brought it up to the padlock until both items touched: iron and gold.

Nothing.

"What's the matter?" Reed asked. The hurt blinded him again. The need overrode everything in his mind. He just became frustrated. "Why won't it work?" "It must be cursed," Chayse said. "Maybe lined with quicksilver."

Reed felt like he had only seconds to get the right answer to the last Math question on a semester test before time ran out or he'd flunk and have to go to summer school. Again. His mind had gone blank from stress.

"You need the key!" Chayse said.

Well, duh! Why hadn't Reed realized that? And what good did it do to know that anyway? He didn't have a key or anything like a key. And he didn't even know where the key might be.

"Up there!" Chayse pointed. "On that table!"

She was trying to help! Just like old times! Together they would find a way out of this mess!

Reed stood up and saw a long skeleton key lying on top of the rickety table. Laid down fresh because he could a trace had been made through the sea of dust covering the tabletop.

"Better just hold up, now," Cyrus said again. "This is all just too cozy."

Reed felt Rancor's heat. Why should he listen to anything the blacksmith had to say about anything? Not only did he see the bad in everything, but the man had also betrayed Reed and had left him to fend for himself. He should be the one in the cage.

"Get me out!" Chayse pleaded and shook the cage door.

Reed did what he thought was the right thing. He took up the key and stuck into the keyhole on the bottom of the padlock and turned the key so that it sprung open and the cage door unlatched. Then Reed pulled the cage door open.

His sister Chayse duck walked out and stood up.

The twins stared at each other.

"Dear Judge, she looks like Frehley," Cyrus said. "And kid, you look like the queen."

Reed wanted to lash out at Cyrus for calling him "kid" again. But Chayse refocused him when she opened her arms and said. "Reed."

His hurt was like a magnet. And Chayse was family. He wanted his family back worse than anything.

He hugged her. Harder than she hugged him.

Chayse kissed his forehead. Strange. She had never done that before.

Not ever. In fact, it would be the last thing Chayse would want to do: kiss her own brother. That was just too good to be true.

What had Cyrus warned him: too cozy?

It was cozy all right but somehow it felt all wrong.

All.

Wrong.

So Reed hugged her around the shoulders with his gold ingot wrapped in his fist. Chayse's arms dropped down to encircle his waist. Then she took his fist in one hand and opened it up.

Reed noticed something in her other hand. It looked like a rock. Or a lump of coal that had been taken out of the fire: twisted and fused.

Chayse held up the rock next to his open palm and the ingot seed flew out of his hand and across the Assembly Hall towards the center door.

His sister leered at him. Only she wasn't Chayse. She was Wice. "Silly kid, tricks are for me."

Reed's hand was empty and his heart was heavy. The old hurt washed over him like an old friend. He felt stupid and helpless.

All three doors under the archways opened in unison. Out from behind the right door came Rancor laughing at them. Out from behind the center came Elfwitch who snatched up the gold ingot in a small iron box.

And bursting out from the left door came Colonel Graves with this sword drawn and leading a small squad of troopers—all of them had taken off their red tunics.

"Traitor!" the Elfwitch said and took out her double silver necklace. A silver wall filled the space in front of her and her acolyte stretching from the pillar back to the center door on one side and then from the pillar to the door from where the colonel and his loyal men had come from. They had been cordoned off.

Sergeant Hood and half of the Deadcoats left in his detail came back through the gates. Both the escape attempt and the insurrection were over. Wice gave her Dark Lady a nod.

"Like I've told you all along, my pet," the Dark Lady said hefting the box in her open palm, "men are just pawns. Playthings who bore me quick.

Then she gave orders. "Sergeant, take the colonel to the dungeon. Round up any more turncoats and do the same. Watch for the other renegades. They will turn up.

"Call for all my servants to assemble in the Circle Chamber. And bring these two along with you."

"We both screwed up this time, kid," Cyrus said.

***

Chapter Fifty-Six: Lair and Liar

Instead of being reunited with his sister and trying to find a way home, Reed stood alone with his hurt.

His only companion, Cyrus. Who had lost his own family.

Now they had something in common.

They were both losers. Outcasts. No more than insects in the eye of the Elfwitch.

Neither one of them belonged in the Domain. The Dark Lady had no use for them.

Sergeant Hood got busy with his orders. He called for more loyal Deadcoats to come and take the weapons from Colonel Graves and his detail. Then they were escorted through the door on the right down to the dungeon.

Reed was stunned. His hurt was still fresh in his heart. His throat choked. "Why?"

Wice, because she was no longer Chayse in her mien, asked, "Why what?"

Reed pointed to the Elfwitch who came to stand beside her acolyte. "She's evil."

"She's awesome," Wice said.

"She's mean," Reed said.

"She's tough," Wice said.

"She's cruel," Reed said.

"Only when people don't listen," Wice said.

"She's hateful, that's why they don't wanna listen," Reed said.

"They hate her because they fear her," Wice said.

"No, they fear her because she might kill them. Sooner or later, she hates on everybody. 'Cuz she's just a bully!" Reed said.

"People have to be made to obey. If they did what they are told, there wouldn't be any problems," Wice said.

"Are you saying it's ok for the Elfwitch to kill someone because they won't listen to her?" Reed asked. "Is that what Mom would want us to do? Just go along because we're afraid?" Wice became angry. And she became Chayse again: "Mom was afraid of Miss Elsie Crutch. Look what happened then? Mom couldn't keep us. So the Elfwitch took us."

"No, the Elfwitch kidnapped us!" Reed said. "That was wrong! And from what I've seen of the Realm, the Elfwitch's turned everything upside down. On purpose. I'm not afraid to stop her. That's what Mom and Dad would want."

"Mom and Dad aren't here," Wice said.

"Yes, they are! Didn't you meet Queen Regina? That's Mom, you idiot! How about Frehley? That's Dad! Don't you think there's something else goin' on here that the Elfwitch doesn't want us to know?" Reed demanded.

"If you try to stop her, I'll have to stop you," Wice said.

"How? You gonna kill me?" Reed wanted to know.

"You want to kill the Elfwitch. You're no better," Wice condemned.

"You don't even know what's right and wrong anymore!" Reed said. "The Elfwitch's jacked your mind all up! She's not Mom. She's not Dad. She's not me. The Elfwitch is not even family. She hates us!"

Wice paused and the smiled. "Good things run from those who hate."

Reed's face fell.

"You're arguin' with a fence post, kid," Cyrus said.

"Quit callin' me, kid," Reed growled.

The Elfwitch smiled and talked once more as Miss Elsie Crutch. "This has been a really good session. A lot of authentic emotions. But you might stand to use some 'I feel' statements.

"Notice that Rancor did not have to use his spell? These two just naturally hate each other."

"I don't hate my sister," Reed said. "I hate what you've done to her."

"Then hand over your silver necklace and I'll send you back home," the Elfwitch said.

"I keep on tellin' you, I don't have the necklace anymore," Reed said. Then he crossed his arms. "So I'll guess you'll have to kill me."

"Oh, good. You want to play martyr," the Elfwitch said. "Wice, my pet, what do we need to free my fellow Dark Rider?"

"Silver," Wice said.

"And?" the Elfwitch asked.

"Blood," Wice said.

The Elfwitch pointed to the door on the right. "Lead them to the Circle Chamber, my pet."

"Follow me, you wretches," Wice commanded and walked across the Assembly Hall to the door on the right.

Cyrus gestured for Reed to follow her and the blacksmith fell into step. Behind the two prisoners came Rancor and the Elfwitch.

They proceeded through the door on the right of the Assembly Hall into a hall broad enough for four men to walk abreast. It led to a cascading stairwell that switchbacked downwards from the silver daylight into orange-hued darkness.

Down they went passing landings that led to open doors to rooms filled with bunk beds and hammocks. These were the Deadcoats' dormitories but the beds looked dusty and unused. Reed guessed that when you were cursed with living death, you didn't need to sleep a whole lot.

He was surprised he could find anything humorous. But thinking about it made him laugh.

"What's so funny, kid?" Cyrus asked.

"Deadcoats," Reed said.

"They're a joke now," Cyrus said. "But Colonel Graves just came up a notch or two on my list. I think he cannoned the Destroyer on purpose."

"Good," Reed said. "I hope he blew that Dark Rider to kingdom come."

"There is no kingdom!" the Elfwitch snapped. "There is no more Realm! There is only my Domain!"

"Yeah, yeah," Cyrus quipped. "You've already said that before."

"Soon, you will see the Dark Riders in all their power and know the Darkness in full," the Elfwitch intoned.

Soon the stone of the Keep gave way to carved rock as the stairs themselves became gutted steps of stone. The stairs ended at a hallway encased in brick running back under the Keep. They were beneath it now. And from the dank air and the pitiful sounds bouncing off the walls, Reed knew this was the dungeon level.

"My home away from home," Cyrus grumbled. "We've come full circle."

The blacksmith was right. This is where Reed had first met Moor Kreed and Strap, both of whom he knew back in his own World. But it was when Frehley had popped up his shaggy head, Reed had felt a ray of hope.

To Reed, Frehley was Dad. Only just a little different.

And Queen Regina was becoming more like Mom every hour.

Reed knew there was no way that the Elfwitch had anything to do with that. These people were true. And all the Elfwitch could do was try to twist the truth and confuse him.

Hadn't Moor Kreed said that the Judge is not the author of confusion?

As they came into the main hallway of the dungeon, Packy sat up with its paw against Reed's ear. The rat was back home, too.

They proceeded straight down the cellblock where Sergeant Hood's troopers were ushering in Colonel Graves and the turncoats. Neither group with red tunics or white vests looked all that spry. All the troopers looked besotted and with one foot in the grave, already.

Then they went down a slick slope to a lower level with niches carved out of gut rock. This was solitary confinement with very little light in the walkway and none penetrating back into the inner cells. Reed did not know if anybody still lay in the dark shadows without hope.

The passage narrowed into cut rock and ahead was a light coming through an opening. Wice led them toward the light. It came from a single source. A tripod set up in the center of the room with a band of blue atop a black base.

Circle Chamber. The Elfwitch's lair. They proceeded into the cavern of curved walls set with shelves of stone jars and racks of tubes and tables full of small caged animals and implements.

Above the tripod was a centrifuge pod attached to a large metal hook. And next to the tripod was an empty perch. Reed knew it was for that freak of a bird—the double-headed vulture.

Reed watched the Elfwitch put the iron box with his gold ingot on a table next to a second iron box. Wice placed the rock she had used to knock the ingot out of his hand down on the table between the two boxes. Both boxes jerked and scooted away from the rock.

That was interesting.

Very interesting.

Gold wasn't magnetic. But somehow something in that rock had become anti-magnetic. Reed could have won last year's Science Fair contest with that rock.

Strange to be thinking of that now.

Cyrus whistled. "Quite a workshop."

They noticed a blueish glow exuding from the tunnel on the other side of the Circle Chamber.

"That's the way to Ice Prison," Reed explained.

"I'd like to find a different way out," Cyrus said.

"There is no 'way out,'" the Elfwitch said. "Surrender to me what I want and you'll go free."

Cyrus harrumphed in his throat. "Your word's no good to me. I've learned that the hard way."

The Elfwitch laughed. "You caught me on that one! It's true. I can only let one of you go. We will require the life of the other. And the silver necklace. Precious metal is required and blood must be shed. That is the price of freeing a Dark Rider."

"If you find my silver necklace, then you can have me," Reed said. "I doubt you find it."

The Elfwitch nodded.

"All the kid wants to do is get back home. You took my home. So take my life," Cyrus said. "Do it now and get it over with."

The Elfwitch shrugged. "I am impressed. I've never had to choose before. Wice, you choose."

Reed's shoulders slumped. His hope dimmed. And his hurt came back.

There were many ways to be tortured, Reed had learned. And the Elfwitch relished every which way she could think up.

Wice took up a slicing knife from the table with the boxes and the rock. She smiled as she made her choice quick. Walking over to Reed she reached out her hand and plucked Packy upside down off of Reed's shoulder.

Packy kicked and scratched as it shook its whiskers.

"Please," Reed urged. "Don't."

"Good choice, my pet," the Elwitch laughed. "There's not much difference between a man and a rat. That's why I keep them for experiments. Now we can keep the boy twin instead."

"You're the meanest woman ever!" Reed shouted.

"I've watched whole nations be wiped out in a blink of an eye," the Elfwitch bragged. "Do you think your pitiful cries move me?"

"You've got a heart of stone," Cyrus said. "That's why."

"At least I didn't sell my soul for my family," the Elfwitch said.

"That was my choice, I admit it," Cyrus said. "And I repented. I done saved one life already. That was for my wife. And I owe one more for my daughter."

"If you don't talk yourself to death first," Wice grumbled.

Rancor laughed and crossed his arms over his leather duster.

"Proceed, my pet," the Elfwitch said.

Reed didn't want to lose Packy. He didn't want to lose anyone or anything dear to him anymore. When would it stop?

Wice put the edge of the knife against Packy's throat. The rat became still though Reed could see its ribs flexing from rapid breathing. Just as helpless as Reed was.

God help me! Jesus, stop her! He prayed his quiet desperate plea. The rat was small and insignificant. Back in his own World, Reed was just a rat, too.

What did it matter?

Was God even listening?

But Reed had asked from out of his heart. And the Spirit answered: *this is the time and the place.*

"'When you see your sister again, tell her the Judge says, "I desire mercy and not sacrifice,"'" Reed said. "Oh, Chayse. I've seen him. Face to face. He said he was just a beekeeper. But it was the Judge. Or God. Or his Son. Or Jesus. He was all of them. He made this world. And he is the Light."

Wice became Chayse. And Chayse took the knife away and flung both arms in frustration. "What does that even mean?"

Both the Elfwitch winced and Rancor groaned.

"Do not speak the Law here!" the Dark Lady snapped.

"The Judge! Light! The Son! Life!" Cyrus laughed. "I wished I'd seen him. I've got a question to ask him."

"Oh, shut up, you insufferable fool!" the Elfwitch said.

Packy bit Wice on the side of her thumb. Wice screamed out and the rat jumped down out of her hand to scramble across the floor.

The Elfwitch became incensed. "Stop! That! Rat!"

Rancor wasn't of much use in trying to halt Packy. It could only disperse into a swarm of flies and try to mass around the rat. Wice rushed over to stamp it with the heel of her shoe.

But Packy was in his element. He darted to and fro. Back and forth. Between their legs. Under their noses. Out the tunnel leading to the dungeon. And to safety.

Cyrus began to belly laugh.

Reed was shocked. In his weakness and desperation, the Spirit had given him the words to speak. And he never could have guessed the consequences.

Packy was safe.

So Reed joined in with laughing.

They both laughed from their heads to their toes. Until they couldn't breathe and had to bend over with hands on each other's shoulders to try and draw a breath.

The Elfwitch stepped over and slapped them both. Both of them were so winded they began to cry. But it wasn't from the slaps which they hardly felt.

Reed got it. The Elfwitch was a bully. And bullies don't like to be laughed at. To be reminded of what they truly were: small and insignificant.

And yet the weakest thing in the whole Keep, maybe even in the whole Realm, had just gotten the best of the Elfwitch.

Cyrus finished laughing and wiped the tears from his face.

Reed felt victorious. Anything could happen now. Or they would happen just as the Son had said they would which gave him even greater comfort.

"The first one to bring me the silver necklace will go free," the Elfwitch said. "That is my final offer."

But that just started Cyrus laughing anew. And Reed couldn't help himself so he joined back in.

The fit didn't last as long this time. As Reed's side went straight to stitches. But it felt good to have laughed so hard. He couldn't remember the last time he'd laughed that hard.

The Destroyer led the other servants into the Chamber Circle through the tunnel leading from the dungeon. The lycanthrope twins in their human form limped in with burn marks around their throats. Behind them came Sergeant Hood and a squad of Deadcoats along with the ladies-in-waiting. All bore the moon-snake tattoo.

"You didn't happen to see a rat out there did you?" Cyrus asked.

Reed giggled.

The Destroyer ignored the blacksmith and reported to the Elfwitch with sign language.

"The other renegades are in the dungeon cell with the traitors," she told Wice.

"There ain't no reason to be afraid anymore, kid," Cyrus said. "The Elfwitch's afraid no one's gonna believe her lies anymore."

"You don't know everything. You can't do everything. You couldn't even stop Packy!" Reed said.

The Elfwitch's face turned as dark as the Destroyer's hair. "You dare mock me?! You will take the rat's place! Both of you! I'll have enough blood to fill this room!"

"We'll get that necklace! Then you'll shut up!" Wice said.

Reed stepped closer to the table. "Am I gettin' under your skin? Mom always says I'm the last straw that's always breakin' her back. She says I was born to give her grief!"

Rancor stepped forward as if it were hearing melodious sounds. The Destroyer crossed its arms. The Elfwitch frowned.

Wice became Chayse again. "Shut yer little pie hole!"

"Wice," the Elfwitch said in a stern voice.

Rancor breathed in the aroma of vile hatred deep inside.

"You come here and shut it for me!" Reed said.

That did the trick. Wice raised the slicing knife high and stepped forward. And Reed stepped a little closer to the table.

"Wice!" the Elfwitch said. But through her Spell Speak, Reed and Cyrus heard *Never lose your temper. Stand down.*

Wice threw the slicing knife to the ground and crossed her arms. Pouting just like Chayse would. Which she learned from Mom whenever she got mad at Dad for not listening.

A squeak came from the exit tunnel to the dungeon. Packy padded its way back in. Dragging a necklace on a chain.

The rat laid the necklace at Reed's feet and climbed up to perch again on his shoulder.

The Elfwitch crossed her arms and nodded.

Wice put her hands on her hips and smiled.

While Rancor roared with laughter almost spitting up in the process.

Reed picked up the heart necklace. It was his last connection to his own World. Both Mom and Sis. And who they all really were.

And the one thing the Elfwitch had most wanted all along. Reed felt good to know he had been a thorn in her side this whole time. Packy was safe and that's what he had prayed for. What good would the silver necklace do him now?

Reed tried to focus on the open heart. It gleamed under the tripod's cold blue fire. But nothing happened. At least not like when he held gold.

"Good try," Wice beamed. "But silver is for healing and vows."

"And curses, don't forget, my pet," the Elfwitch said.

Reed shrugged. "I'll trade you for it."

"This should be interesting, my pet," the Elfwitch said. "What do you think I'd give you for it? You got your rat back."

"That rock," Reed said keeping the necklace in his fist and pointing to the rock on the table between the two iron boxes.

"Kid," Cyrus said. "That's a horrible trade."

"I like rocks," Reed shrugged again.

The Elfwitch growled. "Wice, make the exchange."

Wice picked up the rock off the table and held it out in one hand as he held her other expecting to receive the silver open heart necklace. Reed stepped forward and picked up the rock and dropped the necklace in Wice's other hand.

All the Dark Riders nodded in assent.

Then Reed tossed the rock back onto the table. It rolled between the two iron boxes and repelled them off the table. Sent them tumbling down over the floor.

"Wice!" the Elfwitch hissed. "The gold!"

The boxes were tumbling dice going in different directions.

Reed snatched up one box.

And Cyrus the other.

Before the blacksmith knew it, the Destroyer had him in a headlock so tight that Cyrus could not open the iron box and use the gold.

All Sergeant Hood and the Deadcoat squad could do was hold their muskets at the ready.

Reed popped open the iron ring box.

Something else the Beekeeper had said spoke again inside him. *Since gold is Light, it will dispel the cold fire of Darkness. Just bring the two together.*

Reed took the gold ingot out of the iron box between his fingers and raced to the tripod. Wice grabbed onto his arm and tried to hold him back. But Reed stretched out enough to thumb flick the ingot into the tripod.

When Light and Truth met Darkness and Lies, something ignited and set off a chain reaction.

A wave of white light expanded across the whole room in the blink of an eye.

Sweeping over Reed and everyone and everything.

Wiping out all sound.

Washing out every color.

***

Chapter Fifty-Seven: Keep and Crypt

It was like Reed was under an ocean of warm white.

He could not hear.

There was no color or depth. Everything was a silver outline against the white. It was like the time Reed had seen an x-ray of his lungs when he'd been sick with bronchitis for over a month.

It was an afterglow. Like images burned against the back of his eyelids.

That was because his eyes were closed.

Reed opened his eyes.

All was chaos.

Everything in the Circle Chamber was wreck and ruin.

People and Deadcoats and creatures lay on the ground on their backsides.

Tables overturned.

Tubes shattered.

Racks collapsed.

Herbs spread about and potions spilled out.

Cages demolished.

And animals scattered and scampered to and fro with malformed appendages.

Groups of black flies buzzed around the spillage.

His ears felt stopped up. The frequency in his ear turned back on. Static blared down his ear canal.

Reed felt something crawling down the side of his face. He wiped at it and looked at his fingertips.

They were smeared with blood. Dad had told him the time his eardrum had ruptured in his left ear when Uncle Buddy hadn't cleaned a rifle well and tried to shoot it and it had exploded next to Dad's ear.

That's what must have happened.

All this because of that little bit of gold.

Reed was unhurt then. Besides not being able to hear. But he couldn't shake the buzzing from his head.

First, Reed checked on Packy. The rat washed its head and whiskers with its arms and paws. Trying to get the smell of Wice's hands off of itself.

Next, he spotted the Elfwitch sitting with her back against a curved wall between the exit tunnels. Her eyes were open but didn't focus. Reed hoped that she was dead—now that would indeed be a miracle.

Wice rolled about on the ground next to the table. She had been winded. Not unlike what had happened to Reed back at the Martello tower.

The ladies-in-waiting waited on their backsides. Sergeant Hood and his squad were at ease on the floor. Black flies flew in solitary orbits as Rancor had dissolved. And the Destroyer had been flung into a rack of shelves knocking over jars and wore their many contents.

Cyrus had been blown back against the curved wall not far from the Elfwitch. He sat up and shook his head. He said something but when he realized he couldn't hear himself, the blacksmith brought up his fist and opened it.

Inside was the second iron ring box. It contained the half dollar that Creedmore had given Reed that had turned into a regent's gold coin here in the Realm that the Destroyer had put into the box when Cyrus had betrayed Reed.

Cyrus clutched it and nodded. Then he pushed himself up from the floor.

Reed knew what Cyrus had tried to say.

Time to go.

Reed ran to the man and together they found a path through the wreckage. Sergeant Hood came to his dead senses and tried to grab Reed's heel. Experimental animals scurried back and forth across the floor at various speeds while some found the exit tunnel leading back to the dungeons.

Cyrus pulled Reed into the tunnel. He slapped the ring box into the boy's hand. "So that's what gold does when it's unleashed!"

"That was absolutely awesome!" Reed said.

"We gotta find the others," Cyrus said. They followed the rock tunnel as it sloped up to a cavern lit with dim torches.

Reed felt a pull back the way they had come. "Sissy."

"Look," Cyrus said. "If you wanna help your sister we gotta find the Law. And we'll need quicksilver."

"I'm not leavin' here without her," Reed said.

"I hear ya," Cyrus said. "Well, I'm not leavin' here until we find the crypt of the Son."

"Why?" Reed asked. "He's alive. I've seen him."

"Well, I ain't yet," Cyrus said. "So, I wanna see for myself."

As they came into the solitary niches, Packy called out. Another rat screeched in reply from inside a dark recess. They were back under the Keep.

"This is its home, understand?" Cyrus said to Reed. "It used one of these niches as its nest. That's where it stashed your necklace. I doubt anyone would've ever found it."

"Safer than a bank, Dad would've said," Reed said.

As always, the solitary level was dark and quiet. As silent as a grave. A place hidden away from all life—sound and taste and movement.

They reached the other end of the level and trotted up the ramp leading to the next one. Behind them, they could hear shouts and orders and running feet. The Elfwitch and her servants were back on the move. There was no rest from the wicked.

The rock walls turned back into mason-crafted stone. This level was well lit with torches in the sconces. There were three cellblocks arranged back to back in the middle like large stalls in a barn holding beasts with burdens.

Only the middle one held prisoners. Several Deadcoats who had shed their red tunics down to their white shirts and breeches. And a large man with greasy black hair. Two other men, one in leather buckskin and the other in a blue and black uniform. And a woman in a royal gown—Queen Regina, Captain Michael, Frehley, and Strap.

Deadcoat soldiers stood on guard at either end. Two of the troopers were close to Reed and Cyrus as they came up the ramp. Surprised at seeing renegade prisoner roaming around free they shouted "Halt!" as they got their weapons at the ready.

"Time to get busy," Cyrus said.

Reed stood and delivered. He opened the ring box and took out his coin. Holding it up vertical between thumb and forefinger Reed showed the guards the heads side up.

A golden arm reached out and knocked the Deadcoat guards off their feet. Cyrus pounced on them and ripped a musket from out of one trooper's hands and shot pointblank at the other. The musket ball delivered a mortal blow but the trooper could not die so Cyrus had to pin him to the ground with his own bayonet.

Cyrus put his foot on the second trooper's neck as the Deadcoat kept his musket against his chest while the other Deadcoat tried to grab the blacksmith's ankle.

"They just don't know when to quit!" Cyrus shouted.

The Deadcoat guards at the other end of the cellblock ran towards the commotion.

A circle twirled out of the coin growing in shape to become a collar around the second fallen Deadcoat. Cyrus indicated to Reed they should move forward and take on the other two guards rushing down at them. Two spinning gold discs shot out of the coin and took out the feet of the Deadcoats. The limbs snapped away from the dead soldiers who crawled on their stomachs towards their enemies.

Reed and Cyrus ran over their backs like stepping stones in a river, Cyrus taking the opportunity to wrest away a musket from one of the wiggling Deadcoats.

The two came to the middle cellblock door as the others inside gathered around.

"Reed!" Frehley called. "You got away from the Elfwitch!"

"Did you see your sister?" Queen Regina asked.

Reed nodded. "The Elfwitch still has her under a spell. And now she has my silver necklace. Packy brought it back to save our lives."

Packy screeched from its perch on Reed's shoulder.

Strap slapped Frehley in the shoulder to get his attention so the ex-Royal Huntsman could see the giant sign an argument to him.

"I know, I know," Frehley said. "Packrats are smart."

Packy screeched again.

"Get us out before more Deadcoats come," Captain Michael said.

"I don't know why you chose to come back, but we will all have to fight our way out," Colonel Graves said. "There is an armory on the next level."

"Be quick then, kid," Cyrus said.

"For the last time, quit calling me kid!" Reed said as he brought the gold coin up to the lock on the jail cell door. The whole door shook as the lock's cylinder fell away from the mounting plate. Strap put his fingers through the gap in the lock to grip the door. It came off its hinges and he cast it against the stone wall.

Frehley complimented his giant companion. "Just like old times. We get busted and then we bust out."

The company let Colonel Graves and his loyal troopers take the lead out of the cellblock and up the stairs to the next landing. A short hallway dead-ended off the landing with four closed doors, two on either side. The colonel led them down the hallway to the second door on the left.

It was locked. But not for long as Strap lifted his leg and stomped it in.

Colonel Graves took a torch out of the hallway sconce and gave light to the room.

The walls were lined with racks of weapons as others were stacked in standing bundles in stations throughout the small room. There were weapons of every sort and size. From pistol to musket bores to long arquebuses to dagger blades and bowie knives and rapier blades. There were even hatchets and maces and spears and halberds.

"The Black Watch has only the best," Colonel Graves said as he and the loyal troopers picked out their weapons of choice. "Crafted by the best."

"Sweet Son," Cyrus whistled. "What couldn't we use?"

"My queen," Colonel Graves said in a husky tone as he took a pistol and rapier blade down. "We must hurry."

"Yes, colonel," Queen Regina said. "Gentlemen, prepare our defense."

Each of the company took their pick. Frehley took himself a bowie knife, two pistols, and a musket and set about priming them. Reed chose a pistol and a dagger, he didn't feel the need for a musket, not with his gold coin in his possession. Captain Michael chose two pistols and a rapier. Strap picked two pistols, a mace, and a halberd. The Queen took a pistol and a rapier.

After testing its balance and sweep, Frehley told her, "It looks good on ya."

She nodded and thrust with the blade.

Cyrus pulled down a hatchet. Then the blacksmith spied a wall of armor pieces: breastplates, gauntlets, helmets, and greaves that covered each arm. He moved over to that wall and had Reed help him pull down a greave for his missing left arm that had studded braces and brass knuckles for a hand.

"Help tie this on me," Cyrus said as he held the shoulder pad up to his severed armpit.

Reed tied the leather thongs around the right side of the blacksmith's neck. Then he asked, "Don't you want a firearm, too?"

Cyrus chose the strangest musket on the rack. It looked like a short single barrel shotgun although the barrel was as thick as Cyrus' forearm and the muzzle flanged out at the end.

"What kinda gun is that?" Reed asked.

"A thunder stick, kid," Cyrus said as he had the boy help him load it. Then he unrolled an arm's length of chain from off a cylinder and slung a loop around his neck and wrapped the other end around the butt of his 'thunder stick.' Now he had a hatchet in his belt and a short gun hanging against his side.

"Colonel Graves, is there another way out of the Keep? A secret passage, perhaps?" Queen Regina asked.

The colonel nodded. "There is an escape tunnel. It's been locked for ages."

"I just wanna know where's the crypt of the Son?" Cyrus asked.

Colonel Graves shrugged. "There is another tunnel away from the Elfwitch's lair. It has an old door. But the Porter guards it."

"Cyrus, we probably saw it on our way out the first time," Frehley said. "But we can't go back down there. We're no match for the Dark Riders without quicksilver."

Cyrus shrugged. "The Bee Keeper told you to find the law. So we find the law."

"One thing at a time," the queen said. "It took years for everything to get tied up in a knot. It won't all be unraveled at once.

"Colonel Graves, where is the secret passage?"

The Colonel thought. "It should be on the next level above us. We will have to fight our way there and then hold off the Elfwitch's servants while we search for it."

"If that's what we gotta do, then let's get to it," Frehley said.

He nodded to Strap and they opened the hall door again.

There were shouts and footfalls. The Elfwitch's servants were on the stairs. Coming up and going down in their search.

Frehley and Strap led the company out as Colonel Graves led his troopers.

They filled the hallway.

The landing was empty. The Elfwitch's servants had gone by them. Passing them over in their search.

All they had to do was make the landing and get to the next level without being seen or heard.

A fly buzzed off the stairwell. Followed by another. And another. Until a swarm of them blocked the stairs.

Down the stairs came the Destroyer. It strode through the buzzing mass of black flies that coalesced into the shape of the Rancor behind it. The Destroyer tapped its iron gauntlets and then put its fingers to its lips and whistled high and sharp.

Up the stairs came the snarls and padding feet of the lycanthropes. The twin werewolves padded behind the two Dark Riders. They snarled and bore their fangs.

Something was different about their manes. Each bore two iron-studded collars around the burn marks made onto their hide by the gold loops. They took the lead in the advance.

The Elfwitch's servants had come ready to fight.

***

Chapter Fifty-Eight: Despair and Hope

The Elfwitch became woke. Full in her self-knowledge. Alert and self-aware.

Pointing to her feet as she bent down, Wice picked up the thing the Elfwitch had long coveted. The thing she had crossed over to another world to seek out. Reed's silver open heart necklace.

"Where are my servants?" the Elfwitch demanded.

"I sent them to find the renegades," Wice said.

The Elfwitch rose and smoothed her black raven gown and the back of her hair. After patting her brow with her gown sleeve, she took out her own double twisted silver necklace.

"Next time, wait for me," she said. But through Spell Speak, Wice heard the words twist into *Here, I issue the commands.*

"I didn't do anything wrong," Wice said.

"But you could have," the Elfwitch said.

"But I didn't," Wice said.

"There is a hierarchy," the Elfwitch. "And you are not at the top. Not even close."

"What if I had a silver necklace?" Wice asked. "Like this one?"

She held out Reed's dispossessed silver open heart necklace. "It belonged to the boy twin. His mother gave it to him. I claim right of by kinship."

The Elfwitch took out her own double twisted silver necklace. "That is not how the hierarchy works. You don't even have the mark."

The six remaining ladies-in-waiting helped rouse each other and get one another to their feet.

The boy twin had made a surprise move. He had sacrificed the gold the blacksmith had smelted out of his phone and dropped it into the tripod. Wice had been amazed and terrified at the result. The tripod was fed by the Heart of Darkness. And it couldn't withstand gold.

"Servants," the Elfwitch commanded at the clap of her hands, "bring me the silver necklace."

But through Spell Speak, the command shifted into *Take hold of my pet and take away the silver necklace.*

The ladies-in-waiting circled the young girl before she could attempt to escape. Where she would run to? *After the boy twin.* Who would help her? *The boy twin. He has gold.*

Did she need to run?

Did she even need the boy twin and his gold?

She held silver.

Wice held the necklace high in her hand.

The Elfwitch crossed her arms and held her double necklace out. "Do. Not. Even. Try. Me."

Wice shrugged in defeat. The necklaces had to be given freely for their power to be wielded by the next owner. Simply possessing the necklace did ensure the necklace's power would work. Those were the boundaries.

The rat must have stolen it from Reed. But the rat wasn't a person. Did animals have to obey the same boundaries? And hadn't the rat brought the necklace back and offered it in exchange for its master's life?

The gold's dissipation had set off an incredible chain reaction. It was like time had stopped and everything in the room had withstood a silent explosion.

Hadn't that reset the rules? Or something? Could Wice use the silver necklace at all?

The ladies-in-waiting who once served Queen Regina and now served the Elfwitch all had the same look of resolve. They were going to obey the Elfwitch's command forfeiture of their lives. But Wice was beginning to have other ideas.

Still clutching the silver necklace high, she reached out to touch the metal. Hadn't she been able to do it before in the guest quarters? And even in the foundation tunnels of Tower Reign?

There was hesitation among the six ladies-in-waiting. They tightened their circle by making a step forward.

Now was the time for the silver necklace to do it work.

Nothing happened.

Wice closed her eyes tight and gritted her teeth.

She felt many hands grip her shoulders. Then grab her arm and fist. Then open her fist and take away the silver necklace.

Wice opened her eyes and found the Elfwitch beaming as she now held the boy twin's silver open heart necklace.

The rat had meant the silver necklace for the Elfwitch.

Well, if Wice couldn't use gold and if there was no chance of the Elfwitch giving over the silver necklace there was still quicksilver.

What would have happened if quicksilver had been dropped inside the tripod instead?

The Elfwitch gathered her stature and self-rule. "Come. Bring my pet. I will deal with her afterward."

"After what?" Wice asked.

"After we free the last Dark Rider, Shadow. He will spread fear far and wide. And the Heart of Darkness will come. Once the Judge sees that this world has been turned over to evil he will come to destroy it. Either way, we win. It is inevitable," the Elfwitch explained.

The Elfwitch signaled to the circle of women surrounding Wice to follow her out of the wrecked Circle Chamber and down the exit tunnel to Ice Prison.

"So everything gets destroyed. You call that a win?" Wice asked.

The rock tunnel gave way to carved crystal blue ice. Vapors filled the tunnel from the frozen wall as their body heat and breath interacted with the glacial wall.

The Elfwitch shook her head and laughed. "Oh, my pet, you do not understand. There are many worlds in this one universe. And there many strands to the universe. The battle will rage on.

"The Judge is too stubborn to surrender but eventually he will just go away."

Then Chayse put a thought in Wice's head. *The Judge is God. And in the beginning God made the heavens and the Earth. God did it. Not the Elfwitch.* "Just where will the Judge go?"

"My pet, did you not listen to my story of everything?" the Elfwitch rebuked her. "The Judge will have to come crawling back on his knees begging for the Darkness to take him back. Once that happens, then the struggle will be over and the universe strands will have one master.

"Just think! This world is just the beginning! Next will be the world you came from! There are worlds beyond count to turnover to the Darkness. We will be busy for an eternity! Isn't that wonderful?"

The procession went down the ice tunnel to the parallel junction. The cavern's size never failed to impress Wice. Its breadth and depth made her feel small. Its cool air chilled her lungs.

The cavern was a space carved out between the mass of glacier and the wall of rock that was the foundation of the Keep. The only light came from the diffused blue glare of the ice. Millions of square inches of frozen water.

The wall of ice lay about fifty yards ahead. Stretching storeys above them. Reaching even beyond the limit of the rock.

Here the Elfwitch stopped and turned to Wice. "My pet, you must take the mark if you are to join us. You have seen. You have known. You have even helped. After the release of Shadow, you must choose."

The Elfwitch anticipated winning. She had waited centuries. Plotting all the ways she could bring down the Realm. To ruin all that the Judge had created. To bring everything into Darkness.

But she wasn't all-powerful or she would have won long ago. What was different about now then? The twins and their silver heart necklaces.

The Elfwitch had sought her own release and then had gone to another world to seek her advantage. To find a world where the Queen and this Frehley had been different people and had gotten married and had twins and those twins had been given two silver necklaces. Then the Elfwitch had crossed back over with the twins and had used one silver necklace to free a Dark Rider.

Now she was about to free the last remaining Dark Rider.

Would that do it? Would it ensure victory? Would that be the revenge of the Darkness? But, at best, it would only get the Darkness even.

What came after vengeance?

What would happen to the Darkness when it had won and had no enemies left to fight or no more beasts to torture or no more worlds to destroy?

It would be all alone. With nothing. And no one.

Wasn't that a kind of hell? To win by taking everything away from your enemy and then destroying your enemy just to find out you are all alone with nothing.

That was a hollow victory.

Getting the last word that would never be heard.

Wice felt empty.

She felt cheated.

They continued down the frozen passage to where the four niches stood inside the glacial wall. The last occupied niche stood to the right of three empty niches. Of all the Dark Riders, this one had the least human features. Just a skeletal frame wrapped in a black robe with a frayed cloth over its hands and feet and a cowl over its head hiding its face.

How could any human emotion—love or hate—penetrate its black coverings?

Before this last niche stood the same cloth-covered altar that had been used twice before. Serving to focus the worship of the Dark Riders to the Heart of Darkness that sustained them.

One of the six remaining ladies-in-waiting pulled the black cloth away from the altar revealing what lay beneath it.

Wice had to look twice. Because the first time she did not believe it.

It was another chest. A twin to the first chest with its strange contents that the Elfwitch carried with her everywhere. But that chest had been marked with the word WICE.

A different word had been burned into this wooden lid. WEIK.

A second chest. And a second word.

What if Wice had seen this chest first? What if she had chosen this for a name?

She had begun to understand what WICE might mean. And she had an inkling as to what WEIK meant.

The Elfwitch stood before the chest and raised the silver necklace. "O my servants, we are on the cusp of victory. We are about to free the last of my family.

"But there are boundaries to overcome. And they can only be overcome with the sacrifice of blood and precious metal."

As a group, the six ladies-in-waiting stepped forward, chins out and arms crossed over ending in fists. "We saw what happened to our sister. We have taken the mark. We have obeyed you every step of the way. Sacrifice your pet. She has not taken the mark."

The Elfwitch lowered the silver necklace and looked down her long thin nose. She looked from the group of six women to Wice. And then from Wice back to the six women, who not long ago had been seven women.

Wice straightened her shoulders and did not blink. She told herself not to be afraid. There was only one way to be certain she knew what the word Weik meant and that was to use it.

The Elfwitch reached into her sleeve and pulled out seven pieces of hay. Seven straws. She held them up so that no one could see their total length.

"You will draw straws. The short straw will decide the sacrifice. My pet will go first," the Elfwitch commanded.

Wice took a straw and pinched it between the fingers of her closed fist. One by one the ladies-in-waiting each took a straw and compared each one among the others as they drew until all seven straws had been chosen. Then the women arranged themselves by the longest to the shortest certain of victory because the shortest straw among them was longer than the piece held between Wice's fingers.

The ladies-in-waiting chose the one who had the next shortest straw to speak for them. "Again, we have done what you have asked. Do what you say you will do. You must sacrifice your pet."

Wice smiled and keeping the piece of straw pinched between her first two fingers she opened her fist. Now she held the longest piece of straw. And the speaker's face fell.

The Elfwitch drew up her shoulders causing her neck to bulge. Her eyes became slits and her skin became scaly. Her long nose flattened and her mouth widened. "I said that the short straw would decide."

As her arms receded the Elfwitch grasped the silver necklace in her serpentine mouth. Then she lashed out and hugged the speaker of the ladies-in-waiting. As the muscles under the scales began to constrict, the lady-in-waiting gasped for air.

The Elfwitch used her coils to raise the crushed lady-in-waiting up to the fourth niche. The silver necklace glowed bright argent as the lady-in-waiting's face turned a dull blue. The ice covering the fourth Dark Rider dissolved into mist and vapor as the robed figured stirred.

As the ice fell away and the figure became free, Shadow did not step down like the other two Dark Riders. Instead, Shadow passed out of the niche and streamed across the corridor. For this Dark Rider had no form.

Wice felt her heart sink. Somewhere deep inside her, Chayse turned her face. She wanted to jump into a deep well. Never again would she see her own World. Never again would she see her bubbie. Her twin brother. Mom was lost to her forever. And Dad…that was her greatest hurt. She had never named it until now. She missed Dad most of all. And hated him. For rejecting her.

But now it was too late.

--Shadow's robe was a shadow.

There was no hope for anything.

--It's hood a cloud.

All was lost.

--And it's skeletal face a nightmare.

Wice had been robbed of everything. Except for one emotion. Something like steel that took root in Chayse's hurt.

She may have chosen not to call herself Chayse anymore. She may have wanted not to remember everything that had happened to Chayse anymore. But she was still angry.

Along with that anger, she knew a secret.

A revelation that was no longer a secret to her anymore.

She filtered that knowledge through her anger.

"Weik, Lycanthrope twins," Wice called out. "You are to weik. Vic, come back to the Circle Chamber. Nick chase down the renegades."

The Elfwitch transmogrified into her human form dropping the lifeless lady-in-waiting at the base of the fourth and last empty niche. She was both impressed and incensed at what Wice had just said.

Wice had used this second word of power. But what she said had become twisted and stretched out in echoes with different pitches. The words had become: *Lycanthrope twins DIVIDE. Divide your combined strength and identity. Victor, return to the Circle Chamber. Nicolai, pursue the renegades but DO NOT harm them.*

Wice saw that the look on the Elfwitch's face was the same as what Wice felt inside herself: amazed.

She had just used Spell Speak.

***

Chapter Fifty-Nine: Coupe and Grace

Except for Rancor, all of the Elfwitch's servants bore iron. All the better to shield themselves from the effects of Reed's gold coin.

This battle would be different. It would be hard-won. For either side.

"Why? Why do I always run into this guy?" Cyrus moaned about the hulking Destroyer.

The Lycanthrope twins were the closest to the company and Colonel Graves' mutineers. But the Destroyer strode behind them with his shoulders hunched down and his massive arms spread out like oak limbs. Anyone of the company could be snatched and crushed in its grasping claws.

A sound came up the stairwell.

It was a voice.

Pouring through the stone masonry.

"Weik, Lycanthrope twins!"

A feminine voice.

"You are to weik!"

Not a woman's.

"Vic, come back to the Circle Chamber. Nick, chase down the renegades."

It was the voice of a girl.

All present heard the words. And how they twisted and stretched into a deeper pitch with a darker tone. The girl was using Spell Speak.

Lycanthrope twins began to DIVIDE.

Both the lycanthropes transmogrified back to their human selves. They blinked their eyes in disbelief. The only thing they retained from their werewolf form were the two iron collars around their necks.

"We have always…" Victor began.

"…worked in tandem," Nicolai finished.

Divide your combined strength and identity.

"This is not…" Victor intoned.

"A wise command," Nicolai chimed.

Victor, return to the Circle Chamber. Nicolai, pursue the renegades but DO NOT harm them.

"We hear," Victor grumbled.

"And obey," Nicolai snapped.

Victor turned and mounted the stairs to begin his descent while Nicolai scowled.

"Well, look at that," Frehley said.

"That wasn't the Elfwitch," Queen Regina said.

"It was Sissy," Reed said.

Nicolai yelled from the top of his throat until he went hoarse. Then he began the attack with a mad dash at the company.

Cyrus set his stance and raised the hatchet over his head. "This is for my wife and daughter."

He threw the hatchet end over end. It whistled through the air. And glanced off Nicolai's forehead.

The Elfwitch's servant stumbled and fumbled. The dazed Nicolai wandered into the path of the Destroyer who knocked him aside. Nicolai's shoulder crashed into the stone wall and his legs buckled. Down he went like a drunk sitting to gather a thought that wouldn't come.

Quicker than a hungry bear, the Destroyer was upon them. It gave Cyrus an elbow to his stomach taking the wind out of his bellows. Cyrus bowled over to suck in another breath.

Strap stepped up to grapple with the Destroyer. Head to head. Toe to toe. Until the beast pushed the giant down to his knees while crushing his hands in its iron grip.

Reed pulled out his coin and wrapped his forefinger and thumb around it. Flashing it at the Destroyer, golden circles pulsed out at the beast. It knocked the golden circles away with the top of its iron braceleted wrists.

Then the beast rushed like a bull through the company. Pushing aside Frehley and Captain Michael. Ready to collide straight into both Reed and Queen Regina.

"Reed!" Cyrus called as he tried to straighten back up. Pulling something out of his belt he tossed the object over to Reed.

The boy caught it. The object was heavy. It was the fused rock that Reed had found in the Circle Chamber. The magnetized metal that had been re-polarized.

As the Destroyer's brought his fist down to batter Reed's head, the boy brought up the magnetic rock as his only defense. When the beast's iron bracelet came near to the rock, it bounced away. In fury, the Destroyer swung both his fists at Reed, but the boy moved the rock into the path of both swings and the Destroyer missed its mark by a mile.

The Destroyer raged and punched out to the wall on either side knocking out two large holes that brought down broken masonry and debris. It was still very much a danger and a threat. But it was not covered in iron from head to toe.

Reed focused his coin and flicked golden circles at the Destroyer's boots. Two gold circles entwined the beast's feet and knotted themselves. The Destroyer's boots were drawn together and the beast toppled to the floor. It thrashed over onto its back trying to tear off the golden rope.

From its safe perch on Reed's shoulder, Packy squeaked at the Destroyer. The Dark Rider had gotten a little of its own back. Its face seemed more twisted with wounded pride than hurt. Reed didn't even know if it could feel the kind of pain that it gave out. He only knew that the Destroyer would never stop hurting people until it was either back in Ice Prison or obliterated.

That only left Rancor blocking the stairwell. The Dark Rider brought up its claws and hissed. Out of its fingertips flew a squadron of red bodied wasps like darts.

Reed made a large circle with his gold coin in front of the queen who was the intended target. The circle in the air became ringed with fire and as the wasps tried to pass through their bodies were consumed so that ash came out the other side and fell like dirty snow at Queen Regina's feet.

Strap pulled himself up by his boots and raced at the Dark Rider with his mace to smash through the entity. It dissolved into a swarm of black flies that Strap could only knock about or swat at. But now the stairwell was clear.

"Let us take the lead!" Colonel Graves said as he directed his troopers past the company and up the stairs.

Queen Regina helped up Frehley and Strap picked up Captain Michael by his armpits and the company fell in step behind the Black Watch mutineers. No longer were they Deadcoats. They were fighting for their honor once again.

Reed was hopeful. He could feel that same hope building in all the company. They had made it past their first obstacle.

They met the second on the next landing. The hallway that Colonel Graves said held a secret passage was blocked by Sergeant Hood and a score of Deadcoats arranged in four rows. They were armed to their rotten teeth with fresh oiled muskets, bayonets, pistols, swords, and daggers.

Colonel Graves lined his troopers into a wedge and stood at their point. "Sergeant, stand down."

"None shall pass," Sergeant Hood said and leveled a rapier at his old commanding officer.

Colonel Graves saluted him and led the charge. The wedge of Black Watch troopers clashed with the rows of Deadcoats. Colonel Graves drove through the first two rows like butter but the last two rows parted to the sides and hinged in the troopers on either side. In response, the colonel signaled for his men to make a tight circle.

The fighting became hand to hand. Since the troopers were already dead, mortal wounds could not stop them. Each side could only whittle away at limbs and extremities.

Sergeant Hood slashed and bashed his way to challenge Colonel Graves. Locking arms to afford no ground to either opponent they dueled with their rapiers. Thrusting and slicing. Wounding each other and pulling one another back to the fray.

The sergeant pulled back enough to make a broad sweep at Colonel Graves' shoulders. The pass of Sergeant Hood's blade took the colonel's head. From the floor, the colonel glared at his opponent as his headless body fought on and even took Sergeant Hood's left arm off at the elbow.

The maimed sergeant kicked the Colonel Graves' body in the abdomen sending it crashing to the floor. Sergeant Hood sprang on top of it and thrust his rapier down into the kicking colonel's chest and twisted the blade. Leaving the body impaled on the floor, the sergeant took up his musket and bayonet and stalked back through the fray toward the company.

"None shall pass," he repeated as he approached them.

The company had bested the lycanthropes, the Destroyer, and even Rancor but the Deadcoats could only be stopped one at a time. Piece by piece.

Having won their individual contests, four more Deadcoats turned to stalk after their inglorious sergeant. Three came with bayonets at the ready. The fourth aimed at the queen.

"Defend, gentlemen," the Queen said with a cool eye.

Frehley took a dead bead and shot the trooper in the neck. Had it not been a cursed enemy who could not die because Death had rejected him, the enemy combatant would have collapsed and bled out. But this was a Deadcoat. With blood turned to sand. Heart to stone.

Spinning in a pirouette, the Deadcoat's shot went wild. Whizzing over the shoulder of Cyrus' missing arm.

Captain Michael took aim with both pistols and shot the front two Deadcoats in the face blinding them both. Still, they lurched on. A walking wall of animated dead flesh.

"Reed," Cyrus said to the boy. "Use your coin to light this wick if you please."

The blacksmith pulled on the chain wrapped around the butt of the arquebus. The massive gun that reminded Reed of a shotgun and what Cyrus had called a "thunderstick." The wick stood out of the matchlock. Reed used his gold coin as a punk to light the tip of the wick.

Captain Michael sprang at one of the blinded Deadcoats. Knocking the bayonet aside with his rapier, the captain crashed into the trooper to knock him aside. He grappled to take the musket out of the dead man's hands.

Strap bounded forward holding his halberd to the side as he knocked another two Deadcoats upside their heads with his mace. In just two whacks, he cracked their heads and broke their jaws but still the Deadcoats did not relent.

The fourth Deadcoat stabbed at Frehley who staved it off with the length of his bowie knife. Keeping the blade along his wrist, he turned the knife over and stabbed under the Deadcoat's armpit. Which should have been a mortal blow but to a Deadcoat was like stabbing into old leather.

That left Sergeant Hood unchallenged. The non-commissioned officer moved forward slicing at the air with his rapier. Making straight for Reed, Queen Regina, and Cyrus.

The waxed rope sizzled away as Cyrus pulled on the slack of the chain to secure his grip and hold on the gunstock. The blacksmith opened his stance to steady his aim. He leveled the flanged opening at Sergeant Hood.

"Your time has finally come, ol' Cy," Sergeant Hood said. "There's still enough of me left to do you in."

"Any blacksmith will tell ya, Hoodie," Cyrus said. "It's all about usin' the right tool to get the job done. Now say goodbye."

As the sergeant sprang forward with a bent knee to swing down his curved rapier, the wick burned down to the pan holding the powder on the arquebus. The pan flashed like an old-time photo being taken and the musket roared. Out came unchoked shot that spread out about three feet with hundreds of iron pellets from a thunderous blast.

The musket kicked back and up in Cyrus' arm sending the shot a few feet up on the target. More than enough iron balls found their mark: the sergeant's abdomen and chest and face. The force of the blast slammed into the Deadcoat and sent part of him flying back down the hall.

All that was left standing of the sergeant was his two smoking boots.

The melee in the hall was over.

Neither the Deadcoats nor the mutineers had taken the advantage even with both their leaders haven been taken out of action. There were two left from each side.

Queen Regina stepped forward and gave Sergeant Hood a coup de grace with a downward cut of her rapier to avenge Colonel Graves' sacrifice who had once more fought for her as well as truth and justice and liberty.

The two Deadcoats came at her. She parried one of their bayonet thrusts and took a leg off at the knee. That Deadcoat having been disarmed and gone down, Strap swept the last remaining Deadcoat away with the tip of the halberd.

"Colonel Graves mentioned a secret passage located in this hall, do you know of it?" Queen Regina asked the last two loyal troopers.

They both shook their heads.

"Gentlemen, tear this hall apart," the queen ordered.

Strap chinked against the stone masonry with the butt of his halberd. Frehley pried against loose stone with the point of his bowie knife. And Captain Michael moved his hands across the walls. They searched for a hollow spot or a false covering or a breeze coming from a tunnel.

But Cyrus had another thought. "Reed, get that magnet out. Let's use that."

The fused rock had proved itself quite handy. Reed pulled it out of his belt.

"Move it over the walls," Cyrus instructed.

"What are you hopin' to find?" Frehley asked him.

"If it's a secret passage, then it's locked tight. Not just covered over," Cyrus said as he watched the boy move the magnet rock across the wall.

"What is that rock?" Captain Michael asked.

"Some kind of reversed magnet we found in the Circle Chamber," Reed said.

Queen Regina nodded her approval. "If the lock or door is made of iron, this will show us."

The rock bucked against the left wall halfway down the hall.

Cyrus pointed. "There."

Frehley and Strap tapped out the dimensions of the door with the tips of their weapons being able to detect it from the differing reverberations coming from their probing. Still obscured by the masonry, the door purported to be as tall as Strap and as wide as Cyrus.

"There is no way we can chisel through it, my queen," Captain Michael said.

"Reed," Frehley said. "You're our best hope. Use that coin like you did to get us out of the cell."

"But I could see that door!" Reed complained. How could he open something when it was already blocked?

A growl came upstairs. Pounding feet hit the steps below.

"The Dark Riders have recovered," Captain Michael.

"You're capable of much more than you think," Queen Regina said. "I used to believe what others said about me was true. But now I realize that when they said that I couldn't do something that they really just wanted me to fail. And so I wouldn't do it out of fear of failing.

"Well, that's just not true. Failure is something we do and not who we are. I believe in you, Reed."

Reed took a deep breath like he did the first time he was facing the deep end of the diving pool off the low diving board at the Raccoon Springs Recreational Center.

He had survived that jump.

Reaching out with the golden coin safe in his grasp, he mimed turning an imaginary knob. A rumble came from behind the wall. Something heavy shifted. Iron pieces grated.

Reed turned the imaginary knob again and pulled an imaginary door back.

The masonry began to crack. Something pushed against the stone from behind. Scraping metal against rock.

Brick by brick, a part of the wall collapsed as the metal panel of an iron door swung open revealing the mouth of a passage covered with dirty cobwebs.

"That was amazing, kid!" Cyrus said.

"We couldn't have done it without you," Frehley said and clapped Reed on the shoulder.

"It all starts with faith," Queen Regina said. "Faith that the Judge will help us."

***

Chapter Sixty: Lock and Key

Before they entered the dark passage, the company pillaged what weapons they could from the fallen and twitching Deadcoats and mutineer troopers. Frehley took only a pistol along with a bowie knife. Captain Michael kept his rapier and picked up a musket. Strap augmented his weapon cache by grabbing two more pistols and keeping the halberd while putting down his mace. Queen Regina took a pistol along with her rapier. Cyrus picked up two pistols and unchained the arquebus to leave it behind and sling the chain around his neck. And Reed still had his pistol and dagger along with the gold coin.

The two remaining mutineer troopers used their bayonets to clear the passageway of cobwebs. Colonel Graves had called it a secret tunnel. Where did it lead? Why had it been sealed?

The passage was as quiet as a grave. The air smelled of forgotten years. Even spiders had abandoned this solitary path long ago.

Mystery stared them full in the face. The dark recess promised to reveal something great and wonderful. True and dangerous.

There was a hope of finding something.

"We'll need light," Queen Regina said.

Both Frehley and Captain Michael took torches out of sconces on the wall.

Strap entered first having to duck his massive frame under the door frame. The two remaining troopers walked on either side.

Frehley investigated the door and threshold. It was red flaking iron. Old and rusted out.

Whatever had been stashed down here had seen ancient internment. Meant to hide something forever. Even as the means to keep the mystery a secret dissolved and faded away.

Like Dad would say, "Nothing stays a secret for long."

"Have you ever heard of this place?" Frehley asked the queen.

She shook her head.

"No one has been here since it was sealed," Captain Michael said as he showed their back trail through the dust mounded on the floor like loose dirt.

The passageway proved a short run into another larger cavern. Carved by time and nature. Most of the rock was rough. Even the stalactites were a dull color. The only differentiation was a long ledge near to the cave wall. There was a glaze on the surface. A pattern to the texture.

A blueish glow emanated from a far off chamber on the right. Reed breathed in the cool air blowing down from it. He felt like he had been here before. "This is where we ended up when we first escaped."

"The kid's right, Frehley," Cyrus said.

Frehley pointed to the right. "Then that way leads to Ice Prison and Glacier Mountains." Then he pointed to the left. "And that way…"

Something felt wrong. Something had been overlooked. Everyone picked up on it.

Strap named it first. By signing. He made a side to side waving motion with his hand and wrist.

"What does he mean?" Queen Regina asked.

"The Porter," Frehley said and began to look around with his torch.

The glazed ledge near the cave floor moved without a sound. A shape rose in the torchlight. Like an albino tree trunk with scales instead of bark.

Asheroth. The Porter. Guardian of doors and passageways.

A hungry snake.

Its triangular head swooped down out of the darkness. Striking one of the mutineer troopers. The head brushed past Reed with the trooper's kicking legs poking out of the snake's mouth.

"Run!" Cyrus shouted.

Frehley looked around. "To where?"

But the blacksmith was already running away. Like he had time and time again.

The great serpent struck again. This time aiming for Queen Regina. It bowled over the last remaining mutineer trooper crushing him under its massive weight.

The queen slashed across the albino snake's scaly nose while Strap ran alongside its chin and jabbed it in the lip with the halberd. Then he shoved the head aside. It was too strong for the giant to pin it against the wall and the snake jerked its head back snapping the staff of the halberd.

Reed did what he had done the very first time he had used the gold coin. He read the inscription on the heads side. "'TRUST IN THE JUDGE!'" Then he flipped the coin over to read the tails side. "'TOWER REIGN!'"

The snake shook its great head and shrank back from the company. Its massive forked tongue tasting the air. It coiled its body beneath its triangular head as its slitted eyes fixed on Reed and his gold coin.

Then it struck again.

Straight at Reed.

Blocking the boy in with its midsection.

Wrapping itself around him it turned the boy over and smothered him.

And began to squeeze.

It should have broken Reed's ribs in a heartbeat. It should have crushed him within a shake of its snake's tail. But that didn't happen.

Reed had time to take a breath before the wall of muscle had started to constrict. He couldn't breathe. His hot breath was trapped in his lungs. Nor could he speak. Nor free his hand to hit the scaly hide of the snake with the golden coin. He panicked. It was like the time he had almost drowned in the Spring River. To be in the grip of something powerful and unstoppable.

All Reed could do was wiggle his palm a little.

And the great serpent responded. It trembled and its hold slacked.

Reed was able to wiggle his wrist this time.

The snake had to respond. It released its hold even more.

This time Reed turned his hand in a counter-clockwise motion.

The coils fell away as the snake receded into the shadows. It turned its great head and retreated into a side hole. To lick its hurts and shed its wounded pride somewhere down in its labyrinthine lair.

"How was that even possible?" Captain Michael asked as Strap came over to check on the boy. "There was no way we could have even helped you!"

"That was the Judge, Reed," Frehley said as he joined Strap in examining Reed. "There ain't even a scratch on you."

Reed took a couple of breaths: sweet and deep. "I didn't even know I could do it!"

Queen Regina came over and lifted his face with a gentle finger on his chin. "You see? With the Judge's help, you overcame the Porter. What have we to fear?"

"Hey!" Cyrus called from further up the chamber. "You'd better come and look at this!"

Satisfied that Reed was hale and well, Frehley led the company further up the cavern.

There was a light coming from the other end. Enough that Cyrus had been able to discover something without the aid of a torch.

The light had a silver tinged hue. An exit tunnel leading to the backside of the Keep. A way out.

But Cyrus had not followed it outside. Something had kept him rooted in place. He stood transfixed.

All of the company joined him and stared at the sight.

It was not a tunnel. But it had a large round opening. That had once been covered with a large stone that could be moved back and forth in carved grooves in the rock.

The stone now stood rolled away to the side in the grooves. Carved into the rock were symbols that the company had seen before. But not quite in this fashion.

There was a symbol of a snake's tail at the top and coils winding down to a snake head's that rested on a downturned crescent moon as if the selenite object were frowning.

Reed had to look at it again before he realized that it was the snake-moon symbol of the Elfwitch but it had been turned upside down.

The rock covering the chamber having been rolled back it made the interior naked to their eyes.

The inside chamber was tall and round. In the middle stood a large stone box. Heavy and flat like a slab. Carved with reliefs along its four smooth sides.

Cyrus could barely keep his voice from giggling. "Do you know what that is?"

"It looks like a sarcophagus," Queen Regina said.

"This is it!" Cyrus said with glee. "This is the crypt of the Son! This is where he was buried!"

"The Beekeeper told us that the Elfwitch buried him," Frehley said. "And that the Judge raised him from the grave."

Cyrus walked inside first. He ran his hands along the sides of the sarcophagus. Then he bent down and picked up folded cloth. "What's this?"

"A funeral shroud," Queen Regina said.

"If this is the Son's crypt then the sarcophagus should be empty," Captain Michael said.

Everyone ran to the side of the sarcophagus.

It was almost as tall as Reed. He had to stand on his tiptoes to peer inside.

The cover was broken off at the top. Captain Michael put his torch through the opening.

"There's nothing inside!" Cyrus jumped up and down. "There's nothing inside!"

"No, there's something down there," Frehley said and reached through the jagged stone opening.

"There's something down there! There's something down there!" Cyrus sang.

Frehley brought that something out of the sarcophagus. Captain Michael brought his torch out and held it above the item.

It was cylindrical. With handles like a rolling pin. It was a wooden rod with old parchment still wrapped around it.

Frehley unrolled the first length. Looking it over under torchlight he offered it to Queen Regina so she might see. And read.

After she had the ex-Royal Huntsman unroll more of the pages, she read a passage aloud.

"'Your Word, a lamp to my foot, and a light to my path.'"

"More!" Cyrus shouted dancing about in front of the sarcophagus. "Read some more!"

Queen Regina nodded and Frehley unrolled about half of the scroll. She read on,"'Thus My word shall be that goes out of My mouth, it shall not turn back to me empty handed, but surely it does the thing that I please and accomplishes that for which I have sent it.'"

"More!" Cyrus said as he fist-pumped the air. "I want to hear more!"

So Frehley unrolled the length he had already taken and unrolled more of the scroll until it was almost two-thirds unrolled.

Then the queen read, "'In the origin the Word had been existing and the Word had been existing with the Judge and the Word was himself the Judge.'"

"This is the Law, your highness," Frehley said as he rolled all the length back around the rod.

"Aha!" Cyrus shouted in joy. "He is alive! The Son is alive! And he is the Word! He is the Son of the living Judge! And the Elfwitch ain't nothin' but a liar!"

"A stinkin' liar," Frehley added.

"A stinkin' evil liar," Queen Regina further qualified.

"A stinkin' evil loser-liar," Reed finished.

Packy squealed.

Captain Michael crossed his arms and smiled.

Strap shook his head along with each qualified pronouncement.

They shouted out praise to the Judge and then got down on their knees and each gave a prayer of gratitude.

Queen Regina wiped tears from her eyes. "My whole life, my father talked about the Law instead of reading it. He may have meant well, but if we don't read the Law how we will ever know what's in the Law and we will never know how to keep the Law as the Judge intended.

"Otherwise, everyone will just do what they think is right in their own eyes. And that's the mess we've got now."

"We are undoing the trap," Frehley said. "Inch by inch. We are freeing ourselves. Now we have the Law again."

"And I will read from it every day at Court. At the beginning of every council," the queen promised.

"Well, the Beekeeper told you to find the Law and you did," Cyrus said. "Now what's next?"

"The Dark Riders must be imprisoned again. Then we will have to deal with any turncoats. We are few for such a large job. It's long from over," Captain Michael said.

"Many have taken the mark," Queen Regina said. "As long as the Elfwitch is free and the Darkness rules, they are our enemies. We stand with the Judge. With truth. And the Light. The Beekeeper said that the Darkness can only take the space that the Light has left. If we bring back the Light, the Darkness will flee."

Reed listened. He felt that same feeling of peace and rest that had bound them in unity at the Beekeeper's table. It had been a kind of fulfillment and rest.

But he still had his hurts. "I want my sister back. And then I want to get back home. I helped you find the Law. Will you please help me get my sister back?"

Queen Regina took the scroll from Frehley and handed it to Strap for him to tuck into his belt. Then she held out her rapier. "I vow to face the Dark Riders. I vow to bring the Light back to the Realm. And I vow to help you restore your sister and return you both to your home."

Frehley took out his bowie knife and touched the queen's blade. Then Captain Michael joined their blades with the foible of his rapier. Reed joined their blades with his dagger point. And both Strap and Cyrus put their hands on the nexus of the blades.

The queen had them swear on the Law to do what they had promised so help them the Judge.

"I've seen the boy's golden coin stop the Dark Riders," Captain Michael said. "But can it imprison them back in the ice?"

Frehley shook his head, "The Beekeeper said that gold has authority and that silver was for vows, binding, and healing. But they seem to cancel each other out."

"Quicksilver!" Reed urged. "It can do just about anything. But it's different."

Frehley nodded. "Quicksilver has to bind to something. Since it turns gold and silver to paste, only iron can contain it. We'll have to use something iron. Then you have to touch something directly with the quicksilver. Then it works like a charm."

Cyrus whistled. "Woohoo. Like a charm he says."

"The Law is our cage to hold the Dark Riders," Queen Regina proclaimed.

"And quicksilver is the key that locks the cage," Frehley said.

"This means we will have to face the Dark Riders," Captain Michael said.
"First, we'll have to go back to Quicksilver Lake," Frehley said.
"No!" Captain Michael said. "It is forbidden!"

***

Chapter Sixty-One: Brother and Sister

Captain Michael was adamant. Taking his rapier out and pointing at Frehley, he forswore the oath he had just made. Their unity was broken.

Reed stepped forward. "Then I'll go. I'm an outsider. How can it be against the law for me?"

The captain of the Queen's Men curled his mustached lip. "No one goes. This is what caused this whole mess in the first place."

"What caused this mess was when we abandoned the Law," Queen Regina said. She came to stand with Reed between the captain and Frehley.

"You will not fight my battles," Frehley said as he unsheathed his bowie knife. Holding the blade down along his wrist he came stepped forward to challenge the captain of the Queen's Men.

"Guys!" Reed said. "Don't fight! We just all promised!"

But the two did not listen. They feinted and lunged at each other. Daring each other to try to draw first blood.

In retrospect, Reed realized they should have laid their hands on the scroll of the Law and then take their vow, which was what the fight was about between Judge Hart and Miss Elsie Crutch. Reed didn't understand then why the CASA agent had been so against the bible being in the courtroom. But he understood now.

"Do not fight! This gets us nowhere!" Queen Regina said.

But nobody listened and neither the queen nor Strap waded in to stop them.

Reed felt a cold wind behind him. The temperature dropped ten degrees in a heartbeat. Pinpricks chased each other up his spine.

Someone was behind.

Or something.

He turned and saw an erect figure in a leather duster and a broad rim hat had entered the crypt in stealth.

Rancor. With its twisted scowl. He huffed out his vile steaming breath onto his palm and then he blew it at them.

The breath expanded into a hazy mist that enveloped them.

"You took my arm!" Cyrus yelled and pulled out his pistol and aimed it straight at Frehley.

"I will not let you go back to Quicksilver Lake!" Captain Michael yelled and thrust at Frehley's wrist to disarm him.

"Come on, both of you!" Frehley taunted them. "You're gonna have to kill me to keep from Quicksilver Lake!"

Reed was beginning to feel helpless again. Like when Mom and Dad would argue. And like when Mom would tear into Reed about every little thing because Dad wasn't there to catch the heat.

"Stop it!" Reed screamed. He was mad at letting himself feel helpless. He had a gold coin. Shouldn't he use it against these knuckleheads before they hurt one another?

These were adults. Maybe they were from another world but they weren't acting any different than adults Reed had seen in his own World.

But Reed wasn't helpless. He had choices. He could be mad at Mom for always yelling at him and not listening. Yes, that hurt. He could be mad for Dad for leaving him and not being around. That hurt worse.

Reed found that he was the maddest at the Elfwitch. For stealing Sissy. Chayse was his twin sister. She couldn't leave him. Not like Mom and Dad had.

This all had to stop.

"If you kill Frehley, then I'll go to Quicksilver Lake!" Reed said. "Then you'll have to kill me, too."

The combatants paused as that sank in.

"I'm going to Quicksilver Lake, too," Queen Regina said. "So you'll have to kill me as well."

Strap bounded into the midst of the company. He crashed into Cyrus and knocked him aside with his shoulder. Then he grabbed both Frehley and Captain Michael by the back of their collars and put them both in a headlock.

"This all needs to stop," Reed pleaded.

But the queen took Reed right in hand and marched towards Rancor. "Leave, demon! Run while you can. You're going back into the ice."

The creature's scowl turned into a growl.

Reed took out his coin. "You may not obey me! But you have to obey Truth and Justice!"

Queen Regina held up the scroll of Law. "You'll have to obey the Judge and his Law!"

At the mention of the holy names and the truth, the Rancor took off his hat and howled at the ceiling of the crypt.

"Go!" Reed commanded.

"Leave!" Queen Regina proclaimed. "We banish you!"

Rancor lurched forward. But a golden flash radiating out from the coin and pushed the creature back.

Strap let go of those in his double headlock and bounded towards the Dark Rider but the creature's form dissolved into black flies and streamed back out of the crypt.

"We can't stay here," Frehley said.

"Which way to Quicksilver Lake?" Queen Regina asked.

Reed pointed to the wall of the crypt opposite the entrance. "It should be that way. It's beyond the Keep."

The wall blocked them. No one knew what lay behind it. Had the crypt been placed inside a cave under Glacier Mountains? No one knew because no one had been here besides the ones who made the crypt long ago.

On the wall heading in the direction of Quicksilver Lake, a niche had been crafted large enough to hold a statue and votive candle. It lay empty. Full of dust with a large notch in the lower brick shelf.

Reed investigated it close up. The notch was not from a crack. Someone had chiseled the triangular notch into the brick shelf. On purpose.

"What did you find?" Frehley asked as he came over. The ex-Royal Huntsman's keen eye was useful in the layout of a room as much as on game trails in the forest. Though he professed to hate the confinement of four walls, he was adept at spelunking, and as much as having a crypt inside a cave was an anomaly, the crypt's masonry would be by design and not by accident.

"It seems out of place," Reed said.

Frehley agreed. "In a crypt that is out of place. Tucked away. Out of sight."

Reed rested his forefinger above the notch and held his breath. So much of the Realm and the Domain was familiar, yet odd. Making it all so strange. No, beyond strange.

"Only way to find out," Frehley urged. "I'd push it."

Reed tapped the notch on the brick with his forefinger.

A spring hinge turned. And then the masonry began to pull back as it scraped against the grooved floor. Revealing a false wall as a door.

Fresh daytime/nighttime air rushed in. Cool with the scent of glacial ice. Massive shadows rose up a rocky path.

"Reed found a secret opening!" Cyrus called.

Captain Michael took out his rapier again and stood next to the queen. "We still have enemies on the prowl for us."

"And they'll be wanting to even the score," Frehley added.

"Gentlemen, they are desperate," Queen Regina said. "No matter how they might taunt us, they know this will be their last stand. They are looking at being back in Ice Prison. For them, the Darkness is Freedom. They revel in all its chaos and hate and murder. But we have the Law. We have the truth. We will bring the Light back. Because we are on the Judge's side."

"Time to slowdown for the showdown," Cyrus said as he popped his thumb knuckle and then squeezed his other fingers into his palm to pop those knuckles. Then he arched his shoulders and turned his neck from side to side.

The queen led the company out of the secret exit from the crypt into the silver light of the day and night. The large moon blocked the natural light of the sky with its selenite glare. Reed felt like cursing the Lesser Light. It had usurped its place.

He wanted to help the queen and Frehley restore order.

He wanted to get Sissy back.

He wanted them both to get back home.

He wanted to see Dad again. Mom, too.

He wanted them all to be a family again.

Having first met Frehley and then Queen Regina had just whetted his appetite for those wants.

The path took the company through a narrow pass strewn with rocks and pebbles. Leftovers from the ancient landslides. Once on this narrow path, they squeezed through the rock base that had been used as the base of the Keep keeping their backs to Glacier Mountains. The massive barrier made all that area of land impassable.

Reed reflected upon what the Beekeeper had told them. Lands of the east stretching to the coast had once been full of milk and honey. And they had fallen into decline and corruption and then had come under judgment.

That judgment hadn't been an invading army. It had been an act of nature that had brought disaster and changed the landscape in the blink of an eye.

With the Keep just behind them and Glacier Mountains hedging in their right, Reed knew where they were. They were on the right track. Just ahead the pass broadened out to a bowl surrounded by a rim of rock that slipped under into a cave at the back and sloped down to a beach of sand and rock and clamshell on the other end.

The overhang of the rock lip hid the portcullis that guarded the exit tunnel that led towards Outlaw Forest. Below the beach lay Quicksilver Lake. Still and full of viscous mercurial fluid.

And down on the beach stood their enemies. Haters of Law. Rebels against the Light.

There were six enemies. Two to one side: Shadow who floated above the beach with its frayed black robe. Rancor with his hands on the hips of his black leather duster. Two to the other side: Victor, the last surviving lycanthrope twin, caught in his human form and still in his iron collar. The Destroyer who stood with his iron gauntleted arms crossed.

And two in the middle: the Elfwitch with her double twisted silver necklace in hand. Wice with her brown hair down and her blue eyes reflected the frozen crystals of Glacier Mountains.

Not a word was spoken.

None needed to be.

Both sides faced each other. Waiting for one side to make the first move.

Shadow moved first. The creature rose up letting its frayed black robes furl out. It rode the wild wind of despair like a tattered sail.

The company felt their hearts sink. And their courage drop. Doubt spoke to them like Spell Speak: *Better to turn tail and run. Why not surrender? You'll never win.*

Why did Reed expect to win Sissy back? How could he expect any of the company to defeat anyone of these foes?

Cyrus stepped forward. "I've lost so much that I've got nothin' left to lose. But I still got a choice. I will choose how I will live."

He jumped up and grabbed the bottom of Shadow's robe. The Dark Rider tried to pull away. Cyrus was lifted off his feet as he yanked at the creature and even grabbed a higher handhold below its bony knees.

The rest of the Darkness' line-up swept against the defenders of the Light like an onrushing tide. Victor boxed with Frehley each ducking and blocking some punches while landing a few on the sides or shoulders of their opponent. The Destroyer and Strap clashed like two bricks smashing together. Rancor dissolved into a swarm of flies and surrounded Captain Michael. The Elfwitch brandished her double entwined necklace against the queen's rapier as they paced around each other.

Reed came face to face with the girl who had forgotten she was his twin sister.

Wice's chestnut hair blew around her as she held the silver snake comb with the twines pointed out like a dagger. She stabbed at the boy who should have been her brother. But Reed turned his gold coin toward the blow and a golden flash pushed her hand back.

"Please, Chayse, stop," Reed called. "We don't belong here. We've got to get back home."

"Chayse is gone!" Wice yelled.

Reed stood straight and put the gold coin back into his belt.

"If that's true then we are enemies," Reed said. "And you must kill me. So if you're gonna do it, then do it. 'Cuz I don't wanna leave here without you."

Wice screamed with fury and launched herself at the boy. She beat at him with one hand and scratched at him with the silver comb. Reed grabbed her hand with the silver comb but Wice tripped him down into the sand.

Again, she tried to sit on his chest and gain some leverage. But Reed wouldn't give her the advantage and turned onto his side. He would not let go of her arm.

"I've killed others! I can kill you! There can be no forgiveness for me!" Wice declared.

"That's not true!" Reed argued as he tried to hold her free hand. "There's the Judge! The Beekeeper! The queen found the Law! It's all real! Light and love are ruh--!"

But Wice cut Reed off by getting a chokehold on him with her free hand.

The others struggled with their counterparts.

The black flies swarmed over Captain Michael's face and sword arm until their shape was covered. The flies made his face into a grimace as his black blade rose up. With a bellow, the hate covered captain rushed at Strap's blindside as the giant pushed back against the Destroyer.

The giant hip tossed the Destroyer into the rushing Captain Michael. The blow of the blade fell against the ribs of the beast. Strap backhanded the captain knocking most of the flies loose.

Captain Michael's face returned: human and determined.

Frehley and Victor danced around each other. Trading blows. Landing haymakers and uppercuts. Beating each into a pulp. Their eyes blackened and cheeks swollen.

Focusing on each other they turned about faster and faster. Their feet slid in the sand of the sloping shore. Each waiting for the other to lose their balance.

When Victor had his back to the lip of the rock bowl, Frehley turned and ran down the sloping shore. Towards Quicksilver Lake. Even in human form, Victor was fast as he dashed after the ex-Royal Huntsman.

Tackling Frehley at the shoreline, Victor kept him from his goal. He clutched one of Frehley's legs as the man kicked and tried to pull himself closer to the body of quicksilver just beyond his fingers.

Shadow could not shake its human weight. It began to sink. Cyrus was able to put both his feet on the ground as raised his reach to the creature's hips.

Strap locked arms again with the Destroyer as they flipped each other over. But Strap let himself be flipped this time. The two began to tumble down the sloping beach. Whenever one of them sat upon the other's chest they wrapped their feet around the other's head and pulled them back off into a leg scissor hold until the other pulled their head free.

"You lost your Realm long ago," the Elfwitch said as she made a feint toward the queen with her necklace. Silver was more for protection. The only weapon the Elfwitch had was her lies.

"Then you would have ruled long ago. But you didn't," Queen Regina said. "Why didn't you rule? Because the only power you had was what I let you take from me.

"I'm taking it back now."

"You are incompetent! Weak! I rule here!" the Elfwitch said.

"You are a liar!" Queen Regina said. "You were a liar at the beginning!"

The lake was inches away. Frehley pulled out his bowie knife and scrapped the top of it against the surface of the viscous lake. Victor yelled in defiance as the liquid coalesced along the blade.

Frehley stabbed at Victor who caught the other's wrist. Staring at the point of the quicksilver covered blade, the lycanthrope tried to pull Frehley's arm down. But Frehley stood up and putting his foot into the rocky sand, pushed back.

The blade touched Victor's iron collar. The quicksilver bound around it.

"Down, doggie, down!" Frehley commanded.

The quicksilver collar pulled the lycanthrope down. Victor curled up into a ball.

Shadow clutched Cyrus' greaves shoulder and tore it from him.

"Wrong one!" Cyrus laughed as he pulled Shadow down to his own height. Still grinning, the blacksmith reached over and yanked the silver necklace off of the creature's neck.

Rancor gathered itself into its anamorphic self, the black flies becoming the black leather duster and broad brim hat once again. Captain Michael spied a flash of quicksilver upon its chest. Quick as light, he thrust the rapier inwards and upwards, then pulled the blade back.

The rapier's blade cut through the chain and the quicksilver heart necklace fell from around Rancor's neck. Captain Michael dove down the sloped shore after it while Rancor screamed and sent wasps flying out of its fingertips. But the captain rolled over in the sand. Whipping the broken chain around him, he slapped at the wasps as they turned to ash.

Strap and the Destroyer were even in falls. The giant slammed into the beast and pushed it further down the sloping beach. It grabbed Strap's leg in order to toss him over but the giant yanked back on one of the Destroyer's fingers breaking its hold so he could put his leg back down on the sand.

Then Strap grabbed the Destroyer's belt and leather shirt by the collar. He turned and fell back tossing the Destroyer over his head. The beast flipped over and landed on its chest in the lapping liquid of Quicksilver Lake.

The beast jumped up as its silver necklace now saturated with quicksilver was eaten away and fell in globs back into the surf. The Destroyer cocked its arms back but quicksilver was all both gauntleted hands. Strings of the liquid bonded between its hands and hardened. The lake began to boil as quicksilver rose up inch by inch over the Destroyer's frame from its leather boots to its mane of wild hair. The liquid metal encased the beast.

The Elfwitch encircled herself with the double twisted necklace. "I have quicksilver, too! Come at me and you will be destroyed!"

Queen Regina rested the rapier at her feet with both hands. "You have said your lies. Now let me speak the truth. It is not my truth. It is not a truth. It is the Law. This is what the Judge says: 'Woe to those who call evil good and good evil. Who put darkness for light and light for darkness. Who put bitter for sweet and sweet for bitter!'

"And again this is what the Judge says: 'The Judge uses the foolish things of this world to confound the wise. And the weak to shame the strong.'

"Your rule here has come to an end. You have a jail cell of ice waiting for you."

The queen dipped the end of her sword into Quicksilver Lake. The liquid rose up like a thermometer expanding the blade and making it glow a silver-blue. Taking a wide stance, Queen Regina brought her sword arm back and swung the blade down to smash the evil that had sickened her Realm. She meant to take the Elfwitch's head, though that was not how the Law had prophesied the end of all evil.

Still, Queen Regina had to try.

The Elfwitch saw an end coming. She put her arm up to shield the coming blow. Her silver shield would not hold up, she knew.

She had read the Law and knew it by heart. Or at least the parts that mentioned her. She knew where she stood with Judge and knew when her time would come

But then she straightened up. And smiled.

Why should the Elfwitch smile? Queen Regina thought to herself.

Because today was not her time.

But even though she knew the Law that didn't mean she believed it or revered it.

The Elfwitch did not cower but defied the coming blow and ensuing death or imprisonment by lifting her fist to the sky.

In answer, a sweeping shadow covered both the Elfwitch and Queen Regina. Talons grasped the Elfwitch by wrist and forearm. And the double-headed vulture made away with its master. Up over the rim of the rock bowl and back towards the Keep and to the Circle Chamber.

Captain Michael had Rancor at bay with his sword point and broken silver heart necklace.

Cyrus still had a grip on Shadow and held its silver necklace by its mouth.

Frehley had Victor by his quicksilver collar.

The only loose end was Wice.

And she was not a Dark Rider.

Nor a servant who had taken the moon-snake tattoo mark.

Reed had to trip Wice to break her chokehold. He wasn't going to go down again.

She flew at him smacking and slapping with vicious nails.

He grabbed her up in a bear hug so that they were face to face.

"Chayse!" he urged. "Listen to me!"

"I'm Wice!" the hurt girl screamed. "And I've killed!"

"It's me, Bubba!" Reed said. "Stop it!"

"You can't forgive me! You won't forgive me! I'll kill you, too!" the desperate girl cried out.

"It doesn't matter!" Reed said as he held to the bucking and screaming girl that was his sister. His twin sister. She had been a part of him since they had been formed in the same womb at the same time.

Wice was gone. She was leaving Chayse behind.

Chayse screamed. Everything was dark.

Pitch black perfect blindness.

Fingers found her.

She kept screaming.

They were warm and tender fingers. Meaning to offer solace and shelter. Not harm.

Chayse was beside herself. She was in a perfect storm of fear and hate. With nowhere to go and no one to help her. Not Dad. Not even Mom.

Except one person.

And that person was with her here and now.

The fingers were attached to kind hands.

The hands were connected to encircling arms.

The arms were a part of a body that had arrived in their own World just five minutes after her own. A heartbeat sharing the womb with her. A silver necklace that fit into hers.

Her brother. Her twin self. Who was her complete opposite.

It was Reed. And he was hugging her. His body warmth soft and comforting.

"There, there. It'll be alright, Sissy. We are still alive. We still have each other. We still have hope," Reed said. He offered a truth: love, hope, and family.

Chayse knew what Mom would say back in their own World: *"Either we define our circumstances or we let our circumstances define us."*

Instead, Reed said something even more true and way more powerful: "I'll tell you what Dad told me after he had left Mom. *'There's nothing you could ever do or say that would make me stop loving you.'* After he told me that, I just forgave him.'"

Chayse returned to herself. "I wish he'd tell that to Mom and I wish she'd believe him."

They both shed tears and hugged each other.

Their tears ran down each other's cheeks.

"Praise! Chayse has been restored to us!" Queen Regina said.

"Don't you two want your necklaces back from these Dark Riders?" Frehley asked.

"It's about time to get you both home. Your family is waiting," Cyrus said.

"We can make things right here?" Chayse asked.

Reed nodded. "We have the power. We have friends here. We have gold and metal and quicksilver."

"And we have the Law!" Queen Regina proclaimed. "But how do we banish the Dark Riders?"

"After a hunt, hunters gather in a circle and show their trophies," Frehley said. "Everyone make a circle and bring your necklaces or metal."

The company made a circle holding onto their prey with one hand and touching silver and quicksilver necklaces and gold coin and the scroll of law to Victor's quicksilver collar.

"Back to your prison cell!" said Queen Regina.

"Back to your icy dreams!" said Frehley.

"Back to your station!" said Captain Michael.

"Back to your real home!" said Cyrus.

Strap indicated with a nod where the Dark Riders could go.

"Go back to the shadows," said Chayse.

"Where they run from themselves," said Reed.

A ball of lightning radiating out from the combined metal and enveloped the three Dark Riders and condensing them all down into a nucleus inside floating orbs. The three orbs whisked away back to Keep and Glacier Mountains. Their destination: Ice Prison.

***

Chapter Sixty-Two: Spell and Speak

All of the Dark Riders were gone.

Only Victor was left cowering in his human form.

"What are you going. To do with me?" he asked in a hesitant voice. It was the first time he ever had to finish his own sentence.

The queen pointed her rapier at him. "Where will your Dark Mistress flee?"

Victor put his chin up. "She is older than you know. She has her ways. She has doors. To everywhere in the universe."

"This servant is dangerous. He should be dealt with, your highness," Captain Michael said.

"We will have our hands full with all the other traitors and turncoats. This one might be useful in helping them hunt them down," Frehley suggested.

Victor puffed up his chest and slapped his moon-snake tattoo. "I am bound to the Darkness."

Queen Regina, who had taken in Victor's words and the others' suggestions, nodded. "That tells me much."

She slapped the lycanthrope on the arm with the side of her mercurial coated rapier. The quicksilver slathered over his moon-snake tattoo. Filling in the traces. Obliterating the design.

Victor shook with the quickening. The irises of his eyes changed their hue from blue to a dull silver.

"Lead us in the quickest way to the Circle Chamber or wherever the Elfwitch may be hiding," Queen Regina said.

"I can travel. Faster in my. True form," Victor pleaded. He, too, was not used to having to finish his own sentences.

"Aren't you a werewolf?" Reed asked.

Victor shook his head.

"Doesn't a lycanthrope change back and forth from wolf to man and man to wolf?" Frehley asked.

Again Victor shook his head.

"Dear Judge!" Cyrus gasped. "He's a wolf trapped in a man's body!"

Victor gave a slow nod.

"Free him then," Queen Regina commanded.

Strap reached out and touched the man's head with the quicksilver bonded collar. Victor smiled and transmogrified into a regal grey timber wolf before their eyes. He looked over the company before putting his head up to howl at the enormous moon face that obscured the Greater Light.

The wolf leaped back up the beach to find another passage cleft in the rock bowl.

"Everyone, follow," the queen urged.

The narrow led to a cave mouth where they followed the wolf single file. The wolf would stop along its run to let the company sight it. Then it would leap on ahead.

The way ran crooked. It was a natural path. Not man-made. Perhaps a mere animal trail.

When it began to descend into the depths of the bedrock of the Keep, Reed held forth his gold coin to give a warm yellow light to their path. Holding the precious coin in one hand, he held his twin sister by the other hand.

They did not become lost. On occasion, they would see the two yellow orbs of the wolf's eyes up ahead. He was not leading them astray.

The way proved short.

The company met the wolf at a closed door where tiny pinpoints of light slipped out under the threshold. They parted to give Reed room as he and Chayse moved up to the door. The boy touched the back of the door with the cold coin and it pushed itself open.

The wolf padded into the room first. Followed by the twins. Then the rest of the company.

They stood in the wreckage of the Circle Chamber. The light coming from sconces set along the circular wall. The door they had entered through had been through a false door behind one of the many bookcases filled with jars which now was a sloppy mess.

The room was empty of anyone. And anything. Except for ruined cages and broken jars and crushed vials.

The only thing that lay untouched was the chest marked WICE.

Running steps came from the tunnel leading back to the dungeon level.

In came the Elfwitch.

Chayse had never seen her run away. Or retreat. But now the Elfwitch was in full flight.

She was a dangerous creature with few limitations.

Behind the Dark Lady flapped the large wings of the double-headed vulture. The wolf snarled and leaped at the bird. It could not light anywhere. Instead, it had to make a tight bank and get what altitude it could in the chamber to fly back through the exit tunnel.

The wolf tore off after the bird. Now the Elfwitch was all alone. Reed had never seen her by herself. She seemed smaller somehow. Diminished.

The only thing between the company and the Dark Lady was the old wooden chest. The thing that held an endless mystery. The Elfwitch made a mad dash for freedom by going straight for the chest.

"Quick!" Chayse warned. "Help me stop her, Reed! Keep that lid closed!"

The twin girl ran to intercept the Elfwitch with her twin brother at her heels.

The Elfwitch was faster. She reached the chest and had the lid open before the twins could get there. It creaked back on ancient hinges. There was no telling what metal they once were.

With a smile, she prepared to step into the chest. Escaping to freedom. To spread her seeds of evil.

Chayse grabbed the other side of the lid and with Reed coming behind her both the twins fell on top of the lid and used their body weight to shut it tight.

The Elfwitch snarled and pulled out her double twisted heart-moon-snake necklace. There was much she could still do with it.

"Reed!" Cyrus called. "Do what you did last time!"

Reed reached into his belt and taking out his gold coin, he urged Chayse to slide off the lid. "Just open it a hair!"

The Elfwitch tried to keep it shut from her end but her necklace was only good for defense. She could not come up against Reed as long as he held the gold coin.

Chayse cracked the lid wide enough for Reed to drop in the gold coin.

The Elfwitch just had time to hiss, "You little fool!"

Then the eruption hit not unlike a tsunami wave making landfall.

It was different than the time before. Much more intense. Space and reality were tugged on.

The chest lifted and sucked itself in before bursting out in an expanding cloud of gas and light and chain lightning. Star nurseries and nebula leaped out into the small space of the Circle Chamber which became as big as the universe in a single flash. The light of a thousand suns shone through a myriad of precious stones: red wavelength through rubies, green wavelength through emeralds, orange wavelength through citrine, blue wavelength through sapphire, light blue wavelength through aquamarine, violet wavelength through amethyst, and bright white light wavelength through diamonds.

The air was sucked out of the room.

The room was sucked out of the earth.

The earth disappeared.

The spectral colors of the rainbow arched over them all.

Revealing a cold fire at the heart of the chest like a black burning diamond. A heart of Darkness kept hard against the warmth of love. A pearl of night kept secret from the Light.

Exposed in all its deeds under the wavelength of the light spectrum.

Caught naked in the Light of truth.

The cold fire whisked out of existence. Like it had never been at all. A shadow that had covered the cornerstone of the rainbow disappeared.

Revealing the true nature and shape of the center of all things.

So that all could revel in the glorious Light. Feel Peace. Hold Truth in their hearts.

Something was passing by. The tail of something incomprehensible. And immeasurable.

The Judge. His Son. And their Spirit.

Just the tail of the magnificent presence swept by. As the presence was everywhere at once and in all things, its entirety could be seen in full measure.

Then even stranger things began to happen.

The Keep came down in pieces above them.

The jail doors of the cells above all came off their hinges and fell against the wall.

And the moon was pulled back into its proper orbit.

Darkness settled onto the land and the rubble of the Keep.

A stillness came over the space where the Elfwitch and the company were. Tucked into a cleft of eternity. Time and place came back to them. Returned them to Circle Chamber now free of a single vestige of the Elfwitch's arcane art.

Out of the darkness nimbuses of light focused around the two remaining sconces.

Chayse opened her eyes.

Reed took a breath.

The other members of the company looked at their hands and felt their faces to make sure they were complete and whole.

"That was amazing," Chayse said.

"It was clothed in rainbows!" Cyrus gasped.

"That was the Judge," Frehley said. "At least just his tail as he passed us."

"Only the Judge is clothed in rainbows," Queen Regina confirmed.

Both Strap and Captain Michael nodded.

The Elfwitch looked paler. Her shoulders slumped. For now, she held only a silver moon-snake necklace. Queen Regina's open heart quicksilver necklace was no more.

"You cannot stop me! You do not have the authority! I will not be bested by a couple of kids!" the Elfwitch said. She lifted her skirts and rushed past the rest of the company more like an old woman with a hitch in her step.

No-one stopped her for the company was dazed from the revelation that had proceeded with the gold coin had diffused the cold heart of darkness that had powered the chest.

The Elfwitch made a harried and slow escape through the exit tunnel to Ice Prison.

"Why is she headed back that way?" Reed asked his twin.

"There's another chest at Ice Prison!" Chayse told him.

Reed was incredulous, "A second chest?"

"It's called WEIK," Chayse told him.

The word resounded throughout the chamber. Changing and stretching into different words and voices with different pitches. *DIVIDE. LIGHT AND DARKNESS. TRUTH AND LIE. LOVE AND HATE.*

"Chayse! You can do Spell Speak!" Reed said.

"And you know how to use gold!" Chayse said.

"Children," Queen Regina chided them. "If there is a second chest at Ice Prison, we can't let the Elfwitch escape!"

Frehley and Strap grabbed the torches from out of the sconces as the twins led the company out the exit tunnel to Ice Prison. The carved rock passage was a too familiar path. One that always brought dread because of its destination.

Glacier Mountains had not changed. Their judgment still stood. Three of the Dark Riders were again imprisoned in their frozen niches.

The Elfwitch had made it there before them to the second chest. She had the lid propped open with both hands and one leg into its dimension. She sat on the edge smiling.

She was waiting for them.

Surrounded by what was left of her loyal servants. Five Huntsman spiders moving slow but sure. Their footpads sticking to the ice.

"The both of you have no idea what waits for you," the Elfwitch smiled. "You think the Judge is loving and good and kind. But he lets the Darkness do what it wills.

"You'll have to go to sleep sometime. And that's when I come out to play. I live in the shadows. Way down deep where I can creep. You can go all day and think me away. But when you lay down to rest is the time I like best.

"Boy twin, without that gold coin you are nothing. You came into this world five minutes too late. And you, girl, are full of blood guilt. Kyphus' face will always be before you."

Before their eyes, her black raven robe melded into pantsuits and a sweater and jacket. Her red hair became tied into a bun and thick square librarian glasses appeared on her eyes. She was Miss Elsie Crutch again.

"I go to make sure you will never see your parents again," she threatened.

With that, she slipped into the chest. The lid creaking shut. There was no way her body could have fit into the chest but she had disappeared down it like a rabbit down its hole.

Three of the spiders picked up the chest and began to carry it further down the narrow space between the wall of ice and rock cavern.

Chasing after the retreating spiders and their cargo, Cyrus promised, "She's not gettin' away from me! Not after all her lyin' and hurtin'!"

The last two arachnids acted as a rearguard and scuttled forwards to stop the blacksmith's approach. Frehley and Strap came at them from both sides and put their torches to both Huntsman spiders. The flame caught their hairy legs and spread to their gristly abdomens. They ran in circles like twirling flames in ever wilder orbits until they bounced into the three Huntsmen spiders carrying the chest. The burning two touched the legs of the fleeing three and the spread to all five.

The planks of the chest began to smoke. The spider troop dropped the chest and shriveled up into burning balls. Carbonized into lumps and hulks.

Cyrus ran to the chest and beat at the flames and kicked at the smoking edges. "You won't get away from me!"

Frehley and Strap helped to smother the smoking planks.

They were further down the glacier than anyone had ever been before. The frigid air had already frosted the burned edges of the chest. None of them could survive for too much longer this far into the glacial wall.

Strap and Frehley tried to do what three Huntsman Spiders had done with ease: pick up the end of the chest. They didn't hold it for long before putting the chest down and blowing on their hands. The company stamped their feet and brushed crystals out of their hair.

"It's too heavy and it's too cold," Frehley told the queen.

"Better to just leave it here, your highness," Captain Michael said. "We can close off the passage and no one will be able to ever find it again."

After a moment, Queen Regina nodded. "We have done all we can. We have done more than enough. Now we need to tend to the healing of the Realm."

Cyrus was incredulous. "You're gonna let the Elfwitch go free?"

"Leave vengeance to the Judge. You keep chasing after her and you will destroy your future," Queen Regina said.

The twins didn't like that the Elfwitch was free to spin her machinations across the universe.

"We've got to get home," Chayse said.

"We've got to help our parents," Reed said.

"They must think we've been kidnapped," Chayse said.

"Or worse," Reed said.

Frehley grabbed the queen's hand. "I wish that we were your parents."

Reed smiled. "You kinda are."

Chayse nodded. "Here, at least."

Cyrus shook his head. "I can't just sit here when evil is runnin' free. Someone's got to stop her."

He ran to the chest and opened it with his good arm. "Y'all got a home. I've got nothin' left to lose." Putting one leg into the chest he sat on the lip and turned back. "Hey, there's water in here!"

Without another word or complaint, Cyrus slipped down into the chest and the lid creaked closed behind him. In a second he was gone, too.

Reed shook his head. "There he goes again."

"I pray he does well," Frehley said. "Wherever he ends up."

***

Chapter Sixty-Three: King and Queen

"Children, we must go. There is nothing here for the living," Queen Regina said.

Everyone was in unity with that.

When they got back to the tunnel leading to the Circle Chamber they had to by-pass it because there would be no way to go any further up the Keep past the dungeon level. So Frehley led them away from Ice Prison. Again traversing along the rock wall on the left while keeping the glacial mass on their right.

They hurried as fast as they could. Frehley holding a torch out front and Strap bringing up the rear with the second torch. If they strayed too far or stayed too long this close to the glacier they would freeze to death. Already the frigid mass of immovable ice was sucking away their body warmth.

Up ahead a black crack appeared in the space between the rock wall and the glacier. It could not be another chamber as lights twinkled in its canopy.

It was the outside night sky.

They had found another opening out of the bedrock.

For the first time since coming to the Realm, the twins looked up to the sky and could determine that it was true night. The darkened firmament held the third heaven. One full of stars in constellations that would determine the time of the seasons.

Receded to its proper position in the night time sky sat the Lesser Light.

"My Judge," Queen Regina said. "Things are returning back to their proper place."

"It is because the Elfwitch has been banished," Captain Michael said.

"It's because we have the Law again," Frehley said.

Strap patted the rolled up scroll still sung in his belt.

The company trudged on.

They had reached the naked hills that ran along the escarpment before the great Glacier Mountains. Somewhere up ahead lay Outlaw Forest.

"How are we going to return home?" Chayse asked.

"I've been thinkin' on it the whole time," Reed said. "Those chests are definite doors to another dimension."

"But there's no way of tellin' where we'd end up if we just climbed in," Chayse said as the company winded through traces and runs between the small denuded hills.

"I think we're gettin' pretty close to our own World, sis," Reed said.

"I've been thinkin' on that, too, Reed," Frehley said.

"Yes," the queen added. "You say we are your parents in your own World. And that the Elfwitch passed as someone different."

"Not just her, but Strap is my best friend by another name," Frehley said. "And the Revelator was there. And even that snake Kyphus was a greasy advocate there."

"You were there, too, Captain Michael," Chayse said. "You were an officer of the court. And you were so kind to us."

Captain Michael raised his eyebrows. "Naturally. It seems that our doubles are not that all dissimilar from our true selves."

"Or vice versa," Chayse said. "Since we are from there and have come here."

"Maybe there are mirrors of people's true selves in many worlds," Reed surmised.

"If we exist in eternity then all things are possible," Queen Regina said.

"Y'all are makin' my head hurt, now," Frehley said. "Better to stick to the problem at hand. The twins don't belong here. But they could stay here. That would make me very happy. But they would want to go back to their true home at some point.

"Their world is a mirror of the world here.

"So, my thought is if we try to find the place where you two crossed over, we might have a better chance of sending them back."

"That's what I was thinkin', Da--" Reed caught himself. "I mean, Frehley."

The ex-Royal Huntsman, who was once again doing his job, smiled. "I would be proud to have you as my son. To tell the truth, I have claimed you as my own in my heart."

"Queen Regina, I am sorry I didn't tell you everything when we were first alone. I kinda wanted to but I was kinda afraid," Chayse said.

"You were enthralled by the Elfwitch. She took great lengths to keep the truth hidden from you and me. She may even have tried to kill me if you had told me the truth of who you were and where you came from," Queen Regina said. "But she made a great mistake of even bringing you both here."

"Why did she take the risk?" Captain Michael asked.

"For the same reason she wanted our quicksilver heart necklaces," Frehley said.

"She wanted all our heart necklaces," Queen Regina said.

"Because we are family," Chayse said.

"Because we are Lyftwyches here," Reed said.

Chayse's heart fell. "We're not even a family anymore back in our own World."

"I wish we could use gold and silver back home like it can be used here," Reed said.

"You can't make people do what they don't want to do," Frehley said.

Queen Regina finished the thought, "They will resent you."

"How do we get our family back?" Chayse asked.

"Your parents will have to remember why they fell in love. And what a true blessing you as children have been to them," Queen Regina said.

"They'll have to ask the Judge to forgive themselves and heal their family," Frehley said. "Do you not have the Law in your own World?"

"Yes," Chayse said. "It's called the Bible."

"What does the 'Bible' mean?" Frehley asked.

"The 'Book,'" Reed said.

"I didn't know that," Chayse said. "And I didn't know you knew that."

Reed shrugged. "I actually read during on Accelerated Reader days. You should try it."

Chayse bristled. "I should try to tear your ears off, is what I should do."

"Children," Queen Regina scolded.

Frehley laughed. "Yes, all things are returning back to their proper places."

"What will y'all do now?" Reed asked.

"Bring the Law back to Tower Reign," Queen Regina said in her official tone. "We will rule the Realm as our father wished."

"And the traitors and turncoats?" Captain Michael asked. "There will be many to hunt down and arrest."

"Even if with the Dark Riders back in Ice Prison," Chayse said, "the traitors will remain loyal to the Darkness as long as they have their moon-snake tattoo. It's like a poison in their system."

"Some no doubt will flee and fight to the death," Captain Michael conceded. "But even if they do surrender we won't be able to trust them again, your highness."

"We will not order mass executions," Queen Regina said. "That is what the Elfwitch would do."

"Ol' Cy hid his moon-snake tattoo from us," Frehley pointed out. "It wasn't until the quicksilver necklace took his arm that he was right as rain. And you couldn't turn Victor until his rightful form until you used quicksilver to wipe away his tattoo."

"If you are proposing we take quicksilver with us back to Tower Reign, it is forbidden," Captain Michael said.

"Just why is it forbidden?" Chayse asked.

"Because that's the way it's always been," Captain Michael said.

"Not always," Reed pointed out. "The Judge made quicksilver the same as he made gold and silver."

"Those two metals have a purpose. So quicksilver must have one, too," Chayse pointed out.

"Captain Michael, with all due respect," Frehley began, "when the queen dipped her sword blade into Quicksilver Lake she was not struck dead and she did not turn to the Darkness."

"What other concerns do you have, captain?" Queen Regina asked.

"Once this secret of how to bind quicksilver onto iron comes out, any fool could come and grab some and do whatever he wanted for good or ill," Captain Michael said. "That was another purpose of the Black Watch. Though, Colonel Graves reclaimed his honor by dying for our cause, we will have to make a new Watch."

"Then this, I do by decree," Queen Regina said. "Captain Michael, I promote you to colonel and give you the honor of establishing and maintaining a new watch, the Law Watch. You will build a new Keep, free of any dungeon, with no secret tunnels to Ice Prison. You will enlist such men as you deem fit for service. Your garrison will make sure to keep Ice Prison and the Sepulcher of the Son sealed. You will also guard all approaches to Quicksilver Lake."

"Then I must make two requests, my highness," Colonel Mike said.

The queen inclined her head.

"I ask that you take what quicksilver you need for the time being and make an edict forbidding anyone to come and take whatever they would venture," Captain Michael said.

The queen paused. Then gave her assent. "Done. And the second?"

"Asheroth," Captain Michael said. "We should send Frehley to hunt it down and kill it."

The queen turned to Frehley who shook his head.

"Not so, my queen," Frehley said. "The Judge made Asheroth. It is an animal. It serves a purpose. It guards those tunnels. It has done so up to now and the only reason we bested it twice was because of Reed's gold coin."

Queen Regina gave her ruling. "I concur."

"Who shall lead your bodyguard, my highness?" Colonel Michael asked.

Queen Regina reached out her hand and beckoned Strap to approach. The mute giant stepped forward and took her tiny regal hand in his huge mitt. She squeezed it as she placed him before her and motioned him to kneel.

"I hereby commission you, Strap, captain of my personal bodyguard and household. You shall watch over the defense of Tower Reign and of my family," Queen Regina proclaimed and touched his shoulders with the flat of the rapier.

Captain Michael arched his brows but then shrugged.

Frehley gainsaid to speak for himself, "And I suppose I am free and clear to be the official Royal Huntsman?"

The queen shook her head.

"No?" Frehley asked.

"That is correct. My answer is no," Queen Regina said.

Frehley was stunned. Reed felt sorry for him. He loved to hunt and to be outside in the woods. And after twelve long years in prison, he wasn't going to be restored to his former rank.

"I'm at a loss," Frehley said.

Queen Regina cocked her eyebrow. "I have a new task for you. You are to find the next best blacksmith to Cyrus since we have lost him for the time being. This blacksmith is to make two iron bands which you will bring back and under Captain Michael's supervision, bond quicksilver unto them.

"Then you are to bring the quicksilver rings to Tower Reign and present them to me with a special request."

The twins could not believe their ears.

Frehley managed, "What request will you have of me then?"

"That is what I plan to ask you. And I will give you my answer now," Queen Regina said. "Yes."

"Yes?" Frehley asked. "To what?"

Strap hit his friend on the shoulder. Then he mimicked putting a ring on his finger.

"Oh," Frehley said. Then he paused to reflect and his jaw dropped. "Oh, my!"

"Hooray!" the twins cheered.

Strap smiled.

Captain Michael's shoulders slumped.

"You're gonna be a Lyftwych," Reed told the man who looked like his dad, Frederick Leftwich, in his own World.

"King Lyftwych," Chayse said.

"Dear Judge," Frehley said in his own defense.

"Indeed," Captain Michael said.

***

Chapter Sixty-Four: Lake and Karst

"Children, it would please our heart if you both chose to stay," Queen Regina told them using the royal personage. "But we deem you both free to do what your heart tells you."

Reed and Chayse turned to each other as they had so much in life. For decisions. For laughs. For tears. For fears.

"The queen and Frehley look just like Mom and Dad," Reed said.

"But they're different here," Chayse said. "They've overcome."

Reed nodded. "They had their problems. But they found out they still love each other."

"That's the best thing we found in this place, Reed," Chayse said. "Everything else was a nightmare."

"Well, ol' Cy found himself again," Reed said. "So, that was a good thing."

"I'm sorry I didn't get to meet him," Chayse said.

"Oh, he was a toot," Reed said.

"We can't stay here," Chayse said.

"We could stay here," Reed said.

"But we can't. They aren't our Mom and Dad," Chayse said.

"Mom and Dad still got their problems," Reed said.

"Mom and Dad still need us," Chayse said.

The twins turned to the company.

"We have to get back to Our World," Chayse said.

"It's what the Judge would want," Reed said.

Frehley came to them and put his arms around their shoulders and hugged them both. Then the queen gave them royal kisses on each cheek. Strap wrapped them both up in a double bear hug. And Captain Michael took their hands while giving them a deep bow of respect.

"You will be welcome in our court anytime," Queen Regina said.

"Here, you're Lyftwyches," Frehley said. "You're regents."

The twins nodded and both said, "Thank you, your royal majesties."

The queen saluted them. And the others gave their goodbyes.

Above the lake and beyond Glacier Mountains, the sky in the east changed. No longer was it a midnight blue full of millions of cold fires. Softer hues began to light up the horizon. Soft pink which turned to a vibrant red. Out of that came a calming blue. Behind that came a pleasing green.

At last, a glorious orb rose. Bigger than the moon could ever be. Filling the sky with a gentle orange.

It was the coming dawn. Night had been banished. Day ruled again.

It was the one time that the twins and all the company could look at the sun and not be blinded.

To the company, it was a magnificent sight.

For the twins, it was about the most beautiful thing they had ever seen.

"Things are comin' back to where they belong," Frehley said.

They basked in the warm glow of sunlight. Peaceful beams danced through the sky pushing back the purple curtains of night after twelve long years. Mists rose to the sky as clouds floated on their way across the Realm.

"Right," Chayse said. "Now just how close are we to our own World?"

"The typography isn't exactly the same but the Realm looks very much like back home. Raccoon Springs Village. Shiloh," Reed said.

"And Osage Cave!" Chayse said.

Reed nodded and pointed back up the shore to the portcullis cave hidden beneath the overhanging rock ledge. "It's not exactly Osage Cave, but if it was then Quicksilver Lake would be the…"

"The sinkhole!"Chayse said.

Reed nodded again. "A door."

"Isn't it poisonous?   Quicksilver helped change the Elfwitch into an evil person," Chayse asked.

"I think she wanted to become evil long before she messed with quicksilver," Reed said.

"We have no iron to help us," Chayse said.

Strap came to them with the open iron collar that he had taken off Victor. He gave it to them with one of his big smiles.

"Children, this will be dangerous," Queen Regina said. "But I believe that quicksilver is a tool. And matches the heart of the wielder. It will help you."

The twins each took hold of the iron collar and went down the slope of the beach to the shoreline of Quicksilver Lake.

The viscous liquid already lapped at the shoreline. Lying like tufts of cream atop a stagnant lake. They each dipped the iron collar into the quicksilver as the running metal ran over the design.

Then they took their first step onto the surface.

They did not sink down.

The quicksilver collar kept them buoyant.

The twins held onto the collar and to each other.

Out they ventured.

The middle of the lake became agitated. Bucking and rolling. Make grey waves and silver caps.

Riptides and currents began to churn in a circle until a vortex took hold in the lake. The vortex rotated in strength until it became a whirlpool. The twins stepped down into the center of the whirlpool.

The viscous quicksilver greeted them at the bottom of the lake as they sank and passed out of the Realm. The liquid flowed into a dark cavern. Riding the current through the rock, the twins passed into a larger chamber.

The earth became another element.

The chamber became a void.

Time became a flux.

The quicksilver filtered through a membrane.

Where down became up.

The bottom became the top.

Bubbles of water trapped with air filtered out the other side of the membrane.

The buoyant bubbles surrounded them and pulled them up towards the light.

Towards the surface of another body of water.

***

LAW

Chapter Sixty-Five: Lie and Truth

The twins broke surface.

They gasped for breath. Splashing in the deep green karst pool of Osage Cave State Park. After days or maybe weeks, they were back home.

Home was gone.

Broken.

By Miss Elsie Crutch. And her two watchdogs—Nick and Vic. And the FINS order signed by Judge Hart. And supervised by ad-litem Kyler.

A hot mess was waiting for them.

How where they ever going to explain everything that happened to them?

First thing: they had to get to safety.

"Reed!" Chayse called out. She was the strongest swimmer. Being a little taller and having longer legs.

"I'm good!" Reed sputtered when he really wasn't.

Chayse tried to rise. The karst had no beach. Just steeps walls surrounding the sinkhole.

But there was a small oak tree with its roots just under the water line and its boughs spread out over the lake from its perch on the bottom of the wall.

"Swim to the tree!" Chayse called to her younger twin brother. "You see it?" Reed raised his hand out of the water to flash her a soaked thumb's up.

The twins swam to the bent oak. Chayse, arriving first, wrapped her left arm around the lowest bough and grabbed her twin brother with her right arm and pulled him to where he hugged onto to with his life.

They were tired.

They were hungry.

They were homesick.

They took turns crying out "Help!"

Their words bounced off the water and ricocheted off the karst walls. The syllables doubling before dying away. How Spell Speak could help them now.

They didn't have a single precious metal. Not a necklace. Or a coin. Or a drop of quicksilver.

But they had each other.

Up above the karst, the platform deck stretched out from the trail atop the ridge and cave.

Their voices kicked up some crows. Which wasn't a good sign. Later, a vulture glided overhead.

The twins were relieved to see it had only one head.

They kept calling. Until their arms ached. And their wet limbs became heavy.

Someone ran down the wooden walkway. Down the steps to the observation platform. It was a man with an orange vest on.

A volunteer. A searcher. Better than that: a savior.

He did a double-take and grabbed onto the rails. Then he took a walkie-talkie off his belt. After squelching a button, he spoke into it and listened for a reply.

"Hey!" the twins called up to the man.

"Are you okay?" the man called back down.

"Yes!" Reed said.

"Please hurry!" Chayse urged.

The man brought a sheriff's deputy from the Indian Springs area. That man left and returned with deputies from Frazer County. Then a female investigator with a black FBI jacket. Then the local Fire Department.Until at least twenty people were standing on the platform talking on walkie-talkies and texting on their phones and pointing down at the twins.

A water rescue and salvage team had to be called in. They repelled down the sides of the cliff in harnesses wearing dive suits. The team let a few divers out of their harnesses into the water so they could check on the condition of the twin's submerged bodies. Once they determined the twins had both arms and legs and were free-floating in the water and met all the requirements for rescuing they helped the twins into the harnesses.

First, Chayse and then Reed were lifted up the side of karst.

Once they were cliffside, the torrent of questions came. Were they the missing twins? Could they prove it? Where had they been these last seven days? How come they were dressed to go to a Renaissance Fair? Where was Miss Elsie Crutch? Her two assistants, Nick and Vic? Where were the Brazzles? Had they been tied up? Abused? Molested? When was the last time they had eaten?

The twins looked at each other and said they either didn't know or couldn't remember.

At that point, the FBI separated the twins into different tents set up in the parking lot of the Osage Cave State Park to take their depositions.

The twins were each wrapped in blankets and given bottles of water. Chayse asked for bags of Cheetos and Reed asked for Lays original potato chips. After they had munched through a couple of snack bags of their preferred flavor, the FBI interviewers prompted them each to begin.

Without even having prepared a story, the twins gave the same story. They told everything as it happened: their first encounter with Miss Elsie Crutch, being taken into custody, the court hearing, going into foster care with the Brazzles, coming to Osage Cave, and Miss Elsie Crutch showing up with both of her assistants.

The twins' story stayed the same in relating what came next: the twins ran away from their captors and climbed into the cave that fed the spring stream. The cave chambers were extensive and they got lost. They even got separated at one point. They were able to elude their captors. Find each other. But they couldn't find their way out. They saw a cave pool with light coming from beneath. So they jumped in and swam towards it.

To answer how they came to be in these strange clothes, the twins said the Brazzles made them do it once they had arrived down at the bottom of the trail next to the cave.

The FBI pressed them again and again. Trying to trip up their narrative and question their definition of facts. That all stopped when three people arrived.

The first was a DHS court liaison. A blonded woman with a ponytail pulled back at the base of her neck and clad in grey pantsuits and a red-blue windbreaker. The FBI was careful to check her credentials, even going to the Fulton County website to confirm her title and identity.

She identified herself as Kelley Dalton. Carrying a file of recently signed papers from Judge Hart's office, she identified the twins with her court docs app on her phone and gave copies of the court documents releasing the twins into her immediate custody.

The FBI printed the children anyway.

But when they demanded saliva for DNA testing and a more thorough search of their young bodies, the court liaison refused stating that would be up to Judge Hart. If the twins showed no sign of abuse then it was unwarranted. The FBI interviewers stated they saw alarming gaps in the twins' story and were concerned because they were giving the same story. Then the FBI chided the DHS liaison and all the counties represented by their sheriff deputies to find these five people: Miss Elsie Crutch, Nick, Vic, and the Brazzles.

DHS agent Kelley Dalton would not let them leave without a copy of their interview with both twins and pointed out to Judge Hart's court edict and the half dozen sheriff deputies each with a hand on their holstered gun.

Packing up their portable recording devices and field kits, the FBI threatened counter lawsuits and revocations of jobs and ending of careers for any local state or county official who would knowingly try to obstruct their attempt at justice.

No one was sad to see them go.

The other two visitors waited in the local authority command tent accompanied by two Frazer County deputies. Kelley brought the twins to meet these two visitors.

The twins had not seen these two people this close together in years.

It was Mom and Dad.

There were no words.

Just hugs.

And kisses.

And lots of tears.

"What happened to ya?" Mom demanded.

"Where've ya been?" Dad asked.

Reed wiped tears from his eyes. All that time on the run and the long journey was catching up. He didn't feel much like talking right now.

"We got lost in that cave," Chayse said.

"Bull crap," Mom said and pointed her finger at all the deputies. "Someone did something to ya."   "I'll go find those people myself," Dad threatened. "Me and Buddy. We'll bring 'em back. After we've dragged them down the road."

"I have a copy of their sworn statement to the FBI, Mr. and Mrs. Leftwich," Kelley Dalton said. She had been reading over the statements during the twins' reunion with their parents. Holding it out, the parents turned to her. "They do not once mention any kind of abuse other than some threats. Once the Brazzles took them here and the three CASA agents showed up, the twins escaped their captors."

"And we've been hidin' out ever since," Reed said.

Chayse gave her younger and smaller brother a poke in the ribs. "We got lost in that cave."

"Yeah, for a long while," Reed said.

"You've been missin' seven days, kids," Dad said.

"Yeah, for seven days," Reed clarified.

"I don't feel good knowin' all these people were in on it," Mom said. "All of them workin' for the court. They coulda been doin' this for years."

"Human traffickin'," Dad said.

"Human traffickin'," Mom shook her head. "It's gotta stop."

Two EMTs entered the command tent and checked over the twins one by one.

"Are you hungry?" Mom asked.

"You kids gotta be hungry," Dad said.

Chayse shrugged. "We ate last--"

"The last of our snacks days ago," Reed said. "The Brazzles gave us some candy and chips and leftover pizza when we're in their SUV. But it was just to get us to trust them."

Chayse gave Reed a look. She hoped he didn't go too far. Next, he'd be saying the Brazzles gave them a sack lunch for the cave trip.

After the EMTs had finished their preliminary check-up, they turned to the parents.

"Your children are well. Just some cuts and bruises on them," the first one said.

"Probably from being lost in the cave," the second one said.

"So, they ain't hurt?" Mom asked.

The EMTs shook their heads. "No, ma'am. They're quite healthy. Hardly dehydrated or malnourished."

"Really?" Kelley asked and made a note on an app on her phone.

"So, y'all stocked up on junk food for seven days?" Dad asked. "Oh, I forget. You took a leftover pizza with you into the cave."

"And where did you get those clothes?" Mom asked. "That's not what you were wearin' at court last week."

Chayse shrugged. "They made us changed once we got here."

"Yeah, they're sickos," Reed said.

"Did you find water to drink in the cave?" Kelley Dalton asked.

Chayse thought a moment. "Yeah, we did."

"Lots of water in that cave," Reed said.

"The FBI must have asked you all these questions," Kelley Dalton said. "You tell them the same thing you're telling us?"

"Sure," Chayse said.

"Yes, ma'am," Reed said.

Kelley Dalton punched in notes on her phone. The app probably let her add notes the twins' electronic court file on a shared drive. "Mr. and Mrs. Leftwich, we will have a court psychologist look at the twins before the next hearing."

"*Next* court hearing?" Dad echoed.

"I thought this was a done deal," Mom said. "It should be cut and dry. My kids were taken away. By the court. Then they were almost kidnapped. By the court. I want my kids back."

"It's just not that easy," Kelley Dalton said.

"What's not easy?" Mom argued. "I had them. I take care of them. If everybody would quit stickin' their nose in our business and just let us raise our kids the best we can, we'd do just fine."

"But then you'd have to get a whole new job," Dad pointed out to Kelley Dalton.

Kelley Dalton put her phone down and looked at the twins' parents for a moment. "I understand your concern. I truly do. This is a dereliction of duty and will demand a whole separate investigation.

"But there is also the legality of the whole thing. Your family is in FINS. There was a custody component. And a foster care request--"

Mom pointed her finger at Kelley Dalton. "Look, that's not happening again. I am not ever givin' my kids up to you or anyone. I don't care if you send a Navy Seal Team after me. I. Am. Not. Givin'. Them. Up. Again. Ever."

"Y'all had yer chance," Dad said. "We played along. And you screwed it up. Royal."

Kelley Dalton took a moment and dropped her tone. "The FINS will have to be closed out, is what I'm saying, Mr. and Mrs. Leftwich. It is a formality. But it's the law. The twins may be interviewed again during a separate investigation."

Dad spoke up. "The kids ain't leavin' my sight. They ain't gonna be alone with no one. I don't care how many government jobs or degrees the person's got."

Mom was proud of that and stuck her chin up. "I want a lawyer. My own lawyer."

"That is your certainly you're right, Mrs. Leftwich. But the kids will still have a lawyer ad-litem," Kelley Dalton said.

"No!" Chayse said.

"We don't want that Kyph--" Reed started.

"Ad-litem Kyler," Chayse finished giving her brother the stink eye.

"I agree. You can't fool kids, Miss Dalton," Mom said. "They know when someone's bein' fake or real."

"Meaning what, Mrs. Leftwich?" Kelley Dalton said.

"Meanin' y'all better talk to lawyer ad-litem Alexander Kyler durin' yer 'internal investigation,'" Dad said.

Kelley Dalton said nothing as Mom and Dad let that sink in.

"Are we finished here?" Mom asked. "I'd like to take my kids home."

A sheriff's deputy took Kelley Dalton aside and talked into her ear behind his hand.

The twins shuffled their feet. Mom looked at Dad who gave her one of his winning smiles. She just rolled her eyes at him.

Then Kelley Dalton approached the waiting and very tired family. She coughed into her hand. "The sheriff is concerned for your well being. They have five suspects who have committed federal felonies still at large."

"Do ya think we're in any danger?" Mom asked.

"I can handle these jokers," Dad said. "Got a twenty ought six. Sawed-off. I'll bag all these turkeys."

That reminded Reed of how Cyrus had taken Sergeant Hood out. *I bet his boots are still standin' there.*

"The CASA agents have made threats against your children. They are the only witnesses to what all might have happened. I'm afraid the suspects might still target them," Kelley Dalton said.

"So what are ya sayin'?" Mom asked. "We can't go home?"

A Frazer County deputy stepped forward. "We have sent a deputy to patrol your house, ma'am. We think the twins are targets. Until all these suspects are in custody, you and your whole family are in imminent danger."

"I have arranged for a hotel room for y'all here in town," Kelley said. She pulled out a paper receipt from a manila folder and handed it to Mom. "You have a two queen bedroom with a pullout sleeper at the Sleepy Inn. That's the best room they got."

Dad rubbernecked to try to look it over. Until Mom held the receipt so they both could look.

"You want us both to stay here tonight?" Dad asked.

"With your children," Kelley said.

"You get the pullout," Mom told Dad.

The twins were excited. Coming home. Seeing both Mom and Dad. All good things. Miss Elsie Crutch and her whole crew on the run. A plus.

But getting to stay in a hotel room.

Now, that was special.

The twins loaded into Mom's Saturn Vue and Dad followed them in his beat up Dodge.

They drove to the hotel and found it less than what Kelley Dalton had made it out to be. The Sleepy Inn was an old fashioned motor inn.

"This is not a hotel," Mom said.

It was just a row of single-story rooms attached to an office with a brick facade. Built in the 1960s or '70s at the height of American car culture. For transients and traveling salesmen.

"This is a drug haven. A flophouse," she said as she pulled her car up to the room number written on the receipt Kelley Dalton had given her.

Dad pulled up beside them in his pick-up and winked at them.

Behind him came a sheriff's deputy's car on patrol.

"Don't it make you feel safe? Cared for like little children?" Dad asked Mom as they opened the door to the best suite of the Sleepy Inn.

"Guess you're not used to havin' a police escort," Mom said as she took her gathered family's belongings inside.

"Ha, ha," Dad said as he closed the door.

And like that, Reed got his wish.

They were a family again.

At least for one night.

It was like a try-out.

Mom took the queen bed next to the bathroom. She put the twins in the bed next to the door and Dad took the sleeper couch against the wall by the door.

Reed wanted the TV on.

Mom didn't want him to have it on.

Dad told her to let him have it on if it would keep him quiet.

Mom turned it on the National Geographic channel. And when Reed complained it was a boring channel Mom said it would put him to sleep faster.

Dad snored.

No one else slept.

"Reed," Chayse whispered.

Reed was still awake. "Yeah, Sissy."

"Do you remember the last time we were all in a hotel room together?" Chayse asked him.

"I sure do. We went to St. Louis. That's the time we went to the zoo," Reed said. He had loved the St. Louis Zoo.

"You got scared when we saw those big cats," Chayse teased. "You were afraid you'd fall in and get eaten."

Reed hated whenever she brought that up. "I was only five."

"So was I," Chayse teased him.

"Were you scared back in the Realm?" Reed asked you.

"At first," Chayse said. "But the Elfwitch made everything so fascinating. I guess I just got. Confused. Were you scared?"

"Most of the time. I just wanted to get back home," Reed said.

***

Chapter Sixty-Six: Father and Son

No one slept in the next morning.

The twins woke to Mom fussing at Dad's snoring. It was like stepping back into the past. Of all the things Reed wanted: time with Dad, joking with Dad, hunting with Dad, this is one thing he didn't want—Mom fighting with Dad.

"I can't help it," Dad said as he sat upon the sleeper couch.

Mom walked around with a curling iron in her hand. Back and forth from the bathroom. Fussing at Dad. Hurrying the twins to finish getting ready.

It was just like home.

Reed had gotten his wish.

"You could get one of those nose strips," Mom said. "You used to wear those all the time."

Dad noticed Reed watching him. "Yeah, the whole football team did. We wore them during the games."

"And it helped you breathe better, right?" Mom asked.

"Don't know about that," Dad said as he got up. He still hadn't gotten ready yet. "But we did hit harder." He mimicked rushing with an elbow.

Reed laughed.

Mom rushed back in once again. "Get your crap off the beds. All of you. So I can make them."

"Reggie, you don't have to make beds in a hotel!" Dad argued.

"Motel," Mom reminded.

"They got housin' staff that does it," Dad said.

"I don't want no tweakers goin' through my stuff," Mom said.

"We ain't got no stuff they'd want," Dad said. "Just the kids."

"Ha, ha, funny," Mom said.

Chayse looked behind the curtains at the parking lot. "The deputy's still sitting out in his car in the parking lot. Got his shades on."

"Hope that made you feel sake," Dad said.

"Nah, the Destroyer woulda got him easy," Reed said and felt Chayse's eyes like knives as soon as he said it.

"That some new wrestler's name?" Mom asked.

"Yeah," Reed said as he jumped to Mom's unmade bed.

"Why don't the cops go after the tweakers, Dad?" Chayse asked.

"Cuz they're too busier with their manhunt for that crazy CASA woman," Mom said.

Dad shook his head. "Tweakers are low priority cuz what they do is a lower class felony and kidnappin' kids is a far worse crime. Since doin' meth is a lower class felony, the fines are lower. The worse the crime, the higher the fines. More money for the courts to go for the big time crooks.

"The worse crimes don't happen every day now. When the chance comes for a big fine, the cops gotta take it. That's why all these different counties got deputies out there in a dragnet.

"But it don't matter no how. Cuz if these people got money, they'll pay the fines and walk. Rich people don't go to jail. They pay to make trouble go away. Jail is for people who can't make bail."

Mom came back in. She wore a black dress with a t-shirt had a towel around her neck like a bib as she applied make-up. Chayse knew Mom wouldn't put her shirt on until she was done with her make-up. "Freddie, don't be sayin' such around the kids."

"Ain't you still payin' on yer fines?" Chayse said.

Reed defended Dad. "No, he ain't in trouble anymore."

Dad shrugged. "I ain't been in trouble since I got popped for drivin' without a license. And yes, I'm still payin' on it. Pretty soon, I'll be done payin' and I won't have to see Judge Hart's face again."

"You said that last month," Chayse said.

"Yeah, well, there's even less to pay now," Dad said.

"He's been payin' Chayse," Mom said. "I've been checkin'. Cuz he's supposed to be payin' me for you guys, too."

Dad shrugged. "I'm livin' just to pay the bills. Your mom's got some now cuz of all this FINS business."

"But she ain't done nothin' wrong," Reed said. "Ever."

"You gotta pay to file papers. You gotta pay for a lawyer. You gotta pay for the fines," Mom read off an imaginary list. "Court gets expensive."

"Like goin' to the doctor?"Chayse asked.

Mom nodded. Then to Dad, she asked, "So, if we find out how much we gotta pay to get the kids back, would you help me?" Mom asked.

Dad's eyes went up. "Of course. Means we gotta rob a bank. Or sell meth." When he saw her roll her eyes, he got serious and asked, "Could we talk about custody, too?"

"I'm here. You're here. Let's talk," Mom said.

The twins' jaw dropped.'

There was a knock at the door.

It was Kelley Dalton in a black dress and with her hair down. They hadn't heard her pull up but she had parked her black Titanium Ford Edge next to Mom and Dad's vehicles. The deputy watched them with his wind rolled down and shades on.

Mom greeted the court liaison like it was the front door of her own home rather than a fleabag motel. "Yes, Miss Dalton?"

"Is everyone decent?" the woman asked.

"No one's cookin' meth at the moment," Dad called out from the couch sleeper.

Mom gave Dad the stink eye. "Come in, Miss Dalton."

The blonde woman came in. She looked around the room at the open suitcases and empty snack bags and unmade beds. "I trust everyone got a good night's sleep."

"Sure did, how 'bout yourself?" Dad asked.

"Any word on the manhunt?" Mom asked.

Kelley Dalton shook her head.

"You ain't caught a one of them?" Dad asked.

"Bet they all disappeared," Chayse said.

"Right off the face of the earth," Reed said.

Kelley looked at the twins. "Do you know something? Did the kidnappers mention a rendezvous?"

"They only mentioned they was crazy, was all, ma'am," Reed said.

Chayse nodded in affirmation.

"You didn't come just to tell us you haven't found this human trafficking ring," Mom said.

"No, I didn't. I came to escort you, along with the deputy, to a meeting with the lawyer ad-litem," Kelley said.

"I'm just saying upfront, I am no fan of Alexander Kyler," Mom said.

"He's in on it, I'm tellin' ya," Dad said.

"He's been reassigned," Kelley said.

Everyone sat up, except for Mom, and became still.

"May I ask why?" Mom asked.

"He's on sick leave, is all I know," Kelley said. "A new lawyer ad-litem has been assigned to us from the Federal District Court out of Searcy. I am to take y'all to meet with him this morning."

"When?" Mom asked.

"At ten-thirty," Kelley Dalton.

"That's in just forty-five minutes!" Mom said. "Kids you'd better hurry and get ready."

Both twins ran to the bathroom but Chayse got there first. Reed complained that he had to pee and that she took too long. Sissy told him to go outside and pee.

Dad laughed.

"What you laughin' at?" Mom asked him. "You're goin' too. So you best get cleaned up."

Reed was holding the crotch of his shorts and jumping up and down.

Dad sighed and got off the sleeper couch. "Come on, Reed. There's a bathroom in the motel lobby."

"How come you know that less you been here?" Mom asked.

Reed ran up to Dad as he held the motel room door open. "That's right. I've been here."

"With some girl, no doubt!" Mom said.

"No, with Buddy," Dad said.

"Buddy?" Mom argued.

Dad nodded as he walked outside with Reed. "We done some plumbin' work for the owner a while back."

Reed still had to make long strides to keep up with Dad. There was a hitch in his step. They might have just been going to the bathroom but he was with his Dad again. His real father. It almost felt the same as when Reed had trekked with Frehley.

Strange.

"Listen, now that we're actually alone, I gotta ask ya something, Bubba," Dad said.

Reed was an eager beaver and would have told his Dad anything. Even the truth.

Dad slouched down to ask, "Did you really help your sister get out of that cave?"

Reed nodded. Because, in a way, they had come through a cave, to get to Quicksilver Lake.

"Son, I'm proud of ya," Dad said. "That's what a man does. Whatever it takes to help his family."

Breathing in until his chest was about to burst, Reed held his head high.

"Now tell the truth," Dad said as they reached the motor lodge office. "Were you ever scared?"

The question made Reed uncomfortable. How should he answer? What did Dad want him to say?

Dad held the door open as Reed got stuck on how he should answer. "It's ok to be scared. Men don't ever say that. Won't ever admit it. But I'm tellin' ya, everyone gets scared, so it's ok."

Reed shrugged. He still didn't want to answer. He didn't want to have to tell his Dad just how much and how often he had been scared in the Realm.

"But don't ever let being afraid stop you from helping yer sister or yer momma," Dad said.

The manager came out from his office where he had been laying on an old army cot.

Dad answered his bed head stare, "My son needs to use your bathroom."

The family got ready at the quick.

Mom had taken a long time to get ready while chiding everyone else that they were taking their own sweet time.

"Come on, everybody," she scowled. "Let's get this over with."

Chayse didn't look too happy either over having to go back to court. "That's where this whole mess started."

"No, it didn't," Reed said. "There's the 'whole mess' and then there's our mess."

"What do you mean?" Chayse asked.

"It started didn't start when Miss Elsie Crutch came to our door. And it didn't start when we were born. The 'whole mess' started when the Darkness turned away from the Light. So, there is a God. Or Judge. I truly do believe that. If we seen him in the Realm then he's here in this world, too. He has to be in every world there is cuz he made them all," Reed said.

"Then why doesn't he come down here and straighten this mess out?" Chayse asked.

Reed pointed at Dad as he talked with Mom. Kelley Dalton walked over to join them but she stood at an angle with her foot pointed toward her car and her hands down by her side. "God doesn't make mistake. He undoes them. Our mess started when Dad left. So they'll have to be the ones to wanna make it right."

"Let's just take my truck," Dad offered. Then he turned to Kelley. "Or is that against the order."

"Of course not," Kelley said. "As long as Reggie is there with them."

"Y'all act like I've some kind of registered offender. I've never done anything hurtful to my kids," Dad said.

Mom harrumphed. "'Cept leave 'em."

"No, I left you," Dad said. "And ever since you been tryin' to take them away from me. 'Cept you can't afford them kids without askin' me for money."

Mom started spitting out vitriol, "Maybe if you kept a job long enough--" But then she caught herself and took a breath. "If you had a steady job, we could split these bills better."

The twins were ready for another fight to kick up. But it didn't boil over. Something happened.

Mom didn't ramp up her words. And Dad didn't yell back.

"I've been meanin' to tell ya, I talked to Tate Hill. He's agreed to take me back on as an apprentice and help me get my plumbin' license again. Then I can get square with my fines and help you guys out more," Dad said.

Mom blinked. Her eyes softened. "That would be. Great!"

Kelley laughed. "Well, this has been a good session. I like that you're both talking and listening and offering solutions. Real progress."

"What's this new lawyer ad-litem like?" Chayse asked. "He isn't as weird as the last one, is he?"

"He's a licensed professional employee of the court. And he will conduct himself in that manner or he will have to answer to that same court," Kelley said.

Mom looked her full in the face. "Oh, I like that answer."

"Well, God is no respecter of persons. And it says in the good book that if a judge is a respecter of persons, then he's taking bribes," Dad said.

"I understand your distrust in this situation," Kelley said. "The entire court will be investigated at the highest level."

Dad guffawed, "Yeah, by another court." Then he opened the back driver's down of his king cab. "Kids, pile in."

The twins fell over themselves trying to get in. They giggled as Dad opened the passenger door for Mom and helped her up. They hadn't all been for a ride together as a family in dogs' years.

Dad revved up his Cummins diesel as Kelley Dalton got into her blue four-door car with the official government plates. He followed Kelley back down the highway to the main light in Shiloh. They made a right at Alpha Auto Sales--"Your FIRST place for the BEST deal!"—and drove down to the square.

The federal building was on the south side of the courthouse next to the police station. As they climbed out of Dad's Dodge, Reed noticed something different in the In-Season Thrift store window. Two somethings: one something was gone and one something was new.

At least five Shadows hung from the eaves and the colonial British soldier still stood in the main window. But the life-size animated revenant ghoul biker sitting on a chopper that had been parked on the sidewalk next to the store door was gone.

Another figure stood just inside the shop past the threshold.

Tall and lithe.

A hint of fluttering black raven feathers.

"Mom, can I go look in that store?" Reed asked.

Chayse looked at her twin brother. He indicated the store window. She looked again and then shrugged. "I guess Reed wants me to go with him."

"That ok, Miss Kelley?" Mom asked and looked at her phone. "We've still got ten minutes."

Kelley shrugged and lifted her eyebrows. "Sure."

"You wanna come, Dad?" Chayse asked as she followed after Reed who was running across the street without looking both ways.

Dad thought about it. "Sure. Give me a couple of minutes, tho'."

"'Kay!"Chayse said as she ran to catch up with Reed.

They ran into the shop. It was warm. As if the air conditioner was never turned on. It was stuffy. As if the air never stirred. All of the decorations were used. Taken out of closets and attics and never dusted down. Some of the items were still sealed having been 'Made in China' sometime late in the last century but never opened in this one. Dust had discolored the plastic bags and dulled the shelf card.

Neither sister had been outside and neither one seemed to be at the front of the store. The store was quiet. Except for the twins' own footsteps creaking on the wood floor.

"What is it?" Chayse asked.

"I thought I saw someone in the doorway," Reed said. "And that biker's gone."

"Well, maybe someone bought it," Chayse said.

Reed was glad it was gone so he didn't have to look at it. He wouldn't let himself think of what it reminded him of. Something he never wanted to name again.

A floorboard creaked. Toward the back of the store.

"Hello!" Chayse called out.

Reed shh-ed her.

Another board creaked.

There was an open doorway to the back of the store behind the cash register. The twins went past the counter and peered through the doorway. The back of the store was a narrow storage space that followed the layout of the store floor. And every inch was full of old boxes taken from peoples' yard sales and closets. The smell of dust and years and shut-in people was even stronger here.

"That's some kind of funk," Chayse said and held her nose.

The back door to the store was open. A back alley ran behind the store and beyond it lay an open lot with grass and weeds. Something scraped against the back wall.

Reed walked through the storage space and to the open door frame.

"Reed!" Chayse called. "Don't go out there!"

But she noticed he had a healthy dose of Dad: a bad combination of being stubborn and curious. Reed didn't listen to Mom so why should he listen to his twin sister. He was going to go outside just to see what he could see.

He stood at the threshold and turned back. "I don't see nothin'."

The doorway darkened.

Two shadows filled it. Anthromorphic. About the same height and body size.

Two people. In faded blue jeans and striped button-down shirts. And the same spiky hair cut.

It was the Brazzles. Payton and Shawn. With the same daring smile.

"Stupid kids," said Mrs. Brazzle.

"Tricks are for the Elfwitch," Mr. Brazzle said.

Chayse froze. The Brazzles shouldn't be here. But here they were.

She wasn't going to let them take Reed.

"You haven't won, you know," Mr. Brazzle said.

"You can't beat her. Ever," Mrs. Brazzle said.

"She couldn't beat us," Reed said.

Chayse stood behind her twin brother. "We're family. That's why she won't ever win."

"We have a message," Mr. Brazzle said.

"From the Dark Lady," Mrs. Brazzle said.

"Many worlds there are…

"…To travel near and far," said Mr. Brazzle.

"All of them I own…

"…I make them my home," said Mrs. Brazzle.

"In secret and shadow…

'…Where only fear can grow," said Mr. Brazzle.

"When you tire and try to rest…

"…That's when I open my chest," said Mrs. Brazzle.

"I will give terror in the night…

"…As I drive out the light," ended Mr. Brazzle.

There was nothing else to be said.

There was nothing else the twins could do.

They stood together as a family and in love. And faced the pair of servants who posed as a married couple. But whose vow was to the Darkness.

"Kids!" Dad called from the front of the shop. "Quit playin'. If you make me come get you I'll tan yer hide."

"If you think this is the end," Mr. Brazzle said.

"It has yet to begin," Mrs. Brazzle said.

Chayse intoned, "Go away." But the words whispered to each other and went in four directions and came back like the wind. They stretched out into different words: *Return to your Dark Mistress and leave us alone.*"

In a breath, they were gone.

Dad found them. "What are you doin' back here? There's nothing but garbage in this store. Come on out front before them crazy sisters who own this place think we're stealin' some of this garbage!"

But he did not tan their hides.

***

Chapter Sixty-Seven: Family and Stranger

Dad led them out of the store. Everyone was glad to quit it. Who would leave their shop open and unattended? There being no shoppers was eerie enough. But not even the owners being there was creepier.

Kelley Dalton waited on the stoop to the Federal Building. Mom was halfway across the street.

"It's time! Let's not be late! We don't need any more fines!" she called.

"We definitely don't need any junk in there," Dad told them.

The twins looked around for either the Brazzles or their SUV.

Besides the lycanthrope twins, the Brazzles were the only servants of the Darkness who had crossed back over to the Realm. And now they had disappeared again once the twins had crossed over.

Another mystery.

And where was the Elfwitch? Or Miss Elsie Crutch? Where had she gone?

The biggest mystery of them all.

The twins knew if the Dark Lady did not want to be found in their World or any other then she did not want to be found.

It wasn't a total victory. It was more of a stand-off. But there was something else the twins wanted even more than for the Elfwitch to be destroyed. And if God would grant them that one desire then they would have something that the Elfwitch or Elsie Crutch could never destroy. Something that would make the Elfwitch run straight back to her shadow Domain once she realized that she could not destroy it.

And wouldn't that be an even better victory?

When the twins caught up with Mom, she took Chayse's hand as they crossed the other side of the street and went up the steps of the Federal Building while Reed's hand found Dad's. Hand in hand the family entered the building and traversed the narrow paneled hallway. The darkened hallway held pictures of current officer holders and posters promising that the federal government had zero tolerance for human trafficking while upholding the right for women's health.

Kelley Dalton met them half way down the corridor and led them to the other end of the building to an even smaller waiting area with small three chairs that did not look designed to give comfort while waiting for an agent of the United States government.

The court liaison knocked on the last door on the hall and poked her head through. "The Leftwichs are here, Mr. Walker."

"Good!" boomed a voice from inside. "Send them right in!"

Mom rolled her eyes and Dad motored with his lips. Chayse grabbed Reed's hand. The longer they were all around each, the more things were returning back to normal.

Kelley pushed the door open and in the Leftwichs went.

The office had the same dark paneling as the hallway. Licenses and degrees lined the wall all bearing the same name: Cornelius Kane Walker. A large man with a barrel chest sat behind the desk that occupied most of the small room.

Mr. Cornelius Kane Walker himself. The man was in his mid to late thirties. With curly hair receding well back on the top of his head while taking the time to stick out over his ears.

He wore dark navy pants that could not contain his massive legs and a blue button-down shirt with white pinstripes. He had a wide gold tie with silver stripes. One beefy hand-typed on his laptop. The other was tucked into his pants pocket.

Mr. Cornelius Kane Walker greeted them all with a huge smile spread from ear to ear.

Both the twins had to blink.

"Cyrus!" Reed blurted out.

This time Chayse was too stunned to stop him.

Without missing a beat, Mr. Cornelius Kane Walker stood up from behind his desk and offered a burly hand to both Mom and Dad while keeping the other tucked in his pants pocket.

"Mr. Frederick Leftwich and Mrs. Regina Leftwich," he said and gave them each a firm handshake. "I'm very honored to meet you both." And then he slouched to extend a burly hand to the twins. "And this must be Chayse Leftwich. And you. You must be Reed."

"I must," Reed said.

"Reed?" Mom asked. "Do you know this man?"

Reed shook his head. The same as when she asked about if he had taken the family size bag of Lay's potato chips that Mom had just bought. "I…uh…I…"

"My picture is out in the hall, Mrs. Leftwich," said Mr. Cornelius Kane Walker. "They use it to scare the rats away."

Rats. Reed had forgotten all about Packy. Somehow he knew Packy could look out for himself. There would be other rats who had survived the fall of the Keep.

Both the twins were sure they caught a wink from Mr. Cornelius Kane Walker.

That strange feeling that a prank was being played on the twins came over them. It was not like before. This had been a pleasant surprise.

They had a quite different feeling about how things would go in court now.

Mom and Dad could sense the twins had relaxed but they weren't going to let their guard down. Not again. They were both tired of always being on the losing side.

Mr. Cornelius Kane Walker began, "I just got done reading your file and--"

Mom held up her hand. "Please, Mr. Walker. We don't want to relive everything we've just been through. Just tell me true. Will I be able to get my kids back?"

Mr. Walker nodded to himself while he thought on how to give a summary of possible outcomes. "Yes, it is very possible, Mrs. Leftwich. No matter what you might think, the Federal government is not in the business of tearing families apart."

"Do you have a family of your own, Mr. Walker?" Mom asked.

Mr. Walker looked down to the right. Back at the corner of his desk. There were two small picture frames. One was a twin frame and sat open like a book. The other was more of a small commemorative stand with an oval setting.

"I did," Mr. Walker said. "Once."

"Did you have a wife and daughter?" Reed asked.

"Why, yes," Mr. Walker said.

"Forgive him, Mr. Walker," Mom said. "He must have seen the pictures on your desk."

"Of course, ma'am," Mr. Walker said.

"How did they die, if you don't mind me asking," Dad asked.

"Of course not, sir," Mr. Walker said. "It was a fire. I was not at home at the time to be of much help."

"So you felt helpless?" Dad asked.

"Yes," Mr. Walker said.

"Guilty?" Dad asked.

"Naturally," Mr. Walker said.

"So, you can understand what your clients go through in this FINS process," Dad said.

"Most definitely," Mr. Walker said. "My tragedy gave me a choice. I could grow cold and stay full of my hurt or I could help others. I chose to help others. So, I went back to school and got my law degree. Now I specialize in family court issues."

"You became a lawyer after you lost your family?" Mom asked.

"Yes, ma'am," Mr. Walker said. "That is correct."

The twins nodded. Reed even gave Mr. Walker a thumbs up. Again, he gave them a wink when Mom and Dad were not looking.

Mom and Dad relaxed.

"How do we get our kids back?" Dad asked.

"Get married," Mr. Walker said. "Married couples with stable jobs who can provide a good home have the strongest chance, really."

Mom and Dad dropped their jaws.

"It's just not that simp--" was all Mom could get out.

"I don't think she would ever--" was all Dad could manage.

Mom focused herself again. "Will Judge Hart be our judge again?"

Mr. Walker shook his head and smiled. "Judge Hart will not be presiding over this session. He has moved it to the Federal District Court in Searcy. We will be making motions under Judge Stone."

"What do we say?" Mom asked.

"What do we ask?" Dad asked.

Mr. Walker held up his hand as he sat on the edge of the desk and spread his thick thighs. "Leave that to me. I know what Judge Stone likes to hear."

"When is our court date?" Mom asked.

Mr. Walker looked at his apple watch. "In about fifteen minutes."

Dad had to catch Mom and then he had to sit down.

After Dad got Mom to open her eyes and breathe slower, she asked. "Why so fast?"

"There will be a separate motion based on your children's testimony that may lead to arrest warrants," Mr. Walker said. "That will happen after your FINS deposition."

"Aren't they on the hunt for these people now?" Mom asked.

"This would be for federal prosecution. Which would entail the U.S. Marshalls. The FBI. Homeland Defense. The works," Mr. Walker said.

Mom shook her head, "All of those people after her."

"They won't find the Elfwitch," Reed murmured.

"The 'who-witch?'" Dad asked.

Chayse covered for him. "He said, 'Elsie Crutch.'"

"No, he didn't. He called her a witch," Dad said.

"Reed, don't talk about adults like that," Mom said.

"Well, he's right," Dad said. "That woman is a witch."

The twins smiled.

"Mr. and Mrs. Leftwich, I see no reason why Judge Stone wouldn't rescind Judge Hart's order and dismiss the FINS case if you two let me talk for you and say what I tell you," Mr. Walker said. "Now, once we are out of court, you must promise to follow my advice. It won't be easy. There will be court hearings for follow-ups. So, we all must do what we say we will do.

"First, Mr. Leftwich, will you seek gainful employment? Preferably, a job that withholds taxes? One that even offers benefits would be great."

Dad nodded. "I'm serious about getting my plumbing license."

"Good. Tell the judge exactly what you just told me," Mr. Walker said. "Now, Mrs. Leftwich, would you seek employment that pays at least eleven or twelve an hour instead of two part-time jobs?"

"How am I supposed to make it on one job?" Mom asked.

"If Mr. Leftwich is giving the correct amount of payments every month, you shouldn't have to. And the next thing, will both of you agree to go to counseling?" Mr. Walker asked.

Mom waited for Dad to answer first.

"I'm not sayin' I haven't done my share of mistakes. But if it means havin' my wife—the mother of children—keep my kids, then yes," Dad said.

Mom gave a slow nod. "If he's agreein' then I can agree to it."

"Good," Mr. Walker smiled and took both of their hands in one of his beefy ones. "Now, when I suggest these things to the Judge and state you are willing, he will ask you to say it in your own words, for the record understand. So, you both are to say just what you told me here in my office and it will go well."

"It's about our time for things to start goin' good, Mr. Walker," Mom said and squeezed both Dad's hand and Mr. Walker's.

"Way past due," Dad said not taking his hand back yet.

The twins each put a hand on top of the hand pile.

Then Mr. Walker took out his hand he had kept tucked in his pocket and put it on top of the hand pile. It was a full above arm prosthetic. The clenched hand was gloved and the rest was hard, clear plastic.

The twins' eyes went wide.

For a third time, Mr. Walker winked at them.

"If you don't mind me askin', Mr. Walker," Mom said. "But how did you lose yer arm?"

"By tryin' to take somethin' that didn't belong to me," Mr. Walker said but in the tone and cadence of Cyrus the blacksmith. "Trust, Mr. and Mrs. Leftwich, this will all work out."

Mom and Dad shuffled out. Chayse was next.

"Reed," Mr. Walker called.

The boy twin turned. The Federal lawyer ad-litem turned the small commemorative stand around and took the object out that it had housed. The lawyer offered the item to Reed.

It was a coin.

It shone.

With something familiar.

Reed took it. It was heavy. Made of real gold.

Etched into the gold on the heads side was the portrait of a man with long tousled hair. One word stamped above in arc: LIBERTY. And under the man's neck was stamped the phrase: TRUST IN THE JUDGE.

On the tails side was a building that Reed never did get to see but had heard plenty about. It was a round castle with a large central tower atop which flew a single pennon. Etched into the bottom was the two-word phrase: TOWER REIGN.

"You are Cyrus? Aren't you?" Reed asked.

"Here, I am just who I said I am," Mr. Walker said. "When I climbed into that chest, I saw a small light. It was coming from your coin. I was in some kind of cave. I prayed and the Judge used the coin to lead me out and I found myself here. Now my task is to help you…and others. To let you know that the Judge has not forgotten about you. And I am to help you out now and then."

"The Elfwitch?" Reed asked.

"My job is to see that she never bothers your family again," Mr. Walker/Cyrus said as he took his jacket which had been lying on the back of his office chair.

Leading Reed out of his office, they gathered with the rest of the family and Kelley Dalton.

Mr. Walker gave them all a warm smile as he put his prosthetic arm into a sleeve of the jacket. "It's time. Do be nervous. This will be an end to it,"

They walked out of the Federal building and crossed back over the south side of the square to enter the Shiloh Court House. Mr. Walker and Kelley Dalton took the COURT EMPLOYEE entrance on the south side of the courthouse as the family went around to the west entrance and then up the stairwell on the right to the second floor to the courtroom.

Someone was waiting for them on the next floor.

Bailiff Mike stood on the landing next to the metal detector. Instead of a blue and black livery of the Queen's Men and a handlebar mustache, Bailiff Mike wore a black policeman's clothes and had a very trim mustache.

The twins smiled at him.

"Welcome back, you two yardapes," Bailiff Mike smiled as the family passed through the metal detector. "Step right in. There's a winner every time."

The family came in and sat at the table on the left of the court.

Bailiff Mike followed and took his spot along the west wall.

"All rise," he announced.

The family rose.

Out of the judge's chamber came first the reporter who took her spot in the cubicle below the judge's bench. Next came Kelley Dalton with an iPad as she stood at the prosecutor's table. Last came Mr. Cornelius Kane Walker followed by Judge Stone.

Judge Stone was a young man.

"This court is now in session, the honorable Judge Stone now presiding," Bailiff Mike finished.

Everyone sat only after Judge Stone took his seat.

He was a young judge. Not much older looking than Dad himself, Reed noted. Chayse thought you had to be old to be a judge because you had finished at least sixteen years of law school.

Black bushy hair surrounded his regal head. His nose was hawk-like. His eyes were like pearls of peaceful wisdom.

Reed did a double-take.

Was he not looking at the Beekeeper?

Some people here in his own World seemed to have a double in the Realm. But others seemed to be in two places. At once.

Judge Stone read off the docket and asked Kelley Dalton to present the old FINS case. It was all legal jargon that no one could understand. Double talk and archaic words that had to be said for the "record."

As the lawyers presented all that had happened to Judge Stone, the twins watched their parents. They each sat on at one end of the table with the kids behind them. Dad surprised them by pulling out a length of chain from under his striped shirt. Cascading down from his thumb was a trinket at the end of the chain.

An open silver heart with tiny brackets to hold another one inside its design.

Mom's eyes softened. Her cheeks blushed. Then she pulled out her own chain and held her own open heart silver necklace between her thumb and forefinger.

Mr. Walker, acting as lawyer ad-litem, called each of the twins up to give their testimony as to all what had happened at the last FINS hearing and their attempted abduction by the Brazzles abetted by court agents Nic and Vic and directed by CASA agent Miss Elsie Crutch. Then the judge had Mom and Dad each stand and ask their intentions and each gave their answer as near and direct as they had to Mr. Walker.

Judge Stone had the lawyers craft an order to rescind Judge Hart's FINS custody plan and gave joint-custody of the twins back to both parents provided Dad show proof of his plumbing journeymanship and Mom's full-time job and a record of their joint counseling.

And like that, Judge Stone banged his gavel and dismissed the hearing.

Everyone rose as the Judge left first.

A weight had been lifted.

All the officers of the court smiled.

The twins hugged Mom and then they hugged Dad.

Dad looked at Mom and Mom looked at Dad.

"I mean it," Dad said. "This time."

"I don't know, Freddie," Mom said shaking her head. "I'm afraid it'll just end up like it always does."

"I mean it, Reggie," Dad promised. "I come home and no one's there. If I'm not out doing something then I'm just staring at four walls. A house is not a home without a family.

"I barely get to see the kids. It's like when I get them they are already back out the door. I'm tired of being alone. I miss you.

"What did I do that made you so mad? Couldn't you ever forgive me?"

Mom sighed, "It's just not that simple. Things have to change."

"I can only change so much. A little at a time, maybe," Dad said. "But I need you to forgive me. I miss not having my family."

Mom grimaced. Then she wiped a tear out of her eye. "Why don't you come over for dinner Saturday?"

"Why not tonight?" Dad asked. "Why not start now?"

Mom gave a slow nod.

The twins were excited.

"Kids, you'll have to help," Mom said.

"You help your mom now, hear?" Dad said.

"Chayse's got the dishes. I'll sweep the floor!" Reed called out.

"Half those dishes are always yours!" Chayse argued. "You clean up your own mess!"

"Mom says you gotta!" Reed said.

"And Dad says you gotta do what Mom says!" Chayse shot back.

"Some things never change," Mom said.

Dad gave one of his free and high laughs.

***

About the Author

Jeffrey Cummins is very grateful for the blessings and dreams and hardships that have come his way. Over the years, he has worked in retail, the banking industry, as a mental health paraprofessional, and as a public school teacher. This is his first published book, and prior to this, he won an Editor's Choice for a short story in the *Arkansas Anthology*. He currently lives in the Ozarks with his wife and family and their many dogs.